M is for MONSTER

M is for MONSTER

A Modern Bestiary of Classic Monsters

Compiled by

Michael Kelahan

FALL RIVER PRESS

New York

FALL RIVER PRESS

New York

An Imprint of Sterling Publishing
387 Park Avenue South
New York, NY 10016

FALL RIVER PRESS and the distinctive Fall River Press logo are registered trademarks of Barnes & Noble, Inc.

This 2011 edition published by Fall River Press.

ISBN 978-1-4351-3073-9

Manufactured in the United States of America

2 4 6 8 10 9 7 5 3 1

www.sterlingpublishing.com

FOR PETER STRAUB

Gentleman, scholar, and a man among the monsters

Contents

Introduction

"Here Be Monsters!"

In days of old, when cartographers wanted to indicate *terra incognita*—that is, unknown country—or oceans that had yet to be explored, they would write this phrase directly on their maps, and often complement it with the illustration of a frightening serpent or hideous sea monster. In doing so, they gave the Unknown a shape and form, something that incarnated the uncertainty and apprehension that people of their time and place felt toward things unfamiliar and unpredictable.

Horror is a fiction whose writers regularly attempt to give form and substance to the Unknown, and monsters are among the most useful tools they have for shaping it into nightmarish creations that capture our worst fears and strike terror into the hearts of readers. *M is for Monster* is a celebration of the many varieties of monster that horror writers have imagined into being. In its pages, you will find twenty-six of the most horrifying monsters ever conceived of on the printed page, and brought to life as only some of the most inventive writers of horror fiction in the last two centuries could achieve. Insofar as each of these monsters represents a species whose name begins with a different letter of the alphabet, the volume serves as a basic bestiary or field guide to horror literature's most frightening fauna.

Indeed, some of the creatures abroad in this book are genuine fauna, made monstrous by circumstances of their stories. In "The Valley of Spiders," H.G. Wells plays upon the average person's squeamishness about spiders. If one spider is unsettling, he speculates, imagine an entire wilderness full of spiders that have grown to somewhat larger than normal size. The creature in Morgan Robertson's "From the Darkness and the Depths" is an entity of genuine biological reality, though sailors feared it as a sea monster long before the age of scientific enlightenment. In "The Purple Terror," Fred M. White evokes the monstrous by endowing exotic flora with the habits of predatory fauna.

Just as some of these monsters have one foot (or other appendage) firmly planted in the natural world, so do others have an existence that significantly predates their treatment in horror fiction. It says much about us as a species that many of the most fearsome monsters in this volume are creatures of myth and legend distilled from folktales that the respective cultures that told them believed to be true. The air elemental known as the Wendigo in Algernon Blackwood's tale of the same name is one of the pantheon of supernatural beings in Native North American lore. Though never actually described in the story, the Wendigo manifests through unearthly sounds and smells, and its monstrousness is unmistakable in the terrifying transformations it inflicts on human victims. Likewise, the ghoulish creature in Lafacadio Hearn's "Jikininki" is an entity well-known in eastern folklore, while the more benign creature in Robert Louis Stevenson's "The Bottle Imp" will be instantly recognized as belonging to the same family of fantastic beings most readers know from the tale of Aladdin and his lamp in the *Arabian Nights.* In his "Novel of the Black Seal," Arthur Machen looks to the lore and legendry of the British Isles pertaining to the "little people," and suggests that the charming fairy tales about them that have come down to us through the ages are garblings that have obscured the truth about their utter malignity.

The majority of stories in this volume were written in the late nineteenth and early twentieth centuries, arguably the golden age of the monster tale. It was in these decades that horror's iconic monsters came into being and flourished under a variety of guises that even non-horror readers would recognize. The animated mummy in Arthur Conan Doyle's "Lot No. 249," the werewolf in Bernard Capes's "The Thing in the Forest," and the zombies in Vivian Meik's "White Zombie" cut the same figures in these stories as they do in cinematic depictions that entertained mass audiences beginning in the 1930s. Somewhat less familiar are Ulric Daubeny's treatment of the vampire in "The Sumach," in which the vampire assumes a form *not* struck from the template established by Bram Stoker's *Dracula* only two decades earlier. The best writers of ghost fiction were especially inventive in finding interesting and unusual approaches to their themes, and both J. Sheridan Le Fanu, in "Squire Toby's Will," and M.R. James, in "The Ash-Tree," find particularly imaginative ways to suggest the ghostly without showing ghosts themselves.

In his study *The Philosophy of Horror,* Noel Carroll defines the monster of horror fiction and film as "a being in violation of the natural order, where the perimeter of the natural order is determined by contemporary science." No story in this volume more thoroughly expresses the idea of the monster as a travesty of nature than H.P. Lovecraft's "The Call of Cthulhu," whose monster, which exists outside of space or time as humankind understands it, appears as a gross violation of the natural order as known by human science. Where Lovecraft attempts to give the incomprehensibility of the monstrous a describable appearance, Ambrose Bierce, in "The Damned Thing," and Barry Pain, in "The Tower," enjoin readers to employ their imaginations in envisioning what shape monsters invisible to the naked eye might take, based on the carnage and destruction they cause.

So here you have a veritable zoo-full of wild and weird monsters that literally run the gamut from A to Z. Some are grotesque distortions of familiar human, animal, or plant forms. Others are notable for how thoroughly they deviate from the norms by which we classify natural life. It is worth keeping in mind, as you acquaint yourself with the monsters that populate this book, that ultimately our measure of the monstrous is a measure of ourselves—how we look, what we know, and how horrifyingly different some things can be from those parameters. Perhaps the monsters in these pages are so frightening because they show us the limits of our understanding about just what strange life forms the world as we know it *might* support.

MICHAEL KELAHAN
New York, 2011

A is for Alien

The stories of American writer H.P. Lovecraft (1890–1937) abound with alien monsters and extradimensional life-forms that are more indifferent than hostile to the human beings who are unfortunate enough to cross their paths. This story, first published in the February 1928 issue of *Weird Tales*, fuses elements of supernatural fiction and science fiction for a story type that Lovecraft referred to as the tale of cosmic horror. Inasmuch as it lays the foundations of the myth pattern uniting Lovecraft's stories that has come to be known as the Cthulhu Mythos, it is regarded as one of the most important horror stories of the twentieth century.

H.P. LOVECRAFT

The Call of Cthulhu

(Found among the papers of the late Francis Wayland Thurston, of Boston)

"Of such great powers or beings there may be conceivably a survival. . .a survival of a hugely remote period when. . .consciousness was manifested, perhaps, in shapes and forms long since withdrawn before the tide of advancing humanity. . .forms of which poetry and legend alone have caught a flying memory and called them gods, monsters, mythical beings of all sorts and kinds. . . ."

—ALGERNON BLACKWOOD

I
The Horror in Clay

The most merciful thing in the world, I think, is the inability of the human mind to correlate all its contents. We live on a placid island of ignorance in the midst of black seas of infinity, and it was not meant that we should voyage far. The sciences, each straining in its own direction, have hitherto harmed us little; but some day the piecing together of dissociated knowledge will open up such terrifying vistas of reality, and of our frightful position therein, that we shall either go mad from the revelation or flee from the deadly light into the peace and safety of a new dark age.

Theosophists have guessed at the awesome grandeur of the cosmic cycle wherein our world and human race form transient incidents. They have hinted at strange survivals in terms which would freeze the blood if not masked by a bland optimism. But it is not from them that there came the single glimpse of forbidden aeons which chills me when I think of it and maddens me when I dream of it. That glimpse, like all dread glimpses of truth, flashed out from an accidental piecing together of separated things—in this case an old newspaper item and the notes of a dead professor. I hope that no one else will accomplish this piecing out; certainly, if I live, I shall never knowingly supply a link in so hideous a chain. I think that the professor, too, intended to keep silent regarding the part he knew, and that he would have destroyed his notes had not sudden death seized him.

My knowledge of the thing began in the winter of 1926–27 with the death of my grand-uncle George Gammell Angell, Professor Emeritus of Semitic Languages in Brown University, Providence, Rhode Island. Professor Angell was widely known as an authority on ancient inscriptions, and had frequently been resorted to by the heads of prominent museums; so that his passing at the age of ninety-two may be recalled by many. Locally, interest was intensified by the obscurity of the cause of death. The professor had been stricken whilst returning from the Newport boat; falling suddenly, as witnesses said, after having been jostled by a nautical-looking negro who had come from one of the queer dark courts on the precipitous hillside which formed a short cut from the waterfront to the deceased's home in Williams Street. Physicians were unable to find any visible disorder, but concluded after perplexed debate that some obscure lesion of the heart, induced by the brisk ascent of so steep a hill by so elderly a man, was responsible for the end. At the time I saw no reason to dissent from this dictum, but latterly I am inclined to wonder—and more than wonder.

As my grand-uncle's heir and executor, for he died a childless widower, I was expected to go over his papers with some thoroughness; and for that purpose moved his entire set of files and boxes to my quarters in Boston. Much of the material which I correlated will be later published by the American Archaeological Society, but there was one box which I found exceedingly puzzling, and which I felt much averse from shewing to other eyes. It had been locked, and I did not find the key till it occurred to me to examine the personal ring which the professor carried always in his pocket. Then indeed I succeeded in opening it, but when I did so seemed only to be confronted by a greater and more closely locked barrier. For what could be the meaning of the queer clay bas-relief and the disjointed jottings, ramblings, and cuttings which I found? Had my uncle, in his latter years, become credulous of the most superficial impostures? I resolved to search out the eccentric sculptor responsible for this apparent disturbance of an old man's peace of mind.

The bas-relief was a rough rectangle less than an inch thick and about five by six inches in area; obviously of modern origin. Its designs, however, were far from modern in atmosphere and suggestion; for although the vagaries of cubism and futurism are many and wild, they do not often reproduce that cryptic regularity which lurks in prehistoric writing. And writing of some kind the bulk of these designs seemed certainly to be; though my memory, despite much familiarity with the papers and collections of my uncle, failed in any way to identify this particular species, or even to hint at its remotest affiliations.

Above these apparent hieroglyphics was a figure of evidently pictorial intent, though its impressionistic execution forbade a very clear idea of its nature. It seemed to be a sort of monster, or symbol representing a monster, of a form which only a diseased fancy could conceive. If I say that my somewhat extravagant imagination yielded simultaneous pictures of an octopus, a dragon, and a human caricature, I shall not be unfaithful to the spirit of the thing. A pulpy, tentacled head surmounted a grotesque and scaly body with rudimentary wings; but it was the *general outline* of the whole which made it most shockingly frightful. Behind the figure was a vague suggestion of a Cyclopean architectural background.

The writing accompanying this oddity was, aside from a stack of press cuttings, in Professor Angell's most recent hand; and made no pretence to literary style. What seemed to be the main document was headed "CTHULHU CULT" in characters painstakingly printed to avoid the erroneous reading of a word so unheard-of. The manuscript was divided into two sections, the first of which was headed "1925—Dream and Dream Work of H. A. Wilcox, 7 Thomas St., Providence, R.I.", and the second, "Narrative of Inspector John R. Legrasse, 121 Bienville St., New Orleans, La., at 1908 A. A. S. Mtg.—Notes on Same, & Prof. Webb's Acct." The other manuscript papers were all brief notes, some of them accounts of the queer dreams of different persons, some of them citations from theosophical books and magazines (notably W. Scott-Elliot's *Atlantis and the Lost Lemuria*), and the rest comments on long-surviving secret societies and hidden cults, with references to passages in such mythological and anthropological source-books as Frazer's *Golden Bough* and Miss Murray's *Witch-Cult in Western Europe*. The cuttings largely alluded to outré, mental illnesses and outbreaks of group folly or mania in the spring of 1925.

The first half of the principal manuscript told a very peculiar tale. It appears that on March 1st, 1925, a thin, dark young man of neurotic and excited aspect had called upon Professor Angell bearing the singular clay bas-relief, which was then exceedingly damp and fresh. His card bore the name of Henry Anthony Wilcox, and my uncle had recognised him as the youngest son of an excellent family slightly known to him, who had latterly been studying sculpture at the Rhode Island School of Design and living alone at the Fleur-de-Lys Building near that institution. Wilcox was a precocious youth of known genius but great eccentricity, and had from childhood excited attention through the strange stories and odd dreams he was in the habit of relating. He called himself "psychically hypersensitive," but the staid folk of the ancient commercial city dismissed him as merely "queer." Never mingling much with his kind, he had dropped gradually from social visibility, and was now known only to a small group of aesthetes from other towns. Even the Providence Art Club, anxious to preserve its conservatism, had found him quite hopeless.

On the occasion of the visit, ran the professor's manuscript, the sculptor abruptly asked for the benefit of his host's archaeological knowledge in identifying the hieroglyphics on the bas-relief. He spoke in a dreamy, stilted manner which suggested pose and alienated sympathy; and my uncle shewed some sharpness in replying, for the conspicuous freshness of the tablet implied kinship with anything but archaeology. Young Wilcox's rejoinder, which impressed my uncle enough to make him recall and record it verbatim, was of a fantastically poetic cast which must have typified his whole conversation, and which I have since found highly characteristic of him. He said, "It is new, indeed, for I made it last night in a dream of strange cities; and dreams are older than brooding Tyre, or the contemplative Sphinx, or garden-girdled Babylon."

It was then that he began that rambling tale which suddenly played upon a sleeping memory and won the fevered interest of my uncle. There had been a slight earthquake tremor the night before, the most considerable felt in New England for some years; and Wilcox's imagination had been keenly affected. Upon retiring, he had had an unprecedented dream of great Cyclopean cities of titan blocks and sky-flung monoliths, all dripping with green ooze and sinister with latent horror. Hieroglyphics had covered the walls and pillars, and from some undetermined point below had come a voice that was not a voice; a chaotic sensation which only fancy could transmute into sound, but which he attempted to render by the almost unpronounceable jumble of letters, *"Cthulhu fhtagn."*

This verbal jumble was the key to the recollection which excited and disturbed Professor Angell. He questioned the sculptor with scientific minuteness; and studied with almost frantic intensity the bas-relief on which the youth had found himself working, chilled and clad only in his night-clothes, when waking had stolen bewilderingly over him. My uncle blamed his old age, Wilcox afterward said, for his slowness in recognising both hieroglyphics and pictorial design. Many of his questions seemed highly out-of-place to his visitor, especially those which tried to connect the latter with strange cults or societies; and Wilcox could not understand the repeated promises of silence which he was offered in exchange for an admission of membership in some widespread mystical or paganly religious body. When Professor Angell became convinced that the sculptor was indeed ignorant of any cult or system of cryptic lore, he besieged his visitor with demands for future reports of dreams. This bore regular fruit, for after the first interview the manuscript records daily calls of the young man, during which he related startling fragments of nocturnal imagery whose burden was always some terrible Cyclopean vista of dark and dripping stone, with a subterrene voice or intelligence shouting monotonously in enigmatical sense-impacts unin-scribable save as gibberish. The two sounds most frequently repeated are those rendered by the letters "Cthulhu" and "R'lyeh."

On March 23d, the manuscript continued, Wilcox failed to appear; and inquiries at his quarters revealed that he had been stricken with an obscure sort of fever and taken to the home of his family in Waterman Street. He had cried out in the night, arousing several other artists in the building, and had manifested since then only alternations of unconsciousness and delirium. My uncle at once telephoned the family, and from that time forward kept close watch of the case; calling often at the Thayer Street office of Dr. Tobey, whom he learned to be in charge. The youth's febrile mind, apparently, was dwelling on strange things; and the doctor shuddered now and then as he spoke of them. They included not only a repetition of what he had formerly dreamed, but touched wildly on a gigantic thing "miles high" which walked or lumbered about. He at no time fully described this object, but occasional frantic words, as repeated by Dr. Tobey, convinced the professor that it must be identical with the nameless monstrosity he had sought to depict in his dream-sculpture. Reference to this object, the doctor added, was invariably a prelude to the young man's subsidence into lethargy. His temperature, oddly enough, was not greatly above normal; but his whole condition was other-wise such as to suggest true fever rather than mental disorder.

On April 2nd at about 3 p.m. every trace of Wilcox's malady suddenly ceased. He sat upright in bed, astonished to find himself at home and com-pletely ignorant of what had happened in dream or reality since the night of March 22nd. Pronounced well by his physician, he returned to his quarters in three days; but to Professor Angell he was of no further assistance. All traces of strange dreaming had vanished with his recovery, and my uncle kept no record of his night-thoughts after a week of pointless and irrelevant accounts of thoroughly usual visions.

Here the first part of the manuscript ended, but references to certain of the scattered notes gave me much material for thought—so much, in fact, that only the ingrained scepticism then forming my philosophy can account for my continued distrust of the artist. The notes in question were those descriptive of the dreams of various persons covering the same period as that in which young Wilcox had had his strange visitations. My uncle, it seems, had quickly instituted a prodigiously far-flung body of inquiries amongst nearly all the friends whom he could question without impertinence, asking for nightly reports of their dreams, and the dates of any notable visions for some time past. The reception of his request seems to have been varied; but he must, at the very least, have received more responses than any ordinary man could have handled without a secretary. This original correspondence was not preserved, but his notes formed a thorough and really significant digest. Average people in society and business—New England's traditional "salt of the earth"—gave an almost completely negative result, though scattered cases of uneasy but formless nocturnal impressions appear here and there, always between March 23d and April 2nd—the period of young Wilcox's delirium. Scientific men were little more affected, though four cases of vague description suggest fugitive glimpses of strange landscapes, and in one case there is mentioned a dread of something abnormal.

It was from the artists and poets that the pertinent answers came, and I know that panic would have broken loose had they been able to compare notes. As it was, lacking their original letters, I half suspected the compiler of having asked leading questions, or of having edited the correspondence in corroboration of what he had latently resolved to see. That is why I continued to feel that Wilcox, somehow cognisant of the old data which my uncle had possessed, had been imposing on the veteran scientist. These responses from aesthetes told a disturbing tale. From February 28th to April 2nd a large proportion of them had dreamed very bizarre things, the intensity of the dreams being immeasurably the stronger during the period of the sculptor's delirium. Over a fourth of those who reported anything, reported scenes and half-sounds not unlike those which Wilcox had described; and some of the dreamers confessed acute fear of the gigantic nameless thing visible toward the last. One case, which the note describes with emphasis, was very sad. The subject, a widely known architect with leanings toward theosophy and occultism, went violently insane on the date of young Wilcox's seizure, and expired several months later after incessant screamings to be saved from some escaped denizen of hell. Had my uncle referred to these cases by name instead of merely by number, I should have attempted some corroboration and personal investigation; but as it was, I succeeded in tracing down only a few. All of these, however, bore out the notes in full. I have often wondered if all the objects of the professor's questioning felt as puzzled as did this fraction. It is well that no explanation shall ever reach them.

The press cuttings, as I have intimated, touched on cases of panic, mania, and eccentricity during the given period. Professor Angell must have employed a cutting bureau, for the number of extracts was tremendous and the sources scattered throughout the globe. Here was a nocturnal suicide in London, where a lone sleeper had leaped from a window after a shocking cry. Here likewise a rambling letter to the editor of a paper in South America, where a fanatic deduces a dire future from visions he has seen. A despatch from California describes a theosophist colony as donning white robes en masse for some "glorious fulfilment" which never arrives, whilst items from India speak guardedly of serious native unrest toward the end of March. Voodoo orgies multiply in Hayti, and African outposts report ominous mutterings. American officers in the Philippines find certain tribes bothersome about this time, and New York policemen are mobbed by hysterical Levantines on the night of March 22–23. The west of Ireland, too, is full of wild rumour and legendry, and a fantastic painter named Ardois-Bonnot hangs a blasphemous "Dream Landscape" in the Paris spring salon of 1926. And so numerous are the recorded troubles in insane asylums, that only a miracle can have stopped the medical fraternity from noting strange parallelisms and drawing mystified conclusions. A weird bunch of cuttings, all told; and I can at this date scarcely envisage the callous rationalism with which I set them aside. But I was then convinced that young Wilcox had known of the older matters mentioned by the professor.

II
The Tale of Inspector Legrasse

The older matters which had made the sculptor's dream and bas-relief so significant to my uncle formed the subject of the second half of his long manuscript. Once before, it appears, Professor Angell had seen the hellish outlines of the nameless monstrosity, puzzled over the unknown hieroglyphics, and heard the ominous syllables which can be rendered only as *"Cthulhu"*; and all this in so stirring and horrible a connexion that it is small wonder he pursued young Wilcox with queries and demands for data.

The earlier experience had come in 1908, seventeen years before, when the American Archaeological Society held its annual meeting in St. Louis.

Professor Angell, as befitted one of his authority and attainments, had had a prominent part in all the deliberations; and was one of the first to be approached by the several outsiders who took advantage of the convocation to offer questions for correct answering and problems for expert solution.

The chief of these outsiders, and in a short time the focus of interest for the entire meeting, was a commonplace-looking middle-aged man who had travelled all the way from New Orleans for certain special information unobtainable from any local source. His name was John Raymond Legrasse, and he was by profession an Inspector of Police. With him he bore the subject of his visit, a grotesque, repulsive, and apparently very ancient stone statuette whose origin he was at a loss to determine. It must not be fancied that Inspector Legrasse had the least interest in archaeology. On the contrary, his wish for enlightenment was prompted by purely professional considerations. The statuette, idol, fetish, or whatever it was, had been captured some months before in the wooded swamps south of New Orleans during a raid on a supposed voodoo meeting; and so singular and hideous were the rites connected with it, that the police could not but realise that they had stumbled on a dark cult totally unknown to them, and infinitely more diabolic than even the blackest of the African voodoo circles. Of its origin, apart from the erratic and unbelievable tales extorted from the captured members, absolutely nothing was to be discovered; hence the anxiety of the police for any antiquarian lore which might help them to place the frightful symbol, and through it track down the cult to its fountain-head.

Inspector Legrasse was scarcely prepared for the sensation which his offering created. One sight of the thing had been enough to throw the assembled men of science into a state of tense excitement, and they lost no time in crowding around him to gaze at the diminutive figure whose utter strangeness and air of genuinely abysmal antiquity hinted so potently at unopened and archaic vistas. No recognised school of sculpture had animated this terrible object, yet centuries and even thousands of years seemed recorded in its dim and greenish surface of unplaceable stone.

The figure, which was finally passed slowly from man to man for close and careful study, was between seven and eight inches in height, and of exquisitely artistic workmanship. It represented a monster of vaguely anthropoid outline, but with an octopus-like head whose face was a mass of feelers, a scaly, rubbery-looking body, prodigious claws on hind and fore feet, and long, narrow wings behind. This thing, which seemed instinct with a fearsome and unnatural malignancy, was of a somewhat bloated corpulence, and squatted evilly on a rectangular block or pedestal covered with undecipherable characters. The tips of the wings touched the back edge of the block, the seat occupied the centre, whilst the long, curved claws of the doubled-up, crouching hind legs gripped the front edge and extended a quarter of the way down toward the bottom of the pedestal. The cephalopod head was bent forward, so that the ends of the facial feelers brushed the backs of huge fore paws which clasped the croucher's elevated knees. The aspect of the whole was abnormally life-like, and the more subtly fearful because its source was so totally unknown. Its vast, awesome, and incalculable age was unmistakable; yet not one link did it shew with any known type of art belonging to civilisation's youth—or indeed to any other time. Totally separate and apart, its very material was a mystery; for the soapy, greenish-black stone with its golden or iridescent flecks and striations resembled nothing familiar to geology or mineralogy. The characters along the base were equally baffling; and no member present, despite a representation of half the world's expert learning in this field, could form the least notion of even their remotest linguistic kinship. They, like the subject and material, belonged to something horribly remote and distinct from mankind as we know it; something frightfully suggestive of old and unhallowed cycles of life in which our world and our conceptions have no part.

And yet, as the members severally shook their heads and confessed defeat at the Inspector's problem, there was one man in that gathering who suspected a touch of bizarre familiarity in the monstrous shape and writing, and who presently told with some diffidence of the odd trifle he knew. This person was the late William Channing Webb, Professor of Anthropology in Princeton University, and an explorer of no slight note. Professor Webb had been engaged, forty-eight years before, in a tour of Greenland and Iceland in search of some Runic inscriptions which he failed to unearth; and whilst high up on the West Greenland coast had encountered a singular tribe or cult of degenerate Esquimaux whose religion, a curious form of devil-worship, chilled him with its deliberate bloodthirstiness and repulsiveness. It was a faith of which other Esquimaux knew little, and which they mentioned only with shudders, saying that it had come down from horribly ancient aeons before ever the world was made. Besides nameless rites and human sacrifices there were certain queer hereditary rituals addressed to a supreme elder devil or *tornasuk*; and of this Professor Webb had taken a careful phonetic copy from an aged *angekok* or wizard-priest, expressing the sounds in Roman letters as best he knew how. But just now of prime significance was the fetish which this cult had cherished, and around which they danced when the aurora leaped high over the ice cliffs. It was, the professor stated, a very crude bas-relief of stone, comprising a hideous picture and some cryptic writing. And so far as he could tell, it was a rough parallel in all essential features of the bestial thing now lying before the meeting.

This data, received with suspense and astonishment by the assembled members, proved doubly exciting to Inspector Legrasse; and he began at once to ply his informant with questions. Having noted and copied an oral ritual among the swamp cult-worshippers his men had arrested, he besought the professor to remember as best he might the syllables taken down amongst the diabolist Esquimaux. There then followed an exhaustive comparison of details, and a moment of really awed silence when both detective and scientist agreed on the virtual identity of the phrase common to two hellish rituals so many worlds of distance apart. What, in substance, both the Esquimaux wizards and the Louisiana swamp-priests had chanted to their kindred idols was something very like this—the word-divisions being guessed at from traditional breaks in the phrase as chanted aloud:

"Ph'nglui mglw'nafh Cthulhu R'lyeh wgah'nagl fhtagn."

Legrasse had one point in advance of Professor Webb, for several among his mongrel prisoners had repeated to him what older celebrants had told them the words meant. This text, as given, ran something like this:

"In his house at R'lyeh dead Cthulhu waits dreaming."

And now, in response to a general and urgent demand, Inspector Legrasse related as fully as possible his experience with the swamp worshippers; telling a story to which I could see my uncle attached profound significance. It savoured of the wildest dreams of myth-maker and theosophist, and disclosed an astonishing degree of cosmic imagination among such half-castes and pariahs as might be least expected to possess it.

On November 1st, 1907, there had come to the New Orleans police a frantic summons from the swamp and lagoon country to the south. The squatters there, mostly primitive but good-natured descendants of Lafitte's men, were in the grip of stark terror from an unknown thing which had stolen upon them in the night. It was voodoo, apparently, but voodoo of a more terrible sort than they had ever known; and some of their women and children had disappeared since the malevolent tom-tom had begun its incessant beating far within the black haunted woods where no dweller ventured. There were insane shouts and harrowing screams, soul-chilling chants and dancing devil-flames; and, the frightened messenger added, the people could stand it no more.

So a body of twenty police, filling two carriages and an automobile, had set out in the late afternoon with the shivering squatter as a guide. At the end of the passable road they alighted, and for miles splashed on in silence through the terrible cypress woods where day never came. Ugly roots and malignant hanging nooses of Spanish moss beset them, and now and then a pile of dank stones or fragment of a rotting wall intensified by its hint of morbid habitation a depression which every malformed tree and every fungous islet combined to create. At length the squatter settlement, a miserable huddle of huts, hove in sight; and hysterical dwellers ran out to cluster around the group of bobbing lanterns. The muffled beat of tom-toms was now faintly audible far, far ahead; and a curdling shriek came at infrequent intervals when the wind shifted. A reddish glare, too, seemed to filter through the pale undergrowth beyond endless avenues of forest night. Reluctant even to be left alone again, each one of the cowed squatters refused point-blank to advance another inch toward the scene of unholy worship, so Inspector Legrasse and his nineteen colleagues plunged on unguided into black arcades of horror that none of them had ever trod before.

The region now entered by the police was one of traditionally evil repute, substantially unknown and untraversed by white men. There were legends of a hidden lake unglimpsed by mortal sight, in which dwelt a huge, formless white polypous thing with luminous eyes; and squatters whispered that bat-winged devils flew up out of caverns in inner earth to worship it at midnight. They said it had been there before D'Iberville, before La Salle, before the Indians, and before even the wholesome beasts and birds of the woods. It was nightmare itself, and to see it was to die. But it made men dream, and so they knew enough to keep away. The present voodoo orgy was, indeed, on the merest fringe of this abhorred area, but that location was bad enough; hence perhaps the very place of the worship had terrified the squatters more than the shocking sounds and incidents.

Only poetry or madness could do justice to the noises heard by Legrasse's men as they ploughed on through the black morass toward the red glare and the muffled tom-toms. There are vocal qualities peculiar to men, and vocal qualities peculiar to beasts; and it is terrible to hear the one when the source should yield the other. Animal fury and orgiastic licence here whipped themselves to daemoniac heights by howls and squawking ecstasies that tore and reverberated through those nighted woods like pestilential tempests from the gulfs of hell. Now and then the less organised ululation would cease, and from what seemed a well-drilled chorus of hoarse voices would rise in sing-song chant that hideous phrase or ritual:

"Ph'nglui mglw'nafh Cthulhu R'lyeh wgah'nagl fhtagn."

Then the men, having reached a spot where the trees were thinner, came suddenly in sight of the spectacle itself. Four of them reeled, one fainted, and two were shaken into a frantic cry which the mad cacophony of the orgy fortunately deadened. Legrasse dashed swamp water on the face of the fainting man, and all stood trembling and nearly hypnotised with horror.

In a natural glade of the swamp stood a grassy island of perhaps an acre's extent, clear of trees and tolerably dry. On this now leaped and twisted a more indescribable horde of human abnormality than any but a Sime or an Angarola could paint. Void of clothing, this hybrid spawn were braying, bellowing, and writhing about a monstrous ring-shaped bonfire; in the centre of which, revealed by occasional rifts in the curtain of flame, stood a great granite monolith some eight feet in height; on top of which, incongruous with its diminutiveness, rested the noxious carven statuette. From a wide circle of ten scaffolds set up at regular intervals with the flame-girt monolith as a centre hung, head downward, the oddly marred bodies of the helpless squatters who had disappeared. It was inside this circle that the ring of worshippers jumped and roared, the general direction of the mass motion being from left to right in endless Bacchanal between the ring of bodies and the ring of fire.

It may have been only imagination and it may have been only echoes which induced one of the men, an excitable Spaniard, to fancy he heard antiphonal responses to the ritual from some far and unillumined spot deeper within the wood of ancient legendry and horror. This man, Joseph D. Galvez, I later met and questioned; and he proved distractingly imaginative. He indeed went so far as to hint of the faint beating of great wings, and of a glimpse of shining eyes and a mountainous white bulk beyond the remotest trees—but I suppose he had been hearing too much native superstition.

Actually, the horrified pause of the men was of comparatively brief duration. Duty came first; and although there must have been nearly a hundred mongrel celebrants in the throng, the police relied on their firearms and plunged determinedly into the nauseous rout. For five minutes the resultant din and chaos were beyond description. Wild blows were struck, shots were fired, and escapes were made; but in the end Legrasse was able to count some forty-seven sullen prisoners, whom he forced to dress in haste and fall into line between two rows of policemen. Five of the worshippers lay dead, and two severely wounded ones were carried away on improvised stretchers by their fellow-prisoners. The image on the monolith, of course, was carefully removed and carried back by Legrasse.

Examined at headquarters after a trip of intense strain and weariness, the prisoners all proved to be men of a very low, mixed-blooded, and mentally aberrant type. Most were seamen, and a sprinkling of negroes and mulattoes, largely West Indians or Brava Portuguese from the Cape Verde Islands, gave a colouring of voodooism to the heterogeneous cult. But before many questions were asked, it became manifest that something far deeper and older than negro fetichism was involved. Degraded and ignorant as they were, the creatures held with surprising consistency to the central idea of their loathsome faith.

They worshipped, so they said, the Great Old Ones who lived ages before there were any men, and who came to the young world out of the sky. Those Old Ones were gone now, inside the earth and under the sea; but their dead bodies had told their secrets in dreams to the first men, who formed a cult which had never died. This was that cult, and the prisoners said it had always existed and always would exist, hidden in distant wastes and dark places all over the world until the time when the great priest Cthulhu, from his dark house in the mighty city of R'lyeh under the waters, should rise and bring the earth again beneath his sway. Some day he would call, when the stars were ready, and the secret cult would always be waiting to liberate him.

Meanwhile no more must be told. There was a secret which even torture could not extract. Mankind was not absolutely alone among the conscious things of earth, for shapes came out of the dark to visit the faithful few. But these were not the Great Old Ones. No man had ever seen the Old Ones.

The carven idol was great Cthulhu, but none might say whether or not the others were precisely like him. No one could read the old writing now, but things were told by word of mouth. The chanted ritual was not the secret—that was never spoken aloud, only whispered. The chant meant only this: "In his house at R'lyeh dead Cthulhu waits dreaming."

Only two of the prisoners were found sane enough to be hanged, and the rest were committed to various institutions. All denied a part in the ritual murders, and averred that the killing had been done by Black Winged Ones which had come to them from their immemorial meeting-place in the haunted wood. But of those mysterious allies no coherent account could ever be gained. What the police did extract, came mainly from an immensely aged mestizo named Castro, who claimed to have sailed to strange ports and talked with undying leaders of the cult in the mountains of China.

Old Castro remembered bits of hideous legend that paled the speculations of theosophists and made man and the world seem recent and transient indeed. There had been aeons when other Things ruled on the earth, and They had had great cities. Remains of Them, he said the deathless Chinamen had told him, were still to be found as Cyclopean stones on islands in the Pacific. They all died vast epochs of time before men came, but there were arts which could revive Them when the stars had come round again to the right positions in the cycle of eternity. They had, indeed, come themselves from the stars, and brought Their images with Them.

These Great Old Ones, Castro continued, were not composed altogether of flesh and blood. They had shape—for did not this star-fashioned image prove it?—but that shape was not made of matter. When the stars were right, They could plunge from world to world through the sky; but when the stars were wrong, They could not live. But although They no longer lived, They would never really die. They all lay in stone houses in Their great city of R'lyeh, preserved by the spells of mighty Cthulhu for a glorious resurrection when the stars and the earth might once more be ready for Them. But at that time some force from outside must serve to liberate Their bodies. The spells that preserved Them intact likewise prevented Them from making an initial move, and They could only lie awake in the dark and think whilst uncounted millions of years rolled by. They knew all that was occurring in the universe, but Their mode of speech was transmitted thought. Even now They talked in Their tombs. When, after infinities of chaos, the first men came, the Great Old Ones spoke to the sensitive among them by moulding their dreams; for only thus could Their language reach the fleshly minds of mammals.

Then, whispered Castro, those first men formed the cult around small idols which the Great Ones shewed them; idols brought in dim aeras from dark stars. That cult would never die till the stars came right again, and the secret priests would take great Cthulhu from His tomb to revive His subjects and resume His rule of earth. The time would be easy to know, for then mankind would have become as the Great Old Ones; free and wild and beyond good and evil, with laws and morals thrown aside and all men shouting and killing and revelling in joy. Then the liberated Old Ones would teach them new ways to shout and kill and revel and enjoy themselves, and all the earth would flame with a holocaust of ecstasy and freedom. Meanwhile the cult, by appropriate rites, must keep alive the memory of those ancient ways and shadow forth the prophecy of their return.

In the elder time chosen men had talked with the entombed Old Ones in dreams, but then something had happened. The great stone city R'lyeh, with its monoliths and sepulchres, had sunk beneath the waves; and the deep waters, full of the one primal mystery through which not even thought can pass, had cut off the spectral intercourse. But memory never died, and high-priests said that the city would rise again when the stars were right. Then came out of the earth the black spirits of earth, mouldy and shadowy, and full of dim rumours picked up in caverns beneath forgotten sea-bottoms. But of them old Castro dared not speak much. He cut himself off hurriedly, and no amount of persuasion or subtlety could elicit more in this direction. The size of the Old Ones, too, he curiously declined to mention. Of the cult, he said that he thought the centre lay amid the pathless deserts of Arabia, where Irem, the City of Pillars, dreams hidden and untouched. It was not allied to the European witch-cult, and was virtually unknown beyond its members. No book had ever really hinted of it, though the deathless Chinamen said that there were double meanings in the Necronomicon of the mad Arab Abdul Alhazred which the initiated might read as they chose, especially the much-discussed couplet:

"That is not dead which can eternal lie,
And with strange aeons even death may die."

Legrasse, deeply impressed and not a little bewildered, had inquired in vain concerning the historic affiliations of the cult. Castro, apparently, had told the truth when he said that it was wholly secret. The authorities at Tulane University could shed no light upon either cult or image, and now the detective had come to the highest authorities in the country and met with no more than the Greenland tale of Professor Webb.

The feverish interest aroused at the meeting by Legrasse's tale, corroborated as it was by the statuette, is echoed in the subsequent correspondence of those who attended; although scant mention occurs in the formal publications of the society. Caution is the first care of those accustomed to face occasional charlatanry and imposture. Legrasse for some time lent the image to Professor Webb, but at the latter's death it was returned to him and remains in his possession, where I viewed it not long ago. It is truly a terrible thing, and unmistakably akin to the dream-sculpture of young Wilcox.

That my uncle was excited by the tale of the sculptor I did not wonder, for what thoughts must arise upon hearing, after a knowledge of what Legrasse had learned of the cult, of a sensitive young man who had *dreamed* not only the figure and exact hieroglyphics of the swamp-found image and the Greenland devil tablet, but had come *in his dreams* upon at least three of the precise words of the formula uttered alike by Esquimaux diabolists and mongrel Louisianans? Professor Angell's instant start on an investigation of the utmost thoroughness was eminently natural; though privately I suspected young Wilcox of having heard of the cult in some indirect way, and of having invented a series of dreams to heighten and continue the mystery at my uncle's expense. The dream-narratives and cuttings collected by the professor were, of course, strong corroboration; but the rationalism of my mind and the extravagance of the whole subject led me to adopt what I thought the most sensible conclusions. So, after thoroughly studying the manuscript again and correlating the theosophical and anthropological notes with the cult narrative of Legrasse, I made a trip to Providence to see the sculptor and give him the rebuke I thought proper for so boldly imposing upon a learned and aged man.

Wilcox still lived alone in the Fleur-de-Lys Building in Thomas Street, a hideous Victorian imitation of seventeenth-century Breton architecture which flaunts its stuccoed front amidst the lovely colonial houses on the ancient hill, and under the very shadow of the finest Georgian steeple in America. I found him at work in his rooms, and at once conceded from the specimens scattered about that his genius is indeed profound and authentic. He will, I believe, some time be heard from as one of the great decadents; for he has crystallised in clay and will one day mirror in marble those nightmares and phantasies which Arthur Machen evokes in prose, and Clark Ashton Smith makes visible in verse and in painting.

Dark, frail, and somewhat unkempt in aspect, he turned languidly at my knock and asked me my business without rising. When I told him who I was, he displayed some interest; for my uncle had excited his curiosity in probing his strange dreams, yet had never explained the reason for the study. I did not enlarge his knowledge in this regard, but sought with some subtlety to draw him out. In a short time I became convinced of his absolute sincerity, for he spoke of the dreams in a manner none could mistake. They and their subconscious residuum had influenced his art profoundly, and he shewed me a morbid statue whose contours almost made me shake with the potency of its black suggestion. He could not recall having seen the original of this thing except in his own dream bas-relief, but the outlines had formed themselves insensibly under his hands. It was, no doubt, the giant shape he had raved of in delirium. That he really knew nothing of the hidden cult, save from what my uncle's relentless catechism had let fall, he soon made clear; and again I strove to think of some way in which he could possibly have received the weird impressions.

He talked of his dreams in a strangely poetic fashion; making me see with terrible vividness the damp Cyclopean city of slimy green stone—whose geometry, he oddly said, was *all wrong*—and hear with frightened expectancy the ceaseless, half-mental calling from underground: *"Cthulhu fhtagn," "Cthulhu fhtagn."* These words had formed part of that dread ritual which told of dead Cthulhu's dream-vigil in his stone vault at R'lyeh, and I felt deeply moved despite my rational beliefs. Wilcox, I was sure, had heard of the cult in some casual way, and had soon forgotten it amidst the mass of his equally weird reading and imagining. Later, by virtue of its sheer impressiveness, it had found subconscious expression in dreams, in the bas-relief, and in the terrible statue I now beheld; so that his imposture upon my uncle had been a very innocent one. The youth was of a type, at once slightly affected and slightly ill-mannered, which I could never like; but I was willing enough now to admit both his genius and his honesty. I took leave of him amicably, and wish him all the success his talent promises.

The matter of the cult still remained to fascinate me, and at times I had visions of personal fame from researches into its origin and connexions. I visited New Orleans, talked with Legrasse and others of that old-time raiding-party, saw the frightful image, and even questioned such of the mongrel prisoners as still survived. Old Castro, unfortunately, had been dead for some years. What I now heard so graphically at first-hand, though it was really no more than a detailed confirmation of what my uncle had written, excited me afresh; for I felt sure that I was on the track of a very real, very secret, and very ancient religion whose discovery would make me an anthropologist of note. My attitude was still one of absolute materialism, *as I wish it still were,* and I discounted with almost inexplicable perversity the coincidence of the dream notes and odd cuttings collected by Professor Angell.

One thing I began to suspect, and which I now fear I *know,* is that my uncle's death was far from natural. He fell on a narrow hill street leading up from an ancient waterfront swarming with foreign mongrels, after a careless push from a negro sailor. I did not forget the mixed blood and marine pursuits of the cult-members in Louisiana, and would not be surprised to learn of secret methods and poison needles as ruthless and as anciently known as the cryptic rites and beliefs. Legrasse and his men, it is true, have been let alone; but in Norway a certain seaman who saw things is dead. Might not the deeper inquiries of my uncle after encountering the sculptor's data have come to sinister ears? I think Professor Angell died because he knew too much, or because he was likely to learn too much. Whether I shall go as he did remains to be seen, for I have learned much now.

III
The Madness from the Sea

If heaven ever wishes to grant me a boon, it will be a total effacing of the results of a mere chance which fixed my eye on a certain stray piece of shelf-paper. It was nothing on which I would naturally have stumbled in the course of my daily round, for it was an old number of an Australian journal, the *Sydney Bulletin* for April 18, 1925. It had escaped even the cutting bureau which had at the time of its issuance been avidly collecting material for my uncle's research.

I had largely given over my inquiries into what Professor Angell called the "Cthulhu Cult," and was visiting a learned friend in Paterson, New Jersey; the curator of a local museum and a mineralogist of note. Examining one day the reserve specimens roughly set on the storage shelves in a rear room of the museum, my eye was caught by an odd picture in one of the old papers spread beneath the stones. It was the *Sydney Bulletin* I have mentioned, for my friend has wide affiliations in all conceivable foreign parts; and the picture was a half-tone cut of a hideous stone image almost identical with that which Legrasse had found in the swamp.

Eagerly clearing the sheet of its precious contents, I scanned the item in detail; and was disappointed to find it of only moderate length. What it suggested, however, was of portentous significance to my flagging quest; and I carefully tore it out for immediate action. It read as follows:

MYSTERY DERELICT FOUND AT SEA

Vigilant Arrives With Helpless Armed New Zealand Yacht in Tow.
One Survivor and Dead Man Found Aboard. Tale of
Desperate Battle and Deaths at Sea.
Rescued Seaman Refuses
Particulars of Strange Experience.
Odd Idol Found in His Possession. Inquiry
to Follow.

The Morrison Co.'s freighter *Vigilant*, bound from Valparaiso, arrived this morning at its wharf in Darling Harbour, having in tow the battled and disabled but heavily armed steam yacht *Alert* of Dunedin, N. Z., which was sighted April 12th in S. Latitude 34° 21', W. Longitude 152° 17' with one living and one dead man aboard.

The *Vigilant* left Valparaiso March 25th, and on April 2nd was driven considerably south of her course by exceptionally heavy storms and monster waves. On April 12th the derelict was sighted; and though apparently deserted, was found upon boarding to contain one survivor in a half-delirious condition and one man who had evidently been dead for more than a week. The living man was clutching a horrible stone idol of unknown origin, about a foot in height, regarding whose nature authorities at Sydney University, the Royal Society, and the Museum in College Street all profess complete bafflement, and which the survivor says he found in the cabin of the yacht, in a small carved shrine of common pattern.

> This man, after recovering his senses, told an exceedingly strange story of piracy and slaughter. He is Gustaf Johansen, a Norwegian of some intelligence, and had been second mate of the two-masted schooner *Emma* of Auckland, which sailed for Callao February 20th with a complement of eleven men. The *Emma*, he says, was delayed and thrown widely south of her course by the great storm of March 1st, and on March 22nd, in S. Latitude 49° 51', W. Longitude 128° 34', encountered the *Alert*, manned by a queer and evil-looking crew of Kanakas and half-castes. Being ordered peremptorily to turn back, Capt. Collins refused; whereupon the strange crew began to fire savagely and without warning upon the schooner with a peculiarly heavy battery of brass cannon forming part of the yacht's equipment. The *Emma*'s men shewed fight, says the survivor, and though the schooner began to sink from shots beneath the waterline they managed to heave alongside their enemy and board her, grappling with the savage crew on the yacht's deck, and being forced to kill them all, the number being slightly superior, because of their particularly abhorrent and desperate though rather clumsy mode of fighting.
>
> Three of the *Emma*'s men, including Capt. Collins and First Mate Green, were killed; and the remaining eight under Second Mate Johansen proceeded to navigate the captured yacht, going ahead in their original direction to see if any reason for their ordering back had existed. The next day, it appears, they raised and landed on a small island, although none is known to exist in that part of the ocean; and six of the men somehow died ashore, though Johansen is queerly reticent about this part of his story, and speaks only of their falling into a rock chasm. Later, it seems, he and one companion boarded the yacht and tried to manage her, but were beaten about by the storm of April 2nd. From that time till his rescue on the 12th the man remembers little, and he does not even recall when William Briden, his companion, died. Briden's death reveals no apparent cause, and was probably due to excitement or exposure. Cable advices from Dunedin report that the *Alert* was well known there as an island trader, and bore an evil reputation along the waterfront. It was owned by a curious group of half-castes whose frequent meetings and night trips to the woods attracted no little curiosity; and it had set sail in great haste just after the storm and earth tremors of March 1st. Our Auckland correspondent gives the *Emma* and her crew an excellent reputation, and Johansen is described as a sober and worthy man. The admiralty will institute an inquiry on the whole matter beginning tomorrow, at which every effort will be made to induce Johansen to speak more freely than he has done hitherto.

This was all, together with the picture of the hellish image; but what a train of ideas it started in my mind! Here were new treasuries of data on the Cthulhu Cult, and evidence that it had strange interests at sea as well as on land. What motive prompted the hybrid crew to order back the *Emma* as they sailed about with their hideous idol? What was the unknown island on which six of the *Emma*'s crew had died, and about which the mate Johansen was so secretive? What had the vice-admiralty's investigation brought out, and what was known of the noxious cult in Dunedin? And most marvellous of all, what deep and more than natural linkage of dates was this which gave a malign and now undeniable significance to the various turns of events so carefully noted by my uncle?

March 1st—our February 28th according to the International Date Line—the earthquake and storm had come. From Dunedin the *Alert* and her noisome crew had darted eagerly forth as if imperiously summoned, and on the other side of the earth poets and artists had begun to dream of a strange, dank Cyclopean city whilst a young sculptor had moulded in his sleep the form of the dreaded Cthulhu. March 23d the crew of the *Emma* landed on an unknown island and left six men dead; and on that date the dreams of sensitive men assumed a heightened vividness and darkened with dread of a giant monster's malign pursuit, whilst an architect had gone mad and a sculptor had lapsed suddenly into delirium! And what of this storm of April 2nd—the date on which all dreams of the dank city ceased, and Wilcox emerged unharmed from the bondage of strange fever? What of all this—and of those hints of old Castro about the sunken, star-born Old Ones and their coming reign; their faithful cult *and their mastery of dreams*? Was I tottering on the brink of cosmic horrors beyond man's power to bear? If so, they must be horrors of the mind alone, for in some way the second of April had put a stop to whatever monstrous menace had begun its siege of mankind's soul.

That evening, after a day of hurried cabling and arranging, I bade my host adieu and took a train for San Francisco. In less than a month I was in Dunedin; where, however, I found that little was known of the strange cult-members who had lingered in the old sea-taverns. Waterfront scum was far too common for special mention; though there was vague talk about one inland trip these mongrels had made, during which faint drumming and red flame were noted on the distant hills. In Auckland I learned that Johansen had returned with *yellow hair turned white* after a perfunctory and inconclusive questioning at Sydney, and had thereafter sold his cottage in West Street and sailed with his wife to his old home in Oslo. Of his stirring experience he would tell his friends no more than he had told the admiralty officials, and all they could do was to give me his Oslo address.

After that I went to Sydney and talked profitlessly with seamen and members of the vice-admiralty court. I saw the *Alert,* now sold and in commercial use, at Circular Quay in Sydney Cove, but gained nothing from its non-committal bulk. The crouching image with its cuttlefish head, dragon body, scaly wings, and hieroglyphed pedestal, was preserved in the Museum at Hyde Park; and I studied it long and well, finding it a thing of balefully exquisite workmanship, and with the same utter mystery, terrible antiquity, and unearthly strangeness of material which I had noted in Legrasse's smaller specimen. Geologists, the curator told me, had found it a monstrous puzzle; for they vowed that the world held no rock like it. Then I thought with a shudder of what old Castro had told Legrasse about the primal Great Ones: "They had come from the stars, and had brought Their images with Them."

Shaken with such a mental revolution as I had never before known, I now resolved to visit Mate Johansen in Oslo. Sailing for London, I reëmbarked at once for the Norwegian capital; and one autumn day landed at the trim wharves in the shadow of the Egeberg. Johansen's address, I discovered, lay in the Old Town of King Harold Haardrada, which kept alive the name of Oslo during all the centuries that the greater city masqueraded as "Christiana." I made the brief trip by taxicab, and knocked with palpitant heart at the door of a neat and ancient building with plastered front. A sad-faced woman in black answered my summons, and I was stung with disappointment when she told me in halting English that Gustaf Johansen was no more.

He had not survived his return, said his wife, for the doings at sea in 1925 had broken him. He had told her no more than he had told the public, but had left a long manuscript—of "technical matters" as he said—written in English, evidently in order to safeguard her from the peril of casual perusal. During a walk through a narrow lane near the Gothenburg dock, a bundle of papers falling from an attic window had knocked him down. Two Lascar sailors at once helped him to his feet, but before the ambulance could reach him he was dead. Physicians found no adequate cause for the end, and laid it to heart trouble and a weakened constitution.

I now felt gnawing at my vitals that dark terror which will never leave me till I, too, am at rest; "accidentally" or otherwise. Persuading the widow that my connexion with her husband's "technical matters" was sufficient to entitle me to his manuscript, I bore the document away and began to read it on the London boat. It was a simple, rambling thing—a naive sailor's effort at a post-facto diary—and strove to recall day by day that last awful voyage. I cannot attempt to transcribe it verbatim in all its cloudiness and redundance, but I will tell its gist enough to shew why the sound of the water against the vessel's sides became so unendurable to me that I stopped my ears with cotton.

Johansen, thank God, did not know quite all, even though he saw the city and the Thing, but I shall never sleep calmly again when I think of the horrors that lurk ceaselessly behind life in time and in space, and of those unhallowed blasphemies from elder stars which dream beneath the sea, known and favoured by a nightmare cult ready and eager to loose them on the world whenever another earthquake shall heave their monstrous stone city again to the sun and air.

Johansen's voyage had begun just as he told it to the vice-admiralty. The *Emma,* in ballast, had cleared Auckland on February 20th, and had felt the full force of that earthquake-born tempest which must have heaved up from the sea-bottom the horrors that filled men's dreams. Once more under control, the ship was making good progress when held up by the *Alert* on March 22nd, and I could feel the mate's regret as he wrote of her bombardment and sinking. Of the swarthy cult-fiends on the *Alert* he speaks with significant horror. There was some peculiarly abominable quality about them which made their destruction seem almost a duty, and Johansen shews ingenuous wonder at the charge of ruthlessness brought against his party during the proceedings of the court of inquiry. Then, driven ahead by curiosity in their captured yacht under Johansen's command, the men sight a great stone pillar sticking out of the sea, and in S. Latitude 47° 9', W. Longitude 126° 43' come upon a coast-line of mingled mud, ooze, and weedy Cyclopean masonry which can be nothing less than the tangible substance of earth's supreme terror—the nightmare corpse-city of R'lyeh, that was built in measureless aeons behind history by the vast, loathsome shapes that seeped down from the dark stars. There lay great Cthulhu and his hordes, hidden in green slimy vaults and sending out at last, after cycles incalculable, the thoughts that spread fear to the dreams of the sensitive and called imperiously to the faithful to come on a pilgrimage of liberation and restoration. All this Johansen did not suspect, but God knows he soon saw enough!

I suppose that only a single mountain-top, the hideous monolith-crowned citadel whereon great Cthulhu was buried, actually emerged from the waters. When I think of the *extent* of all that may be brooding down there I almost wish to kill myself forthwith. Johansen and his men were awed by the cosmic majesty of this dripping Babylon of elder daemons, and must have guessed without guidance that it was nothing of this or of any sane planet. Awe at the unbelievable size of the greenish stone blocks, at the dizzying height of the great carven monolith, and at the stupefying identity of the colossal statues and bas-reliefs with the queer image found in the shrine on the *Alert,* is poignantly visible in every line of the mate's frightened description.

Without knowing what futurism is like, Johansen achieved something very close to it when he spoke of the city; for instead of describing any definite structure or building, he dwells only on broad impressions of vast angles and stone surfaces—surfaces too great to belong to any thing right or proper for this earth, and impious with horrible images and hieroglyphs. I mention his talk about angles because it suggests something Wilcox had told me of his awful dreams. He had said that the geometry of the dream-place he saw was abnormal, non-Euclidean, and loathsomely redolent of spheres and dimensions apart from ours. Now an unlettered seaman felt the same thing whilst gazing at the terrible reality.

Johansen and his men landed at a sloping mud-bank on this monstrous Acropolis, and clambered slipperily up over titan oozy blocks which could have been no mortal staircase. The very sun of heaven seemed distorted when viewed through the polarising miasma welling out from this sea-soaked perversion, and twisted menace and suspense lurked leeringly in those crazily elusive angles of carven rock where a second glance shewed concavity after the first shewed convexity.

Something very like fright had come over all the explorers before anything more definite than rock and ooze and weed was seen. Each would have fled had he not feared the scorn of the others, and it was only half-heartedly that they searched—vainly, as it proved—for some portable souvenir to bear away.

It was Rodriguez the Portuguese who climbed up the foot of the monolith and shouted of what he had found. The rest followed him, and looked curiously at the immense carved door with the now familiar squid-dragon bas-relief. It was, Johansen said, like a great barn-door; and they all felt that it was a door because of the ornate lintel, threshold, and jambs around it, though they could not decide whether it lay flat like a trap-door or slantwise like an outside cellar-door. As Wilcox would have said, the geometry of the place was all wrong. One could not be sure that the sea and the ground were horizontal, hence the relative position of everything else seemed phantasmally variable.

Briden pushed at the stone in several places without result. Then Donovan felt over it delicately around the edge, pressing each point separately as he went. He climbed interminably along the grotesque stone moulding—that is, one would call it climbing if the thing was not after all horizontal—and the men wondered how any door in the universe could be so vast. Then, very softly and slowly, the acre-great panel began to give inward at the top; and they saw that it was balanced. Donovan slid or somehow propelled himself down or along the jamb and rejoined his fellows, and everyone watched the queer recession of the monstrously carven portal. In this phantasy of prismatic distortion it moved anomalously in a diagonal way, so that all the rules of matter and perspective seemed upset.

The aperture was black with a darkness almost material. That tenebrousness was indeed a *positive quality;* for it obscured such parts of the inner walls as ought to have been revealed, and actually burst forth like smoke from its aeon-long imprisonment, visibly darkening the sun as it slunk away into the shrunken and gibbous sky on flapping membraneous wings. The odour arising from the newly opened depths was intolerable, and at length the quick-eared Hawkins thought he heard a nasty, slopping sound down there. Everyone listened, and everyone was listening still when It lumbered slobberingly into sight and gropingly squeezed Its gelatinous green immensity through the black doorway into the tainted outside air of that poison city of madness.

Poor Johansen's handwriting almost gave out when he wrote of this. Of the six men who never reached the ship, he thinks two perished of pure fright in that accursed instant. The Thing cannot be described—there is no language for such abysms of shrieking and immemorial lunacy, such eldritch contradictions of all matter, force, and cosmic order. A mountain walked or stumbled. God! What wonder that across the earth a great architect went mad, and poor Wilcox raved with fever in that telepathic instant? The Thing of the idols, the green, sticky spawn of the stars, had awaked to claim his own. The stars were right again, and what an age-old cult had failed to do by design, a band of innocent sailors had done by accident. After vigintillions of years great Cthulhu was loose again, and ravening for delight.

Three men were swept up by the flabby claws before anybody turned. God rest them, if there be any rest in the universe. They were Donovan, Guerrera, and Ångstrom. Parker slipped as the other three were plunging frenziedly over endless vistas of green-crusted rock to the boat, and Johansen swears he was swallowed up by an angle of masonry which shouldn't have been there; an angle which was acute, but behaved as if it were obtuse. So only Briden and Johansen reached the boat, and pulled desperately for the *Alert* as the mountainous monstrosity flopped down the slimy stones and hesitated floundering at the edge of the water.

Steam had not been suffered to go down entirely, despite the departure of all hands for the shore; and it was the work of only a few moments of feverish rushing up and down between wheel and engines to get the *Alert* under way. Slowly, amidst the distorted horrors of that indescribable scene, she began to churn the lethal waters; whilst on the masonry of that charnel shore that was not of earth the titan Thing from the stars slavered and gibbered like Polypheme cursing the fleeing ship of Odysseus. Then, bolder than the storied Cyclops, great Cthulhu slid greasily into the water and began to pursue with vast wave-raising strokes of cosmic potency. Briden looked back and went mad, laughing shrilly as he kept on laughing at intervals till death found him one night in the cabin whilst Johansen was wandering deliriously.

But Johansen had not given out yet. Knowing that the Thing could surely overtake the *Alert* until steam was fully up, he resolved on a desperate chance; and, setting the engine for full speed, ran lightning-like on deck and reversed the wheel. There was a mighty eddying and foaming in the noisome brine, and as the steam mounted higher and higher the brave Norwegian drove his vessel head on against the pursuing jelly which rose above the unclean froth like the stern of a daemon galleon. The awful squid-head with writhing feelers came nearly up to the bowsprit of the sturdy yacht, but Johansen drove on relentlessly. There was a bursting as of an exploding bladder, a slushy nastiness as of a cloven sunfish, a stench as of a thousand opened graves, and a sound that the chronicler would not put on paper. For an instant the ship was befouled by an acrid and blinding green cloud, and then there was only a venomous seething astern; where—God in heaven!—the scattered plasticity of that nameless sky-spawn was nebulously *recombining* in its hateful original form, whilst its distance widened every second as the *Alert* gained impetus from its mounting steam.

That was all. After that Johansen only brooded over the idol in the cabin and attended to a few matters of food for himself and the laughing maniac by his side. He did not try to navigate after the first bold flight, for the reaction had taken something out of his soul. Then came the storm of April 2nd, and a gathering of the clouds about his consciousness. There is a sense of spectral whirling through liquid gulfs of infinity, of dizzying rides through reeling universes on a comet's tail, and of hysterical plunges from the pit to the moon and from the moon back again to the pit, all livened by a cachinnating chorus of the distorted, hilarious elder gods and the green, bat-winged mocking imps of Tartarus.

Out of that dream came rescue—the *Vigilant,* the vice-admiralty court, the streets of Dunedin, and the long voyage back home to the old house by the Egeberg. He could not tell—they would think him mad. He would write of what he knew before death came, but his wife must not guess. Death would be a boon if only it could blot out the memories.

That was the document I read, and now I have placed it in the tin box beside the bas-relief and the papers of Professor Angell. With it shall go this record of mine—this test of my own sanity, wherein is pieced together that which I hope may never be pieced together again. I have looked upon all that the universe has to hold of horror, and even the skies of spring and the flowers of summer must ever afterward be poison to me. But I do not think my life will be long. As my uncle went, as poor Johansen went, so I shall go. I know too much, and the cult still lives.

Cthulhu still lives, too, I suppose, again in that chasm of stone which has shielded him since the sun was young. His accursed city is sunken once more, for the *Vigilant* sailed over the spot after the April storm; but his ministers on earth still bellow and prance and slay around idol-capped monoliths in lonely places. He must have been trapped by the sinking whilst within his black abyss, or else the world would by now be screaming with fright and frenzy. Who knows the end? What has risen may sink, and what has sunk may rise. Loathsomeness waits and dreams in the deep, and decay spreads over the tottering cities of men. A time will come—but I must not and cannot think! Let me pray that, if I do not survive this manuscript, my executors may put caution before audacity and see that it meets no other eye.

B is for Banshee

In the folklore of Ireland, the banshee is a spirit, usually female in form, whose wail is a forewarning of death. In this story, first published in the Christmas issue of *London Society* for 1867, British writer Charlotte Riddell (1832–1906), who signed her distinguished ghost stories as Mrs. J.H. Riddell, makes the banshee's cry something much more nuanced than just a harbinger of horrors.

MRS. J.H. RIDDELL

Hertford O'Donnell's Warning

Many a year ago, before chloroform was thought of, there lived in an old, rambling house, in Gerard Street, Soho, a young Irishman called Hertford O'Donnell.

After Hertford O'Donnell he was entitled to write M.R.C.S., for he had studied hard to gain this distinction, and the older surgeons at Guy's (his hospital) considered him, in their secret hearts, one of the most rising operators of the day.

Having said chloroform was unknown at the time this story opens, it will strike my readers that, if Hertford O'Donnell were a rising and successful operator in those days, of necessity he combined within himself a larger number of striking qualities than are by any means necessary to form a successful operator in these.

There was more than mere hand skill, more than even thorough knowledge of his profession, needful for the man who, dealing with conscious subjects, essayed to rid them of some of the diseases to which flesh is heir. There was greater courage required in the manipulator of old than is altogether essential now. Then, as now, a thorough mastery of his instruments—a steady hand—a keen eye—a quick dexterity were indispensable to a good operator; but, added to all these things, there formerly required a pulse which knew no quickening—a mental strength which never faltered—a ready power of adaptation in unexpected circumstances—fertility of resource in difficult cases, and a brave front under all emergencies.

If I refrain from adding that a hard as well as a courageous heart was an important item in the programme, it is only out of deference to general opinion, which, amongst other delusions, clings to the belief that courage and hardness are antagonistic qualities.

Hertford O'Donnell, however, was hard as steel. He understood his work, and he did it thoroughly; but he cared no more for quivering nerves and contracting muscles, for screams of agony, for faces white with pain, and teeth clenched in the extremity of anguish, than he did for the stony countenances of the dead which sometimes in the dissecting room appalled younger and less experienced men.

He had no sentiment, and he had no sympathy. The human body was to him an ingenious piece of mechanism which it was at once a pleasure and a profit to understand. Precisely as Brunel loved the Thames Tunnel, or any other singular engineering feat, so O'Donnell loved a patient on whom he operated successfully, more especially if the ailment possessed by the patient were of a rare and difficult character.

And for this reason he was much liked by all who came under his hands, for patients are apt to mistake a surgeon's interest in their cases for interest in themselves; and it was gratifying to John Dicks, plasterer, and Timothy Began, labourer, to be the happy possessors of remarkable diseases, which produced a cordial understanding between them and the handsome Irishman.

If he were hard and cool at the moment of hewing them to pieces, that was all forgotten, or remembered only as a virtue, when, after being discharged from hospital like soldiers who have served in a severe campaign, they met Mr. O'Donnell in the street, and were accosted by that rising individual, just as though he considered himself nobody.

He had a royal memory, this stranger in a strange land, both for faces and cases; and like the rest of his countrymen he never felt it beneath his dignity to talk cordially to corduroy and fustian.

In London, as at Calgillan, he never held back his tongue from speaking a cheery or a kindly word. His manners were pliable enough if his heart were not; and the porters, and the patients, and the nurses, and the students at Guy's all were pleased to see Hertford O'Donnell.

Rain, hail, sunshine, it was all the same; there was a life and a brightness about the man which communicated itself to those with whom he came in contact. Let the mud out in Smithfield be a foot deep, or the London fog thick as pea-soup, Mr. O'Donnell never lost his temper, never muttered a surly reply to the gatekeeper's salutation, but spoke out blithely and cheerfully to his pupils and his patients, to the sick and to the well, to those below and to those above him.

And yet, spite of all these good qualities—spite of his handsome face, his fine figure, his easy address, and his unquestionable skill as an operator, the dons, who acknowledged his talent, shook their heads gravely when two or three of them in private and solemn conclave talked confidentially of their younger brother.

If there were many things in his favour, there were more in his disfavour. He was Irish—not merely by the accident of birth, which might have been forgiven, since a man cannot be held accountable for such caprices of Nature, but by every other accident and design which is objectionable to the orthodox and respectable and representative English mind.

In speech, appearance, manner, habits, modes of expression, habits of life, Hertford O'Donnell was Irish. To the core of his heart he loved the island which he, nevertheless, declared he never meant to revisit; and amongst the English he moved to all intents and purposes a foreigner, who was resolved, so said the great prophets at Guy's, to go to destruction as fast as he could, and let no man hinder him.

"He means to go the whole length of his tether," observed one of the ancient wiseacres to another; which speech implied a conviction that Hertford O'Donnell, having sold himself to the Evil One, had determined to dive the full length of his rope into wickedness before being pulled to the shore where even wickedness is negative—where there are no mad carouses, no wild, sinful excitement, nothing but impotent wailing and gnashing of teeth.

A reckless, graceless, clever, wicked devil—going to his natural home as fast as in London a man can possibly progress thither: this was the opinion his superiors held of the man who lived all alone with a housekeeper and her husband (who acted as butler) in his big house near Soho.

Gerrard Street was not then an utterly shady and forgotten locality: carriage patients found their way to the rising young surgeon—some great personages thought it not beneath them to fee an individual whose consulting rooms were situated on what was even then the wrong side of Regent Street. He was making money, and he was spending it; he was over head and ears in debt—useless, vulgar debt—senselessly contracted, never bravely faced. He had lived at an awful pace ever since he came to London, at a pace which only a man who hopes and expects to die young can ever travel.

Life, what good was it? death, was he a child, or a woman, or a coward, to be afraid of that hereafter? God knew all about the trifle which had upset his coach better than the dons at Guy's; and he did not dread facing his Maker, and giving an account to Him even of the disreputable existence he had led since he came to London.

Hertford O'Donnell knew the world pretty well, and the ways thereof were to him as roads often traversed; therefore, when he said that at the day of judgment he felt certain he should come off better than many of those who censured him, it may be assumed that, although his views of post-mortem punishment were vague, unsatisfactory, and infidel, still his information as to the peccadilloes of his neighbours was such as consoled himself.

And yet, living all alone in the old house near Soho Square, grave thoughts would intrude frequently into the surgeon's mind—thoughts which where, so to say, italicized by peremptory letters, and still more peremptory visits from people who wanted money.

Although he had many acquaintances he had no single friend, and accordingly these thoughts were received and brooded over in solitude, in those hours when, after returning from dinner or supper, or congenial carouse, he sat in his dreary room smoking his pipe and considering means and ways, chances and certainties.

In good truth he had started in London with some vague idea that as his life in it would not be of long continuance, the pace at which he elected to travel could be of little consequence; but the years since his first entry into the metropolis were now piled one on the top of another, his youth was behind him, his chances of longevity, spite of the way he had striven to injure his constitution, quite as good as ever. He had come to that time in existence, to that narrow strip of tableland whence the ascent of youth and the descent of age are equally discernible—when, simply because he has lived for so many years, it strikes a man as possible he may have to live for just as many more, with the ability for hard work gone, with the boon companions scattered abroad, with the capacity for enjoying convivial meetings a mere memory, with small means perhaps, with no bright hopes, with the pomp and the equipage, and the fairy carriages, and the glamour which youth flings over earthly objects faded away like the pageant of yesterday, while the dreary ceremony of living has to be gone through today and to-morrow and the morrow after, as though the gay cavalcade and the martial music, and the glittering helmets and the prancing steeds, were still accompanying the wayfarer to his journey's end.

Ah! my friends, there comes a moment when we must all leave the coach, with its four bright bays, its pleasant outside freight, its cheery company, its guard who blows the horn so merrily through villages and along lonely country roads.

Long before we reach that final stage, where the black business claims us for its own especial property, we have to bid good-bye to all easy, thoughtless journeying, and betake ourselves, with what zest we will, to traversing the common of Reality. There is no royal road across it that ever I heard of. From the king on his throne to the labourer who vaguely imagines what manner of being a king is, we have all to tramp across that desert at one period of our lives, at all events; and that period usually is when, as I have said, a man starts to find the hopes, and the strength, and the buoyancy of youth left behind, while years and years of life lie stretching out before him.

The coach he has travelled by drops him here. There is no appeal, there is no help; therefore let him take off his hat and wish the new passengers good speed, without either envy or repining.

Behold, he has had his turn, and let whosoever will, mount on the box-seat of life again, and tip the coachman and handle the ribbons, he shall take that pleasant journey no more—no more for ever.

Even supposing a man's spring-time to have been a cold and ungenial one, with bitter easterly winds and nipping frosts, biting the buds and retarding the blossoms, still it was spring for all that—spring with the young green leaves sprouting forth, with the flowers unfolding tenderly, with the songs of birds and the rush of waters, with the summer before and the autumn afar off, and winter remote as death and eternity; but when once the trees have donned their summer foliage, when the pure white blossoms have disappeared, and a gorgeous red and orange and purple blaze of many-coloured flowers fills the gardens, then if there come a wet, dreary day, the idea of autumn and winter is not so difficult to realise. When once twelve o'clock is reached, the evening and night become facts, not possibilities; and it was of the afternoon, and the evening and the night, Hertford O'Donnell sat thinking on the Christmas Eve when I crave permission to introduce him to my readers.

A good-looking man ladies considered him. A tall, dark-complexioned, black-haired, straight-limbed, deeply, divinely blue-eyed fellow, with a soft voice, with a pleasant brogue, who had ridden like a Centaur over the loose stone walls in Connemara, who had danced all night at the Dublin balls, who had walked over the Bennebeola mountains, gun in hand, day after day without weariness, who had fished in every one of the hundred lakes you can behold from the top of that mountain near the Recess Hotel, who had led a mad, wild life in Trinity College, and a wilder, perhaps, while 'studying for a doctor'—as the Irish phrase goes—in Dublin, and who, after the death of his eldest brother left him free to return to Calgillan and pursue the usual utterly useless, utterly purposeless, utterly pleasant life of an Irish gentleman possessed of health, birth, and expectations, suddenly kicked over the paternal traces, bade adieu to Calgillan Castle and the blandishments of a certain beautiful Miss Clifden, beloved of his mother, and laid out to be his wife, walked down the avenue without even so much company as a gossoon to carry his carpet-bag, shook the dust from his feet at the lodge-gates, and took his seat on the coach, never once looking back at Calgillan, where his favourite mare was standing in the stable, his greyhounds chasing one another round the home paddock, his gun at half-cock in his dressing-room, and his fishing-tackle all in order and ready for use.

He had not kissed his mother nor asked for his father's blessing; he left Miss Clifden arrayed in her brand-new riding-habit without a word of affection or regret; he had spoken no syllable of farewell to any servant about the place; only when the old woman at the lodge bade him good morning and

God-blessed his handsome face, he recommended her bitterly to look well at it, for she would never see it more.

Twelve years and a half had passed since then without either Nancy Blake or any other one of the Calgillan people having set eyes on Master Hertford's handsome face. He had kept his vow to himself; he had not written home; he had not been indebted to mother or father for even a tenpenny-piece during the whole of that time; he had lived without friends, and he had lived without God—so far as God ever lets a man live without him—and his own private conviction was that he could get on very well without either. One thing only he felt to be needful—money, money to keep him when the evil days of sickness, or age, or loss of practice came upon him. Though a spendthrift, he was not a simpleton. Around him he saw men who, having started with fairer prospects than his own, were nevertheless reduced to indigence; and he knew that what had happened to others might happen to himself.

An unlucky cut, slipping on a bit of orange-peel in the street, the merest accident imaginable, is sufficient to change opulence to beggary in the life's programme of an individual whose income depends on eye, on nerve, on hand; and besides the consciousness of this fact, Hertford O'Donnell knew that beyond a certain point in his profession progress was not easy.

It did not depend quite on the strength of his own bow or shield whether he counted his earnings by hundreds or thousands. Work may achieve competence; but mere work cannot, in a profession at all events, compass wealth.

He looked around him, and he perceived that the majority of great men—great and wealthy—had been indebted for their elevation more to the accidents of birth, patronage, connection, or marriage, than to personal ability.

Personal ability, no doubt, they possessed; but then, little Jones, who lived in Frith Street, and who could barely keep himself and his wife and family, had ability, too, only he lacked the concomitants of success.

He wanted something or some one to puff him into notoriety—a brother at court—a lord's leg to mend—a rich wife to give him prestige in society; and, lacking this something or some one, he had grown grey-haired and fainthearted in the service of that world which utterly despises its most obsequious servants.

"Clatter along the streets with a pair of hired horses, snub the middle classes, and drive over the commonalty—that is the way to compass wealth and popularity in England," said Hertford O'Donnell, bitterly; and, as the man desired wealth and popularity, he sat before his fire, with a foot on each hob, and a short pipe in his mouth, considering how he might best obtain the means to clatter along the streets in his carriage, and splash plebeians with mud from his wheels like the best.

In Dublin he could, by means of his name and connection, have done well; but then he was not in Dublin, neither did he want to be. The bitterest memories of his life were inseparable from the name of the Green Island, and he had no desire to return to it.

Besides, in Dublin heiresses are not quite so plentiful as in London; and an heiress Hertford O'Donnell had decided would do more for him than years of steady work.

A rich wife could clear him of debt, introduce him to fashionable practice, afford him that measure of social respectability which a medical bachelor invariably lacks, deliver him from the loneliness of Gerrard Street, and the domination of Mr. and Mrs. Coles.

To most men, deliberately bartering away their independence for money seems so prosaic a business that they strive to gloss it over even to themselves, and to assign every reason for their choice, save that which is really the influencing one.

Not so, however, with Hertford O'Donnell. He sat beside the fire scoffing over his proposed bargain—thinking of the lady's age—her moneybags—her desirable house in town—her seat in the country—her snobbishness—her folly.

"It would be a fitting ending," he sneered; "and why I did not settle the matter to-night passes my comprehension. I am not a fool, to be frightened with old women's tales; and yet I must have turned white. I felt I did, and she asked me whether I was ill. And then to think of my being such an idiot as to ask her if she had heard anything like a cry, as though she would be likely to hear that—she, with her poor parvenu blood, which, I often imagine, must have been mixed with some of her father's strong pickling vinegar. What the deuce could I have been dreaming about? I wonder what it really was"; and Hertford O'Donnell pushed his hair back from his forehead, and took another draught from the too familiar tumbler, which was placed conveniently on the chimneypiece.

"After expressly making up my mind to propose, too!" he mentally continued. "Could it have been conscience—that myth, which somebody, who knew nothing of the matter, said, 'makes cowards of us all?' I don't believe in conscience; and even if there be such a thing capable of being developed by sentiment and cultivation, why should it trouble me? I have no intention of wronging Miss Janet Price Ingot—not the least. Honestly and fairly I shall marry her; honestly and fairly I shall act by her. An old wife is not exactly an ornamental article of furniture in a man's house; and I do not know that the fact of her being well gilded makes her look any more ornamental. But she shall have no cause for complaint; and I will go and dine with her tomorrow, and settle the matter."

Having arrived at which resolution, Mr. O'Donnell arose, kicked down the fire—burning hollow—with the heel of his boot, knocked the ashes out of his pipe, emptied his tumbler, and bethought him it was time to go to bed. He was not in the habit of taking his rest so early as quarter to twelve o'clock; but he felt unusually weary—tired mentally and bodily—and lonely beyond all power of expression.

"The fair Janet would be better than this," he said, half aloud; and then with a start and a shiver, and a blanched face, he turned sharply round, whilst a low, sobbing, wailing cry echoed mournfully through the room. No form of words could give an idea of the sound. The plaintiveness of the Eolian harp—that plaintiveness which so soon affects and lowers the highest spirits—would have seemed wildly gay in comparison to the sadness of the cry which seemed floating in the air. As the summer wind comes and goes amongst the trees, so that mournful wail came and went—came and went. It came in a rush of sound, like a gradual crescendo managed by a skilful musician, and it died away like a lingering note, so that the listener could scarcely tell the exact moment when it faded away into silence.

I say faded away, for it disappeared as the coast line disappears in the twilight, and there was utter stillness in the apartment.

Then, for the first time, Hertford O'Donnell looked at his dog, and beholding the creature crouched into a corner beside the fireplace, called upon him to come out.

His voice sounded strange even to himself, and apparently the dog thought so too, for he made no effort to obey the summons.

"Come out, sir," his master repeated, and then the animal came crawling reluctantly forward, with his hair on end, his eyes almost starting from his head, trembling violently, as the surgeon, who caressed him, felt.

"So you heard it, Brian?" he said to the dog. "And so your ears are sharper than hers, old fellow? It's a mighty queer thing to think of, being favoured with a visit from a banshee in Gerrard Street; and as the lady has travelled so far, I only wish I knew whether there is any sort of refreshment she would like to take after her long journey."

He spoke loudly, and with a certain mocking defiance, seeming to think the phantom he addressed would reply; but when he stopped at the end of his sentence, no sound came through the stillness. There was utter silence in the room—silence broken only by the falling of the cinders on the hearth and the breathing of his dog.

"If my visitor would tell me," he proceeded, "for whom this lamentation is being made, whether for myself, or for some member of my illustrious family, I should feel immensely obliged. It seems too much honour for a poor surgeon to have such attention paid him. Good heavens! What is that?" he exclaimed, as a ring, loud and peremptory, woke all the echoes in the house, and brought his housekeeper, in a state of distressing dishabille, "out of her warm bed," as she subsequently stated, to the head of the staircase.

Across the hall Hertford O'Donnell strode, relieved at the prospect of speaking to any living being. He took no precaution of putting up the chain, but flung the door wide. A dozen burglars would have proved welcome in comparison to that ghostly intruder; and, as I have said, he threw the door open, admitting a rush of wet, cold air, which made poor Mrs. Coles's few remaining teeth chatter in her head.

"Who is there?—what do you want?" asked the surgeon, seeing no person, and hearing no voice. "Who is there?—why the devil can't you speak?"

But when even this polite exhortation failed to elicit an answer, he passed out into the night, and looked up the street, and down the street, to see nothing but the driving rain and the blinking lights.

"If this goes on much longer I shall soon think I must be either mad or drunk," he muttered, as he re-entered the house, and locked and bolted the door once more.

"Lord's sake! what is the matter, sir?" asked Mrs. Coles, from the upper flight, careful only to reveal the borders of her nightcap to Mr. O'Donnell's admiring gaze. "Is anybody killed?— have you to go out, sir?"

"It was only a runaway ring," he answered, trying to reassure himself with an explanation he did not in his heart believe.

"Runaway I—I'd runaway them," murmured Mrs. Coles, as she retired to the conjugal couch, where Coles was, to quote her own expression, "snoring like a pig through it all." Almost immediately afterwards she heard her master ascend the stairs and close his bedroom-door.

"Madam will surely be too much of a gentlewoman to intrude here," thought the surgeon, scoffing even at his own fears; but when he lay down he did not put out his light, and he made Brian leap up and crouch on the coverlet beside him.

The man was fairly frightened, and would have thought it no discredit to his manhood to acknowledge as much. He was not afraid of death, he was not afraid of trouble, he was not afraid of danger; but he was afraid of the banshee; and as he lay with his hand on the dog's head, he thought over all the stories he had ever heard about this family retainer in the days of his youth. He had not thought about her for years and years. Never before had he heard her voice himself. When his brother died, she had not thought it necessary to travel up to Dublin and give him notice of the impending catastrophe. "If she had, I would have gone down to Calgillan, and perhaps saved his life," considered the surgeon. "I wonder who this is for! If for me, that will settle my debts and my marriage. If I could be quite certain it was either of the old people, I would start for Ireland tomorrow." And then vaguely his mind wandered on to think of every banshee story he had ever heard in his life—about the beautiful lady with the wreath of flowers, who sat on the rocks below Red Castle, in the County Antrim, crying till one of the sons died for love of her; about the Round Chamber at Dunluce, which was swept clean by the banshee every night; about the bed in a certain great house in Ireland, which was slept in constantly, although no human being ever passed in or out after dark; about that general officer who, the night before Waterloo, said to a friend, "I have heard the banshee, and shall not come off the field alive to-morrow; break the news gently to poor Carry"; and who, nevertheless, coming safe off the field, had subsequently news about poor Carry broken tenderly and pitifully to him; about the lad who, aloft in the rigging, hearing through the night a sobbing and wailing coming over the waters, went down to the captain and told him he was afraid they were somehow out of their reckoning, just in time to save the ship, which, when morning broke, they found but for his warning would have been on the rocks. It was blowing great guns, and the sea was all in a fret and turmoil, and they could sometimes see in the trough of the waves, as down a valley, the cruel black reefs they had escaped.

On deck the captain stood speaking to the boy who had saved them, and asking how he knew of their danger; and when the lad told him, the captain laughed, and said her ladyship had been outwitted that time.

But the boy answered, with a grave shake of his head, that the warning was either for him or his, and that if he got safe to port there would be bad tidings waiting for him from home: whereupon the captain bade him go below, and get some brandy and lie down.

He got the brandy, and he lay down, but he never rose again; and when the storm abated—when a great calm succeeded to the previous tempest—there was a very solemn funeral at sea; and on their arrival at Liverpool the captain took a journey to Ireland to tell a widowed mother how her only son died, and to bear his few effects to the poor desolate soul.

And Hertford O'Donnell thought again about his own father riding full-chase across country, and hearing, as he galloped by a clump of plantation, something like a sobbing and wailing. The hounds were in full cry; but he still felt, as he afterwards expressed it, that there was something among those trees he could not pass; and so he jumped off his horse, and hung the reins over the branch of a fir, and beat the cover well, but not a thing could he find in it.

Then, for the first time in his life, Miles O'Donnell turned his horse's head *from* the hunt, and, within a mile of Calgillan, met a man running to tell him Mr. Martin's gun had burst, and hurt him badly.

And he remembered the story also, of how Mary O'Donnell, his great-aunt, being married to a young Englishman, heard the banshee as she sat one evening waiting for his return; and of how she, thinking the bridge by which he often came home unsafe for horse and man, went out, in a great panic, to meet and entreat him to go round by the main road for her sake. Sir Everard was riding along in the moonlight, making straight for the bridge, when he beheld a figure dressed all in white upon it. Then there was a crash, and the figure disappeared.

The lady was rescued and brought back to the hall; but next morning there were two dead bodies within its walls—those of Lady Eyreton and her still-born son.

Quicker than I write them, these memories chased one another through Hertford O'Donnell's brain; and there was one more terrible memory than any which would recur to him, concerning an Irish nobleman who, seated alone in his great town-house in London, heard the banshee, and rushed out to get rid of the phantom, which wailed in his ear, nevertheless, as he strode down Piccadilly. And then the surgeon remembered how he went with a friend to the Opera, feeling sure that there no banshee, unless she had a box, could find admittance, until suddenly he heard her singing up amongst the highest part of the scenery, with a terrible mournfulness, with a pathos which made the prima donna's tenderest notes seem harsh by comparison.

As he came out, some quarrel arose between him and a famous fire-eater, against whom he stumbled; and the result was that the next afternoon there was a new Lord ——, *vice* Lord ——, killed in a duel with Captain Bravo.

Memories like these are not the most enlivening possible; they are apt to make a man fanciful, and nervous, and wakeful; but as time ran on, Hertford O'Donnell fell asleep, with his candle still burning, and Brian's cold nose pressed against his hand.

He dreamt of his mother's family—the Hertfords, of Artingbury, Yorkshire, far-off relatives of Lord Hertford—so far off that even Mrs. O'Donnell held no clue to the genealogical maze.

He thought he was at Artingbury, fishing; that it was a misty summer's morning, and the fish rising beautifully. In his dream he hooked one after another, and the boy who was with him threw them into the basket.

At last there was one more difficult to land than the others; and the boy, in his eagerness to watch the sport, drew nearer and nearer to the brink, while the fisher, intent on his prey, failed to notice his companion's danger.

Suddenly there was a cry, a splash, and the boy disappeared from sight.

Next instant he rose again, however, and then, for the first time, Hertford O'Donnell saw his face.

It was one he knew well.

In a moment he plunged into the water, and struck out for the lad. He had him by the hair, he was turning to bring him back to land, when the stream suddenly changed into a wide, wild, shoreless sea, where the billows were chasing one another with a mad demoniac mirth.

For a while O'Donnell kept the lad and himself afloat. They were swept under the waves, and came forth again, only to see larger waves rushing towards them; but through all the surgeon never loosened his hold until a tremendous billow engulphing them both, tore the boy from him.

With the horror of that he awoke, to hear a voice saying quite distinctly:

"Go to the hospital!—go at once!"

The surgeon started up in bed, rubbed his eyes, and looked about him. The candle was flickering faintly in its socket. Brian, with his ears pricked forward, had raised his head at his master's sudden jump.

Everything was quiet, but still those words were ringing in his ear—

"Go to the hospital!—go at once!"

The tremendous peal of the bell overnight, and this sentence, seemed to be simultaneous.

That he was wanted at Guy's—wanted imperatively—came to O'Donnell like an inspiration.

Neither sense nor reason had anything to do with the conviction that roused him out of bed, and made him dress as speedily as possible, and grope his way down the staircase, Brian following.

He opened the front door, and passed out into the darkness. The rain was over, and the stars were shining as he pursued his way down Newport Market, and thence, winding in and out in a south-east direction, through Lincoln's Inn Fields and Old Square to Chancery Lane, whence he proceeded to St. Paul's.

Along the deserted streets he resolutely continued his walk. He did not know what he was going to Guy's for. Some instinct was urging him on, and he neither strove to combat nor control it. Only once had the thought of turning back occurred, and that was at the archway leading into Old Square. There he had paused for a moment, asking himself whether he were not gone stark, staring mad; but Guy's seemed preferable to the haunted house in Gerrard Street, and he walked resolutely on, determining to say, if any surprise were expressed at his appearance, that he had been sent for.

Sent for?—yes, truly; but by whom?

On through Cannon Street; on over London Bridge, where the lights flickered in the river, and the sullen plash of the water flowing beneath the arches, washing the stone piers could be heard, now the human din was hushed and lulled to sleep. On, thinking of many things: of the days of his youth; of his dead brother; of his father's heavily encumbered estate; of the fortune his mother had vowed she would leave to some charity rather than to him, if he refused to marry according to her choice; of his wild life in London; of the terrible cry he had heard overnight—that terrible wail which he could not drive away from his memory even as he entered Guy's, and confronted the porter, who said—

"You have just been sent for, sir; did you meet the messenger?"

Like one in a dream, Hertford O'Donnell heard him; like one in a dream, also, he asked what was the matter.

"Bad accident, sir; fire: fell off a balcony—unsafe—old building. Mother and child—a son; child with compound fracture of thigh." This, the joint information of porter and house-surgeon, mingled together, and made a roar in Mr. O'Donnell's ears like the sound of the sea breaking on a shingly shore.

Only one sentence he understood perfectly—"Immediate amputation necessary." At this point he grew cool; he was the careful, cautious, successful surgeon in a moment.

"The child, you say?" he answered; "let me see him."

The Guy's Hospital of to-day may be different to the Guy's Hertford O'Donnell knew so well. Railways have, I believe, swept away the old operating room; railways may have changed the position of the old accident ward, to reach which, in the days of which I am writing, the two surgeons had to pass a staircase leading to the upper stories.

On the lower step of this staircase, partially in shadow, Hertford O'Donnell beheld, as he came forward, an old woman seated.

An old woman with streaming grey hair, with attenuated arms, with head bowed forward, with scanty clothing, with bare feet; who never looked up at their approach, but sat unnoticing, shaking her head and wringing her hands in an extremity of grief.

"Who is that?" asked Mr. O'Donnell, almost involuntarily.

"Who is what?" demanded his companion.

"That—that woman," was the reply.

"What woman?"

"There—are you blind?—seated on the bottom step of the staircase. What is she doing?" persisted Mr. O'Donnell.

"There is no woman near us," his companion answered, looking at the rising surgeon very much as though he suspected him of seeing double.

"No woman!" scoffed Hertford. "Do you expect me to disbelieve the evidence of my own eyes?" and he walked up to the figure, meaning to touch it.

But as he essayed to do so, the woman seemed to rise in the air and float away, with her arms stretched high up over her head, uttering such a wail of pain, and agony, and distress, as caused the Irishman's blood to curdle.

"My God! Did you hear that?" he said to his companion.

"What?" was the reply.

Then, although he knew the sound had fallen on deaf ears, he answered—

"The wail of the banshee! Some of my people are doomed!"

"I trust not,"' answered the house-surgeon, who had an idea, nevertheless, that Hertford O'Donnell's banshee lived in a whisky-bottle, and that she would some day make an end of that rising and clever operator.

With nerves utterly shaken, Mr. O'Donnell walked forward to the accident ward. There, with his face shaded from the light, lay his patient—a young boy, with a compound fracture of the thigh.

In that ward, in the face of actual pain or danger capable of relief, the surgeon had never known faltering nor fear; and now he carefully examined the injury, felt the pulse, inquired as to the treatment pursued, and ordered the sufferer to be carried to the operating room.

While he was looking over his instruments he heard the boy lying on the table murmur faintly—

"Tell her not to cry so—tell her not to cry."

"What is he talking about?" Hertford O'Donnell inquired.

"The nurse says he has been speaking about some woman crying ever since he came in—his mother, most likely," answered one of the attendants.

"He is delirious, then?" observed the surgeon.

"No, sir," pleaded the boy, excitedly. "No; it is that woman—that woman with the grey hair. I saw her looking from the upper window before the balcony gave way. She has never left me since, and she won't be quiet, wringing her hands and crying."

"Can you see her now?" Hertford O'Donnell inquired, stepping to the side of the table. "Point out where she stands."

Then the lad stretched forth a feeble finger in the direction of the door, where clearly, as he had seen her seated on the stairs, the surgeon saw a woman standing—a woman with grey hair and scanty clothing, and upstretched arms and bare feet.

"A word with you, sir," O'Donnell said to the house-surgeon, drawing him back from the table. "I cannot perform this operation: send for some other person. I am ill: I am incapable."

"But," pleaded the other, "there is no time to get any one else. We sent for Mr. —— before we troubled you, but he was out of town, and all the rest of the surgeons live so far away. Mortification may set in at any moment, and—"

"Do you think you require to teach me my business?" was the reply. "I know the boy's life hangs on a thread, and that is the very reason I cannot operate. I am not fit for it. I tell you I have seen to-night that which unnerves me for anything. My hand is not steady. Send for some one else without delay. Say I am ill—dead!—what you please. Heavens! there she is again, right over the boy! Do you hear her?" and Hertford O'Donnell fell fainting on the floor.

How long he lay in that death-like swoon I cannot say; but when he returned to consciousness, the principal physician of Guy's was standing beside him in the cold grey light of the Christmas morning.

"The boy?" murmured O'Donnell, faintly.

"Now, my dear fellow, keep yourself quiet," was the reply.

"The boy?" he repeated, irritably. "Who operated?"

"No one," Dr. —— answered. "It would have been useless cruelty. Mortification had set in, and—"

Hertford O'Donnell turned his face to the wall, and his friend could not see it.

"Do not distress yourself," went on the physician, kindly. "Allington says he could not have survived the operation in any case. He was quite delirious from the first, raving about a woman with grey hair, and—"

"Yes, I know," Hertford O'Donnell interrupted; "and the boy had a mother, they told me, or I dreamt it."

"Yes, bruised and shaken, but not seriously injured."

"Has she blue eyes and fair hair—fair hair all rippling and wavy? Is she white as a lily, with just a faint flush of colour in her cheek? Is she young, and trusting, and innocent? No; I am wandering. She must be nearly thirty, now. Go, for God's sake, and tell me if you can find a woman that you could imagine having been as a girl such as I describe."

"Irish?" asked the doctor; and O'Donnell made a gesture of assent.

"It is she, then," was the reply; "a woman with the face of an angel."

"A woman who should have been my wife," the surgeon answered; "whose child was my son."

"Lord help you!" ejaculated the doctor. Then Hertford O'Donnell raised himself from the sofa where they had laid him, and told his companion the story of his life—how there had been bitter feud between his people and her people—how they were divided by old animosities and by difference of religion—how they had met by stealth, and exchanged rings and vows, all for nought—how his family had insulted hers, so that her father, wishful for her to marry a kinsman of his own, bore her off to a far-away land, and made her write him a letter of eternal farewell—how his own parents had kept all knowledge of the quarrel from him till she was utterly beyond his reach—how they had vowed to discard him unless he agreed to marry according to their wishes—how he left his home, and came to London, and pushed his fortune. All this Hertford O'Donnell repeated; and when he had finished the bells were ringing for morning service—ringing loudly—ringing joyfully. "Peace on earth, good will towards men."

But there was little peace that morning for Hertford O'Donnell. He had to look on the face of his dead son, wherein he beheld, as though reflected, the face of the boy in his dream.

Stealthily he followed his friend, and beheld, with her eyes closed, her cheeks pale and pinched, her hair thinner, but still falling like a veil over her, the love of his youth, the only woman he had ever loved devotedly and unselfishly.

There is little space left here, to tell of how the two met at last—of how the stone of the years seemed suddenly rolled away from the tomb of their past, and their youth arose and returned to them even amid their tears.

She had been true to him, through persecution, through contumely, through kindness, which was more trying: through shame, and grief, and poverty, she had been loyal to the lover of her youth; and before the new year dawned there came a letter from Calgillan, saying that the banshee had been heard there, and praying Hertford, if he were still alive, to let bygones be bygones, in consideration of the long years of estrangement—the anguish and remorse of his afflicted parents.

More than that. Hertford O'Donnell, if a reckless man, was honourable; and so, on the Christmas Day when he was to have proposed for Miss Ingot, he went to that lady, and told her how he had wooed and won in the years of his youth one who after many days was miraculously restored to him; and from the hour in which he took her into his confidence he never thought her either vulgar or foolish, but rather he paid homage to the woman who, when she had heard the whole tale repeated, said, simply, "Ask her to come to me till you claim her—and God bless you both!"

C *is for* Carnivorous Plant

British writer Frederick Merrick White (1859–?) contributed several tales of horror and science fiction to *Pearson's* and other popular fiction magazines around the turn of the twentieth century. In this story, which was published in the September 1899 issue of *The Strand,* he imagines a plant with the qualities of a Venus Flytrap—but on a scale large enough to menace humans.

FRED M. WHITE

The Purple Terror

I

Lieutenant Will Scarlett's instructions were devoid of problems, physical or otherwise. To convey a letter from Captain Driver of the Yankee Doodle, in Porto Rico Bay, to Admiral Lake on the other side of the isthmus, was an apparently simple matter.

"All you have to do," the captain remarked, "is to take three or four men with you in case of accidents, cross the isthmus on foot, and simply give this letter into the hands of Admiral Lake. By so doing we shall save at least four days, and the aborigines are presumedly friendly."

The aborigines aforesaid were Cuban insurgents. Little or no strife had taken place along the neck lying between Porto Rico and the north bay where Lake's flagship lay, though the belt was known to be given over to the disaffected Cubans.

"It is a matter of fifty miles through practically unexplored country," Scarlett replied; "and there's a good deal of the family quarrel in this business, sir. If the Spaniards hate us, the Cubans are not exactly enamoured of our flag."

Captain Driver roundly denounced the whole pack of them.

"Treacherous thieves to a man," he said. " I don't suppose your progress will have any brass bands and floral arches to it. And they tell me the forest is pretty thick. But you'll get there all the same. There is the letter, and you can start as soon as you like."

"I may pick my own men, sir? "

"My dear fellow, take whom you please. Take the mastiff, if you like."

"I'd like the mastiff," Scarlett replied; "as he is practically my own, I thought you would not object."

Will Scarlett began to glow as the prospect of adventure stimulated his imagination. He was rather a good specimen of West Point naval dandyism. He had brains at the back of his smartness, and his geological and botanical knowledge were going to prove of considerable service to a grateful country when said grateful country should have passed beyond the rudimentary stages of colonization. And there was some disposition to envy Scarlett on the part of others floating for the past month on the liquid prison of the sapphire sea.

A warrant officer, Tarrer by name, *plus* two A.B.'s of thews and sinews, to say nothing of the dog, completed the exploring party. By the time that the sun kissed the tip of the feathery hills they had covered some six miles of their journey. From the first Scarlett had been struck by the absolute absence of the desolation and horror of civil strife. Evidently the fiery cross had not been carried here; huts and houses were intact; the villagers stood under sloping eaves, and regarded the Americans with a certain sullen curiosity.

"We'd better stop for the night here," said Scarlett.

They had come at length to a village that boasted some pretensions. An adobe chapel at one end of the straggling street was faced by a wine-house at the other. A padre, with hands folded over a bulbous, greasy gabardine, bowed gravely to Scarlett's salutation. The latter had what Tarrer called "considerable Spanish."

"We seek quarters for the night," said Scarlett. " Of course, we are prepared to pay for them."

The sleepy padre nodded towards the wine-house.

"You will find fair accommodation there," he said. " We are friends of the Americanos."

Scarlett doubted the fact, and passed on with florid thanks. So far, little signs of friendliness had been encountered on the march. Coldness, suspicion, a suggestion of fear, but no friendliness to be embarrassing.

The keeper of the wine-shop had his doubts. He feared his poor accommodation for guests so distinguished. A score or more of picturesque, cut-throat-looking rascals with cigarettes in their mouths lounged sullenly in the bar. The display of a brace of gold dollars enlarged mine host's opinion of his household capacity.

"I will do my best, señors," he said. "Come this way."

So it came to pass that an hour after twilight Tarrer and Scarlett were seated in the open amongst the oleanders and the trailing gleam of the fireflies, discussing cigars of average merit and a native wine that was not without virtues. The long bar of the wine-house was brilliantly illuminated; from within came shouts of laughter mingled with the ting, tang of the guitar and the rollicking clack of the castanets.

"They seem to be happy in there," Tarrer remarked. "It isn't all daggers and ball in this distressful country."

A certain curiosity came over Scarlett.

"It is the duty of a good officer," he said, "to lose no opportunity of acquiring useful information. Let us join the giddy throng, Tarrer."

Tarrer expressed himself with enthusiasm in favour of any amusement that might be going. A month's idleness on shipboard increases the appetite for that kind of thing wonderfully. The long bar was comfortable, and filled with Cubans who took absolutely no notice of the intruders. Their eyes were turned towards a rude stage at the far end of the bar, whereon a girl was gyrating in a dance with a celerity and grace that caused the wreath of flowers around her shoulders to resemble a trembling zone of purple flame.

"A wonderfully pretty girl and a wonderfully pretty dance," Scarlett murmured, when the motions ceased and the girl leapt gracefully to the ground. "Largesse, I expect. I thought so. Well, I'm good for a quarter."

The girl came forward, extending a shell prettily. She curtsied before Scarlett and fixed her dark, liquid eyes on his. As he smiled and dropped his quarter-dollar into the shell a coquettish gleam came into the velvety eyes. An ominous growl came from the lips of a bearded ruffian close by.

"Othello's jealous," said Tarrer. "Look at his face."

"I am better employed," Scarlett laughed. "That was a graceful dance, pretty one. I hope you are going to give us another one presently"

Scarlett paused suddenly. His eyes had fallen on the purple band of flowers the girl had twined round her shoulder. Scarlett was an enthusiastic botanist; he knew most of the gems in Flora's crown, but he had never looked upon such a vivid wealth of blossom before.

The flowers were orchids, and orchids of a kind unknown to collectors anywhere. On this point Scarlett felt certain. And yet this part of the world was by no means a difficult one to explore in comparison with New Guinea and Sumatra, where the rarer varieties had their homes.

The blooms were immensely large, far larger than any flower of the kind known to Europe or America, of a deep pure purple, with a blood-red centre. As Scarlett gazed upon them he noticed a certain cruel expression on the flower. Most orchids have a kind of face of their own; the purple blooms had a positive expression of ferocity and cunning. They exhumed, too, a queer, sickly fragrance. Scarlett had smelt something like it before, after the Battle of Manila. The perfume was the perfume of a corpse.

"And yet they are magnificent flowers," said Scarlett. "Won't you tell me where you got them from, pretty one?"

The girl was evidently flattered by the attention bestowed upon her by the smart young American. The bearded Othello alluded to edged up to her side.

"The señor had best leave the girl alone," he said, insolently.

Scarlett's fist clenched as he measured the Cuban with his eyes. The Admiral's letter crackled in his breast-pocket, and discretion got the best of valour.

"You are paying yourself a poor compliment, my good fellow," he said, "though I certainly admire your good taste. Those flowers interested me."

The man appeared to be mollified. His features corrugated in a smile.

"The señor would like some of those blooms?" he asked. "It was I who procured them for little Zara here. I can show you where they grow."

Every eye in the room was turned in Scarlett's direction. It seemed to him that a kind of diabolical malice glistened on every dark face there, save that of the girl, whose features paled under her healthy tan.

"If the señor is wise," she began, "he will not—"

"Listen to the tales of a silly girl," Othello put in, menacingly. He grasped the girl by the arm, and she winced in positive pain. "Pshaw, there is no harm where the flowers grow, if one is only careful. I will take you there, and I will be your guide to Port Anna, where you are going, for a gold dollar."

All Scarlett's scientific enthusiasm was aroused. It is not given to every man to present a new orchid to the horticultural world. And this one would dwarf the finest plant hitherto discovered.

"Done with you," he said; "we start at daybreak. I shall look to you to be ready. Your name is Tito? Well, good-night, Tito."

As Scarlett and Tarrer withdrew the girl suddenly darted forward. A wild word or two fluttered from her lips. Then there was a sound as of a blow, followed by a little, stifled cry of pain.

"No, no," Tarrer urged, as Scarlett half turned. "Better not. They are ten to one, and they are no friends of ours. It never pays to interfere in these family quarrels. I daresay, if you interfered, the girl would be just as ready to knife you as her jealous lover."

"But a blow like that, Tarrer!"

"It's a pity, but I don't see how we can help it. Your business is the quick dispatch of the Admiral's letter, not the squiring of dames."

Scarlett owned with a sigh that Tarrer was right.

II

It was quite a different Tito who presented himself at daybreak the following morning. His insolent manner had disappeared. He was cheerful, alert, and he had a manner full of the most winning politeness.

"You quite understand what we want," Scarlett said. "My desire is to reach Port Anna as soon as possible. You know the way?"

"Every inch of it, señor. I have made the journey scores of times. And I shall have the felicity of getting you there early on the third day from now."

"Is it so far as that?"

"The distance is not great, señor. It is the passage through the woods. There are parts where no white man has been before."

"And you will not forget the purple orchids?"

A queer gleam trembled like summer lightning in Tito's eyes. The next instant it had gone. A time was to come when Scarlett was to recall that look, but for the moment it was allowed to pass.

"The señor shall see the purple orchid," he said; "thousands of them. They have a bad name amongst our people, but that is all nonsense. They grow in the high trees, and their blossoms cling to long, green tendrils. These tendrils are poisonous to the flesh, and great care should be taken in handling them. And the flowers are quite harmless, though we call them the devil's poppies."

To all of this Scarlett listened eagerly. He was all-impatient to see and handle the mysterious flower for himself. The whole excursion was going to prove a wonderful piece of luck. At the same time he had to curb his impatience. There would be no chance of seeing the purple orchid to-day.

For hours they fought their way along through the dense tangle. A heat seemed to lie over all the land like a curse—a blistering, sweltering, moist heat with no puff of wind to temper its breathlessness. By the time that the sun was sliding down, most of the party had had enough of it.

They passed out of the underwood at length, and, striking upwards, approached a clump of huge forest trees on the brow of a ridge. All kinds of parasites hung from the branches: there were ropes and bands of green, and high up a fringe of purple glory that caused Scarlett's pulses to leap a little faster.

"Surely that is the purple orchid?" he cried.

Tito shrugged his shoulders contemptuously.

"A mere straggler or two," he said, "and out of our reach in any case. The señor will have all he wants and more to-morrow."

"But it seems to me," said Scarlett, "that I could—"

Then he paused. The sun like a great glowing shield was shining full behind the tree with its crown of purple, and showing up every green rope and thread clinging to the branches with the clearness of liquid crystal. Scarlett saw a network of green cords like a huge spider's web, and in the centre of it was not a fly, but a human skeleton!

The arms and legs were stretched apart as if the victim had been crucified. The wrists and ankles were bound in the cruel web. Fragments of tattered clothing fluttered in the faint breath of the evening breeze.

"Horrible," Scarlett cried, "absolutely horrible!"

"You may well say that," Tarrer exclaimed, with a shudder. "Like the fly in the amber or the apple in the dumpling, the mystery is how he got there."

"Perhaps Tito can explain the mystery," Scarlett suggested.

Tito appeared to be uneasy and disturbed. He looked furtively from one to the other of his employers as a culprit might who feels he has been found out. But his courage returned as he noted the absence of suspicion in the faces turned upon him.

"I can explain," he exclaimed, with teeth that chattered from some unknown terror or guilt. "It is not the first time that I have seen the skeleton. Some plant-hunter doubtless who came here alone. He climbed into the tree without a knife, and those green ropes got twisted round his limbs, as a swimmer gets entangled in the weeds. The more he struggled, the more the cords bound him. He would call in vain for anyone to assist him here. And so he must have died."

The explanation was a plausible one, but by no means detracted from the horror of the discovery. For some time the party pushed their way on in the twilight, till the darkness descended suddenly like a curtain.

"We will camp here," Tito said; "it is high, dry ground, and we have this belt of trees above us. There is no better place than this for miles around. In the valley the miasma is dangerous."

As Tito spoke he struck a match, and soon a torch flamed up. The little party were on a small plateau, fringed by trees. The ground was dry and hard, and. as Scarlett and his party saw to their astonishment, littered with bones. There were skulls of animals and skulls of human beings, the skeletons of birds, the frames of beasts both great and small. It was a weird, shuddering sight.

"We can't possibly stay here," Scarlett exclaimed.

Tito shrugged his shoulders.

"There is nowhere else," he replied. "Down in the valley there are many dangers. Further in the woods are the snakes and jaguars. Bones are nothing. Peuf, they can be easily cleared away."

They had to be cleared away, and there was an end of the matter. For the most part the skeletons were white and dry as air and sun could make them. Over the dry, calcined mass the huge fringe of trees nodded mournfully. With the rest, Scarlett was busy scattering the mocking frames aside.

A perfect human skeleton lay at his feet. On one finger something glittered—a signet ring. As Scarlett took it in his hand he started.

"I know this ring!" he exclaimed; "it belonged to Pierre Anton, perhaps the most skilled and intrepid plant-hunter the *Jardin des Plantes* ever employed. The poor fellow was by way of being a friend of mine. He met the fate that he always anticipated."

"There must have been a rare holocaust here," said Tarrer.

"It beats me," Scarlett responded. By this time a large circle had been shifted clear of human and other remains. By the light of the fire loathsome insects could be seen scudding and straddling away. "It beats me entirely. Tito, can you offer any explanation? If the bones were all human I could get some grip of the problem. But when one comes to birds and animals as well! Do you see that the skeletons lie in a perfect circle, starting from the centre of the clump of trees above us? What does it mean?"

Tito professed utter ignorance of the subject. Some years before a small tribe of natives invaded the peninsula for religious rites. They came from a long way off in canoes, and wild stories were told concerning them. They burnt sacrifices, no doubt.

Scarlett turned his back contemptuously on this transparent tale. His curiosity was aroused. There must be some explanation, for Pierre Anton had been seen of men within the last ten years.

"There's something uncanny about this," he said, to Tarrer. "I mean to get to the bottom of it, or know why."

"As for me," said Tarrer, with a cavernous yawn, "I have but one ambition, and that is my supper, followed by my bed."

III

Scarlett lay in the light of the fire looking about him. He felt restless and uneasy, though he would have found it difficult to explain the reason. For one thing, the air trembled to strange noises. There seemed to be something moving, writhing in the forest trees above his head. More than once it seemed to his distorted fancy that he could see a squirming knot of green snakes in motion.

Outside the circle, in a grotto of bones, Tito lay sleeping. A few moments before his dark, sleek head had been furtively raised, and his eyes seemed to gleam in the flickering firelight with malignant cunning. As he met Scarlett's glance he gave a deprecatory gesture and subsided.

"What the deuce does it all mean?" Scarlett muttered. "I feel certain yonder rascal is up to some mischief. Jealous still because I paid his girl a little attention. But he can't do us any real harm. Quiet, there!"

The big mastiff growled and then whined uneasily. Even the dog seemed to be conscious of some unseen danger. He lay down again, cowed by the stern command, but he still whimpered in his dreams.

"I fancy I'll keep awake for a spell," Scarlett told himself.

For a time he did so. Presently he began to slide away into the land of poppies. He was walking amongst a garden of bones which bore masses of purple blossoms. Then Pierre Anton came on the scene, pale and resolute as Scarlett had always known him; then the big mastiff seemed in some way to be mixed up with the phantasm of the dream, barking as if in pain, and Scarlett came to his senses.

He was breathing short, a beady perspiration stood on his forehead, his heart hammered in quick thuds—all the horrors of nightmare were still upon him. In a vague way as yet he heard the mastiff howl, a real howl of real terror, and Scarlett knew that he was awake.

Then a strange thing happened. In the none too certain light of the fire, Scarlett saw the mastiff snatched up by some invisible hand, carried far on high towards the trees, and finally flung to the earth with a crash. The big dog lay still as a log.

A sense of fear born of the knowledge of impotence came over Scarlett; what in the name of evil did it all mean? The smart scientist had no faith in the occult, and yet what did it all mean?

Nobody stirred. Scarlett's companions were soaked and soddened with fatigue; the rolling thunder of artillery would have scarce disturbed them. With teeth set and limbs that trembled, Scarlett crawled over to the dog.

The great, black-muzzled creature was quite dead. The full chest was stained and soaked in blood; the throat had been cut apparently with some jagged, saw-like instrument away to the bone. And, strangest thing of all, scattered all about the body was a score or more of the great purple orchid flowers broken off close to the head. A hot, pricking sensation travelled slowly up Scarlett's spine and seemed to pass out at the tip of his skull. He felt his hair rising.

He was frightened. As a matter of honest fact, he had never been so horribly scared in his life before. The whole thing was so mysterious, so cruel, so bloodthirsty.

Still, there must be some rational explanation. In some way the matter had to do with the purple orchid. The flower had an evil reputation. Was it not known to these Cubans as the devil's poppy?

Scarlett recollected vividly now Zara's white, scared face when Tito had volunteered to show the way to the resplendent bloom; he remembered the cry of the girl and the blow that followed. He could see it all now. The girl had meant to warn him against some nameless horror to which Tito was leading the small party. This was the jealous Cuban's revenge.

A wild desire to pay this debt to the uttermost fraction filled Scarlett, and shook him with a trembling passion. He crept along in the drenching dew to where Tito lay, and touched his forehead with the chill blue rim of a revolver barrel. Tito stirred slightly.

"You dog! " Scarlett cried. "I am going to shoot you."

Tito did not move again. His breathing was soft and regular. Beyond a doubt the man was sleeping peacefully. After all he might be innocent; and yet, on the other hand, he might be so sure of his quarry that he could afford to slumber without anxiety as to his vengeance.

In favour of the latter theory was the fact that the Cuban lay beyond the limit of what had previously been the circle of dry bones. It was just possible that there was no danger outside that pale. In that case it would be easy to arouse the rest, and so save them from the horrible death which had befallen the mastiff. No doubt these were a form of upas tree, but that would not account for the ghastly spectacle in mid-air.

"I'll let this chap sleep for the present," Scarlett muttered.

He crawled back, not without misgivings, into the ring of death. He meant to wake the others and then wait for further developments. By now his senses were more alert and vigorous than they had ever been before. A preternatural clearness of brain and vision possessed him. As he advanced he saw suddenly falling a green bunch of cord that straightened into a long, emerald line. It was triangular in shape, fine at the apex, and furnished with hooked spines. The rope appeared to dangle from the tree overhead; the broad, sucker-like termination was evidently soaking up moisture.

A natural phenomenon evidently, Scarlett thought. This was some plant new to him, a parasite living amongst the tree-tops and drawing life and vigour by means of these green, rope-like antennae designed by Nature to soak and absorb the heavy dews of night.

For a moment the logic of this theory was soothing to Scarlett's distracted nerves, but only for a moment, for then he saw at regular intervals along the green rope the big purple blossoms of the devil's poppy.

He stood gasping there, utterly taken aback for the moment. There must be some infernal juggling behind all this business. He saw the rope slacken and quiver, he saw it swing forward like a pendulum, and the next minute it had passed across the shoulders of a sleeping seaman.

Then the green root became as the arm of an octopus. The line shook from end to end like the web of an angry spider when invaded by a wasp. It seemed to grip the sailor and tighten, and then, before Scarlett's affrighted eyes, the sleeping man was raised gently from the ground.

Scarlett jumped forward with a desire to scream hysterically. Now that a comrade was in danger he was no longer afraid. He whipped a jack-knife from his pocket and slashed at the cruel cord. He half expected to meet with the stoutness of a steel strand, but to his surprise the feeler snapped like a carrot, bumping the sailor heavily on the ground.

He sat up, rubbing his eyes vigorously.

"That you, sir?" he asked. "What is the matter?"

"For the love of God, get up at once and help me to arouse the others," Scarlett said, hoarsely. We have come across the devil's workshop. All the horrors of the inferno are invented here."

The bluejacket struggled to his feet. As he did so, the clothing from his waist downwards slipped about his feet, clean cut through by the teeth of the green parasite. All around the body of the sailor blood oozed from a zone of teeth-marks.

Two-o'clock-in-the-morning courage is a virtue vouchsafed to few. The tar, who would have faced an ironclad cheerfully, fairly shivered with fright and dismay.

"What does it mean, sir?" he cried. "I've been—"

"Wake the others," Scarlett screamed; "wake the others."

Two or three more green tangles of rope came tumbling to the ground, straightening and quivering instantly. The purple blossoms stood out like a frill upon them. Like a madman Scarlett shouted, kicking his companions without mercy.

They were all awake at last, grumbling and moaning for their lost slumbers. All this time Tito had never stirred.

"I don't understand it at all," said Tarrer.

"Come from under those trees," said Scarlett, "and I will endeavour to explain. Not that you will believe me for a moment. No man can be expected to believe the awful nightmare I am going to tell you."

Scarlett proceeded to explain. As he expected, his story was followed with marked incredulity, save by the wounded sailor, who had strong evidence to stimulate his otherwise defective imagination.

"I can't believe it," Tarrer said, at length. They were whispering together beyond earshot of Tito, whom they had no desire to arouse for obvious reasons. "This is some diabolical juggling of yonder rascally Cuban. It seems impossible that those slender green cords could—"

Scarlett pointed to the centre of the circle.

"Call the dog," he said, grimly, "and see if he will come."

"I admit the point as far as the poor old mastiff is concerned. But at the same time I don't—however, I'll see for myself."

By this time a dozen or more of the slender cords were hanging pendent from the trees. They moved from spot to spot as if jerked up by some unseen hand and deposited a foot or two farther. With the great purple bloom fringing the stem, the effect was not unlovely save to Scarlett, who could see only the dark side of it. As Tarrer spoke he advanced in the direction of the trees.

"What are you going to do?" Scarlett asked.

"Exactly what I told you. I am going to investigate this business for myself."

Without wasting further words Scarlett sprang forward. It was no time for the niceties of an effete civilization. Force was the only logical argument to be used in a case like this, and Scarlett was the more powerful man of the two.

Tarrer saw and appreciated the situation.

"No, no," he cried; "none of that. Anyway, you're too late."

He darted forward and threaded his way between the slender emerald columns. As they moved slowly and with a certain stately deliberation there was no great danger to an alert and vigorous individual. As Scarlett entered the avenue he could hear the soak and suck as the dew was absorbed.

"For Heaven's sake, come out of it," he cried.

The warning came too late. A whip-like trail of green touched Tarrer from behind, and in a lightning flash he was in the coils. The tendency to draw up anything and everything gave the cords a terrible power. Tarrer evidently felt it, for his breath came in great gasps.

"Cut me free," he said, hoarsely; "cut me free. I am being carried off my feet."

He seemed to be doomed for a moment, for all the cords there were apparently converging in his direction. This, as a matter of fact, was a solution of the whole sickening, horrible sensation. Pulled here and there, thrust in one direction and another, Tarrer contrived to keep his feet.

Heedless of possible danger to himself Scarlett darted forward, calling to his companions to come to the rescue. In less time than it takes to tell, four knives were at work ripping and slashing in all directions.

"Not all of you," Scarlett whispered. So tense was the situation that no voice was raised above a murmur. "You two keep your eyes open for fresh cords, and cut them as they fall, instantly. Now then."

The horrible green spines were round Tarrer's body like snakes. His face was white, his breath came painfully, for the pressure was terrible. It seemed to Scarlett to be one horrible dissolving view of green, slimy cords and great weltering, purple blossoms. The whole of the circle was strewn with them. They were wet and slimy underfoot.

Tarrer had fallen forward half unconscious. He was supported now by but two cords above his head. The cruel pressure had been relieved. With one savage sweep of his knife Scarlett cut the last of the lines, and Tarrer fell like a log unconscious to the ground. A feeling of nausea, a yellow dizziness, came over Scarlett as he staggered beyond the dread circle. He saw Tarrer carried to a place of safety, and then the world seemed to wither and leave him in the dark.

"I feel a bit groggy and weak," said Tarrer an hour or so later: "but beyond that this idiot of a Richard is himself again. So far as I am concerned, I should like to get even with our friend Tito for this."

"Something with boiling oil in it," Scarlett suggested, grimly. "The callous scoundrel has slept soundly through the whole of this business. I suppose he felt absolutely certain that he had finished with us."

"Upon my word, we ought to shoot the beggar!" Tarrer exclaimed.

"I have a little plan of my own," said Scarlett, "which I am going to put in force later on. Meanwhile we had better get on with breakfast. When Tito wakes a pleasant little surprise will await him."

Tito roused from his slumbers in due course and looked around him. His glance was curious, disappointed, then full of a white and yellow fear. A thousand conflicting emotions streamed across his dark face. Scarlett read them at a glance as he called the Cuban over to him.

"I am not going into any unnecessary details with you," he said. "It has come to my knowledge that you are playing traitor to us. Therefore we prefer to complete our journey alone. We can easily find the way now."

"The señor may do as he pleases," he replied. "Give me my dollar and let me go."

Scarlett replied grimly that he had no intention of doing anything of the kind. He did not propose to place the lives of himself and his comrades in the power of a rascally Cuban who had played false.

"We are going to leave you here till we return," he said. "You will have plenty of food, you will be perfectly safe under the shelter of these trees, and there is no chance of anybody disturbing you. We are going to tie you up to one of these trees for the next four-and-twenty hours."

All the insolence died out of Tito's face. His knees bowed, a cold dew came out over the ghastly green of his features. From the shaking of his limbs he might have fared disastrously with ague.

"The trees," he stammered, "the trees, señor! There is danger from snakes, and—and from many things. There are other places—"

"If this place was safe last night it is safe to-day," Scarlett said, grimly. "I have quite made up my mind."

Tito fought no longer. He fell forward on his knees, he howled for mercy, till Scarlett fairly kicked him up again.

"Make a clean breast of it," he said, "or take the consequences. You know perfectly well that we have found you out, scoundrel."

Tito's story came in gasps. He wanted to get rid of the Americans. He was jealous. Besides, under the Americanos would Cuba be any better off? By no means and assuredly not. Therefore it was the duty of every good Cuban to destroy the Americanos where possible.

"A nice lot to fight for," Scarlett muttered. "Get to the point."

Hastened to the point by a liberal application of stout shoe-leather, Tito made plenary confession. The señor himself had suggested death by medium of the devil's poppies. More than one predatory plant-hunter had been lured to his destruction in the same way. The skeleton hung on the tree was a Dutchman who had walked into the clutch of the purple terror innocently. And Pierre Anton had done the same. The suckers of the devil's poppy only came down at night to gather moisture; in the day they were coiled up like a spring. And anything that they touched they killed. Tito had watched more than one bird or small beast crushed and mauled by these cruel spines with their fringe of purple blossoms.

"How do you get the blooms?" Scarlett asked.

"That is easy," Tito replied. "In the daytime I moisten the ground under the trees. Then the suckers unfold, drawn by the water. Once the suckers unfold one cuts several of them off with long knives. There is danger, of course, but not if one is careful."

"I'll not trouble the devil's poppy any further at present," said Scarlett, "but I shall trouble you to accompany me to my destination as a prisoner."

Tito's eyes dilated.

"They will not shoot me?" he asked, hoarsely.

"I don't know," Scarlett replied. "They may hang you instead. At any rate, I shall be bitterly disappointed if they don't end you one way or the other. Whichever operation it is, I can look forward to it with perfect equanimity."

D *is for* Demon

Demons come in all shapes and sizes, and they don't always issue from the underworld. The otherworldly creatures American writer Clark Ashton Smith (1893–1961) conjures in this tale, first published in the October 1932 issue of the pulp magazine *Strange Tales of Mystery and Terror*, have all the endowments of infernal demons, and woe betide the person who doesn't treat them with the caution such monsters warrant.

CLARK ASHTON SMITH

The Hunters from Beyond

I have seldom been able to resist the allurement of a bookstore, particularly one that is well supplied with rare and exotic items. Therefore I turned in at Toleman's to browse around for a few minutes. I had come to San Francisco for one of my brief, biannual visits, and had started early that idle forenoon to an appointment with Cyprian Sincaul, the sculptor, a second or third cousin of mine, whom I had not seen for several years.

His studio was only a block from Toleman's, and there seemed to be no especial object in reaching it ahead of time. Cyprian had offered to show me his collection of recent sculptures; but, remembering the smooth mediocrity of his former work, amid which were a few banal efforts to achieve horror and grotesquerie, I did not anticipate anything more than an hour or two of dismal boredom.

The little shop was empty of customers. Knowing my proclivities, the owner and his one assistant became tacitly non-attentive after a word of recognition, and left me to rummage at will among the curiously laden shelves. Wedged in between other but less alluring titles, I found a deluxe edition of Goya's *Proverbes.* I began to turn the heavy pages, and was soon engrossed in the diabolic art of these nightmare-nurtured drawings.

It has always been incomprehensible to me that I did not shriek aloud with mindless, overmastering terror, when I happened to look up from the volume, and saw the thing that was crouching in a corner of the bookshelves before me. I could not have been more hideously startled if some hellish conception of Goya had suddenly come to life and emerged from one of the pictures in the folio.

What I saw was a forward-slouching, vermin-gray figure, wholly devoid of hair or down or bristles, but marked with faint, etiolated rings like those of a serpent that has lived in darkness. It possessed the head and brow of an anthropoid ape, a semi-canine mouth and jaw, and arms ending in twisted hands whose black hyena talons nearly scraped the floor. The thing was infinitely bestial, and, at the same time, macabre; for its parchment skin was shriveled, corpselike, mummified, in a manner impossible to convey; and from eye sockets well-nigh deep as those of a skull, there glimmered evil slits of yellowish phosphorescence, like burning sulphur. Fangs that were stained as if with poison or gangrene, issued from the slavering, half-open mouth; and the whole attitude of the creature was that of some maleficent monster in readiness to spring.

Though I had been for years a professional writer of stories that often dealt with occult phenomena, with the weird and the spectral, I was not at this time possessed of any clear and settled belief regarding such phenomena. I had never before seen anything that I could identify as a phantom, nor even an hallucination; and I should hardly have said offhand that a bookstore on a busy street, in full summer daylight, was the likeliest of places in which to see one. But the thing before me was assuredly nothing that could ever exist among the permissible forms of a sane world. It was too horrific, too atrocious, to be anything but a creation of unreality.

Even as I stared across the Goya, sick with a half-incredulous fear, the apparition moved toward me. I say that it moved, but its change of position was so instantaneous, so utterly without effort or visible transition, that the verb is hopelessly inadequate. The foul specter had seemed five or six feet away. But now it was stooping directly above the volume that I still held in my hands, with its loathsomely lambent eyes peering upward at my face, and a gray-green slime drooling from its mouth on the broad pages. At the same time I breathed an insupportable fetor, like a mingling of rancid serpent-stench with the moldiness of antique charnels and the fearsome reek of newly decaying carrion.

In a frozen timelessness that was perhaps no more than a second or two, my heart appeared to suspend its beating, while I beheld the ghastly face. Gasping, I let the Goya drop with a resonant bang on the floor, and even as it fell, I saw that the vision had vanished.

Toleman, a tonsured gnome with shell-rimmed goggles, rushed forward to retrieve the fallen volume, exclaiming: "What is wrong, Mr. Hastane? Are you ill?" From the meticulousness with which he examined the binding in search of possible damage, I knew that his chief solicitude was concerning the Goya. It was plain that neither he nor his clerk had seen the phantom; nor could I detect aught in their demeanor to indicate that they had noticed the mephitic odor that still lingered in the air like an exhalation from broken graves. And, as far as I could tell, they did not even perceive the grayish slime that still polluted the open folio.

I do not remember how I managed to make my exit from the shop. My mind had become a seething blur of muddled horror, of crawling, sick revulsion from the supernatural vileness I had beheld, together with the direst apprehension for my own sanity and safety. I recall only that I found myself on the street above Toleman's, walking with feverish rapidity toward my cousin's studio, with a neat parcel containing the Goya volume under my arm. Evidently, in an effort to atone for my clumsiness, I must have bought and paid for the book by a sort of automatic impulse, without any real awareness of what I was doing.

I came to the building in which was my destination, but went on around the block several times before entering. All the while I fought desperately to regain my self-control and equipoise. I remember how difficult it was even to moderate the pace at which I was walking, or refrain from breaking into a run; for it seemed to me that I was fleeing all the time from an invisible pursuer. I tried to argue with myself, to convince the rational part of my mind that the apparition had been the product of some evanescent trick of light and shade, or a temporary dimming of eyesight. But such sophistries were useless; for I had seen the gargoylish terror all too distinctly, in an unforgettable fullness of grisly detail.

What could the thing mean? I had never used narcotic drugs or abused alcohol. My nerves, as far as I knew, were in sound condition. But either I had suffered a visual hallucination that might mark the beginning of some obscure cerebral disorder, or had been visited by a spectral phenomenon, by something from realms and dimensions that are past the normal scope of human perception. It was a problem either for the alienist or the occultist.

Though I was still damnably upset, I contrived to regain a nominal composure of my faculties. Also, it occurred to me that the unimaginative portrait busts and tamely symbolic figure-groups of Cyprian Sincaul might serve admirably to sooth my shaken nerves. Even his grotesques would seem sane and ordinary by comparison with the blasphemous gargoyle that had drooled before me in the bookshop.

I entered the studio building, and climbed a worn stairway to the second floor, where Cyprian had established himself in a somewhat capacious suite of rooms. As I went up the stairs, I had the peculiar feeling that somebody was climbing them just ahead of me; but I could neither see nor hear anyone, and the hall above was no less silent and empty than the stairs.

Cyprian was in his atelier when I knocked. After an interval which seemed unduly long, I heard him call out, telling me to enter. I found him wiping his hands on an old cloth, and surmised that he had been modeling. A sheet of light burlap had been thrown over what was plainly an ambitious but unfinished group of figures, which occupied the center of the long room. All around were other sculptures, in clay, bronze, marble, and even the terra cotta and steatite which he sometimes employed for his less conventional conceptions. At one end of the room there stood a heavy Chinese screen.

At a single glance I realized that a great change had occurred, both in Cyprian Sincaul and his work. I remembered him as an amiable, somewhat flabby-looking youth, always dapperly dressed, with no trace of the dreamer or visionary. It was hard to recognize him now, for he had become lean, harsh, vehement. with an air of pride and penetration that was almost Luciferian. His unkempt mane of hair was already shot with white, and his eyes were electrically brilliant with a strange knowledge, and yet somehow were vaguely furtive, as if there dwelt behind them a morbid and macabre fear.

The change in his sculpture was no less striking. The respectable tameness and polished mediocrity were gone, and in their place, incredibly, was something little short of genius. More unbelievable still, in view of the laboriously ordinary grotesques of his earlier phase, was the trend that his art had now taken. All around me were frenetic, murderous demons, satyrs mad with nympholepsy, ghouls that seemed to sniff the odors of the charnel, lamias voluptuously coiled about their victims, and less namable things that belonged to the outland realms of evil myth and malign superstition.

Sin, horror, blasphemy, diablerie—the lust and malice of pandemonium—all had been caught with impeccable art. The potent nightmarishness of these creations was not calculated to reassure my trembling nerves; and all at once I felt an imperative desire to escape from the studio, to flee from the baleful throng of frozen cacodemons and chiseled chimeras.

My expression must have betrayed my feelings to some extent.

"Pretty strong work, aren't they?" said Cyprian, in a loud, vibrant voice, with a note of harsh pride and triumph. "I can see that you are surprised—you didn't look for anything of the sort, I dare say."

"No, candidly, I didn't," I admitted. "Good Lord, man, you will become the Michelangelo of diabolism if you go on at this rate. Where on earth do you get such stuff?"

"Yes, I've gone pretty far," said Cyprian, seeming to disregard my question. "Further even than you think, probably. If you could know what I know, could see what I have seen, you might make something really worth-while out of your weird fiction, Philip. You are very clever and imaginative, of course. But you've never had any experience."

I was startled and puzzled. "Experience? What do you mean?"

"Precisely that. You try to depict the occult and the supernatural without even the most rudimentary first-hand knowledge of them. I tried to do something of the same sort in sculpture, years ago, without knowledge; and doubtless you recall the mediocre mess that I made of it. But I've learned a thing or two since then."

"Sounds as if you had made the traditional bond with the devil, or something of the sort," I observed, with a feeble and perfunctory levity.

Cyprian's eyes narrowed slightly, with a strange, secret look.

"I know what I know. Never mind how or why. The world in which we live isn't the only world; and some of the others lie closer at hand than you think. The boundaries of the seen and the unseen are sometimes interchangeable."

Recalling the malevolent phantom, I felt a peculiar disquietude as I listened to his words. An hour before, his statement would have impressed me as mere theorizing, but now it assumed an ominous and terrifying significance.

"What makes you think I have had no experience of the occult?" I asked.

"Your stories hardly show anything of the kind—anything factual or personal. They are all palpably made up. When you've argued with a ghost, or watched the ghouls at meal-time, or fought with an incubus, or suckled a vampire, you may achieve some genuine characterization and color along such lines."

For reasons that should be fairly obvious, I had not intended to tell anyone of the unbelievable thing at Toleman's. Now, with a singular mixture of emotions, of compulsive, eerie terrors and desire to refute the animadversions of Cyprian, I found myself describing the phantom.

He listened with an inexpressive look, as if his thoughts were occupied with other matters than my story. Then, when I had finished:

"You are becoming more psychic than I imagined. Was your apparition anything like one of these?"

With the last words, he lifted the sheet of burlap from the muffled group of figures beside which he had been standing.

I cried out involuntarily with the shock of that appalling revelation, and almost tottered as I stepped back.

Before me, in a monstrous semicircle, were seven creatures who might all have been modeled from the gargoyle that had confronted me across the folio of Goya drawings. Even in several that were still amorphous or incomplete, Cyprian had conveyed with a damnable art the peculiar mingling of primal bestiality and mortuary putrescence that had signalized the phantom. The seven monsters had closed in on a cowering, naked girl, and were all clutching foully toward her with their hyena claws. The stark, frantic, insane terror on the face of the girl, and the slavering hunger of her assailants, were alike unbearable. The group was a masterpiece, in its consummate power of technique—but a masterpiece that inspired loathing rather than admiration. And following my recent experience, the sight of it affected me with indescribable alarm. It seemed to me that I had gone astray from the normal, familiar world into a land of detestable mystery, of prodigious and unnatural menace.

Held by an abhorrent fascination, it was hard for me to wrench my eyes away from the figure-piece. At last I turned from it to Cyprian himself. He was regarding me with a cryptic air, beneath which I suspected a covert gloating.

"How do you like my little pets?" he inquired. "I am going to call the composition *The Hunters from Beyond*."

Before I could answer, a woman suddenly appeared from behind the Chinese screen. I saw that she was the model for the girl in the unfinished group. Evidently she had been dressing, and she was now ready to leave, for she wore a tailored suit and a smart toque. She was beautiful, in a dark, semi-Latin fashion; but her mouth was sullen and reluctant, and her wide, liquid eyes were wells of strange terror as she gazed at Cyprian, myself, and the uncovered statue-piece.

Cyprian did not introduce me. He and the girl talked together in low tones for a minute or two, and I was unable to overhear more than half of what they said. I gathered, however, that an appointment was being made for the next sitting. There was a pleading, frightened note in the girl's voice, together with an almost maternal concern; and Cyprian seemed to be arguing with her or trying to reassure her about something. At last she went out, with a queer, supplicative glance at me—a glance whose meaning I could only surmise and could not wholly fathom.

"That was Marta," said Cyprian. "She is half Irish, half Italian. A good model; but my new sculptures seem to be making her a little nervous." He laughed abruptly, with a mirthless, jarring note that was like the cachinnation of a sorcerer.

"In God's name, what are you trying to do here?" I burst out. "What does it all mean? Do such abominations really exist, on earth or in any hell?"

He laughed again, with an evil subtlety, and became evasive all at once. "Anything may exist, in a boundless universe with multiple dimensions. Anything may be real—or unreal. Who knows? It is not for me to say. Figure it out for yourself, if you can—there's a vast field for speculation—and perhaps for more than speculation."

With this, he began immediately to talk of other topics. Baffled, mystified, with a sorely troubled mind and nerves that were more unstrung than ever by the black enigma of it all, I ceased to question him. Simultaneously, my desire to leave the studio became almost overwhelming—a mindless, whirwind panic that prompted me to run pell-mell from the room and down the stairs into the wholesome normality of the common, Twentieth Century streets. It seemed to me that the rays which fell through the skylight were not those of the sun, but of some darker orb; that the room was touched with unclean webs of shadow where shadow should not have been; that the stone Satans, the bronze lamias, the terracotta satyrs, and the clay gargoyles had somehow increased in number and might spring to malignant life at any instant.

Hardly knowing what I said, I continued to converse for a while with Cyprian. Then, excusing myself on the score of a nonexistent luncheon appointment, and promising vaguely to return for another visit before my departure from the city, I took my leave.

I was surprised to find my cousin's model in the lower hall, at the foot of the stairway. From her manner, and her first words, it was plain that she had been waiting.

"You are Mr. Philip Hastane, aren't you?" she said, in an eager, agitated voice. "I am Marta Fitzgerald. Cyprian has often mentioned you, and I believe that he admires you a lot.

"Maybe you'll think me crazy," she went on, "but I had to speak to you. I can't stand the way that things are going here, and I'd refuse to come to the place any more, if it wasn't that I—like Cyprian so much.

"I don't know what he has done—but he is altogether different from what he used to be. His new work is so horrible—you can't imagine how it frightens me. The sculptures he does are more hideous, more hellish all the time. Ugh! those drooling, dead-gray monsters in that new group of his—I can hardly bear to be in the studio with them. It isn't right for anyone to depict such things. Don't you think they are awful, Mr. Hastane? They look as if they had broken loose from hell—and make you think that hell can't be very far away. It is wrong and wicked for anyone to—even imagine them; and I wish that Cyprian would stop. I am afraid that something will happen to him—to his mind—if he goes on. And I'll go mad, too, if I have to see those monsters many more times. My God! No one could keep sane in that studio."

She paused, and appeared to hesitate. Then:

"Can't you do something, Mr. Hastane? Can't you talk to him, and tell him how wrong it is, and how dangerous to his mental health? You must have a lot of influence with Cyprian—you are his cousin, aren't you? And he thinks you are very clever, too. I wouldn't ask you, if I hadn't been forced to notice so many things that aren't as they should be.

"I wouldn't bother you, either, if I knew anyone else to ask. He has shut himself up in that awful studio for the past year, and he hardly ever sees anybody. You are the first person that he has invited to see his new sculptures. He wants them to be a complete surprise for the critics and the public, when he holds his next exhibition.

"But you'll speak to Cyprian, won't you, Mr. Hastane? I can't do anything to stop him—he seems to exult in the mad horrors he creates. And he merely laughs at me when I try to tell him the danger. However, I think that those things are making him a little nervous sometimes—that he is growing afraid of his own morbid imagination. Perhaps he will listen to you."

If I had needed anything more to unnerve me, the desperate pleading of the girl and her dark, obscurely baleful hintings would have been enough. I could see that she loved Cyprian, that she was frantically anxious concerning him, and hysterically afraid; otherwise, she would not have approached an utter stranger in this fashion.

"But I haven't any influence with Cyprian," I protested, feeling a queer embarrassment. "And what am I to say to him, anyway? Whatever he is doing is his own affair, not mine. His new sculptures are magnificent—I have never seen anything more powerful of the kind. And how could I advise him to stop doing them? There would be no legitimate reason; he would simply laugh me out of the studio. An artist has the right to choose his own subject-matter, even if he takes it from the nether pits of Limbo and Erebus."

* * *

The girl must have pleaded and argued with me for many minutes in that deserted hall. Listening to her, and trying to convince her of my inability to fulfill her request, was like a dialog in some futile and tedious nightmare. During the course of it, she told me a few details that I am unwilling to record in this narrative; details that were too morbid and too shocking for belief, regarding the mental alteration of Cyprian, and his new subject-matter and method of work. There were direct and oblique hints of a growing perversion; but somehow it seemed that much more was being held back; that even in her most horrifying disclosures she was not wholly frank with me. At last, with some sort of hazy promise that I would speak to Cyprian, would remonstrate with him, I succeeded in getting away from her, and returned to my hotel.

The afternoon and evening that followed were tinged as by the tyrannous adumbration of an ill dream. I felt that I had stepped from the solid earth into a gulf of seething, menacing, madness-haunted shadow, and was lost henceforward to all rightful sense of location or direction. It was all too hideous—and too doubtful and unreal. The change in Cyprian himself was no less bewildering, and hardly less horrifying, than the vile phantom of the bookshop, and the demon sculptures that displayed a magisterial art. It was as if the man had become possessed by some satanic energy or entity.

Everywhere that I went, I was powerless to shake off the feeling of an intangible pursuit, of a frightful, unseen vigilance. It seemed to me that the worm-gray face and sulphurous eyes would reappear at any moment; that the semi-canine mouth with its gangrene-dripping fangs might come to slaver above the restaurant table at which I ate, or upon the pillow of my bed. I did not dare to reopen the purchased Goya volume, for fear of finding that certain pages were still defiled with a spectral slime.

I went out and spent the evening in cafés, in theaters, wherever people thronged and lights were bright. It was after midnight when I finally ventured to brave the solitude of my hotel bedroom. Then there were endless hours of nerve-wrung insomnia, of shivering, sweating apprehension beneath the electric bulb that I had left burning. Finally, a little before dawn, by no conscious transition and with no premonitory drowsiness, I fell asleep.

I remember no dreams—only the vast, incubus-like oppression that persisted even in the depth of slumber, as if to drag me down with its formless, ever-clinging weight into gulfs beyond the reach of created flight or the fathoming of organized entity.

It was almost noon when I awoke, and found myself staring into the verminous, apish, mummy-dead face and hell-illumined eyes of the gargoyle that had crouched before me in the corner at Toleman's. The thing was standing at the foot of my bed; and behind it as I stared, the wall of the room, which was covered with a floral paper, dissolved in an infinite vista of grayness, teeming with ghoulish forms that emerged like monstrous, misshapen bubbles from plains of undulant ooze and skies of serpentining vapor. It was another world, and my very sense of equilibrium was disturbed by an evil vertigo as I gazed. It seemed to me that my bed was heaving dizzily, was turning slowly, deliriously toward the gulf; that the feculent vista and the vile apparition were swimming beneath me; that I would fall toward them in another moment and be precipitated forever into that world of abysmal monstrosity and obscenity.

In a start of profound alarm, I fought my vertigo, fought the sense that another will than mine was drawing me, that the unclean gargoyle was luring me by some unspeakable mesmeric spell, as a serpent is said to lure its prey. I seemed to read a nameless purpose in its yellow-slitted eyes, in the soundless moving of its oozy lips; and my very soul recoiled with nausea and revulsion as I breathed its pestilential fetor.

Apparently, the mere effort of mental resistance was enough. The vista and the face receded; they went out in a swirl of daylight. I saw the design of tea roses on the wallpaper beyond; and the bed beneath me was sanely horizontal once more. I lay sweating with my terror, all adrift on a sea of nightmare surmise of unearthly threat and whirlpool madness, till the ringing of the telephone bell recalled me automatically to the known world.

I sprang to answer the call. It was Cyprian, though I should hardly have recognized the dead, hopeless tones of his voice, from which the mad pride and self-assurance of the previous day had wholly vanished.

"I must see you at once," he said. "Can you come to the studio?"

I was about to refuse, to tell him that I had been called home suddenly, that there was no time, that I must catch the noon train—anything to avert the ordeal of another visit to that place of mephitic evil—when I heard his voice again.

"You simply must come, Philip. I can't tell you about it over the phone, but a dreadful thing has happened: Marta had disappeared."

I consented, telling him that I would start for the studio as soon as I had dressed. The whole nightmare had closed in, had deepened immeasurably with his last words; but remembering the haunted face of the girl, her hysteric fears, her frantic plea and my vague promise, I could not very well decline to go.

I dressed and went out with my mind in a turmoil of abominable conjecture of ghastly doubt, and apprehension all the more hideous because I was unsure of its object. I tried to imagine what had happened, tried to piece together the frightful, evasive, half-admitted hints of unknown terror into a tangible coherent fabric, but found myself involved in a chaos of shadowy menace.

I could not have eaten any breakfast, even if I had taken the necessary time. I went at once to the studio, and found Cyprian standing aimlessly amid his baleful statuary. His look was that of a man who has been stunned by the blow of some crushing weapon, or has gazed on the very face of Medusa. He greeted me in a vacant manner, with dull, toneless words. Then, like a charged machine, as if his body rather than his mind were speaking, he began at once to pour forth the atrocious narrative.

"They took her," he said, simply. "Maybe you didn't know it, or weren't sure of it; but I have been doing all my new sculptures from life—even that last group. Marta was posing for me this forenoon—only an hour ago—or less. I had hoped to finish her part of the modeling today; and she wouldn't have had to come again for this particular piece. I hadn't called the Things this time, since I knew she was beginning to fear them more and more. I think she feared them on my account more than her own—and they were making me a little uneasy too, by the boldness with which they sometimes lingered when I had ordered them to leave, and the way they would sometimes appear when I didn't want them.

"I was busy with some of the final touches on the girl figure, and wasn't even looking at Marta, when suddenly I knew that the Things were there. The smell told me, if nothing else—I guess you know what the smell is like. I looked up, and found that the studio was full of them—they had never before appeared in such numbers. They were surrounding Marta, were crowding and jostling each other, were all reaching toward her with their filthy talons; but even then, I didn't think that they could harm her. They aren't material beings, in the sense that we are, and they really have no physical power outside their own plane. All that they do have is a sort of snaky mesmerism, and they'll always try to drag you down to their own dimension by means of it. God help anyone who yields to them; but you don't have to go, unless you are weak, or willing. I've never had any doubt of my power to resist them, and I didn't really dream they could do anything to Marta.

"It startled me, though, when I saw the whole crowding hell-pack, and I ordered them to go pretty sharply. I was angry—and somewhat alarmed, too. But they merely grimaced and slavered, with that slow, twisting movement of their lips that is like a voiceless gibbering, and then they closed in on Marta, just as I represented them doing in that accursed group of sculpture. Only there were scores of them now, instead of merely seven.

"I can't describe how it happened, but all at once their foul talons had reached the girl; they were pawing her, were pulling at her hands, her arms, her body. She screamed and I hope I'll never hear another scream so full of black agony and soul-unhinging fright. Then I knew that she had yielded to them—either from choice, or from excess of terror—and knew that they were taking her away.

"For a moment, the studio wasn't there at all—only a long, gray, oozing plain, beneath skies where the fumes of hell were writhing like a million ghostly and distorted dragons. Marta was sinking into that ooze, and the Things were all about her, gathering in fresh hundreds from every side, fighting each other for place, sinking with her like bloated, misshaped fen-creatures into their native slime. Then everything vanished—and I was standing here in the studio, all alone with these damned sculptures."

He paused for a little, and stared with dreary, desolate eyes at the floor. Then:

"It was awful, Philip, and I'll never forgive myself for having anything to do with those monsters. I must have been a little mad, but I've always had a strong ambition to create some real stuff in the field of the grotesque and visionary and macabre. I don't suppose you ever suspected, back in my stodgy phase, that I had a veritable appetence for such things. I wanted to do in sculpture what Poe and Lovecraft and Baudelaire have done in literature, what Rops and Goya did in pictorial art.

"That was what led me into the occult, when I realized my limitations. I knew that I had to see the dwellers of the invisible worlds before I could depict them. I wanted to do it. I longed for this power of vision and representation more than anything else. And then, all at once, I found that I had the power of summoning the unseen. . . .

"There was no magic involved, in the usual sense of the word—no spells and circles, no pentacles and burning gums from old sorcery books. At bottom, it was just will power, I guess—a will to divine the satanic, to summon the innumerable malignities and grotesqueries that people other planes than ours, or mingle unperceived with humanity.

"You've no idea what I have beheld, Philip. These statues of mine—these devils, vampires, lamias, satyrs—were all done from life, or, at least from recent memory. The originals are what the occultists would call elementals, I suppose. There are endless worlds, contiguous to our own, or coexisting with it, that such beings inhabit. All the creations of myth and fantasy, all the familiar spirits that sorcerers have evoked, are resident in these worlds.

"I made myself their master, I levied upon them at will. Then, from a dimension that must be a little lower than all others, a little nearer the ultimate nadir of hell, I called the innominate beings who posed for this new figure-piece.

"I don't know what they are, but I have surmised a good deal. They are hateful as the worms of the Pit, they are malevolent as harpies, they drool with a poisonous hunger not to be named or imagined. But I believed that they were powerless to do anything outside their own sphere, and I've always laughed at them when they tried to entice me—even though that snakish mental pull of theirs was rather creepy at times. It was as if soft, invisible, gelatinous arms were trying to drag you down from the firm shore into a bottomless bog.

"They are hunters—I am sure of that—the hunters from Beyond. God knows what they will do to Marta now that they have her at their mercy. That vast, viscid, miasma-haunted place to which they took her is awful beyond the imagining of a Satan. Perhaps—even there—they couldn't harm her body. But bodies aren't what they want—it isn't for human flesh that they grope with those ghoulish claws, and gape and slaver with those gangrenous mouths. The brain itself—and the soul, too—is their food: they are the creatures who prey on the minds of madmen and madwomen, who devour the disembodied spirits that have fallen from the cycles of incarnation, have gone down beyond the possibility of rebirth.

"To think of Marta in their power—it is worse than hell or madness. Marta loved me, and I loved her, too, though I didn't have the sense to realize it, wrapped as I was in my dark, baleful ambition and impious egotism. She was afraid for me, and I believe she surrendered voluntarily to the Things. She must have thought that they would leave me alone if they secured another victim in my place."

He ceased, and began to pace idly and feverishly about, I saw that his hollow eyes were alight with torment, as if the mechanical telling of his horrible story had in some manner served to re-quicken his crushed mind. Utterly and starkly appalled by his hideous revelations, I could say nothing, but could only stand and watch his torture-twisted face.

Incredibly, his expression changed, with a wild, startled look that was instantly transfigured into joy. Turning to follow his gaze, I saw that Marta was standing in the center of the room. She was nude, except for a Spanish shawl that she must have worn while posing. Her face was bloodless as the marble of a tomb, and her eyes were wide and blank, as if she had been drained of all life, of all thought or emotion or memory, as if even the knowledge of horror had been taken away from her. It was the face of the living dead, and the soulless mask of ultimate idiocy; and the joy faded from Cyprian's eyes as he stepped toward her.

He took her in his arms, he spoke to her with a desperate, loving tenderness, with cajoling and caressing words. She made no answer, however, no movement of recognition or awareness, but stared beyond him with her blank eyes, to which the daylight and the darkness, the void air and her lover's face, would henceforward be the same. He and I both knew, in that instant, that she would never again respond to any human voice, or to human love or terror; that she was like an empty cerement, retaining the outward form of that which the worms have eaten in their mausolean darkness. Of the noisome pits wherein she had been, of that bournless realm and its pullulating phantoms, she could tell us nothing: her agony had ended with the terrible mercy of complete forgetfulness.

* * *

Like one who confronts the Gorgon, I was frozen by her wide and sightless gaze. Then, behind her, where stood an array of carven Satans and lamias, the room seemed to recede, the walls and floor dissolved in a seething, unfathomable gulf, amid whose pestilential vapors the statues were mingled in momentary and loathsome ambiguity with the ravening faces, the hunger-contorted forms that swirled toward us from their ultra-dimensional limbo like a devil-laden hurricane from Malebolge. Outlined against that boiling, measureless cauldron of malignant storm, Marta stood like an image of glacial death and silence in the arms of Cyprian. Then, once more, after a little, the abhorrent vision faded, leaving only the diabolic statuary.

I think that I alone had beheld it; that Cyprian had seen nothing but the dead face of Marta. He drew her close, he repeated his hopeless words of tenderness and cajolery. Then, suddenly, he released her with a vehement sob of despair. Turning away, while she stood and still looked on with unseeing eyes, he snatched a heavy sculptor's mallet from the table on which it was lying, and proceeded to smash with furious blows the newly-modeled group of gargoyles, till nothing was left but the figure of the terror-maddened girl, crouching above a mass of cloddish fragments and formless, half-dried clay.

E is for Elemental

The Wendigo, a creature of Native North American folklore, is sometimes portrayed as an elemental spirit whose element is the air. British writer Algernon Blackwood (1869–1951) excelled at depictions of the forces of nature as awesome and inscrutable supernatural presences, and in this tale, first published in his 1910 collection *The Lost Valley and Other Stories,* the Wendigo is as malicious as it is mischievous.

ALGERNON BLACKWOOD

The Wendigo

I

A considerable number of hunting parties were out that year without finding so much as a fresh trail; for the moose were uncommonly shy, and the various Nimrods returned to the bosoms of their respective families with the best excuses the facts of their imaginations could suggest. Dr. Cathcart, among others, came back without a trophy; but he brought instead the memory of an experience which he declares was worth all the bull moose that had ever been shot. But then Cathcart, of Aberdeen, was interested in other things besides moose—amongst them the vagaries of the human mind. This particular story, however, found no mention in his book on *Collective Hallucination* for the simple reason (so he confided once to a fellow colleague) that he himself played too intimate a part in it to form a competent judgment of the affair as a whole. . . .

Besides himself and his guide, Hank Davis, there was young Simpson, his nephew, a divinity student destined for the "Wee Kirk" (then on his first visit to Canadian backwoods), and the latter's guide, Défago. Joseph Défago was a French "Canuck," who had strayed from his native Province of Quebec years before, and had got caught in Rat Portage when the Canadian Pacific Railway was a-building; a man who, in addition to his unparalleled knowledge of woodcraft and bush-lore, could also sing the old *voyageur* songs and tell a capital hunting yarn into the bargain. He was deeply susceptible, moreover, to that singular spell which the wilderness lays upon certain lonely natures, and he loved the wild solitudes with a kind of romantic passion that amounted almost to an obsession. The life of the backwoods fascinated him—whence, doubtless, his surpassing efficiency in dealing with their mysteries.

On this particular expedition he was Hank's choice. Hank knew him and swore by him. He also swore at him, "jest as a pal might," and since he had a vocabulary of picturesque, if utterly meaningless, oaths, the conversation between the two stalwart and hardy woodsmen was often of a rather lively description. This river of expletives, however, Hank agreed to dam a little out of respect for his old "hunting boss," Dr. Cathcart, whom of course he addressed after the fashion of the country as "Doc," and also because he understood that young Simpson was already a "bit of a parson." He had, however, one objection to Défago, and one only—which was, that the French Canadian sometimes exhibited what Hank described as "the output of a cursed and dismal mind," meaning apparently that he sometimes was true to type, Latin type, and suffered fits of a kind of silent moroseness when nothing could induce him to utter speech. Défago, that is to say, was imaginative and melancholy. And, as a rule, it was too long a spell of "civilisation" that induced the attacks, for a few days of the wilderness invariably cured them.

This, then, was the party of four that found themselves in camp the last week in October of that "shy moose year" 'way up in the wilderness north of Rat Portage—a forsaken and desolate country. There was also Punk, an Indian, who had accompanied Dr. Cathcart and Hank on their hunting trips in previous years, and who acted as cook. His duty was merely to stay in camp, catch fish, and prepare venison steaks and coffee at a few minutes' notice. He dressed in the worn-out clothes bequeathed to him by former patrons, and, except for his coarse black hair and dark skin, he looked in these city garments no more like a real redskin than a stage Negro looks like a real African. For all that, however, Punk had in him still the instincts of his dying race; his taciturn silence and his endurance survived; also his superstition.

The party round the blazing fire that night were despondent, for a week had passed without a single sign of recent moose discovering itself. Défago had sung his song and plunged into a story, but Hank, in bad humour, reminded him so often that "he kep' mussing-up the fac's so, that it was 'most all nothin' but a petered-out lie," that the Frenchman had finally subsided into a sulky silence which nothing seemed likely to break. Dr. Cathcart and his nephew were fairly done after an exhausting day. Punk was washing up the dishes, grunting to himself under the lean-to of branches, where he later also slept. No one troubled to stir the slowly dying fire. Overhead the stars were brilliant in a sky quite wintry, and there was so little wind that ice was already forming stealthily along the shores of the still lake behind them. The silence of the vast listening forest stole forward and enveloped them.

Hank broke in suddenly with his nasal voice.

"I'm in favour of breaking new ground to-morrow, Doc," he observed with energy, looking across at his employer. "We don't stand a dead Dago's chance around here."

"Agreed," said Cathcart, always a man of few words. "Think the idea's good."

"Sure pop, it's good," Hank resumed with confidence. "S'pose, now, you and I strike west, up Garden Lake way for a change! None of us ain't touched that quiet bit o' land yet—"

"I'm with you."

"And you, Défago, take Mr. Simpson along in the small canoe, skip across the lake, portage over into Fifty Island Water, and take a good squint down that thar southern shore. The moose 'yarded' there like hell last year, and for all we know they may be doin' it agin this year jest to spite us."

Défago, keeping his eyes on the fire, said nothing by way of reply. He was still offended, possibly, about his interrupted story.

"No one's been up that way this year, an' I'll lay my bottom dollar on *that!*" Hank added with emphasis, as though he had a reason for knowing. He looked over at his partner sharply. "Better take the little silk tent and stay away a couple o' nights," he concluded, as though the matter were definitely settled. For Hank was recognised as general organiser of the hunt, and in charge of the party.

It was obvious to anyone that Défago did not jump at the plan, but his silence seemed to convey something more than ordinary disapproval, and across his sensitive dark face there passed a curious expression like a flash of firelight—not so quickly, however, that the three men had not time to catch it. "He funked for some reason, *I* thought," Simpson said afterwards in the tent he shared with his uncle. Dr. Cathcart made no immediate reply, although the look had interested him enough at the time for him to make a mental note of it. The expression had caused him a passing uneasiness he could not quite account for at the moment.

But Hank, of course, had been the first to notice it, and the odd thing was that instead of becoming explosive or angry over the other's reluctance, he at once began to humour him a bit.

"But there ain't no *speshul* reason why no one's been up there this year," he said with a perceptible hush in his tone; "not the reason you mean, anyway! Las' year it was the fires that kep' folks out, and this year I guess—I guess it jest happened so, that's all!" His manner was clearly meant to be encouraging.

Joseph Défago raised his eyes a moment, then dropped them again. A breath of wind stole out of the forest and stirred the embers into a passing blaze. Dr. Cathcart again noticed the expression in the guide's face, and again he did not like it. But this time the nature of the look betrayed itself. In those eyes, for an instant, he caught the gleam of a man scared in his very soul. It disquieted him more than he cared to admit.

"Bad Indians up that way?" he asked, with a laugh to ease matters a little, while Simpson, too sleepy to notice this subtle by-play, moved off to bed with a prodigious yawn; "or—or anything wrong with the country?" he added, when his nephew was out of hearing.

Hank met his eye with something less than his usual frankness.

"He's jest skeered," he replied good-humouredly. "Skeered stiff about some ole feery tale! That's all, ain't it, ole pard?" And he gave Défago a friendly kick on the moccasined foot that lay nearest the fire.

Défago looked up quickly, as from an interrupted reverie, a reverie, however, that had not prevented his seeing all that went on about him.

"Skeered—*nuthin'!*" he answered, with a flush of defiance. "There's nuthin' in the Bush that can skeer Joseph Défago, and don't you forget it!" And the natural energy with which he spoke made it impossible to know whether he told the whole truth or only a part of it.

Hank turned towards the doctor. He was just going to add something when he stopped abruptly and looked round. A sound close behind them in the darkness made all three start. It was old Punk, who had moved up from his lean-to while they talked and now stood there just beyond the circle of firelight—listening.

"'Nother time, Doc!" Hank whispered, with a wink, "when the gallery ain't stepped down into the stalls!" And, springing to his feet, he slapped the Indian on the back and cried noisily, "Come up t' the fire an' warm yer dirty red skin a bit." He dragged him towards the blaze and threw more wood on. "That was a mighty good feed you give us an hour or two back," he continued heartily, as though to set the man's thoughts on another scent, "and it ain't Christian to let you stand out there freezin' yer ole soul to hell while we're gettin' all good an' toasted!" Punk moved in and warmed his feet, smiling darkly at the other's volubility which he only half understood, but saying nothing. And presently Dr. Cathcart, seeing that further conversation was impossible, followed his nephew's example and moved off to the tent, leaving the three men smoking over the now blazing fire.

It is not easy to undress in a small tent without waking one's companion, and Cathcart, hardened and warm-blooded as he was in spite of his fifty odd years, did what Hank would have described as "considerable of his twilight" in the open. He noticed, during the process, that Punk had meanwhile gone back to his lean-to, and that Hank and Défago were at it hammer and tongs, or, rather, hammer and anvil, the little French Canadian being the anvil. It was all very like the conventional stage picture of Western melodrama: the fire lighting up their faces with patches of alternate red and black; Défago, in slouch hat and moccasins in the part of the "badlands" villain; Hank, open-faced and hatless, with that reckless fling of his shoulders, the honest and deceived hero; and old Punk, eavesdropping in the background, supplying the atmosphere of mystery. The doctor smiled as he noticed the details; but at the same time something deep within him—he hardly knew what—shrank a little, as though an almost imperceptible breath of warning had touched the surface of his soul and was gone again before he could seize it. Probably it was traceable to that "scared expression" he had seen in the eyes of Défago; "probably"—for this hint of fugitive emotion otherwise escaped his usually so keen analysis. Défago, he was vaguely aware, might cause trouble somehow. . . . He was not as steady a guide as Hank, for instance. . . . Further than that he could not get. . . .

He watched the men a moment longer before diving into the stuffy tent where Simpson already slept soundly. Hank, he saw, was swearing like a mad African in a New York nigger saloon; but it was the swearing of "affection." The ridiculous oaths flew freely now that the cause of their obstruction was asleep. Presently he put his arm almost tenderly upon his comrade's shoulder, and they moved off together into the shadows where their tent stood faintly glimmering. Punk, too, a moment later followed their example and disappeared between his odorous blankets in the opposite direction.

Dr. Cathcart then likewise turned in, weariness and sleep still fighting in his mind with an obscure curiosity to know what it was that had scared Défago about the country up Fifty Island Water way—wondering, too, why Punk's presence had prevented the completion of what Hank had to say. Then sleep overtook him. He would know tomorrow. Hank would tell him the story while they trudged after the elusive moose.

Deep silence fell about the little camp, planted there so audaciously in the jaws of the wilderness. The lake gleamed like a sheet of black glass beneath the stars. The cold air pricked. In the draughts of night that poured their silent tide from the depths of the forest, with messages from distant ridges and from lakes just beginning to freeze, there lay already the faint, bleak odours of coming winter. White men, with their dull scent, might never have divined them; the fragrance of the wood fire would have concealed from them these almost electrical hints of moss and bark and hardening swamp a hundred miles away. Even Hank and Défago, subtly in league with the soul of the woods as they were, would probably have spread their delicate nostrils in vain. . . .

But an hour later, when all slept like the dead, old Punk crept from his blankets and went down to the shore of the lake like a shadow—silently, as only Indian blood can move. He raised his head and looked about him. The thick darkness rendered sight of small avail, but, like the animals, he possessed other senses that darkness could not mute. He listened—then sniffed the air. Motionless as a hemlock stem he stood there. After five minutes again he lifted his head and sniffed, and yet once again. A tingling of the wonderful nerves that betrayed itself by no outer sign, ran through him as he tasted the keen air. Then, merging his figure into the surrounding blackness in a way that only wild men and animals understand, he turned, still moving like a shadow, and went stealthily back to his lean-to and his bed.

And soon after he slept, the change of wind he had divined stirred gently the reflection of the stars within the lake. Rising among the far ridges of the country beyond Fifty Island Water, it came from the direction in which he had stared, and it passed over the sleeping camp with a faint and sighing murmur through the tops of the big trees that was almost too delicate to be audible. With it, down the desert paths of night, though too faint, too high even for the Indian's hair-like nerves, there passed a curious, thin odour, strangely disquieting, an odour of something that seemed unfamiliar—utterly unknown.

The French Canadian and the man of Indian blood each stirred uneasily in his sleep just about this time, though neither of them woke. Then the ghost of that unforgettably strange odour passed away and was lost among the leagues of tenantless forest beyond.

II

In the morning the camp was astir before the sun. There had been a light fall of snow during the night and the air was sharp. Punk had done his duty betimes, for the odours of coffee and fried bacon reached every tent. All were in good spirits.

"Wind's shifted!" cried Hank vigorously, watching Simpson and his guide already loading the small canoe. "It's across the lake—dead right for you fellers. And the snow'll make bully trails! If there's any moose mussing around up thar, they'll not get so much as a tail-end scent of you with the wind as it is. Good luck, Monsieur Défago!" he added, facetiously giving the name its French pronunciation for once, *"bonne chance!"*

Défago returned the good wishes, apparently in the best of spirits, the silent mood gone. Before eight o'clock old Punk had the camp to himself, Cathcart and Hank were far along the trail that led westwards, while the canoe that carried Défago and Simpson, with silk tent and grub for two days, was already a dark speck bobbing on the bosom of the lake, going due east.

The wintry sharpness of the air was tempered now by a sun that topped the wooded ridges and blazed with a luxurious warmth upon the world of lake and forest below; loons flew skimming through the sparkling spray that the wind lifted; divers shook their dripping heads to the sun and popped smartly out of sight again; and as far as eye could reach rose the leagues of endless, crowding Bush, desolate in its lonely sweep and grandeur, untrodden by foot of man, and stretching its mighty and unbroken carpet right up to the frozen shores of Hudson Bay.

Simpson, who saw it all for the first time as he paddled hard in the bows of the dancing canoe, was enchanted by its austere beauty. His heart drank in the sense of freedom and great spaces just as his lungs drank in the cool and perfumed wind. Behind him in the stern seat, singing fragments of his native chanteys, Défago steered the craft of birch bark like a thing of life, answering cheerfully all his companion's questions. Both were gay and light-hearted. On such occasions men lose the superficial, worldly distinctions; they become human beings working together for a common end. Simpson, the employer, and Défago the employed, among these primitive forces, were simply—two men, the "guider" and the "guided." Superior knowledge, of course, assumed control, and the younger man fell without a second thought into the quasi-subordinate position. He never dreamed of objecting when Défago dropped the "Mr.," and addressed him as "Say, Simpson," or "Simpson, boss," which was invariably the case before they reached the farther shore after a stiff paddle of twelve miles against a head wind. He only laughed, and liked it; then ceased to notice it at all.

For this "divinity student" was a young man of parts and character, though as yet, of course, untravelled; and on this trip—the first time he had seen any country but his own and little Switzerland—the huge scale of things somewhat bewildered him. It was one thing, he realised, to hear about primeval forests, but quite another to see them. While to dwell in them and seek acquaintance with their wild life was, again, an initiation that no intelligent man could undergo without a certain shifting of personal values hitherto held for permanent and sacred.

Simpson knew the first faint indication of this emotion when he held the new .303 rifle in his hands and looked along its pair of faultless, gleaming barrels. The three days' journey to their headquarters, by lake and portage, had carried the process a stage farther. And now that he was about to plunge beyond even the fringe of wilderness where they were camped into the virgin heart of uninhabited regions as vast as Europe itself, the true nature of the situation stole upon him with an effect of delight and awe that his imagination was fully capable of appreciating. It was himself and Défago against a multitude—at least, against a Titan!

The bleak splendors of these remote and lonely forests rather overwhelmed him with the sense of his own littleness. That stern quality of the tangled backwoods which can only be described as merciless and terrible, rose out of these far blue woods swimming upon the horizon, and revealed itself. He understood the silent warning. He realised his own utter helplessness. Only Défago, as a symbol of a distant civilisation where man was master, stood between him and a pitiless death by exhaustion and starvation.

It was thrilling to him, therefore, to watch Défago turn over the canoe upon the shore, pack the paddles carefully underneath, and then proceed to "blaze" the spruce stems for some distance on either side of an almost invisible trail, with the careless remark thrown in, "Say, Simpson, if anything happens to me, you'll find the canoe all correc' by these marks;—then strike doo west into the sun to hit the home camp agin, see?"

It was the most natural thing in the world to say, and he said it without any noticeable inflexion of the voice, only it happened to express the youth's emotions at the moment with an utterance that was symbolic of the situation and of his own helplessness as a factor in it. He was alone with Défago in a primitive world: that was all. The canoe, another symbol of man's ascendancy, was now to be left behind. Those small yellow patches, made on the trees by the axe, were the only indications of its hiding place.

Meanwhile, shouldering the packs between them, each man carrying his own rifle, they followed the slender trail over rocks and fallen trunks and across half-frozen swamps; skirting numerous lakes that fairly gemmed the forest, their borders fringed with mist; and towards five o'clock found themselves suddenly on the edge of the woods, looking out across a large sheet of water in front of them, dotted with pine-clad islands of all describable shapes and sizes.

"Fifty Island Water," announced Défago wearily, "and the sun jest goin' to dip his bald old head into it!" he added, with unconscious poetry; and immediately they set about pitching camp for the night.

In a very few minutes, under those skilful hands that never made a movement too much or a movement too little, the silk tent stood taut and cozy, the beds of balsam boughs ready laid, and a brisk cooking fire burned with the minimum of smoke. While the young Scotchman cleaned the fish they had caught trolling behind the canoe, Défago "guessed" he would "jest as soon" take a turn through the Bush for indications of moose. "*May* come across a trunk where they bin and rubbed horns," he said, as he moved off, "or feedin' on the last of the maple leaves,"—and he was gone.

His small figure melted away like a shadow in the dusk, while Simpson noted with a kind of admiration how easily the forest absorbed him into herself. A few steps, it seemed, and he was no longer visible.

Yet there was little underbrush hereabouts; the trees stood somewhat apart, well spaced; and in the clearings grew silver birch and maple, spearlike and slender, against the immense stems of spruce and hemlock. But for occasional prostrate monsters, and the boulders of grey rock that thrust uncouth shoulders here and there out of the ground, it might well have been a bit of park in the Old Country. Almost, one might have seen in it the hand of man. A little to the right, however, began the great burnt section, miles in extent, proclaiming its real character—*brulé,* as it is called, where the fires of the previous year had raged for weeks, and the blackened stumps now rose gaunt and ugly, bereft of branches, like gigantic match heads stuck into the ground, savage and desolate beyond words. The perfume of charcoal and rain-soaked ashes still hung faintly about it.

The dusk rapidly deepened; the glades grew dark; the crackling of the fire and the wash of little waves along the rocky lake shore were the only sounds audible. The wind had dropped with the sun, and in all that vast world of branches nothing stirred. Any moment, it seemed, the woodland gods, who are to be worshipped in silence and loneliness, might stretch their mighty and terrific outlines among the trees. In front, through doorways pillared by huge straight stems, lay the stretch of Fifty Island Water, a crescent-shaped lake some fifteen miles from tip to tip, and perhaps five miles across where they were camped. A sky of rose and saffron, more clear than any atmosphere Simpson had ever known, still dropped its pale streaming fires across the waves, where the islands—a hundred, surely, rather than fifty—floated like the fairy barques of some enchanted fleet. Fringed with pines, whose crests fingered most delicately the sky, they almost seemed to move upwards as the light faded—about to weigh anchor and navigate the pathways of the heavens instead of the currents of their native and desolate lake.

And strips of colored cloud, like flaunting pennons, signaled their departure to the stars. . . .

The beauty of the scene was strangely uplifting. Simpson smoked the fish and burnt his fingers into the bargain in his efforts to enjoy it and at the same time tend the frying pan and the fire. Yet, ever at the back of his thoughts, lay that other aspect of the wilderness: the indifference to human life, the merciless spirit of desolation which took no note of man. The sense of his utter loneliness, now that even Défago had gone, came close as he looked about him and listened for the sound of his companion's returning footsteps.

There was pleasure in the sensation, yet with it a perfectly comprehensible alarm. And instinctively the thought stirred in him: "What should I—*could* I, do—if anything happened and he did not come back—?"

They enjoyed their well-earned supper, eating untold quantities of fish, and drinking unmilked tea strong enough to kill men who had not covered thirty miles of hard "going," eating little on the way. And when it was over, they smoked and told stories round the blazing fire, laughing, stretching weary limbs, and discussing plans for the morrow. Défago was in excellent spirits, though disappointed at having no signs of moose to report. But it was dark and he had not gone far. The *brulé,* too, was bad. His clothes and hands were smeared with charcoal. Simpson, watching him, realised with renewed vividness their position—alone together in the wilderness.

"Défago," he said presently, "these woods, you know, are a bit too big to feel quite at home in—to feel comfortable in, I mean!. . . Eh?" He merely gave expression to the mood of the moment; he was hardly prepared for the earnestness, the solemnity even, with which the guide took him up.

"You've hit it right, Simpson, boss," he replied, fixing his searching brown eyes on his face, "and that's the truth, sure. There's no end to 'em—no end at all." Then he added in a lowered tone as if to himself, "There's lots found out *that,* and gone plumb to pieces!"

But the man's gravity of manner was not quite to the other's liking; it was a little too suggestive for this scenery and setting; he was sorry he had broached the subject. He remembered suddenly how his uncle had told him that men were sometimes stricken with a strange fever of the wilderness, when the seduction of the uninhabited wastes caught them so fiercely that they went forth, half fascinated, half deluded, to their death. And he had a shrewd idea that his companion held something in sympathy with that queer type. He led the conversation on to other topics, on to Hank and the doctor, for instance, and the natural rivalry as to who should get the first sight of moose.

"If they went doo west," observed Défago carelessly, "there's sixty miles between us now—with ole Punk at halfway house eatin' himself full to bustin' with fish and coffee." They laughed together over the picture. But the casual mention of those sixty miles again made Simpson realise the prodigious scale of this land where they hunted; sixty miles was a mere step; two hundred little more than a step. Stories of lost hunters rose persistently before his memory. The passion and mystery of homeless and wandering men, seduced by the beauty of great forests, swept his soul in a way too vivid to be quite pleasant. He wondered vaguely whether it was the mood of his companion that invited the unwelcome suggestion with such persistence.

"Sing us a song, Défago, if you're not too tired," he asked; "one of those old *voyageur* songs you sang the other night." He handed his tobacco pouch to the guide and then filled his own pipe, while the Canadian, nothing loth, sent his light voice across the lake in one of those plaintive, almost melancholy chanties with which lumbermen and trappers lessen the burden of their labor. There was an appealing and romantic flavor about it, something that recalled the atmosphere of the old pioneer days when Indians and wilderness were leagued together, battles frequent, and the Old Country farther off than it is today. The sound travelled pleasantly over the water, but the forest at their backs seemed to swallow it down with a single gulp that permitted neither echo nor resonance.

It was in the middle of the third verse that Simpson noticed something unusual—something that brought his thoughts back with a rush from faraway scenes. A curious change had come into the man's voice. Even before he knew what it was, uneasiness caught him, and looking up quickly, he saw that Défago, though still singing, was peering about him into the Bush, as though he heard or saw something. His voice grew fainter—dropped to a hush—then ceased altogether. The same instant, with a movement amazingly alert, he started to his feet and stood upright—*sniffing the air.* Like a dog scenting game, he drew the air into his nostrils in short, sharp breaths, turning quickly as he did so in all directions, and finally "pointing" down the lake shore, eastwards. It was a performance unpleasantly suggestive and at the same time singularly dramatic. Simpson's heart fluttered disagreeably as he watched it.

"Lord, man! How you made me jump!" he exclaimed, on his feet beside him the same instant, and peering over his shoulder into the sea of darkness. "What's up? Are you frightened—?"

Even before the question was out of his mouth he knew it was foolish, for any man with a pair of eyes in his head could see that the Canadian had turned white down to his very gills. Not even sunburn and the glare of the fire could hide that.

The student felt himself trembling a little, weakish in the knees. "What's up?" he repeated quickly. "D'you smell moose? Or anything queer, anything—wrong?" He lowered his voice instinctively.

The forest pressed round them with its encircling wall; the nearer tree stems gleamed like bronze in the firelight; beyond that—blackness, and, so far as he could tell, a silence of death. Just behind them a passing puff of wind lifted a single leaf, looked at it, then laid it softly down again without disturbing the rest of the covey. It seemed as if a million invisible causes had combined just to produce that single visible effect. Other life pulsed about them—and was gone.

Défago turned abruptly; the livid hue of his face had turned to a dirty grey.

"I never said I heered—or smelt—nuthin'," he said slowly and emphatically, in an oddly altered voice that conveyed somehow a touch of defiance. "I was only—takin' a look round—so to speak. It's always a mistake to be too previous with yer questions." Then he added suddenly with obvious effort, in his more natural voice, "Have you got the matches, Boss Simpson?" and proceeded to light the pipe he had half filled just before he began to sing.

Without speaking another word they sat down again by the fire. Défago changing his side so that he could face the direction the wind came from. For even a tenderfoot could tell that. Défago changed his position in order to hear and smell—all there was to be heard and smelt. And, since he now faced the lake with his back to the trees it was evidently nothing in the forest that had sent so strange and sudden a warning to his marvellously trained nerves.

"Guess now I don't feel like singing any," he explained presently of his own accord. "That song kinder brings back memories that's troublesome to me; I never oughter've begun it. It sets me on t' imagining things, see?"

Clearly the man was still fighting with some profoundly moving emotion. He wished to excuse himself in the eyes of the other. But the explanation, in that it was only a part of the truth, was a lie, and he knew perfectly well that Simpson was not deceived by it. For nothing could explain away the livid terror that had dropped over his face while he stood there sniffing the air. And nothing—no amount of blazing fire, or chatting on ordinary subjects—could make that camp exactly as it had been before. The shadow of an unknown horror, naked if unguessed, that had flashed for an instant in the face and gestures of the guide, had also communicated itself, vaguely and therefore more potently, to his companion. The guide's visible efforts to dissemble the truth only made things worse. Moreover, to add to the younger man's uneasiness, was the difficulty, nay, the impossibility he felt of asking questions, and also his complete ignorance as to the cause. . . . Indians, wild animals, forest fires—all these, he knew, were wholly out of the question. His imagination searched vigorously, but in vain. . . .

Yet, somehow or other, after another long spell of smoking, talking and roasting themselves before the great fire, the shadow that had so suddenly invaded their peaceful camp began to lift. Perhaps Défago's efforts, or the return of his quiet and normal attitude accomplished this; perhaps Simpson himself had exaggerated the affair out of all proportion to the truth; or possibly the vigorous air of the wilderness brought its own powers of healing. Whatever the cause, the feeling of immediate horror seemed to have passed away as mysteriously as it had come, for nothing occurred to feed it. Simpson began to feel that he had permitted himself the unreasoning terror of a child. He put it down partly to a certain subconscious excitement that this wild and immense scenery generated in his blood, partly to the spell of solitude, and partly to overfatigue. That pallor in the guide's face was, of course, uncommonly hard to explain, yet it *might* have been due in some way to an effect of firelight, or his own imagination. . . . He gave it the benefit of the doubt; he was Scotch.

When a somewhat unordinary emotion has disappeared, the mind always finds a dozen ways of explaining away its causes. . . . Simpson lit a last pipe and tried to laugh to himself. On getting home to Scotland it would make quite a good story. He did not realise that this laughter was a sign that terror still lurked in the recesses of his soul—that, in fact, it was merely one of the conventional signs by which a man, seriously alarmed, tries to persuade himself that he is *not so*.

Défago, however, heard that low laughter and looked up with surprise on his face. The two men stood, side by side, kicking the embers about before going to bed. It was ten o'clock—a late hour for hunters to be still awake.

"What's ticklin' yer?" he asked in his ordinary tone, yet gravely.

"I—I was thinking of our little toy woods at home, just at that moment," stammered Simpson, coming back to what really dominated his mind, and startled by the question, "and comparing them to—to all this," and he swept his arm round to indicate the Bush.

A pause followed in which neither of them said anything.

"All the same I wouldn't laugh about it, if I was you," Défago added, looking over Simpson's shoulder into the shadows. "There's places in there nobody won't never see into—nobody knows what lives in there either."

"Too big—too far off?" The suggestion in the guide's manner was immense and horrible.

Défago nodded. The expression on his face was dark. He, too, felt uneasy. The younger man understood that in a *hinterland* of this size there might well be depths of wood that would never in the life of the world be known or trodden. The thought was not exactly the sort he welcomed. In a loud voice, cheerfully, he suggested that it was time for bed. But the guide lingered, tinkering with the fire, arranging the stones needlessly, doing a dozen things that did not really need doing. Evidently there was something he wanted to say, yet found it difficult to "get at."

"Say, you, Boss Simpson," he began suddenly, as the last shower of sparks went up into the air, "you don't—smell nothing, do you—nothing pertickler, I mean?" The commonplace question, Simpson realised, veiled a dreadfully serious thought in his mind. A shiver ran down his back.

"Nothing but burning wood," he replied firmly, kicking again at the embers. The sound of his own foot made him start.

"And all the evenin' you ain't smelt—nothing?" persisted the guide, peering at him through the gloom; "nothing extrordiny, and different to anything else you ever smelt before?"

"No, no, man; nothing at all!" he replied aggressively, half angrily.

Défago's face cleared. "That's good!" he exclaimed with evident relief. "That's good to hear."

"Have *you?*" asked Simpson sharply, and the same instant regretted the question.

The Canadian came closer in the darkness. He shook his head. "I guess not," he said, though without overwhelming conviction. "It must've been just that song of mine that did it. It's the song they sing in lumber camps and godforsaken places like that, when they're skeered the Wendigo's somewhere around, doin' a bit of swift travellin'—"

"And what's the Wendigo, pray?" Simpson asked quickly, irritated because again he could not prevent that sudden shiver of the nerves. He knew that he was close upon the man's terror and the cause of it. Yet a rushing passionate curiosity overcame his better judgment, *and* his fear.

Défago turned swiftly and looked at him as though he were suddenly about to shriek. His eyes shone, but his mouth was wide open. Yet all he said, or whispered rather, for his voice sank very low, was—

"It's nuthin'—nuthin' but what those lousy fellers believe when they've bin hittin' the bottle too long—a sort of great animal that lives up yonder," he jerked his head northwards, "quick as lightning in its tracks, an' bigger'n anything else in the Bush, an' ain't supposed to be very good to look at—that's *all!*"

"A backwoods superstition—" began Simpson, moving hastily toward the tent in order to shake off the hand of the guide that clutched his arm. "Come, come, hurry up for God's sake, and get the lantern going! It's time we were in bed and asleep if we're going to be up with the sun tomorrow. . . ."

The guide was close on his heels. "I'm coming," he answered out of the darkness, "I'm coming." And after a slight delay he appeared with the lantern and hung it from a nail in the front pole of the tent. The shadows of a hundred trees shifted their places quickly as he did so, and when he stumbled over the rope, diving swiftly inside, the whole tent trembled as though a gust of wind struck it.

The two men lay down, without undressing, upon their beds of soft balsam boughs, cunningly arranged. Inside, all was warm and cosy, but outside the world of crowding trees pressed close about them, marshalling their million shadows, and smothering the little tent that stood there like a wee white shell facing the ocean of tremendous forest.

Between the two lonely figures within, however, there pressed another shadow that was *not* a shadow from the night. It was the Shadow cast by the strange Fear, never wholly exorcised, that had leaped suddenly upon Défago in the middle of his singing. And Simpson, as he lay there, watching the darkness through the open flap of the tent, ready to plunge into the fragrant abyss of sleep, knew first that unique and profound stillness of a primeval forest when no wind stirs. . .and when the night has weight and substance that enters into the soul to bind a veil about it. . . . Then sleep took him. . . .

III

Thus, it seemed to him, at least. Yet it was true that the lap of the water, just beyond the tent door, still beat time with his lessening pulses when he realised that he was lying with his eyes open and that another sound had recently introduced itself with cunning softness between the splash and murmur of the little waves.

And, long before he understood what this sound was, it had stirred in him the centres of pity and alarm. He listened intently, though at first in vain, for the running blood beat all its drums too noisily in his ears. Did it come, he wondered, from the lake, or from the woods?. . .

Then, suddenly, with a rush and a flutter of the heart, he knew that it was close beside him in the tent; and, when he turned over for a better hearing, it focused itself unmistakably not two feet away. It was a sound of weeping; Défago upon his bed of branches was sobbing in the darkness as though his heart would break, the blankets evidently stuffed against his mouth to stifle it.

And his first feeling, before he could think or reflect, was the rush of a poignant and searching tenderness. This intimate, human sound, heard amid the desolation about them, woke pity. It was so incongruous, so pitifully incongruous—and so vain! Tears—in this vast and cruel wilderness: of what avail? He thought of a little child crying in mid-Atlantic. . . . Then, of course, with fuller realisation, and the memory of what had gone before, came the descent of the terror upon him, and his blood ran cold.

"Défago," he whispered quickly, "what's the matter?" He tried to make his voice very gentle. "Are you in pain—unhappy—?" There was no reply, but the sounds ceased abruptly. He stretched his hand out and touched him. The body did not stir.

"Are you awake?" for it occurred to him that the man was crying in his sleep. "Are you cold?" He noticed that his feet, which were uncovered, projected beyond the mouth of the tent. He spread an extra fold of his own blankets over them. The guide had slipped down in his bed, and the branches seemed to have been dragged with him. He was afraid to pull the body back again, for fear of waking him.

One or two tentative questions he ventured softly, but though he waited for several minutes there came no reply, nor any sign of movement. Presently he heard his regular and quiet breathing, and putting his hand again gently on the breast, felt the steady rise and fall beneath.

"Let me know if anything's wrong," he whispered, "or if I can do anything. Wake me at once if you feel—queer."

He hardly knew what to say. He lay down again, thinking and wondering what it all meant. Défago, of course, had been crying in his sleep. Some dream or other had afflicted him. Yet never in his life would he forget that pitiful sound of sobbing, and the feeling that the whole awful wilderness of woods listened. . . .

His own mind busied itself for a long time with the recent events, of which *this* took its mysterious place as one, and though his reason successfully argued away all unwelcome suggestions, a sensation of uneasiness remained, resisting ejection, very deep-seated—peculiar beyond ordinary.

IV

But sleep, in the long run, proves greater than all emotions. His thoughts soon wandered again; he lay there, warm as toast, exceedingly weary; the night soothed and comforted, blunting the edges of memory and alarm. Half an hour later he was oblivious of everything in the outer world about him.

Yet sleep, in this case, was his great enemy, concealing all approaches, smothering the warning of his nerves.

As, sometimes, in a nightmare events crowd upon each other's heels with a conviction of dreadfulest reality, yet some inconsistent detail accuses the whole display of incompleteness and disguise, so the events that now followed, though they actually happened, persuaded the mind somehow that the detail which could explain them had been overlooked in the confusion, and that therefore they were but partly true, the rest delusion. At the back of the sleeper's mind something remains awake, ready to let slip the judgment. "All this is not *quite* real; when you wake up you'll understand."

And thus, in a way, it was with Simpson. The events, not wholly inexplicable or incredible in themselves, yet remain for the man who saw and heard them a sequence of separate facts of cold horror, because the little piece that might have made the puzzle clear lay concealed or overlooked.

So far as he can recall, it was a violent movement, running downwards through the tent towards the door, that first woke him and made him aware that his companion was sitting bolt upright beside him—quivering. Hours must have passed, for it was the pale gleam of the dawn that revealed his outline against the canvas. This time the man was not crying; he was quaking like a leaf; the trembling he felt plainly through the blankets down the entire length of his own body. Défago had huddled down against him for protection, shrinking away from something that apparently concealed itself near the door flaps of the little tent.

Simpson thereupon called out in a loud voice some question or other—in the first bewilderment of waking he does not remember exactly what—and the man made no reply. The atmosphere and feeling of true nightmare lay horribly about him, making movement and speech both difficult. At first, indeed, he was not sure where he was—whether in one of the earlier camps, or at home in his bed at Aberdeen. The sense of confusion was very troubling.

And next—almost simultaneous with his waking, it seemed—the profound stillness of the dawn outside was shattered by a most uncommon sound. It came without warning, or audible approach; and it was unspeakably dreadful. It was a voice, Simpson declares, possibly a human voice; hoarse yet plaintive—a soft, roaring voice close outside the tent, overhead rather than upon the ground, of immense volume, while in some strange way most penetratingly and seductively sweet. It rang out, too, in three separate and distinct notes, or cries, that bore in some odd fashion a resemblance, farfetched yet recognisable, to the name of the guide: *"Dé-fa-go!"*

The student admits he is unable to describe it quite intelligently, for it was unlike any sound he had ever heard in his life, and combined a blending of such contrary qualities. "A sort of windy, crying voice," he calls it, "as of something lonely and untamed, wild and of abominable power. . . ."

And, even before it ceased, dropping back into the great gulfs of silence, the guide beside him had sprung to his feet with an answering though unintelligible cry. He blundered against the tent pole with violence, shaking the whole structure, spreading his arms out frantically for more room, and kicking his legs impetuously free of the clinging blankets. For a second, perhaps two, he stood upright by the door, his outline dark against the pallor of the dawn; then, with a furious, rushing speed, before his companion could move a hand to stop him, he shot with a plunge through the flaps of canvas—and was gone. And as he went—so astonishingly fast that the voice could actually be heard dying in the distance—he called aloud in tones of anguished terror that at the same time held something strangely like the frenzied exultation of delight:

"Oh! oh! My feet of fire! My burning feet of fire! Oh! oh! This height and fiery speed!"

And then the distance quickly buried it, and the deep silence of very early morning descended upon the forest as before.

It had all come about with such rapidity that, but for the evidence of the empty bed beside him, Simpson could almost have believed it to have been the memory of a nightmare carried over from sleep. He still felt the warm pressure of that vanished body against his side; there lay the twisted blankets in a heap; the very tent yet trembled with the vehemence of the impetuous departure. The strange words rang in his ears, as though he still heard them in the distance—wild language of a suddenly stricken mind. Moreover, it was not only the senses of sight and hearing that reported uncommon things to his brain, for even while the man cried and ran, he had become aware that a strange perfume, faint yet pungent, pervaded the interior of the tent. And it was at this point, it seems, brought to himself by the consciousness that his nostrils were taking this distressing odour down into his throat, that he found his courage, sprang quickly to his feet—and went out.

The grey light of dawn that dropped, cold and glimmering, between the trees revealed the scene tolerably well. There stood the tent behind him, soaked with dew; the dark ashes of the fire, still warm; the lake, white beneath a coating of mist, the islands rising darkly out of it like objects packed in wool; and patches of snow beyond among the clearer spaces of the Bush—everything cold, still, waiting for the sun. But nowhere a sign of the vanished guide—still, doubtless, flying at frantic speed through the frozen woods. There was not even the sound of disappearing footsteps, nor the echoes of the dying voice. He had gone—utterly.

There was nothing; nothing but the sense of his recent presence, so strongly left behind about the camp; and—this penetrating, all-pervading odour.

And even this was now rapidly disappearing in its turn. In spite of his exceeding mental perturbation, Simpson struggled hard to detect its nature, and define it, but the ascertaining of an elusive scent, not recognised subconsciously and at once, is a very subtle operation of the mind. And he failed. It was gone before he could properly seize or name it. Approximate description, even, seems to have been difficult, for it was unlike any smell he knew. Acrid rather, not unlike the odour of a lion, he thinks, yet softer and not wholly unpleasing, with something almost sweet in it that reminded him of the scent of decaying garden leaves, earth, and the myriad, nameless perfumes that make up the odour of a big forest. Yet the "odour of lions" is the phrase with which he usually sums it all up.

Then—it was wholly gone, and he found himself standing by the ashes of the fire in a state of amazement and stupid terror that left him the helpless prey of anything that chose to happen. Had a muskrat poked its pointed muzzle over a rock, or a squirrel scuttled in that instant down the bark of a tree, he would most likely have collapsed without more ado and fainted. For he felt about the whole affair the touch somewhere of a great Outer Horror—and his scattered powers had not as yet had time to collect themselves into a definite attitude of fighting self-control.

Nothing did happen, however. A great kiss of wind ran softly through the awakening forest, and a few maple leaves here and there rustled tremblingly to earth. The sky seemed to grow suddenly much lighter. Simpson felt the cool air upon his cheek and uncovered head; realised that he was shivering with the cold; and, making a great effort, realised next that he was alone in the Bush—*and* that he was called upon to take immediate steps to find and succor his vanished companion.

Make an effort, accordingly, he did, though an ill-calculated and futile one. With that wilderness of trees about him, the sheet of water cutting him off behind, and the horror of that wild cry in his blood, he did what any other inexperienced man would have done in similar bewilderment: he ran about, without any sense of direction, like a frantic child, and called loudly without ceasing the name of the guide:

"Défago! Défago! Défago!" he yelled, and the trees gave him back the name as often as he shouted, only a little softened—"Défago! Défago! Défago!"

He followed the trail that lay a short distance across the patches of snow, and then lost it again where the trees grew too thickly for snow to lie. He shouted till he was hoarse, and till the sound of his own voice in all that unanswering and listening world began to frighten him. His confusion increased in direct ratio to the violence of his efforts. His distress became formidably acute, till at length his exertions defeated their own object, and from sheer exhaustion he headed back to the camp again. It remains a wonder that he ever found his way. It was with great difficulty, and only after numberless false clues, that he at last saw the white tent between the trees, and so reached safety.

Exhaustion then applied its own remedy, and he grew calmer. He made the fire and breakfasted. Hot coffee and bacon put a little sense and judgment into him again, and he realised that he had been behaving like a boy. He now made another, and more successful attempt to face the situation collectedly, and, a nature naturally plucky coming to his assistance, he decided that he must first make as thorough a search as possible, failing success in which, he must find his way into the home camp as best he could and bring help.

And this was what he did. Taking food, matches and rifle with him, and a small axe to blaze the trees against his return journey, he set forth. It was eight o'clock when he started, the sun shining over the tops of the trees in a sky without clouds. Pinned to a stake by the fire he left a note in case Défago returned while he was away.

This time, according to a careful plan, he took a new direction, intending to make a wide sweep that must sooner or later cut into indications of the guide's trail; and, before he had gone a quarter of a mile he came across the tracks of a large animal in the snow, and beside it the light and smaller tracks of what were beyond question human feet—the feet of Défago. The relief he at once experienced was natural, though brief; for at first sight he saw in these tracks a simple explanation of the whole matter: these big marks had surely been left by a bull moose that, wind against it, had blundered upon the camp, and uttered its singular cry of warning and alarm the moment its mistake was apparent. Défago, in whom the hunting instinct was developed to the point of uncanny perfection, had scented the brute coming down the wind hours before. His excitement and disappearance were due, of course, to—to his—

Then the impossible explanation at which he grasped faded, as common sense showed him mercilessly that none of this was true. No guide, much less a guide like Défago, could have acted in so irrational a way, going off even without his rifle. . . ! The whole affair demanded a far more complicated elucidation, when he remembered the details of it all—the cry of terror, the amazing language, the grey face of horror when his nostrils first caught the new odour; that muffled sobbing in the darkness, and—for this, too, now came back to him dimly—the man's original aversion for this particular bit of country. . . .

Besides, now that he examined them closer, these were not the tracks of a bull moose at all! Hank had explained to him the outline of a bull's hoofs, of a cow's or calf's, too, for that matter; he had drawn them clearly on a strip of birch bark. And these were wholly different. They were big, round, ample, and with no pointed outline as of sharp hoofs. He wondered for a moment whether bear tracks were like that. There was no other animal he could think of, for caribou did not come so far south at this season, and, even if they did, would leave hoof marks.

They were ominous signs—these mysterious writings left in the snow by the unknown creature that had lured a human being away from safety—and when he coupled them in his imagination with that haunting sound that broke the stillness of the dawn, a momentary dizziness shook his mind, distressing him again beyond belief. He felt the *threatening* aspect of it all. And, stooping down to examine the marks more closely, he caught a faint whiff of that sweet yet pungent odour that made him instantly straighten up again, fighting a sensation almost of nausea.

Then his memory played him another evil trick. He suddenly recalled those uncovered feet projecting beyond the edge of the tent, and the body's appearance of having been dragged towards the opening; the man's shrinking from something by the door when he woke later. The details now beat against his trembling mind with concerted attack. They seemed to gather in those deep spaces of the silent forest about him, where the host of trees stood waiting, listening, watching to see what he would do. The woods were closing round him.

With the persistence of true pluck, however, Simpson went forward, following the tracks as best he could, smothering these ugly emotions that sought to weaken his will. He blazed innumerable trees as he went, ever fearful of being unable to find the way back, and calling aloud at intervals of a few seconds the name of the guide. The dull tapping of the axe upon the massive trunks, and the unnatural accents of his own voice became at length sounds that he even dreaded to make, dreaded to hear. For they drew attention without ceasing to his presence and exact whereabouts, and if it were really the case that something was hunting himself down in the same way that he was hunting down another—

With a strong effort, he crushed the thought out the instant it rose. It was the beginning, he realised, of a bewilderment utterly diabolical in kind that would speedily destroy him.

Although the snow was not continuous, lying merely in shallow flurries over the more open spaces, he found no difficulty in following the tracks for the first few miles. They went straight as a ruled line wherever the trees permitted. The stride soon began to increase in length, till it finally assumed proportions that seemed absolutely impossible for any ordinary animal to have made. Like huge flying leaps they became. One of these he measured, and though he knew that "stretch" of eighteen feet must be somehow wrong, he was at a complete loss to understand why he found no signs on the snow between the extreme points. But what perplexed him even more, making him feel his vision had gone utterly awry, was that Défago's stride increased in the same manner, and finally covered the same incredible distances. It looked as if the great beast had lifted him with it and carried him across these astonishing intervals. Simpson, who was much longer in the limb, found that he could not compass even half the stretch by taking a running jump.

And the sight of these huge tracks, running side by side, silent evidence of a dreadful journey in which terror or madness had urged to impossible results, was profoundly moving. It shocked him in the secret depths of his soul. It was the most horrible thing his eyes had ever looked upon. He began to follow them mechanically, absentmindedly almost, ever peering over his shoulder to see if he, too, were being followed by something with a gigantic tread. . . . And soon it came about that he no longer quite realised what it was they signified—these impressions left upon the snow by something nameless and untamed, always accompanied by the footmarks of the little French Canadian, his guide, his comrade, the man who had shared his tent a few hours before, chatting, laughing, even singing by his side. . . .

V

For a man of his years and inexperience, only a canny Scot, perhaps, grounded in common sense and established in logic, could have preserved even that measure of balance that this youth somehow or other did manage to preserve through the whole adventure. Otherwise, two things he presently noticed, while forging pluckily ahead, must have sent him headlong back to the comparative safety of his tent, instead of only making his hands close more tightly upon the rifle stock, while his heart, trained for the Wee Kirk, sent a wordless prayer winging its way to heaven. Both tracks, he saw, had undergone a change, and this change, so far as it concerned the footsteps of the man, was in some undecipherable manner—appalling.

It was in the bigger tracks he first noticed this, and for a long time he could not quite believe his eyes. Was it the blown leaves that produced odd effects of light and shade, or that the dry snow, drifting like finely ground rice about the edges, cast shadows and high lights? Or was it actually the fact that the great marks had become faintly colored? For round about the deep, plunging holes of the animal there now appeared a mysterious, reddish tinge that was more like an effect of light than of anything that dyed the substance of the snow itself. Every mark had it, and had it increasingly—this indistinct fiery tinge that painted a new touch of ghastliness into the picture.

But when, wholly unable to explain or to credit it, he turned his attention to the other tracks to discover if they, too, bore similar witness, he noticed that these had meanwhile undergone a change that was infinitely worse, and charged with far more horrible suggestion. For, in the last hundred yards or so, he saw that they had grown gradually into the semblance of the parent tread. Imperceptibly the change had come about, yet unmistakably. It was hard to see where the change first began. The result, however, was beyond question. Smaller, neater, more cleanly modeled, they formed now an exact and careful duplicate of the larger tracks beside them. The feet that produced them had, therefore, also changed. And something in his mind reared up with loathing and with terror as he saw it.

Simpson, for the first time, hesitated; then, ashamed of his alarm and indecision, took a few hurried steps ahead; the next instant stopped dead in his tracks. Immediately in front of him all signs of the trail ceased; both tracks came to an abrupt end. On all sides, for a hundred yards and more, he searched in vain for the least indication of their continuance. There was—nothing.

The trees were very thick just there, big trees all of them, spruce, cedar, hemlock; there was no underbrush. He stood, looking about him, all distraught; bereft of any power of judgment. Then he set to work to search again, and again, and yet again, but always with the same result: *nothing.* The feet that printed the surface of the snow thus far had now, apparently, left the ground!

And it was in that moment of distress and confusion that the whip of terror laid its most nicely calculated lash about his heart. It dropped with deadly effect upon the sorest spot of all, completely unnerving him. He had been secretly dreading all the time that it would come—and come it did.

Far overhead, muted by great height and distance, strangely thinned and wailing, he heard the crying voice of Défago, the guide.

The sound dropped upon him out of that still, wintry sky with an effect of dismay and terror unsurpassed. The rifle fell to his feet. He stood motionless an instant, listening as it were with his whole body, then staggered back against the nearest tree for support, disorganised hopelessly in mind and spirit. To him, in that moment, it seemed the most shattering and dislocating experience he had ever known, so that his heart emptied itself of all feeling whatsoever as by a sudden draught.

"Oh! oh! This fiery height! Oh, my feet of fire! My burning feet of fire. . . !" ran in far, beseeching accents of indescribable appeal this voice of anguish down the sky. Once it called—then silence through all the listening wilderness of trees.

And Simpson, scarcely knowing what he did, presently found himself running wildly to and fro, searching, calling, tripping over roots and boulders, and flinging himself in a frenzy of undirected pursuit after the Caller. Behind the screen of memory and emotion with which experience veils events, he plunged, distracted and half-deranged, picking up false lights like a ship at sea, terror in his eyes and heart and soul. For the Panic of the Wilderness had called to him in that far voice—the Power of untamed Distance—the Enticement of the Desolation that destroys. He knew in that moment all the pains of someone hopelessly and irretrievably lost, suffering the lust and travail of a soul in the final Loneliness. A vision of Défago, eternally hunted, driven and pursued across the skiey vastness of those ancient forests fled like a flame across the dark ruin of his thoughts. . . .

It seemed ages before he could find anything in the chaos of his disorganised sensations to which he could anchor himself steady for a moment, and think. . . .

The cry was not repeated; his own hoarse calling brought no response; the inscrutable forces of the Wild had summoned their victim beyond recall—and held him fast.

Yet he searched and called, it seems, for hours afterwards, for it was late in the afternoon when at length he decided to abandon a useless pursuit and return to his camp on the shores of Fifty Island Water. Even then he went with reluctance, that crying voice still echoing in his ears. With difficulty he found his rifle and the homeward trail. The concentration necessary to follow the badly blazed trees, and a biting hunger that gnawed, helped to keep his mind steady. Otherwise, he admits, the temporary aberration he had suffered might have been prolonged to the point of positive disaster. Gradually the ballast shifted back again, and he regained something that approached his normal equilibrium.

But for all that the journey through the gathering dusk was miserably haunted. He heard innumerable following footsteps; voices that laughed and whispered; and saw figures crouching behind trees and boulders, making signs to one another for a concerted attack the moment he had passed. The creeping murmur of the wind made him start and listen. He went stealthily, trying to hide where possible, and making as little sound as he could. The shadows of the woods, hitherto protective or covering merely, had now become menacing, challenging; and the pageantry in his frightened mind masked a host of possibilities that were all the more ominous for being obscure. The presentiment of a nameless doom lurked ill-concealed behind every detail of what had happened.

It was really admirable how he emerged victor in the end; men of riper powers and experience might have come through the ordeal with less success. He had himself tolerably well in hand, all things considered, and his plan of action proves it. Sleep being absolutely out of the question and travelling an unknown trail in the darkness equally impracticable, he sat up the whole of that night, rifle in hand, before a fire he never for a single moment allowed to die down. The severity of the haunted vigil marked his soul for life; but it was successfully accomplished; and with the very first signs of dawn he set forth upon the long return journey to the home camp to get help. As before, he left a written note to explain his absence, and to indicate where he had left a plentiful *cache* of food and matches—though he had no expectation that any human hands would find them!

How Simpson found his way alone by the lake and forest might well make a story in itself, for to hear him tell it is to *know* the passionate loneliness of soul that a man can feel when the Wilderness holds him in the hollow of its illimitable hand—and laughs. It is also to admire his indomitable pluck.

He claims no skill, declaring that he followed the almost invisible trail mechanically, and without thinking. And this, doubtless, is the truth. He relied upon the guiding of the unconscious mind, which is instinct. Perhaps, too, some sense of orientation, known to animals and primitive men, may have helped as well, for through all that tangled region he succeeded in reaching the exact spot where Défago had hidden the canoe nearly three days before with the remark, "Strike doo west across the lake into the sun to find the camp."

There was not much sun left to guide him, but he used his compass to the best of his ability, embarking in the frail craft for the last twelve miles of his journey with a sensation of immense relief that the forest was at last behind him. And, fortunately, the water was calm; he took his line across the centre of the lake instead of coasting round the shores for another twenty miles. Fortunately, too, the other hunters were back. The light of their fires furnished a steering point without which he might have searched all night long for the actual position of the camp.

It was close upon midnight all the same when his canoe grated on the sandy cove, and Hank, Punk and his uncle, disturbed in their sleep by his cries, ran quickly down and helped a very exhausted and broken specimen of Scotch humanity over the rocks toward a dying fire.

VI

The sudden entrance of his prosaic uncle into this world of wizardry and horror that had haunted him without interruption now for two days and two nights, had the immediate effect of giving to the affair an entirely new aspect. The sound of that crisp "Hulloa, my boy! And what's up now?" and the grasp of that dry and vigorous hand introduced another standard of judgment. A revulsion of feeling washed through him. He realised that he had let himself "go" rather badly. He even felt vaguely ashamed of himself. The native hard-headedness of his race reclaimed him.

And this doubtless explains why he found it so hard to tell that group round the fire—everything. He told enough, however, for the immediate decision to be arrived at that a relief party must start at the earliest possible moment, and that Simpson, in order to guide it capably, must first have food and, above all, sleep. Dr. Cathcart observing the lad's condition more shrewdly than his patient knew, gave him a very slight injection of morphine. For six hours he slept like the dead.

From the description carefully written out afterwards by this student of divinity, it appears that the account he gave to the astonished group omitted sundry vital and important details. He declares that, with his uncle's wholesome, matter-of-fact countenance staring him in the face, he simply had not the courage to mention them. Thus, all the search party gathered, it would seem, was that Défago had suffered in the night an acute and inexplicable attack of mania, had imagined himself "called" by someone or something, and had plunged into the bush after it without food or rifle, where he must die a horrible and lingering death by cold and starvation unless he could be found and rescued in time. "In time," moreover, meant "at once."

In the course of the following day, however—they were off by seven, leaving Punk in charge with instructions to have food and fire always ready—Simpson found it possible to tell his uncle a good deal more of the story's true inwardness, without divining that it was drawn out of him as a matter of fact by a very subtle form of cross examination. By the time they reached the beginning of the trail, where the canoe was laid up against the return journey, he had mentioned how Défago spoke vaguely of "something he called a 'Wendigo' "; how he cried in his sleep; how he imagined an unusual scent about the camp; and had betrayed other symptoms of mental excitement. He also admitted the bewildering effect of "that extraordinary odour" upon himself, "pungent and acrid like the odour of lions." And by the time they were within an easy hour of Fifty Island Water he had let slip the further fact—a foolish avowal of his own hysterical condition, as he felt afterwards—that he had heard the vanished guide call "for help." He omitted the singular phrases used, for he simply could not bring himself to repeat the preposterous language. Also, while describing how the man's footsteps in the snow had gradually assumed an exact miniature likeness of the animal's plunging tracks, he left out the fact that they measured a *wholly* incredible distance. It seemed a question, nicely balanced between individual pride and honesty, what he should reveal and what suppress. He mentioned the fiery tinge in the snow, for instance, yet shrank from telling that body and bed had been partly dragged out of the tent. . . .

With the net result that Dr. Cathcart, adroit psychologist that he fancied himself to be, had assured him clearly enough exactly where his mind, influenced by loneliness, bewilderment and terror, had yielded to the strain and invited delusion. While praising his conduct, he managed at the same time to point out where, when, and how his mind had gone astray. He made his nephew think himself finer than he was by judicious praise, yet more foolish than he was by minimising the value of the evidence. Like many another materialist, that is, he lied cleverly on the basis of insufficient knowledge, *because* the knowledge supplied seemed to his own particular intelligence inadmissible.

"The spell of these terrible solitudes," he said, "cannot leave any mind untouched, any mind, that is, possessed of the higher imaginative qualities. It has worked upon yours exactly as it worked upon my own when I was your age. The animal that haunted your little camp was undoubtedly a moose, for the 'belling' of a moose may have, sometimes, a very peculiar quality of sound. The colored appearance of the big tracks was obviously a defect of vision in your own eyes produced by excitement. The size and stretch of the tracks we shall prove when we come to them. But the hallucination of an audible voice, of course, is one of the commonest forms of delusion due to mental excitement—an excitement, my dear boy, perfectly excusable, and, let me add, wonderfully controlled by you under the circumstances. For the rest, I am bound to say, you have acted with a splendid courage, for the terror of feeling oneself lost in this wilderness is nothing short of awful, and, had I been in your place, I don't for a moment believe I could have behaved with one quarter of your wisdom and decision. The only thing I find it uncommonly difficult to explain is—that—damned odour."

"It made me feel sick, I assure you," declared his nephew, "positively dizzy!" His uncle's attitude of calm omniscience, merely because he knew more psychological formulae, made him slightly defiant. It was so easy to be wise in the explanation of an experience one has not personally witnessed. "A kind of desolate and terrible odour is the only way I can describe it," he concluded, glancing at the features of the quiet, unemotional man beside him.

"I can only marvel," was the reply, "that under the circumstances it did not seem to you even worse." The dry words, Simpson knew, hovered between the truth, and his uncle's interpretation of "the truth."

And so at last they came to the little camp and found the tent still standing, the remains of the fire, and the piece of paper pinned to a stake beside it—untouched. The *cache,* poorly contrived by inexperienced hands, however, had been discovered and opened—by muskrats, mink and squirrel. The matches lay scattered about the opening, but the food had been taken to the last crumb.

"Well, fellers, he ain't here," exclaimed Hank loudly after his fashion. "And that's as sartain as the coal supply down below! But whar he's got to by this time is 'bout as unsartain as the trade in crowns in t'other place." The presence of a divinity student was no barrier to his language at such a time, though for the reader's sake it may be severely edited. "I propose," he added, "that we start out at once an' hunt for'm like hell!"

The gloom of Défago's probable fate oppressed the whole party with a sense of dreadful gravity the moment they saw the familiar signs of recent occupancy. Especially the tent, with the bed of balsam branches still smoothed and flattened by the pressure of his body, seemed to bring his presence near to them. Simpson, feeling vaguely as if his world were somehow at stake, went about explaining particulars in a hushed tone. He was much calmer now, though overwearied with the strain of his many journeys. His uncle's method of explaining—"explaining away," rather—the details still fresh in his haunted memory helped, too, to put ice upon his emotions.

"And that's the direction he ran off in," he said to his two companions, pointing in the direction where the guide had vanished that morning in the grey dawn. "Straight down there he ran like a deer, in between the birch and the hemlock. . . . "

Hank and Dr. Cathcart exchanged glances.

"And it was about two miles down there, in a straight line," continued the other, speaking with something of the former terror in his voice, "that I followed his trail to the place where—it stopped—dead!"

"And where you heered him callin' an' caught the stench, an' all the rest of the wicked entertainment," cried Hank, with a volubility that betrayed his keen distress.

"And where your excitement overcame you to the point of producing illusions," added Dr. Cathcart under his breath, yet not so low that his nephew did not hear it.

It was early in the afternoon, for they had travelled quickly, and there were still a good two hours of daylight left. Dr. Cathcart and Hank lost no time in beginning the search, but Simpson was too exhausted to accompany them. They would follow the blazed marks on the trees, and where possible, his footsteps. Meanwhile the best thing he could do was to keep a good fire going, and rest.

But after something like three hours' search, the darkness already down, the two men returned to camp with nothing to report. Fresh snow had covered all signs, and though they had followed the blazed trees to the spot where Simpson had turned back, they had not discovered the smallest indication of a human being—or for that matter, of an animal. There were no fresh tracks of any kind; the snow lay undisturbed.

It was difficult to know what was best to do, though in reality there was nothing more they *could* do. They might stay and search for weeks without much chance of success. The fresh snow destroyed their only hope, and they gathered round the fire for supper, a gloomy and despondent party. The facts, indeed, were sad enough, for Défago had a wife at Rat Portage, and his earnings were the family's sole means of support.

Now that the whole truth in all its ugliness was out, it seemed useless to deal in further disguise or pretense. They talked openly of the facts and probabilities. It was not the first time, even in the experience of Dr. Cathcart, that a man had yielded to the singular seduction of the Solitudes and gone out of his mind; Défago, moreover, was predisposed to something of the sort, for he already had a touch of melancholia in his blood, and his fiber was weakened by bouts of drinking that often lasted for weeks at a time. Something on this trip—one might never know precisely what—had sufficed to push him over the line, that was all. And he had gone, gone off into the great wilderness of trees and lakes to die by starvation and exhaustion. The chances against his finding camp again were overwhelming; the delirium that was upon him would also doubtless have increased, and it was quite likely he might do violence to himself and so hasten his cruel fate. Even while they talked, indeed, the end had probably come. On the suggestion of Hank, his old pal, however, they proposed to wait a little longer and devote the whole of the following day, from dawn to darkness, to the most systematic search they could devise. They would divide the territory between them. They discussed their plan in great detail. All that men could do they would do.

And, meanwhile, they talked about the particular form in which the singular Panic of the Wilderness had made its attack upon the mind of the unfortunate guide. Hank, though familiar with the legend in its general outline, obviously did not welcome the turn the conversation had taken. He contributed little, though that little was illuminating. For he admitted that a story ran over all this section of country to the effect that several Indians had "seen the Wendigo" along the shores of Fifty Island Water in the "fall" of last year, and that this was the true reason of Défago's disinclination to hunt there. Hank doubtless felt that he had in a sense helped his old pal to death by overpersuading him. "When an Indian goes crazy," he explained, talking to himself more than to the others, it seemed, "it's always put that he's 'seen the Wendigo.' An' pore old Défaygo was superstitious down to his very heels . . . !"

And then Simpson, feeling the atmosphere more sympathetic, told over again the full story of his astonishing tale; he left out no details this time; he mentioned his own sensations and gripping fears. He only omitted the strange language used.

"But Défago surely had already told you all these details of the Wendigo legend, my dear fellow," insisted the doctor. "I mean, he had talked about it, and thus put into your mind the ideas which your own excitement afterwards developed?"

Whereupon Simpson again repeated the facts. Défago, he declared, had barely mentioned the beast. He, Simpson, knew nothing of the story, and, so far as he remembered, had never even read about it. Even the word was unfamiliar.

Of course he was telling the truth, and Dr. Cathcart was reluctantly compelled to admit the singular character of the whole affair. He did not do this in words so much as in manner, however. He kept his back against a good, stout tree; he poked the fire into a blaze the moment it showed signs of dying down; he was quicker than any of them to notice the least sound in the night about them—a fish jumping in the lake, a twig snapping in the bush, the dropping of occasional fragments of frozen snow from the branches overhead where the heat loosened them. His voice, too, changed a little in quality, becoming a shade less confident, lower also in tone. Fear, to put it plainly, hovered close about that little camp, and though all three would have been glad to speak of other matters, the only thing they seemed able to discuss was this—the source of their fear. They tried other subjects in vain; there was nothing to say about them. Hank was the most honest of the group; he said next to nothing. He never once, however, turned his back to the darkness. His face was always to the forest, and when wood was needed he didn't go farther than was necessary to get it.

VII

A wall of silence wrapped them in, for the snow, though not thick, was sufficient to deaden any noise, and the frost held things pretty tight besides. No sound but their voices and the soft roar of the flames made itself heard. Only, from time to time, something soft as the flutter of a pine moth's wings went past them through the air. No one seemed anxious to go to bed. The hours slipped towards midnight.

"The legend is picturesque enough," observed the doctor after one of the longer pauses, speaking to break it rather than because he had anything to say, "for the Wendigo is simply the Call of the Wild personified, which some natures hear to their own destruction."

"That's about it," Hank said presently. "An' there's no misunderstandin' when you hear it. It calls you by name right 'nough."

Another pause followed. Then Dr. Cathcart came back to the forbidden subject with a rush that made the others jump.

"The allegory is significant," he remarked, looking about him into the darkness, "for the Voice, they say, resembles all the minor sounds of the

Bush—wind, falling water, cries of the animals, and so forth. And, once the victim hears *that*—he's off for good, of course! His most vulnerable points, moreover, are said to be the feet and the eyes; the feet, you see, for the lust of wandering, and the eyes for the lust of beauty. The poor beggar goes at such a dreadful speed that he bleeds beneath the eyes, and his feet burn."

Dr. Cathcart, as he spoke, continued to peer uneasily into the surrounding gloom. His voice sank to a hushed tone.

"The Wendigo," he added, "is said to burn his feet—owing to the friction, apparently caused by its tremendous velocity—till they drop off, and new ones form exactly like its own."

Simpson listened in horrified amazement; but it was the pallor on Hank's face that fascinated him most. He would willingly have stopped his ears and closed his eyes, had he dared.

"It don't always keep to the ground neither," came in Hank's slow, heavy drawl, "for it goes so high that he thinks the stars have set him all a-fire. An' it'll take great thumpin' jumps sometimes, an' run along the tops of the trees, carrying its partner with it, an' then droppin' him jest as a fish hawk'll drop a pickerel to kill it before eatin'. An' its food, of all the muck in the whole Bush is—moss!" And he laughed a short, unnatural laugh. "It's a moss eater, is the Wendigo," he added, looking up excitedly into the faces of his companions, "moss eater," he repeated, with a string of the most outlandish oaths he could invent.

But Simpson now understood the true purpose of all this talk. What these two men, each strong and "experienced" in his own way, dreaded more than anything else was—silence. They were talking against time. They were also talking against darkness, against the invasion of panic, against the admission reflection might bring that they were in an enemy's country—against anything, in fact, rather than allow their inmost thoughts to assume control. He himself, already initiated by the awful vigil with terror, was beyond both of them in this respect. He had reached the stage where he was immune. But these two, the scoffing, analytical doctor, and the honest, dogged backwoodsman, each sat trembling in the depths of his being.

Thus the hours passed; and thus, with lowered voices and a kind of taut inner resistance of spirit, this little group of humanity sat in the jaws of the wilderness and talked foolishly of the terrible and haunting legend. It was an unequal contest, all things considered, for the wilderness had already the advantage of first attack—and of a hostage. The fate of their comrade hung over them with a steadily increasing weight of oppression that finally became insupportable.

It was Hank, after a pause longer than the preceding ones that no one seemed able to break, who first let loose all this pent-up emotion in very unexpected fashion, by springing suddenly to his feet and letting out the most ear-shattering yell imaginable into the night. He could not contain himself any longer, it seemed. To make it carry even beyond an ordinary cry he interrupted its rhythm by shaking the palm of his hand before his mouth.

"That's for Défago," he said, looking down at the other two with a queer, defiant laugh, "for it's my belief"—the sandwiched oaths may be omitted—"that my ole partner's not far from us at this very minute."

There was a vehemence and recklessness about his performance that made Simpson, too, start to his feet in amazement, and betrayed even the doctor into letting the pipe slip from between his lips. Hank's face was ghastly, but Cathcart's showed a sudden weakness—a loosening of all his faculties, as it were. Then a momentary anger blazed into his eyes, and he too, though with deliberation born of habitual self-control, got upon his feet and faced the excited guide. For this was unpermissible, foolish, dangerous, and he meant to stop it in the bud.

What might have happened in the next minute or two one may speculate about, yet never definitely know, for in the instant of profound silence that followed Hank's roaring voice, and as though in answer to it, something went past through the darkness of the sky overhead at terrific speed—something of necessity very large, for it displaced much air, while down between the trees there fell a faint and windy cry of a human voice, calling in tones of indescribable anguish and appeal—

"Oh, oh! This fiery height! Oh, oh! My feet of fire! My burning feet of fire!"

White to the very edge of his shirt, Hank looked stupidly about him like a child. Dr. Cathcart uttered some kind of unintelligible cry, turning as he did so with an instinctive movement of blind terror towards the protection of the tent, then halting in the act as though frozen. Simpson, alone of the three, retained his presence of mind a little. His own horror was too deep to allow of any immediate reaction. He had heard that cry before.

Turning to his stricken companions, he said almost calmly—

"That's exactly the cry I heard—the very words he used!"

Then, lifting his face to the sky, he cried aloud, "Défago, Défago! Come down here to us! Come down—!"

And before there was time for anybody to take definite action one way or another, there came the sound of something dropping heavily between the trees, striking the branches on the way down, and landing with a dreadful thud upon the frozen earth below. The crash and thunder of it was really terrific.

"That's him, s'help me the good Gawd!" came from Hank in a whispering cry half choked, his hand going automatically toward the hunting knife in his belt. "And he's coming! He's coming!" he added, with an irrational laugh of horror, as the sounds of heavy footsteps crunching over the snow became distinctly audible, approaching through the blackness towards the circle of light.

And while the steps, with their stumbling motion, moved nearer and nearer upon them, the three men stood round that fire, motionless and dumb. Dr. Cathcart had the appearance of a man suddenly withered; even his eyes did not move. Hank, suffering shockingly, seemed on the verge again of violent action; yet did nothing. He, too, was hewn of stone. Like stricken children they seemed. The picture was hideous. And, meanwhile, their owner still invisible, the footsteps came closer, crunching the frozen snow. It was endless—too prolonged to be quite real—this measured and pitiless approach. It was accursed.

VIII

Then at length the darkness, having thus laboriously conceived, brought forth—a figure. It drew forward into the zone of uncertain light where fire and shadows mingled, not ten feet away; then halted, staring at them fixedly. The same instant it started forward again with the spasmodic motion as of a thing moved by wires, and coming up closer to them, full into the glare of the fire, they perceived then that—it was a man; and apparently that this man was—Défago.

Something like a skin of horror almost perceptibly drew down in that moment over every face, and three pairs of eyes shone through it as though they saw across the frontiers of normal vision into the Unknown.

Défago advanced, his tread faltering and uncertain; he made his way straight up to them as a group first, then turned sharply and peered close into the face of Simpson. The sound of a voice issued from his lips—

"Here I am, Boss Simpson. I heered someone calling me." It was a faint, dried up voice, made wheezy and breathless as by immense exertion. "I'm havin' a reg'lar hellfire kind of a trip, I am." And he laughed, thrusting his head forward into the other's face.

But that laugh started the machinery of the group of waxwork figures with the wax-white skins. Hank immediately sprang forward with a stream of oaths so far-fetched that Simpson did not recognise them as English at all, but thought he had lapsed into Indian or some other lingo. He only realised that Hank's presence, thrust thus between them, was welcome—uncommonly welcome. Dr. Cathcart, though more calmly and leisurely, advanced behind him, heavily stumbling.

Simpson seems hazy as to what was actually said and done in those next few seconds, for the eyes of that detestable and blasted visage peering at such close quarters into his own utterly bewildered his senses at first. He merely stood still. He said nothing. He had not the trained will of the older men that forced them into action in defiance of all emotional stress. He watched them moving as behind a glass that half destroyed their reality; it was dream-like; perverted. Yet, through the torrent of Hank's meaningless phrases, he remembers hearing his uncle's tone of authority—hard and forced—saying several things about food and warmth, blankets, whisky and the rest . . . and, further, that whiffs of that penetrating, unaccustomed odour, vile yet sweetly bewildering, assailed his nostrils during all that followed.

It was no less a person than himself, however—less experienced and adroit than the others though he was—who gave instinctive utterance to the sentence that brought a measure of relief into the ghastly situation by expressing the doubt and thought in each one's heart.

"It *is*—YOU, isn't it, Défago?" he asked under his breath, horror breaking his speech.

And at once Cathcart burst out with the loud answer before the other had time to move his lips. "Of course it is! Of course it is! Only—can't you see—he's nearly dead with exhaustion, cold and terror! Isn't that enough to change a man beyond all recognition?" It was said in order to convince himself as much as to convince the others. The overemphasis alone proved that. And continually, while he spoke and acted, he held a handkerchief to his nose. That odour pervaded the whole camp.

For the "Défago" who sat huddled by the big fire, wrapped in blankets, drinking hot whisky and holding food in wasted hands, was no more like the guide they had last seen alive than the picture of a man of sixty is like a daguerreotype of his early youth in the costume of another generation. Nothing really can describe that ghastly caricature, that parody, masquerading there in the firelight as Défago. From the ruins of the dark and awful memories he still retains, Simpson declares that the face was more animal than human, the features drawn about into wrong proportions, the skin loose and hanging, as though he had been subjected to extraordinary pressures and tensions. It made him think vaguely of those bladder faces blown up by the hawkers on Ludgate Hill, that change their expression as they swell, and as they collapse emit a faint and wailing imitation of a voice. Both face and voice suggested some such abominable resemblance. But Cathcart long afterwards, seeking to describe the indescribable, asserts that thus might have looked a face and body that had been in air so rarified that, the weight of atmosphere being removed, the entire structure threatened to fly asunder and become—*incoherent*. . . .

It was Hank, though all distraught and shaking with a tearing volume of emotion he could neither handle nor understand, who brought things to a head without much ado. He went off to a little distance from the fire, apparently so that the light should not dazzle him too much, and shading his eyes for a moment with both hands, shouted in a loud voice that held anger and affection dreadfully mingled—

"You ain't Défaygo! You ain't Défaygo at all! I don't give a ——damn, but that ain't you, my ole pal of twenty years!" He glared upon the huddled figure as though he would destroy him with his eyes. "An' if it is I'll swab the floor of hell with a wad of cotton wool on a toothpick, s'help me the good Gawd!" he added, with a violent fling of horror and disgust.

It was impossible to silence him. He stood there shouting like one possessed, horrible to see, horrible to hear—*because it was the truth*. He repeated himself in fifty different ways, each more outlandish than the last. The woods rang with echoes. At one time it looked as if he meant to fling himself upon "the intruder," for his hand continually jerked towards the long hunting knife in his belt.

But in the end he did nothing, and the whole tempest completed itself very shortly with tears. Hank's voice suddenly broke, he collapsed on the ground, and Cathcart somehow or other persuaded him at last to go into the tent and lie quiet. The remainder of the affair, indeed, was witnessed by him from behind the canvas, his white and terrified face peeping through the crack of the tent door flap.

Then Dr. Cathcart, closely followed by his nephew who so far had kept his courage better than all of them, went up with a determined air and stood opposite to the figure of Défago huddled over the fire. He looked him squarely in the face and spoke. At first his voice was firm.

"Défago, tell us what's happened—just a little, so that we can know how best to help you?" he asked in a tone of authority, almost of command. And at that point, it was command. At once afterwards, however, it changed in quality, for the figure turned up to him a face so piteous, so terrible and so little like humanity, that the doctor shrank back from him as from something spiritually unclean. Simpson, watching close behind him, says he got the impression of a mask that was on the verge of dropping off, and that underneath they would discover something black and diabolical, revealed in utter nakedness. "Out with it, man, out with it!" Cathcart cried, terror running neck and neck with entreaty. "None of us can stand this much longer. . . !" It was the cry of instinct over reason.

And then "Défago," smiling *whitely,* answered in that thin and fading voice that already seemed passing over into a sound of quite another character—

"I seen that great Wendigo thing," he whispered, sniffing the air about him exactly like an animal. "I been with it too—"

Whether the poor devil would have said more, or whether Dr. Cathcart would have continued the impossible cross-examination cannot be known, for at that moment the voice of Hank was heard yelling at the top of his voice from behind the canvas that concealed all but his terrified eyes. Such a howling was never heard.

"His feet! Oh, Gawd, his feet! Look at his great changed—feet!"

Défago, shuffling where he sat, had moved in such a way that for the first time his legs were in full light and his feet were visible. Yet Simpson had no time, himself, to see properly what Hank had seen. And Hank has never seen fit to tell. That same instant, with a leap like that of a frightened tiger, Cathcart was upon him, bundling the folds of blanket about his legs with such speed that the young student caught little more than a passing glimpse of something dark and oddly massed where moccasined feet ought to have been, and saw even that but with uncertain vision.

Then, before the doctor had time to do more, or Simpson time to even think a question, much less ask it, Défago was standing upright in front of them, balancing with pain and difficulty, and upon his shapeless and twisted visage an expression so dark and so malicious that it was, in the true sense, monstrous.

"Now *you* seen it too," he wheezed, "you seen my fiery, burning feet! And now—that is, unless you kin save me an' prevent—it's 'bout time for—"

His piteous and beseeching voice was interrupted by a sound that was like the roar of wind coming across the lake. The trees overhead shook their tangled branches. The blazing fire bent its flames as before a blast. And something swept with a terrific, rushing noise about the little camp and seemed to surround it entirely in a single moment of time. Défago shook the clinging blankets from his body, turned towards the woods behind, and with the same stumbling motion that had brought him—was gone: gone, before anyone could move muscle to prevent him, gone with an amazing, blundering swiftness that left no time to act. The darkness positively swallowed him; and less than a dozen seconds later, above the roar of the swaying trees and the shout of the sudden wind, all three men, watching and listening with stricken hearts, heard a cry that seemed to drop down upon them from a great height of sky and distance—

"Oh, oh! This fiery height! Oh, oh! My feet of fire! My burning feet of fire . . . !" then died away, into untold space and silence.

Dr. Cathcart—suddenly master of himself, and therefore of the others—was just able to seize Hank violently by the arm as he tried to dash headlong into the Bush.

"But I want ter know, —— you!" shrieked the guide. "I want ter see! That ain't him at all, but some —— devil that's shunted into his place . . . !"

Somehow or other—he admits he never quite knew how he accomplished it—he managed to keep him in the tent and pacify him. The doctor, apparently, had reached the stage where reaction had set in and allowed his own innate force to conquer. Certainly he "managed" Hank admirably. It was his nephew, however, hitherto so wonderfully controlled, who gave him most cause for anxiety, for the cumulative strain had now produced a condition of lachrymose hysteria which made it necessary to isolate him upon a bed of boughs and blankets as far removed from Hank as was possible under the circumstances.

And there he lay, as the watches of that haunted night passed over the lonely camp, crying startled sentences, and fragments of sentences, into the folds of his blanket. A quantity of gibberish about speed and height and fire mingled oddly with biblical memories of the classroom. "People with broken faces all on fire are coming at a most awful, awful, pace towards the camp!" he would moan one minute; and the next would sit up and stare into the woods, intently listening, and whisper, "How terrible in the wilderness are—are the feet of them that—" until his uncle came across to change the direction of his thoughts and comfort him.

The hysteria, fortunately, proved but temporary. Sleep cured him, just as it cured Hank.

Till the first signs of daylight came, soon after five o'clock, Dr. Cathcart kept his vigil. His face was the colour of chalk, and there were strange flushes beneath the eyes. An appalling terror of the soul battled with his will all through those silent hours. These were some of the outer signs. . . .

At dawn he lit the fire himself, made breakfast, and woke the others, and by seven they were well on their way back to the home camp—three perplexed and afflicted men, but each in his own way having reduced his inner turmoil to a condition of more or less systematised order again.

IX

They talked little, and then only of the most wholesome and common things, for their minds were charged with painful thoughts that clamoured for explanation, though no one dared refer to them. Hank, being nearest to primitive conditions, was the first to find himself, for he was also less complex. In Dr. Cathcart "civilisation" championed his forces against an attack singular enough. To this day, perhaps, he is not *quite* sure of certain things. Anyhow, he took longer to "find himself."

Simpson, the student of divinity, it was who arranged his conclusions probably with the best, though not most scientific, appearance of order. Out there, in the heart of unreclaimed wilderness, they had surely witnessed something crudely and essentially primitive. Something that had survived somehow the advance of humanity had emerged terrifically, betraying a scale of life still monstrous and immature. He envisaged it rather as a glimpse into prehistoric ages, when superstitions, gigantic and uncouth, still oppressed the hearts of men; when the forces of nature were still untamed, the Powers that may have haunted a primeval universe not yet withdrawn. To this day he thinks of what he termed years later in a sermon "savage and formidable Potencies lurking behind the souls of men, not evil perhaps in themselves, yet instinctively hostile to humanity as it exists."

With his uncle he never discussed the matter in detail, for the barrier between the two types of mind made it difficult. Only once, years later, something led them to the frontier of the subject—of a single detail of the subject, rather:

"Can't you even tell me what—*they* were like?" he asked; and the reply, though conceived in wisdom, was not encouraging, "It is far better you should not try to know, or to find out."

"Well—that odour—?" persisted the nephew. "What do you make of that?"

Dr. Cathcart looked at him and raised his eyebrows.

"Odours," he replied, "are not so easy as sounds and sights of telepathic communication. I make as much, or as little, probably, as you do yourself."

He was not quite so glib as usual with his explanations. That was all.

At the fall of day, cold, exhausted, famished, the party came to the end of the long portage and dragged themselves into a camp that at first glimpse seemed empty. Fire there was none, and no Punk came forward to welcome them. The emotional capacity of all three was too over-spent to recognise either surprise or annoyance; but the cry of spontaneous affection that burst from the lips of Hank, as he rushed ahead of them towards the fireplace, came probably as a warning that the end of the amazing affair was not quite yet. And both Cathcart and his nephew confessed afterwards that when they saw him kneel down in his excitement and embrace something that reclined, gently moving, beside the extinguished ashes, they felt in their very bones that this "something" would prove to be Défago—the true Défago, returned.

And so, indeed, it was.

It is soon told. Exhausted to the point of emaciation, the French Canadian—what was left of him, that is—fumbled among the ashes, trying to make a fire. His body crouched there, the weak fingers obeying feebly the instinctive habit of a lifetime with twigs and matches. But there was no longer any mind to direct the simple operation. The mind had fled beyond recall. And with it, too, had fled memory. Not only recent events, but all previous life was a blank.

This time it was the real man, though incredibly and horribly shrunken. On his face was no expression of any kind whatever—fear, welcome, or recognition. He did not seem to know who it was that embraced him, or who it was that fed, warmed and spoke to him the words of comfort and relief. Forlorn and broken beyond all reach of human aid, the little man did meekly as he was bidden. The "something" that had constituted him "individual" had vanished forever.

In some ways it was more terribly moving than anything they had yet seen—that idiot smile as he drew wads of coarse moss from his swollen cheeks and told them that he was "a damned moss-eater"; the continued vomiting of even the simplest food; and, worst of all, the piteous and childish voice of complaint in which he told them that his feet pained him—"burn like fire"—which was natural enough when Dr. Cathcart examined them and found that both were dreadfully frozen. Beneath the eyes there were faint indications of recent bleeding.

The details of how he survived the prolonged exposure, of where he had been, or of how he covered the great distance from one camp to the other, including an immense detour of the lake on foot since he had no canoe—all this remains unknown. His memory had vanished completely. And before the end of the winter whose beginning witnessed this strange occurrence, Défago, bereft of mind, memory and soul, had gone with it. He lingered only a few weeks.

And what Punk was able to contribute to the story throws no further light upon it. He was cleaning fish by the lake shore about five o'clock in the evening—an hour, that is, before the search party returned—when he saw this shadow of the guide picking its way weakly into camp. In advance of him, he declares, came the faint whiff of a certain singular odour.

That same instant old Punk started for home. He covered the entire journey of three days as only Indian blood could have covered it. The terror of a whole race drove him. He knew what it all meant. Défago had "seen the Wendigo."

F
is for
Familiar

Familiars are the traditional companions and servants of witches and sorceresses. In folklore, they often take the form of a cat. British writer Arthur Sarsfield Ward (1883–1959), who under his pseudonym Sax Rohmer achieved literary renown for his popular tales of the sinister Fu Manchu, gives the sorceress's familiars in this tale an interesting twist appropriate for its Egyptian setting. The story was first published in the January 1916 issue of *The Premier Magazine.*

SAX ROHMER

In the Valley of the Sorceress

I

Condor wrote to me three times before the end (said Neville, Assistant-Inspector of Antiquities, staring vaguely from his open window at a squad drilling before the Kasr-en-Nil Barracks). He dated his letters from the camp at Deir-el-Bahari. Judging from these, success appeared to be almost within his grasp. He shared my theories, of course, respecting Queen Hatasu, and was devoting the whole of his energies to the task of clearing up the great mystery of Ancient Egypt which centres around that queen.

For him, as for me, there was a strange fascination about those defaced walls and roughly obliterated inscriptions. That the queen under whom

Egyptian art came to the apogee of perfection should thus have been treated by her successors; that no perfect figure of the wise, famous, and beautiful Hatasu should have been spared to posterity; that her very cartouche should have been ruthlessly removed from every inscription upon which it appeared, presented to Condor's mind a problem only second in interest to the immortal riddle of Gizeh.

You know my own views upon the matter? My monograph, "Hatasu, the Sorceress," embodies my opinion. In short, upon certain evidences, some adduced by Theodore Davis, some by poor Condor, and some resulting from my own inquiries, I have come to the conclusion that the source—real or imaginary—of this queen's power was an intimate acquaintance with what nowadays we term, vaguely, magic. Pursuing her studies beyond the limit which is lawful, she met with a certain end, not uncommon, if the old writings are to be believed, in the case of those who penetrate too far into the realms of the Borderland.

For this reason—the practice of black magic—her statues were dishonored, and her name erased from the monuments. Now, I do not propose to enter into any discussion respecting the reality of such practices; in my monograph I have merely endeavored to show that, according to contemporary belief, the queen was a sorceress. Condor was seeking to prove the same thing; and when I took up the inquiry, it was in the hope of completing his interrupted work.

He wrote to me early in the winter of 1908, from his camp by the Rock Temple. Davis's tomb, at Bibân el-Mulûk, with its long, narrow passage, apparently had little interest for him; he was at work on the high ground behind the temple, at a point one hundred yards or so due west of the upper platform. He had an idea that he should find there the mummies of Hatasu—and another; the latter, a certain Sen-Mût, who appears in the inscriptions of the reign as an architect high in the queen's favor. The archaeological points of the letter do not concern us in the least, but there was one odd little paragraph which I had cause to remember afterwards.

"A girl belonging to some Arab tribe," wrote Condor, "came racing to the camp two nights ago to claim my protection. What crime she had committed, and what punishment she feared, were far from clear; but she clung to me, trembling like a leaf, and positively refused to depart. It was a difficult situation, for a camp of fifty native excavators, and one highly respectable

European enthusiast, affords no suitable quarters for an Arab girl—and a very personable Arab girl. At any rate, she is still here; I have had a sort of lean-to rigged up in a little valley east of my own tent, but it is very embarrassing."

Nearly a month passed before I heard from Condor again; then came a second letter, with the news that on the eve of a great discovery—as he believed—his entire native staff—the whole fifty—had deserted one night in a body! "Two days' work," he wrote, "would have seen the tomb opened—for I am more than ever certain that my plans are accurate. Then I woke up one morning to find every man Jack of my fellows missing! I went down into the village where a lot of them live, in a towering rage, but not one of the brutes was to be found, and their relations professed entire ignorance respecting their whereabouts. "What caused me almost as much anxiety as the check in my work was the fact that Mahâra—the Arab girl—had vanished also. I am wondering if the thing has any sinister significance."

Condor finished with the statement that he was making tremendous efforts to secure a new gang. "But," said he, "I shall finish the excavation, if I have to do it with my own hands."

His third and last letter contained even stranger matters than the two preceding it. He had succeeded in borrowing a few men from the British Archaeological camp in the Fáyûm. Then, just as the work was restarting, the Arab girl, Mahâra, turned up again, and entreated him to bring her down the Nile, "at least as far as Dendera. For the vengeance of her tribesmen," stated Condor, "otherwise would result not only in her own death, but in mine! At the moment of writing I am in two minds what to do. If Mahâra is to go upon this journey, I do not feel justified in sending her alone, and there is no one here who could perform the duty," etc.

I began to wonder, of course; and I had it in mind to take the train to Luxor merely in order to see this Arab maiden, who seemed to occupy so prominent a place in Condor's mind. However, Fate would have it otherwise; and the next thing I heard was that Condor had been brought into Cairo, and was at the English hospital.

He had been bitten by a cat—presumably from the neighboring village; and although the doctor at Luxor dealt with the bite at once, traveled down with him, and placed him in the hand of the Pasteur man at the hospital, he died, as you remember, in the night of his arrival, raving mad; the Pasteur treatment failed entirely.

I never saw him before the end, but they told me that his howls were horribly like those of a cat. His eyes changed in some way, too, I understand; and, with his fingers all contracted, he tried to scratch everyone and everything within reach.

They had to strap the poor beggar down, and even then he tore the sheets into ribbons.

Well, as soon as possible, I made the necessary arrangements to finish Condor's inquiry. I had access to his papers, plans, etc., and in the spring of the same year I took up my quarters near Deirel-Bahari, roped off the approaches to the camp, stuck up the usual notices, and prepared to finish the excavation, which, I gathered, was in a fairly advanced state.

My first surprise came very soon after my arrival, for when, with the plan before me, I started out to find the shaft, I found it, certainly, but only with great difficulty.

It had been filled in again with sand and loose rock right to the very top!

II

All my inquiries availed me nothing. With what object the excavation had been thus closed I was unable to conjecture. That Condor had not reclosed it I was quite certain, for at the time of his mishap he had actually been at work at the bottom of the shaft, as inquiries from a native of Suefee, in the Fáyûm, who was his only companion at the time, had revealed.

In his eagerness to complete the inquiry, Condor, by lantern light, had been engaged upon a solitary night-shift below, and the rabid cat had apparently fallen into the pit; probably in a frenzy of fear, it had attacked Condor, after which it had escaped.

Only this one man was with him, and he, for some reason that I could not make out, had apparently been sleeping in the temple—quite a considerable distance from Condor's camp. The poor fellow's cries had aroused him, and he had met Condor running down the path and away from the shaft.

This, however, was good evidence of the existence of the shaft at the time, and as I stood contemplating the tightly packed rubble which alone marked its site, I grew more and more mystified, for this task of reclosing the cutting represented much hard labor.

Beyond perfecting my plans in one or two particulars, I did little on the day of my arrival. I had only a handful of men with me, all of whom I knew, having worked with them before, and beyond clearing Condor's shaft I did not intend to excavate further.

Hatasu's Temple presents a lively enough scene in the daytime during the winter and early spring months, with the streams of tourists constantly passing from the white causeway to Cook's Rest House on the edge of the desert. There had been a goodly number of visitors that day to the temple below, and one or two of the more curious and venturesome had scrambled up the steep path to the little plateau which was the scene of my operations. None had penetrated beyond the notice boards, however, and now, with the evening sky passing through those innumerable shades which defy palette and brush, which can only be distinguished by the trained eye, but which, from palest blue melt into exquisite pink, and by some magical combination form that deep violet which does not exist to perfection elsewhere than in the skies of Egypt, I found myself in the silence and the solitude of "the Holy Valley."

I stood at the edge of the plateau, looking out at the rosy belt which marked the course of the distant Nile, with the Arabian hills vaguely sketched beyond. The rocks stood up against that prospect as great black smudges, and what I could see of the causeway looked like a gray smear upon a drab canvas. Beneath me were the chambers of the Rock Temple, with those wall paintings depicting events in the reign of Hatasu which rank among the wonders of Egypt.

Not a sound disturbed my reverie, save a faint clatter of cooking utensils from the camp behind me—a desecration of that sacred solitude. Then a dog began to howl in the neighboring village. The dog ceased, and faintly to my ears came the note of a reed pipe. The breeze died away, and with it the piping.

I turned back to the camp, and, having partaken of a frugal supper, turned in upon my campaigner's bed, thoroughly enjoying my freedom from the routine of official life in Cairo, and looking forward to the morrow's work pleasurably.

Under such circumstances a man sleeps well; and when, in an uncanny gray half-light, which probably heralded the dawn, I awoke with a start, I knew that something of an unusual nature alone could have disturbed my slumbers.

Firstly, then, I identified this with a concerted howling of the village dogs. They seemed to have conspired to make night hideous; I have never heard such an eerie din in my life. Then it gradually began to die away, and I realized, secondly, that the howling of the dogs and my own awakening might be due to some common cause. This idea grew upon me, and as the howling subsided, a sort of disquiet possessed me, and, despite my efforts to shake it off, grew more urgent with the passing of every moment.

In short, I fancied that the thing which had alarmed or enraged the dogs was passing from the village through the Holy Valley, upward to the Temple, upward to the plateau, and was approaching *me.*

I have never experienced an identical sensation since, but I seemed to be audient of a sort of psychic patrol, which, from a remote *pianissimo,* swelled *fortissimo,* to an intimate but silent clamor, which beat in some way upon my brain, but not through the faculty of hearing, for now the night was deathly still.

Yet I was persuaded of some *approach*—of the coming of something sinister, and the suspense of waiting had become almost insupportable, so that I began to accuse my Spartan supper of having given me nightmares, when the tent-flap was suddenly raised, and, outlined against the paling blue of the sky, with a sort of reflected elfin light playing upon her face, I saw an Arab girl looking in at me!

By dint of exerting all my self-control I managed to restrain the cry and upward start which this apparition prompted. Quite still, with my fists tightly clenched, I lay and looked into the eyes which were looking into mine.

The style of literary work which it has been my lot to cultivate fails me in describing that beautiful and evil face. The features were severely classical and small, something of the Bisharîn type, with a cruel little mouth and a rounded chin, firm to hardness. In the eyes alone lay the languor of the Orient; they were exceedingly—indeed, excessively—long and narrow. The ordinary ragged, picturesque finery of a desert girl bedecked this midnight visitant, who, motionless, stood there watching me.

I once read a work by Pierre de l'Ancre, dealing with the Black Sabbaths of the Middle Ages, and now the evil beauty of this Arab face threw my memory back to those singular pages, for, perhaps owing to the reflected light which I have mentioned, although the explanation scarcely seemed adequate, those long, narrow eyes shone catlike in the gloom.

Suddenly I made up my mind. Throwing the blanket from me, I leapt to the ground, and in a flash had gripped the girl by the wrists. Confuting some lingering doubts, she proved to be substantial enough. My electric torch lay upon a box at the foot of the bed, and, stooping, I caught it up and turned its searching rays upon the face of my captive.

She fell back from me, panting like a wild creature trapped, then dropped upon her knees and began to plead—began to plead in a voice and with a manner which touched some chord of consciousness that I could swear had never spoken before, and has never spoken since.

She spoke in Arabic, of course, but the words fell from her lips as liquid music in which lay all the beauty and all the deviltry of the "Siren's Song." Fully opening her astonishing eyes, she looked up at me, and, with her free hand pressed to her bosom, told me how she had fled from an unwelcome marriage; how, an outcast and a pariah, she had hidden in the desert places for three days and three nights, sustaining life only by means of a few dates which she had brought with her, and quenching her thirst with stolen watermelons.

"I can bear it no longer, *effendim*. Another night out in the desert, with the cruel moon beating, beating, beating upon my brain, with creeping things coming out from the rocks, wriggling, wriggling, their many feet making whisperings in the sand—ah, it will kill me! And I am for ever outcast from my tribe, from my people. No tent of all the Arabs, though I fly to the gates of Damascus, is open to me, save I enter in shame, as a slave, as a plaything, as a toy. My heart"—furiously she beat upon her breast—"is empty and desolate, *effendim*. I am meaner than the lowliest thing that creeps upon the sand; yet the God that made that creeping thing made me also—and you, you, who are merciful and strong, would not crush any creature because it was weak and helpless."

I had released her wrist now, and was looking down at her in a sort of stupor. The evil which at first I had seemed to perceive in her was effaced, wiped out as an artist wipes out an error in his drawing. Her dark beauty was speaking to me in a language of its own; a strange language, yet one so intelligible that I struggled in vain to disregard it. And her voice, her gestures, and the witch-fire of her eyes were whipping up my blood to a fever heat of passionate sorrow—of despair. Yes, incredible as it sounds, despair!

In short, as I see it now, this siren of the wilderness was playing upon me as an accomplished musician might play upon a harp, striking this string and that at will, and sounding each with such full notes as they had rarely, if ever, emitted before.

Most damnable anomaly of all, I—Edward Neville, archaeologist, most prosy and matter-of-fact man in Cairo, perhaps—*knew* that this nomad who had burst into my tent, upon whom I had set eyes for the first time scarce three minutes before, held me enthralled; and yet, with her wondrous eyes upon me, I could summon up no resentment, and could offer but poor resistance.

"In the Little Oasis, *effendim,* I have a sister who will admit me into her household, if only as a servant. There I can be safe, there I can rest. O *Inglîsi,* at home in England you have a sister of your own! Would you see her pursued, a hunted thing from rock to rock, crouching for shelter in the lair of some jackal, stealing that she might live—and flying always, never resting, her heart leaping for fear, flying, flying, with nothing but dishonor before her?"

She shuddered and clasped my left hand in both her own convulsively, pulling it down to her bosom.

"There can be only one thing, *effendim,*" she whispered. "Do you not see the white bones bleaching in the sun?"

Throwing all my resolution into the act, I released my hand from her clasp, and, turning aside, sat down upon the box which served me as chair and table, too.

A thought had come to my assistance, had strengthened me in the moment of my greatest weakness; it was the thought of that Arab girl mentioned in Condor's letters. And a scheme of things, an incredible scheme, that embraced and explained some, if not all, of the horrible circumstances attendant upon his death, began to form in my brain.

Bizarre it was, stretching out beyond the realm of things natural and proper, yet I clung to it, for there, in the solitude, with this wildly beautiful creature kneeling at my feet, and with her uncanny powers of fascination yet enveloping me like a cloak, I found it not so improbable as inevitably it must have seemed at another time.

I turned my head, and through the gloom sought to look into the long eyes. As I did so they closed and appeared as two darkly luminous slits in the perfect oval of the face.

"You are an impostor!" I said in Arabic, speaking firmly and deliberately. "To Mr. Condor"—I could have sworn that she started slightly at sound of the name—"you called yourself Mahâra. I know you, and I will have nothing to do with you."

But in saying it I had to turn my head aside, for the strangest, maddest impulses were bubbling up in my brain in response to the glances of those half-shut eyes.

I reached for my coat, which lay upon the foot of the bed, and, taking out some loose money, I placed fifty piastres in the nerveless brown hand.

"That will enable you to reach the Little Oasis, if such is your desire," I said. "It is all I can do for you, and now—you must go."

The light of the dawn was growing stronger momentarily, so that I could see my visitor quite clearly. She rose to her feet, and stood before me, a straight, slim figure, sweeping me from head to foot with such a glance of passionate contempt as I had never known or suffered.

She threw back her head magnificently, dashed the money on the ground at my feet, and, turning, leaped out of the tent.

For a moment I hesitated, doubting, questioning my humanity, testing my fears; then I took a step forward, and peered out across the plateau. Not a soul was in sight. The rocks stood up gray and eerie, and beneath lay the carpet of the desert stretching unbroken to the shadows of the Nile Valley.

III

We commenced the work of clearing the shaft at an early hour that morning. The strangest ideas were now playing in my mind, and in some way I felt myself to be in opposition to definite enmity. My excavators labored with a will, and, once we had penetrated below the first three feet or so of tightly packed stone, it became a mere matter of shoveling, for apparently the lower part of the shaft had been filled up principally with sand.

I calculated that four days' work at the outside would see the shaft clear to the base of Condor's excavation. There remained, according to his own notes, only another six feet or so; but it was solid limestone—the roof of the passage, if his plans were correct, communicating with the tomb of Hatasu.

With the approach of night, tired as I was, I felt little inclination for sleep. I lay down on my bed with a small Browning pistol under the pillow, but after an hour or so of nervous listening drifted off into slumber. As on the night before, I awoke shortly before the coming of dawn.

Again the village dogs were raising a hideous outcry, and again I was keenly conscious of some ever-nearing menace. This consciousness grew stronger as the howling of the dogs grew fainter, and the sense of *approach* assailed me as on the previous occasion.

I sat up immediately with the pistol in my hand, and, gently raising the tent flap, looked out over the darksome plateau. For a long time I could perceive nothing; then, vaguely outlined against the sky, I detected something that moved above the rocky edge.

It was so indefinite in form that for a time I was unable to identify it, but as it slowly rose higher and higher, two luminous eyes—obviously feline eyes, since they glittered greenly in the darkness—came into view. In character and in shape they were the eyes of a cat, but in point of size they were larger than the eyes of any cat I had ever seen. Nor were they jackal eyes. It occurred to me that some predatory beast from the Sûdan might conceivably have strayed thus far north.

The presence of such a creature would account for the nightly disturbance amongst the village dogs; and, dismissing the superstitious notions which had led me to associate the mysterious Arab girl with the phenomenon of the howling dogs, I seized upon this new idea with a sort of gladness.

Stepping boldly out of the tent, I strode in the direction of the gleaming eyes. Although my only weapon was the Browning pistol, it was a weapon of considerable power, and, moreover, I counted upon the well-known cowardice of nocturnal animals. I was not disappointed in the result.

The eyes dropped out of sight, and as I leaped the edge of rock overhanging the temple a lithe shape went streaking off in the greyness beneath me. Its coloring appeared to be black, but this appearance may have been due to the bad light. Certainly it was no cat, was no jackal; and once, twice, thrice my Browning spat into the darkness.

Apparently I had not scored a hit, but the low reports of the weapon aroused the men sleeping in the camp, and soon I was surrounded by a ring of inquiring faces.

But there I stood on the rock-edge, looking out across the desert in silence. Something in the long, luminous eyes, something in the sinuous, flying shape had spoken to me intimately, horribly.

Hassan es-Sugra, the headman, touched my arm and I knew that I must offer some explanation.

"Jackals," I said shortly. And with no other word I walked back to my tent.

The night passed without further event, and in the morning we addressed ourselves to the work with such a will that I saw, to my satisfaction, that by noon of the following day the labor of clearing the loose sand would be completed.

During the preparation of the evening meal I became aware of a certain disquiet in the camp, and I noted a disinclination on the part of the native laborers to stray far from the tents. They hung together in a group, and whilst individually they seemed to avoid meeting my eye, collectively they watched me in a furtive fashion.

A gang of Moslem workmen calls for delicate handling, and I wondered if, inadvertently, I had transgressed in some way their iron-bound code of conduct. I called Hassan es-Sugra aside.

"What ails the men?" I asked him. "Have they some grievance?"

Hassan spread his palms eloquently.

"If they have," he replied, "they are secret about it, and I am not in their confidence. Shall I thrash three or four of them in order to learn the nature of this grievance?"

"No thanks all the same," I said, laughing at this characteristic proposal. "If they refuse to work to-morrow, there will be time enough for you to adopt those measures."

On this, the third night of my sojourn in the Holy Valley by the Temple of Hatasu, I slept soundly and uninterruptedly. I had been looking forward with the keenest zest to the morrow's work, which promised to bring me within sight of my goal, and when Hassan came to awaken me, I leaped out of bed immediately.

Hassan es-Sugra, having performed his duty, did not, as was his custom, retire; he stood there, a tall, angular figure, looking at me strangely.

"Well?" I said.

"There is trouble," was his simple reply. "Follow me, Neville Effendi."

Wondering greatly, I followed him across the plateau and down the slope to the excavation. There I pulled up short with a cry of amazement.

Condor's shaft was filled in to the very top, and presented, to my astonished gaze, much the same aspect that had greeted me upon my first arrival!

"The men—" I began.

Hassan es-Sugra spread wide his palms.

"Gone!" he replied. "Those Coptic dogs, those eaters of carrion, have fled in the night."

"And this"—I pointed to the little mound of broken granite and sand—"is their work?"

"So it would seem," was the reply; and Hassan sniffed his sublime contempt.

I stood looking bitterly at this destruction of my toils. The strangeness of the thing at the moment did not strike me, in my anger; I was only concerned with the outrageous impudence of the missing workmen, and if I could have laid hands upon one of them it had surely gone hard with him.

As for Hassan es-Sugra, I believe he would cheerfully have broken the necks of the entire gang. But he was a man of resource.

"It is so newly filled in," he said, "that you and I, in three days, or in four, can restore it to the state it had reached when those nameless dogs, who regularly prayed with their shoes on, those devourers of pork, began their dirty work."

His example was stimulating. *I* was not going to be beaten, either.

After a hasty breakfast, the pair of us set to work with pick and shovel and basket. We worked as those slaves must have worked whose toil was directed by the lash of the Pharaoh's overseer. My back acquired an almost permanent crook, and every muscle in my body seemed to be on fire. Not even in the midday heat did we slacken or stay our toils; and when dusk fell that night a great mound had arisen beside Condor's shaft, and we had excavated to a depth it had taken our gang double the time to reach.

When at last we threw down our tools in utter exhaustion, I held out my hand to Hassan, and wrung his brown fist enthusiastically. His eyes sparkled as he met my glance.

"Neville Effendi," he said, "you are a true Moslem!"

And only the initiated can know how high was the compliment conveyed.

That night I slept the sleep of utter weariness, yet it was not a dreamless sleep, or perhaps it was not so deep as I supposed, for blazing cat-eyes encircled me in my dreams, and a constant feline howling seemed to fill the night.

When I awoke the sun was blazing down upon the rock outside my tent, and, springing out of bed, I perceived, with amazement, that the morning was far advanced. Indeed, I could hear the distant voices of the donkey-boys and other harbingers of the coming tourists.

Why had Hassan es-Sugra not awakened me?

I stepped out of the tent and called him in a loud voice. There was no reply. I ran across the plateau to the edge of the hollow.

Condor's shaft had been reclosed to the top!

Language fails me to convey the wave of anger, amazement, incredulity, which swept over me. I looked across to the deserted camp and back to my own tent; I looked down at the mound, where but a few hours before had been a pit, and seriously began to question whether I was mad or whether madness had seized upon all who had been with me. Then, pegged down upon the heap of broken stones I perceived, fluttering, a small piece of paper.

Dully I walked across and picked it up. Hassan, a man of some education, clearly was the writer. It was a pencil scrawl in doubtful Arabic, and, not without difficulty, I deciphered it as follows:

"Fly, Neville Effendi! This is a haunted place."

Standing there by the mound, I tore the scrap of paper into minute fragments, bitterly casting them from me upon the ground. It was incredible; it was insane.

The man who had written that absurd message, the man who had undone his own work, had the reputation of being fearless and honorable. He had been with me before a score of times, and had quelled petty mutinies in the camp in a manner which marked him a born overseer. I could not understand; I could scarcely believe the evidence of my own senses.

What did I do?

I suppose there are some who would have abandoned the thing at once and for always, but I take it that the national traits are strong within me. I went over to the camp and prepared my own breakfast; then, shouldering pick and shovel, I went down into the valley and set to work. What ten men could not do, what two men had failed to do, one man was determined to do.

It was about half an hour after commencing my toils, and when, I suppose, the surprise and rage occasioned by the discovery had begun to wear off, that I found myself making comparisons between my own case and that of Condor. It became more and more evident to me that events—mysterious events—were repeating themselves.

The frightful happenings attendant upon Condor's death were marshaling in my mind. The sun was blazing down upon me, and distant voices could be heard in the desert stillness. I knew that the plain below was dotted with pleasure-seeking tourists, yet nervous tremors shook me. Frankly, I dreaded the coming of the night.

Well, tenacity or pugnacity conquered, and I worked on until dusk. My supper despatched, I sat down on my bed and toyed with the Browning.

I realized already that sleep, under existing conditions, was impossible. I perceived that on the morrow I must abandon my one-man enterprise, pocket my pride, in a sense, and seek new assistants, new companions.

The fact was coming home to me conclusively that a menace, real and not mythical, hung over that valley. Although, in the morning sunlight and filled with indignation, I had thought contemptuously of Hassan es-Sugra, now, in the mysterious violet dusk so conducive to calm consideration, I was forced to admit that he was at least as brave a man as I. And he had fled! What did that night hold in keeping for me?

I will tell you what occurred, and it is the only explanation I have to give of why Condor's shaft, said to communicate with the real tomb of Hatasu, to this day remains unopened.

There, on the edge of my bed, I sat far into the night, not daring to close my eyes. But physical weariness conquered in the end, and, although I have no recollection of its coming, I must have succumbed to sleep, since I remember—can never forget—a repetition of the dream, or what I had assumed to be a dream, of the night before.

A ring of blazing green eyes surrounded me. At one point this ring was broken, and in a kind of nightmare panic I leaped at that promise of safety, and found myself outside the tent.

Lithe, slinking shapes hemmed me in—cat shapes, ghoul shapes, veritable figures of the pit. And the eyes, the shapes, although they were the eyes and shapes of cats, sometimes changed elusively, and became the wicked eyes and the sinuous, writhing shapes of women. Always the ring was incomplete, and always I retreated in the only direction by which retreat was possible. I retreated from those cat-things.

In this fashion I came at last to the shaft, and there I saw the tools which I had left at the end of my day's toil.

Looking around me, I saw also, with such a pang of horror as I cannot hope to convey to you, that the ring of green eyes was now unbroken about me.

And it was closing in.

Nameless feline creatures were crowding silently to the edge of the pit, some preparing to spring down upon me where I stood. A voice seemed to speak in my brain; it spoke of capitulation, telling me to accept defeat, lest, resisting, my fate be the fate of Condor.

Peals of shrill laughter rose upon the silence. The laughter was mine.

Filling the night with this hideous, hysterical merriment, I was working feverishly with pick and with shovel filling in the shaft.

The end? The end is that I awoke, in the morning, lying, not on my bed, but outside on the plateau, my hands torn and bleeding and every muscle in my body throbbing agonisingly. Remembering my dream—for even in that moment of awakening I thought I had dreamed—I staggered across to the valley of the excavation.

Condor's shaft was reclosed to the top.

G *is for* Ghoul

Ghouls—semi-human eaters of the dead—are creatures in the folklore of many lands, and play a prominent role in the tales collected under the title *The Arabian Nights.* American writer Henry S. Whitehead (1882–1932) acknowledges the Eastern pedigree of the ghoul in this story, first published in the February 1933 issue of *Weird Tales.* It is one of several stories to feature Whitehead's fictional avatar, Gerald Canevin, whose encounters with the supernatural span the globe from the West Indies to England and America.

HENRY S. WHITEHEAD

The Chadbourne Episode

Perhaps the most fortunate circumstance of the well-nigh incredible Chadbourne affair is that little Abby Chandler was not quite seven years of age on the evening when she came back home and told her mother her story about the old sow and the little pigs. It was July, and Abby with her big tin pail had been up in the high ridge near the Old Churchyard after low-bush blueberries. She had not even been especially frightened, her mother had said. That is what I mean by the fortunate aspect of it. Little Abby was altogether too young to be devastated, her sweet little soul prematurely blasted, her mentality wrenched and twisted away from normality even by seeing with her round, China-blue eyes what she had seen up there on the steep hillside.

Little Abby had not noticed particularly the row of eight or nine pushing, squeaking, grunting little pigs at their early evening meal because her attention had been entirely concentrated on the curious appearance, as it seemed to her, of the source of that meal. That old sow, little Abby had told her mother, had had "a lady's head. . . ."

There was, of course, a *raison d'être*—a solution—back of this reported marvel. That solution occurred to Mrs. Chandler almost at once. Abby must have heard something, in the course of her six and three-quarter years of life here in Chadbourne among the little town's permanent inhabitants, some old-wives' gossip for choice, about "marked" people; whispered "cases" of people born with some strange anatomical characteristics of a domestic animal—freaks—or even farm animals "marked" with some human streak—a calf with a finger growing out of its left hind fetlock—things like that; animals quickly destroyed and buried out of sight. Such statements can be heard in many New England rural settlements which have never wholly let go the oddments in tradition brought over from Cornwall and the West Country of Old England. Everybody has heard them.

Chadbourne would be no exception to anything like this. The old town lies nestling among the granite-bouldered ridges and dimpling hills of deep, rural, eastern Connecticut. In any such old New England town the older people talk much about all such affairs as Black Sabbaths, and Charmed Cattle, and Marked People.

All of that Mrs. Chandler knew and sensed in her blood and bones. She had been a Grantham before she had married Silas Chandler, and the Grantham family had been quietly shrinking and deteriorating for nine generations in Chadbourne along with the process of the old town's gradual dry rotting, despite the efforts of such of the old-time gentry as may have survived in such places.

For gentry they are, deeply imbedded in New England, people who had never forgotten the meaning of the old *noblesse oblige*, people who have never allowed their fine sense of duty and obligation to lapse. In Chadbourne we had such a family, the Merritts; *Mayflower* passengers to Plymouth in the Massachusetts Colony in 1620; officers and trustees for generations of Dartmouth College in New Hampshire and of Trinity College, Hartford, Connecticut. We Canevins, Virginians, were not, of course, of this stock. My father, Alexander Canevin, had bought up an abandoned farm on a

Chadbourne ridge-top about the time of the Spanish War. In that high air, among those rugged hills and to the intoxicating summer scents of bayberry-blossoms and sweet-fern—which the Connecticut farmers name appropriately, "hardhack"—I had sojourned summers since my early childhood.

Tom Merritt and I had grown up together, and he, following the family tradition, had gone to Dartmouth, thence to the Harvard Medical School. At the time of little Abby's adventure he was serving his community well as the Chadbourne general practitioner. But for the four years previous to his coming back and settling down to this useful if humdrum professional career, Thomas Bradford Merritt, M.D., had been in the diplomatic service as a career consul, chiefly in Persia where, before his attachment as a step up to our legation in Teheran, he had held consular posts at Jask, a town in the far south on the Gulf of Oman; at Kut-el-Amara in the west, just south of Baghdad; and finally at Shiraz, where he had collected some magnificent rugs.

The autumn before little Abby Chandler's blueberrying expedition Tom, who acted as my agent, had rented my Chadbourne farmhouse just as I was leaving New York for my customary winter's sojourn in the West Indies. That my tenants were Persians had, it appeared, no connection at all with Tom's long residence in that land. They had been surprised, Tom told me, when they found out that the New England gentleman whose advertisement of my place they had answered from New York City was familiar with their country, had resided there, and even spoke its language passably.

In spite of this inducement to some sort of sociability, the Persian family, according to Tom, had comported themselves, toward him and everybody else in Chadbourne, with a high degree of reticence and reserve. The womenfolk had kept themselves altogether secluded, rarely leaving the house that winter. When they did venture forth they were always heavily muffled up—actually veiled, Tom thought—and only the edges, so to speak, of the mother and two daughters were ever to be observed by any inhabitant of Chadbourne curious to know how Persian ladies might look through the windows of Mr. Rustum Dadh's big limousine.

Besides the stout mother and the two stout, "yellowish-complected," sloe-eyed daughters, there was Mr. Rustum Dadh himself, and two servants. These were the chauffeur, a square-built, tight-lipped, rather grim-looking fellow, who made all his own repairs to the big car and drove wrapped up in a fur-lined livery overcoat; and a woman, presumably the wife of the chauffer, who never appeared outside at all, even on Friday nights when there were movies in Chadbourne's Palace Opera House.

All that I knew about my tenants Tom Merritt told me. I never saw any of the Rustum Dadh family from first to last. I had, in fact, completely forgotten all about them until I arrived in Chadbourne the following June some time after their departure and learned from Tom the bare facts I have set out here.

On a certain night in July that summer the Rustum Dadhs were farthest from my thoughts. It was nine o'clock, and I was sitting in the living-room reading. My telephone rang insistently. I laid down my book with a sigh at being interrupted. I found Thomas Bradford Merritt, M.D., on the other end of the wire.

"Come down here as soon as you can, Gerald," said Tom without any preliminaries, and there was a certain unusual urgency in his voice.

"What's happened?" I inquired.

"It may be—ah—something in your line, so to speak," said Doctor Merritt; "something—well—out of the ordinary. Bring that Männlicher rifle of yours!"

"I'll be right down," said I, snapped up the receiver, got the Männlicher out of my case in the hall where it is in with my shotguns, and raced out to the garage. Here, of a certainty, was something quite strange and new for Chadbourne, where the nearest thing to anything like excitement from year's end to year's end would be an altercation between a couple of robins over a simultaneously discovered worm! "Bring your rifle!" On the way down to the village I did not try to imagine what could possibly lie behind such a summons—from conservative Tom Merritt. I concentrated upon my driving, down the winding country road from my rugged hilltop into town, speeding on the short stretches, easing around treacherous turns at a great speed. . . .

I dashed into Tom's house eight minutes after hanging up the receiver. There was a light I had observed, in the library as well as in the office, and I went straight in there and found Tom sitting on the edge of a stiff chair, plainly waiting for my arrival.

"Here I am," said I, and laid my rifle on the library table. Tom plunged into his story. . . .

"I'm tied up—a confinement case. They'll be calling me now any minute. Listen to this, Gerald—this is probably a new one on you—even in the face of all the queer things you know—your West Indian experiences; *vodu;* all the rest of it; something *I* know, and—have always kept my mouth shut about! That is—if this is what I'm afraid it is. You'll have to take my word for it. I haven't lost my mind or anything of the sort—you'll probably think that if it turns out to be what I think it is—get this, now:

"Dan Curtiss' little boy, Truman, disappeared, late this afternoon, about sundown. Truman is five years old, a little fellow. He was last seen by some older kids coming back to town with berries from the Ridge about suppertime. Little Truman, they said, was 'with a lady,' just outside the Old Cemetery.

"Two lambs and a calf have disappeared within the last week. Traced up there. A bone or two and a wisp of wool or so—the calf's ears, in different places, but both up there, and part of its tail; found 'em scattered around when they got up there to look.

"Some are saying 'a cattymount.' Most of 'em say dogs."

"But—it isn't dogs, Gerald. 'Sheep-killers' tear up their victims on the spot. They don't drag 'em three miles up a steep hill before they eat 'em. They run in a pack, too. Everybody knows that. Nothing like that has been seen—no pack, no evidences of a pack. Those lost animals have disappeared singly—more evidence that it isn't 'dogs.' They've been taken up and, presumably, eaten, up on top of the Cemetery Ridge. Sheep-killing dogs don't take calves, either, and there's that calf to be accounted for. You see—I've been thinking it all out, pretty carefully. As for the catamount, well, catamounts don't commonly live—and eat—out in the open. A catamount would drag off a stolen animal far into the deep woods."

I nodded.

"I've heard something about animals disappearing; only the way I heard it was that it's been going on for quite a long time, and somewhat more intensively during the past month or so."

Tom Merritt nodded at that. "Right," said he. "It's been going on ever since those Persians left, Gerald. All the time they were here—six months it was—they always bought their house supply of meat and poultry alive, 'on the hoof.' Presumably they preferred to kill and dress their meat themselves. I don't know, for a fact, of course. Anyhow, that was one of the peculiarities of the 'foreigners up at the Canevin Place,' and it got plenty of comment in the town, as you may well imagine. And—since they left—it hasn't been only lambs and calves. I know of at least four dogs. Cats, maybe, too! Nobody would keep much account of lost cats in Chadbourne."

This, somehow, surprised me. I had failed to hear about the dogs and possible cats.

"Dogs, too, eh?" I remarked.

Then Tom Merritt got up abruptly, off his stiff chair, and came over and stood close behind and spoke low and intensively, and very convincingly, directly into my ear.

"And now—it's a child, Gerald. That's too much—for this, or any other decent town. You've never lived in Persia. I have. I'm going to tell you in plain words what I think is going on. Try to believe me, Gerald. Literally, I mean. You've got to believe me—trust me—to do what you've got to do tonight because I can't come right now. It's going to be an ordeal for you. It would be for anybody. Listen to this, now:

"This situation only came to me, clearly, just before I called you up, Gerald. I'd been sitting here after supper, tied up on this Grantham case—waiting for them to call me. It was little Truman Curtiss's disappearance that brought the thing to a head, of course. The whole town's buzzing with it, naturally. No such thing ever happened here before. A child has always been perfectly safe in Chadbourne since they killed the last Indian a hundred and fifty years ago. I hadn't seen the connection before. I've been worked to death for one thing. I naturally hadn't been very much steamed up about a few lambs and dogs dropping out of sight.

"That might mean a camp of tramps somewhere. But—tramps don't steal five-year-old kids. It isn't tramps that do kidnapping for ransom.

"It all fitted together as soon as I really put my mind on it. Those Rustum Dadhs and their unaccountable reticence—the live animals that went up to that house of yours all winter—what I'd heard, and even seen a glimpse of—out there in Kut and Shiraz—that grim-jawed, tight-lipped chauffeur of theirs, with the wife that nobody ever got a glimpse of—finally that story of little Abby Chandler—"

And the incredible remainder of what Doctor Thomas Merritt had to tell me was said literally in my ear, in a tense whisper, as though the teller were actually reluctant that the walls and chairs and books of that mellow old New England library should overhear the utterly monstrous thing he had to tell. . . .

I was shaken when he had finished. I looked long into my lifelong friend Tom Merritt's honest eyes as he stood before me when he had finished, his two firm, capable hands resting on my two shoulders. There was conviction, certainty, in his look. There was no slightest doubt in my mind but that he believed what he had been telling me. But—could he, or any one, by any possible chance, be right on the facts? Here in Chadbourne, of all places on top of the globe!

"I've read about—them—in the *Arabian Nights*," I managed to murmur.

Tom Merritt nodded decisively. "I've seen—two," he said, quietly. "Get going, Gerald," he added; "it's action from now on."

I stepped over to the table and picked up my rifle.

"And remember," he added, as we walked across the room to the door, "what I've told you about them. Shoot them down. Shoot to kill—if you see them. Don't hesitate. Don't wait. Don't—er—talk! No hesitation. That's the rule—in Persia. And remember how to prove it—*remember the marks!* You may have to prove it—to anybody who may be up there still, hunting for poor little Truman Curtiss."

The office telephone rang.

Doctor Merritt opened the library door and looked out into the wide hallway. Then he shouted in the direction of the kitchen.

"Answer it, Mehitabel. Tell 'em I've left. It'll be Seymour Grantham, for his wife." Then to me: "There are two search parties up there, Gerald."

And as we ran down the path from the front door to where our two cars were standing in the road I heard Doctor Merritt's elderly housekeeper at the telephone explaining in her high, nasal twang of the born Yankee, imparting the information that the doctor was on his way to the agitated Grantham family.

I drove up to the old cemetery on the Ridge even faster than I had come down from my own hill fifteen minutes earlier that evening.

The late July moon, one night away from full, bathed the fragrant hill in her clear, serene light. Half-way up the hill road to the Ridge I passed one search party returning. I encountered the other coming out of the cemetery gate as I stopped my steaming engine and set my brakes in front of the entrance. The three men of this party, armed with a lantern, a rifle, and two sizeable clubs, gathered around me. The youngest, Jed Peters, was the first to speak. It was precisely in the spirit of Chadbourne that this first remark would have no direct reference to the pressing affair motivating all of us. Jed had pointed to my rifle, interest registered plainly in his heavy, honest countenance.

"Some weepon—thet-thar, I'd reckon, Mr. Canevin."

I have had a long experience with my Chadbourne neighbors.

"It's a Männlicher," said I, "what is called 'a weapon of precision.' It is accurate to the point of nicking the head off a pin up to about fourteen hundred yards."

These three fellows, one of them the uncle of the missing child, had discovered nothing. They turned back with me, however, without being asked. I could have excused them very gladly. After what Tom Merritt had told me, I should have preferred being left alone to deal with the situation unaided. There was no avoiding it, however. I suggested splitting up the party and had the satisfaction of seeing this suggestion put into effect. The three of them walked off slowly to the left while I waited, standing inside the cemetery gate, until I could just hear their voices.

Then I took up my stand with my back against the inside of the cemetery wall, directly opposite the big Merritt family mausoleum.

The strong moonlight made it stand out clearly. I leaned against the stone wall, my rifle cuddled in my arms, and waited. I made no attempt to watch the mausoleum continuously, but ranged my eyes over the major portion of the cemetery, an area which, being only slightly shrubbed, and sloping upward gently from the entrance, was plainly visible. From time to time as I stood there, ready, I would catch a faint snatch of the continuous conversation going on among the three searchers, as they walked along on a long course which I had suggested to them, all the way around the cemetery, designed to cover territory which, in the local phraseology, ran "down through," "up across," and "over around." I had been waiting, and the three searchers had been meandering, for perhaps twenty minutes—the ancient town clock in the Congregational church tower had boomed ten about five minutes before—when I heard a soft, grating sound in the direction of the Merritt mausoleum. My eyes came back to it sharply.

There, directly before the now half-open bronze door, stood a strange, even a grotesque figure. It was short, squat, thick-set. Upon it, I might say accurately, hung—as though pulled on in the most hurried and slack fashion imaginable—a coat and trousers. The moonlight showed it up clearly and it was plain, even in such light, that these two were the only garments in use. The trousers hung slackly, bagging thickly over a pair of large bare feet. The coat, unbuttoned, sagged and slithered lopsidedly. The coat and trousers were the standardized, unmistakable, diagonal gray material of a chauffer's livery. The head was bare and on it a heavy, bristle-like crop of unkempt hair stood out absurdly. The face was covered with an equally bristle-like growth, unshaven for a month by the appearance. About the tight-shut, menacing mouth, which divided a pair of square, iron-like broad jaws, the facial hairs merged or blended in what seemed from my view point a kind of vague smear, as though the hair were heavily matted.

From this sinister figure there emerged a thick, guttural, repressed voice, as though the speaker were trying to express himself in words without opening his lips:

"Come—come he-ar. Come—I will show you what you look for."

Through my head went everything that Tom Merritt had whispered in my ear. This was my test—my test, with a very great deal at stake—of my trust in what he had said—in him—in the rightness of his information; and it had been information, based on his deduction, such as few men have had to decide upon. I said a brief prayer in that space of a few instants. I observed that the figure was slowly approaching me.

"Come," it repeated—*"come now—I show you—what you, a-seek—here."*

I pulled myself together. I placed my confidence, and my future, in Tom Merritt's hands.

I raised my Männlicher, took careful aim, pulled the trigger. I repeated the shot. Two sharp cracks rang out on that still summer air, and then I lowered the deadly little weapon and watched while the figure crumpled and sagged down, two little holes one beside the other in its forehead, from which a dark stain was spreading over bristly face, matting it all together the way the region of the mouth had looked even before it lay quiet and crumpled up on the ground half-way between the mausoleum and where I stood.

I had done it. I had done what Tom Merritt had told me to do, ruthlessly, without any hesitation, the way Tom had said they did it in Persia around Teheran, the capital, and Shiraz, and in Kut-el-Amara, and down south in Jask.

And then, having burned my bridges, and, for all I knew positively, made myself eligible for a noose at Wethersfield, I walked across to the mausoleum, and straight up to to the opened bronze door, and looked inside.

A frightful smell—a smell like all the decayed meat in the world all together in one place—took me by the throat. A wave of quick nausea invaded me. But I stood my ground and forced myself to envisage what was inside; and when I had seen, despite my short retchings and coughings I resolutely raised my Männlicher and shot and shot and shot at moving, scampering targets; shot again and again and again until nothing moved inside there. I had seen, besides those moving targets, something else; some things I will not attempt to describe beyond using the word "fragments." Poor little five-year-old Truman Curtiss who had last been seen just outside the cemetery gate "with a lady" would never climb that hill again, never pick any more blueberries in Chadbourne or any other place. . . .

I looked without regret on the shambles I had wrought within the old Merritt tomb. The Männlicher is a weapon of precision. . . .

I was brought to a sense of things going on outside the tomb by the sound of running feet, the insistent clipping drawl of three excited voices asking questions. The three searchers, snapped out of their leisurely walk around the cemetery, and quite near by the time my shooting had begun, arrived at the seen of action.

"What's it all about, Mr. Canevin?"

"We heard ye a-shooting away."

"Good Cripes! Gerald's shot a *man!*"

I blew the smoke out of the barrel of my Männlicher, withdrew the clip. I walked toward the group, bending now over the crumpled figure on the ground halfway to the cemetery gate.

"Who's this man you shot, Gerald? Good Cripes! It's the fella that druv the car for them-there Persians. Good Cripes, Gerald—are ye crazy? You can't shoot down a man like that!"

"It's not a man," said I, coming up to them and looking down on the figure.

There was a joint explosion at that. I waited, standing quietly by, until they had exhausted themselves. They were, plainly, more concerned with what consequences I should have to suffer than with the fate of the chauffeur.

"You say it ain't no man! Are ye crazy, Gerald?"

"It's not a man," I repeated. "Reach down and press his jaws together so that he opens his mouth, and you'll see what I mean."

Then, as they naturally enough I suppose hesitated to fill this order, I stooped down, pressed together the buccinator muscles in the middle of the broad Mongol-like cheeks. The mouth came open, and thereat there was another chorus from the three. It was just as Tom Merritt had described it! The teeth were the teeth of one of the great carnivores, only flat, fang-like, like a shark's teeth. No mortal man ever wore such a set within his mouth, or ever needed such a set, the fangs of a tearer of flesh. . . .

"Roll him over," said I, "and loosen the coat so that you can see his back."

To this task young Jed addressed himself.

"Good Cripes!" This from the Curtiss fellow, the lost child's uncle. Along the back, sewn thickly in the dark brown skin, ran a band of three-inch coal-black bristles, longer and stiffer than those of any prize hog. We gazed down in silence for a long moment. Then:

"Come," said I, "and look inside the Merritt tomb—but—brace yourselves! It won't be a pleasant sight."

I turned, led the way, the others falling in behind me. Then, from young Jed Peters:

"You say this-here ain't no man—an'—I believe ye, Mr. Canevin! But—Cripes Almighty!—ef this'n hain't no man, what, a-God's Name, is it?"

"It is a ghoul," said I over my shoulder, "and inside the tomb there are ten more of them—the dam and nine whelps. And what is left of the poor little Curtiss child. . . ."

Looking into the mausoleum that second time, in cold blood, so to speak, was a tough experience even for me who had wrought that havoc in there. As for the others—Eli Curtiss, the oldest of the three, was very sick. Bert Blatchford buried his face in his arms against the door's lintel, and when I shook him by the shoulder in fear lest he collapse, the face he turned to me was blank and ghastly, and his ruddy cheeks had gone the color of lead.

Only young Jed Peters really stood up to it. He simply swore roundly, repeating his "Good Cripes!" over and over again—an articulate youth.

The whelps, with their flattish, human-like faces and heads, equipped with those same punishing, overmuscled jaws like their sire's—like the jaws of a fighting bulldog—their short, thick legs and arms, and their narrow, bristly backs, resembled young pigs more than human infants. All, being of one litter, were of about the same size; all were sickeningly bloody-mouthed from their recent feast. These things lay scattered about the large, circular, marble-walled chamber where they had dropped under the merciless impact of my bullets.

Near the entrance lay sprawled the repulsive, heavy carcass of the dam, her dreadful, fanged mouth open, her sow-like double row of dugs uppermost, these dragged flaccid and purplish and horrible from the recent nursing of the lately-weaned litter. All these unearthly-looking carcasses were naked. The frightful stench still prevailed, still poured out through the open doorway. Heaps and mounds of nauseous offal cluttered the place.

It was young Jed who grasped first and most firmly my suggestion that these horrors be buried out of sight, that a curtain of silence should be drawn down tight by the four of us, fastened permanently against any utterance of the dreadful things we had seen that night. It was young Jed who organized the three into a digging party, who fetched the grave tools from the unfastened cemetery shed.

We worked in a complete silence, as fast as we could. It was not until we were hastily throwing back the loose earth over what we had placed in the sizable pit we had made that the sound of a car's engine, coming up the hill, caused our first pause. We listened.

"It's Doc Merritt's car," I said, somewhat relieved. I looked at my wristwatch. It was a quarter past midnight.

To the four of us, leaning there on our spades, Doctor Merritt repeated something of the history of the Persian tombs, a little of what he had come to know of those mysterious, semi-mythical dwellers among the half-forgotten crypts of ancient burial-grounds, eaters of the dead, which yet preferred the bodies of the living, furtive shapes shot down when glimpsed—in ancient, mysterious Persia. . . .

I left my own car for the three fellows to get home in, young Jed promising to have it back in my garage later in the morning, and drove home with Doctor Merritt.

"There was another thing which I didn't take the time to tell you," said Tom, as we slipped down the winding hill road under the pouring moonlight. "That was that the Rustum Dadh's servants were never seen to leave Chadbourne; although, of course, it was assumed they had done so. The family went by train. I went down to the station to see them off and I found old Rustum Dadh even less communicative than usual.

"'I suppose your man is driving your car down to New York,' I said. It had arrived six months before, when they came to Chadbourne, with both the servants in it, and the inside all piled up with the family's belongings. The old boy merely grunted unintelligibly, in a way he had.

"That afternoon, when I went up to your place to see that everything was ship-shape, there stood the car in the garage, empty. And, while I was wondering what had become of the chauffeur and his wife, and why they hadn't been sent off in the car the way they came, up drives Bartholomew Wade from his garage, and he has the car-key and a letter from Rustum Dadh with directions, and a check for ten dollars and his carfare back from New York. His instructions were to drive the car to New York and leave it there. He did so that afternoon."

"What was the New York address?" I inquired. "That might take some looking into if you think—"

"I don't know what to think—about Rustum Dadh's connection with it all, Gerald," said Tom. "The address was merely the Cunard Line Docks. Whether Rustum Dadh and his family were—the same—there's simply no telling. There's the evidence of the live animals sent up to the house. That live meat may have been for the chauffeur and his wife—seems unlikely, somehow. There was a rumor around town about some dispute or argument between the old man and his chauffeur, over their leaving all together—just a rumor, something picked up or overheard by some busybody. You can take that for what it's worth, of course. The two of 'em, desirous to break away from civilization, revert, here in Chadbourne—that, I imagine, is the probability. There are many times the number of people below ground in the three old cemeteries than going about their affairs—and other people's!—here in Chadbourne. But, whatever Rustum Dadh's connection with—what we know—whatever share of guilt rests on him—he's gone, Gerald, and we can make any one of the three or four possible guesses; but it won't get us anywhere." Then, a little weariness showing in his voice, for Tom Merritt, too, had had a pretty strenuous evening, he added:

"I hired young Jed Peters to spend tomorrow cleaning out the old tomb-house of the ancestors!"

I cleaned my rifle before turning in that night. When I had got this job done and had taken a boiling-hot shower bath, it was close to two o'clock a.m. before I rolled in between the sheets. I had been dreading a sleepless night with the edge of my mind, after that experience up there on Old Cemetery Ridge. I lay in bed for a while, wakeful, going over snatches of it in my mind. Young Jed! No deterioration there at any rate. There was a fellow who would stand by you in a pinch. The old yeoman stock had not run down appreciably in young Jed.

I feel asleep at last after assuring myself all over again that I had done a thorough job up there on the hill. Ghouls! Not merely *Arabian Nights* creatures, like the Afreets and the Djinn. No. Real—those jaws! They shot them down, on sight, over there in Persia when they were descried coming out of their holes among the old tomb-places. . . .

Little, reddish, half-gnawed bones, scattered about that fetid shambles—little bones that had never been torn out of the bodies of calves or lambs—little bones that had been—

I wonder if I shall ever be able to forget those little bones, those little, pitiful bones. . . .

I awoke to the purr of an automobile engine in second speed, coming up the steep hill to my farmhouse, and it was a glorious late-summer New England morning. Young Jed Peters was arriving with my returned car.

I jumped out of bed, pulled on a bathrobe, stepped into a pair of slippers. It was seven-thirty. I went out to the garage and brought young Jed back inside with me for a cup of coffee. It started that new day propitiously to see the boy eat three fried eggs and seven pieces of breakfast bacon. . . .

H *is for* Haunt

British writer Montague Rhodes James (1862–1936) is credited with having laid down the ground rules of the modern ghost story, and his menacing haunts often assume a distinctly repugnant form. In this story, part of his landmark 1904 collection *Ghost Stories of an Antiquary*, a ghostly survival exerts its influence through a repellant physical intermediary.

M.R. James

The Ash-Tree

Everyone who has travelled over Eastern England knows the smaller country-houses with which it is studded—the rather dank little buildings, usually in the Italian style, surrounded with parks of some eighty to a hundred acres. For me they have always had a very strong attraction, with the grey paling of split oak, the noble trees, the meres with their reed-beds, and the line of distant woods. Then, I like the pillared portico—perhaps stuck on to a red-brick Queen Anne house which has been faced with stucco to bring it into line with the "Grecian" taste of the end of the eighteenth century; the hall inside, going up to the roof, which hall ought always to be provided with a gallery and a small organ. I like the library, too, where you may find anything from a Psalter of the thirteenth century to a Shakespeare quarto. I like the pictures, of course; and perhaps most of all I like fancying what life in such a house was when it was first built, and in the piping times of landlords' prosperity, and not least now, when, if money is not so plentiful, taste is more varied and life quite as interesting. I wish to have one of these houses, and enough money to keep it together and entertain my friends in it modestly.

But this is a digression. I have to tell you of a curious series of events which happened in such a house as I have tried to describe. It is Castringham Hall in Suffolk. I think a good deal has been done to the building since the period of my story, but the essential features I have sketched are still there—Italian portico, square block of white house, older inside than out, park with fringe of woods, and mere. The one feature that marked out the house from a score of others is gone. As you looked at it from the park, you saw on the right a great old ash-tree growing within half a dozen yards of the wall, and almost or quite touching the building with its branches. I suppose it had stood there ever since Castringham ceased to be a fortified place, and since the moat was filled in and the Elizabethan dwelling-house built. At any rate, it had well-nigh attained its full dimensions in the year 1690.

In that year the district in which the Hall is situated was the scene of a number of witch-trials. It will be long, I think, before we arrive at a just estimate of the amount of solid reason—if there was any—which lay at the root of the universal fear of witches in old times. Whether the persons accused of this offence really did imagine that they were possessed of unusual power of any kind; or whether they had the will at least, if not the power, of doing mischief to their neighbours; or whether all the confessions, of which there are so many, were extorted by the cruelty of the witch-finders—these are questions which are not, I fancy, yet solved. And the present narrative gives me pause. I cannot altogether sweep it away as mere invention. The reader must judge for himself.

Castringham contributed a victim to the *auto-da-fé*. Mrs. Mothersole was her name, and she differed from the ordinary run of village witches only in being rather better off and in a more influential position. Efforts were made to save her by several reputable farmers of the parish. They did their best to testify to her character, and showed considerable anxiety as to the verdict of the jury.

But what seems to have been fatal to the woman was the evidence of the then proprietor of Castringham Hall—Sir Matthew Fell. He deposed to having watched her on three different occasions from his window, at the full of the moon, gathering sprigs "from the ash-tree near my house." She had climbed into the branches, clad only in her shift, and was cutting off small twigs with a peculiarly curved knife, and as she did so she seemed to be talking to herself. On each occasion Sir Matthew had done his best to capture the woman, but she had always taken alarm at some accidental noise he had made, and all he could see when he got down to the garden was a hare running across the path in the direction of the village.

On the third night he had been at the pains to follow at his best speed, and had gone straight to Mrs. Mothersole's house; but he had had to wait a quarter of an hour battering at her door, and then she had come out very cross, and apparently very sleepy, as if just out of bed; and he had no good explanation to offer of his visit.

Mainly on this evidence, though there was much more of a less striking and unusual kind from other parishioners, Mrs. Mothersole was found guilty and condemned to die. She was hanged a week after the trial, with five or six more unhappy creatures, at Bury St. Edmunds.

Sir Matthew Fell, then Deputy-Sheriff, was present at the execution. It was a damp, drizzly March morning when the cart made its way up the rough grass hill outside Northgate, where the gallows stood. The other victims were apathetic or broken down with misery; but Mrs. Mothersole was, as in life so in death, of a very different temper. Her "poysonous Rage," as a reporter of the time puts it, "did so work upon the Bystanders—yea, even upon the Hangman—that it was constantly affirmed of all that saw her that she presented the living Aspect of a mad Divell. Yet she offer'd no Resistance to the Officers of the Law; onely she looked upon those that laid Hands upon her with so direfull and venomous an Aspect that—as one of them afterwards assured me—the meer Thought of it preyed inwardly upon his Mind for six Months after."

However, all that she is reported to have said were the seemingly meaningless words: "There will be guests at the Hall." Which she repeated more than once in an undertone.

Sir Matthew Fell was not unimpressed by the bearing of the woman. He had some talk upon the matter with the Vicar of his parish, with whom he travelled home after the assize business was over. His evidence at the trial had not been very willingly given; he was not specially infected with the witch-finding mania, but he declared, then and afterwards, that he could not give any other account of the matter than that he had given, and that he could not possibly have been mistaken as to what he saw. The whole transaction had been repugnant to him, for he was a man who liked to be on pleasant terms with those about him; but he saw a duty to be done in this business, and he had done it. That seems to have been the gist of his sentiments, and the Vicar applauded it, as any reasonable man must have done.

A few weeks after, when the moon of May was at the full, Vicar and Squire met again in the park, and walked to the Hall together. Lady Fell was with her mother, who was dangerously ill, and Sir Matthew was alone at home; so the Vicar, Mr. Crome, was easily persuaded to take a late supper at the Hall.

Sir Matthew was not very good company this evening. The talk ran chiefly on family and parish matters, and, as luck would have it, Sir Matthew made a memorandum in writing of certain wishes or intentions of his regarding his estates, which afterwards proved exceedingly useful.

When Mr. Crome thought of starting for home, about half past nine o'clock, Sir Matthew and he took a preliminary turn on the gravelled walk at the back of the house. The only incident that struck Mr. Crome was this: they were in sight of the ash-tree which I described as growing near the windows of the building, when Sir Matthew stopped and said:

"What is that that runs up and down the stem of the ash? It is never a squirrel? They will all be in their nests by now."

The Vicar looked and saw the moving creature, but he could make nothing of its colour in the moonlight. The sharp outline, however, seen for an instant, was imprinted on his brain, and he could have sworn, he said, though it sounded foolish, that, squirrel or not, it had more than four legs.

Still, not much was to be made of the momentary vision, and the two men parted. They may have met since then, but it was not for a score of years.

Next day Sir Matthew Fell was not downstairs at six in the morning, as was his custom, nor at seven, nor yet at eight. Hereupon the servants went and knocked at his chamber door. I need not prolong the description of their anxious listenings and renewed batterings on the panels. The door was opened at last from the outside, and they found their master dead and black. So much you have guessed. That there were any marks of violence did not at the moment appear; but the window was open.

One of the men went to fetch the parson, and then by his directions rode on to give notice to the coroner. Mr. Crome himself went as quick as he might to the Hall, and was shown to the room where the dead man lay. He has left some notes among his papers which show how genuine a respect and sorrow was felt for Sir Matthew, and there is also this passage, which I transcribe for the sake of the light it throws upon the course of events, and also upon the common beliefs of the time:

"There was not any the least Trace of an Entrance having been forc'd to the Chamber: but the Casement stood open, as my poor Friend would always have it in this Season. He had his Evening Drink of small Ale in a silver vessel of about a pint measure, and tonight had not drunk it out. This Drink was examined by the Physician from Bury, a Mr. Hodgkins, who could not, however, as he afterwards declar'd upon his Oath, before the Coroner's quest, discover that any matter of a venomous kind was present in it. For, as was natural, in the great Swelling and Blackness of the Corpse, there was talk made among the Neighbours of Poyson. The Body was very much Disorder'd as it laid in the Bed, being twisted after so extream a sort as gave too probable Conjecture that my worthy Friend and Patron had expir'd in great Pain and Agony. And what is as yet unexplain'd, and to myself the Argument of some Horrid and Artfull Designe in the Perpetrators of this Barbarous Murther, was this, that the Women which were entrusted with the laying-out of the Corpse and washing it, being both sad Persons and very well Respected in their Mournfull Profession, came to me in a great Pain and Distress both of Mind and Body, saying, what was indeed confirmed upon the first View, that they had no sooner touch'd the Breast of the Corpse with their naked Hands than they were sensible of a more than ordinary violent Smart and Acheing in their Palms, which, with their whole Forearms, in no long time swell'd so immoderately, the Pain still continuing, that, as afterwards proved, during many weeks they were forc'd to lay by the exercise of their Calling; and yet no mark seen on the Skin.

"Upon hearing this, I sent for the Physician, who was still in the House, and we made as carefull a Proof as we were able by the Help of a small Magnifying Lens of Crystal of the condition of the Skinn on this Part of the Body: but could not detect with the Instrument we had any Matter of Importance beyond a couple of small Punctures or Pricks, which we then concluded were the Spotts by which the Poyson might be introduced, remembering that Ring of *Pope Borgia,* with other known Specimens of the Horrid Art of the Italian Poysoners of the last age.

"So much is to be said of the Symptoms seen on the Corpse. As to what I am to add, it is meerly my own Experiment, and to be left to Posterity to judge whether there be anything of Value therein. There was on the Table by the Beddside a Bible of the small size, in which my Friend—punctuall as in Matters of less Moment, so in this more weighty one—used nightly, and upon his First Rising, to read a sett Portion. And I taking it up—not without a Tear duly paid to him which from the Study of this poorer Adumbration was now pass'd to the contemplation of its great Originall—it came into my Thoughts, as at such moments of Helplessness we are prone to catch at any the least Glimmer that makes promise of Light, to make trial of that old and by many accounted Superstitious Practice of drawing the *Sortes*; of which a Principall Instance, in the case of his late Sacred Majesty the Blessed Martyr King *Charles* and my Lord *Falkland,* was now much talked of. I must needs admit that by my Trial not much Assistance was afforded me: yet, as the Cause and Origin of these Dreadfull Events may hereafter be search'd out, I set down the Results, in the case it may be found that they pointed the true Quarter of the Mischief to a quicker Intelligence than my own.

"I made, then, three trials, opening the Book and placing my Finger upon certain Words: which gave in the first these words, from Luke xiii. 7, *Cut it down*; in the second, Isaiah xiii. 20, *It shall never be inhabited*; and upon the third Experiment, Job xxxix. 30, *Her young ones also suck up blood.*"

This is all that need be quoted from Mr. Crome's papers. Sir Matthew Fell was duly coffined and laid into the earth, and his funeral sermon, preached by Mr. Crome on the following Sunday, has been printed under the title of "The Unsearchable Way; or, England's Danger and the Malicious Dealings of Antichrist," it being the Vicar's view, as well as that most commonly held in the neighbourhood, that the Squire was the victim of a recrudescence of the Popish Plot.

His son, Sir Matthew the second, succeeded to the title and estates. And so ends the first act of the Castringham tragedy. It is to be mentioned, though the fact is not surprising, that the new Baronet did not occupy the room in which his father had died. Nor, indeed, was it slept in by anyone but an occasional visitor during the whole of his occupation. He died in 1735, and I do not find that anything particular marked his reign, save a curiously constant mortality among his cattle and live-stock in general, which showed a tendency to increase slightly as time went on.

Those who are interested in the details will find a statistical account in a letter to the *Gentleman's Magazine* of 1772, which draws the facts from the Baronet's own papers. He put an end to it at last by a very simple expedient, that of shutting up all his beasts in sheds at night, and keeping no sheep in his park. For he had noticed that nothing was ever attacked that spent the night indoors. After that the disorder confined itself to wild birds, and beasts of chase. But as we have no good account of the symptoms, and as all-night watching was quite unproductive of any clue, I do not dwell on what the Suffolk farmers called the "Castringham sickness."

The second Sir Matthew died in 1735, as I said, and was duly succeeded by his son, Sir Richard. It was in his time that the great family pew was built out on the north side of the parish church. So large were the Squire's ideas that several of the graves on that unhallowed side of the building had to be disturbed to satisfy his requirements. Among them was that of Mrs. Mothersole, the position of which was accurately known, thanks to a note on a plan of the church and yard, both made by Mr. Crome.

A certain amount of interest was excited in the village when it was known that the famous witch, who was still remembered by a few, was to be exhumed. And the feeling of surprise, and indeed disquiet, was very strong when it was found that, though her coffin was fairly sound and unbroken, there was no trace whatever inside it of body, bones, or dust. Indeed, it is a curious phenomenon, for at the time of her burying no such things were dreamt of as resurrection-men, and it is difficult to conceive any rational motive for stealing a body otherwise than for the uses of the dissecting-room.

The incident revived for a time all the stories of witch-trials and of the exploits of the witches, dormant for forty years, and Sir Richard's orders that the coffin should be burnt were thought by a good many to be rather foolhardy, though they were duly carried out.

Sir Richard was a pestilent innovator, it is certain. Before his time the Hall had been a fine block of the mellowest red brick; but Sir Richard had travelled in Italy and become infected with the Italian taste, and, having more money than his predecessors, he determined to leave an Italian palace where he had found an English house. So stucco and ashlar masked the brick; some indifferent Roman marbles were planted about in the entrance-hall and gardens; a reproduction of the Sibyl's temple at Tivoli was erected on the opposite bank of the mere; and Castringham took on an entirely new, and, I must say, a less engaging, aspect. But it was much admired, and served as a model to a good many of the neighbouring gentry in after-years.

One morning (it was in 1754) Sir Richard woke after a night of discomfort. It had been windy, and his chimney had smoked persistently, and yet it was so cold that he must keep up a fire. Also something had so rattled about the window that no man could get a moment's peace. Further, there was the prospect of several guests of position arriving in the course of the day, who would expect sport of some kind, and the inroads of the distemper (which continued among his game) had been lately so serious that he was afraid for his reputation as a game-preserver. But what really touched him most nearly was the other matter of his sleepless night. He could certainly not sleep in that room again.

That was the chief subject of his meditations at breakfast, and after it he began a systematic examination of the rooms to see which would suit his notions best. It was long before he found one. This had a window with an eastern aspect and that with a northern; this door the servants would be always passing, and he did not like the bedstead in that. No, he must have a room with a western look-out, so that the sun could not wake him early, and it must be out of the way of the business of the house. The housekeeper was at the end of her resources.

"Well, Sir Richard," she said, "you know that there is but the one room like that in the house."

"Which may that be?" said Sir Richard.

"And that is Sir Matthew's—the West Chamber."

"Well, put me in there, for there I'll lie tonight," said her master. "Which way is it? Here, to be sure"; and he hurried off.

"Oh, Sir Richard, but no one has slept there these forty years. The air has hardly been changed since Sir Matthew died there."

Thus she spoke, and rustled after him.

"Come, open the door, Mrs. Chiddock. I'll see the chamber, at least."

So it was opened, and, indeed, the smell was very close and earthy. Sir Richard crossed to the window, and, impatiently, as was his wont, threw the shutters back, and flung open the casement. For this end of the house was one which the alterations had barely touched, grown up as it was with the great ash-tree, and being otherwise concealed from view.

"Air it, Mrs. Chiddock, all today, and move my bed-furniture in in the afternoon. Put the Bishop of Kilmore in my old room."

"Pray, Sir Richard," said a new voice, breaking in on this speech, "might I have the favour of a moment's interview?"

Sir Richard turned round and saw a man in black in the doorway, who bowed.

"I must ask your indulgence for this intrusion, Sir Richard. You will, perhaps, hardly remember me. My name is William Crome, and my grandfather was Vicar in your grandfather's time."

"Well, sir," said Sir Richard, "the name of Crome is always a passport to Castringham. I am glad to renew a friendship of two generations' standing. In what can I serve you? for your hour of calling—and, if I do not mistake you, your bearing—shows you to be in some haste."

"That is no more than the truth, sir. I am riding from Norwich to Bury St. Edmunds with what haste I can make, and I have called in on my way to leave with you some papers which we have but just come upon in looking over what my grandfather left at his death. It is thought you may find some matters of family interest in them."

"You are mighty obliging, Mr. Crome, and, if you will be so good as to follow me to the parlour, and drink a glass of wine, we will take a first look at these same papers together. And you, Mrs. Chiddock, as I said, be about airing this chamber. . . . Yes, it is here my grandfather died. . . . Yes, the tree, perhaps, does make the place a little dampish. . . . No; I do not wish to listen to any more. Make no difficulties, I beg. You have your orders—go. Will you follow me, sir?"

They went to the study. The packet which young Mr. Crome had brought—he was then just become a Fellow of Clare Hall in Cambridge, I may say, and subsequently brought out a respectable edition of Polyaenus—contained among other things the notes which the old Vicar had made upon the occasion of Sir Matthew Fell's death. And for the first time Sir Richard was confronted with the enigmatical *Sortes Biblicæ* which you have heard. They amused him a good deal.

"Well," he said, "my grandfather's Bible gave one prudent piece of advice—*Cut it down*. If that stands for the ash-tree, he may rest assured I shall not neglect it. Such a nest of catarrhs and agues was never seen."

The parlour contained the family books, which, pending the arrival of a collection which Sir Richard had made in Italy, and the building of a proper room to receive them, were not many in number.

Sir Richard looked up from the paper to the bookcase.

"I wonder," says he, "whether the old prophet is there yet? I fancy I see him."

Crossing the room, he took out a dumpy Bible, which, sure enough, bore on the flyleaf the inscription: "To Matthew Fell, from his Loving Godmother, Anne Aldous, 2 September 1659."

"It would be no bad plan to test him again, Mr. Crome. I will wager we get a couple of names in the Chronicles. H'm! what have we here? 'Thou shalt seek me in the morning, and I shall not be.' Well, well! Your grandfather would have made a fine omen of that, hey? No more prophets for me! They are all in a tale. And now, Mr. Crome, I am infinitely obliged to you for your packet. You will, I fear, be impatient to get on. Pray allow me—another glass."

So with offers of hospitality, which were genuinely meant (for Sir Richard thought well of the young man's address and manner), they parted.

In the afternoon came the guests—the Bishop of Kilmore, Lady Mary Hervey, Sir William Kentfield, etc. Dinner at five, wine, cards, supper, and dispersal to bed.

Next morning Sir Richard is disinclined to take his gun with the rest. He talks with the Bishop of Kilmore. This prelate, unlike a good many of the Irish Bishops of his day, had visited his see, and, indeed, resided there, for some considerable time. This morning, as the two were walking along the terrace and talking over the alterations and improvements in the house, the Bishop said, pointing to the window of the West Room:

"You could never get one of my Irish flock to occupy that room, Sir Richard."

"Why is that, my lord? It is, in fact, my own."

"Well, our Irish peasantry will always have it that it brings the worst of luck to sleep near an ash-tree, and you have a fine growth of ash not two yards from your chamber window. Perhaps," the Bishop went on, with a smile, "it has given you a touch of its quality already, for you do not seem, if I may say it, so much the fresher for your night's rest as your friends would like to see you."

"That, or something else, it is true, cost me my sleep from twelve to four, my lord. But the tree is to come down tomorrow, so I shall not hear much more from it."

"I applaud your determination. It can hardly be wholesome to have the air you breathe strained, as it were, through all that leafage."

"Your lordship is right there, I think. But I had not my window open last night. It was rather the noise that went on—no doubt from the twigs sweeping the glass—that kept me open-eyed."

"I think that can hardly be, Sir Richard. Here—you see it from this point. None of these nearest branches even can touch your casement unless there were a gale, and there was none of that last night. They miss the panes by a foot."

"No, sir, true. What, then, will it be, I wonder, that scratched and rustled so—ay, and covered the dust on my sill with lines and marks?"

At last they agreed that the rats must have come up through the ivy. That was the Bishop's idea, and Sir Richard jumped at it.

So the day passed quietly, and night came, and the party dispersed to their rooms, and wished Sir Richard a better night.

And now we are in his bedroom, with the light out and the Squire in bed. The room is over the kitchen, and the night outside still and warm, so the window stands open.

There is very little light about the bedstead, but there is a strange movement there; it seems as if Sir Richard were moving his head rapidly to and fro with only the slightest possible sound. And now you would guess, so deceptive is the half-darkness, that he had several heads, round and brownish, which move back and forward, even as low as his chest. It is a horrible illusion. Is it nothing more? There! something drops off the bed with a soft plump, like a kitten, and is out of the window in a flash; another—four—and after that there is quiet again.

"Thou shall seek me in the morning, and I shall not be."

As with Sir Matthew, so with Sir Richard—dead and black in his bed!

A pale and silent party of guests and servants gathered under the window when the news was known. Italian poisoners, Popish emissaries, infected air—all these and more guesses were hazarded, and the Bishop of Kilmore looked at the tree, in the fork of whose lower boughs a white tom-cat was crouching, looking down the hollow which years had gnawed in the trunk. It was watching something inside the tree with great interest.

Suddenly it got up and craned over the hole. Then a bit of the edge on which it stood gave way, and it went slithering in. Everyone looked up at the noise of the fall.

It is known to most of us that a cat can cry; but few of us have heard, I hope, such a yell as came out of the trunk of the great ash. Two or three screams there were—the witnesses are not sure which—and then a slight and muffled noise of some commotion or struggling was all that came. But Lady Mary Hervey fainted outright, and the housekeeper stopped her ears and fled till she fell on the terrace.

The Bishop of Kilmore and Sir William Kentfield stayed. Yet even they were daunted, though it was only at the cry of a cat; and Sir William swallowed once or twice before he could say:

"There is something more than we know of in that tree, my lord. I am for an instant search."

And this was agreed upon. A ladder was brought, and one of the gardeners went up, and, looking down the hollow, could detect nothing but a few dim indications of something moving. They got a lantern, and let it down by a rope.

"We must get at the bottom of this. My life upon it, my lord, but the secret of these terrible deaths is there."

Up went the gardener again with the lantern, and let it down the hole cautiously. They saw the yellow light upon his face as he bent over, and saw his face struck with an incredulous terror and loathing before he cried out in a dreadful voice and fell back from the ladder—where, happily, he was caught by two of the men—letting the lantern fall inside the tree.

He was in a dead faint, and it was some time before any word could be got from him.

By then they had something else to look at. The lantern must have broken at the bottom, and the light in it caught upon dry leaves and rubbish that lay there for in a few minutes a dense smoke began to come up, and then flame; and, to be short, the tree was in a blaze.

The bystanders made a ring at some yards' distance, and Sir William and the Bishop sent men to get what weapons and tools they could; for, clearly, whatever might be using the tree as its lair would be forced out by the fire.

So it was. First, at the fork, they saw a round body covered with fire—the size of a man's head—appear very suddenly, then seem to collapse and fall back. This, five or six times; then a similar ball leapt into the air and fell on the grass, where after a moment it lay still. The Bishop went as near as he dared to it, and saw—what but the remains of an enormous spider, veinous and seared! And, as the fire burned lower down, more terrible bodies like this began to break out from the trunk, and it was seen that these were covered with greyish hair.

All that day the ash burned, and until it fell to pieces the men stood about it, and from time to time killed the brutes as they darted out. At last there was a long interval when none appeared, and they cautiously closed in and examined the roots of the tree.

"They found," says the Bishop of Kilmore, "below it a rounded hollow place in the earth, wherein were two or three bodies of these creatures that had plainly been smothered by the smoke; and, what is to me more curious, at the side of this den, against the wall, was crouching the anatomy or skeleton of a human being, with the skin dried upon the bones, having some remains of black hair, which was pronounced by those that examined it to be undoubtedly the body of a woman, and clearly dead for a period of fifty years."

I *is for* Invisible

What you can't see *can* hurt you—at least that's what American writer Ambrose Bierce (1842–1914?) would have you believe in this tale, which was first published in the December 7, 1893, issue of *Tales from New York Town Topics.* It is one of many stories he wrote in which a tone of sardonic humor makes the horrors stand out in sharp relief.

AMBROSE BIERCE

The Damned Thing

I

One Does Not Always Eat What Is on the Table

By the light of a tallow candle, which had been placed on one end of a rough table, a man was reading something written in a book. It was an old account book, greatly worn; and the writing was not, apparently, very legible, for the man sometimes held the page close to the flame of the candle to get a stronger light upon it. The shadow of the book would then throw into obscurity a half of the room, darkening a number of faces and figures; for besides the reader, eight other men were present. Seven of them sat against the rough log walls, silent and motionless, and, the room being small, not very far from the table. By extending an arm any one of them could have touched the eighth man, who lay on the table, face upward, partly covered by a sheet, his arms at his sides. He was dead.

The man with the book was not reading aloud, and no one spoke; all seemed to be waiting for something to occur; the dead man only was without expectation. From the blank darkness outside came in, through the aperture that served for a window, all the ever unfamiliar noises of night in the wilderness—the long, nameless note of a distant coyote; the stilly pulsing thrill of tireless insects in trees; strange cries of night birds, so different from those of the birds of day; the drone of great blundering beetles, and all that mysterious chorus of small sounds that seem always to have been but half heard when they have suddenly ceased, as if conscious of an indiscretion. But nothing of all this was noted in that company; its members were not overmuch addicted to idle interest in matters of no practical importance; that was obvious in every line of their rugged faces—obvious even in the dim light of the single candle. They were evidently men of the vicinity—farmers and woodsmen.

The person reading was a trifle different; one would have said of him that he was of the world, worldly, albeit there was that in his attire which attested a certain fellowship with the organisms of his environment. His coat would hardly have passed muster in San Francisco: his foot-gear was not of urban origin, and the hat that lay by him on the floor (he was the only one uncovered) was such that if one had considered it as an article of mere personal adornment he would have missed its meaning. In countenance the man was rather prepossessing, with just a hint of sternness; though that he may have assumed or cultivated, as appropriate to one in authority. For he was a coroner. It was by virtue of his office that he had possession of the book in which he was reading; it had been found among the dead man's effects—in his cabin, where the inquest was now taking place.

When the coroner had finished reading he put the book into his breast pocket. At that moment the door was pushed open and a young man entered. He, clearly, was not of mountain birth and breeding: he was clad as those who dwell in cities. His clothing was dusty, however, as from travel. He had, in fact, been riding hard to attend the inquest.

The coroner nodded; no one else greeted him.

"We have waited for you," said the coroner. "It is necessary to have done with this business to-night."

The young man smiled. "I am sorry to have kept you," he said. "I went away, not to evade your summons, but to post to my newspaper an account of what I suppose I am called back to relate."

The coroner smiled.

"The account that you posted to your newspaper," he said, "differs probably from that which you will give here under oath."

"That," replied the other, rather hotly and with a visible flush, "is as you choose. I used manifold paper and have a copy of what I sent. It was not written as news, for it is incredible, but as fiction. It may go as a part of my testimony under oath."

"But you say it is incredible."

"That is nothing to you, sir, if I also swear that it is true."

The coroner was apparently not greatly affected by the young man's manifest resentment. He was silent for some moments, his eyes upon the floor. The men about the sides of the cabin talked in whispers, but seldom withdrew their gaze from the face of the corpse. Presently the coroner lifted his eyes and said: "We will resume the inquest."

The men removed their hats. The witness was sworn.

"What is your name?" the coroner asked.

"William Harker."

"Age?"

"Twenty-seven."

"You knew the deceased, Hugh Morgan?"

"Yes."

"You were with him when he died?"

"Near him."

"How did that happen—your presence, I mean?"

"I was visiting him at this place to shoot and fish. A part of my purpose, however, was to study him, and his odd, solitary way of life. He seemed a good model for a character in fiction. I sometimes write stories."

"I sometimes read them."

"Thank you."

"Stories in general—not yours."

Some of the jurors laughed. Against a sombre background humor shows high lights. Soldiers in the intervals of battle laugh easily, and a jest in the death chamber conquers by surprise.

"Relate the circumstances of this man's death," said the coroner. "You may use any notes or memoranda that you please."

The witness understood. Pulling a manuscript from his breast pocket he held it near the candle, and turning the leaves until he found the passage that he wanted, began to read.

II
What May Happen in a Field of Wild Oats

". . . The sun had hardly risen when we left the house. We were looking for quail, each with a shotgun, but we had only one dog. Morgan said that our best ground was beyond a certain ridge that he pointed out, and we crossed it by a trail through the *chaparral.* On the other side was comparatively level ground, thickly covered with wild oats. As we emerged from the *chaparral,* Morgan was but a few yards in advance. Suddenly, we heard, at a little distance to our right, and partly in front, a noise as of some animal thrashing about in the bushes, which we could see were violently agitated.

" 'We've started a deer,' I said. 'I wish we had brought a rifle.'

"Morgan, who had stopped and was intently watching the agitated *chaparral,* said nothing, but had cocked both barrels of his gun, and was holding it in readiness to aim. I thought him a trifle excited, which surprised me, for he had a reputation for exceptional coolness, even in moments of sudden and imminent peril.

" 'O, come!' I said. 'You are not going to fill up a deer with quail-shot, are you?'

"Still he did not reply; but, catching a sight of his face as he turned it slightly toward me, I was struck by the pallor of it. Then I understood that we had serious business on hand, and my first conjecture was that we had 'jumped' a grizzly. I advanced to Morgan's side, cocking my piece as I moved.

"The bushes were now quiet, and the sounds had ceased, but Morgan was as attentive to the place as before.

" 'What is it? What the devil is it?' I asked.

" 'That Damned Thing!' he replied, without turning his head. His voice was husky and unnatural. He trembled visibly.

"I was about to speak further, when I observed the wild oats near the place of the disturbance moving in the most inexplicable way. I can hardly describe it. It seemed as if stirred by a streak of wind, which not only bent it, but pressed it down—crushed it so that it did not rise, and this movement was slowly prolonging itself directly toward us.

"Nothing that I had ever seen had affected me so strangely as this unfamiliar and unaccountable phenomenon, yet I am unable to recall any sense of fear. I remember—and tell it here because, singularly enough, I recollected it then—that once, in looking carelessly out of an open window, I momentarily mistook a small tree close at hand for one of a group of larger trees at a little distance away. It looked the same size as the others, but, being more distinctly and sharply defined in mass and detail, seemed out of harmony with them. It was a mere falsification of the law of aerial perspective, but it startled, almost terrified me. We so rely upon the orderly operation of familiar natural laws that any seeming suspension of them is noted as a menace to our safety, a warning of unthinkable calamity. So now the apparently causeless movement of the herbage, and the slow, undeviating approach of the line of disturbance were distinctly disquieting. My companion appeared actually frightened, and I could hardly credit my senses when I saw him suddenly throw his gun to his shoulders and fire both barrels at the agitated grass! Before the smoke of the discharge had cleared away I heard a loud savage cry—a scream like that of a wild animal—and, flinging his gun upon the ground, Morgan sprang away and ran swiftly from the spot. At the same instant I was thrown violently to the ground by the impact of something unseen in the smoke—some soft, heavy substance that seemed thrown against me with great force.

"Before I could get upon my feet and recover my gun, which seemed to have been struck from my hands, I heard Morgan crying out as if in mortal agony, and mingling with his cries were such hoarse savage sounds as one hears from fighting dogs. Inexpressibly terrified, I struggled to my feet and looked in the direction of Morgan's retreat; and may heaven in mercy spare me from another sight like that! At a distance of less than thirty yards was my friend, down upon one knee, his head thrown back at a frightful angle, hatless, his long hair in disorder and his whole body in violent movement from side to side, backward and forward. His right arm was lifted and seemed to lack the hand—at least, I could see none. The other arm was invisible. At times, as my memory now reports this extraordinary scene, I could discern but a part of his body; it was as if he had been partly blotted out—I can not otherwise express it—then a shifting of his position would bring it all into view again.

"All this must have occurred within a few seconds, yet in that time Morgan assumed all the postures of a determined wrestler vanquished by superior weight and strength. I saw nothing but him, and him not always distinctly. During the entire incident his shouts and curses were heard, as if through an enveloping uproar of such sounds of rage and fury as I had never heard from the throat of man or brute!

"For a moment only I stood irresolute, then, throwing down my gun, I ran forward to my friend's assistance. I had a vague belief that he was suffering from a fit or some form of convulsion. Before I could reach his side he was down and quiet. All sounds had ceased, but, with a feeling of such terror as even these awful events had not inspired, I now saw the same mysterious movement of the wild oats prolonging itself from the trampled area about the prostrate man toward the edge of a wood. It was only when it had reached the wood that I was able to withdraw my eyes and look at my companion. He was dead."

III
A Man though Naked May Be in Rags

The coroner rose from his seat and stood beside the dead man. Lifting an edge of the sheet he pulled it away, exposing the entire body, altogether naked and showing in the candle-light a claylike yellow. It had, however, broad maculations of bluish black, obviously caused by extravasated blood from contusions. The chest and sides looked as if they had been beaten with a bludgeon. There were dreadful lacerations; the skin was torn in strips and shreds.

The coroner moved round to the end of the table and undid a silk handkerchief, which had been passed under the chin and knotted on the top of the head. When the handkerchief was drawn away it exposed what had been the throat. Some of the jurors who had risen to get a better view repented their curiosity, and turned away their faces. Witness Harker went to the open window and leaned out across the sill, faint and sick. Dropping the handkerchief upon the dead man's neck, the coroner stepped to an angle of the room, and from a pile of clothing produced one garment after another, each of which he held up a moment for inspection. All were torn, and stiff with blood. The jurors did not make a closer inspection. They seemed rather uninterested. They had, in truth, seen all this before; the only thing that was new to them being Harker's testimony.

"Gentlemen," the coroner said, "we have no more evidence, I think. Your duty has been already explained to you; if there is nothing you wish to ask you may go outside and consider your verdict."

The foreman rose—a tall, bearded man of sixty, coarsely clad.

"I should like to ask one question, Mr. Coroner," he said. "What asylum did this yer last witness escape from?"

"Mr. Harker," said the coroner, gravely and tranquilly, "from what asylum did you last escape?"

Harker flushed crimson again, but said nothing, and the seven jurors rose and solemnly filed out of the cabin.

"If you have done insulting me, sir," said Harker, as soon as he and the officer were left alone with the dead man, "I suppose I am at liberty to go?"

"Yes."

Harker started to leave, but paused, with his hand on the door latch. The habit of his profession was strong in him—stronger than his sense of personal dignity. He turned about and said:

"The book that you have there—I recognize it as Morgan's diary. You seemed greatly interested in it; you read in it while I was testifying. May I see it? The public would like—"

"The book will cut no figure in this matter," replied the official, slipping it into his coat pocket; "all the entries in it were made before the writer's death."

As Harker passed out of the house the jury reentered and stood about the table on which the now covered corpse showed under the sheet with sharp definition. The foreman seated himself near the candle, produced from his breast pocket a pencil and scrap of paper, and wrote rather laboriously the following verdict, which with various degrees of effort all signed:

"We, the jury, do find that the remains come to their death at the hands of a mountain lion, but some of us thinks, all the same, they had fits."

IV

An Explanation from the Tomb

In the diary of the late Hugh Morgan are certain interesting entries having, possibly, a scientific value as suggestions. At the inquest upon his body the book was not put in evidence; possibly the coroner thought it not worth while to confuse the jury. The date of the first of the entries mentioned cannot be ascertained; the upper part of the leaf is torn away; the part of the entry remaining is as follows:

"...would run in a half circle, keeping his head turned always toward the centre and again he would stand still, barking furiously. At last he ran away into the brush as fast as he could go. I thought at first that he had gone mad, but on returning to the house found no other alteration in his manner than what was obviously due to fear of punishment.

"Can a dog see with his nose? Do odors impress some cerebral centre with images of the thing that emitted them?...

"Sept 2.—Looking at the stars last night as they rose above the crest of the ridge east of the house, I observed them successively disappear—from left to right. Each was eclipsed but an instant, and only a few at the same time, but along the entire length of the ridge all that were within a degree or two of the crest were blotted out. It was as if something had passed along between me and them; but I could not see it, and the stars were not thick enough to define its outline. Ugh! I don't like this." ...

Several weeks' entries are missing, three leaves being torn from the book.

"Sept. 27.—It has been about here again—I find evidences of its presence every day. I watched again all last night in the same cover, gun in hand, double-charged with buckshot. In the morning the fresh footprints were there, as before. Yet I would have sworn that I did not sleep—indeed, I hardly sleep at all. It is terrible, insupportable! If these amazing experiences are real I shall go mad; if they are fanciful I am mad already.

"Oct. 3.—I shall not go—it shall not drive me away. No, this is *my* house, *my* land. God hates a coward....

"Oct. 5.—I can stand it no longer; I have invited Harker to pass a few weeks with me—he has a level head. I can judge from his manner if he thinks me mad.

"Oct. 7.—I have the solution of the problem; it came to me last night—suddenly, as by revelation. How simple—how terribly simple!

"There are sounds that we can not hear. At either end of the scale are notes that stir no chord of that imperfect instrument, the human ear. They are too high or too grave. I have observed a flock of blackbirds occupying an entire treetop—the tops of several trees—and all in full song. Suddenly—in a moment—at absolutely the same instant—all spring into the air and fly away. How? They could not all see one another—whole treetops intervened. At no point could a leader have been visible to all. There must have been a signal of warning or command, high and shrill above the din, but by me unheard. I have observed, too, the same simultaneous flight when all were silent, among not only blackbirds, but other birds—quail, for example, widely separated by bushes—even on opposite sides of a hill.

"It is known to seamen that a school of whales basking or sporting on the surface of the ocean, miles apart, with the convexity of the earth between them, will sometimes dive at the same instant—all gone out of sight in a moment. The signal has been sounded—too grave for the ear of the sailor at the masthead and his comrades on the deck—who nevertheless feel its vibrations in the ship as the stones of a cathedral are stirred by the bass of the organ.

"As with sounds, so with colors. At each end of the solar spectrum the chemist can detect the presence of what are known as 'actinic' rays. They represent colors—integral colors in the composition of light—which we are unable to discern. The human eye is an imperfect instrument; its range is but a few octaves of the real 'chromatic scale.' I am not mad; there are colors that we cannot see.

"And, God help me! the Damned Thing is of such a color!"

J
is for
Jinn

"Jinn" is one of many names given to genies, creatures of Arabic folklore. The best known jinn in all literature is, perhaps, the genie trapped in a lamp who granted Aladdin wishes in *The Arabian Nights*. British writer Robert Louis Stevenson (1850-1894) gives the wish-granting jinn of this story, first published in the February 8 through March 1 issues of *New York Herald*, a character more appropriate for the tale's Hawaiian setting.

ROBERT LOUIS STEVENSON

The Bottle Imp

Note.*—Any student of that very unliterary product, the English drama of the early part of the century, will here recognise the name and the root idea of a piece once rendered popular by the redoubtable B. Smith. The root idea is there and identical, and yet I believe I have made it a new thing. And the fact that the tale has been designed and written for a Polynesian audience may lend it some extraneous interest nearer home.*

—R. L. S.

There was a man of the Island of Hawaii, whom I shall call Keawe; for the truth is, he still lives, and his name must be kept secret; but the place of his birth was not far from Honaunau, where the bones of Keawe the Great lie hidden in a cave. This man was poor, brave, and active; he could read and write like a schoolmaster; he was a first-rate mariner besides, sailed for some time in the island steamers, and steered a whale-boat on the Hamakua coast. At length it came in Keawe's mind to have a sight of the great world and foreign cities, and he shipped on a vessel bound to San Francisco.

This is a fine town, with a fine harbour, and rich people uncountable; and, in particular, there is one hill which is covered with palaces. Upon this hill Keawe was one day taking a walk with his pocket full of money, viewing the great houses upon either hand with pleasure. "What fine houses these are!" he was thinking, "and how happy must these people be who dwell in them, and take no care for the morrow!" The thought was in his mind when he came abreast of a house that was smaller than some others, but all finished and beautified like a toy; the steps of that house shone like silver, and the borders of the garden bloomed like garlands, and the windows were bright like diamonds; and Keawe stopped and wondered at the excellence of all he saw. So stopping, he was aware of a man that looked forth upon him through a window so clear that Keawe could see him as you see a fish in a pool upon the reef. The man was elderly, with a bald head and a black beard; and his face was heavy with sorrow, and he bitterly sighed. And the truth of it is, that as Keawe looked in upon the man, and the man looked out upon Keawe, each envied the other.

All of a sudden, the man smiled and nodded, and beckoned Keawe to enter, and met him at the door of the house.

"This is a fine house of mine," said the man, and bitterly sighed. "Would you not care to view the chambers?"

So he led Keawe all over it, from the cellar to the roof, and there was nothing there that was not perfect of its kind, and Keawe was astonished.

"Truly," said Keawe, "this is a beautiful house; if I lived in the like of it, I should be laughing all day long. How comes it, then, that you should be sighing?"

"There is no reason," said the man, "why you should not have a house in all points similar to this, and finer, if you wish. You have some money, I suppose?"

"I have fifty dollars," said Keawe; "but a house like this will cost more than fifty dollars."

The man made a computation. "I am sorry you have no more," said he, "for it may raise you trouble in the future; but it shall be yours at fifty dollars."

"The house?" asked Keawe.

"No, not the house," replied the man; "but the bottle. For, I must tell you, although I appear to you so rich and fortunate, all my fortune, and this house itself and its garden, came out of a bottle not much bigger than a pint. This is it."

And he opened a lockfast place, and took out a round-bellied bottle with a long neck; the glass of it was white like milk, with changing rainbow colours in the grain. Withinsides something obscurely moved, like a shadow and a fire.

"This is the bottle," said the man; and, when Keawe laughed, "You do not believe me?" he added. "Try, then, for yourself. See if you can break it."

So Keawe took the bottle up and dashed it on the floor till he was weary; but it jumped on the floor like a child's ball, and was not injured.

"This is a strange thing," said Keawe. "For by the touch of it, as well as by the look, the bottle should be of glass."

"Of glass it is," replied the man, sighing more heavily than ever; "but the glass of it was tempered in the flames of hell. An imp lives in it, and that is the shadow we behold there moving: or so I suppose. If any man buy this bottle the imp is at his command; all that he desires—love, fame, money, houses like this house, ay, or a city like this city—all are his at the word uttered. Napoleon had this bottle, and by it he grew to be the king of the world; but he sold it at the last and fell. Captain Cook had this bottle, and by it he found his way to so many islands; but he, too, sold it, and was slain upon Hawaii. For, once it is sold, the power goes and the protection; and unless a man remain content with what he has, ill will befall him."

"And yet you talk of selling it yourself?" Keawe said.

"I have all I wish, and I am growing elderly," replied the man. "There is one thing the imp cannot do—he cannot prolong life; and, it would not be fair to conceal from you, there is a drawback to the bottle; for if a man die before he sells it, he must burn in hell forever."

"To be sure, that is a drawback and no mistake," cried Keawe. "I would not meddle with the thing. I can do without a house, thank God; but there is one thing I could not be doing with one particle, and that is to be damned."

"Dear me, you must not run away with things," returned the man. "All you have to do is to use the power of the imp in moderation, and then sell it to someone else, as I do to you, and finish your life in comfort."

"Well, I observe two things," said Keawe. "All the time you keep sighing like a maid in love, that is one; and, for the other, you sell this bottle very cheap."

"I have told you already why I sigh," said the man. "It is because I fear my health is breaking up; and, as you said yourself, to die and go to the devil is a pity for anyone. As for why I sell so cheap, I must explain to you there is a peculiarity about the bottle. Long ago, when the devil brought it first upon earth, it was extremely expensive, and was sold first of all to Prester John for many millions of dollars; but it cannot be sold at all, unless sold at a loss. If you sell it for as much as you paid for it, back it comes to you again like a homing pigeon. It follows that the price has kept falling in these centuries, and the bottle is now remarkably cheap. I bought it myself from one of my great neighbours on this hill, and the price I paid was only ninety dollars. I could sell it for as high as eighty-nine dollars and ninety-nine cents, but not a penny dearer, or back the thing must come to me. Now, about this there are two bothers. First, when you offer a bottle so singular for eighty odd dollars, people suppose you to be jesting. And second—but there is no hurry about that—and I need not go into it. Only remember it must be coined money that you sell it for."

"How am I to know that this is all true?" asked Keawe.

"Some of it you can try at once," replied the man. "Give me your fifty dollars, take the bottle, and wish your fifty dollars back into your pocket. If that does not happen, I pledge you my honour I will cry off the bargain and restore your money."

"You are not deceiving me?" said Keawe.

The man bound himself with a great oath.

"Well, I will risk that much," said Keawe, "for that can do no harm." And he paid over his money to the man, and the man handed him the bottle.

"Imp of the bottle," said Keawe, "I want my fifty dollars back." And sure enough he had scarce said the word before his pocket was as heavy as ever.

"To be sure this is a wonderful bottle," said Keawe.

"And now good-morning to you, my fine fellow, and the devil go with you for me!" said the man.

"Hold on," said Keawe, "I don't want any more of this fun. Here, take your bottle back."

"You have bought it for less than I paid for it," replied the man, rubbing his hands. "It is yours now; and, for my part, I am only concerned to see the back of you." And with that he rang for his Chinese servant, and had Keawe shown out of the house.

Now, when Keawe was in the street, with the bottle under his arm, he began to think. "If all is true about this bottle, I may have made a losing bargain," thinks he. "But perhaps the man was only fooling me." The first thing he did was to count his money; the sum was exact—forty-nine dollars American money, and one Chili piece. "That looks like the truth," said Keawe. "Now I will try another part."

The streets in that part of the city were as clean as a ship's decks, and though it was noon, there were no passengers. Keawe set the bottle in the gutter and walked away. Twice he looked back, and there was the milky, round-bellied bottle where he left it. A third time he looked back, and turned a corner; but he had scarce done so, when something knocked upon his elbow, and behold! It was the long neck sticking up; and as for the round belly, it was jammed into the pocket of his pilot-coat.

"And that looks like the truth," said Keawe.

The next thing he did was to buy a corkscrew in a shop, and go apart into a secret place in the fields. And there he tried to draw the cork, but as often as he put the screw in, out it came again, and the cork as whole as ever.

"This is some new sort of cork," said Keawe, and all at once he began to shake and sweat, for he was afraid of that bottle.

On his way back to the port-side, he saw a shop where a man sold shells and clubs from the wild islands, old heathen deities, old coined money, pictures from China and Japan, and all manner of things that sailors bring in their sea-chests. And here he had an idea. So he went in and offered the bottle for a hundred dollars. The man of the shop laughed at him at first, and offered him five; but, indeed, it was a curious bottle—such glass was never blown in any human glassworks, so prettily the colours shone under the milky white, and so strangely the shadow hovered in the midst; so, after he had disputed awhile after the manner of his kind, the shop-man gave Keawe sixty silver dollars for the thing, and set it on a shelf in the midst of his window.

"Now," said Keawe, "I have sold that for sixty which I bought for fifty—or, to say truth, a little less, because one of my dollars was from Chili. Now I shall know the truth upon another point."

So he went back on board his ship and when he opened his chest, there was the bottle, and had come more quickly than himself. Now Keawe had a mate on board whose name was Lopaka.

"What ails you?" said Lopaka, "that you stare in your chest?"

They were alone in the ship's forecastle, and Keawe bound him to secrecy, and told all.

"This is a very strange affair," said Lopaka; "and I fear you will be in trouble about this bottle. But there is one point very clear—that you are sure of the trouble, and you had better have the profit in the bargain. Make up your mind what you want with it; give the order, and if it is done as you desire, I will buy the bottle myself; for I have an idea of my own to get a schooner, and go trading through the islands."

"That is not my idea," said Keawe; "but to have a beautiful house and garden on the Kona Coast, where I was born, the sun shining in at the door, flowers in the garden, glass in the windows, pictures on the walls, and toys and fine carpets on the tables, for all the world like the house I was in this day—only a story higher, and with balconies all about like the King's palace; and to live there without care and make merry with my friends and relatives."

"Well," said Lopaka, "let us carry it back with us to Hawaii; and if all comes true, as you suppose, I will buy the bottle, as I said, and ask a schooner."

Upon that they were agreed, and it was not long before the ship returned to Honolulu, carrying Keawe and Lopaka, and the bottle. They were scarce come ashore when they met a friend upon the beach, who began at once to condole with Keawe

"I do not know what I am to be condoled about," said Keawe.

"Is it possible you have not heard," said the friend, "your uncle—that good old man—is dead, and your cousin—that beautiful boy—was drowned at sea?"

Keawe was filled with sorrow, and, beginning to weep and to lament, he forgot about the bottle. But Lopaka was thinking to himself, and presently, when Keawe's grief was a little abated, "I have been thinking," said Lopaka. "Had not your uncle lands in Hawaii, in the district of Kau?"

"No," said Keawe, "not in Kau; they are on the mountain-side—a little way south of Hookena."

"These lands will now be yours?" asked Lopaka.

"And so they will," says Keawe, and began again to lament for his relatives.

"No," said Lopaka, "do not lament at present. I have a thought in my mind. How if this should be the doing of the bottle? For here is the place ready for your house."

"If this be so," cried Keawe, "it is a very ill way to serve me by killing my relatives. But it may be, indeed; for it was in just such a station that I saw the house with my mind's eye."

"The house, however, is not yet built," said Lopaka.

"No, nor like to be!" said Keawe; "for though my uncle has some coffee and ava and bananas, it will not be more than will keep me in comfort; and the rest of that land is the black lava."

"Let us go to the lawyer," said Lopaka; "I have still this idea in my mind."

Now, when they came to the lawyer's, it appeared Keawe's uncle had grown monstrous rich in the last days, and there was a fund of money.

"And here is the money for the house!" cried Lopaka.

"If you are thinking of a new house," said the lawyer, "here is the card of a new architect, of whom they tell me great things."

"Better and better!" cried Lopaka. "Here is all made plain for us. Let us continue to obey orders."

So they went to the architect, and he had drawings of houses on his table.

"You want something out of the way," said the architect. "How do you like this?" and he handed a drawing to Keawe.

Now, when Keawe set eyes on the drawing, he cried out aloud, for it was the picture of his thought exactly drawn.

"I am in for this house," thought he. "Little as I like the way it comes to me, I am in for it now, and I may as well take the good along with the evil."

So he told the architect all that he wished, and how he would have that house furnished, and about the pictures on the wall and the knick-knacks on the tables; and he asked the man plainly for how much he would undertake the whole affair.

The architect put many questions, and took his pen and made a computation; and when he had done he named the very sum that Keawe had inherited.

Lopaka and Keawe looked at one another and nodded.

"It is quite clear," thought Keawe, "that I am to have this house, whether or no. It comes from the devil, and I fear I will get little good by that; and of one thing I am sure, I will make no more wishes as long as I have this bottle. But with the house I am saddled, and I may as well take the good along with the evil."

So he made his terms with the architect, and they signed a paper; and Keawe and Lopaka took ship again and sailed to Australia; for it was concluded between them they should not interfere at all, but leave the architect and the bottle imp to build and to adorn that house at their own pleasure.

The voyage was a good voyage, only all the time Keawe was holding in his breath, for he had sworn he would utter no more wishes, and take no more favours from the devil. The time was up when they got back. The architect told them that the house was ready, and Keawe and Lopaka took a passage in the *Hall,* and went down Kona way to view the house, and see if all had been done fitly according to the thought that was in Keawe's mind.

Now the house stood on the mountain-side, visible to ships. Above, the forest ran up into the clouds of rain; below, the black lava fell in cliffs, where the kings of old lay buried. A garden bloomed about that house with every hue of flowers; and there was an orchard of papaia on the one hand and an orchard of herdprint on the other, and right in front, toward the sea, a ship's mast had been rigged up and bore a flag. As for the house, it was three stories high, with great chambers and broad balconies on each. The windows were of glass, so excellent that it was as clear as water and as bright as day. All manner of furniture adorned the chambers. Pictures hung upon the wall in golden frames—pictures of ships, and men fighting, and of the most beautiful women, and of singular places; nowhere in the world are there pictures of so bright a colour as those Keawe found hanging in his house. As for the knick-knacks, they were extraordinarily fine; chiming clocks and musical boxes, little men with nodding heads, books filled with pictures, weapons of price from all quarters of the world, and the most elegant puzzles to entertain the leisure of a solitary man. And as no one would care to live in such chambers, only to walk through and view them, the balconies were made so broad that a whole town might have lived upon them in delight; and Keawe knew not which to prefer, whether the back porch, where you got the land-breeze, and looked upon the orchards and the flowers, or the front balcony, where you could drink the wind of the sea, and look down the steep wall of the mountain and see the *Hall* going by once a week or so between Hookena and the hills of Pele, or the schooners plying up the coast for wood and ava and bananas.

When they had viewed all, Keawe and Lopaka sat on the porch.

"Well," asked Lopaka, "is it all as you designed?"

"Words cannot utter it," said Keawe. "It is better than I dreamed, and I am sick with satisfaction."

"There is but one thing to consider," said Lopaka; "all this may be quite natural, and the bottle imp have nothing whatever to say to it. If I were to buy the bottle, and got no schooner after all, I should have put my hand in the fire for nothing. I gave you my word, I know; but yet I think you would not grudge me one more proof."

"I have sworn I would take no more favours," said Keawe. "I have gone already deep enough."

"This is no favour I am thinking of," replied Lopaka. "It is only to see the imp himself. There is nothing to be gained by that, and so nothing to be ashamed of; and yet, if I once saw him, I should be sure of the whole matter. So indulge me so far, and let me see the imp; and, after that, here is the money in my hand, and I will buy it."

"There is only one thing I am afraid of," said Keawe. "The imp may be very ugly to view; and if you once set eyes upon him you might be very undesirous of the bottle."

"I am a man of my word," said Lopaka. "And here is the money betwixt us."

"Very well," replied Keawe. "I have a curiosity myself. So come, let us have one look at you, Mr. Imp."

Now as soon as that was said, the imp looked out of the bottle, and in again, swift as a lizard; and there sat Keawe and Lopaka turned to stone. The night had quite come, before either found a thought to say or voice to say it with; and then Lopaka pushed the money over and took the bottle.

"I am a man of my word," said he, "and had need to be so, or I would not touch this bottle with my foot. Well, I shall get my schooner and a dollar or two for my pocket; and then I will be rid of this devil as fast as I can. For to tell you the plain truth, the look of him has cast me down."

"Lopaka," said Keawe, "do not you think any worse of me than you can help; I know it is night, and the roads bad, and the pass by the tombs an ill place to go by so late, but I declare since I have seen that little face, I cannot eat or sleep or pray till it is gone from me. I will give you a lantern and a basket to put the bottle in, and any picture or fine thing in all my house that takes your fancy; and be gone at once, and go sleep at Hookena with Nahinu."

"Keawe," said Lopaka, "many a man would take this ill; above all, when I am doing you a turn so friendly, as to keep my word and buy the bottle; and for that matter, the night and the dark, and the way by the tombs, must be all tenfold more dangerous to a man with such a sin upon his conscience, and such a bottle under his arm. But for my part, I am so extremely terrified myself, I have not the heart to blame you. Here I go then; and I pray God you may be happy in your house, and I fortunate with my schooner, and both get to heaven in the end in spite of the devil and his bottle."

So Lopaka went down the mountain; and Keawe stood in his front balcony, and listened to the clink of the horse's shoes, and watched the lantern go shining down the path, and along the cliff of caves where the old dead are buried; and all the time he trembled and clasped his hands, and prayed for his friend, and gave glory to God that he himself was escaped out of that trouble.

But the next day came very brightly, and that new house of his was so delightful to behold that he forgot his terrors. One day followed another, and Keawe dwelt there in perpetual joy. He had his place on the back porch; it was there he ate and lived, and read the stories in the Honolulu newspapers; but when anyone came by they would go in and view the chambers and the pictures. And the fame of the house went far and wide; it was called *Ka-Hale Nui*—the Great House—in all Kona; and sometimes the Bright House, for Keawe kept a Chinaman, who was all day dusting and furbishing; and the glass, and the gilt, and the fine stuffs, and the pictures, shone as bright as the morning. As for Keawe himself, he could not walk in the chambers without singing, his heart was so enlarged; and when ships sailed by upon the sea, he would fly his colours on the mast.

So time went by, until one day Keawe went upon a visit as far as Kailua to certain of his friends. There he was well feasted; and left as soon as he could the next morning, and rode hard, for he was impatient to behold his beautiful house; and, besides, the night then coming on was the night in which the dead of old days go abroad in the sides of Kona; and having already meddled with the devil, he was the more chary of meeting with the dead. A little beyond Honaunau, looking far ahead, he was aware of a woman bathing in the edge of the sea; and she seemed a well-grown girl, but he thought no more of it. Then he saw her white shift flutter as she put it on, and then her red holoku; and by the time he came abreast of her she was done with her toilet, and had come up from the sea, and stood by the track-side in her red holoku, and she was all freshened with the bath, and her eyes shone and were kind. Now Keawe no sooner beheld her than he drew rein.

"I thought I knew everyone in this country," said he. "How comes it that I do not know you?"

"I am Kokua, daughter of Kiano," said the girl, "and I have just returned from Oahu. Who are you?"

"I will tell you who I am in a little," said Keawe, dismounting from his horse, "but not now. For I have a thought in my mind, and if you knew who I was, you might have heard of me, and would not give me a true answer. But tell me, first of all, one thing: Are you married?"

At this Kokua laughed out aloud. "It is you who ask questions," she said. "Are you married yourself?"

"Indeed, Kokua, I am not," replied Keawe, "and never thought to be until this hour. But here is the plain truth. I have met you here at the road-side, and I saw your eyes, which are like the stars, and my heart went to you as swift as a bird. And so now, if you want none of me, say so, and I will go on to my own place; but if you think me no worse than any other young man, say so, too, and I will turn aside to your father's for the night, and to-morrow I will talk with the good man."

Kokua said never a word, but she looked at the sea and laughed.

"Kokua," said Keawe, "if you say nothing, I will take that for the good answer; so let us be stepping to your father's door."

She went on ahead of him, still without speech; only sometimes she glanced back and glanced away again, and she kept the strings of her hat in her mouth.

Now, when they had come to the door, Kiano came out on his veranda, and cried out and welcomed Keawe by name. At that the girl looked over, for the fame of the great house had come to her ears; and, to be sure, it was a great temptation. All that evening they were very merry together; and the girl was as bold as brass under the eyes of her parents, and made a mock of

Keawe, for she had a quick wit. The next day he had a word with Kiano, and found the girl alone.

"Kokua," said he, "you made a mock of me all the evening; and it is still time to bid me go. I would not tell you who I was, because I have so fine a house, and I feared you would think too much of that house and too little of the man that loves you. Now you know all, and if you wish to have seen the last of me, say so at once."

"No," said Kokua; but this time she did not laugh, nor did Keawe ask for more.

This was the wooing of Keawe; things had gone quickly; but so an arrow goes, and the ball of a rifle swifter still, and yet both may strike the target. Things had gone fast, but they had gone far also, and the thought of Keawe rang in the maiden's head; she heard his voice in the breach of the surf upon the lava, and for this young man that she had seen but twice she would have left father and mother and her native islands. As for Keawe himself, his horse flew up the path of the mountain under the cliff of tombs, and the sound of the hoofs, and the sound of Keawe singing to himself for pleasure, echoed in the caverns of the dead. He came to the Bright House, and still he was singing. He sat and ate in the broad balcony, and the Chinaman wondered at his master, to hear how he sang between the mouthfuls. The sun went down into the sea, and the night came; and Keawe walked the balconies by lamplight, high on the mountains, and the voice of his singing startled men on ships.

"Here am I now upon my high place," he said to himself. "Life may be no better; this is the mountain top; and all shelves about me toward the worse. For the first time I will light up the chambers, and bathe in my fine bath with the hot water and the cold, and sleep alone in the bed of my bridal chamber."

So the Chinaman had word, and he must rise from sleep and light the furnaces; and as he wrought below, beside the boilers, he heard his master singing and rejoicing above him in the lighted chambers. When the water began to be hot the Chinaman cried to his master; and Keawe went into the bathroom; and the Chinaman heard him sing as he filled the marble basin; and heard him sing, and the singing broken, as he undressed; until of a sudden, the song ceased. The Chinaman listened, and listened; he called up the house to Keawe to ask if all were well, and Keawe answered him "Yes," and bade him go to bed; but there was no more singing in the Bright House; and all night long, the Chinaman heard his master's feet go round and round the balconies without repose.

Now the truth of it was this: as Keawe undressed for his bath, he spied upon his flesh a patch like a patch of lichen on a rock, and it was then that he stopped singing. For he knew the likeness of that patch, and knew that he was fallen in the Chinese Evil.

Now, it is a sad thing for any man to fall into this sickness. And it would be a sad thing for anyone to leave a house so beautiful and so commodious, and depart from all his friends to the north coast of Molokai between the mighty cliff and the sea-breakers. But what was that to the case of the man Keawe, he who had met his love but yesterday, and won her but that morning, and now saw all his hopes break, in a moment, like a piece of glass?

Awhile he sat upon the edge of the bath; then sprang, with a cry, and ran outside; and to and fro, to and fro, along the balcony, like one despairing.

"Very willingly could I leave Hawaii, the home of my fathers," Keawe was thinking. "Very lightly could I leave my house, the high-placed, the many-windowed, here upon the mountains. Very bravely could I go to Molokai, to Kalaupapa by the cliffs, to live with the smitten and to sleep there, far from my fathers. But what wrong have I done, what sin lies upon my soul, that I should have encountered Kokua coming cool from the sea-water in the evening? Kokua, the soul ensnarer! Kokua, the light of my life! Her may I never wed, her may I look upon no longer, her may I no more handle with my loving hand; and it is for this, it is for you, O Kokua! that I pour my lamentations!"

Now you are to observe what sort of a man Keawe was, for he might have dwelt there in the Bright House for years, and no one been the wiser of his sickness; but he reckoned nothing of that, if he must lose Kokua. And again, he might have wed Kokua even as he was; and so many would have done, because they have the souls of pigs; but Keawe loved the maid manfully, and he would do her no hurt and bring her in no danger.

A little beyond the midst of the night, there came in his mind the recollection of that bottle. He went round to the back porch, and called to memory the day when the devil had looked forth; and at the thought ice ran in his veins.

"A dreadful thing is the bottle," thought Keawe, "and dreadful is the imp, and it is a dreadful thing to risk the flames of hell. But what other hope have I to cure my sickness or to wed Kokua? What!" he thought, "would I beard the devil once, only to get me a house, and not face him again to win Kokua?"

Thereupon he called to mind it was the next day the *Hall* went by on her return to Honolulu. "There must I go first," he thought, "and see Lopaka. For the best hope that I have now is to find that same bottle I was so pleased to be rid of."

Never a wink could he sleep; the food stuck in his throat; but he sent a letter to Kiano, and about the time when the steamer would be coming, rode down beside the cliff of the tombs. It rained; his horse went heavily; he looked up at the black mouths of the caves, and he envied the dead that slept there and were done with trouble; and called to mind how he had galloped by the day before, and was astonished. So he came down to Hookena, and there was all the country gathered for the steamer as usual. In the shed before the store they sat and jested and passed the news; but there was no matter of speech in Keawe's bosom, and he sat in their midst and looked without on the rain falling on the houses, and the surf beating among the rocks, and the sighs arose in his throat.

"Keawe of the Bright House is out of spirits," said one to another. Indeed, and so he was, and little wonder.

Then the *Hall* came, and the whale-boat carried him on board. The after-part of the ship was full of Haoles—whites—who had been to visit the volcano, as their custom is; and the midst was crowded with Kanakas, and the fore-part with wild bulls from Hilo and horses from Kau; but Keawe sat apart from all in his sorrow, and watched for the house of Kiano. There it sat, low upon the shore in the black rocks, and shaded by the coron palms, and there by the door was a red holoku, no greater than a fly, and going to and fro with a fly's busyness. "Ah, queen of my heart," he cried, "I'll venture my dear soul to win you!"

Soon after darkness fell, and the cabins were lit up, and the Haoles sat and played at the cards and drank whiskey as their custom is; but Keawe walked the deck all night; and all the next day, as they steamed under the lea of Maui or of Molokai, he was still pacing to and fro like a wild animal in a menagerie.

Towards evening they passed Diamond Head, and came to the pier of Honolulu. Keawe stepped out among the crowd and began to ask for Lopaka. It seemed he had become the owner of a schooner—none better in the islands—and was gone upon an adventure as far as Pola-Pola or Kahiki; so there was no help to be looked for from Lopaka. Keawe called to mind a friend of his, a lawyer in the town (I must not tell his name), and inquired of him. They said he was grown suddenly rich, and had a fine new house upon Waikiki shore; and this put a thought in Keawe's head, and he called a hack and drove to the lawyer's house.

The house was all brand new, and the trees in the garden no greater than walking-sticks, and the lawyer, when he came, had the air of a man well pleased

"What can I do to serve you?" said the lawyer.

"You are a friend of Lopaka's," replied Keawe, "and Lopaka purchased from me a certain piece of goods that I thought you might enable me to trace."

The lawyer's face became very dark. "I do not profess to misunderstand you, Mr. Keawe," said he, "though this is an ugly business to be stirring in. You may be sure I know nothing, but yet I have a guess, and if you would apply in a certain quarter I think you might have news."

And he named the name of a man, which, again, I had better not repeat. So it was for days, and Keawe went from one to another, finding everywhere new clothes and carriages, and fine new houses and men everywhere in great contentment, although, to be sure, when he hinted at his business their faces would cloud over.

"No doubt I am upon the track," thought Keawe. "These new clothes and carriages are all the gifts of the little imp, and these glad faces are the faces of men who have taken their profit and got rid of the accursed thing in safety. When I see pale cheeks and hear sighing, I shall know that I am near the bottle."

So it befell at last that he was recommended to a Haole in Beritania Street. When he came to the door, about the hour of the evening meal, there were the usual marks of the new house, and the young garden, and the electric light shining in the windows; but when the owner came, a shock of hope and fear ran through Keawe; for here was a young man, white as a corpse, and black about the eyes, the hair shedding from his head, and such a look in his countenance as a man may have when he is waiting for the gallows.

"Here it is, to be sure," thought Keawe, and so with this man he noways veiled his errand. "I am come to buy the bottle," said he.

At the word, the young Haole of Beritania Street reeled against the wall.

"The bottle!" he gasped. "To buy the bottle!" Then he seemed to choke, and seizing Keawe by the arm carried him into a room and poured out wine in two glasses.

"Here is my respects," said Keawe, who had been much about with Haoles in his time. "Yes," he added, "I am come to buy the bottle. What is the price by now?"

At that word the young man let his glass slip through his fingers, and looked upon Keawe like a ghost.

"The price," says he; "the price! You do not know the price?"

"It is for that I am asking you," returned Keawe. "But why are you so much concerned? Is there anything wrong about the price?"

"It has dropped a great deal in value since your time, Mr. Keawe," said the young man stammering.

"Well, well, I shall have the less to pay for it," says Keawe. "How much did it cost you?"

The young man was as white as a sheet. "Two cents," said he.

"What?" cried Keawe, "two cents? Why, then, you can only sell it for one. And he who buys it—" The words died upon Keawe's tongue; he who bought it could never sell it again, the bottle and the bottle imp must abide with him until he died, and when he died must carry him to the red end of hell.

The young man of Beritania Street fell upon his knees. "For God's sake buy it!" he cried. "You can have all my fortune in the bargain. I was mad when I bought it at that price. I had embezzled money at my store; I was lost else; I must have gone to jail."

"Poor creature," said Keawe, "you would risk your soul upon so desperate an adventure, and to avoid the proper punishment of your own disgrace; and you think I could hesitate with love in front of me. Give me the bottle, and the change which I make sure you have all ready. Here is a five-cent piece."

It was as Keawe supposed; the young man had the change ready in a drawer; the bottle changed hands, and Keawe's fingers were no sooner clasped upon the stalk than he had breathed his wish to be a clean man. And, sure enough, when he got home to his room, and stripped himself before a glass, his flesh was whole like an infant's. And here was the strange thing: he had no sooner seen this miracle, than his mind was changed within him, and he cared naught for the Chinese Evil, and little enough for Kokua; and had but the one thought, that here he was bound to the bottle imp for time and for eternity, and had no better hope but to be a cinder forever in the flames of hell. Away ahead of him he saw them blaze with his mind's eye, and his soul shrank, and darkness fell upon the light.

When Keawe came to himself a little, he was aware it was the night when the band played at the hotel. Thither he went, because he feared to be alone; and there, among happy faces, walked to and fro, and heard the tunes go up and down, and saw Berger beat the measure, and all the while he heard the flames crackle, and saw the red fire burning in the bottomless pit. Of a sudden the band played *Hiki-ao-ao;* that was a song that he had sung with Kokua, and at the strain courage returned to him.

"It is done now," he thought, "and once more let me take the good along with the evil."

So it befell that he returned to Hawaii by the first steamer, and as soon as it could be managed he was wedded to Kokua, and carried her up the mountain-side to the Bright House.

Now it was so with these two, that when they were together, Keawe's heart was stilled; but as soon as he was alone he fell into a brooding horror, and heard the flames crackle, and saw the red fire burn in the bottomless pit. The girl, indeed, had come to him wholly; her heart leapt in her side at sight of him, her hand clung to his; and she was so fashioned, from the hair upon her head to the nails upon her toes, that none could see her without joy. She was pleasant in her nature. She had the good word always. Full of song she was, and went to and fro in the Bright House, the brightest thing in its three stories, carolling like the birds. And Keawe beheld and heard her with delight, and then must shrink upon one side, and weep and groan to think upon the price that he had paid for her; and then he must dry his eyes, and wash his face, and go and sit with her on the broad balconies, joining in her songs, and, with a sick spirit, answering her smiles.

There came a day when her feet began to be heavy and her songs more rare; and now it was not Keawe only that would weep apart, but each would sunder from the other and sit in opposite balconies with the whole width of the Bright House betwixt. Keawe was so sunk in his despair, he scarce observed the change, and was only glad he had more hours to sit alone and brood upon his destiny, and was not so frequently condemned to pull a smiling face on a sick heart. But one day, coming softly through the house, he heard the sound of a child sobbing, and there was Kokua rolling her face upon the balcony floor, and weeping like the lost.

"You do well to weep in this house, Kokua," he said. "And yet I would give the head off my body that you (at least) might have been happy."

"Happy!" she cried. "Keawe, when you lived alone in your Bright House, you were the word of the island for a happy man; laughter and song were in your mouth, and your face was as bright as the sunrise. Then you wedded poor Kokua; and the good God knows what is amiss in her—but from that day you have not smiled. Oh!" she cried, "what ails me? I thought I was pretty, and I knew I loved him. What ails me that I throw this cloud upon my husband?"

"Poor Kokua," said Keawe. He sat down by her side, and sought to take her hand; but that she plucked away. "Poor Kokua," he said, again. "My poor child—my pretty. And I had thought all this while to spare you! Well, you shall know all. Then, at least, you will pity poor Keawe; then you will understand how much he loved you in the past—that he dared hell for your possession—and how much he loves you still (the poor condemned one), that he can yet call up a smile when he beholds you."

With that, he told her all, even from the beginning.

"You have done this for me?" she cried. "Ah, well, then what do I care!"—and she clasped and wept upon him.

"Ah, child!" said Keawe, "and yet, when I consider of the fire of hell, I care a good deal!"

"Never tell me," said she; "no man can be lost because he loved Kokua, and no other fault. I tell you, Keawe, I shall save you with these hands, or perish in your company. What! you loved me, and gave your soul, and you think I will not die to save you in return?"

"Ah, my dear! you might die a hundred times, and what difference would that make?" he cried, "except to leave me lonely till the time comes of my damnation?"

"You know nothing," said she. "I was educated in a school in Honolulu; I am no common girl. And I tell you, I shall save my lover. What is this you say about a cent? But all the world is not American. In England they have a piece they call a farthing, which is about half a cent. Ah! sorrow!" she cried, "that makes it scarcely better, for the buyer must be lost, and we shall find none so brave as my Keawe! But, then, there is France; they have a small coin there which they call a centime, and these go five to the cent or thereabout. We could not do better. Come, Keawe, let us go to the French islands; let us go to Tahiti, as fast as ships can bear us. There we have four centimes, three centimes, two centimes, one centime; four possible sales to come and go on; and two of us to push the bargain. Come, my Keawe! kiss me, and banish care. Kokua will defend you."

"Gift of God!" he cried. "I cannot think that God will punish me for desiring aught so good! Be it as you will, then; take me where you please: I put my life and my salvation in your hands."

Early the next day Kokua was about her preparations. She took Keawe's chest that he went with sailoring; and first she put the bottle in a corner; and then packed it with the richest of their clothes and the bravest of the knick-knacks in the house. "For," said she, "we must seem to be rich folks, or who will believe in the bottle?" All the time of her preparation she was as gay as a bird; only when she looked upon Keawe, the tears would spring in her eye, and she must run and kiss him. As for Keawe, a weight was off his soul; now that he had his secret shared, and some hope in front of him, he seemed like a new man, his feet went lightly on the earth, and his breath was good to him again. Yet was terror still at his elbow; and ever and again, as the wind blows out a taper, hope died in him, and he saw the flames toss and the red fire burn in hell.

It was given out in the country they were gone pleasuring to the States, which was thought a strange thing, and yet not so strange as the truth, if any could have guessed it. So they went to Honolulu in the *Hall,* and thence in the *Umatilla* to San Francisco with a crowd of Haoles, and at San Francisco took their passage by the mail brigantine, the *Tropic Bird,* for Papeete, the chief place of the French in the south islands. Thither they came, after a pleasant voyage, on a fair day of the Trade wind, and saw the reef with the surf breaking, and Motuiti with its palms, and the schooner riding withinside, and the white houses of the town low down along the shore among green trees, and overhead the mountains and the clouds of Tahiti, the wise island.

It was judged the most wise to hire a house, which they did accordingly, opposite the British Consul's, to make a great parade of money, and themselves conspicuous with carriages and horses. This it was very easy to do, so long as they had the bottle in their possession; for Kokua was more bold than Keawe, and, whenever she had a mind, called on the imp for twenty or a hundred dollars. At this rate they soon grew to be remarked in the town; and the strangers from Hawaii, their riding and their driving, the fine holokus and the rich lace of Kokua, became the matter of much talk.

They got on well after the first with the Tahitian language, which is indeed like to the Hawaiian, with a change of certain letters; and as soon as they had any freedom of speech, began to push the bottle. You are to consider it was not an easy subject to introduce; it was not easy to persuade people you were in earnest, when you offered to sell them for four centimes the spring of health and riches inexhaustible. It was necessary besides to explain the dangers of the bottle; and either people disbelieved the whole thing and laughed, or they thought the more of the darker part, became overcast with gravity, and drew away from Keawe and Kokua, as from persons who had dealings with the devil. So far from gaining ground, these two began to find they were avoided in the town; the children ran away from them screaming, a thing intolerable to Kokua; Catholics crossed themselves as they went by; and all persons began with one accord to disengage themselves from their advances.

Depression fell upon their spirits. They would sit at night in their new house, after a day's weariness, and not exchange one word, or the silence would be broken by Kokua bursting suddenly into sobs. Sometimes they would pray together; sometimes they would have the bottle out upon the floor, and sit all evening watching how the shadow hovered in the midst. At such times they would be afraid to go to rest. It was long ere slumber came to them, and, if either dozed off, it would be to wake and find the other silently weeping in the dark, or, perhaps, to wake alone, the other having fled from the house and the neighbourhood of that bottle, to pace under the bananas in the little garden, or to wander on the beach by moonlight.

One night it was so when Kokua awoke. Keawe was gone. She felt in the bed and his place was cold. Then fear fell upon her, and she sat up in bed. A little moonshine filtered through the shutters. The room was bright, and she could spy the bottle on the floor. Outside it blew high, the great trees of the avenue cried aloud, and the fallen leaves rattled in the veranda. In the midst of this Kokua was aware of another sound; whether of a beast or of a man she could scarce tell, but it was as sad as death, and cut her to the soul. Softly she arose, set the door ajar, and looked forth into the moonlit yard.

There, under the bananas, lay Keawe, his mouth in the dust, and as he lay he moaned.

It was Kokua's first thought to run forward and console him; her second potently withheld her. Keawe had borne himself before his wife like a brave man; it became her little in the hour of weakness to intrude upon his shame. With the thought she drew back into the house.

"Heaven," she thought, "how careless have I been—how weak! It is he, not I, that stands in this eternal peril; it was he, not I, that took the curse upon his soul. It is for my sake, and for the love of a creature of so little worth and such poor help, that he now beholds so close to him the flames of hell—ay, and smells the smoke of it, lying without there in the wind and moonlight. Am I so dull of spirit that never till now I have surmised my duty, or have I seen it before and turned aside? But now, at least, I take up my soul in both the hands of my affection; now I say farewell to the white steps of heaven and the waiting faces of my friends. A love for a love, and let mine be equalled with Keawe's! A soul for a soul, and be it mine to perish!"

She was a deft woman with her hands, and was soon apparelled. She took in her hands the change—the precious centimes they kept ever at their side; for this coin is little used, and they had made provision at a Government office. When she was forth in the avenue clouds came on the wind, and the moon was blackened. The town slept, and she knew not whither to turn till she heard one coughing in the shadow of the trees.

"Old man," said Kokua, "what do you here abroad in the cold night?"

The old man could scarce express himself for coughing, but she made out that he was old and poor, and a stranger in the island.

"Will you do me a service?" said Kokua. "As one stranger to another, and as an old man to a young woman, will you help a daughter of Hawaii?"

"Ah," said the old man. "So you are the witch from the eight islands, and even my old soul you seek to entangle. But I have heard of you, and defy your wickedness."

"Sit down here," said Kokua, "and let me tell you a tale." And she told him the story of Keawe from the beginning to the end.

"And now," said she, "I am his wife, whom he bought with his soul's welfare. And what should I do? If I went to him myself and offered to buy it, he would refuse. But if you go, he will sell it eagerly; I will await you here; you will buy it for four centimes, and I will buy it again for three. And the Lord strengthen a poor girl!"

"If you meant falsely," said the old man, "I think God would strike you dead."

"He would!" cried Kokua. "Be sure he would. I could not be so treacherous—God would not suffer it."

"Give me the four centimes and await me here," said the old man.

Now, when Kokua stood alone in the street, her spirit died. The wind roared in the trees, and it seemed to her the rushing of the flames of hell; the shadows tossed in the light of the street lamp, and they seemed to her the snatching hands of evil ones. If she had had the strength, she must have run away, and if she had had the breath she must have screamed aloud; but, in truth, she could do neither, and stood and trembled in the avenue, like an affrighted child.

Then she saw the old man returning, and he had the bottle in his hand.

"I have done your bidding," said he. "I left your husband weeping like a child; to-night he will sleep easy." And he held the bottle forth.

"Before you give it me," Kokua panted, "take the good with the evil—ask to be delivered from your cough."

"I am an old man," replied the other, "and too near the gate of the grave to take a favour from the devil. But what is this? Why do you not take the bottle? Do you hesitate?"

"Not hesitate!" cried Kokua. "I am only weak. Give me a moment. It is my hand resists, my flesh shrinks back from the accursed thing. One moment only!"

The old man looked upon Kokua kindly. "Poor child!" said he, "you fear; your soul misgives you. Well, let me keep it. I am old, and can never more be happy in this world, and as for the next—"

"Give it me!" gasped Kokua. "There is your money. Do you think I am so base as that? Give me the bottle."

"God bless you, child," said the old man.

Kokua concealed the bottle under her holoku, said farewell to the old man, and walked off along the avenue, she cared not whither. For all roads were now the same to her, and led equally to hell. Sometimes she walked, and sometimes ran; sometimes she screamed out loud in the night, and sometimes lay by the wayside in the dust and wept. All that she had heard of hell came back to her; she saw the flames blaze, and she smelt the smoke, and her flesh withered on the coals.

Near day she came to her mind again, and returned to the house. It was even as the old man said—Keawe slumbered like a child. Kokua stood and gazed upon his face.

"Now, my husband," said she, "it is your turn to sleep. When you wake it will be your turn to sing and laugh. But for poor Kokua, alas! that meant no evil—for poor Kokua no more sleep, no more singing, no more delight, whether in earth or Heaven."

With that she lay down in the bed by his side, and her misery was so extreme that she fell in a deep slumber instantly.

Late in the morning her husband woke her and gave her the good news. It seemed he was silly with delight, for he paid no heed to her distress, ill though she dissembled it. The words stuck in her mouth, it mattered not; Keawe did the speaking. She ate not a bite, but who was to observe it? for Keawe cleared the dish. Kokua saw and heard him, like some strange thing in a dream; there were times when she forgot or doubted, and put her hands to her brow; to know herself doomed and hear her husband babble, seemed so monstrous.

All the while Keawe was eating and talking, and planning the time of their return, and thanking her for saving him, and fondling her, and calling her the true helper after all. He laughed at the old man that was fool enough to buy that bottle.

"A worthy old man he seemed," Keawe said. "But no one can judge by appearances. For why did the old reprobate require the bottle?"

"My husband," said Kokua, humbly, "his purpose may have been good."

Keawe laughed like an angry man.

"Fiddle-de-dee!" cried Keawe. "An old rogue, I tell you; and an old ass to boot. For the bottle was hard enough to sell at four centimes; and at three it will be quite impossible. The margin is not broad enough, the thing begins to smell of scorching—brrr!" said he, and shuddered. "It is true I bought it myself at a cent, when I knew not there were smaller coins. I was a fool for my pains; there will never be found another: and whoever has that bottle now will carry it to the pit."

"O my husband!" said Kokua. "Is it not a terrible thing to save oneself by the eternal ruin of another? It seems to me I could not laugh. I would be humbled. I would be filled with melancholy. I would pray for the poor holder."

Then Keawe, because he felt the truth of what she said, grew the more angry. "Heighty-teighty!" cried he. "You may be filled with melancholy if you please. It is not the mind of a good wife. If you thought at all of me, you would sit shamed."

Thereupon he went out, and Kokua was alone.

What chance had she to sell that bottle at two centimes? None, she perceived. And if she had any, here was her husband hurrying her away to a country where there was nothing lower than a cent. And here—on the morrow of her sacrifice—was her husband leaving her and blaming her.

She would not even try to profit by what time she had, but sat in the house, and now had the bottle out and viewed it with unutterable fear, and now, with loathing, hid it out of sight.

By and by, Keawe came back, and would have her take a drive.

"My husband, I am ill," she said. "I am out of heart. Excuse me, I can take no pleasure."

Then was Keawe more wroth than ever. With her, because he thought she was brooding over the case of the old man; and with himself, because he thought she was right, and was ashamed to be so happy.

"This is your truth," cried he, "and this your affection! Your husband is just saved from eternal ruin, which he encountered for the love of you—and you can take no pleasure! Kokua, you have a disloyal heart."

He went forth again furious, and wandered in the town all day. He met friends, and drank with them; they hired a carriage and drove into the country, and there drank again. All the time Keawe was ill at ease, because he was taking this pastime while his wife was sad, and because he knew in his heart that she was more right than he; and the knowledge made him drink the deeper.

Now there was an old brutal Haole drinking with him, one that had been a boatswain of a whaler—a runaway, a digger in gold mines, a convict in prisons. He had a low mind and a foul mouth; he loved to drink and to see others drunken; and he pressed the glass upon Keawe. Soon there was no more money in the company.

"Here, you!" says the boatswain, "you are rich, you have been always saying. You have a bottle or some foolishness."

"Yes," says Keawe, "I am rich; I will go back and get some money from my wife, who keeps it."

"That's a bad idea, mate," said the boatswain. "Never you trust a petticoat with dollars. They're all as false as water; you keep an eye on her."

Now, this word struck in Keawe's mind; for he was muddled with what he had been drinking.

"I should not wonder but she was false, indeed," thought he. "Why else should she be so cast down at my release? But I will show her I am not the man to be fooled. I will catch her in the act."

Accordingly, when they were back in town, Keawe bade the boatswain wait for him at the corner, by the old calaboose, and went forward up the avenue alone to the door of his house. The night had come again; there was a light within, but never a sound; and Keawe crept about the corner, opened the back door softly, and looked in.

There was Kokua on the floor, the lamp at her side; before her was a milk-white bottle, with a round belly and a long neck; and as she viewed it, Kokua wrung her hands.

A long time Keawe stood and looked in the doorway. At first he was struck stupid; and then fear fell upon him that the bargain had been made amiss, and the bottle had come back to him as it came at San Francisco; and at that his knees were loosened, and the fumes of the wine departed from his head like mists off a river in the morning. And then he had another thought; and it was a strange one, that made his cheeks to burn.

"I must make sure of this," thought he.

So he closed the door, and went softly round the corner again, and then came noisily in, as though he were but now returned. And, lo! by the time he opened the front door no bottle was to be seen; and Kokua sat in a chair and started up like one awakened out of sleep.

"I have been drinking all day and making merry," said Keawe. "I have been with good companions, and now I only come back for money, and return to drink and carouse with them again."

Both his face and voice were as stern as judgment, but Kokua was too troubled to observe.

"You do well to use your own, my husband," said she, and her words trembled.

"Oh, I do well in all things," said Keawe, and he went straight to the chest and took out money. But he looked besides in the corner where they kept the bottle, and there was no bottle there.

At that the chest heaved upon the floor like a sea-billow, and the house span about him like a wreath of smoke, for he saw he was lost now, and there was no escape. "It is what I feared," he thought. "It is she who has bought it."

And then he came to himself a little and rose up; but the sweat streamed on his face as thick as the rain and as cold as the well-water.

"Kokua," said he, "I said to you to-day what ill became me. Now I return to carouse with my jolly companions," and at that he laughed a little quietly. "I will take more pleasure in the cup if you forgive me."

She clasped his knees in a moment; she kissed his knees with flowing tears.

"Oh," she cried, "I asked but a kind word!"

"Let us never one think hardly of the other," said Keawe, and was gone out of the house.

Now, the money that Keawe had taken was only some of that store of centime pieces they had laid in at their arrival. It was very sure he had no mind to be drinking. His wife had given her soul for him, now he must give his for hers; no other thought was in the world with him.

At the corner, by the old calaboose, there was the boatswain waiting.

"My wife has the bottle," said Keawe, "and, unless you help me to recover it, there can be no more money and no more liquor to-night."

"You do not mean to say you are serious about that bottle?" cried the boatswain.

"There is the lamp," said Keawe. "Do I look as if I was jesting?"

"That is so," said the boatswain. "You look as serious as a ghost."

"Well, then," said Keawe, "here are two centimes; you must go to my wife in the house, and offer her these for the bottle, which (if I am not much mistaken) she will give you instantly. Bring it to me here, and I will buy it back from you for one; for that is the law with this bottle, that it still must be sold for a less sum. But whatever you do, never breathe a word to her that you have come from me."

"Mate, I wonder are you making a fool of me?" asked the boatswain.

"It will do you no harm if I am," returned Keawe.

"That is so, mate," said the boatswain.

"And if you doubt me," added Keawe, "you can try. As soon as you are clear of the house, wish to have your pocket full of money, or a bottle of the best rum, or what you please, and you will see the virtue of the thing."

"Very well, Kanaka," says the boatswain. "I will try; but if you are having your fun out of me, I will take my fun out of you with a belaying-pin."

So the whaler-man went off up the avenue; and Keawe stood and waited. It was near the same spot where Kokua had waited the night before; but Keawe was more resolved, and never faltered in his purpose; only his soul was bitter with despair.

It seemed a long time he had to wait before he heard a voice singing in the darkness of the avenue. He knew the voice to be the boatswain's; but it was strange how drunken it appeared upon a sudden.

Next, the man himself came stumbling into the light of the lamp. He had the devil's bottle buttoned in his coat; another bottle was in his hand; and even as he came in view he raised it to his mouth and drank.

"You have it," said Keawe. "I see that."

"Hands off!" cried the boatswain, jumping back. "Take a step near me, and I'll smash your mouth. You thought you could make a cat's paw of me, did you?"

"What do you mean?" cried Keawe.

"Mean?" cried the boatswain. "This is a pretty good bottle, this is; that's what I mean. How I got it for two centimes I can't make out; but I'm sure you shan't have it for one."

"You mean you won't sell?" gasped Keawe.

"No, sir!" cried the boatswain. "But I'll give you a drink of the rum, if you like."

"I tell you," said Keawe, "the man who has that bottle goes to hell."

"I reckon I'm going anyway," returned the sailor; "and this bottle's the best thing to go with I've struck yet. No, sir!" he cried again, "this is my bottle now, and you can go and fish for another."

"Can this be true?" Keawe cried. "For your own sake, I beseech you, sell it me!"

"I don't value any of your talk," replied the boatswain. "You thought I was a flat; now you see I'm not; and there's an end. If you won't have a swallow of the rum, I'll have one myself. Here's your health, and good-night to you!"

So off he went down the avenue towards town, and there goes the bottle out of the story.

But Keawe ran to Kokua light as the wind; and great was their joy that night; and great, since then, has been the peace of all their days in the Bright House.

K *is for* Kraken

Over the centuries, "kraken" has become an almost generic name for immense monsters of the ocean depths, including giant squid. American writer Morgan Robertson (1851–1916) specialized in tales of the sea, some of them borderline fantasy and science fiction, and in this one, first published in the January 1913 issue of *The New Story* magazine, credible scientific description of the sea monster does not dispel its awesome frightfulness.

MORGAN ROBERTSON

From the Darkness and the Depths

I had known him for a painter of renown—a master of his art, whose pictures, which sold for high prices, adorned museums, the parlors of the rich, and, when on exhibition, were hung low and conspicuous. Also, I knew him for an expert photographer—an "art photographer," as they say, one who dealt with this branch of industry as a fad, an amusement, and who produced pictures that in composition, light, and shade rivaled his productions with the brush.

His cameras were the best that the market could supply, yet he was able, from his knowledge of optics and chemistry, to improve them for his own uses far beyond the ability of the makers. His studio was filled with examples of his work, and his mind was stocked with information and opinions on all subjects ranging from international policies to the servant-girl problem.

He was a man of the world, gentlemanly and successful, about sixty years old, kindly and gracious of manner, and out of this kindliness and graciousness had granted me the compliment of his friendship, and access to his studio whenever I felt like calling upon him.

Yet it never occurred to me that the wonderful and technically correct marines hanging on his walls were due to anything but the artist's conscientious study of his subject, and only his casual mispronunciation of the word "leeward," which landsmen pronounce as spelled, but which rolls off the tongue of a sailor, be he former dock rat or naval officer, as "looward," and his giving the long sounds to the vowels of the words "patent" and "tackle," that induced me to ask if he had ever been to sea.

"Why, yes," he answered. "Until I was thirty I had no higher ambition than to become a skipper of some craft; but I never achieved it. The best I did was to sign first mate for one voyage—and that one was my last. It was on that voyage that I learned something of the mysterious properties of light, and it made me a photographer, then an artist. You are wrong when you say that a searchlight cannot penetrate fog."

"But it has been tried," I remonstrated.

"With ordinary light. Yes, of course, subject to refraction, reflection, and absorption by the millions of minute globules of water it encounters."

We had been discussing the wreck of the *Titanic*, the most terrible marine disaster of history, the blunders of construction and management, and the later proposed improvements as to the lowering of boats and the location of ice in a fog.

Among these considerations was also the plan of carrying a powerful searchlight whose beam would illumine the path of a twenty-knot liner and render objects visible in time to avoid them. In regard to this I had contended that a searchlight could not penetrate fog, and if it could, would do as much harm as good by blinding and confusing the watch officers and lookouts on other craft.

"But what other kind of light can be used?" I asked, in answer to his mention of ordinary light.

"Invisible light," he answered. "I do not mean the Röntgen ray, nor the emanation from radium, both of which are invisible, but neither of which is light, in that neither can be reflected nor refracted. Both will penetrate many different kinds of matter, but it needs reflection or refraction to make visible an object on which it impinges. Understand?"

"Hardly," I answered dubiously. "What kind of visible light is there, if not radium or the Röntgen ray? You can photograph with either, can't you?"

"Yes, but to see what you have photographed you must develop the film. And there is no time for that aboard a fast steamer running through the ice and the fog. No, it is mere theory, but I have an idea that the ultraviolet light—the actinic rays beyond the violet end of the spectrum, you know—will penetrate fog to a great distance, and in spite of its higher refractive power, which would distort and magnify an object, it is better than nothing."

"But what makes you think that it will penetrate fog?" I queried. "And if it is invisible itself, how will it illumine an object?"

"As to your first question," he answered, with a smile, "it is well known to surgeons that ultraviolet light will penetrate the human body to the depth of an inch, while the visible rays are reflected at the surface. And it has been known to photographers for fifty years that this light—easily isolated by dispersion through prisms—will act on a sensitized plate in an utterly dark room."

"Granted," I said. "But how about the second question? How can you see by this light?"

"There you have me," he answered. "It will need a quicker development than any now known to photography—a traveling film, for instance, that will show the picture of an iceberg or a ship before it is too late to avoid it—a traveling film sensitized by a quicker acting chemical than any now used."

"Why not puzzle it out?" I asked. "It would be a wonderful invention."

"I am too old," he answered dreamily. "My life work is about done. But other and younger men will take it up. We have made great strides in optics. The moving picture is a fact. Colored photographs are possible. The ultraviolet microscope shows us objects hitherto invisible because smaller than the wave length of visible light. We shall ultimately use this light to see through opaque objects. We shall see colors never imagined by the human mind, but which have existed since the beginning of light.

"We shall see new hues in the sunset, in the rainbow, in the flowers and foliage of forest and field. We may possibly see creatures in the air above never seen before.

"We shall certainly see creatures from the depths of the sea, where visible light cannot reach—creatures whose substance is of such a nature that it will not respond to the light it has never been exposed to—a substance which is absolutely transparent because it will not absorb, and appear black; will not reflect, and show a color of some kind; and will not refract, and distort objects seen through it."

"What!" I exclaimed. "Do you think there are invisible creatures?"

He looked gravely at me for a moment, then said: "You know that there are sounds that are inaudible to the human ear because of their too rapid vibration, others that are audible to some, but not to all. There are men who cannot hear the chirp of a cricket, the tweet of a bird, or the creaking of a wagon wheel.

"You know that there are electric currents much stronger in voltage than is necessary to kill us, but of wave frequency so rapid that the human tissue will not respond, and we can receive such currents without a shock. And *I know*"—he spoke with vehemence—"that there are creatures in the deep sea of color invisible to the human eye, for I have not only felt such a creature, but seen its photograph taken by the ultraviolet light."

"Tell me," I asked breathlessly. "Creatures solid, but invisible?"

"Creatures solid, and invisible because absolutely transparent. It is long since I have told the yarn. People would not believe me, and it was so horrible an experience that I have tried to forget it. However, if you care for it, and are willing to lose your sleep to-night, I'll give it to you."

He reached for a pipe, filled it, and began to smoke; and as he smoked and talked, some of the glamor and polish of the successful artist and clubman left him. He was an old sailor, spinning a yarn.

"It was about thirty years ago," he began, "or, to be explicit, twenty-nine years this coming August, at the time of the great Java earthquake. You've heard of it—how it killed seventy thousand people, thirty thousand of whom were drowned by the tidal wave.

"It was a curious phenomenon; Krakatoa Island, a huge conical mountain rising from the bottom of Sunda Strait, went out of existence, while in Java a mountain chain was leveled, and up from the bowels of the earth came an iceberg—as you might call it—that floated a hundred miles on a stream of molten lava before melting.

"I was not there; I was two hundred miles to the sou'west, first mate of one of those old-fashioned, soft-pine, centerboard barkentines—three sticks the same length, you know—with the mainmast stepped on the port side of the keel to make room for the centerboard—a craft that would neither stay, nor wear, nor scud, nor heave to, like a decent vessel.

"But she had several advantages; she was new, and well painted, deck, top-sides, and bottom. Hence her light timbers and planking were not water-soaked. She was fastened with 'trunnels,' not spikes and bolts, and hemp rigged.

"Perhaps there was not a hundredweight of iron aboard of her, while her hemp rigging, though heavier than water, was lighter than wire rope, and so, when we were hit by the back wash of that tidal wave, we did not sink, even though butts were started from one end to the other of the flimsy hull, and all hatches were ripped off.

"I have called it the back wash, yet we may have had a tidal wave of our own; for, though we had no knowledge of the frightful catastrophe at Java, still there had been for days several submarine earthquakes all about us, sending fountains of water, steam bubbles, and mud from the sea bed into the air.

"As the soundings were over two thousand fathoms in that neighborhood, you can imagine the seismic forces at work beneath us. There had been no wind for days, and no sea, except the agitation caused by the upheavals. The sky was a dull mud color, and the sun looked like nothing but a dark, red ball, rising day by day in the east, to move overhead and set in the west. The air was hot, sultry, and stifling, and I had difficulty in keeping the men—a big crew—at work.

"The conditions would try anybody's temper, and I had my own troubles. There was a passenger on board, a big, fat, highly educated German—a scientist and explorer—whom we had taken aboard at some little town on the West Australian coast, and who was to leave us at Batavia, where he could catch a steamer for Germany.

"He had a whole laboratory with him, with scientific instruments that I didn't know the names of, with maps he had made, stuffed beasts and birds he had killed, and a few live ones which he kept in cages and attended to himself in the empty hold; for we were flying light, you know, without even ballast aboard, and bound to Batavia for a cargo.

"It was after a few eruptions from the bottom of the sea that he got to be a nuisance; he was keenly interested in the strange dead fish and nondescript creatures that had been thrown up. He declared them new, unknown to science, and wore out my patience with entreaties to haul them aboard for examination and classification.

"I obliged him for a time, until the decks stank with dead fish, and the men got mutinous. Then I refused to advance the interests of science any farther, and, in spite of his excitement and pleadings, refused to litter the decks any more. But he got all he wanted of the unclassified and unknown before long.

"Tidal wave, you know, is a name we give to any big wave, and it has no necessary connection with the tides. It may be the big third wave of a series—just a little bigger than usual; it may be the ninth, tenth, and eleventh waves merged into one huge comber by uneven wind pressure; it may be the back wash from an earthquake that depresses the nearest coast, and it may be—as I think it was in our case—a wave sent out by an upheaval from the sea bed. At any rate, we got it, and we got it just after a tremendous spouting of water and mud, and a thick cloud of steam on the northern horizon.

"We saw a seeming rise to the horizon, as though caused by refraction, but which soon eliminated refraction as a cause by its becoming visible in its details—its streaks of water and mud, its irregular upper edge, the occasional combers that appeared on this edge, and the terrific speed of its approach. It was a wave, nothing else, and coming at forty knots at least.

"There was little that we could do; there was no wind, and we headed about west, showing our broadside; yet I got the men at the downhauls, clewlines, and stripping lines of the lighter kites; but before a man could leave the deck to furl, that moving mountain hit us, and buried us on our beam ends just as I had time to sing out: 'Lash yourselves, every man.'

"Then I needed to think of my own safety and passed a turn of the mizzen gaff-topsail downhaul about me, belaying to a pin as the cataclysm hit us. For the next two minutes—although it seemed an hour, I did not speak, nor breathe, nor think, unless my instinctive grip on the turns of the downhaul on the pin may have been an index of thought. I was under water; there was roaring in my ears, pain in my lungs, and terror in my heart.

"Then there came a lessening of the turmoil, a momentary quiet, and I roused up, to find the craft floating on her side, about a third out of water, but apt to turn bottom up at any moment from the weight of the water-soaked gear and canvas, which will sink, you know, when wet.

"I was hanging in my bight of rope from a belaying pin, my feet clear of the perpendicular deck, and my ears tortured by the sound of men overboard crying for help—men who had not lashed themselves. Among them I knew was the skipper, a mild-mannered little fellow, and the second mate, an incompetent tough from Portsmouth, who had caused me lots of trouble by his abuse of the men and his depending upon me to stand by him.

"Nothing could be done for them; they were adrift on the back wall of a moving mountain that towered thirty degrees above the horizon to port; and another moving mountain, as big as the first, was coming on from starboard—caused by the tumble into the sea of the uplifted water.

"Did you ever fall overboard in a full suit of clothes? If you did, you know the mighty exercise of strength required to climb out. I was a strong, healthy man at the time, but never in my life was I so tested. I finally got a grip on the belaying pin and rested; then, with an effort that caused me physical pain, I got my right foot up to the pinrail and rested again; then, perhaps more by mental strength than physical—for I loved life and wanted to live—I hooked my right foot over the rail, reached higher on the rope, rested again, and finally hove myself up to the mizzen rigging, where I sat for a few moments to get my breath, and think, and look around.

"Forward, I saw men who had lashed themselves to the starboard rail, and they were struggling, as I had struggled, to get up to the horizontal side of the vessel. They succeeded, but at the time I had no use for them. Sailors will obey orders, if they understand the orders, but this was an exigency outside the realm of mere seamanship.

"Men were drowning off to port; men, like myself, were climbing up to temporary safety afforded by the topsides of a craft on her beam ends; and aft, in the alleyway, was the German professor, unlashed, but safe and secure in his narrow confines, one leg through a cabin window, and both hands gripping the rail, while he bellowed like a bull, not for himself, however—but for his menagerie in the empty hold.

"There was small chance for the brutes—smaller than for ourselves, left on the upper rail of an over-turned craft, and still smaller than the chance of the poor devils off to port, some of whom had gripped the half-submerged top-hamper, and were calling for help.

"We could not help them; she was a Yankee craft, and there was not a life buoy or belt on board; and who, with another big wave coming, would swim down to looward with a line?

"Landsmen, especially women and boys, have often asked me why a wooden ship, filled with water, sinks, even though not weighted with cargo. Some sailors have pondered over it, too, knowing that a small boat, built of wood, and fastened with nails, will float if water-logged.

"But the answer is simple. Most big craft are built of oak or hard pine, and fastened together with iron spikes and bolts—sixty tons at least to a three-hundred-ton schooner. After a year or two this hard, heavy wood becomes water-soaked, and, with the iron bolts and spikes, is heavier than water, and will sink when the hold is flooded.

"This craft of ours was like a small boat—built of soft light wood, with trunnels instead of bolts, and no iron on board except the anchors and one capstan. As a result, though ripped, twisted, broken, and disintegrated, she still floated even on her beam ends.

"But the soaked hemp rigging and canvas might be enough to drag the craft down, and with this fear in my mind I acted quickly. Singing out to the men to hang on, I made my way aft to where we had an ax, lodged in its beckets on the after house. With this I attacked the mizzen lanyards, cutting everything clear, then climbed forward to the main.

"Hard as I worked I had barely cut the last lanyard when that second wave loomed up and crashed down on us. I just had time to slip into the bight of a rope, and save myself; but I had to give up the ax; it slipped from my hands and slid down to the port scuppers.

"That second wave, in its effect, was about the same as the first, except that it righted the craft. We were buried, choked, and half drowned; but when the wave had passed on, the main and mizzenmasts, unsupported by the rigging that I had cut away, snapped cleanly about three feet above the deck, and the broad, flat-bottomed craft straightened up, lifting the weight of the foremast and its gear, and lay on an even keel, with foresail, staysail, and jib set, the fore gaff-topsail, flying jib, and jib-topsail clewed down and the wreck of the masts bumping against the port side.

"We floated, but with the hold full of water, and four feet of it on deck amidships that surged from one rail to the other as the craft rolled, pouring over and coming back. All hatches were ripped off, and our three boats were carried away from their chocks on the house.

"Six men were clearing themselves from their lashings at the fore rigging, and three more, who had gone overboard with the first sea, and had caught the upper gear to be lifted as the craft righted, were coming down, while the professor still declaimed from the alley.

" 'Hang on all,' I yelled; 'there's another sea coming.'

"It came, but passed over us without doing any more damage, and though a fourth, fifth, and sixth followed, each was of lesser force than the last, and finally it was safe to leave the rail and wade about, though we still rolled rails under in what was left of the turmoil.

"Luckily, there was no wind, though I never understood why, for earthquakes are usually accompanied by squalls. However, even with wind, our canvas would have been no use to us; for, waterlogged as we were, we couldn't have made a knot an hour, nor could we have steered, even with all sail set. All we could hope for was the appearance of some craft that would tow the ripped and shivered hull to port, or at least take us off.

"So, while I searched for the ax, and the professor searched into the depths under the main hatch for signs of his menagerie—all drowned, surely—the remnant of the crew lowered the foresail and jibs, stowing them as best they could.

"I found the ax, and found it just in time; for I was attacked by what could have been nothing but a small-sized sea serpent, that had been hove up to the surface and washed aboard us. It was only about six feet long, but it had a mouth like a bulldog, and a row of spikes along its back that could have sawed a man's leg off.

"I managed to kill it before it harmed me, and chucked it overboard against the protests of the professor, who averred that I took no interest in science.

" 'No, I don't,' I said to him. 'I've other things to think of. And you, too. You'd better go below and clean up your instruments, or you'll find them ruined by salt water.'

"He looked sorrowfully and reproachfully at me, and started to wade aft; but he halted at the forward companion, and turned, for a scream of agony rang out from the forecastle deck, where the men were coming in from the jibs, and I saw one of them writhing on his back, apparently in a fit, while the others stood wonderingly around.

"The forecastle deck was just out of water, and there was no wash; but in spite of this, the wriggling, screaming man slid head-first along the break and plunged into the water on the main deck.

"I scrambled forward, still carrying the ax, and the men tumbled down into the water after the man; but we could not get near him. We could see him under water, feebly moving, but not swimming; and yet he shot this way and that faster than a man ever swam; and once, as he passed near me, I noticed a gaping wound in his neck, from which the blood was flowing in a stream—a stream like a current, which did not mix with the water and discolor it.

"Soon his movements ceased, and I waded toward him; but he shot swiftly away from me, and I did not follow, for something cold, slimy, and firm touched my hand—something in the water, but which I could not see.

"I floundered back, still holding the ax, and sang out to the men to keep away from the dead man; for he was surely dead by now. He lay close to the break of the topgallant forecastle, on the starboard side; and as the men mustered around me I gave one my ax, told the rest to secure others, and to chop away the useless wreck pounding our port side—useless because it was past all seamanship to patch up that basketlike hull, pump it out, and raise jury rigging.

"While they were doing it, I secured a long pike pole from its beckets, and, joined by the professor, cautiously approached the body prodding ahead of me.

"As I neared the dead man, the pike pole was suddenly torn from my grasp, one end sank to the deck, while the other raised above the water; then it slid upward, fell, and floated close to me. I seized it again and turned to the professor.

" 'What do you make of this, Herr Smidt?' I asked. 'There is something down there that we cannot see—something that killed that man. See the blood?'

"He peered closely at the dead man, who looked curiously distorted and shrunken, four feet under water. But the blood no longer was a thin stream issuing from his neck; it was gathered into a misshapen mass about two feet away from his neck.

" 'Nonsense,' he answered. 'Something alive which we cannot see is contrary to all laws of physics. Der man must have fallen und hurt himself, which accounts for der bleeding. Den he drowned in der water. Do you see?—mine Gott! What iss?'

"He suddenly went under water himself, and dropping the pike pole, I grabbed him by the collar and braced myself. Something was pulling him away from me, but I managed to get his head out, and he spluttered:

" 'Help! Holdt on to me. Something haf my right foot.'

" 'Lend a hand here,' I yelled to the men, and a few joined me, grabbing him by his clothing. Together we pulled against the invisible force, and finally all of us went backward, professor and all, nearly to drown ourselves before regaining our feet. Then, as the agitated water smoothed, I distinctly saw the mass of red move slowly forward and disappear in the darkness under the forecastle deck.

" 'You were right, mine friend,' said the professor, who, in spite of his experience, held his nerve. 'Dere is something invisible in der water—something dangerous, something which violates all laws of physics und optics. Oh, mine foot, how it hurts!'

" 'Get aft,' I answered, 'and find out what ails it. And you fellows,' I added to the men, 'keep away from the forecastle deck. Whatever it is, it has gone under it.'

"Then I grabbed the pike pole again, cautiously hooked the barb into the dead man's clothing, and, assisted by the men, pulled him aft to the poop, where the professor had preceded, and was examining his ankle. There was a big, red wale around it, in the middle of which was a huge blood blister. He pricked it with his knife, then rearranged his stocking and joined us as we lifted the body.

" 'Great God, sir!' exclaimed big Bill, the bosun. 'Is that Frank? I wouldn't know him.'

"Frank, the dead man, had been strong, robust, and full-blooded. But he bore no resemblance to his living self. He lay there, shrunken, shortened, and changed, a look of agony on his emaciated face, and his hands clenched—not extended like those of one drowned.

" 'I thought drowned men swelled up,' ventured one of the men.

" 'He was not drowned,' said Herr Smidt. 'He was sucked dry, like a lemon. Perhaps in his whole body there is not an ounce of blood, nor lymph, nor fluid of any kind.'

"I secured an iron belaying pin, tucked it inside his shirt, and we hove him overboard at once; for, in the presence of this horror, we were not in the mood for a burial service. There we were, eleven men on a waterlogged hulk, adrift on a heaving, greasy sea, with a dark-red sun showing through a muddy sky above, and an invisible *thing* forward that might seize any of us at any moment it chose, in the water or out; for Frank had been caught and dragged down.

"Still, I ordered the men, cook, steward, and all, to remain on the poop and—the galley being forward—to expect no hot meals, as we could subsist for a time on the cold, canned food in the storeroom and lazaret.

"Because of an early friction between the men and the second mate, the mild-mannered and peace-loving skipper had forbidden the crew to wear sheath knives; but in this exigency I overruled the edict. While the professor went down into his flooded room to doctor his ankle and attend to his instruments, I raided the slop chest, and armed every man of us with a sheath knife and belt; for while we could not see the creature, we could feel it—and a knife is better than a gun in a hand-to-hand fight.

"Then we sat around, waiting, while the sky grew muddier, the sun darker, and the northern horizon lighter with a reddish glow that was better than the sun. It was the Java earthquake, but we did not know it for a long time.

"Soon the professor appeared and announced that his instruments were in good condition, and stowed high on shelves above the water.

" 'I must resensitize my plates, however,' he said. 'Der salt water has spoiled them; but mine camera merely needs to dry out; und mine telescope, und mine static machine und Leyden jars—why, der water did not touch them.'

" 'Well,' I answered. 'That's all right. But what good are they in the face of this emergency? Are you thinking of photographing anything now?'

" 'Perhaps. I haf been thinking some.'

" 'Have you thought out what that creature is—forward, there?'

" 'Partly. It is some creature thrown up from der bottom of der sea, und washed on board by der wave. Light, like wave motion, ends at a certain depth, you know; und we have over twelve thousand feet beneath us. At that depth dere is absolute darkness, but we know that creatures live down dere, und fight, und eat, und die.'

"'But what of it? Why can't we see that thing?'

"'Because, in der ages that haf passed in its evolution from der original moneron, it has never been exposed to light—I mean visible light, der light that contains der seven colors of der spectrum. Hence it may not respond to der three properties of visible light—reflection, which would give it a color of some kind; absorption, which would make it appear black; or refraction, which, in der absence of der other two, would distort things seen through it. For it would be transparent, you know.'

"'But what can be done?' I asked helplessly, for I could not understand at the time what he meant.

"'Nothing, except that der next man attacked must use his knife. If he cannot see der creature, he can feel it. Und perhaps—I do not know yet—perhaps, in a way, we may see it—its photograph.'

"I looked blankly at him, thinking he might have gone crazy, but he continued.

"'You know,' he said, 'that objects too small to be seen by the microscope, because smaller than der amplitude of der shortest wave of visible light, can be seen when exposed to der ultraviolet light—der dark light beyond der spectrum? Und you know that this light is what acts der most in photography? That it exposes on a sensitized plate new stars in der heavens invisible to der eye through the strongest telescope?'

"'Don't know anything about it,' I answered. 'But if you can find a way out of this scrape we're in, go ahead.'

"'I must think,' he said dreamily. 'I haf a rock-crystal lens which is permeable to this light, und which I can place in mine camera. I must have a concave mirror, not of glass, which is opaque to this light, but of metal.'

"'What for?' I asked.

"'To throw der ultraviolet light on der beast. I can generate it with mine static machine.'

"'How will one of our lantern reflectors do? They are of polished tin, I think.'

"'Good! I can repolish one.'

"We had one deck lantern larger than usual, with a metallic reflector that concentrated the light into a beam, much as do the present day searchlights. This I procured from the lazaret, and he pronounced it available. Then he disappeared, to tinker up his apparatus.

"Night came down, and I lighted three masthead lights, to hoist at the fore to inform any passing craft that we were not under command; but, as I would not send a man forward on that job, I went myself, carefully feeling my way with the pike pole. Luckily, I escaped contact with the creature, and returned to the poop, where we had a cold supper of canned cabin stores.

"The top of the house was dry, but it was cold, especially so as we were all drenched to the skin. The steward brought up all the blankets there were in the cabin—for even a wet blanket is better than none at all—but there were not enough to go around, and one man volunteered, against my advice, to go forward and bring aft bedding from the forecastle.

"He did not come back; we heard his yell, that finished with a gurgle; but in that pitch black darkness, relieved only by the red glow from the north, not one of us dared to venture to his rescue. We knew that he would be dead, anyhow, before we could get to him; so we stood watch, sharing the blankets we had when our time came to sleep.

"It was a wretched night that we spent on the top of that after house. It began to rain before midnight, the heavy drops coming down almost in solid waves; then came wind, out of the south, cold and biting, with real waves, that rolled even over the house, forcing us to lash ourselves. The red glow to the north was hidden by the rain and spume, and, to add to our discomfort, we were showered with ashes, which, even though the surface wind was from the south, must have been brought from the north by an upper air current.

"We did not find the dead man when the faint daylight came; and so could not tell whether or not he had used his knife. His body must have washed over the rail with a sea, and we hoped the invisible killer had gone, too. But we hoped too much. With courage born of this hope a man went forward to lower the masthead lights, prodding his way with the pike pole.

"We watched him closely, the pole in one hand, his knife in the other. But he went under at the fore rigging without even a yell, and the pole went with him, while we could see, even at the distance and through the disturbed water, that his arms were close to his sides, and that he made no movement, except for the quick darting to and fro. After a few moments, however, the pike pole floated to the surface, but the man's body, drained, no doubt, of its buoyant fluids, remained on the deck.

"It was an hour later, with the pike pole for a feeler, before we dared approach the body, hook on to it, and tow it aft. It resembled that of the first victim, a skeleton clothed with skin, with the same look of horror on the face. We buried it like the other, and held to the poop, still drenched by the downpour of rain, hammered by the seas, and choked by ashes from the sky.

"As the shower of ashes increased it became dark as twilight, and though the three lights aloft burned out at about midday, I forbade a man to go forward to lower them, contenting myself with a turpentine flare lamp that I brought up from the lazaret, and filled, ready to show if the lights of a craft came in view. Before the afternoon was half gone it was dark as night, and down below, up to his waist in water, the German professor was working away.

"He came up at supper time, humming cheerfully to himself, and announced that he had replaced his camera lens with the rock crystal, that the lantern, with its reflector and a blue spark in the focus, made an admirable instrument for throwing the invisible rays on the beast, and that he was all ready, except that his plates, which he had resensitized—with some phosphorescent substance that I forget the name of, now—must have time to dry. And then, he needed some light to work by when the time came, he explained.

" 'Also another victim,' I suggested bitterly; for he had not been on deck when the last two men had died.

" 'I hope not,' he said. 'When we can see, it may be possible to stir him up by throwing things forward; then when he moves der water we can take shots.'

" 'Better devise some means of killing him,' I answered. 'Shooting won't do, for water stops a bullet before it goes a foot into it.'

" 'Der only way I can think of,' he responded, 'is for der next man—you hear me all, you men—to stick your knife at the end of the blood—where it collects in a lump. Dere is der creature's stomach, and a vital spot.'

" 'Remember this, boys,' I laughed, thinking of the last poor devil, with his arms pinioned to his side. 'When you've lost enough blood to see it in a lump, stab for it.'

"But my laugh was answered by a shriek. A man lashed with a turn of rope around his waist to the stump of the mizzenmast, was writhing and heaving on his back, while he struck with his knife, apparently at his own body. With my own knife in my hand I sprang toward him, and felt for what had seized him. It was something cold, and hard, and leathery, close to his waist.

"Carefully gauging my stroke, I lunged with the knife, but I hardly think it entered the invisible fin, or tail, or paw of the monster; but it moved away from the screaming man, and the next moment I received a blow in the face that sent me aft six feet, flat on my back. Then came unconsciousness.

"When I recovered my senses the remnant of the crew were around me, but the man was gone—dragged out of the bight of the rope that had held him against the force of breaking seas, and down to the flooded main deck, to die like the others. It was too dark to see, or do anything; so, when I could speak I ordered all hands but one into the flooded cabin where, in the upper berths and on the top of the table, were a few dry spots.

"I filled and lighted a lantern, and gave it to the man on watch with instructions to hang it to the stump of the mizzen and to call his relief at the end of four hours. Then, with doors and windows closed, we went to sleep, or tried to go to sleep. I succeeded first, I think, for up to the last of consciousness I could hear the mutterings of the men; when I awakened, they were all asleep, and the cabin clock, high above the water, told me that, though it was still dark, it was six in the morning.

"I went on deck; the lantern still burned at the stump of mizzenmast but the lookout was gone. He had not lived long enough to be relieved, as I learned by going below and finding that no one had been called.

"We were but six, now—one sailor and the bos'n, the cook and steward, the professor and myself."

The old artist paused, while he refilled and lighted his pipe. I noticed that the hand that held the match shook perceptibly, as though the memories of that awful experience had affected his nerves. I know that the recital had affected mine; for I joined him in a smoke, my hands shaking also.

"Why," I asked, after a moment of silence, "if it was a deep-sea creature, did it not die from the lesser pressure at the surface?"

"Why do not men die on the mountaintops?" he answered. "Or up in balloons? The record is seven miles high, I think; but they lived. They suffered from cold, and from lack of oxygen—that is, no matter how fast, or deeply they breathed, they could not get enough. But the lack of pressure did not trouble them; the human body can adjust itself.

"Conversely, however, an increase of pressure may be fatal. A man dragged down more than one hundred and fifty feet may be crushed; and a surface fish sent to the bottom of the sea may die from the pressure.

It is simple; it is like the difference between a weight lifted from us and a weight added."

"Did this thing kill any more men?" I asked.

"All but the professor and myself, and it almost killed me. Look here."

He removed his cravat and collar, pulled down his shirt, and exposed two livid scars about an inch in diameter, and two apart.

"I lost all the blood I could spare through those two holes," he said, as he readjusted his apparel; "but I saved enough to keep me alive."

"Go on with the yarn," I asked. "I promise you I will not sleep to-night."

"Perhaps I will not sleep myself," he answered, with a mournful smile. "Some things should be forgotten, but as I have told you this much I may as well finish, and be done with it.

"It was partly due to a sailor's love for tobacco, partly to our cold, drenched condition. A sailor will starve quietly, but go crazy if deprived of his smoke. This is so well known at sea that a skipper, who will not hesitate to sail from port with rotten or insufficient food for his men, will not dare take a chance without a full supply of tobacco in the slop chest.

"But our slop chest was under water, and the tobacco utterly useless. I did not use it at the time, but I fished some out for the others. It did not do; it would not dry out to smoke, and the salt in it made it unfit to chew. But the bos'n had an upper bunk in the forward house, in which was a couple of pounds of navy plug, and he and the sailor talked this over until their craving for a smoke overcame their fear of death.

"Of course, by this time, all discipline was ended, and all my commands and entreaties went for nothing. They sharpened their knives, and, agreeing to go forward, one on the starboard rail, the other on the port, and each to come to the other's aid if called, they went up into the darkness of ashes and rain. I opened my room window, which overlooked the main deck, but could see nothing.

"Yet I could hear; I heard two screams for help, one after the other—one from the starboard side, the other from the port, and knew that they were caught. I closed the window, for nothing could be done. What manner of thing it was that could grab two men so far apart nearly at the same time was beyond all imagining.

"I talked to the steward and cook, but found small comfort. The first was a Jap, the other a Chinaman, and they were the old-fashioned kind—what they could not see with their eyes, they could not believe. Both thought that all those men who had met death had either drowned or died by falling. Neither understood—and, in fact, I did not myself—the theories of Herr Smidt. He had stopped his cheerful humming to himself now, and was very busy with his instruments.

" 'This thing,' I said to him, 'must be able to see in the dark. It certainly could not have heard those two men, over the noise of the wind, sea, and rain.'

" 'Why not?' he answered, as he puttered with his wires. 'Cats and owls can see in the dark, und the accepted explanation is that by their power of enlarging der pupils they admit more light to the retina. But that explanation never satisfied me. You haf noticed, haf you not, that a cat's eyes shine in der dark, but only when der cat is looking at you?—that is, when it looks elsewhere you do not see der shiny eyes.'

" 'Yes,' I answered, 'I have noticed that.'

" 'A cat's eyes are searchlights, but they send forth a visible light, such as is generated by fireflies, und some fish. Und dere are fish in der upper tributaries of der Amazon which haf four eyes, der two upper of which are searchlights, der two lower of which are organs of percipience or vision. But visible light is not der only light. It is possible that the creature out on deck generates the invisible light, and can see by it.'

" 'But what does it all amount to?' I asked impatiently.

" 'I haf told you,' he answered calmly. 'Der creature may live in an atmosphere of ultraviolet light, which I can generate mineself. When mine plates dry, und it clears off so I can see what I am doing, I may get a picture of it. When we know what it is, we may find means of killing it.'

" 'God grant that you succeed,' I answered fervently. 'It has killed enough of us.'

"But, as I said, the thing killed all but the professor and myself. And it came about through the other reason I mentioned—our cold, drenched condition. If there is anything an Oriental loves above his ancestors, it is his stomach; and the cold, canned food was palling upon us all. We had a little light through the downpour of ashes and rain about mid-day, and the steward and cook began talking about hot coffee.

"We had the turpentine torch for heating water, and some coffee, high and dry on a shelf in the steward's storeroom, but not a pot, pan, or cooking utensil of any kind in the cabin. So these two poor heathens, against my expostulations—somewhat faint, I admit, for the thought of hot coffee took away some of my common sense—went out on the deck and waded forward, waist-deep in the water, muddy now, from the downfall of ashes.

"I could see them as they entered the galley to get the coffeepot, but, though I stared from my window until the blackness closed down, I did not see them come out. Nor did I hear even a squeal. The thing must have been in the galley.

"Night came on, and, with its coming, the wind and rain ceased, though there was still a slight shower of ashes. But this ended toward midnight, and I could see stars overhead and a clear horizon. Sleep, in my nervous, overwrought condition, was impossible; but the professor, after the bright idea of using the turpentine torch to dry out his plates, had gone to his fairly dry berth, after announcing his readiness to take snapshots about the deck in the morning.

"But I roused him long before morning. I roused him when I saw through my window the masthead and two side lights of a steamer approaching from the starboard, still about a mile away. I had not dared to go up and rig that lantern at the mizzen stump; but now I nerved myself to go up with the torch, the professor following with his instruments.

" 'You cold-blooded crank,' I said to him, as I waved the torch. 'I admire your devotion to science, but are you waiting for that thing to get me?'

"He did not answer, but rigged his apparatus on the top of the cabin. He had a Wimshurst machine—to generate a blue spark, you know—and this he had attached to the big deck light, from which he had removed the opaque glass. Then he had his camera, with its rock-crystal lens.

"He trained both forward, and waited, while I waved the torch, standing near the stump with a turn of rope around me for safety's sake in case the thing seized me; and to this idea I added the foolish hope, aroused by the professor's theories, that the blinding light of the torch would frighten the thing away from me as it does wild animals.

"But in this last I was mistaken. No sooner was there an answering blast of a steam whistle, indicating that the steamer had seen the torch, than something cold, wet, leathery, and slimy slipped around my neck. I dropped the torch, and drew my knife, while I heard the whir of the static machine as the professor turned it.

" 'Use your knife, mine friend,' he called. 'Use your knife, und reach for any blood what you see.'

"I knew better than to call for help, and I had little chance to use the knife. Still, I managed to keep my right hand, in which I held it, free, while that cold, leathery thing slipped farther around my neck and waist. I struck as I could, but could make no impression; and soon I felt another stricture around my legs, which brought me on my back.

"Still another belt encircled me, and, though I had come up warmly clad in woolen shirts and monkey jacket, I felt these garments being torn away from me. Then I was dragged forward, but the turn of rope had slipped down toward my waist, and I was merely bent double.

"And all the time that German was whirling his machine, and shouting to strike for any blood I saw. But I saw none. I felt it going, however. Two spots on my chest began to smart, then burn as though hot irons were piercing me. Frantically I struck, right and left, sometimes at the coils encircling me, again in the air. Then all became dark.

"I awakened in a stateroom berth, too weak to lift my hands, with the taste of brandy in my mouth and the professor standing over me with a bottle in his hand.

" 'Ach, it is well,' he said. 'You will recover. You haf merely lost blood, but you did the right thing. You struck with your knife at the blood, and you killed the creature. I was right. Heart, brain, und all vital parts were in der stomach.'

" 'Where are we now?' I asked, for I did not recognize the room.

" 'On board der steamer. When you got on your feet und staggered aft, I knew you had killed him, and gave you my assistance. But you fainted away. Then we were taken off. Und I haf two or three beautiful negatives, which I am printing. They will be a glorious contribution to der scientific world.'

"I was glad that I was alive, yet not alive enough to ask any more questions. But next day he showed me the photographs he had printed."

"In Heaven's name, what was it?" I asked excitedly, as the old artist paused to empty and refill his pipe.

"Nothing but a giant squid, or octopus. Except that it was bigger than any ever seen before, and invisible to the eye, of course. Did you ever read Hugo's terrible story of Gilliat's fight with a squid?"

I had, and nodded.

"Hugo's imagination could not give him a creature—no matter how formidable—larger than one of four feet stretch. This one had three tentacles around me, two others gripped the port and starboard pin-rails, and three were gripping the stump of the mainmast. It had a reach of forty feet, I should think, comparing it with the beam of the craft.

"But there was one part of each picture, ill defined and missing. My knife and right hand were not shown. They were buried in a dark lump, which could be nothing but the blood from my veins. Unconscious, but still struggling, I had struck into the soft body of the monster, and struck true."

L is for Little People

In a number of his weird tales, Welsh writer Arthur Machen (1863–1947) explored the idea that legends of fairies and other creatures of folklore are watered down accounts of supernatural species from the past that still exist in out-of-the-way places and are far from benign. This story, which is often excerpted from his episodic 1895 novel *The Three Impostors,* is memorable for its depiction of the "Little People" as anything *but* friendly and pleasant beings.

ARTHUR MACHEN

Novel of the Black Seal

I am the daughter of a civil engineer, Steven Lally by name, who was so unfortunate as to die suddenly at the outset of his career, and before he had accumulated sufficient means to support his wife and her two children. My mother contrived to keep the small household going on resources which must have been incredibly small; we lived in a remote country village, because most of the necessaries of life were cheaper than in a town, but even so we were brought up with the severest economy. My father was a clever and well-read man, and left behind him a small but select collection of books, containing the best Greek, Latin, and English classics, and these books were the only amusement we possessed. My brother, I remember, learnt Latin out of Descartes's *Meditationes,* and I, in place of the little tales which children are usually told to read, had nothing more charming than a translation of the *Gesta Romanorum*. We grew up thus, quiet and studious children, and in course of time my brother provided for himself in the manner I have mentioned. I continued to live at home: my poor mother had become an invalid, and demanded my continual care, and about two years ago she died after many months of painful illness. My situation was a terrible one; the shabby furniture barely sufficed to pay the debts I had been forced to contract, and the books I despatched to my brother, knowing how he would value them. I was absolutely alone; I was aware how poorly my brother was paid; and though I came up to London in the hope of finding employment, with the understanding that he would defray my expenses, I swore it should only be for a month, and that if I could not in that time find some work I would starve rather than deprive him of the few miserable pounds he had laid by for his day of trouble. I took a little room in a distant suburb; the cheapest that I could find; I lived on bread and tea, and I spent my time in vain answering of advertisements, and vainer walks to addresses I had noted. Day followed on day, and week on week, and still I was unsuccessful, till at last the term I had appointed drew to a close, and I saw before me the grim prospect of slowly dying of starvation. My landlady was good-natured in her way; she knew the slenderness of my means, and I am sure that she would not have turned me out of doors; it remained for me then to go away, and to try to die in some quiet place. It was winter then, and a thick white fog gathered in the early part of the afternoon, becoming more dense as the day wore on; it was a Sunday, I remember, and the people of the house were at chapel. At about three o'clock I crept out and walked away as quickly as I could, for I was weak from abstinence. The white mist wrapped all the streets in silence, a hard frost had gathered thick upon the bare branches of the trees, and frost crystals glittered on the wooden fences, and on the cold, cruel ground beneath my feet. I walked on, turning to right and left in utter haphazard, without caring to look up at the names of the streets, and all that I remember of my walk on that Sunday afternoon seems but the broken fragments of an evil dream. In a confused vision I stumbled on, through roads half-town and half-country, grey fields melting into the cloudy world of mist on one side of me, and on the other comfortable villas with a glow of firelight flickering on the walls, but all unreal; red brick walls and lighted windows, vague trees, and glimmering country, gas-lamps beginning to star the white shadows, the vanishing perspectives of the railway line beneath high embankments, the green and red of the signal lamps,—all these were but momentary pictures flashed on my tired brain and senses numbed by hunger. Now and then I would hear a quick step ringing on the iron road, and men would pass me well wrapped up, walking fast for the sake of warmth, and no doubt eagerly foretasting the pleasures of a glowing hearth, with curtains tightly drawn about the frosted panes, and the welcomes of their friends, but as the early evening darkened and night approached, foot-passengers got fewer and fewer, and I passed through street after street alone. In the white silence I stumbled on, as desolate as if I trod the streets of a buried city; and as I grew more weak and exhausted, something of the horror of death was folding thickly round my heart. Suddenly, as I turned a corner, some one accosted me courteously beneath the lamp-post, and I heard a voice asking if I could kindly point the way to Avon Road. At the sudden shock of human accents I was prostrated, and my strength gave way; I fell all huddled on the sidewalk, and wept and sobbed and laughed in violent hysteria. I had gone out prepared to die, and as I stepped across the threshold that had sheltered me, I consciously bade adieu to all hopes and all remembrances; the door clanged behind me with the noise of thunder, and I felt that an iron curtain had fallen on the brief passage of my life, that henceforth I was to walk a little way in a world of gloom and shadow; I entered on the stage of the first act of death. Then came my wandering in the mist, the whiteness wrapping all things, the void streets, and muffled silence, till when that voice spoke to me it was as if I had died and life returned to me. In a few minutes I was able to compose my feelings, and as I rose I saw that I was confronted by a middle-aged gentleman of specious appearance, neatly and correctly dressed. He looked at me with an expression of great pity, but before I could stammer out my ignorance of the neighbourhood, for indeed I had not the slightest notion of where I had wandered, he spoke.

"My dear madam," he said, "you seem in some terrible distress. You cannot think how you alarmed me. But may I inquire the nature of your trouble? I assure you that you can safely confide in me."

"You are very kind," I replied. "But I fear there is nothing to be done. My condition seems a hopeless one."

"Oh, nonsense, nonsense! You are too young to talk like that. Come, let us walk down here and you must tell me your difficulty. Perhaps I may be able to help you."

There was something very soothing and persuasive in his manner, and as we walked together I gave him an outline of my story, and told of the despair that had oppressed me almost to death.

"You were wrong to give in so completely," he said, when I was silent. "A month is too short a time in which to feel one's way in London. London, let me tell you, Miss Lally, does not lie open and undefended; it is a fortified place, fossed and double-moated with curious intricacies. As must always happen in large towns, the conditions of life have become hugely artificial; no mere simple palisade is run up to oppose the man or woman who would take the place by storm, but serried lines of subtle contrivances, mines, and pitfalls which it needs a strange skill to overcome. You, in your simplicity, fancied you had only to shout for these walls to sink into nothingness, but the time is gone for such startling victories as these. Take courage; you will learn the secret of success before very long."

"Alas! sir," I replied, "I have no doubt your conclusions are correct, but at the present moment I seem to be in a fair way to die of starvation. You spoke of a secret; for Heaven's sake tell it me, if you have any pity for my distress."

He laughed genially. "There lies the strangeness of it all. Those who know the secret cannot tell it if they would; it is positively as ineffable as the central doctrine of Freemasonry. But I may say this, that you yourself have penetrated at least the outer husk of the mystery," and he laughed again.

"Pray do not jest with me," I said. "What have I done, *que sais-je*? I am so far ignorant that I have not the slightest idea of how my next meal is to be provided."

"Excuse me. You ask what you have done? You have met me. Come, we will fence no longer. I see you have self-education, the only education which is not infinitely pernicious, and I am in want of a governess for my two children. I have been a widower for some years; my name is Gregg. I offer you the post I have named, and shall we say a salary of a hundred a year?"

I could only stutter out my thanks, and slipping a card with his address, and a banknote by way of earnest, into my hand, Mr. Gregg bade me good-bye, asking me to call in a day or two.

Such was my introduction to Professor Gregg, and can you wonder that the remembrance of despair and the cold blast that had blown from the gates of death upon me made me regard him as a second father. Before the close of the week I was installed in my new duties. The Professor had leased an old brick manor-house in a western suburb of London, and here, surrounded by pleasant lawns and orchards, and soothed with the murmur of the ancient elms that rocked their boughs above the roof, the new chapter of my life began. Knowing as you do the nature of the professor's occupations, you will not be surprised to hear that the house teemed with books, and cabinets full of strange, and even hideous, objects filled every available nook in the vast low rooms. Gregg was a man whose one thought was for knowledge, and I too before long caught something of his enthusiasm, and strove to enter into his passion for research. In a few months I was perhaps more his secretary than the governess of the two children, and many a night I have sat at the desk in the glow of the shaded lamp while he, pacing up and down in the rich gloom of the firelight, dictated to me the substance of his *Textbook of Ethnology*. But amidst these more sober and accurate studies I always detected a something hidden, a longing and desire for some object to which he did not allude; and now and then he would break short in what he was saying and lapse into reverie, intranced, as it seemed to me, by some distant prospect of adventurous discovery. The textbook was at last finished, and we began to receive proofs from the printers, which were intrusted to me for a first reading, and then underwent the final revision of the professor. All the while his weariness of the actual business he was engaged on increased, and it was with the joyous laugh of a schoolboy when term is over that he one day handed me a copy of the book. "There," he said, "I have kept my word; I promised to write it, and it is done with. Now I shall be free to live for stranger things; I confess it, Miss Lally, I covet the renown of Columbus; you will, I hope, see me play the part of an explorer."

"Surely," I said, "there is little left to explore. You have been born a few hundred years too late for that."

"I think you, are wrong," he replied; "there are still, depend upon it, quaint, undiscovered countries and continents of strange extent. Ah, Miss Lally! believe me, we stand amidst sacraments and mysteries full of awe, and it doth not yet appear what we shall be. Life, believe me, is no simple thing, no mass of grey matter and congeries of veins and muscles to be laid naked by the surgeon's knife; man is the secret which I am about to explore, and before I can discover him I must cross over weltering seas indeed, and oceans and the mists of many thousand years. You know the myth of the lost

Atlantis; what if it be true, and I am destined to be called the discoverer of that wonderful land?"

I could see excitement boiling beneath his words, and in his face was the heat of the hunter; before me stood a man who believed himself summoned to tourney with the unknown. A pang of joy possessed me when I reflected that I was to be in a way associated with him in the adventure, and I, too, burned with the lust of the chase, not pausing to consider that I knew not what we were to unshadow.

The next morning Professor Gregg took me into his inner study, where, ranged against the wall, stood a nest of pigeon-holes, every drawer neatly labelled, and the results of years of toil classified in a few feet of space.

"Here," he said, "is my life; here are all the facts which I have gathered together with so much pains, and yet it is all nothing. No, nothing to what I am about to attempt. Look at this"; and he took me to an old bureau, a piece fantastic and faded, which stood in a corner of the room. He unlocked the front and opened one of the drawers.

"A few scraps of paper," he went on, pointing to the drawer, "and a lump of black stone, rudely annotated with queer marks and scratches—that is all that the drawer holds. Here you see is an old envelope with the dark red stamp of twenty years ago, but I have pencilled a few lines at the back; here is a sheet of manuscript, and here some cuttings from obscure local journals. And if you ask me the subject-matter of the collection, it will not seem extraordinary—a servant-girl at a farmhouse, who disappeared from her place and has never been heard of, a child supposed to have slipped down some old working on the mountains, some queer scribbling on a limestone rock, a man murdered with a blow from a strange weapon; such is the scent I have to go upon. Yes, as you say, there is a ready explanation for all this; the girl may have run away to London, or Liverpool, or New York; the child may be at the bottom of the disused shaft; and the letters on the rock may be the idle whims of some vagrant. Yes, yes, I admit all that; but I know I hold the true key. Look!" and he held me out a slip of yellow paper.

Characters found inscribed on a limestone rock on the Grey Hills, I read, and then there was a word erased, presumably the name of a county, and a date some fifteen years back. Beneath was traced a number of uncouth characters, shaped somewhat like wedges or daggers, as strange and outlandish as the Hebrew alphabet.

"Now the seal," said Professor Gregg, and he handed me the black stone, a thing about two inches long, and something like an old-fashioned tobacco-stopper, much enlarged.

I held it up to the light, and saw to my surprise the characters on the paper repeated on the seal.

"Yes," said the professor, "they are the same. And the marks on the limestone rock were made fifteen years ago, with some red substance. And the characters on the seal are four thousand years old at least. Perhaps much more."

"Is it a hoax?" I said.

"No, I anticipated that. I was not to be led to give my life to a practical joke. I have tested the matter very carefully. Only one person besides myself knows of the mere existence of that black seal. Besides, there are other reasons which I cannot enter into now."

"But what does it all mean?" I said. "I cannot understand to what conclusion all this leads."

"My dear Miss Lally, that is a question that I would rather leave unanswered for some little time. Perhaps I shall never be able to say what secrets are held here in solution; a few vague hints, the outlines of village tragedies, a few marks done with red earth upon a rock, and an ancient seal. A queer set of data to go upon? Half a dozen pieces of evidence, and twenty years before even so much could be got together; and who knows what mirage or *terra incognita* may be beyond all this? I look across deep waters, Miss Lally, and the land beyond may be but a haze after all. But still I believe it is not so, and a few months will show whether I am right or wrong."

He left me, and alone I endeavoured to fathom the mystery, wondering to what goal such eccentric odds and ends of evidence could lead. I myself am not wholly devoid of imagination, and I had reason to respect the professor's solidity of intellect; yet I saw in the contents of the drawer but the materials of fantasy, and vainly tried to conceive what theory could be founded on the fragments that had been placed before me. Indeed, I could discover in what I had heard and seen but the first chapter of an extravagant romance; and yet deep in my heart I burned with curiosity, and day after day I looked eagerly in Professor Gregg's face for some hint of what was to happen.

It was one evening after dinner that the word came.

"I hope you can make your preparations without much trouble," he said suddenly to me. "We shall be leaving here in a week's time."

"Really!" I said in astonishment. "Where are we going?"

"I have taken a country house in the west of England, not far from Caermaen, a quiet little town, once a city, and the headquarters of a Roman legion. It is very dull there, but the country is pretty, and the air is wholesome."

I detected a glint in his eyes, and guessed that this sudden move had some relation to our conversation of a few days before.

"I shall just take a few books with me," said Professor Gregg, "that is all. Everything else will remain here for our return. I have got a holiday," he went on, smiling at me, "and I shan't be sorry to be quit for a time of my old bones and stones and rubbish. Do you know," he went on, "I have been grinding away at facts for thirty years; it is time for fancies."

The days passed quickly; I could see that the professor was all quivering with suppressed excitement, and I could scarce credit the eager appetence of his glance as we left the old manor house behind us and began our journey. We set out at midday, and it was in the dusk of the evening that we arrived at a little country station. I was tired and excited, and the drive through the lanes seems all a dream. First the deserted streets of a forgotten village, while I heard Professor Gregg's voice talking of the Augustan Legion and the clash of arms, and all the tremendous pomp that followed the eagles; then the broad river swimming to full tide with the last afterglow glimmering duskily in the yellow water, the wide meadows, the cornfields whitening, and the deep lane winding on the slope between the hills and the water. At last we began to ascend, and the air grew rarer. I looked down and saw the pure white mist tracking the outline of the river like a shroud, and a vague and shadowy country; imaginations and fantasy of swelling hills and hanging woods, and half-shaped outlines of hills beyond, and in the distance the glare of the furnace fire on the mountain, growing by turns a pillar of shining flame and fading to a dull point of red. We were slowly mounting a carriage drive, and then there came to me the cool breath and the secret of the great wood that was above us; I seemed to wander in its deepest depths, and there was the sound of trickling water, the scent of the green leaves, and the breath of the summer night. The carriage stopped at last, and I could scarcely distinguish the form of the house, as I waited a moment at the pillared porch. The rest of the evening seemed a dream of strange things bounded by the great silence of the wood and the valley and the river.

The next morning, when I awoke and looked out of the bow window of the big, old-fashioned bedroom, I saw under a grey sky a country that was still all mystery. The long, lovely valley, with the river winding in and out below, crossed in mid-vision by a mediæval bridge of vaulted and buttressed stone, the clear presence of the rising ground beyond, and the woods that I had only seen in shadow the night before, seemed tinged with enchantment, and the soft breath of air that sighed in at the opened pane was like no other wind. I looked across the valley, and beyond, hill followed on hill as wave on wave, and here a faint blue pillar of smoke rose still in the morning air from the chimney of an ancient grey farmhouse, there was a rugged height crowned with dark firs, and in the distance I saw the white streak of a road that climbed and vanished into some unimagined country. But the boundary of all was a great wall of mountain, vast in the west, and ending like a fortress with a steep ascent and a domed tumulus clear against the sky.

I saw Professor Gregg walking up and down the terrace path below the windows, and it was evident that he was revelling in the sense of liberty, and the thought that he had for a while bidden good-bye to task-work. When I joined him there was exultation in his voice as he pointed out the sweep of valley and the river that wound beneath the lovely hills.

"Yes," he said, "it is a strangely beautiful country; and to me, at least, it seems full of mystery. You have not forgotten the drawer I showed you, Miss Lally? No; and you have guessed that I have come here not merely for the sake of the children and the fresh air?"

"I think I have guessed as much as that," I replied; "but you must remember I do not know the mere nature of your investigations; and as for the connection between the search and this wonderful valley, it is past my guessing."

He smiled queerly at me. "You must not think I am making a mystery for the sake of mystery," he said. "I do not speak out because, so far, there is nothing to be spoken, nothing definite, I mean, nothing that can be set down in hard black and white, as dull and sure and irreproachable as any blue-book. And then I have another reason: Many years ago a chance paragraph in a newspaper caught my attention, and focussed in an instant the vagrant thoughts and half-formed fancies of many idle and speculative hours into a certain hypothesis. I saw at once that I was treading on a thin crust; my theory was wild and fantastic in the extreme, and I would not for any consideration have written a hint of it for publication. But I thought that in the company of scientific men like myself, men who knew the course of discovery, and were aware that the gas that blazes and flares in the gin-palace was once a wild hypothesis—I thought that with such men as these I might hazard my dream—let us say Atlantis, or the philosopher's stone, or what you like—without danger of ridicule. I found I was grossly mistaken; my friends looked blankly at me and at one another, and I could see something of pity, and something also of insolent contempt, in the glances they exchanged. One of them called on me next day, and hinted that I must be suffering from overwork and brain exhaustion. 'In plain terms,' I said, 'you think I am going mad. I think not'; and I showed him out with some little appearance of heat. Since that day I vowed that I would never whisper the nature of my theory to any living soul; to no one but yourself have I ever shown the contents of that drawer. After all, I may be following a rainbow; I may have been misled by the play of coincidence; but as I stand here in this mystic hush and silence, amidst the woods and wild hills, I am more than ever sure that I am hot on the scent. Come, it is time we went in."

To me in all this there was something both of wonder and excitement; I knew how in his ordinary work Professor Gregg moved step by step, testing every inch of the way, and never venturing on assertion without proof that was impregnable. Yet I divined, more from his glance and the vehemence of his tone than from the spoken word, that he had in his every thought the vision of the almost incredible continually with him; and I, who was with some share of imagination no little of a sceptic, offended at a hint of the marvellous, could not help asking myself whether he were cherishing a monomania, and barring out from this one subject all the scientific method of his other life.

Yet, with this image of mystery haunting my thoughts, I surrendered wholly to the charm of the country. Above the faded house on the hillside began the great forest—a long, dark line seen from the opposing hills, stretching above the river for many a mile from north to south, and yielding in the north to even wilder country, barren and savage hills, and ragged commonland, a territory all strange and unvisited, and more unknown to Englishmen than the very heart of Africa. The space of a couple of steep fields alone separated the house from the wood, and the children were delighted to follow me up the long alleys of undergrowth, between smooth pleached walls of shining beech, to the highest point in the wood, whence one looked on one side across the river and the rise and fall of the country to the great western mountain wall, and on the other over the surge and dip of the myriad trees of the forest, over level meadows and the shining yellow sea to the faint coast beyond. I used to sit at this point on the warm sunlit turf which marked the track of the Roman Road, while the two children raced about hunting for the whinberries that grew here and there on the banks. Here, beneath the deep blue sky and the great clouds rolling, like olden galleons with sails full-bellied, from the sea to the hills, as I listened to the whispered charm of the great and ancient wood, I lived solely for delight, and only remembered strange things when we would return to the house and find Professor Gregg either shut up in the little room he had made his study, or else pacing the terrace with the look, patient and enthusiastic, of the determined seeker.

One morning, some eight or nine days after our arrival, I looked out of my window and saw the whole landscape transmuted before me. The clouds had dipped low and hidden the mountain in the west; a southern wind was driving the rain in shifting pillars up the valley, and the little brooklet that burst the hill below the house now raged, a red torrent, down the river. We were perforce obliged to keep snug within-doors; and when I had attended to my pupils, I sat down in the morning-room, where the ruins of a library still encumbered an old-fashioned bookcase. I had inspected the shelves once or twice, but their contents had failed to attract me; volumes of eighteenth-century sermons, an old book on farriery, a collection of *Poems* by "persons of quality," Prideaux's *Connection,* and an odd volume of Pope, were the boundaries of the library, and there seemed little doubt that everything of interest or value had been removed. Now, however, in desperation, I began to re-examine the musty sheepskin and calf bindings, and found, much to my delight, a fine old quarto printed by the Stephani, containing the three books of Pomponius Mela, *De Situ Orbis,* and other of the ancient geographers. I knew enough of Latin to steer my way through an ordinary sentence, and I soon became absorbed in the odd mixture of fact and fancy—light shining on a little of the space of the world, and beyond, mist and shadow and awful forms. Glancing over the clear-printed pages. my attention was caught by the heading of a chapter in Solinus, and I read the words:—

MIRA DE INTIMIS GENTIBUS LIBYAE, DE LAPIDE HEXECONTALITHO,

—"The wonders of the people that inhabit the inner parts of Libya, and of the stone called Sixtystone."

The odd title attracted me, and I read on: *Gens ista avia er secreta habitat, in montibus horrendis fœda mysteria celebrat. De hominibus nihil aliud illi praeferunt quam figuram, ab humano ritu prorsus exulant, oderunt deum lucis. Stridunt potius quam loquuntur; vox absona nec sine horrore auditur. Lapide quodam gloriantur, quem Hexecontalithon vocant; dicunt enim hunc lapidem sexaginta notas ostendere. Cujus lapidis nomen secretum ineffabile colunt: quod Ixaxar.*

"This folk," I translated to myself, "dwells in remote and secret places, and celebrates foul mysteries on savage hills. Nothing have they in common with men save the face, and the customs of humanity are wholly strange to them; and they hate the sun. They hiss rather than speak; their voices are harsh, and not to be heard without fear. They boast of a certain stone, which they call Sixtystone; for they say that it displays sixty characters. And this stone has a secret unspeakable name; which is Ixaxar."

I laughed at the queer inconsequence of all this, and thought it fit for "Sinbad the Sailor," or other of the supplementary Nights. When I saw Professor Gregg in the course of the day, I told him of my find in the bookcase, and the fantastic rubbish I had been reading. To my surprise he looked up at me with an expression of great interest.

"That is really very curious," he said. "I have never thought it worth while to look into the old geographers, and I dare say I have missed a good deal. Ah, that is the passage, is it. It seems a shame to rob you of your entertainment, but I really think I must carry off the book."

The next day the professor called me to come to the study. I found him sitting at a table in the full light of the window, scrutinizing something very attentively with a magnifying glass.

"Ah, Miss Lally," he began, "I want to use your eyes. This glass is pretty good, but not like my old one that I left in town. Would you mind examining the thing yourself, and telling me how many characters are cut on it?"

He handed me the object in his hand. I saw that it was the black seal he had shown me in London, and my heart began to beat with the thought that I was presently to know something. I took the seal, and, holding it up to the light, checked off the grotesque dagger-shaped characters one by one.

"I make sixty-two," I said at last.

"Sixty-two? Nonsense; it's impossible, Ah, I see what you have done, you have counted that and that," and he pointed to two marks which I had certainly taken as letters with the rest.

"Yes, yes," Professor Gregg went on, "but those are obviously scratches, done accidentally; I saw that at once. Yes, then that's quite right. Thank you very much, Miss Lally."

I was going away, rather disappointed at my having been called in merely to count the number of marks on the black seal, when suddenly there flashed into my mind what I had read in the morning.

"But, Professor Gregg," I cried, breathless, "the seal, the seal. Why, it is the stone Hexecontalithos that Solinus writes of; it is Ixaxar."

"Yes," he said, "I suppose it is. Or it may be a mere coincidence. It never does to be too sure, you know, in these matters. Coincidence killed the professor."

I went away puzzled by what I had heard, and as much as ever at a loss to find the ruling clue in this maze of strange evidence. For three days the bad weather lasted, changing from driving rain to a dense mist, fine and dripping, and we seemed to be shut up in a white cloud that veiled all the world away from us. All the while Professor Gregg was darkling in his room, unwilling, it appeared, to dispense confidences or talk of any kind, and I heard him walking to and fro with a quick, impatient step, as if he were in some way wearied of inaction. The fourth morning was fine, and at breakfast the professor said briskly—

"We want some extra help about the house; a boy of fifteen or sixteen, you know. There are a lot of little odd jobs that take up the maids' time which a boy could do much better."

"The girls have not complained to me in any way," I replied. "Indeed, Anne said there was much less work than in London, owing to there being so little dust."

"Ah, yes, they are very good girls. But I think we shall do much better with a boy. In fact, that is what has been bothering me for the last two days."

"Bothering you?" I said in astonishment, for as a matter of fact the professor never took the slightest interest in the affairs of the house.

"Yes," he said, "the weather, you know. I really couldn't go out in that Scotch mist; I don't know the country very well, and I should have lost my way. But I am going to get the boy this morning."

"But how do you know there is such a boy as you want anywhere about?"

"Oh, I have no doubt as to that. I may have to walk a mile or two at the most, but I am sure to find just the boy I require."

I thought the professor was joking, but, though his tone was airy enough, there was something grim and set about his features that puzzled me. He got his stick, and stood at the door looking meditatively before him, and as I passed through the hall he called to me.

"By the way, Miss Lally, there was one thing I wanted to say to you. I dare say you may have heard that some of these country lads are not over-bright; idiotic would be a harsh word to use, and they are usually called 'naturals,' or something of the kind. I hope you won't mind if the boy I am after should turn out not too keen-witted; he will be perfectly harmless, of course, and blacking boots doesn't need much mental effort."

With that he was gone, striding up the road that led to the wood, and I remained stupefied; and then for the first time my astonishment was mingled with a sudden note of terror, arising I knew not whence, and all unexplained even to myself, and yet I felt about my heart for an instant something of the chill of death, and that shapeless, formless dread of the unknown that is worse than death itself. I tried to find courage in the sweet air that blew up from the sea, and in the sunlight after rain, but the mystic woods seemed to darken around me; and the vision of the river coiling between the reeds, and the silver grey of the ancient bridge, fashioned in my mind symbols of vague dread, as the mind of a child fashions terror from things harmless and familiar.

Two hours later Professor Gregg returned. I met him as he came down the road, and asked quietly if he had been able to find a boy.

"Oh, yes." he answered; "I found one easily enough. His name is Jervase Cradock, and I expect he will make himself very useful. His father has been dead for many years, and the mother, whom I saw, seemed very glad at the prospect of a few shillings extra coming in on Saturday nights. As I expected, he is not too sharp, has fits at times, the mother said; but as he will not be trusted with the china, that doesn't much matter, does it? And he is not in any way dangerous, you know, merely a little weak."

"When is he coming?"

"To-morrow morning at eight o'clock. Anne will show him what he has to do, and how to do it. At first he will go home every night, but perhaps it may ultimately turn out more convenient for him to sleep here, and only go home for Sundays."

I found nothing to say to all this; Professor Gregg spoke in a quiet tone of matter-of-fact, as indeed was warranted by the circumstance; and yet I could not quell my sensation of astonishment at the whole affair. I knew that in reality no assistance was wanted in the housework, and the professor's prediction that the boy he was to engage might prove a little "simple," followed by so exact a fulfilment, struck me as bizarre in the extreme. The next morning I heard from the housemaid that the boy Cradock had come at eight, and that she had been trying to make him useful. "He doesn't seem quite all there, I don't think, miss," was her comment, and later in the day I saw him helping the old man who worked in the garden. He was a youth of about fourteen, with black hair and black eyes and an olive skin, and I saw at once from the curious vacancy of his expression that he was mentally weak. He touched his forehead awkwardly as I went by, and I heard him answering the gardener in a queer, harsh voice that caught my attention; it gave me the impression of some one speaking deep below under the earth, and there was a strange sibilance, like the hissing of the phonograph as the pointer travels over the cylinder. I heard that he seemed anxious to do what he could, and was quite docile and obedient, and Morgan the gardener, who knew his mother, assured me he was perfectly harmless. "He's always been a bit queer," he said, "and no wonder, after what his mother went through before he was born. I did know his father, Thomas Cradock, well, and a very fine workman he was too, indeed. He got something wrong with his lungs owing to working in the wet woods, and never got over it, and went off quite sudden like. And they do say as how Mrs. Cradock was quite off her head; anyhow, she was found by Mr. Hillyer, Ty Coch, all crouched up on the Grey Hills, over there, crying and weeping like a lost soul. And Jervase, he was born about eight months afterwards, and, as I was saying, he was a bit queer always; and they do say when he could scarcely walk he would frighten the other children into fits with the noises he would make."

A word in the story had stirred up some remembrance within me, and, vaguely curious, I asked the old man where the Grey Hills were.

"Up there," he said, with the same gesture he had used before; "you go past the 'Fox and Hounds,' and through the forest, by the old ruins. It's a good five mile from here, and a strange sort of a place. The poorest soil between this and Monmouth, they do say, though it's good feed for sheep. Yes, it was a sad thing for poor Mrs. Cradock."

The old man turned to his work, and I strolled on down the path between the espaliers. gnarled and gouty with age, thinking of the story I had heard, and groping for the point in it that had some key to my memory. In an instant it came before me; I had seen the phrase "Grey Hills" on the slip of yellowed paper that Professor Gregg had taken from the drawer in his cabinet. Again I was seized with pangs of mingled curiosity and fear; I remembered the strange characters copied from the limestone rock, and then again their identity with the inscription of the age-old seal, and the fantastic fables of the Latin geographer. I saw beyond doubt that, unless coincidence had set all the scene and disposed all these bizarre events with curious art, I was to be a spectator of things far removed from the usual and customary traffic and jostle of life. Professor Gregg I noted day by day; he was hot on his trail, growing lean with eagerness; and in the evenings, when the sun was swimming on the verge of the mountain, he would pace the terrace to and fro with his eyes on the ground, while the mist grew white in the valley, and the stillness of the evening brought far voices near, and the blue smoke rose a straight column from the diamond-shaped chimney of the grey farmhouse, just as I had seen it on the first morning. I have told you I was of sceptical habit; but though I understood little or nothing, I began to dread, vainly proposing to myself the iterated dogmas of science that all life is material, and that in the system of things there is no undiscovered land, even beyond the remotest stars, where the supernatural can find a footing. Yet there struck in on this the thought that matter is as really awful and unknown as spirit, that science itself but dallies on the threshold, scarcely gaining more than a glimpse of the wonders of the inner place.

There is one day that stands up from amidst the others as a grim red beacon, betokening evil to come. I was sitting on a bench in the garden, watching the boy Cradock weeding, when I was suddenly alarmed by a harsh and choking sound, like the cry of a wild beast in anguish, and I was unspeakably shocked to see the unfortunate lad standing in full view before me, his whole body quivering and shaking at short intervals as though shocks of electricity were passing through him, his teeth grinding, foam gathering on his lips, and his face all swollen and blackened to a hideous mask of humanity. I shrieked with terror, and Professor Gregg came running; and as I pointed to Cradock, the boy with one convulsive shudder fell face forward, and lay on the wet earth, his body writhing like a wounded blind-worm, and an inconceivable babble of sounds bursting and rattling and hissing from his lips. He seemed to pour forth an infamous jargon, with words, or what seemed words, that might have belonged to a tongue dead since untold ages and buried deep beneath Nilotic mud, or in the inmost recesses of the Mexican forest. For a moment the thought passed through my mind, as my ears were still revolted with that infernal clamour, "Surely this is the very speech of hell," and then I cried out again and again, and ran away shuddering to my inmost soul. I had seen Professor Gregg's face as he stooped over the wretched boy and raised him, and I was appalled by the glow of exultation that shone on every lineament and feature. As I sat in my room with drawn blinds, and my eyes hidden in my hands, I heard heavy steps beneath, and I was told afterwards that Professor Gregg had carried Cradock to his study, and had locked the door. I heard voices murmur indistinctly, and I trembled to think of what might be passing within a few feet of where I sat; I longed to escape to the woods and sunshine, and yet I dreaded the sights that might confront me on the way; and at last, as I held the handle of the door nervously, I heard Professor Gregg's voice calling to me with a cheerful ring. "It's all right now, Miss Lally," he said. "The poor fellow has got over it, and I have been arranging for him to sleep here after tomorrow. Perhaps I may be able to do something for him."

"Yes," he said later, "it was a very painful sight, and I don't wonder you were alarmed. We may hope that good food will build him up a little, but conventional air with which one speaks of hopeless illness; and yet beneath it I detected the delight that leapt up rampant within him, and fought and struggled to find utterance. It was as if one glanced down on the even surface of the sea, clear and immobile, and saw beneath raging depths and a storm of contending billows. It was indeed to me a torturing and offensive problem that this man, who had so bounteously rescued me from the sharpness of death, and showed himself in all the relations of life full of benevolence, and pity, and kindly forethought, should so manifestly be for once on the side of the demons, and take a ghastly pleasure in the torments of an afflicted fellow creature. Apart, I struggled with the horned difficulty, and strove to find the solution; but without the hint of a clue, beset by mystery and contradiction, I saw nothing that might help me, and began to wonder whether, after all, I had not escaped from the white mist of the suburb at too dear a rate. I hinted something of my thought to the professor; I said enough to let him know that I was in the most acute perplexity, but the moment after regretted what I had done when I saw his face contort with a spasm of pain.

"My dear Miss Lally," he said, "you surely do not wish to leave us? No, no, you would not do it. You do not know how I rely on you; how confidently I go forward, assured that you are here to watch over my children. You, Miss Lally, are my rearguard; for let me tell you the business in which I am engaged is not wholly devoid of peril. You have not forgotten what I said the first morning here; my lips are shut by an old and firm resolve till they can open to utter no ingenious hypothesis or vague surmise, but irrefragable fact, as certain as a demonstration in mathematics. Think over it, Miss Lally; not for a moment would I endeavour to keep you here against your own instincts, and yet I tell you frankly that I am persuaded it is here, here amidst the woods, that your duty lies."

I was touched by the eloquence of his tone, and by the remembrance that the man, after all, had been my salvation, and I gave him my hand on a promise to serve him loyally and without question. A few days later the rector of our church—a little church, grey and severe and quaint, that hovered on the very banks of the river and watched the tides swim and return—came to see us, and Professor Gregg easily persuaded him to stay and share our dinner. Mr. Meyrick was a member of an antique family of squires, whose old manor-house stood amongst the hills some seven miles away, and thus rooted in the soil, the rector was a living store of all the old fading customs and lore of the country. His manner, genial, with a deal of retired oddity, won on Professor Gregg; and towards the cheese, when a curious Burgundy had begun its incantations, the two men glowed like the wine, and talked of philology with the enthusiasm of a burgess over the peerage. The parson was expounding the pronunciation of the Welsh *ll*, and producing sounds like the gurgle of his native brooks, when Professor Gregg struck in.

"By the way," he said, "that was a very odd word I met with the other day. You know my boy, poor Jervase Cradock? Well, he has got the bad habit of talking to himself, and the day before yesterday I was walking in the garden here and heard him; he was evidently quite unconscious of my presence. A lot of what he said I couldn't make out, but one word struck me distinctly. It was such an odd sound, half sibilant, half guttural, and as quaint as those double *ls* you have been demonstrating. I do not know whether I can give you an idea of the sound; 'Ishakshar' is perhaps as near as I can get. But the *k* ought to be a Greek *chi* or a Spanish *j*. Now what does it mean in Welsh?"

"In Welsh?" said the parson. "There is no such word in Welsh, nor any word remotely resembling it. I know the book-Welsh, as they call it, and the colloquial dialects as well as any man, but there's no word like that from Anglesea to Usk. Besides, none of the Cradocks speak a word of Welsh; it's dying out about here."

"Really. You interest me extremely, Mr. Meyrick. I confess the word didn't strike me as having the Welsh ring. But I thought it might be some local corruption."

"No, I never heard such a word, or anything like it. Indeed," he added, smiling whimsically, "if it belongs to any language, I should say it must be that of the fairies—the Tylwydd Têg, as we call them."

The talk went on to the discovery of a Roman villa in the neighbourhood; and soon after I left the room, and sat down apart to wonder at the drawing together of such strange clues of evidence. As the professor had spoken of the curious word, I had caught the glint in his eye upon me; and though the pronunciation he gave was grotesque in the extreme, I recognized the name of the stone of sixty characters mentioned by Solinus, the black seal shut up in some secret drawer of the study, stamped for ever by a vanished race with signs that no man could read, signs that might, for all I knew, be the veils of awful things done long ago, and forgotten before the hills were moulded into form.

When the next morning I came down, I found Professor Gregg pacing the terrace in his eternal walk.

"Look at that bridge," he said, when he saw me; "observe the quaint and Gothic design, the angles between the arches, and the silvery grey of the stone in the awe of the morning light. I confess it seems to me symbolic; it should illustrate a mystical allegory of the passage from one world to another."

"Professor Gregg," I said quietly, "it is time that I knew something of what has happened, and of what is to happen."

For the moment he put me off, but I returned again with the same question in the evening, and then Professor Gregg flamed with excitement. "Don't you understand yet?" he cried. "But I have told you a good deal; yes, and shown you a good deal; you have heard pretty nearly all that I have heard, and seen what I have seen; or at least," and his voice chilled as he spoke, "enough to make a good deal clear as noonday. The servants told you, I have no doubt, that the wretched boy Cradock had another seizure the night before last; he awoke me with cries in that voice you heard in the garden, and I went to him, and God forbid you should see what I saw that night. But all this is useless; my time here is drawing to a close; I must be back in town in three weeks, as I have a course of lectures to prepare, and need all my books about me. In a very few days it will be all over, and I shall no longer hint, and no longer be liable to ridicule as a madman and a quack. No, I shall speak plainly, and I shall be heard with such emotions as perhaps no other man has ever drawn from the breasts of his fellows."

He paused, and seemed to grow radiant with the joy of great and wonderful discovery.

"But all that is for the future, the near future certainly, but still the future," he went on at length. "There is something to be done yet; you will remember my telling you that my researches were not altogether devoid of peril? Yes, there, is a certain amount of danger to be faced; I did not know how much when I spoke on the subject before, and to a certain extent I am still in the dark. But it will be a strange adventure, the last of all, the last demonstration in the chain."

He was walking up and down the room as he spoke, and I could hear in his voice the contending tones of exultation and despondence, or perhaps I should say awe, the awe of a man who goes forth on unknown waters, and I thought of his allusion to Columbus on the night he had laid his book before me. The evening was a little chilly, and a fire of logs had been lighted in the study where we were; the remittent flame and the glow on the walls reminded me of the old days. I was sitting silent in an armchair by the fire, wondering over all I had heard, and still vainly speculating as to the secret springs concealed from me under all the phantasmagoria I had witnessed, when I became suddenly aware of a sensation that change of some sort had been at work in the room, and that there was something unfamiliar in its aspect. For some time I looked about me, trying in vain to localize the alteration that I knew had been made; the table by the window, the chairs, the faded settee were all as I had known them. Suddenly, as a sought-for recollection flashes into the mind, I knew what was amiss. I was facing the professor's desk, which stood on the other side of the fire, and above the desk was a grimy-looking bust of Pitt, that I had never seen there before. And then I remembered the true position of this work of art; in the furthest corner by the door was an old cupboard, projecting into the room, and on the top of the cupboard, fifteen feet from the floor, the bust had been, and there, no doubt, it had delayed, accumulating dirt, since the early days of the century.

I was utterly amazed, and sat silent, still in a confusion of thought. There was, so far as I knew, no such thing as a stepladder in the house, for I had asked for one to make some alteration in the curtains of my room, and a tall man standing on a chair would have found it impossible to take down the bust. It had been placed, not on the edge of the cupboard, but far back against the wall; and Professor Gregg was, if anything, under the average height.

"How on earth did you manage to get down Pitt?" I said at last.

The professor looked curiously at me, and seemed to hesitate a little.

"They must have found you a step-ladder, or perhaps the gardener brought in a short ladder from outside?"

"No, I have had no ladder of any kind. Now, Miss Lally," he went on with an awkward simulation of jest, "there is a little puzzle for you; a problem in the manner of the inimitable Holmes; there are the facts, plain and patent: summon your acuteness to the solution of the puzzle. For Heaven's sake," he cried with a breaking voice, "say no more about it! I tell you, I never touched the thing," and he went out of the room with horror manifest on his face, and his hand shook and jarred the door behind him.

I looked round the room in vague surprise, not at all realizing what had happened, making vain and idle surmises by way of explanation, and wondering at the stirring of black waters by an idle word and the trivial change of an ornament. "This is some petty business, some whim on which I have jarred." I reflected; "the professor is perhaps scrupulous and superstitious over trifles, and my question may have outraged unacknowledged fears, as though one killed a spider or spilled the salt before the very eyes of a practical Scotchwoman." I was immersed in these fond suspicions, and began to plume myself a little on my immunity from such empty fears, when the truth fell heavily as lead upon my heart, and I recognized with cold terror that some awful influence had been at work. The bust was simply inaccessible; without a ladder no one could have touched it.

I went out to the kitchen and spoke as quietly as I could to the housemaid.

"Who moved that bust from the top of the cupboard, Anne?" I said to her. "Professor Gregg says he has not touched it. Did you find an old step-ladder in one of the outhouses?"

The girl looked at me blankly.

"I never touched it," she said. "I found it where it is now the other morning when I dusted the room. I remember now, it was Wednesday morning, because it was the morning after Cradock was taken bad in the night. My room is next to his, you know, miss," the girl went on piteously, "and it was awful to hear how he cried and called out names that I couldn't understand. It made me feel all afraid; and then master came, and I heard him speak, and he took down Cradock to the study and gave him something."

"And you found that bust moved the next morning?"

"Yes, miss. There was a queer sort of smell in the study when I came down and opened the windows; a bad smell it was, and I wondered what it could be. Do you know, miss, I went a long time ago to the Zoo in London with my cousin Thomas Barker, one afternoon that I had off, when I was at Mrs. Prince's in Stanhope Gate, and we went into the snake-house to see the snakes, and it was just the same sort of smell; very sick it made me feel, I remember, and I got Barker to take me out. And it was just the same kind of smell in the study, as I was saying, and I was wondering what it could be from, when I see that bust with Pitt cut in it, standing on the master's desk, and I thought to myself, Now who has done that, and how have they done it? And when I came to dust the things, I looked at the bust, and I saw a great mark on it where the dust was gone, for I don't think it can have been touched with a duster for years and years, and it wasn't like finger-marks, but a large patch like, broad and spread out. So I passed my hand over it, without thinking what I was doing, and where that patch was it was all sticky and slimy, as if a snail had crawled over it. Very strange, isn't it, miss? and I wonder who can have done it, and how that mess was made."

The well-meant gabble of the servant touched me to the quick; I lay down upon my bed, and bit my lip that I should not cry out loud in the sharp anguish of my terror and bewilderment. Indeed, I was almost mad with dread; I believe that if it had been daylight I should have fled hot foot, forgetting all courage and all the debt of gratitude that was due to Professor Gregg, not caring whether my fate were that I must starve slowly, so long as I might escape from the net of blind and panic fear that every day seemed to draw a little closer round me. If I knew, I thought, if I knew what there were to dread, I could guard against it; but here, in this lonely house, shut in on all sides by the olden woods and the vaulted hills, terror seems to spring inconsequent from every covert, and the flesh is aghast at the half-hearted murmurs of horrible things. All in vain I strove to summon scepticism to my aid, and endeavoured by cool common-sense to buttress my belief in a world of natural order, for the air that blew in at the open window was a mystic breath, and in the darkness I felt the silence go heavy and sorrowful as a mass of requiem, and I conjured images of strange shapes gathering fast amidst the reeds, beside the wash of the river.

In the morning from the moment that I set foot in the breakfast-room, I felt that the unknown plot was drawing to a crisis; the professor's face was firm and set, and he seemed hardly to hear our voices when we spoke.

"I am going out for a rather long walk," he said, when the meal was over. "You mustn't be expecting me, now, or thinking anything has happened if I don't turn up to dinner. I have been getting stupid lately, and I dare say a miniature walking tour will do me good. Perhaps I may even spend the night in some little inn, if I find any place that looks clean and comfortable."

I heard this, and knew by my experience of Professor Gregg's manner that it was no ordinary business or pleasure that impelled him. I knew not, nor even remotely guessed, where he was bound, nor had I the vaguest notion of his errand, but all the fear of the night before returned; and as he stood, smiling, on the terrace, ready to set out, I implored him to stay, and to forget all his dreams of the undiscovered continent.

"No, no, Miss Lally," he replied, still smiling, "it's too late now. *Vestigia nulla retrorsum,* you know, is the device of all true explorers, though I hope it won't be literally true in my case. But, indeed, you are wrong to alarm yourself so; I look upon my little expedition as quite commonplace; no more exciting than a day with the geological hammers. There is a risk, of course, but so there is on the commonest excursion. I can afford to be jaunty; I am doing nothing so hazardous as 'Arry does a hundred times over in the course of every Bank Holiday. Well, then, you must look more cheerfully; and so good-bye till tomorrow at latest."

He walked briskly up the road, and I saw him open the gate that marks the entrance of the wood, and then he vanished in the gloom of the trees.

All the day passed heavily with a strange darkness in the air, and again I felt as if imprisoned amidst the ancient woods, shut in an olden land of mystery and dread, and as if all was long ago and forgotten by the living outside. I hoped and dreaded; and when the dinner-hour came I waited, expecting to hear the professor's step in the hall, and his voice exulting at I knew not what triumph. I composed my face to welcome him gladly, but the night descended dark, and he did not come.

In the morning, when the maid knocked at my door, I called out to her, and asked if her master had returned; and when she replied that his bedroom stood open and empty, I felt the cold clasp of despair. Still, I fancied he might have discovered genial company, and would return for luncheon, or perhaps in the afternoon, and I took the children for a walk in the forest, and tried my best to play and laugh with them, and to shut out the thoughts of mystery and veiled terror. Hour after hour I waited, and my thoughts grew darker; again the night came and found me watching, and at last, as I was making much ado to finish my dinner, I heard steps outside and the sound of a man's voice.

The maid came in and looked oddly at me. "Please, miss," she began, "Mr. Morgan, the gardener, wants to speak to you for a minute, if you didn't mind."

"Show him in, please," I answered, and set my lips tight.

The old man came slowly into the room, and the servant shut the door behind him.

"Sit down, Mr. Morgan," I said; "what is it that you want to say to me?"

"Well, miss, Mr. Gregg he gave me something for you yesterday morning, just before he went off, and he told me particular not to hand it up before eight o'clock this evening exactly, if so be as he wasn't back again home before, and if he should come home before I was just to return it to him in his own hands. So, you see, as Mr. Gregg isn't here yet, I suppose I'd better give you the parcel directly."

He pulled out something from his pocket, and gave it to me, half rising. I took it silently, and seeing that Morgan seemed doubtful as to what he was to do next, I thanked him and bade him good night, and he went out. I was left alone in the room with the parcel in my hand—a paper parcel, neatly sealed and directed to me, with the instructions Morgan had quoted, all written in the professor's large, loose hand. I broke the seals with a choking at my heart, and found an envelope inside, addressed also, but open, and I took the letter out.

"My dear Miss Lally" it began,—"To quote the old logic manual, the case of your reading this note is a case of my having made a blunder of some sort, and, I am afraid, a blunder that turns these lines into a farewell. It is practically certain that neither you nor any one else will ever see me again. I have made my will with provision for this eventuality, and I hope you will consent to accept the small remembrance addressed to you, and my sincere thanks for the way in which you joined your fortunes to mine. The fate which has come upon me is desperate and terrible beyond the remotest dreams of man; but this fate you have a right to know—if you please. If you look in the left-hand drawer of my dressing-table, you will find the key of the escritoire, properly labelled. In the well of the escritoire is a large envelope sealed and addressed to your name. I advise you to throw it forthwith into the fire; you will sleep better of nights if you do so. But if you must know the history of what has happened, it is all written down for you to read."

The signature was firmly written below, and again I turned the page and read out the words one by one, aghast and white to the lips, my hands cold as ice, and sickness choking me. The dead silence of the room, and the thought of the dark woods and hills closing me in on every side, oppressed me, helpless and without capacity, and not knowing where to turn for counsel. At last I resolved that though knowledge should haunt my whole life and all the days to come, I must know the meaning of the strange terrors that had so long tormented me, rising grey, dim, and awful, like the shadows in the wood at dusk. I carefully carried out Professor Gregg's directions, and not without reluctance broke the seal of the envelope, and spread out his manuscript before me. That manuscript I always carry with me, and I see that I cannot deny your unspoken request to read it. This, then, was what I read that night, sitting at the desk, with a shaded lamp beside me.

The young lady who called herself Miss Lally then proceeded to recite

The Statement of William Gregg, F.R.S., etc.

It is many years since the first glimmer of the theory which is now almost, if not quite, reduced to fact dawned on my mind. A somewhat extensive course of miscellaneous and obsolete reading had done a great deal to prepare the way, and, later, when I became somewhat of a specialist, and immersed myself in the studies known as ethnological, I was now and then startled by facts that would not square with orthodox scientific opinion, and by discoveries that seemed to hint at something still hidden for all our research. More particularly I became convinced that much of the folk-lore of the world is but an exaggerated account of events that really happened, and I was especially drawn to consider the stories of the fairies, the good folk of the Celtic races. Here, I thought I could detect the fringe of embroidery and exaggeration, the fantastic guise, the little people dressed in green and gold sporting in the flowers, and I thought I saw a distinct analogy between the name given to this race (supposed to be imaginary) and the description of their appearance and manners. Just as our remote ancestors called the dreaded beings "fair" and "good" precisely because they dreaded them, so they had dressed them up in charming forms, knowing the truth to be the very reverse. Literature, too, had gone early to work, and had lent a powerful hand in the transformation, so that the playful elves of Shakespeare are already far removed from the true original, and the real horror is disguised in a form of prankish mischief. But in the older tales, the stories that used to make men cross themselves as they sat round the burning logs, we tread a different stage; I saw a widely opposed spirit in certain histories of children and of men and women who vanished strangely from the earth. They would be seen by a peasant in the fields walking towards some green and rounded hillock, and seen no more on earth; and there are stories of mothers who have left a child quietly sleeping, with the cottage door rudely barred with a piece of wood, and have returned, not to find the plump and rosy little Saxon, but a thin and wizened creature, with sallow skin and black, piercing eyes, the child of another race. Then, again, there were myths darker still; the dread of witch and wizard, the lurid evil of the Sabbath, and the hint of demons who mingled with the daughters of men. And just as we have turned the terrible "fair folk" into a company of benignant, if freakish elves, so we have hidden from us the black foulness of the witch and her companions under a popular *diablerie* of old women and broomsticks, and a comic cat with tail on end. So the Greeks called the hideous furies benevolent ladies, and thus the northern nations have followed their example. I pursued my investigations, stealing odd hours from other and more imperative labours, and I asked myself the question: Supposing these traditions to be true, who were the demons who are reported to have attended the Sabbaths? I need not say that I laid aside what I may call the supernatural hypothesis of the Middle Ages, and came to the conclusion that fairies and devils were of one and the same race and origin; invention, no doubt, and the Gothic fancy of old days, had done much in the way of exaggeration and distortion; yet I firmly believe that beneath all this imagery there was a black background of truth. As for some of the alleged wonders, I hesitated. While I should be very loath to receive any one specific instance of modern spiritualism as containing even a grain of the genuine, yet I was not wholly prepared to deny that human flesh may now and then, once perhaps in ten millions cases, be the veil of powers which seem magical to us—powers which, so far from proceeding from the heights and leading men thither, are in reality survivals from the depths of being. The amoeba and the snail have powers which we do not possess; and I thought it possible that the theory of reversion might explain many things which seem wholly inexplicable. Thus stood my position; I saw good reason to believe that much of the tradition, a vast deal of the earliest and uncorrupted tradition of the so-called fairies, represented solid fact, and I thought that the purely supernatural element in these traditions was to be accounted for on the hypothesis that a race which had fallen out of the grand march of evolution might have retained, as a survival, certain powers which would be to us wholly miraculous. Such was my theory as it stood conceived in my mind; and working with this in view, I seemed to gather confirmation from every side, from the spoils of a tumulus or a barrow, from a local paper reporting an antiquarian meeting in the country, and from general literature of all kinds. Amongst other instances, I remember being struck by the phrase "articulate-speaking men" in Homer, as if the writer knew or had heard of men whose speech was so rude that it could hardly be termed articulate; and on my hypothesis of a race who had lagged far behind the rest, I could easily conceive that such a folk would speak a jargon but little removed from the inarticulate noises of brute beasts.

Thus I stood, satisfied that my conjecture was at all events not far removed from fact, when a chance paragraph in a small country print one day arrested my attention. It was a short account of what was to all appearance the usual sordid tragedy of the village—a young girl unaccountably missing, and evil rumour blatant and busy with her reputation. Yet I could read between the lines that all this scandal was purely hypothetical, and in all probability invented to account for what was in any other manner unaccountable. A flight to London or Liverpool, or an undiscovered body lying with a weight about its neck in the foul depths of a woodland pool, or perhaps murder—such were the theories of the wretched girl's neighbours. But as I idly scanned the paragraph, a flash of thought passed through me with the violence of an electric shock: what if the obscure and horrible race of the hills still survived, still remained haunting wild places and barren hills, and now and then repeating the evil of Gothic legend, unchanged and unchangeable as the Turanian Shelta, or the Basques of Spain? I have said that the thought came with violence; and indeed I drew in my breath sharply, and clung with both hands to my elbow-chair, in a strange confusion of horror and elation. It was as if one of my *confrères* of physical science, roaming in a quiet English wood, had been suddenly stricken aghast by the presence of the slimy and loathsome terror of the icthyosaurus, the original of the stories of the awful worms killed by valourous knights, or had seen the sun darkened by the pterodactyl, the dragon of tradition. Yet as a resolute explorer of knowledge, the thought of such a discovery threw me into a passion of joy, and I cut out the slip from the paper and put it in a drawer in my old bureau, resolved that it should be but the first piece in a collection of the strangest significance. I sat long that evening dreaming of the conclusions I should establish, nor did cooler reflection at first dash my confidence. Yet as I began to put the case fairly, I saw that I might be building on an unstable foundation; the facts might possibly be in accordance with local opinion, and I regarded the affair with a mood of some reserve. Yet I resolved to remain perched on the look-out, and I hugged to myself the thought that I alone was watching and wakeful, while the great crowd of thinkers and searchers stood heedless and indifferent, perhaps letting the most prerogative facts pass by unnoticed.

Several years elapsed before I was enabled to add to the contents of the drawer; and the second find was in reality not a valuable one, for it was a mere repetition of the first, with only the variation of another and distant locality. Yet I gained something; for in the second case, as in the first, the tragedy took place in a desolate and lonely country, and so far my theory seemed justified. But the third piece was to me far more decisive. Again, amongst outland hills, far even from a main road of traffic, an old man was found done to death, and the instrument of execution was left beside him. Here, indeed, there were rumour and conjecture, for the deadly tool was a primitive stone axe, bound by gut to the wooden handle, and surmises the most extravagant and improbable were indulged in. Yet, as I thought with a kind of glee, the wildest conjectures went far astray; and I took the pains to enter into correspondence with the local doctor, who was called at the inquest. He, a man of some acuteness, was dumbfounded. "It will not do to speak of these things in country places," he wrote to me; "but frankly, there is some hideous mystery here. I have obtained possession of the stone axe, and have been so curious as to test its powers. I took it into the back garden of my house one Sunday afternoon when my family and the servants were all out, and there, sheltered by the poplar hedges, I made my experiments. I found the thing utterly unmanageable; whether there is some peculiar balance, some nice adjustment of weights, which require incessant practice, or whether an effectual blow can be struck only by a certain trick of the muscles, I do not know; but I can assure you that I went into the house with but a sorry opinion of my athletic capacities. It was like an inexperienced man trying 'putting the hammer'; the force exerted seemed to return on oneself, and I found myself hurled backwards with violence, while the axe fell harmless to the ground. On another occasion I tried the experiment with a clever woodman of the place; but this man, who had handled his axe for forty years, could do nothing with the stone implement, and missed every stroke most ludicrously. In short, if it were not so supremely absurd, I should say that for four thousand years no one on earth could have struck an effective blow with the tool that undoubtedly was used to murder the old man." This, as may be imagined, was to me rare news; and afterwards, when I heard the whole story, and learned that the unfortunate old man had babbled tales of what might be seen at night on a certain wild hillside, hinting at unheard-of wonders, and that he had been found cold one morning on the very hill in question, my exultation was extreme, for I felt I was leaving conjecture far behind me. But the next step was of still greater importance. I had possessed for many years an extraordinary stone seal—a piece of dull black stone, two inches long from the handle to the stamp, and the stamping end a rough hexagon an inch and a quarter in diameter. Altogether, it presented the appearance of an enlarged tobacco stopper of an old-fashioned make. It had been sent to me by an agent in the east, who informed me that it had been found near the site of the ancient Babylon. But the characters engraved on the seal were to me an intolerable puzzle. Somewhat of the cuneiform pattern, there were yet striking differences, which I detected at the first glance, and all efforts to read the inscription on the hypothesis that the rules for deciphering the arrow-headed writing would apply proved futile. A riddle such as this stung my pride, and at odd moments I would take the Black Seal out of the cabinet, and scrutinize it with so much idle perseverance that every letter was familiar to my mind, and I could have drawn the inscription from memory without the slightest error. Judge, then, of my surprise when I one day received from a correspondent in the west of England a letter and an enclosure that positively left me thunderstruck. I saw carefully traced on a large piece of paper the very characters of the Black Seal, without alteration of any kind, and above the inscription my friend had written: *Inscription found on a limestone rock on the Grey Hills, Monmouthshire. Done in some red earth, and quite recent.* I turned to the letter. My friend wrote: "I send you the enclosed inscription with all due reserve. A shepherd who passed by the stone a week ago swears that there was then no mark of any kind. The characters, as I have noted, are formed by drawing some red earth over the stone, and are of an average height of one inch. They look to me like a kind of cuneiform character, a good deal altered, but this, of course, is impossible. It may be either a hoax, or more probably some scribble of the gypsies, who are plentiful enough in this wild country. They have, as you are aware, many hieroglyphics which they use in communicating with one another. I happened to visit the stone in question two days ago in connection with a rather painful incident which has occurred here."

As may be supposed, I wrote immediately to my friend, thanking him for the copy of the inscription, and asking him in a casual manner the history of the incident he mentioned. To be brief, I heard that a woman named Cradock, who had lost her husband a day before, had set out to communicate the sad news to a cousin who lived some five miles away. She took a short cut which led by the Grey Hills. Mrs. Cradock, who was then quite a young woman, never arrived at her relative's house. Late that night a farmer, who had lost a couple of sheep, supposed to have wandered from the flock, was walking over the Grey Hills, with a lantern and his dog. His attention was attracted by a noise, which he described as a kind of wailing, mournful and pitiable to hear; and, guided by the sound, he found the unfortunate Mrs. Cradock crouched on the ground by the limestone rock, swaying her body to and fro, and lamenting and crying in so heart-rending a manner that the farmer was, as he says, at first obliged to stop his ears, or he would have run away. The woman allowed herself to be taken home, and a neighbour came to see to her necessities. All the night she never ceased her crying, mixing her lament with words of some unintelligible jargon, and when the doctor arrived he pronounced her insane. She lay on her bed for a week, now wailing, as people said, like one lost and damned for eternity, and now sunk in a heavy coma; it was thought that grief at the loss of her husband had unsettled her mind, and the medical man did not at one time expect her to live. I need not say that I was deeply interested in this story, and I made my friend write to me at intervals with all the particulars of the case. I heard then that in the course of six weeks the woman gradually recovered the use of her faculties, and some months later she gave birth to a son, christened Jervase, who unhappily proved to be of weak intellect. Such were the facts known to the village; but to me, while I whitened at the suggested thought of the hideous enormities that had doubtless been committed, all this was nothing short of conviction, and I incautiously hazarded a hint of something like the truth to some scientific friends. The moment the words had left my lips I bitterly regretted having spoken, and thus given away the great secret of my life, but with a good deal of relief mixed with indignation I found my fears altogether misplaced, for my friends ridiculed me to my face, and I was regarded as a madman; and beneath a natural anger I chuckled to myself, feeling as secure amidst these blockheads as if I had confided what I knew to the desert sands.

But now, knowing so much, I resolved I would know all, and I concentrated my efforts on the task of deciphering the inscription on the Black Seal. For many years I made this puzzle the sole object of my leisure moments, for the greater portion of my time was, of course, devoted to other duties, and it was only now and then that I could snatch a week of clear research. If I were to tell the full history of this curious investigation, this statement would be wearisome in the extreme, for it would contain simply the account of long and tedious failure. By what I knew already of ancient scripts I was well equipped for the chase, as I always termed it to myself. I had correspondents amongst all the scientific men in Europe, and, indeed, in the world, and I could not believe that in these days any character, however ancient and however perplexed, could long resist the search-light I should bring to bear upon it. Yet in point of fact, it was fully fourteen years before I succeeded. With every year my professional duties increased and my leisure became smaller. This no doubt retarded me a good deal; and yet, when I look back on those years, I am astonished at the vast scope of my investigation of the Black Seal. I made my bureau a centre, and from all the world and from all the ages I gathered transcripts of ancient writing. Nothing, I resolved, should pass me unawares, and the faintest hint should be welcomed and followed up. But as one covert after another was tried and proved empty of result, I began in the course of years to despair, and to wonder whether the Black Seal were the sole relic of some race that had vanished from the world, and left no other trace of its existence—had perished, in fine, as Atlantis is said to have done, in some great cataclysm, its secrets perhaps drowned beneath the ocean or moulded into the heart of the hills. The thought chilled my warmth a little, and though I still persevered, it was no longer with the same certainty of faith. A chance came to the rescue. I was staying in a considerable town in the north of England, and took the opportunity of going over the very creditable museum that had for some time been established in the place. The curator was one of my correspondents; and, as we were looking through one of the mineral cases, my attention was struck by a specimen, a piece of black stone some four inches square, the appearance of which reminded me in a measure of the Black Seal. I took it up carelessly, and was turning it over in my hand, when I saw, to my astonishment, that the under side was inscribed. I said, quietly enough, to my friend the curator that the specimen interested me, and that I should be much obliged if he would allow me to take it with me to my hotel for a couple of days. He, of course, made no objection, and I hurried to my rooms and found that my first glance had not deceived me. There were two inscriptions; one in the regular cuneiform character, another in the character of the Black Seal, and I realized that my task was accomplished. I made an exact copy of the two inscriptions; and when I got to my London study, and had the seal before me, I was able seriously to grapple with the great problem. The interpreting inscription on the museum specimen, though in itself curious enough, did not bear on my quest, but the transliteration made me master of the secret of the Black Seal. Conjecture, of course, had to enter into my calculations; there was here and there uncertainty about a particular ideograph, and one sign recurring again and again on the seal baffled me for many successive nights. But at last the secret stood open before me in plain English, and I read the key of the awful transmutation of the hills. The last word was hardly written, when with fingers all trembling and unsteady I tore the scrap of paper into the minutest fragments, and saw them flame and blacken in the red hollow of the fire, and then I crushed the grey films that remained into finest powder. Never since then have I written those words; never will I write the phrases which tell how man can be reduced to the slime from which he came, and be forced to put on the flesh of the reptile and the snake. There was now but one thing remaining. I knew, but I desired to see, and I was after some time able to take a house in the neighbourhood of the Grey Hills, and not far from the cottage where Mrs. Cradock and her son Jervase resided. I need not go into a full and detailed account of the apparently inexplicable events which have occurred here, where I am writing this. I knew that I should find in Jervase Cradock something of the blood of the "Little People," and I found later that he had more than once encountered his kinsmen in lonely places in that lonely land. When I was summoned one day to the garden, and found him in a seizure speaking or hissing the ghastly jargon of the Black Seal, I am afraid that exultation prevailed over pity. I heard bursting from his lips the secrets of the underworld, and the word of dread, "Ishakshar," the signification of which I must be excused from giving.

But there is one incident I cannot pass over unnoticed. In the waste hollow of the night I awoke at the sound of those hissing syllables I knew so well; and on going to the wretched boy's room, I found him convulsed and foaming at the mouth, struggling on the bed as if he strove to escape the grasp of writhing demons. I took him down to my room and lit the lamp, while he lay twisting on the floor, calling on the power within his flesh to leave him. I saw his body swell and become distended as a bladder, while the face blackened before my eyes; and then at the crisis I did what was necessary according to the directions on the Seal, and putting all scruple on one side, I became a man of science, observant of what was passing. Yet the sight I had to witness was horrible, almost beyond the power of human conception and the most fearful fantasy. Something pushed out from the body there on the floor, and stretched forth a slimy, wavering tentacle, across the room, grasped the bust upon the cupboard, and laid it down on my desk.

When it was over, and I was left to walk up and down all the rest of the night, white and shuddering, with sweat pouring from my flesh, I vainly tried to reason within myself: I said, truly enough, that I had seen nothing really supernatural, that a snail pushing out his horns and drawing them in was but an instance on a smaller scale of what I had witnessed; and yet horror broke through all such reasonings and left me shattered and loathing myself for the share I had taken in the night's work.

There is little more to be said. I am going now to the final trial and encounter; for I have determined that there shall be nothing wanting, and I shall meet the "Little People" face to face. I shall have the Black Seal and the knowledge of its secrets to help me, and if I unhappily do not return from my journey, there is no need to conjure up here a picture of the awfulness of my fate.

Pausing a little at the end of Professor Gregg's statement, Miss Lally continued her tale in the following words:—

Such was the almost incredible story that the professor had left behind him. When I had finished reading it, it was late at night, but the next morning I took Morgan with me, and we proceeded to search the Grey Hills for some trace of the lost professor. I will not weary you with a description of the savage desolation of that tract of country, a tract of utterest loneliness, of bare green hills dotted over with grey limestone boulders, worn by the ravages of time into fantastic semblances of men and beast. Finally, after many hours of weary searching, we found what I told you—the watch and chain, the purse, and the ring—wrapped in a piece of coarse parchment. When Morgan cut the gut that bound the parcel together, and I saw the professor's property, I burst into tears, but the sight of the dreaded characters of the Black Seal repeated on the parchment froze me to silent horror, and I think I understood for the first time the awful fate that had come upon my late employer.

I have only to add that Professor Gregg's lawyer treated my account of what had happened as a fairy tale, and refused even to glance at the documents I laid before him. It was he who was responsible for the statement that appeared in the public press, to the effect that Professor Gregg had been drowned, and that his body must have been swept into the open sea.

M *is for* Mummy

The ancient mummy animated by sorcery to wreak havoc in the modern world is one of the most iconic figures in supernatural horror. At the time that British writer Arthur Conan Doyle (1859–1930)—best known as the creator of Sherlock Holmes—wrote this story, the mummy was a relatively new theme in horror fiction, although it was a fixed presence in newspaper and magazine accounts of western adventurers and explorers uncovering the treasures of ancient Egypt. The story was first published in the September 1892 issue of *Harper's.*

ARTHUR CONAN DOYLE

Lot No. 249

Of the dealings of Edward Bellingham with William Monkhouse Lee, and of the cause of the great terror of Abercrombie Smith, it may be that no absolute and final judgment will ever be delivered. It is true that we have the full and clear narrative of Smith himself, and such corroboration as he could look for from Thomas Styles the servant, from the Reverend Plumptree Peterson, Fellow of Old's, and from such other people as chanced to gain some passing glance at this or that incident in a singular chain of events. Yet, in the main, the story must rest upon Smith alone, and the most will think that it is more likely that one brain, however outwardly sane, has some subtle warp in its texture, some strange flaw in its workings, than that the path of Nature has been overstepped in open day in so famed a centre of learning and light as the University of Oxford. Yet when we think how narrow and how devious this path of Nature is, how dimly we can trace it, for all our lamps of science, and how from the darkness which girds it round great and terrible possibilities loom ever shadowly upwards, it is a bold and confident man who will put a limit to the strange by-paths into which the human spirit may wander.

In a certain wing of what we will call Old College in Oxford there is a corner turret of an exceeding great age. The heavy arch which spans the open door has bent downwards in the centre under the weight of its years, and the grey, lichen-blotched blocks of stone are bound and knitted together with withes and strands of ivy, as though the old mother had set herself to brace them up against wind and weather. From the door a stone stair curves upward spirally, passing two landings, and terminating in a third one, its steps all shapeless and hollowed by the tread of so many generations of the seekers after knowledge. Life has flowed like water down this winding stair, and, waterlike, has left these smooth-worn grooves behind it. From the long-gowned, pedantic scholars of Plantagenet days down to the young bloods of a later age, how full and strong had been that tide of young English life. And what was left now of all those hopes, those strivings, those fiery energies, save here and there in some old-world churchyard a few scratches upon a stone, and perchance a handful of dust in a mouldering coffin? Yet here were the silent stair and the grey old wall, with bend and saltire and many another heraldic device still to be read upon its surface, like grotesque shadows thrown back from the days that had passed.

In the month of May, in the year 1884, three young men occupied the sets of rooms which opened on to the separate landings of the old stair. Each set consisted simply of a sitting-room and of a bedroom, while the two corresponding rooms upon the ground-floor were used, the one as a coal-cellar, and the other as the living-room of the servant, or gyp, Thomas Styles, whose duty it was to wait upon the three men above him. To right and to left was a line of lecture-rooms and of offices, so that the dwellers in the old turret enjoyed a certain seclusion, which made the chambers popular among the more studious undergraduates. Such were the three who occupied them now—Abercrombie Smith above, Edward Bellingham beneath him, and William Monkhouse Lee upon the lowest storey.

It was ten o'clock on a bright spring night, and Abercrombie Smith lay back in his arm-chair, his feet upon the fender, and his briar-root pipe between his lips. In a similar chair, and equally at his ease, there lounged on the other side of the fireplace his old school friend Jephro Hastie. Both men were in flannels, for they had spent their evening upon the river, but apart from their dress no one could look at their hard-cut, alert faces without seeing that they were open-air men—men whose minds and tastes turned naturally to all that was manly and robust. Hastie, indeed, was stroke of his college boat, and Smith was an even better oar, but a coming examination had already cast its shadow over him and held him to his work, save for the few hours a week which health demanded. A litter of medical books upon the table, with scattered bones, models and anatomical plates, pointed to the extent as well as the nature of his studies, while a couple of single-sticks and a set of boxing-gloves above the mantelpiece hinted at the means by which, with Hastie's help, he might take his exercise in its most compressed and least distant form. They knew each other very well—so well that they could sit now in that soothing silence which is the very highest development of companionship.

"Have some whisky," said Abercrombie Smith at last between two cloud-bursts. "Scotch in the jug and Irish in the bottle."

"No, thanks. I'm in for the sculls. I don't liquor when I'm training. How about you?"

"I'm reading hard. I think it best to leave it alone."

Hastie nodded, and they relapsed into a contented silence.

"By-the-way, Smith," asked Hastie, presently, "have you made the acquaintance of either of the fellows on your stair yet?"

"Just a nod when we pass. Nothing more."

"Hum! I should be inclined to let it stand at that. I know something of them both. Not much, but as much as I want. I don't think I should take them to my bosom if I were you. Not that there's much amiss with Monkhouse Lee."

"Meaning the thin one?"

"Precisely. He is a gentlemanly little fellow. I don't think there is any vice in him. But then you can't know him without knowing Bellingham."

"Meaning the fat one?"

"Yes, the fat one. And he's a man whom I, for one, would rather not know."

Abercrombie Smith raised his eyebrows and glanced across at his companion.

"What's up, then?" he asked. "Drink? Cards? Cad? You used not to be censorious."

"Ah! you evidently don't know the man, or you wouldn't ask. There's something damnable about him—something reptilian. My gorge always rises at him. I should put him down as a man with secret vices—an evil liver. He's no fool, though. They say that he is one of the best men in his line that they have ever had in the college."

"Medicine or classics?"

"Eastern languages. He's a demon at them. Chillingworth met him somewhere above the second cataract last long, and he told me that he just prattled to the Arabs as if he had been born and nursed and weaned among them. He talked Coptic to the Copts, and Hebrew to the Jews, and Arabic to the Bedouins, and they were all ready to kiss the hem of his frock-coat. There are some old hermit Johnnies up in those parts who sit on rocks and scowl and spit at the casual stranger. Well, when they saw this chap Bellingham, before he had said five words they just lay down on their bellies and wriggled. Chillingworth said that he never saw anything like it. Bellingham seemed to take it as his right, too, and strutted about among them and talked down to them like a Dutch uncle. Pretty good for an undergrad of Old's, wasn't it?"

"Why do you say you can't know Lee without knowing Bellingham? "

"Because Bellingham is engaged to his sister Eveline. Such a bright little girl, Smith! I know the whole family well. It's disgusting to see that brute with her. A toad and a dove, that's what they always remind me of."

Abercrombie Smith grinned and knocked his ashes out against the side of the grate.

"You show every card in your hand, old chap," said he. "What a prejudiced, green-eyed, evil-thinking old man it is! You have really nothing against the fellow except that."

"Well, I've known her ever since she was as long as that cherry-wood pipe, and I don't like to see her taking risks. And it is a risk. He looks beastly. And he has a beastly temper, a venomous temper. You remember his row with Long Norton?"

"No; you always forget that I am a freshman."

"Ah, it was last winter. Of course. Well, you know the towpath along by the river. There were several fellows going along it, Bellingham in front, when they came on an old market-woman coming the other way. It had been raining—you know what those fields are like when it has rained—and the path ran between the river and a great puddle that was nearly as broad. Well, what does this swine do but keep the path, and push the old girl into the mud, where she and her marketings came to terrible grief. It was a blackguard thing to do, and Long Norton, who is as gentle a fellow as ever stepped, told him what he thought of it. One word led to another, and it ended in Norton laying his stick across the fellow's shoulders. There was the deuce of a fuss about it, and it's a treat to see the way in which Bellingham looks at Norton when they meet now. By Jove, Smith, it's nearly eleven o'clock!"

"No hurry. Light your pipe again."

"Not I. I'm supposed to be in training. Here I've been sitting gossiping when I ought to have been safely tucked up. I'll borrow your skull, if you can share it. Williams has had mine for a month. I'll take the little bones of your ear, too, if you are sure you won't need them. Thanks very much. Never mind a bag, I can carry them very well under my arm. Good-night, my son, and take my tip as to your neighbour."

When Hastie, bearing his anatomical plunder, had clattered off down the winding stair, Abercrombie Smith hurled his pipe into the wastepaper basket, and drawing his chair nearer to the lamp, plunged into a formidable green-covered volume, adorned with great coloured maps of that strange internal kingdom of which we are the hapless and helpless monarchs. Though a freshman at Oxford, the student was not so in medicine, for he had worked for four years at Glasgow and at Berlin, and this coming examination would place him finally as a member of his profession. With his firm mouth, broad forehead, and clear-cut, somewhat hard-featured face, he was a man who, if he had no brilliant talent, was yet so dogged, so patient, and so strong that he might in the end overtop a more showy genius. A man who can hold his own among Scotchmen and North Germans is not a man to be easily set back. Smith had left a name at Glasgow and at Berlin, and he was bent now upon doing as much at Oxford, if hard work and devotion could accomplish it.

He had sat reading for about an hour, and the hands of the noisy carriage clock upon the side table were rapidly closing together upon the twelve, when a sudden sound fell upon the student's ear—a sharp, rather shrill sound, like the hissing intake of a man's breath who gasps under some strong emotion. Smith laid down his book and slanted his ear to listen. There was no one on either side or above him, so that the interruption came certainly from the neighbour beneath—the same neighbour of whom Hastie had given so unsavoury an account. Smith knew him only as a flabby, pale-faced man of silent and studious habits, a man whose lamp threw a golden bar from the old turret even after he had extinguished his own. This community in lateness had formed a certain silent bond between them. It was soothing to Smith when the hours stole on towards dawning to feel that there was another so close who set as small a value upon his sleep as he did. Even now, as his thoughts turned towards him, Smith's feelings were kindly. Hastie was a good fellow, but he was rough, strong-fibred, with no imagination or sympathy. He could not tolerate departures from what he looked upon as the model type of manliness. If a man could not be measured by a public-school standard, then he was beyond the pale with Hastie. Like so many who are themselves robust, he was apt to confuse the constitution with the character, to ascribe to want of principle what was really a want of circulation. Smith, with his stronger mind, knew his friend's habit, and made allowance for it now as his thoughts turned towards the man beneath him.

There was no return of the singular sound, and Smith was about to turn to his work once more, when suddenly there broke out in the silence of the night a hoarse cry, a positive scream—the call of a man who is moved and shaken beyond all control. Smith sprang out of his chair and dropped his book. He was a man of fairly firm fibre, but there was something in this sudden, uncontrollable shriek of horror which chilled his blood and pringled in his skin. Coming in such a place and at such an hour, it brought a thousand fantastic possibilities into his head. Should he rush down, or was it better to wait? He had all the national hatred of making a scene, and he knew so little of his neighbour that he would not lightly intrude upon his affairs. For a moment he stood in doubt and even as he balanced the matter there was a quick rattle of footsteps upon the stairs, and young Monkhouse Lee, half dressed and as white as ashes, burst into his room.

"Come down!" he gasped. "Bellingham's ill."

Abercrombie Smith followed him closely down stairs into the sitting-room which was beneath his own, and intent as he was upon the matter in hand, he could not but take an amazed glance around him as he crossed the threshold. It was such a chamber as he had never seen before—a museum rather than a study. Walls and ceiling were thickly covered with a thousand strange relics from Egypt and the East. Tall, angular figures bearing burdens or weapons stalked in an uncouth frieze round the apartments. Above were bull-headed, stork-headed, cat-headed, owl-headed statues, with viper-crowned, almond-eyed monarchs, and strange, beetle-like deities cut out of the blue Egyptian lapis lazuli. Horus and Isis and Osiris peeped down from every niche and shelf, while across the ceiling a true son of Old Nile, a great, hanging-jawed crocodile, was slung in a double noose.

In the centre of this singular chamber was a large, square table, littered with papers, bottles, and the dried leaves of some graceful, palm-like plant. These varied objects had all been heaped together in order to make room for a mummy case, which had been conveyed from the wall, as was evident from the gap there, and laid across the front of the table. The mummy itself, a horrid, black, withered thing, like a charred head on a gnarled bush, was lying half out of the case, with its clawlike hand and bony forearm resting upon the table. Propped up against the sarcophagus was an old yellow scroll of papyrus, and in front of it, in a wooden arm-chair, sat the owner of the room, his head thrown back, his widely-opened eyes directed in a horrified stare to the crocodile above him, and his blue, thick lips puffing loudly with every expiration.

"My God! he's dying!" cried Monkhouse Lee distractedly.

He was a slim, handsome young fellow, olive-skinned and dark-eyed, of a Spanish rather than of an English type, with a Celtic intensity of manner which contrasted with the Saxon phlegm of Abercrombie Smith.

"Only a faint, I think," said the medical student. "Just give me a hand with him. You take his feet. Now on to the sofa. Can you kick all those little wooden devils off? What a litter it is! Now he will be all right if we undo his collar and give him some water. What has he been up to at all?"

"I don't know. I heard him cry out. I ran up. I know him pretty well, you know. It is very good of you to come down."

"His heart is going like a pair of castanets," said Smith, laying his hand on the breast of the unconscious man. "He seems to me to be frightened all to pieces. Chuck the water over him! What a face he has got on him!"

It was indeed a strange and most repellent face, for colour and outline were equally unnatural. It was white, not with the ordinary pallor of fear but with an absolutely bloodless white, like the under side of a sole. He was very fat, but gave the impression of having at some time been considerably fatter, for his skin hung loosely in creases and folds, and was shot with a meshwork of wrinkles. Short, stubbly brown hair bristled up from his scalp, with a pair of thick, wrinkled ears protruding on either side. His light grey eyes were still open, the pupils dilated and the balls projecting in a fixed and horrid stare. It seemed to Smith as he looked down upon him that he had never seen nature's danger signals flying so plainly upon a man's countenance, and his thoughts turned more seriously to the warning which Hastie had given him an hour before.

"What the deuce can have frightened him so?" he asked.

"It's the mummy."

"The mummy? How, then?"

"I don't know. It's beastly and morbid. I wish he would drop it. It's the second fright he has given me. It was the same last winter. I found him just like this, with that horrid thing in front of him."

"What does he want with the mummy, then?"

"Oh, he's a crank, you know. It's his hobby. He knows more about these things than any man in England. But I wish he wouldn't! Ah, he's beginning to come to."

A faint tinge of colour had begun to steal back into Bellingham's ghastly cheeks, and his eyelids shivered like a sail after a calm. He clasped and unclasped his hands, drew a long, thin breath between his teeth, and suddenly jerking up his head, threw a glance of recognition around him. As his eyes fell upon the mummy, he sprang off the sofa, seized the roll of papyrus, thrust it into a drawer, turned the key, and then staggered back on to the sofa.

"What's up?" he asked. "What do you chaps want?"

"You've been shrieking out and making no end of a fuss," said Monkhouse Lee. "If our neighbour here from above hadn't come down, I'm sure I don't know what I should have done with you."

"Ah, it's Abercrombie Smith," said Bellingham, glancing up at him. "How very good of you to come in! What a fool I am! Oh, my God, what a fool I am!"

He sunk his head on to his hands, and burst into peal after peal of hysterical laughter.

"Look here! Drop it!" cried Smith, shaking him roughly by the shoulder.

"Your nerves are all in a jangle. You must drop these little midnight games with mummies, or you'll be going off your chump. You're all on wires now."

"I wonder," said Bellingham, "whether you would be as cool as I am if you had seen—"

"What then?"

"Oh, nothing. I meant that I wonder if you could sit up at night with a mummy without trying your nerves. I have no doubt that you are quite right. I dare say that I have been taking it out of myself too much lately. But I am all right now. Please don't go, though. Just wait for a few minutes until I am quite myself."

"The room is very close," remarked Lee, throwing open the window and letting in the cool night air.

"It's balsamic resin," said Bellingham. He lifted up one of the dried palmate leaves from the table and frizzled it over the chimney of the lamp. It broke away into heavy smoke wreaths, and pungent, biting odour filled the chamber. "It's the sacred plant—the plant of the priests," he remarked. "Do you know anything of Eastern languages, Smith?"

"Nothing at all. Not a word."

The answer seemed to lift a weight from the Egyptologist's mind.

"By-the-way," he continued, "how long was it from the time that you ran down, until I came to my senses?"

"Not long. Some four or five minutes."

"I thought it could not be very long," said he, drawing a long breath. "But what a strange thing unconsciousness is! There is no measurement to it. I could not tell from my own sensations if it were seconds or weeks. Now that gentleman on the table was packed up in the days of the eleventh dynasty, some forty centuries ago, and yet if he could find his tongue he would tell us that this lapse of time has been but a closing of the eyes and a reopening of them. He is a singularly fine mummy, Smith."

Smith stepped over to the table and looked down with a professional eye at the black and twisted form in front of him. The features, though horribly discoloured, were perfect, and two little nut-like eyes still lurked in the depths of the black, hollow sockets. The blotched skin was drawn tightly from bone to bone, and a tangled wrap of black coarse hair fell over the ears. Two thin teeth, like those of a rat, overlay the shrivelled lower lip. In its crouching position, with bent joints and craned head, there was a suggestion of energy about the horrid thing which made Smith's gorge rise. The gaunt ribs, with their parchment-like covering, were exposed, and the sunken, leaden-hued abdomen, with the long slit where the embalmer had left his mark; but the lower limbs were wrapt round with coarse yellow bandages. A number of little clove-like pieces of myrrh and of cassia were sprinkled over the body, and lay scattered on the inside of the case.

"I don't know his name," said Bellingham, passing his hand over the shrivelled head. "You see the outer sarcophagus with the inscriptions is missing. Lot 249 is all the title he has now. You see it printed on his case. That was his number in the auction at which I picked him up."

"He has been a very pretty sort of fellow in his day," remarked Abercrombie Smith.

"He has been a giant. His mummy is six feet seven in length, and that would be a giant over there, for they were never a very robust race. Feel these great knotted bones, too. He would be a nasty fellow to tackle."

"Perhaps these very hands helped to build the stones into the pyramids," suggested Monkhouse Lee, looking down with disgust in his eyes at the crooked, unclean talons.

"No fear. This fellow has been pickled in natron, and looked after in the most approved style. They did not serve hodsmen in that fashion. Salt or bitumen was enough for them. It has been calculated that this sort of thing cost about seven hundred and thirty pounds in our money. Our friend was a noble at the least. What do you make of that small inscription near his feet, Smith?"

"I told you that I know no Eastern tongue."

"Ah, so you did. It is the name of the embalmer, I take it. A very conscientious worker he must have been. I wonder how many modern works will survive four thousand years?"

He kept on speaking lightly and rapidly, but it was evident to Abercrombie Smith that he was still palpitating with fear. His hands shook, his lower lip trembled, and look where he would, his eye always came sliding round to his gruesome companion. Through all his fear, however, there was a suspicion of triumph in his tone and manner. His eye shone, and his footstep, as he paced the room, was brisk and jaunty. He gave the impression of a man who has gone through an ordeal, the marks of which he still bears upon him, but which has helped him to his end.

"You're not going yet?" he cried, as Smith rose from the sofa.

At the prospect of solitude, his fears seemed to crowd back upon him, and he stretched out a hand to detain him.

"Yes, I must go. I have my work to do. You are all right now. I think that with your nervous system you should take up some less morbid study."

"Oh, I am not nervous as a rule; and I have unwrapped mummies before."

"You fainted last time," observed Monkhouse Lee.

"Ah, yes, so I did. Well, I must have a nerve tonic or a course of electricity. You are not going, Lee?"

"I'll do whatever you wish, Ned."

"Then I'll come down with you and have a shake-down on your sofa. Good-night, Smith. I am so sorry to have disturbed you with my foolishness."

They shook hands, and as the medical student stumbled up the spiral and irregular stair he heard a key turn in a door, and the steps of his two new acquaintances as they descended to the lower floor.

In this strange way began the acquaintance between Edward Bellingham and Abercrombie Smith, an acquaintance which the latter, at least, had no desire to push further. Bellingham, however, appeared to have taken a fancy to his rough-spoken neighbour, and made his advances in such a way that he could hardly be repulsed without absolute brutality. Twice he called to thank Smith for his assistance, and many times afterwards he looked in with books, papers, and such other civilities as two bachelor neighbours can offer each other. He was, as Smith soon found, a man of wide reading, with catholic tastes and an extraordinary memory. His manner, too, was so pleasing and suave that one came, after a time, to overlook his repellent appearance. For a jaded and wearied man he was no unpleasant companion, and Smith found himself, after a time, looking forward to his visits, and even returning them.

Clever as he undoubtedly was, however, the medical student seemed to detect a dash of insanity in the man. He broke out at times into a high, inflated style of talk which was in contrast with the simplicity of his life.

"It is a wonderful thing," he cried, "to feel that one can command powers of good and of evil—a ministering angel or a demon of vengeance." And again, of Monkhouse Lee, he said,—"Lee is a good fellow, an honest fellow, but he is without strength or ambition. He would not make a fit partner for a man with a great enterprise. He would not make a fit partner for me."

At such hints and innuendoes stolid Smith, puffing solemnly at his pipe, would simply raise his eyebrows and shake his head, with little interjections of medical wisdom as to earlier hours and fresher air.

One habit Bellingham had developed of late which Smith knew to be a frequent herald of a weakening mind. He appeared to be forever talking to himself. At late hours of the night, when there could be no visitor with him, Smith could still hear his voice beneath him in a low, muffled monologue, sunk almost to a whisper, and yet very audible in the silence. This solitary babbling annoyed and distracted the student, so that he spoke more than once to his neighbour about it. Bellingham, however, flushed up at the charge, and denied curtly that he had uttered a sound; indeed, he showed more annoyance over the matter than the occasion seemed to demand.

Had Abercrombie Smith had any doubt as to his own ears he had not to go far to find corroboration. Tom Styles, the little wrinkled man-servant who had attended to the wants of the lodgers in the turret for a longer time than any man's memory could carry him, was sorely put to it over the same matter.

"If you please, sir," said he, as he tidied down the top chamber one morning, "do you think Mr. Bellingham is all right, sir?"

"All right, Styles?"

"Yes sir. Right in his head, sir."

"Why should he not be, then?"

"Well, I don't know, sir. His habits has changed of late. He's not the same man he used to be, though I make free to say that he was never quite one of my gentlemen, like Mr. Hastie or yourself, sir. He's took to talkin' to himself something awful. I wonder it don't disturb you. I don't know what to make of him, sir."

"I don't know what business it is of yours, Styles."

"Well, I takes an interest, Mr. Smith. It may be forward of me, but I can't help it. I feel sometimes as if I was mother and father to my young gentlemen. It all falls on me when things go wrong and the relations come. But Mr. Bellingham, sir. I want to know what it is that walks about his room sometimes when he's out and when the door's locked on the outside."

"Eh? you're talking nonsense, Styles."

"Maybe so, sir; but I heard it more'n once with my own ears."

"Rubbish, Styles."

"Very good, sir. You'll ring the bell if you want me."

Abercrombie Smith gave little heed to the gossip of the old man-servant, but a small incident occurred a few days later which left an unpleasant effect upon his mind, and brought the words of Styles forcibly to his memory.

Bellingham had come up to see him late one night, and was entertaining him with an interesting account of the rock tombs of Beni Hassan in Upper Egypt, when Smith, whose hearing was remarkably acute, distinctly heard the sound of a door opening on the landing below.

"There's some fellow gone in or out of your room," he remarked.

Bellingham sprang up and stood helpless for a moment, with the expression of a man who is half incredulous and half afraid.

"I surely locked it. I am almost positive that I locked it," he stammered. "No one could have opened it."

"Why, I hear someone coming up the steps now," said Smith.

Bellingham rushed out through the door, slammed it loudly behind him, and hurried down the stairs. About half-way down Smith heard him stop, and thought he caught the sound of whispering. A moment later the door beneath him shut, a key creaked in a lock, and Bellingham, with beads of moisture upon his pale face, ascended the stairs once more, and re-entered the room.

"It's all right," he said, throwing himself down in a chair. "It was that fool of a dog. He had pushed the door open. I don't know how I came to forget to lock it."

"I didn't know you kept a dog," said Smith, looking very thoughtfully at the disturbed face of his companion.

"Yes, I haven't had him long. I must get rid of him. He's a great nuisance."

"He must be, if you find it so hard to shut him up. I should have thought that shutting the door would have been enough, without locking it."

"I want to prevent old Styles from letting him out. He's of some value, you know, and it would be awkward to lose him."

"I am a bit of a dog-fancier myself," said Smith, still gazing hard at his companion from the corner of his eyes. "Perhaps you'll let me have a look at it."

"Certainly. But I am afraid it cannot be to-night; I have an appointment. Is that clock right? Then I am a quarter of an hour late already. You'll excuse me, I am sure."

He picked up his cap and hurried from the room. In spite of his appointment, Smith heard him re-enter his own chamber and lock his door upon the inside.

This interview left a disagreeable impression upon the medical student's mind. Bellingham had lied to him, and lied so clumsily that it looked as if he had desperate reasons for concealing the truth. Smith knew that his neighbour had no dog. He knew, also, that the step which he had heard upon the stairs was not the step of an animal. But if it were not, then what could it be? There was old Styles's statement about the something which used to pace the room at times when the owner was absent. Could it be a woman? Smith rather inclined to the view. If so, it would mean disgrace and expulsion to Bellingham if it were discovered by the authorities, so that his anxiety and falsehoods might be accounted for. And yet it was inconceivable that an undergraduate could keep a woman in his rooms without being instantly detected. Be the explanation what it might, there was something ugly about it, and Smith determined, as he turned to his books, to discourage all further attempts at intimacy on the part of his soft-spoken and ill-favoured neighbour.

But his work was destined to interruption that night. He had hardly caught up the broken threads when a firm, heavy footfall came three steps at a time from below, and Hastie, in blazer and flannels, burst into the room.

"Still at it!" said he, plumping down into his wonted arm-chair. "What a chap you are to stew! I believe an earthquake might come and knock Oxford into a cocked hat, and you would sit perfectly placid with your books among the ruins. However, I won't bore you long. Three whiffs of baccy, and I am off."

"What's the news, then?" asked Smith, cramming a plug of bird's-eye into his briar with his forefinger.

"Nothing very much. Wilson made 70 for the freshmen against the eleven. They say that they will play him instead of Buddicomb, for Buddicomb is clean off colour. He used to be able to bowl a little, but it's nothing but half-vollies and long hops now."

"Medium right," suggested Smith, with the intense gravity which comes upon a 'varsity man when he speaks of athletics.

"Inclining to fast, with a work from leg. Comes with the arm about three inches or so. He used to be nasty on a wet wicket. Oh, by-the-way, have you heard about Long Norton?"

"What's that?"

"He's been attacked."

"Attacked?"

"Yes, just as he was turning out of the High Street, and within a hundred yards of the gate of Old's."

"But who—"

"Ah, that's the rub! If you said 'what,' you would be more grammatical. Norton swears that it was not human, and, indeed, from the scratches on his throat, I should be inclined to agree with him."

"What, then? Have we come down to spooks?"

Abercrombie Smith puffed his scientific contempt.

"Well, no; I don't think that is quite the idea, either. I am inclined to think that if any showman has lost a great ape lately, and the brute is in these parts, a jury would find a true bill against it. Norton passes that way every night, you know, about the same hour. There's a tree that hangs low over the path—the big elm from Rainy's garden. Norton thinks the thing dropped on him out of the tree. Anyhow, he was nearly strangled by two arms, which, he says, were as strong and as thin as steel bands. He saw nothing; only those beastly arms that tightened and tightened on him. He yelled his head nearly off, and a couple of chaps came running, and the thing went over the wall like a cat. He never got a fair sight of it the whole time. It gave Norton a shake up, I can tell you. I tell him it has been as good as a change at the sea-side for him."

"A garrotter, most likely," said Smith.

"Very possibly. Norton says not; but we don't mind what he says. The garrotter had long nails, and was pretty smart at swinging himself over walls. By-the-way, your beautiful neighbour would be pleased if he heard about it. He had a grudge against Norton, and he's not a man, from what I know of him, to forget his little debts. But hallo, old chap, what have you got in your noddle?"

"Nothing," Smith answered curtly.

He had started in his chair, and the look had flashed over his face which comes upon a man who is struck suddenly by some unpleasant idea.

"You looked as if something I had said had taken you on the raw. By-the-way, you have made the acquaintance of Master B. since I looked in last, have you not? Young Monkhouse Lee told me something to that effect."

"Yes; I know him slightly. He has been up here once or twice."

"Well, you're big enough and ugly enough to take care of yourself. He's not what I should call exactly a healthy sort of Johnny, though, no doubt, he's very clever, and all that. But you'll soon find out for yourself. Lee is all right; he's a very decent little fellow. Well, so long, old chap! I row Mullins for the Vice-Chancellor's pot on Wednesday week, so mind you come down, in case I don't see you before."

Bovine Smith laid down his pipe and turned stolidly to his books once more. But with all the will in the world, he found it very hard to keep his mind upon his work. It would slip away to brood upon the man beneath him, and upon the little mystery which hung round his chambers. Then his thoughts turned to this singular attack of which Hastie had spoken, and to the grudge which Bellingham was said to owe the object of it. The two ideas would persist in rising together in his mind, as though there were some close and intimate connection between them. And yet the suspicion was so dim and vague that it could not be put down in words.

"Confound the chap!" cried Smith, as he shied his book on pathology across the room. "He has spoiled my night's reading, and that's reason enough, if there were no other, why I should steer clear of him in the future."

For ten days the medical student confined himself so closely to his studies that he neither saw nor heard anything of either of the men beneath him. At the hours when Bellingham had been accustomed to visit him, he took care to sport his oak, and though he more than once heard a knocking at his outer door, he resolutely refused to answer it. One afternoon, however, he was descending the stairs when, just as he was passing it, Bellingham's door flew open, and young Monkhouse Lee came out with his eyes sparkling and a dark flush of anger upon his olive cheeks. Close at his heels followed Bellingham, his fat, unhealthy face all quivering with malignant passion.

"You fool!" he hissed. "You'll be sorry."

"Very likely," cried the other. "Mind what I say. It's off! I won't hear of it!"

"You've promised, anyhow."

"Oh, I'll keep that! I won't speak. But I'd rather little Eva was in her grave. Once for all, it's off. She'll do what I say. We don't want to see you again."

So much Smith could not avoid hearing, but he hurried on, for he had no wish to be involved in their dispute. There had been a serious breach between them, that was clear enough, and Lee was going to cause the engagement with his sister to be broken off. Smith thought of Hastie's comparison of the toad and the dove, and was glad to think that the matter was at an end. Bellingham's face when he was in a passion was not pleasant to look upon. He was not a man to whom an innocent girl could be trusted for life. As he walked, Smith wondered languidly what could have caused the quarrel, and what the promise might be which Bellingham had been so anxious that Monkhouse Lee should keep.

It was the day of the sculling match between Hastie and Mullins, and a stream of men were making their way down to the banks of the Isis. A May sun was shining brightly, and the yellow path was barred with the black shadows of the tall elm-trees. On either side the grey colleges lay back from the road, the hoary old mothers of minds looking out from their high, mullioned windows at the tide of young life which swept so merrily past them. Black-clad tutors, prim officials, pale reading men, brown-faced, straw-hatted young athletes in white sweaters or many-coloured blazers, all were hurrying towards the blue winding river which curves through the Oxford meadows.

Abercrombie Smith, with the intuition of an old oarsman, chose his position at the point where he knew that the struggle, if there were a struggle, would come. Far off he heard the hum which announced the start, the gathering roar of the approach, the thunder of running feet, and the shouts of the men in the boats beneath him. A spray of half-clad, deep-breathing runners shot past him, and craning over their shoulders, he saw Hastie pulling a steady thirty-six, while his opponent, with a jerky forty, was a good boat's length behind him. Smith gave a cheer for his friend, and pulling out his watch, was starting off again for his chambers, when he felt a touch upon his shoulder, and found that young Monkhouse Lee was beside him.

"I saw you there," he said, in a timid, deprecating way. "I wanted to speak to you, if you could spare me a half-hour. This cottage is mine. I share it with Harrington of King's. Come in and have a cup of tea."

"I must be back presently," said Smith. "I am hard on the grind at present. But I'll come in for a few minutes with pleasure. I wouldn't have come out only Hastie is a friend of mine."

"So he is of mine. Hasn't he a beautiful style? Mullins wasn't in it. But come into the cottage. It's a little den of a place, but it is pleasant to work in during the summer months."

It was a small, square, white building, with green doors and shutters, and a rustic trellis-work porch, standing back some fifty yards from the river's bank. Inside, the main room was roughly fitted up as a study—deal table, unpainted shelves with books, and a few cheap oleographs upon the wall. A kettle sang upon a spirit-stove, and there were tea things upon a tray on the table.

"Try that chair and have a cigarette," said Lee. "Let me pour you out a cup of tea. It's so good of you to come in, for I know that your time is a good deal taken up. I wanted to say to you that, if I were you, I should change my rooms at once."

"Eh?"

Smith sat staring with a lighted match in one hand and his unlit cigarette in the other.

"Yes; it must seem very extraordinary, and the worst of it is that I cannot give my reasons, for I am under a solemn promise—a very solemn promise. But I may go so far as to say that I don't think Bellingham is a very safe man to live near. I intend to camp out here as much as I can for a time."

"Not safe! What do you mean?"

"Ah, that's what I mustn't say. But do take my advice, and move your rooms. We had a grand row to-day. You must have heard us, for you came down the stairs."

"I saw that you had fallen out."

"He's a horrible chap, Smith. That is the only word for him. I have had doubts about him ever since that night when he fainted—you remember, when you came down. I taxed him to-day, and he told me things that made my hair rise, and wanted me to stand in with him. I'm not strait-laced, but I am a clergyman's son, you know, and I think there are some things which are quite beyond the pale. I only thank God that I found him out before it was too late, for he was to have married into my family."

"This is all very fine, Lee," said Abercrombie Smith curtly. "But either you are saying a great deal too much or a great deal too little."

"I give you a warning."

"If there is real reason for warning, no promise can bind you. If I see a rascal about to blow a place up with dynamite no pledge will stand in my way of preventing him."

"Ah, but I cannot prevent him, and I can do nothing but warn you."

"Without saying what you warn me against."

"Against Bellingham."

"But that is childish. Why should I fear him, or any man?"

"I can't tell you. I can only entreat you to change your rooms. You are in danger where you are. I don't even say that Bellingham would wish to injure you. But it might happen, for he is a dangerous neighbour just now."

"Perhaps I know more than you think," said Smith, looking keenly at the young man's boyish, earnest face. "Suppose I tell you that some one else shares Bellingham's rooms."

Monkhouse Lee sprang from his chair in uncontrollable excitement.

"You know, then?" he gasped.

"A woman."

Lee dropped back again with a groan.

"My lips are sealed," he said. "I must not speak."

"Well, anyhow," said Smith, rising, "it is not likely that I should allow myself to be frightened out of rooms which suit me very nicely. It would be a little too feeble for me to move out all my goods and chattels because you say that Bellingham might in some unexplained way do me an injury. I think that I'll just take my chance, and stay where I am, and as I see that it's nearly five o'clock, I must ask you to excuse me."

He bade the young student adieu in a few curt words, and made his way homeward through the sweet spring evening feeling half-ruffled, half-amused, as any other strong, unimaginative man might who has been menaced by a vague and shadowy danger.

There was one little indulgence which Abercrombie Smith always allowed himself, however closely his work might press upon him. Twice a week, on the Tuesday and the Friday, it was his invariable custom to walk over to Farlingford, the residence of Dr. Plumptree Peterson, situated about a mile and a half out of Oxford. Peterson had been a close friend of Smith's elder brother Francis, and as he was a bachelor, fairly well-to-do, with a good cellar and a better library, his house was a pleasant goal for a man who was in need of a brisk walk. Twice a week, then, the medical student would swing out there along the dark country roads, and spend a pleasant hour in Peterson's comfortable study, discussing, over a glass of old port, the gossip of the 'varsity or the latest developments of medicine or of surgery.

On the day which followed his interview with Monkhouse Lee, Smith shut up his books at a quarter past eight, the hour when he usually started for his friend's house. As he was leaving his room, however, his eyes chanced to fall upon one of the books which Bellingham had lent him, and his conscience pricked him for not having returned it. However repellent the man might be, he should not be treated with discourtesy. Taking the book, he walked downstairs and knocked at his neighbour's door. There was no answer; but on turning the handle he found that it was unlocked. Pleased at the thought of avoiding an interview, he stepped inside, and placed the book with his card upon the table.

The lamp was turned half down, but Smith could see the details of the room plainly enough. It was all much as he had seen it before—the frieze, the animal-headed gods, the hanging crocodile, and the table littered over with papers and dried leaves. The mummy case stood upright against the wall, but the mummy itself was missing. There was no sign of any second occupant of the room, and he felt as he withdrew that he had probably done Bellingham an injustice. Had he a guilty secret to preserve, he would hardly leave his door open so that all the world might enter.

The spiral stair was as black as pitch, and Smith was slowly making his way down its irregular steps, when he was suddenly conscious that something had passed him in the darkness. There was a faint sound, a whiff of air, a light brushing past his elbow, but so slight that he could scarcely be certain of it. He stopped and listened, but the wind was rustling among the ivy outside, and he could hear nothing else.

"Is that you, Styles?" he shouted.

There was no answer, and all was still behind him. It must have been a sudden gust of air, for there were crannies and cracks in the old turret. And yet he could almost have sworn that be heard a footfall by his very side. He had emerged into the quadrangle, still turning the matter over in his head, when a man came running swiftly across the smooth-cropped lawn.

"Is that you, Smith?"

"Hullo, Hastie!"

"For God's sake come at once! Young Lee is drowned! Here's Harrington of King's with the news. The doctor is out. You'll do, but come along at once. There may be life in him."

"Have you brandy?"

"No."

"I'll bring some. There's a flask on my table."

Smith bounded up the stairs, taking three at a time, seized the flask, and was rushing down with it, when, as he passed Bellingham's room, his eyes fell upon something which left him gasping and staring upon the landing.

The door, which he had closed behind him, was now open, and right in front of him, with the lamp-light shining upon it, was the mummy case. Three minutes ago it had been empty. He could swear to that. Now it framed the lank body of its horrible occupant, who stood, grim and stark, with his black shrivelled face towards the door. The form was lifeless and inert, but it seemed to Smith as he gazed that there still lingered a lurid spark of vitality, some faint sign of consciousness in the little eyes which lurked in the depths of the hollow sockets. So astounded and shaken was he that he had forgotten his errand, and was still staring at the lean, sunken figure when the voice of his friend below recalled him to himself.

"Come on, Smith!" he shouted. "It's life and death, you know. Hurry up! Now, then," he added, as the medical student reappeared, "let us do a sprint. It is well under a mile, and we should do it in five minutes. A human life is better worth running for than a pot."

Neck and neck they dashed through the darkness, and did not pull up until, panting and spent, they had reached the little cottage by the river. Young Lee, limp and dripping like a broken water-plant, was stretched upon the sofa, the green scum of the river upon his black hair, and a fringe of white foam upon his leaden-hued lips. Beside him knelt his fellow-student Harrington, endeavouring to chafe some warmth back into his rigid limbs.

"I think there's life in him," said Smith, with his hand to the lad's side. "Put your watch glass to his lips. Yes, there's dimming on it. You take one arm, Hastie. Now work it as I do, and we'll soon pull him round."

For ten minutes they worked in silence, inflating and depressing the chest of the unconscious man. At the end of that time a shiver ran through his body, his lips trembled, and he opened his eyes. The three students burst out into an irrepressible cheer.

"Wake up, old chap. You've frightened us quite enough."

"Have some brandy. Take a sip from the flask."

"He's all right now," said his companion Harrington. "Heavens, what a fright I got! I was reading here, and he had gone for a stroll as far as the river, when I heard a scream and a splash. Out I ran, and by the time that I could find him and fish him out, all life seemed to have gone. Then Simpson couldn't get a doctor, for he has a game-leg, and I had to run, and I don't know what I'd have done without you fellows. That's right, old chap. Sit up."

Monkhouse Lee had raised himself on his hands, and looked wildly about him.

"What's up?" he asked. "I've been in the water. Ah, yes; I remember."

A look of fear came into his eyes, and he sank his face into his hands.

"How did you fall in?"

"I didn't fall in."

"How, then?"

"I was thrown in. I was standing by the bank, and something from behind picked me up like a feather and hurled me in. I heard nothing, and I saw nothing. But I know what it was, for all that."

"And so do I, " whispered Smith.

Lee looked up with a quick glance of surprise. "You've learned, then?" he said. "You remember the advice I gave you?"

"Yes, and I begin to think that I shall take it."

"I don't know what the deuce you fellows are talking about," said Hastie, "but I think, if I were you, Harrington, I should get Lee to bed at once. It will be time enough to discuss the why and the wherefore when he is a little stronger. I think, Smith, you and I can leave him alone now. I am walking back to college; if you are coming in that direction, we can have a chat."

But it was little chat that they had upon their homeward path. Smith's mind was too full of the incidents of the evening, the absence of the mummy from his neighbour's rooms, the step that passed him on the stair, the reappearance—the extraordinary, inexplicable reappearance of the grisly thing—and then this attack upon Lee, corresponding so closely to the previous outrage upon another man against whom Bellingham bore a grudge. All this settled in his thoughts, together with the many little incidents which had previously turned him against his neighbour, and the singular circumstances under which he was first called in to him. What had been a dim suspicion, a vague, fantastic conjecture, had suddenly taken form, and stood out in his mind as a grim fact, a thing not to be denied. And yet, how monstrous it was! how unheard of! how entirely beyond all bounds of human experience. An impartial judge, or even the friend who walked by his side, would simply tell him that his eyes had deceived him, that the mummy had been there all the time, that young Lee had tumbled into the river as any other man tumbles into a river, and that a blue pill was the best thing for a disordered liver. He felt that he would have said as much if the positions had been reversed. And yet he could swear that Bellingham was a murderer at heart, and that he wielded a weapon such as no man had ever used in all the grim history of crime.

Hastie had branched off to his rooms with a few crisp and emphatic comments upon his friend's unsociability, and Abercrombie Smith crossed the quadrangle to his corner turret with a strong feeling of repulsion for his chambers and their associations. He would take Lee's advice, and move his quarters as soon as possible, for how could a man study when his ear was ever straining for every murmur or footstep in the room below? He observed, as he crossed over the lawn, that the light was still shining in Bellingham's window, and as he passed up the staircase the door opened, and the man himself looked out at him. With his fat, evil face he was like some bloated spider fresh from the weaving of his poisonous web.

"Good-evening," said he. "Won't you come in?"

"No," cried Smith, fiercely.

"No? You are busy as ever? I wanted to ask you about Lee. I was sorry to hear that there was a rumour that something was amiss with him."

His features were grave, but there was the gleam of a hidden laugh in his eyes as he spoke. Smith saw it, and he could have knocked him down for it.

"You'll be sorrier still to hear that Monkhouse Lee is doing very well, and is out of all danger," he answered. "Your hellish tricks have not come off this time. Oh, you needn't try to brazen it out. I know all about it."

Bellingham took a step back from the angry student, and half-closed the door as if to protect himself.

"You are mad," he said. "What do you mean? Do you assert that I had anything to do with Lee's accident?"

"Yes," thundered Smith. "You and that bag of bones behind you; you worked it between you. I tell you what it is, Master B., they have given up burning folk like you, but we still keep a hangman, and, by George! if any man in this college meets his death while you are here, I'll have you up, and if you don't swing for it, it won't be my fault. You'll find that your filthy Egyptian tricks won't answer in England."

"You're a raving lunatic," said Bellingham.

"All right. You just remember what I say, for you'll find that I'll be better than my word."

The door slammed, and Smith went fuming up to his chamber, where he locked the door upon the inside, and spent half the night in smoking his old briar and brooding over the strange events of the evening.

Next morning Abercrombie Smith heard nothing of his neighbour, but Harrington called upon him in the afternoon to say that Lee was almost himself again. All day Smith stuck fast to his work, but in the evening he determined to pay the visit to his friend Dr. Peterson upon which he had started upon the night before. A good walk and a friendly chat would be welcome to his jangled nerves.

Bellingham's door was shut as he passed, but glancing back when he was some distance from the turret, he saw his neighbour's head at the window outlined against the lamp-light, his face pressed apparently against the glass as he gazed out into the darkness. It was a blessing to be away from all contact with him, but if for a few hours, and Smith stepped out briskly, and breathed the soft spring air into his lungs. The half-moon lay in the west between two Gothic pinnacles, and threw upon the silvered street a dark tracery from the stone-work above. There was a brisk breeze, and light, fleecy clouds drifted swiftly across the sky. Old's was on the very border of the town, and in five minutes Smith found himself beyond the houses and between the hedges of a May-scented Oxfordshire lane.

It was a lonely and little frequented road which led to his friend's house. Early as it was, Smith did not meet a single soul upon his way. He walked briskly along until he came to the avenue gate, which opened into the long gravel drive leading up to Farlingford. In front of him he could see the cosy red light of the windows glimmering through the foliage. He stood with his hand upon the iron latch of the swinging gate, and he glanced back at the road along which he had come. Something was coming swiftly down it.

It moved in the shadow of the hedge, silently and furtively, a dark, crouching figure, dimly visible against the black background. Even as he gazed back at it, it had lessened its distance by twenty paces, and was fast closing upon him. Out of the darkness he had a glimpse of a scraggy neck, and of two eyes that will ever haunt him in his dreams. He turned, and with a cry of terror he ran for his life up the avenue. There were the red lights, the signals of safety, almost within a stone's throw of him. He was a famous runner, but never had he run as he ran that night.

The heavy gate had swung into place behind him, but he heard it dash open again before his pursuer. As he rushed madly and wildly through the night, he could hear a swift, dry patter behind him, and could see, as he threw back a glance, that this horror was bounding like a tiger at his heels, with blazing eyes and one stringy arm out thrown. Thank God, the door was ajar. He could see the thin bar of light which shot from the lamp in the hall. Nearer yet sounded the clatter from behind. He heard a hoarse gurgling at his very shoulder. With a shriek he flung himself against the door, slammed and bolted it behind him, and sank half-fainting on to the hall chair.

"My goodness, Smith, what's the matter?" asked Peterson, appearing at the door of his study.

"Give me some brandy!"

Peterson disappeared, and came rushing out again with a glass and a decanter.

"You need it," he said, as his visitor drank off what he poured out for him. "Why, man, you are as white as a cheese."

Smith laid down his glass, rose up, and took a deep breath.

"I am my own man again now," said he. "I was never so unmanned before. But, with your leave, Peterson, I will sleep here to-night, for I don't think I could face that road again except by daylight. It's weak, I know, but I can't help it."

Peterson looked at his visitor with a very questioning eye.

"Of course you shall sleep here if you wish. I'll tell Mrs. Burney to make up the spare bed. Where are you off to now?"

"Come up with me to the window that overlooks the door. I want you to see what I have seen."

They went up to the window of the upper hall whence they could look down upon the approach to the house. The drive and the fields on either side lay quiet and still, bathed in the peaceful moonlight.

"Well, really, Smith," remarked Peterson, "it is well that I know you to be an abstemious man. What in the world can have frightened you?"

"I'll tell you presently. But where can it have gone? Ah, now look, look! See the curve of the road just beyond your gate."

"Yes, I see; you needn't pinch my arm off. I saw someone pass. I should say a man, rather thin, apparently, and tall, very tall. But what of him? And what of yourself? You are still shaking like an aspen leaf."

"I have been within hand-grip of the devil, that's all. But come down to your study, and I shall tell you the whole story."

He did so. Under the cheery lamp-light, with a glass of wine on the table beside him, and the portly form and florid face of his friend in front, he narrated, in their order, all the events, great and small, which had formed so singular a chain, from the night on which he had found Bellingham fainting in front of the mummy case until his horrid experience of an hour ago.

"There now," he said as he concluded, "that's the whole black business. It is monstrous and incredible, but it is true."

Dr. Plumptree Peterson sat for some time in silence with a very puzzled expression upon his face.

"I never heard of such a thing in my life, never!" he said at last. "You have told me the facts. Now tell me your inferences."

"You can draw your own."

"But I should like to hear yours. You have thought over the matter, and I have not."

"Well, it must be a little vague in detail, but the main points seem to me to be clear enough. This fellow Bellingham, in his Eastern studies, has got hold of some infernal secret by which a mummy—or possibly only this particular mummy—can be temporarily brought to life. He was trying this disgusting business on the night when he fainted. No doubt the sight of the creature moving had shaken his nerve, even though he had expected it. You remember that almost the first words he said were to call out upon himself as a fool. Well, he got more hardened afterwards, and carried the matter through without fainting. The vitality which he could put into it was evidently only a passing thing, for I have seen it continually in its case as dead as this table. He has some elaborate process, I fancy, by which he brings the thing to pass. Having done it, he naturally bethought him that he might use the creature as an agent. It has intelligence and it has strength. For some purpose he took Lee into his confidence; but Lee, like a decent Christian, would have nothing to do with such a business. Then they had a row, and Lee vowed that he would tell his sister of Bellingham's true character. Bellingham's game was to prevent him, and he nearly managed it, by setting this creature of his on his track. He had already tried its powers upon another man—Norton—towards whom he had a grudge. It is the merest chance that he has not two murders upon his soul. Then, when I taxed him with the matter, he had the strongest reasons for wishing to get me out of the way before I could convey my knowledge to anyone else. He got his chance when I went out, for he knew my habits, and where I was bound for. I have had a narrow shave, Peterson, and it is mere luck you didn't find me on your doorstep in the morning. I'm not a nervous man as a rule, and I never thought to have the fear of death put upon me as it was to-night."

"My dear boy, you take the matter too seriously," said his companion. "Your nerves are out of order with your work, and you make too much of it. How could such a thing as this stride about the streets of Oxford, even at night, without being seen?"

"It has been seen. There is quite a scare in the town about an escaped ape, as they imagine the creature to be. It is the talk of the place."

"Well, it's a striking chain of events. And yet, my dear fellow, you must allow that each incident in itself is capable of a more natural explanation."

"What! even my adventure of to-night?"

"Certainly. You come out with your nerves all unstrung, and your head full of this theory of yours. Some gaunt, half-famished tramp steals after you, and seeing you run, is emboldened to pursue you. Your fears and imagination do the rest."

"It won't do, Peterson; it won't do."

"And again, in the instance of your finding the mummy case empty, and then a few moments later with an occupant, you know that it was lamplight, that the lamp was half turned down, and that you had no special reason to look hard at the case. It is quite possible that you may have overlooked the creature in the first instance."

"No, no; it is out of the question."

"And then Lee may have fallen into the river, and Norton been garrotted. It is certainly a formidable indictment that you have against Bellingham; but if you were to place it before a police magistrate, he would simply laugh in your face."

"I know he would. That is why I mean to take the matter into my own hands."

"Eh?"

"Yes; I feel that a public duty rests upon me, and, besides, I must do it for my own safety, unless I choose to allow myself to be hunted by this beast out of the college, and that would be a little too feeble. I have quite made up my mind what I shall do. And first of all, may I use your paper and pens for an hour?"

"Most certainly. You will find all that you want upon that side table."

Abercrombie Smith sat down before a sheet of foolscap, and for an hour, and then for a second hour his pen travelled swiftly over it. Page after page was finished and tossed aside while his friend leaned back in his arm-chair, looking across at him with patient curiosity. At last, with an exclamation of satisfaction, Smith sprang to his feet, gathered his papers up into order, and laid the last one upon Peterson's desk.

"Kindly sign this as a witness," he said.

"A witness? Of what?"

"Of my signature, and of the date. The date is the most important. Why, Peterson, my life might hang upon it."

"My dear Smith, you are talking wildly. Let me beg you to go to bed."

"On the contrary, I never spoke so deliberately in my life. And I will promise to go to bed the moment you have signed it."

"But what is it?"

"It is a statement of all that I have been telling you to-night. I wish you to witness it."

"Certainly," said Peterson, signing his name under that of his companion. "There you are! But what is the idea?"

"You will kindly retain it, and produce it in case I am arrested."

"Arrested? For what?"

"For murder. It is quite on the cards. I wish to be ready for every event. There is only one course open to me, and I am determined to take it."

"For Heaven's sake, don't do anything rash!"

"Believe me, it would be far more rash to adopt any other course. I hope that we won't need to bother you, but it will ease my mind to know that you have this statement of my motives. And now I am ready to take your advice and to go to roost, for I want to be at my best in the morning."

Abercrombie Smith was not an entirely pleasant man to have as an enemy. Slow and easy-tempered, he was formidable when driven to action. He brought to every purpose in life the same deliberate resoluteness which had distinguished him as a scientific student. He had laid his studies aside for a day, but he intended that the day should not be wasted. Not a word did he say to his host as to his plans, but by nine o'clock he was well on his way to Oxford.

In the High Street he stopped at Clifford's, the gun-maker's, and bought a heavy revolver, with a box of central-fire cartridges. Six of them he slipped into the chambers, and half-cocking the weapon, placed it in the pocket of his coat. He then made his way to Hastie's rooms, where the big oarsman was lounging over his breakfast, with the *Sporting Times* propped up against the coffee-pot.

"Hullo! What's up?" he asked. Have some coffee?"

"No, thank you. I want you to come with me, Hastie, and do what I ask you."

"Certainly, my boy."

"And bring a heavy stick with you."

"Hullo!" Hastie stared. "Here's a hunting-crop that would fell an ox."

"One other thing. You have a box of amputating knives. Give me the longest of them."

"There you are. You seem to be fairly on the war trail. Anything else?"

"No; that will do." Smith placed the knife inside his coat, and led the way to the quadrangle. We are neither of us chickens, Hastie," said he. "I think I can do this job alone, but I take you as a precaution. I am going to have a little talk with Bellingham. If I have only him to deal with, I won't, of course, need you. If I shout, however, up you come, and lam out with your whip as hard as you can lick. Do you understand?"

"All right. I'll come if I hear you bellow."

"Stay here, then. It may be a little time, but don't budge until I come down."

"I'm a fixture."

Smith ascended the stairs, opened Bellingham's door and stepped in. Bellingham was seated behind his table, writing. Beside him, among his litter of strange possessions, towered the mummy case, with its sale number 249 still stuck upon its front, and its hideous occupant stiff and stark within it. Smith looked very deliberately round him, closed the door, locked it, took the key from the inside, and then stepping across to the fireplace, struck a match and set the fire alight. Bellingham sat staring, with amazement and rage upon his bloated face.

"Well, really now, you make yourself at home," he gasped.

Smith sat himself deliberately down, placing his watch upon the table, drew out his pistol, cocked it, and laid it in his lap. Then he took the long amputating knife from his bosom, and threw it down in front of Bellingham.

"Now, then," said he, "just get to work and cut up that mummy."

"Oh, is that it?" said Bellingham with a sneer.

"Yes, that is it. They tell me that the law can't touch you. But I have a law that will set matters straight. If in five minutes you have not set to work, I swear by the God who made me that I will put a bullet through your brain!"

"You would murder me?"

Bellingham had half risen, and his face was the colour of putty.

"Yes."

"And for what?"

"To stop your mischief. One minute has gone."

"But what have I done?"

"I know and you know."

"This is mere bullying."

"Two minutes are gone."

"But you must give reasons. You are a madman—a dangerous madman. Why should I destroy my own property? It is a valuable mummy."

"You must cut it up, and you must burn it."

"I will do no such thing."

"Four minutes are gone."

Smith took up the pistol and he looked towards Bellingham with an inexorable face. As the second-hand stole round, he raised his hand, and the finger twitched upon the trigger.

"There! there! I'll do it!" screamed Bellingham.

In frantic haste he caught up the knife and hacked at the figure of the mummy, ever glancing round to see the eye and the weapon of his terrible visitor bent upon him. The creature crackled and snapped under every stab of the keen blade. A thick yellow dust rose up from it. Spices and dried essences rained down upon the floor. Suddenly, with a rending crack, its backbone snapped asunder, and it fell, a brown heap of sprawling limbs, upon the floor.

"Now into the fire!" said Smith.

The flames leaped and roared as the dried and tinderlike debris was piled upon it. The little room was like the stoke-hole of a steamer and the sweat ran down the faces of the two men; but still the one stooped and worked, while the other sat watching him with a set face. A thick, fat smoke oozed out from the fire, and a heavy smell of burned rosin and singed hair filled the air. In a quarter of an hour a few charred and brittle sticks were all that was left of Lot No. 249.

"Perhaps that will satisfy you," snarled Bellingham, with hate and fear in his little grey eyes as he glanced back at his tormenter.

"No; I must make a clean sweep of all your materials. We must have no more devil's tricks. In with all these leaves! They may have something to do with it."

"And what now?" asked Bellingham, when the leaves also had been added to the blaze.

"Now the roll of papyrus which you had on the table that night. It is in that drawer, I think."

"No, no," shouted Bellingham. " Don't burn that! Why, man, you don't know what you do. It is unique; it contains wisdom which is nowhere else to be found."

"Out with it!"

"But look here, Smith, you can't really mean it. I'll share the knowledge with you. I'll teach you all that is in it. Or, stay, let me only copy it before you burn it!"

Smith stepped forward and turned the key in the drawer. Taking out the yellow, curled roll of paper, he threw it into the fire, and pressed it down with his heel. Bellingham screamed, and grabbed at it; but Smith pushed him back, and stood over it until it was reduced to a formless grey ash.

"Now, Master B.," said he, "I think I have pretty well drawn your teeth. You'll hear from me again, if you return to your old tricks. And now good-morning, for I must go back to my studies."

And such is the narrative of Abercrombie Smith as to the singular events which occurred in Old College, Oxford, in the spring of '84. As Bellingham left the university immediately afterwards, and was last heard of in the Soudan, there is no one who can contradict his statement. But the wisdom of men is small, and the ways of nature are strange, and who shall put a bound to the dark things which may be found by those who seek for them?

N *is for* Necrophage

Necrophages are eaters of the dead who share many traits with more traditional ghouls. American writer Lafcadio Hearn (1850–1904) found a story of just such a creature in the folklore of Japan, where he lived for most of his adult life. Hearn included it in a collection of retold folktales that he gathered just before his death, *Kwaidan: Stories and Studies of Strange Things* (1904).

LAFCADIO HEARN

Jikininki

Once, when Musō Kokushi, a priest of the Zen sect, was journeying alone through the province of Mino, he lost his way in a mountain-district where there was nobody to direct him. For a long time he wandered about helplessly; and he was beginning to despair of finding shelter for the night, when he perceived, on the top of a hill lighted by the last rays of the sun, one of those little hermitages, called *anjitsu,* which are built for solitary priests. It seemed to be in ruinous condition; but he hastened to it eagerly, and found that it was inhabited by an aged priest, from whom he begged the favor of a night's lodging. This the old man harshly refused; but he directed Muso to a certain hamlet, in the valley adjoining, where lodging and food could be obtained.

Musō found his way to the hamlet, which consisted of less than a dozen farm-cottages; and he was kindly received at the dwelling of the headman.

Forty or fifty persons were assembled in the principal apartment, at the moment of Musō's arrival; but he was shown into a small separate room, where he was promptly supplied with food and bedding. Being very tired, he lay down to rest at an early hour; but a little before midnight he was roused from sleep by a sound of loud weeping in the next apartment. Presently the sliding-screens were gently pushed apart; and a young man, carrying a lighted lantern, entered the room, respectfully saluted him, and said:—

"Reverend Sir, it is my painful duty to tell you that I am now the responsible head of this house. Yesterday I was only the eldest son. But when you came here, tired as you were, we did not wish that you should feel embarrassed in any way: therefore we did not tell you that father had died only a few hours before. The people whom you saw in the next room are the inhabitants of this village: they all assembled here to pay their last respects to the dead; and now they are going to another village, about three miles off,—for by our custom, no one of us may remain in this village during the night after a death has taken place. We make the proper offerings and prayers;—then we go away, leaving the corpse alone. Strange things always happen in the house where a corpse has thus been left: so we think that it will be better for you to come away with us. We can find you good lodging in the other village. But perhaps, as you are a priest, you have no fear of demons or evil spirits; and, if you are not afraid of being left alone with the body, you will be very welcome to the use of this poor house. However, I must tell you that nobody, except a priest, would dare to remain here tonight."

Musō made answer:—

"For your kind intention and your generous hospitality, I am deeply grateful. But I am sorry that you did not tell me of your father's death when I came;—for, though I was a little tired, I certainly was not so tired that I should have found any difficulty in doing my duty as a priest. Had you told me, I could have performed the service before your departure. As it is, I shall perform the service after you have gone away; and I shall stay by the body until morning. I do not know what you mean by your words about the danger of staying here alone; but I am not afraid of ghosts or demons: therefore please to feel no anxiety on my account."

The young man appeared to be rejoiced by these assurances, and expressed his gratitude in fitting words. Then the other members of the family, and the folk assembled in the adjoining room, having been told of the priest's kind promises, came to thank him,—after which the master of the house said:—

"Now, reverend Sir, much as we regret to leave you alone, we must bid you farewell. By the rule of our village, none of us can stay here after midnight. We beg, kind Sir, that you will take every care of your honorable body, while we are unable to attend upon you. And if you happen to hear or see anything strange during our absence, please tell us of the matter when we return in the morning."

All then left the house, except the priest, who went to the room where the dead body was lying. The usual offerings had been set before the corpse; and a small Buddhist lamp—*tōmyō*—was burning. The priest recited the service, and performed the funeral ceremonies,—after which he entered into meditation. So meditating he remained through several silent hours; and there was no sound in the deserted village. But, when the hush of the night was at its deepest, there noiselessly entered a Shape, vague and vast; and in the same moment Musō found himself without power to move or speak. He saw that Shape lift the corpse, as with hands, devour it, more quickly than a cat devours a rat,—beginning at the head, and eating everything: the hair and the bones and even the shroud. And the monstrous Thing, having thus consumed the body, turned to the offerings, and ate them also. Then it went away, as mysteriously as it had come.

When the villagers returned next morning, they found the priest awaiting them at the door of the headman's dwelling. All in turn saluted him; and when they had entered, and looked about the room, no one expressed any surprise at the disappearance of the dead body and the offerings. But the master of the house said to Musō:—

"Reverend Sir, you have probably seen unpleasant things during the night: all of us were anxious about you. But now we are very happy to find you alive and unharmed. Gladly we would have stayed with you, if it had been possible. But the law of our village, as I told you last evening, obliges us to quit our houses after a death has taken place, and to leave the corpse alone. Whenever this law has been broken, heretofore, some great misfortune has followed. Whenever it is obeyed, we find that the corpse and the offerings disappear during our absence. Perhaps you have seen the cause."

Then Musō told of the dim and awful Shape that had entered the death-chamber to devour the body and the offerings. No person seemed to be surprised by his narration; and the master of the house observed:—

"What you have told us, reverend Sir, agrees with what has been said about this matter from ancient time."

Musō then inquired:—

"Does not the priest on the hill sometimes perform the funeral service for your dead?"

"What priest?" the young man asked.

"The priest who yesterday evening directed me to this village," answered Musō. "I called at his *anjitsu* on the hill yonder. He refused me lodging, but told me the way here."

The listeners looked at each other, as in astonishment; and, after a moment of silence, the master of the house said:—

"Reverend Sir, there is no priest and there is no *anjitsu* on the hill. For the time of many generations there has not been any resident-priest in this neighborhood."

Musō said nothing more on the subject; for it was evident that his kind hosts supposed him to have been deluded by some goblin. But after having bidden them farewell, and obtained all necessary information as to his road, he determined to look again for the hermitage on the hill, and so to ascertain whether he had really been deceived. He found the *anjitsu* without any difficulty; and, this time, its aged occupant invited him to enter. When he had done so, the hermit humbly bowed down before him, exclaiming:—"Ah! I am ashamed!—I am very much ashamed!—I am exceedingly ashamed!"

"You need not be ashamed for having refused me shelter," said Musō. "You directed me to the village yonder, where I was very kindly treated; and I thank you for that favor.

"I can give no man shelter," the recluse made answer; "—and it is not for the refusal that I am ashamed. I am ashamed only that you should have seen me in my real shape,—for it was I who devoured the corpse and the offerings last night before your eyes. . . . Know, reverend Sir, that I am a *jikininki,*—an eater of human flesh. Have pity upon me, and suffer me to confess the secret fault by which I became reduced to this condition.

"A long, long time ago, I was a priest in this desolate region. There was no other priest for many leagues around. So, in that time, the bodies of the mountain-folk who died used to be brought here,—sometimes from great distances,—in order that I might repeat over them the holy service. But I repeated the service and performed the rites only as a matter of business;—I thought only of the food and the clothes that my sacred profession enabled me to gain. And because of this selfish impiety I was reborn, immediately after my death, into the state of a *jikininki*. Since then I have been obliged to feed upon the corpses of the people who die in this district: every one of them I must devour in the way that you saw last night. . . . Now, reverend Sir, let me beseech you to perform a Segaki-service for me: help me by your prayers, I entreat you, so that I may be soon able to escape from this horrible state of existence." . . .

No sooner had the hermit uttered this petition than he disappeared; and the hermitage also disappeared at the same instant. And Musō Kokushi found himself kneeling alone in the high grass, beside an ancient and moss-grown tomb of the form called *go-rin-ishi*, which seemed to be the tomb of a priest.

O *is for* Occult

Occult entities are rampant in the supernatural fiction of many writers, including the work of British writer William Hope Hodgson (1877–1918), whose tales of Carnacki are among the earliest tales of an occult detective. Carnacki's explorations of the supernatural are always tempered by his sophisticated scientific approach, as in this story, first published in the January 1910 issue of *The Idler.*

WILLIAM HOPE HODGSON

The Gateway of the Monster

In response to Carnacki's usual card of invitation to have dinner and listen to a story, I arrived promptly at Cheyne Walk, to find the three others who were always invited to these happy little times there before me. Five minutes later, Carnacki, Arkright, Jessop, Taylor, and I were all engaged in the "pleasant occupation" of dining.

"You've not been long away this time," I remarked, as I finished my soup; forgetting momentarily Carnacki's dislike of being asked even to skirt the borders of his story until such time as he was ready. Then he would not stint words.

"No," he replied, with brevity, and I changed the subject, remarking that I had been buying a new gun, to which piece of news he gave an intelligent nod and a smile, which I think showed a genuinely good-humoured appreciation of my intentional changing of the conversation.

Later, when dinner was finished, Carnacki snugged himself comfortably down in his big chair, along with his pipe, and began his story, with very little circumlocution:

"As Dodgson was remarking just now, I've only been away a short time, and for a very good reason too—I've only been away a short distance. The exact locality I am afraid I must not tell you; but it is less than twenty miles from here; though, except for changing a name, that won't spoil the story. And it *is* a story too! One of the most extraordinary things I have ever run against.

"I received a letter a fortnight ago from a man I will call Anderson, asking for an appointment. I arranged a time and when he turned up, I found that he wished me to look into and see whether I could not clear up a long-standing and well authenticated case of what he termed 'haunting.' He gave me very full particulars and, finally, as the thing seemed to present something unique, I decided to take it up.

"Two days later, I drove to the house late in the afternoon and discovered it a very old place, standing quite alone in its own grounds.

"Anderson had left a letter with the butler, I found, pleading excuses for his absence, and leaving the whole house at my disposal for my investigations.

"The butler evidently knew the object of my visit, and I questioned him pretty thoroughly during dinner, which I had in rather lonely state. He is an old and privileged servant, and had the history of the Grey Room exact in detail. From him I learned more particulars regarding two things that Anderson had mentioned in but a casual manner. The first was that the door of the Grey Room would be heard in the dead of night to open, and slam heavily, and this when even the butler knew it was locked, and the key on the bunch in his pantry. The second was that the bedclothes would always be found torn off the bed, and hurled in a heap into a corner.

"But it was the door slamming that chiefly bothered the old butler. Many and many a time, he told me, had he lain awake and just got shivering with fright, listening; for at times the door would be slammed time after time—thud! thud! thud!—so that sleep was impossible.

"From Anderson, I knew already that the room had a history extending back over a hundred and fifty years. Three people had been strangled in it—

an ancestor of his and his wife and child. This is authentic, as I had taken very great pains to make sure; so that you can imagine it was with a feeling that I had a striking case to investigate that I went upstairs after dinner to have a look at the Grey Room.

"Peters, the butler, was in rather a state about my going, and assured me with much solemnity that in all the twenty years of his service, no one had ever entered that room after nightfall. He begged me, in quite a fatherly way, to wait till the morning, when there would be no danger, and then he could accompany me himself.

"Of course, I told him not to bother. I explained that I should do no more than look around a bit, and perhaps fix a few seals. He need not fear; I was used to that sort of thing. But he shook his head when I said that.

" 'There isn't many ghosts like ours, sir,' he assured me, with mournful pride. And, by Jove! he was right, as you will see.

"I took a couple of candles, and Peters followed with his bunch of keys. He unlocked the door; but would not come inside with me. He was evidently in quite a fright and renewed his request that I would put off my examination until daylight. Of course, I laughed at him, and told him he could stand sentry at the door and catch anything that came out.

" 'It never comes outside, sir,' he said, in his funny, old, solemn manner. Somehow he managed to make me feel as if I were going to have the creeps right away. Anyway, it was one to him, you know.

"I left him there, and examined the room. It is a big apartment, and well furnished in the grand style, with a huge four-poster, which stands with its head to the end wall. There were two candles on the mantelpiece, and two on each of the three tables that were in the room. I lit the lot, and after that, the room felt a little less inhumanly dreary, though, mind you, it was quite fresh, and well kept in every way.

"After I had taken a good look round, I sealed lengths of *bebe* ribbon across the windows, along the walls, over the pictures, and over the fireplace and the wall closets. All the time, as I worked, the butler stood just without the door and I could not persuade him to enter, though I jested with him a little, as I stretched the ribbons, and went here and there about my work. Every now and again he would say:—'You'll excuse me, I'm sure, sir; but I do wish you would come out, sir. I'm fair in a quake for you.'

"I told him he need not wait; but he was loyal enough in his way what he considered his duty. He said he could not go away and leave me all alone there. He apologised; but made it very clear that I did not realise the danger of the room; and I could see, generally, that he was getting into a really frightened state. All the same I had to make the room so that I should know if anything material entered it; so I asked him not to bother me, unless he really heard something. He was beginning to fret my nerves, and the 'feel' of the room was bad enough already, without making things any nastier.

"For a time further, I worked, stretching ribbons a little above the floor and sealing them so that the merest touch would break the seals, were anyone to venture into the room in the dark with the intention of playing the fool.

"All this had taken me far longer than I had anticipated and, suddenly, I heard a clock strike eleven. I had taken off my coat soon after commencing work; now, however, as I had practically made an end of all that I intended to do, I walked across to the settee and picked it up. I was in the act of getting into it, when the old butler's voice (he had not said a word for the last hour) came sharp and frightened:—'Come out, sir, quick! There's something going to happen!' Jove! but I jumped, and then, in the same moment, one of the candles on the table to the left of the bed went out. Now whether it was the wind, or what, I do not know; but, just for a moment, I was enough startled to make a run for the door; though I am glad to say that I pulled up, before I reached it. I simply could not bunk out, with the butler standing there, after having, as it were, read him a sort of lesson on 'bein' brave, y'know.' So I just turned right round, picked up the two candles off the mantelpiece, and walked across to the table near the bed. Well, I saw nothing. I blew out the candle that was still alight; then I went to those on the two other tables, and blew them out. Then, outside of the door, the old man called again:—'Oh! sir, do be told! Do be told!'

" 'All right, Peters,' I said, and by Jove, my voice was not as steady as I should have liked! I made for the door, and had a bit of work not to start running. I took some thundering long strides, though, as you can imagine. Near the entrance, I had a sudden feeling that there was a cold wind in the room. It was almost as if the window had been suddenly opened a little. I got to the door, and the old butler gave back a step, in a sort of instinctive way.

"'Collar the candles, Peters!' I said, pretty sharply, and shoved them into his hands. I turned, and caught the handle, and slammed the door shut, with a crash. Somehow, do you know, as I did so I thought I felt something pull back on it, but it must have been only fancy. I turned the key in the lock, and then again, double-locking the door.

"I felt easier then, and set-to and sealed the door. In addition I put my card over the keyhole and sealed it there, after which I pocketed the key, and went down-stairs—with Peters who was nervous and silent, leading the way. Poor old beggar! It had not struck me until that moment that he had been enduring a considerable strain during the last two or three hours.

"About midnight I went to bed. My room lay at the end of the corridor upon which opens the door of the Grey Room. I counted the doors between it and mine and found that five rooms lay between. And I am sure you can understand that I was not sorry.

"Just as I was beginning to undress an idea came to me, and I took my candle and sealing-wax, and sealed the doors of all the five rooms. If any door slammed in the night, I should know just which one.

"I returned to my room, locked myself in, and went to bed. I was waked suddenly from a deep sleep by a loud crash somewhere out in the passage. I sat up in bed and listened, but heard nothing. Then I lit my candle. I was in the very act of lighting it when there came the bang of a door being violently slammed along the corridor.

"I jumped out of bed and got my revolver. I unlocked the door and went out into the passage, holding my candle high and keeping the pistol ready. Then a queer thing happened. I could not go a step towards the Grey Room. You all know I am not really a cowardly chap. I've gone into too many cases connected with ghostly things, to be accused of that; but I tell you I funked it, simply funked it, just like any blessed kid. There was something precious unholy in the air that night. I backed into my bedroom and shut and locked the door. Then I sat on the bed all night and listened to the dismal thudding of a door up the corridor. The sound seemed to echo through all the house.

"Daylight came at last, and I washed and dressed. The door had not slammed for about an hour, and I was getting back my nerve again. I felt ashamed of myself, though in some ways it was silly for when you're meddling with that sort of thing your nerve is bound to go, sometimes. And you just have to sit quiet and call yourself a coward until the safety of the day comes. Sometimes it is more than just cowardice, I fancy. I believe at times it is Something warning you, and fighting *for you*. But all the same, I always feel mean and miserable after a time like that.

"When the day came properly I opened my door and, keeping my revolver handy, went quietly along the passage. I had to pass the head of the stairs, along the way, and who should I see coming up, but the old butler, carrying a cup of coffee. He had merely tucked his nightshirt into his trousers and he'd an old pair of carpet slippers on.

"'Hullo, Peters!' I said, feeling suddenly cheerful, for I was as glad as any lost child to have a live human being close to me. 'Where are you off to with the refreshments?'

"The old man gave a start and slopped some of the coffee. He stared up at me, and I could see that he looked white and done-up. He came on up the stairs and held out the little tray to me.

"'I'm very thankful indeed, Sir, to see you safe and well,' he said. 'I feared one time you might risk going into the Grey Room, Sir. I've lain awake all night, with the sound of the Door. And when it came light, I thought I'd make you a cup of coffee. I knew you would want to look at the seals, and somehow it seems safer if there's two, Sir.'

"'Peters,' I said, 'you're a brick. This is very thoughtful of you.' And I drank the coffee. 'Come along,' I told him, and handed him back the tray. 'I'm going to have a look at what the Brutes have been up to. I simply hadn't the pluck to in the night.'

"'I'm very thankful, Sir,' he replied. 'Flesh and blood can do nothing, Sir, against devils, and that's what's in the Grey Room after dark.'

"I examined the seals on all the doors as I went along and found them right, but when I got to the Grey Room, the seal was broken, though the visiting-card over the keyhole was untouched. I ripped it off and unlocked the door and went in, rather cautiously, as you can imagine; but the whole room was empty of anything to frighten one and there was heaps of light. I examined all my seals, and not a single one was disturbed. The old butler had followed me in, and suddenly, he said,—'The bedclothes, Sir!'

"I ran up to the bed and looked over, and surely, they were lying in the corner to the left of the bed. Jove! you can imagine how queer I felt. Something *had* been in the room. I stared for a while from the bed to the clothes on the floor. I had a feeling that I did not want to touch either. Old

Peters, though, did not seem to be affected that way. He went over to the bed-coverings and was going to pick them up, as, doubtless he had done every day these twenty years back, but I stopped him. I wanted nothing touched until I had finished my examination. This, I must have spent a full hour over and then I let Peters straighten up the bed, after which we went out and I locked the door, for the room was getting on my nerves.

"I had a short walk and then breakfast, which made me feel more my own man. Then to the Grey Room again, and, with Peters's help and one of the maids, I had everything taken out except the bed, even the very pictures.

I examined the walls, floor and ceiling then with probe, hammer and magnifying glass, but found nothing unusual. And I can assure you I began to realise, in very truth. that some incredible thing had been loose in the room during the past night.

"I sealed up everything again and went out, locking and sealing the door as before.

"After dinner that night, Peters and I unpacked some of my stuff and I fixed up my camera and flashlight opposite to the door of the Grey Room with a string from the trigger of the flashlight to the door. You see, if the door really opened, the flashlight would blare out and there would be, possibly, a very queer picture to examine in the morning.

"The last thing I did before leaving was to uncap the lens and after that I went off to my bedroom and to bed, for I intended to be up at midnight, and to ensure this, I set my little alarm to call me; also I left my candle burning.

"The clock woke me at twelve and I got up and into my dressing-gown and slippers. I shoved my revolver into my right side-pocket and opened my door. Then, I lit my darkroom lamp and withdrew the slide so that it would give a clear light. I carried it up the corridor about thirty feet and put it down on the floor, with the open side away from me, so that it would show me anything that might approach along the dark passage. Then I went back and sat in the doorway of my room, with my revolver handy, staring up the passage towards the place where I knew my camera stood outside the door of the Grey Room.

"I should think I had watched for about an hour and a half, when suddenly I heard a faint noise away up the corridor. I was immediately conscious of a queer prickling sensation about the back of my head and my hands began to sweat a little. The following instant the whole end of the passage flicked into sight in the abrupt glare of the flashlight. Then came the succeeding darkness and I peered nervously up the corridor, listening tensely, and trying to find what lay beyond the faint, red glow of my dark-lamp, which now seemed ridiculously dim by contrast with the tremendous blaze of the flash-powder. . . . And then, as I stooped forward, staring and listening, there came the crashing thud of the door of the Grey Room. The sound seemed to fill the whole of the large corridor and go echoing hollowly through the house. I tell you, I felt horrible—as if my bones were water. Simply beastly. Jove! how I did stare and how I listened. And then it came again, thud, thud, thud, and then a silence that was almost worse than the noise of the door, for I kept fancying that some brutal thing was stealing upon me along the corridor.

"Suddenly, my lamp was put out, and I could not see a yard before me. I realised all at once that I was doing a very silly thing, sitting there and I jumped up. Even as I did so, I *thought* I heard a sound in the passage, quite *near* to me. I made one backward spring into my room and slammed and locked the door.

"I sat on my bed and stared at the door. I had my revolver in my hand, but it seemed an abominably useless thing. Can you understand? I felt that there was something the other side of my door. For some unknown reason, I *knew* it was pressed up against the door, and it was soft. That was just what I thought. Most extraordinary thing to imagine, when you come to think of it!

"Presently I got hold of myself a bit and marked out a pentacle hurriedly with chalk on the polished floor, and there I sat in it until it was almost dawn. And all the time, away up the corridor, the door of the Grey Room thudded at solemn and horrid intervals. It was a miserable, brutal night.

"When the day began to break, the thudding of the door came gradually to an end, and at last I grabbed together my courage and went along the corridor in the half light, to cap the lens of my camera. I can tell you, it took some doing; but if I had not gone my photograph would have been spoilt, and I was tremendously keen to save it. I got back to my room, and then set-to and rubbed out the five-pointed star in which I had been sitting.

"Half an hour later there was a tap at my door. It was Peters, with my coffee. When I had drunk it we both went along to the Grey Room. As we went, I had a look at the seals on the other doors, but they were untouched. The seal on the door of the Grey Room was broken, as also was the string from the trigger of the flashlight, but the visiting-card over the keyhole was still there. I ripped it off and opened the door.

"Nothing unusual was to be seen, until we came to the bed; then I saw that as on the previous day, the bedclothes had been torn off, and hurled into the left-hand corner, exactly where I had seen them before. I felt very queer, but I did not forget to look at all the seals, only to find that not one had been broken.

"Then I turned and looked at old Peters and he looked at me, nodding his head.

" 'Let's get out of here!' I said. 'It's no place for any living human to enter without proper protection.'

"We went out then and I locked and sealed the door, again.

"After breakfast I developed the negative, but it showed only the door of the Grey Room, half opened. Then I left the house, as I wanted to get certain matters and implements that might be necessary to life, perhaps to the spirit, for I intended to spend the coming night in the Grey Room.

"I got back in a cab about half-past five with my apparatus, and this, Peters and I carried up to the Grey Room, where I piled it carefully in the centre of the floor. When everything was in the room, including a cat which I had brought, I locked and sealed the door and went toward my bedroom, telling Peters I should not be down for dinner. He said, 'Yes, sir,' and went downstairs, thinking that I was going to turn-in, which was what I wanted him to believe, as I knew he would have worried both himself and me, if he had known what I intended.

"But I merely got my camera and flashlight from my bedroom, and hurried back to the Grey Room. I entered and locked and sealed myself in, and set to, for I had a lot to do before it got dark.

"First, I cleared away all the ribbons across the floor; then I carried the cat—still fastened in its basket—over towards the far wall, and left it. I returned then to the centre of the room and measured out a space twenty-one feet in diameter, which I swept with a 'broom of hyssop.' About this, I drew a circle of chalk, taking care never to step over the circle.

"Beyond this I smudged, with a bunch of garlic, a broad belt right around the chalked circle, and when this was complete, I took from among my stores in the centre a small jar of a certain water. I broke away the parchment and withdrew the stopper. Then, dipping my left forefinger in the little jar, I went round the circle again, making upon the floor, just within the line of chalk, the Second Sign of the Saaamaaa Ritual, and joining each Sign most carefully with the left-handed crescent. I can tell you, I felt easier when this was done, and the 'water circle' complete.

"Then, I unpacked some more of the stuff that I had brought, and placed a lighted candle in the 'valley' of each Crescent. After that, I drew a Pentacle so that each of the five points of the defensive star touched the chalk circle. In the five points of the star I placed five portions of a certain bread, each wrapped in linen, and in the five 'vales,' five opened jars of the water I had used to make the 'water circle.' And now I had my first protective barrier complete.

"Now, anyone, except you who know something of my methods of investigation, might consider all this a piece of useless and foolish superstition; but you all remember the Black Veil case, in which I believe my life was saved by a very similar form of protection; whilst Aster, who sneered at it, and would not come inside, died.

"I got the idea from the Sigsand MS., written, so far as I can make out, in the 14th century. At first, naturally, I imagined it was just an expression of the superstition of his time, and it was not until long after my first reading that it occurred to me to test his 'Defence,' which I did, as I've just said, in that horrible Black Veil business. You know how *that* turned out. Later, I used it several times and always I came through safe, until that Noving Fur case. It was only a partial 'Defence' there and I nearly died in the pentacle. After that I came across Professor Garder's 'Experiments with a Medium.' When they surrounded the Medium with a current, of a certain number of vibrations in vacuum, he lost his position—almost as if it cut him off from the Immaterial.

"That made me think and led eventually to the Electric Pentacle, which is a most marvellous 'Defence' against certain manifestations. I used the shape of the defensive star for this protection because I have, personally, no doubt at all but that there is some extraordinary virtue in the old magic figure. Curious thing for a Twentieth Century man to admit, is it not? But, then, as you all know, I never did, and never will allow myself to be blinded by a little cheap laughter. I ask questions, and keep my eyes open!

"In this last case I had little doubt that I had run up against an ab-natural monster, and I meant to take every possible care; for the danger is abominable.

"I turned-to now to fit the Electric Pentacle, setting it so that each of its 'points' and 'vales' coincided exactly with the 'points' and 'vales' of the drawn pentagram upon the floor. Then I connected up the battery, and the next instant the pale blue glare from the intertwining vacuum tubes shone out.

"I glanced about me then, with something of a sigh of relief, and realized suddenly that the dusk was upon me, for the window was grey and unfriendly. Then I stared round at the big, empty room, over the double-barrier of electric and candle light and had an abrupt, extraordinary sense of weirdness thrust upon me—in the air, you know, it seemed; as it were, a sense of something inhuman impending. The room was full of the stench of bruised garlic, a smell I hate.

"I turned now to my camera, and saw that it and the flashlight were in order. Then I tested the action of my revolver carefully, though I had little thought that it would be needed. Yet, to what extent materialisation of an ab-natural creature is possible, given favourable conditions, no one can say, and I had no idea what horrible thing I was going to see, or feel the presence of. I might, in the end, have to fight with a material thing. I did not know and could only be prepared. You see, I never forgot that three other people had been strangled in the bed close to me, and the fierce slamming of the door I had heard myself. I had no doubt that I was investigating a dangerous and ugly case.

"By this time, the night had come (though the room was very light with the burning candles), and I found myself glancing behind me constantly and then all round the room. It was nervy work waiting for that thing to come into the room.

"Suddenly, I was aware of a little, cold wind sweeping over me, coming from behind. I gave one great nerve-thrill, and a prickly feeling went all over the back of my head. Then I hove myself round with a sort of stiff jerk, and stared straight against that queer wind. It seemed to come from the corner of the room to the left of the bed—the place where both times I had found the heap of tossed bedclothes. Yet, I could see nothing unusual; no opening—nothing! . . .

"Abruptly, I was aware that the candles were all a-flicker in that unnatural wind. . . . I believe I just squatted there and stared in a horribly frightened, wooden way for some minutes. I shall never be able to let you know how disgustingly horrible it was sitting in that vile, cold wind! And then, flick! flick! flick! all the candles round the outer barrier went out, and there was I, locked and sealed in that room, and with no light beyond the weakish blue glare of the Electric Pentacle.

"A time of abominable tenseness passed, and still that wind blew upon me, and then, suddenly, I knew that something stirred in the corner to the left of the bed. I was made conscious of it, rather by some inward, unused sense than by either sight or sound; for the pale, short-radius glare of the Pentacle gave but a very poor light for seeing by. Yet, as I stared, something began slowly to grow upon my sight—a moving shadow, a little darker than the surrounding shadows. I lost the thing amid the vagueness, and for a moment or two I glanced swiftly from side to side with a fresh, new-sense of impending danger. Then my attention was directed to the bed. All the coverings were being drawn steadily off, with a hateful, stealthy sort of motion. I heard the slow, dragging slither of the clothes, but I could see nothing of the thing that pulled. I was aware in a funny, subconscious, introspective fashion that the 'creep' had come upon me, prickling all over my head, yet I was cooler mentally than I had been for some minutes; sufficiently so to feel that my hands were sweating coldly and to shift my revolver, half-consciously, whilst I rubbed my right hand dry upon my knee; though never for an instant taking my gaze or my attention from those moving clothes.

"The faint noises from the bed ceased once and there was a most intense silence, with only the dull thudding of the blood beating in my head. Yet, immediately afterwards, I heard again the slurring sound of the bedclothes being dragged off the bed. In the midst of my nervous tension I remembered the camera, and reached round for it; but without looking away from the bed. And then, you know, all in a moment, the whole of the bed-coverings were torn off with extraordinary violence, and I heard the flump they made as they were hurled into the corner.

"There was a time of absolute quietness then for perhaps a couple of minutes; and you can imagine how horrible I felt. The bedclothes had been thrown with such savageness! And, then again, the abominable unnaturalness of the thing that had just been done before me!

"Suddenly, over by the door, I heard a faint noise—a sort of crickling sound, and then a pitter or two upon the floor. A great nervous thrill swept over me, seeming to run up my spine and over the back of my head, for the seal that secured the door had just been broken. Something was there. I could not see the door; at least, I mean to say that it was impossible to say how much I actually saw, and how much my imagination supplied. I made it out, only as a continuation of the grey walls. . . . And then it seemed to me that something dark and indistinct moved and wavered there among the shadows.

"Abruptly I was aware that the door was opening, and with an effort I reached again for my camera; but before I could aim it the door was slammed with a terrific crash that filled the whole room with a sort of hollow thunder. I jumped like a frightened child. There seemed such a power behind the noise, as though a vast, wanton Force were 'out.' Can you understand?

"The door was not touched again; but, directly afterward I heard the basket in which the cat lay, creak. I tell you, I fairly pringled all along my back. I knew that I was going to learn definitely whether what was abroad was dangerous to Life. From the cat there rose suddenly a hideous caterwaul that ceased abruptly; and then—too late—I snapped on the flashlight. In the great glare, I saw that the basket had been overturned and the lid was wrenched open, with the cat lying half in and half out upon the floor. I saw nothing else, but I was full of the knowledge that I was in the presence of some Being or Thing that had power to destroy.

"During the next two or three minutes, there was an odd, noticeable quietness in the room, and you must remember I was half-blinded for the time because of the flashlight, so that the whole place seemed to be pitchy dark just beyond the shine of the Pentacle. I tell you it was most horrible. I just knelt there in the star and whirled round on my knees, trying to see whether anything was coming at me.

"My power of sight came gradually, and I got a little hold of myself and abruptly I saw the thing I was looking for, close to the 'water-circle.' It was big and indistinct and wavered curiously, as though the shadow of a vast spider hung suspended in the air, just beyond the barrier. It passed swiftly round the circle, and seemed to probe ever towards me, but only to draw back with extraordinary jerky movements, as might a living person if they touched the hot bar of a grate.

"Round and round it moved, and round and round I turned. Then, just opposite to one of the 'Vales' in the pentacles, it seemed to pause, as though preliminary to a tremendous effort. It retired almost beyond the glow of the vacuum light and then came straight towards me, appearing to gather form and solidity as it came. There seemed a vast, malign determination behind the movement, that must succeed. I was on my knees, and I jerked back, falling on to my left hand and hip, in a wild endeavor to get back from the advancing thing. With my right hand I was grabbing madly for my revolver which I had let slip. The brutal thing came with one great sweep straight over the garlic and the 'water-circle,' almost to the vale of the pentacle. I believe I yelled. Then, just as suddenly as it had swept over, it seemed to be hurled back by some mighty, invisible force.

"It must have been some moments before I realised that I was safe, and then I got myself together in the middle of the pentacles, feeling horribly gone and shaken, and glancing round and round the barrier, but the thing had vanished. Yet, I had learnt something, for I knew now that the Grey Room was haunted by a monstrous hand.

"Suddenly as I crouched there I saw what had so nearly given the monster an opening through the barrier. In my movements within the pentacle I must have touched one of the jars of water, for just where the thing had made its attack the jar that guarded the 'deep' of the 'vale' had been moved to one side and this had left one of the 'five doorways' unguarded. I put it back quickly and felt almost safe again, for I had found the cause, and the 'Defence' was still good. I began to hope again that I should see the morning come in. When I saw that thing so nearly succeed I had an awful, weak, overwhelming feeling that the 'barriers' could never bring me safe through the night against such a Force. You can understand?

"For a long time I could not see the hand; but presently I thought I saw, once or twice, an odd wavering over among the shadows near the door. A little later, as though in a sudden fit of malignant rage, the dead body of the cat was picked up and beaten with dull, sickening blows against the solid floor. That made me feel rather queer.

"A minute afterwards, the door was opened and slammed twice with tremendous force. The next instant the thing made one swift, vicious dart at me from out of the shadows. Instinctively I started sideways from it, and so plucked my hand from upon the Electric Pentacle where—for a wickedly careless moment—I had placed it. The monster was hurled off from the neighbourhood of the pentacles, though—owing to my inconceivable foolishness—it had been enabled for a second time to pass the outer barriers. I can tell you I shook for a time with sheer funk. I moved right to the centre of the pentacles again and knelt there, making myself as small and compact as possible.

"As I knelt, I began to have presently, a vague wonder at the two 'accidents' which had so nearly allowed the brute to get at me. Was I being *influenced* to unconscious voluntary actions that endangered me? The thought took hold of me and I watched my every movement. Abruptly, I stretched a tired leg and knocked over one of the jars of water. Some was spilled, but because of my suspicious watchfulness, I had it upright and back within the vale while yet some of the water remained. Even as I did so, the vast, black, half-materialised hand beat up at me out of the shadows and seemed to leap almost into my face so nearly did it approach, but for the third time it was thrown back by some altogether enormous, overmastering force. Yet, apart from the dazed fright in which it left me, I had for a moment that feeling of spiritual sickness, as if some delicate, beautiful, inward grace had suffered, which is felt only upon the too near approach of the ab-human and is more dreadful in a strange way, than any physical pain that can be suffered. I knew by this more of the extent and closeness of the danger, and for a long time I was simply cowed by the butt-headed brutality of that Force upon my spirit. I can put it no other way.

"I knelt again in the centre of the pentacles, watching myself with more fear, almost, than the monster; for I knew now that, unless I guarded myself from every sudden impulse that came to me, I might simply work my own destruction. Do you see how horrible it all was?

"I spent the rest of the night in a haze of sick fright and so tense that I could not make a single movement naturally. I was in such fear that any desire for action that came to me might be prompted by the Influence that I knew was at work on me. And outside of the barrier that ghastly thing went round and round, grabbing and grabbing in the air at me. Twice more was the body of the dead cat molested. The second time I heard every bone in its body scrunch and crack. And all the time the horrible wind was blowing upon me from the corner of the room to the left of the bed.

"Then, just as the first touch of dawn came into the sky, that unnatural wind ceased in a single moment and I could see no sign of the hand. The dawn came slowly and presently the wan light filled all the room and made the pale glare of the Electric Pentacle look more unearthly. Yet, it was not until the day had fully come that I made any attempt to leave the barrier, for I did not know but that there was some method abroad in the sudden stopping of that wind to entice me from the pentacles.

"At last, when the dawn was strong and bright, I took one last look round, and ran for the door. I got it unlocked, in a nervous and clumsy fashion then locked it hurriedly and went to my bedroom, where I lay on the bed and tried to steady my nerves. Peters came presently with the coffee and when I had drunk it I told him I meant to have a sleep, as I had been up all night. He took the tray and went out quietly and after I had locked my door I turned in properly and at last got to sleep.

"I woke about midday and after some lunch went up to the Grey Room. I switched off the current from the Pentacle, which I had left on in my hurry; also, I removed the body of the cat. You can understand, I did not want anyone to see the poor brute.

"After that, I made a very careful search of the corner where the bedclothes had been thrown. I made several holes through the woodwork and probed, but found nothing. Then it occurred to me to try with my instrument under the skirting. I did so and heard my wire ring on metal. I turned the hook-end of the probe that way and fished for the thing. At the second go I got it. It was a small object and I took it to the window. I found it to be a curious ring, made of some greyish metal. The curious thing about it was that it was made in the form of a pentagon; that is, the same shape as the inside of the magic pentacle, but without the 'mounts' which form the points of the defensive star. It was free from all chasing or engraving.

"You will understand that I was excited when I tell you that I felt sure I held in my hand the famous Luck Ring of the Anderson family; which, indeed, was of all things the most intimately connected with the history of the haunting. This ring had been handed on from father to son through generations, and always—in obedience to some ancient family tradition—each son had to promise never to wear the ring. The ring, I may say, was brought home by one of the Crusaders under very peculiar circumstances, but the story is too long to go into here.

"It appears that young Sir Hulbert, an ancestor of Anderson's, made a bet one evening, in drink, you know, that he would wear the ring that night. He did so, and in the morning his wife and child were found strangled in the bed in the very room in which I stood. Many people, it would seem, thought young Sir Hulbert was guilty of having done the thing in drunken anger, and he, in an attempt to prove his innocence, slept a second night in the room. He also was strangled.

"Since then, no one has spent a night in the Grey Room until I did so. The ring had been lost so long that its very existence had become almost a myth; and it was most extraordinary to stand there with the actual thing in my hand, as you can understand.

"It was whilst I stood there looking at the ring that I got an idea. Supposing that it were, in a way, a doorway—you see what I mean? A sort of gap in the world-hedge, if I may so phrase my idea. It was a queer thought, I know, and possibly was not my own, but one of those mental nudgings from the Outside. You see, the wind had come from that part of the room where the ring lay. I pondered the thought a lot. Then the shape—the inside of a pentacle. It had no 'mounts,' and without mounts, as the Sigsand MS. has it:—'Thee mownts wych are thee Five Hills of safetie. To lack is to gyve pow'r to thee daemon; and surlie to fayvor the Evill Thynge.' You see, the very shape of the ring was significant. I determined to test it.

"I unmade my pentacle, for it must be 'made' afresh *and around* the one to be protected. Then I went out and locked the door, after which I left the house, to get certain matters, for neither 'yarbs nor fyre nor water' must be used a second time. I returned about seven-thirty and as soon as the things I had brought had been carried up to the Grey Room I dismissed Peters for the night, just as I had done the evening before. When he had gone downstairs I let myself into the room and locked and sealed the door. I went to the place in the centre of the room where all the stuff had been packed and set to work with all my speed to construct a barrier about me and the ring.

"I do not remember whether I explained it to you, but I had reasoned that if the ring were in any way a 'medium of admission,' and it were enclosed with me in the Electric Pentacle it would be, to express it loosely, insulated. Do you see? The Force which had visible expression as a Hand, would have to stay beyond the Barrier which separates the Ab from the Normal, for the 'gateway' would be removed from accessibility.

"As I was saying, I worked with all my speed to get the barrier completed about me and the ring, for it was already later than I cared to be in that room 'unprotected.' Also, I had a feeling that there would be a vast effort made that night to regain the use of the ring. For I had the strongest conviction that the ring was a necessity to materialisation. You will see whether I was right.

"I completed the barriers in about an hour and you can imagine something of the relief I felt when I felt the pale glare of the Electric Pentacle once more all about me. From then, onwards for about two hours, I sat quietly facing the corner from which the wind came.

"About eleven o'clock I had a queer knowledge that something was near to me, yet nothing happened for a whole hour after that. Then suddenly, I felt the cold, queer wind begin to blow upon me. To my astonishment it seemed now to come from behind me, and I shipped round with a hideous quake of fear. The wind met me in the face. It was flowing up from the floor close to me. I stared, in a sickening maze of new frights. What on earth had I done now! The ring was there, close beside me, where I had put it. Suddenly, as I stared, bewildered, I was aware that there was something queer about the ring—funny shadowy movements and convolutions. I looked at them stupidly. And then, abruptly, I knew that the wind was blowing up at me from the ring. A queer indistinct smoke became visible to me, seeming to pour upwards through the ring and mix with the moving shadows. Suddenly, I realised that I was in more than any mortal danger, for the convoluting shadows about the ring were taking shape, and the death-hand was forming *within* the Pentacle. My goodness, do you realise it? I had brought the 'gateway' into the pentacles and the brute was coming through—pouring into the material world, as gas might pour out from the mouth of a pipe.

"I should think that I knelt for a couple of moments in a sort of stunned fright. Then with a mad awkward movement I snatched at the ring, intending to hurl it out of the Pentacle. Yet, it eluded me, as though some invisible, living thing jerked it hither and thither. At last I gripped it, but in the same instant, it was torn from my grasp with incredible and brutal force. A great black shadow covered it and rose into the air and came at me. I saw that it was the Hand, vast and nearly perfect in form. I gave one crazy yell and jumped over the Pentacle and the ring of burning candles and ran despairingly for the door. I fumbled idiotically and ineffectually with the key, and all the time I stared, with the fear that was like insanity, toward the Barriers. The hand was plunging toward me; yet, even as it had been unable to pass into the pentacle when the ring was without; so, now that the ring was within it had no power to pass out. The monster was chained, as surely as any beast would be, were chains rivetted upon it.

"Even then, in that moment, I got a flash of this knowledge, but I was too utterly shaken with fright, to reason and the instant I managed to get the key turned I sprang into the passage and slammed the door with a crash. I locked it and got to my room, somehow; for I was trembling so that I could hardly stand, as you can imagine. I locked myself in and managed to get the candle lit; then I lay down on the bed, and kept quiet for an hour or two, and so I grew steadier.

"I got a little sleep later, but woke when Peters brought my coffee. When I had drunk it I felt altogether better and took the old man along with me whilst I had a look into the Grey Room. I opened the door, and peeped in. The candles were still burning wan against the daylight and behind them was the pale, glowing star of the Electric Pentacle. And there, in the middle, was the ring—the gateway of the monster, lying demure and ordinary.

"Nothing in the room was touched and I knew that the brute had never managed to cross the Pentacles. Then I went out and locked the door.

"After a further sleep of some hours I left the house. I returned in the afternoon in a cab. I had with me an oxy-hydrogen jet, and two cylinders, containing the gases. I carried the things into the Grey Room, and there, in the centre of the Electric Pentacle, I erected the little furnace. Five minutes later the Luck Ring, once the 'luck' but now the 'bane' of the Anderson family, was no more than a little splash of hot metal."

Carnacki felt in his pocket and pulled out something wrapped in tissue paper. He passed it to me. I opened it and found a small circle of greyish metal, something like lead, only harder and rather brighter.

"Well?" I asked, at length, after examining it and handing it round to the others, "did that stop the haunting?"

Carnacki nodded. "Yes," he said. "I slept three nights in the Grey Room, before I left. Old Peters nearly fainted when he knew that I meant to, but by the third night he seemed to realise that the house was just safe and ordinary. And, you know, I believe in his heart he hardly approved."

Carnacki stood up and began to shake hands. "Out you go!" he said, genially.

And presently we went, pondering, to our various homes.

P *is for* Possessed

We usually think of "the possessed" as a person whose thoughts and actions have been taken over by an invading supernatural presence. In this story by British writer William Fryer Harvey (1885–1937), which served as the title tale of his 1928 collection *The Beast with Five Fingers and Other Stories,* the malignant presence claims only one useful part of its intended's body. The story was memorably adapted for the screen under the same title in 1946.

William Fryer Harvey

The Beast with Five Fingers

The story, I suppose, begins with Adrian Borlsover, whom I met when I was a little boy and he an old man. My father had called to appeal for a subscription, and before he left, Mr. Borlsover laid his right hand in blessing on my head. I shall never forget the awe in which I gazed up at his face and realised for the first time that eyes might be dark and beautiful and shining, and yet not able to see.

For Adrian Borlsover was blind.

He was an extraordinary man, who came of an eccentric stock. Borlsover sons for some reason always seemed to marry very ordinary women, which perhaps accounted for the fact that no Borlsover had been a genius and only one Borlsover had been mad. But they were great champions of little causes, generous patrons of odd sciences, founders of querulous sects, trustworthy guides to the bypath meadows of erudition.

Adrian was an authority on the fertilisation of orchids. He had held at one time the family living at Borlsover Conyers, until a congenital weakness of the lungs obliged him to seek a less rigorous climate in the sunny south-coast watering-place where I had seen him. Occasionally he would relieve one or other of the local clergy. My father described him as a fine preacher, who gave long and inspiring sermons from what many men would have considered unprofitable texts. "An excellent proof," he would add, "of the truth of the doctrine of direct verbal inspiration."

Adrian Borlsover was exceedingly clever with his hands. His penmanship was exquisite. He illustrated all his scientific papers, made his own woodcuts, and carved the reredos that is at present the chief feature of interest in the church at Borlsover Conyers. He had an exceedingly clever knack in cutting silhouettes for young ladies and paper pigs and cows for little children, and made more than one complicated wind instrument of his own devising.

When he was fifty years old Adrian Borlsover lost his sight. In a wonderfully short time he adapted himself to the new conditions of life. He quickly learnt to read Braille. So marvellous indeed was his sense of touch, that he was still able to maintain his interest in botany. The mere passing of his long supple fingers over a flower was sufficient means for its identification, though occasionally he would use his lips. I have found several letters of his among my father's correspondence; in no case was there anything to show that he was afflicted with blindness, and this in spite of the fact that he exercised undue economy in the spacing of lines. Towards the close of his life Adrian Borlsover was credited with powers of touch that seemed almost uncanny. It has been said that he could tell at once the colour of a ribbon placed between his fingers. My father would neither confirm nor deny the story.

Adrian Borlsover was a bachelor. His elder brother, Charles, had married late in life, leaving one son, Eustace, who lived in the gloomy Georgian mansion at Borlsover Conyers, where he could work undisturbed in collecting material for his great book on heredity.

Like his uncle, he was a remarkable man. The Borlsovers had always been born naturalists, but Eustace possessed in a special degree the power of systematising his knowledge. He had received his university education in Germany; and then, after post-graduate work in Vienna and Naples, had travelled for four years in South America, and the East, getting together a huge store of material for a new study into the processes of variation.

He lived alone at Borlsover Conyers with Saunders, his secretary, a man who bore a somewhat dubious reputation in the district, but whose powers as a mathematician, combined with his business abilities, were invaluable to Eustace.

Uncle and nephew saw little of each other. The visits of Eustace were confined to a week in the summer or autumn—tedious weeks, that dragged almost as slowly as the bath-chair in which the old man was drawn along the sunny seafront. In their way the two men were fond of each other, though their intimacy would, doubtless, have been greater had they shared the same religious views. Adrian held to the old-fashioned evangelical dogmas of his early manhood; his nephew for many years had been thinking of embracing Buddhism. Both men possessed, too, the reticence the Borlsovers had always shown, and which their enemies sometimes called hypocrisy. With Adrian it was a reticence as to the things he had left undone; but with Eustace it seemed that the curtain which he was so careful to leave undrawn hid something more than a half-empty chamber.

Two years before his death Adrian Borlsover developed, unknown to himself, the not uncommon power of automatic writing. Eustace made the discovery by accident. Adrian was sitting reading in bed, the forefinger of his left hand tracing the Braille characters, when his nephew noticed that a pencil the old man held in his right hand was moving slowly along the opposite page. He left his seat in the window and sat down beside the bed. The right had continued to move and now he could see plainly that they were letters and words which it was forming.

"Adrian Borlsover," wrote the hand, "Eustace Borlsover, Charles Borlsover, Francis Borlsover, Sigismund Borlsover, Adrian Borlsover, Eustace Borlsover, Saville Borlsover. B for Borlsover. Honesty is the Best Policy. Beautiful Belinda Borlsover."

"What curious nonsense!" said Eustace to himself.

"King George ascended the throne in 1760," wrote the hand. "Crowd, a noun of multitude; a collection of individuals. Adrian Borlsover, Eustace Borlsover."

"It seems to me," said his uncle, closing the book, "that you had much better make the most of the afternoon sunshine and take your walk now."

"I think perhaps I will," Eustace answered as he picked up the volume. "I won't go far, and when I come back I can read to you those articles in *Nature* about which we were speaking."

He went along the promenade, but stopped at the first shelter and, seating himself in the corner best protected from the wind, he examined the book at leisure. Nearly every page was scored with a meaningless jumble of pencil-marks; rows of capital letters, short words, long words, complete sentences, copy-book tags. The whole thing, in fact, had the appearance of a copy-book, and, on a more careful scrutiny, Eustace thought that there was ample evidence to show that the handwriting at the beginning of the book, good though it was, was not nearly so good as the handwriting at the end.

He left his uncle at the end of October with a promise to return early in December. It seemed to him quite clear that the old man's power of automatic writing was developing rapidly, and for the first time he looked forward to a visit that would combine duty with interest.

But on his return he was at first disappointed. His uncle, he thought, looked older. He was listless, too, preferring others to read to him and dictating nearly all his letters. Not until the day before he left had Eustace an opportunity of observing Adrian Borlsover's new-found faculty.

The old man, propped up in bed with pillows, had sunk into a light sleep. His two hands lay on the coverlet, his left hand tightly clasping his right. Eustace took an empty manuscript-book and placed a pencil within reach of the fingers of the right hand. They snatched at it eagerly, then dropped the pencil to loose the left hand from its restraining grasp.

"Perhaps to prevent interference I had better hold that hand," said Eustace to himself, as he watched the pencil. Almost immediately it began to write:

"Blundering Borlsovers, unnecessarily unnatural, extraordinarily eccentric, culpably curious."

"Who are you?" asked Eustace in a low voice.

"Never you mind," wrote the hand of Adrian.

"Is it my uncle who is writing?"

"O my prophetic soul, mine uncle!"

"Is it anyone I know?"

"Silly Eustace, you'll see me very soon."

"When shall I see you?"

"When poor old Adrian's dead."

"Where shall I see you?"

"Where shall you not?"

Instead of speaking his next question, Eustace wrote it: "What is the time?"

The fingers dropped the pencil and moved three or four times across the paper. Then, picking up the pencil, they wrote: "Ten minutes before four. Put your book away, Eustace. Adrian mustn't find us working at this sort of thing. He doesn't know what to make of it, and I won't have poor old Adrian disturbed. Au revoir!"

Adrian Borlsover awoke with a start.

"I've been dreaming again," he said; "such queer dreams of leaguered cities and forgotten towns. You were mixed up in this one, Eustace, though I can't remember how. Eustace, I want to warn you. Don't walk in doubtful paths. Choose your friends well. Your poor grandfather . . ."

A fit of coughing put an end to what he was saying, but Eustace saw that the hand was still writing. He managed unnoticed to draw the book away. "I'll light the gas," he said, "and ring for tea." On the other side of the bed-curtain he saw the last sentences that had been written.

"It's too late, Adrian," he read. "We're friends already, aren't we, Eustace Borlsover?"

On the following day Eustace left. He thought his uncle looked ill when he said good-bye, and the old man spoke despondently of the failure his life had been.

"Nonsense, uncle," said his nephew. "You have got over your difficulties in a way not one in a hundred thousand would have done. Everyone marvels at your splendid perseverance in teaching your hands to take the place of your lost sight. To me it's been a revelation of the possibilities of education."

"Education," said his uncle dreamily, as if the word had started a new train of thought. "Education is good so long as you know to whom and for what purpose you give it. But with the lower orders of men, the base and more sordid spirits, I have grave doubts as to its results. Well, good-bye, Eustace; I may not see you again. You are a true Borlsover, with all the

Borlsover faults. Marry, Eustace. Marry some good, sensible girl. And if by any chance I don't see you again, my will is at my solicitor's. I've not left you any legacy, because I know you're well provided for; but I thought you might like to have my books. Oh, and there's just one other thing. You know, before the end people often lose control over themselves and make absurd requests. Don't pay any attention to them, Eustace. Good-bye!" and he held out his hand. Eustace took it. It remained in his a fraction of a second longer than he had expected and gripped him with a virility that was surprising. There was, too, in its touch a subtle sense of intimacy.

"Why, uncle," he said, "I shall see you alive and well for many long years to come."

Two months later Adrian Borlsover died.

Eustace Borlsover was in Naples at the time. He read the obituary notice in the *Morning Post* on the day announced for the funeral.

"Poor old fellow! " he said. "I wonder whether I shall find room for all his books."

The question occurred to him again with greater force when, three days later, he found himself standing in the library at Borlsover Conyers, a huge room built for use and not for beauty in the year of Waterloo by a Borlsover who was an ardent admirer of the great Napoleon. It was arranged on the plan of many college libraries, with tall projecting bookcases forming deep recesses of dusty silence, fit graves for the old hates of forgotten controversy, the dead passions of forgotten lives. At the end of the room, behind the bust of some unknown eighteenth-century divine, an ugly iron corkscrew stair led to a shelf-lined gallery. Nearly every shelf was full.

"I must talk to Saunders about it," said Eustace. "I suppose that we shall have to have the billiard-room fitted up with bookcases."

The two men met for the first time after many weeks in the dining-room that evening.

"Hallo!" said Eustace, standing before the fire with his hands in his pockets. "How goes the world, Saunders? Why these dress togs?" He himself was wearing an old shooting-jacket. He did not believe in mourning, as he had told his uncle on his last visit; and, though he usually went in for quiet-coloured ties, he wore this evening one of an ugly red, in order to shock Morton, the butler, and to make them thrash out the whole question of mourning for themselves in the servants' hall. Eustace was a true Borlsover. "The world," said Saunders, "goes the same as usual, confoundedly slow. The dress togs are accounted for by an invitation from Captain Lockwood to bridge."

"How are you getting there?"

"There's something the matter with the car, so I've told Jackson to drive me round in the dogcart. Any objection?"

"O, dear me, no! We've had all things in common for far too many years for me to raise objections at this hour of the day."

"You'll find your correspondence in the library," went on Saunders. "Most of it I've seen to. There are a few private letters I haven't opened. There's also a box with a rat or something inside it that came by the evening post. Very likely it's the six-toed beast Terry was sending us to cross with the four-toed albino. I didn't look because I didn't want to mess up my things; but I should gather from the way it's jumping about that it's pretty hungry."

"Oh, I'll see to it," said Eustace, "while you and the captain earn an honest penny."

Dinner over and Saunders gone, Eustace went into the library. Though the fire had been lit, the room was by no means cheerful.

"We'll have all the lights on, at any rate," he said, as he turned the switches. "And, Morton," he added, when the butler brought the coffee, "get me a screwdriver or something to undo this box. Whatever the animal is, he's kicking up the deuce of a row. What is it? Why are you dawdling?"

"If you please, sir, when the postman brought it, he told me that they'd bored the holes in the lid at the post office. There were no breathing holes in the lid, sir, and they didn't want the animal to die. That is all, sir."

"It's culpably careless of the man, whoever he was," said Eustace, as he removed the screws, "packing an animal like this in a wooden box with no means of getting air. Confound it all! I meant to ask Morton to bring me a cage to put it in. Now I suppose I shall have to get one myself."

He placed a heavy book on the lid from which the screws had been removed, and went into the billiard-room. As he came back into the library with an empty cage in his hand, he heard the sound of something falling, and then of something scuttling along the floor.

"Bother it! The beast's got out. How in the world am I to find it again in this library?"

To search for it did indeed seem hopeless. He tried to follow the sound of the scuttling in one of the recesses, where the animal seemed to be running behind the books in the shelves; but it was impossible to locate it. Eustace resolved to go on quietly reading. Very likely the animal might gain confidence and show itself. Saunders seemed to have dealt in his usual methodical manner with most of the correspondence. There were still the private letters.

What was that? Two sharp clicks and the lights in the hideous candelabras that hung from the ceiling suddenly went out.

"I wonder if something has gone wrong with the fuse," said Eustace, as he went to the switches by the door. Then he stopped. There was a noise at the other end of the room, as if something was crawling up the iron corkscrew stair. "If it's gone into the gallery," he said, "well and good." He hastily turned on the lights, crossed the room, and climbed up the stair. But he could see nothing. His grandfather had placed a little gate at the top of the stair, so that children could run and romp in the gallery without fear of accident. This Eustace closed, and, having considerably narrowed the circle of his search, returned to his desk by the fire.

How gloomy the library was! There was no sense of intimacy about the room. The few busts that an eighteenth-century Borlsover had brought back from the grand tour might have been in keeping in the old library. Here they seemed out of place. They made the room feel cold in spite of the heavy red damask curtain and great gilt cornices.

With a crash two heavy books fell from the gallery to the floor; then, as Borlsover looked, another, and yet another.

"Very well. You'll starve for this, my beauty!" he said. "We'll do some little experiments on the metabolism of rats deprived of water. Go on! Chuck them down! I think I've got the upper hand." He turned once more to his correspondence. The letter was from the family solicitor. It spoke of his uncle's death, and of the valuable collection of books that had been left to him in the will.

> There was one request [he read] which certainly came as a surprise to me. As you know, Mr. Adrian Borlsover had left instructions that his body was to be buried in as simple a manner as possible at Eastbourne. He expressed a desire that there should be neither wreaths nor flowers of any kind, and hoped that his friends and relatives would not consider it necessary to wear mourning. The day before his death we received a letter cancelling these

> instructions. He wished the body to be embalmed (he gave us the address of the man we were to employ—Pennifer, Ludgate Hill), with orders that his right hand should be sent to you stating that it was at your special request. The other arrangements about the funeral remained unaltered.

"Good Lord," said Eustace, "what in the world was the old boy driving at? And what in the name of all that's holy is that?"

Someone was in the gallery. Someone had pulled the cord attached to one of the blinds, and it had rolled up with a snap. Someone must be in the gallery, for a second blind did the same. Someone must be walking round the gallery, for one after the other the blinds sprang up, letting in the moonlight.

"I haven't got to the bottom of this yet," said Eustace, "but I will do, before the night is very much older"; and he hurried up the corkscrew stair. He had just got to the top, when the lights went out a second time, and he heard again the scuttling along the floor. Quickly he stole on tiptoe in the dim moonshine in the direction of the noise, feeling, as he went, for one of the switches. His fingers touched the metal knob at last. He turned on the electric light.

About ten yards in front of him, crawling along the floor, was a man's hand. Eustace stared at it in utter amazement. It was moving quickly in the manner of a geometer caterpillar, the fingers humped up one moment, flattened out the next; the thumb appeared to give a crablike motion to the whole. While he was looking, too surprised to stir, the hand disappeared round the corner. Eustace ran forward. He no longer saw it, but he could hear it, as it squeezed its way behind the books on one of the shelves. A heavy volume had been displaced. There was a gap in the row of books, where it had got in. In his fear lest it should escape him again, he seized the first book that came to his hand and plugged it into the hole. Then, emptying two shelves of their contents, he took the wooden boards and propped them up in front to make his barrier doubly sure.

"I wish Saunders was back," he said; "one can't tackle this sort of thing alone." It was after eleven, and there seemed little likelihood of Saunders returning before twelve. He did not dare to leave the shelf unwatched, even to run downstairs to ring the bell. Morton, the butler, often used to come round about eleven to see that the windows were fastened, but he might not come. Eustace was thoroughly unstrung. At last he heard steps down below.

"Morton!" he shouted. "Morton!"

"Sir?"

"Has Mr. Saunders got back yet?"

"Not yet, sir."

"Well, bring me some brandy, and hurry up about it. I'm up in the gallery, you duffer."

"Thanks," said Eustace, as he emptied the glass. "Don't go to bed yet, Morton. There are a lot of books that have fallen down by accident. Bring them up and put them back in their shelves."

Morton had never seen Borlsover in so talkative a mood as on that night. "Here," said Eustace, when the books had been put back and dusted, "you might hold up these boards for me, Morton. That beast in the box got out, and I've been chasing it all over the place."

"I think I can hear it chawing at the books, sir. They're not valuable, I hope? I think that's the carriage, sir; I'll go and call Mr. Saunders."

It seemed to Eustace that he was away for five minutes, but it could hardly have been more than one, when he returned with Saunders. "All right, Morton, you can go now. I'm up here, Saunders."

"What's all the row?" asked Saunders, as he lounged forward with his hands in his pockets. The luck had been with him all the evening. He was completely satisfied, both with himself and with Captain Lockwood's taste in wines. "What's the matter? You look to me to be in an absolutely blue funk."

"That old devil of an uncle of mine," began Eustace—"Oh, I can't explain it all. It's his hand that's been playing Old Harry all the evening. But I've got it cornered behind these books. You've got to help me to catch it."

"What's up with you, Eustace? What's the game?"

"It's no game, you silly idiot! If you don't believe me, take out one of those books and put your hand in and feel."

"All right," said Saunders; "but wait till I've rolled up my sleeve. The accumulated dust of centuries, eh?" He took off his coat, knelt down, and thrust his arm along the shelf.

"There's something there right enough," he said. "It's got a funny, stumpy end to it, whatever it is, and nips like a crab. Ah! No, you don't!" He pulled his hand out in a flash. "Shove in a book quickly. Now it can't get out."

"What was it?" asked Eustace.

"Something that wanted very much to get hold of me. I felt what seemed like a thumb and forefinger. Give me some brandy."

"How are we to get it out of there?"

"What about a landing-net?"

"No good. It would be too smart for us. I tell you, Saunders, it can cover the ground far faster than I can walk. But I think I see how we can manage it. The two books at the ends of the shelf are big ones, that go right back against the wall. The others are very thin. I'll take out one at a time, and you slide the rest along until we have it squashed between the end two."

It certainly seemed to be the best plan. One by one as they took out the books, the space behind grew smaller and smaller. There was something in it that was certainly very much alive. Once they caught sight of fingers feeling for a way of escape. At last they had it pressed between the two big books.

"There's muscle there, if there isn't warm flesh and blood," said Saunders, as he held them together. "It seems to be a hand right enough, too. I suppose this is a sort of infectious hallucination. I've read about such cases before."

"Infectious fiddlesticks!" said Eustace, his face white with anger; "bring the thing downstairs. We'll get it back into the box."

It was not altogether easy, but they were successful at last. "Drive in the screws," said Eustace; "we won't run any risks. Put the box in this old desk of mine. There's nothing in it that I want. Here's the key. Thank goodness there's nothing wrong with the lock."

"Quite a lively evening," said Saunders. "Now let's hear more about your uncle."

They sat up together until early morning. Saunders had no desire for sleep. Eustace was trying to explain and to forget; to conceal from himself a fear that he had never felt before—the fear of walking alone down the long corridor to his bedroom.

"Whatever it was," said Eustace to Saunders on the following morning, "I propose that we drop the subject. There's nothing to keep us here for the next ten days. We'll motor up to the Lakes and get some climbing."

"And see nobody all day, and sit bored to death with each other every night. Not for me, thanks. Why not run up to town? Run's the exact word in this case, isn't it? We're both in such a blessed funk. Pull yourself together, Eustace, and let's have another look at the hand."

"As you like," said Eustace; "there's the key."

They went into the library and opened the desk. The box was as they had left it on the previous night.

"What are you waiting for?" asked Eustace.

"I am waiting for you to volunteer to open the lid. However, since you seem to funk it, allow me. There doesn't seem to be the likelihood of any rumpus this morning at all events." He opened the lid and picked out the hand.

"Cold?" asked Eustace.

"Tepid. A bit below blood heat by the feel. Soft and supple too. If it's the embalming, it's a sort of embalming I've never seen before. Is it your uncle's hand?"

"Oh yes, it's his all right," said Eustace. "I should know those long thin fingers anywhere. Put it back in the box, Saunders. Never mind about the screws. I'll lock the desk, so that there'll be no chance of its getting out. We'll compromise by motoring up to town for a week. If we can get off soon after lunch, we ought to be at Grantham or Stamford by night."

"Right," said Saunders, "and to-morrow—oh, well, by to-morrow we shall have forgotten all about this beastly thing."

If, when the morrow came, they had not forgotten, it was certainly true that at the end of the week they were able to tell a very vivid ghost story at the little supper Eustace gave on Hallow E'en.

"You don't want us to believe that it's true, Mr. Borlsover? How perfectly awful!"

"I'll take my oath on it, and so would Saunders here; wouldn't you, old chap?"

"Any number of oaths," said Saunders. "It was a long thin hand, you know, and it gripped me just like that."

"Don't, Mr. Saunders! Don't! How perfectly horrid! Now tell us another one, do! Only a really creepy one, please."

"Here's a pretty mess!" said Eustace on the following day, as he threw a letter across the table to Saunders. "It's your affair, though. Mrs. Merrit, if I understand it, gives a month's notice."

"Oh, that's quite absurd on Mrs. Merrit's part," replied Saunders. "She doesn't know what she's talking about. Let's see what she says."

> Dear Sir [he read]. This is to let you know that I must give you a month's notice as from Tuesday, the 13th. For a long time I've felt the place too big for

me; but when Jane Parfit and Emma Laidlaw go off with scarcely as much as an "If you please," after frightening the wits out of the other girls, so that they can't turn out a room by themselves or walk alone down the stairs for fear of treading on half-frozen toads or hearing it run along the passages at night, all I can say is that it's no place for me. So I must ask you, Mr. Borlsover, sir, to find a new housekeeper, that has no objection to large and lonely houses, which some people do say, not that I believe them for a minute, my poor mother always having been a Wesleyan, are haunted.

Yours faithfully,
ELIZABETH MERRIT

P.S.—I should be obliged if you would give my respects to Mr. Saunders. I hope that he won't run any risks with his cold.

"Saunders," said Eustace, "you've always had a wonderful way with you in dealing with servants. You mustn't let poor old Merrit go."

"Of course she shan't go," said Saunders. "She's probably only angling for a rise in salary. I'll write to her this morning."

"No. There's nothing like a personal interview. We've had enough of town. We'll go back tomorrow, and you must work your cold for all its worth. Don't forget that it's got on to the chest, and will require weeks of feeding up and nursing."

"All right, I think I can manage Mrs. Merrit."

But Mrs. Merrit was more obstinate than he had thought. She was very sorry to hear of Mr. Saunders's cold, and how he lay awake all night in London coughing; very sorry indeed. She'd change his room for him gladly and get the south room aired, and wouldn't he have a hot basin of bread and milk last thing at night? But she was afraid that she would have to leave at the end of the month.

"Try her with an increase of salary," was the advice of Eustace.

It was no use. Mrs. Merrit was obdurate, though she knew of a Mrs. Goddard, who had been housekeeper to Lord Gargrave, who might be glad to come at the salary mentioned.

"What's the matter with the servants, Morton?" asked Eustace that evening, when he brought the coffee into the library. "What's all this about Mrs. Merrit wanting to leave?"

"If you please, sir, I was going to mention it myself. I have a confession to make, sir. When I found your note, asking me to open that desk and take out the box with the rat, I broke the lock as you told me, and was glad to do it, because I could hear the animal in the box making a great noise, and I thought it wanted food. So I took out the box, sir, and got a cage, and was going to transfer it, when the animal got away."

"What in the world are you talking about? I never wrote any such note."

"Excuse me, sir; it was the note I picked up here on the floor on the day you and Mr. Saunders left. I have it in my pocket now."

It certainly seemed to be in Eustace's handwriting. It was written in pencil, and began somewhat abruptly.

"Get a hammer, Morton, [he read] or some other tool and break open the lock in the old desk in the library. Take out the box that is inside. You need not do anything else. The lid is already open. Eustace Borlsover."

"And you opened the desk?"

"Yes, sir; and, as I was getting the cage ready, the animal hopped out."

"What animal?"

"The animal inside the box, sir."

"What did it look like?"

"Well, sir, I couldn't tell you," said Morton, nervously. "My back was turned, and it was half way down the room when I looked up."

"What was its colour?" asked Saunders. "Black?"

"Oh no, sir; a greyish white. It crept along in a very funny way, sir. I don't think it had a tail."

"What did you do then?"

"I tried to catch it; but it was no use. So I set the rat-traps and kept the library shut. Then that girl, Emma Laidlaw, left the door open when she was cleaning, and I think it must have escaped."

"And you think it is the animal that's been frightening the maids?"

"Well, no, sir, not quite. They said it was—you'll excuse me, sir—a hand that they saw. Emma trod on it once at the bottom of the stairs. She thought then it was a half-frozen toad, only white. And then Parfit was washing up the dishes in the scullery. She wasn't thinking about anything in particular. It was close on dusk. She took her hands out of the water and was drying them absent-minded like on the roller towel, when she found she was drying someone else's hand as well, only colder than hers."

"What nonsense!" exclaimed Saunders.

"Exactly, sir; that's what I told her; but we couldn't get her to stop."

"You don't believe all this?" said Eustace, turning suddenly towards the butler.

"Me, sir? Oh no, sir! I've not seen anything."

"Nor heard anything?"

"Well, sir, if you must know, the bells do ring at odd times, and there's nobody there when we go; and when we go round to draw the blinds of a night, as often as not somebody's been there before us. But, as I says to Mrs. Merrit, a young monkey might do wonderful things, and we all know that Mr. Borlsover has had some strange animals about the place."

"Very well, Morton, that will do."

"What do you make of it?" asked Saunders, when they were alone. "I mean of the letter he said you wrote."

"Oh, that's simple enough," said Eustace. "See the paper it's written on? I stopped using that paper years ago, but there were a few odd sheets and envelopes left in the old desk. We never fastened up the lid of the box before locking it in. The hand got out, found a pencil, wrote this note, and shoved it through the crack on to the floor, where Morton found it. That's plain as daylight."

"But the hand couldn't write!"

"Couldn't it? You've not seen it do the things I've seen." And he told Saunders more of what had happened at Eastbourne.

"Well," said Saunders, "in that case we have at least an explanation of the legacy. It was the hand which wrote, unknown to your uncle, that letter to your solicitor bequeathing itself to you. Your uncle had no more to do with that request than I. In fact, it would seem that he had some idea of his automatic writing and feared it."

"Then if it's not my uncle, what is it?"

"I suppose some people might say that a disembodied spirit had got your uncle to educate and prepare a little body for it. Now it's got into that little body and is off on its own."

"Well, what are we to do?"

"We'll keep our eyes open," said Saunders, "and try to catch it. If we can't do that, we shall have to wait till the bally clockwork runs down. After all, if it's flesh and blood, it can't live for ever."

For two days nothing happened. Then Saunders saw it sliding down the banister in the hall. He was taken unawares and lost a full second before he started in pursuit, only to find that the thing had escaped him. Three days later Eustace, writing alone in the library at night, saw it sitting on an open book at the other end of the room. The fingers crept over the page, as if it were reading; but before he had time to get up from his seat, it had taken the alarm, and was pulling itself up the curtains. Eustace watched it grimly, as it hung on to the cornice with three fingers and flicked thumb and forefinger at him in an expression of scornful derision.

"I know what I'll do," he said. "If I only get it into the open, I'll set the dogs on to it."

He spoke to Saunders of the suggestion.

"It's a jolly good idea," he said; "only we won't wait till we find it out of doors. We'll get the dogs. There are the two terriers and the under-keeper's Irish mongrel, that's on to rats like a flash. Your spaniel has not got spirit enough for this sort of game."

They brought the dogs into the house, and the keeper's Irish mongrel chewed up the slippers, and the terriers tripped up Morton, as he waited at table; but all three were welcome. Even false security is better than no security at all.

For a fortnight nothing happened. Then the hand was caught, not by the dogs, but by Mrs. Merrit's grey parrot. The bird was in the habit of periodically removing the pins that kept its seed- and water-tins in place, and of escaping through the holes in the side of the cage. When once at liberty, Peter would show no inclination to return, and would often be about the house for days. Now, after six consecutive weeks of captivity, Peter had again discovered a new way of unloosing his bolts and was at large, exploring the tapestried forests of the curtains and singing songs in praise of liberty from cornice and picture-rail.

"It's no use your trying to catch him," said Eustace to Mrs. Merrit, as she came into the study one afternoon towards dusk with a step-ladder. "You'd much better leave Peter alone. Starve him into surrender, Mrs. Merrit; and don't leave bananas and seed about for him to peck at when he fancies he's hungry. You're far too soft-hearted."

"Well, sir, I see he's right out of reach now on that picture-rail; so, if you wouldn't mind closing the door, sir, when you leave the room, I'll bring his cage in tonight and put some meat inside it. He's that fond of meat, though it does make him pull out his feathers to suck the quills. They *do* say that if you cook—"

"Never mind, Mrs. Merrit," said Eustace, who was busy writing; "that will do; I'll keep an eye on the bird."

For a short time there was silence in the room.

"Scratch poor Peter," said the bird. "Scratch poor old Peter!"

"Be quiet, you beastly bird!"

"Poor old Peter! Scratch poor Peter; do!"

"I'm more likely to wring your neck, if I get hold of you." He looked up at the picture-rail, and there was the hand, holding on to a hook with three fingers, and slowly scratching the head of the parrot with the fourth. Eustace ran to the bell and pressed it hard; then across to the window, which he closed with a bang. Frightened by the noise, the parrot shook its wings preparatory to flight, and, as it did so, the fingers of the hand got hold of it by the throat. There was a shrill scream, from Peter, as he fluttered across the room, wheeling round in circles that ever descended, borne down under the weight that clung to him. The bird dropped at last quite suddenly, and Eustace saw fingers and feathers rolled into an inextricable mass on the floor. The struggle abruptly ceased, as finger and thumb squeezed the neck; the bird's eyes rolled up to show the whites, and there was a faint, half-choked gurgle. But, before the fingers had time to loose their hold, Eustace had them in his own.

"Send Mr. Saunders here at once," he said to the maid who came in answer to the bell. "Tell him I want him immediately."

Then he went with the hand to the fire. There was a ragged gash across the back, where the bird's beak had torn it, but no blood oozed from the wound. He noted with disgust that the nails had grown long and discoloured.

"I'll burn the beastly thing," he said. But he could not burn it. He tried to throw it into the flames, but his own hands, as if impelled by some old primitive feeling, would not let him. And so Saunders found him, pale and irresolute, with the hand still clasped tightly in his fingers.

"I've got it at last," he said, in a tone of triumph.

"Good, let's have a look at it."

"Not when it's loose. Get me some nails and a hammer and a board of some sort."

"Can you hold it all right?"

"Yes, the thing's quite limp; tired out with throttling poor old Peter, I should say."

"And now," said Saunders, when he returned with the things, "what are we going to do?"

"Drive a nail through it first, so that it can't get away. Then we can take our time over examining it."

"Do it yourself," said Saunders. "I don't mind helping you with guinea-pigs occasionally, when there's something to be learned, partly because I don't fear a guinea-pig's revenge. This thing's different."

"Oh, my aunt!" he giggled hysterically, "look at it now." For the hand was writhing in agonized contortions, squirming and wriggling upon the nail like a worm upon the hook.

"Well," said Saunders, "you've done it now. I'll leave you to examine it."

"Don't go, in heaven's name! Cover it up, man; cover it up! Shove a cloth over it! Here!" and he pulled off the antimacassar from the back of a chair and wrapped the board in it. "Now get the keys from my pocket and open the safe. Chuck the other things out. Oh, Lord, it's getting itself into frightful knots! Open it quick!" He threw the thing in and banged the door.

"We'll keep it there till it dies," he said. "May I burn in hell, if I ever open the door of that safe again."

Mrs. Merrit departed at the end of the month. Her successor, Mrs. Handyside, certainly was more successful in the management of the servants. Early in her rule she declared that she would stand no nonsense, and gossip soon withered and died.

"I shouldn't be surprised if Eustace married one of these days," said Saunders. "Well, I'm in no hurry for such an event. I know him far too well for the future Mrs. Borlsover to like me. It will be the same old story again; a long friendship slowly made—marriage—and a long friendship quickly forgotten."

But Eustace did not follow the advice of his uncle and marry. Old habits crept over and covered his new experience. He was, if anything, less morose, and showed a greater inclination to take his natural part in country society.

Then came the burglary. The men, it was said, broke into the house by way of the conservatory. It was really little more than an attempt, for they only succeeded in carrying away a few pieces of plate from the pantry. The safe in the study was certainly found open and empty, but, as Mr. Borlsover informed the police inspector, he had kept nothing of value in it during the last six months.

"Then you're lucky in getting off so easily, sir," the man replied. "By the way they have gone about their business I should say they were experienced cracksmen. They must have caught the alarm when they were just beginning their evening's work."

"Yes," said Eustace, "I suppose I am lucky."

"I've no doubt," said the inspector, "that we shall be able to trace the men. I've said that they must have been old hands at the game. The way they got in and opened the safe shows that. But there's one little thing that puzzles me. One of them was careless enough not to wear gloves, and I'm bothered if I know what he was trying to do. I've traced his finger-marks on the new varnish on the window-sashes in every one of the downstairs rooms. They are very distinctive ones too."

"Right hand or left or both?" asked Eustace.

"Oh, right every time. That's the funny thing. He must have been a foolhardy fellow, and I rather think it was him that wrote that." He took out a slip of paper from his pocket. "That's what he wrote, sir: 'I've got out, Eustace Borlsover, but I'll be back before long.' Some jailbird just escaped, I suppose. It will make it all the easier for us to trace him. Do you know the writing, sir?"

"No," said Eustace. "It's not the writing of any one I know."

"I'm not going to stay here any longer," said Eustace to Saunders at luncheon. "I've got on far better during the last six months than I expected, but I'm not going to run the risk of seeing that thing again. I shall go up to town this afternoon. Get Morton to put my things together, and join me with the car at Brighton on the day after to-morrow. And bring the proofs of those two papers with you. We'll run over them together."

"How long are you going to be away?"

"I can't say for certain, but be prepared to stay for some time. We've stuck to work pretty closely through summer, and I for one need a holiday. I'll engage the rooms at Brighton. You'll find it best to break the journey at Hitchin. I'll wire to you there at the 'Crown' to tell you the Brighton address."

The house he chose at Brighton was in a terrace. He had been there before. It was kept by his old college gyp, a man of discreet silence, who was admirably partnered by an excellent cook. The rooms were on the first floor. The two bedrooms were at the back, and opened out of each other. "Mr. Saunders can have the smaller one, though it is the only one with a fireplace," he said. "I'll stick to the larger of the two, since it's got a bathroom adjoining. I wonder what time he'll arrive with the car."

Saunders came about seven, cold and cross and dirty. "We'll light the fire in the dining-room," said Eustace, "and get Prince to unpack some of the things while we are at dinner. What were the roads like?"

"Rotten. Swimming with mud, and a beastly cold wind against us all day. And this is July. Dear Old England! "

"Yes," said Eustace, "I think we might do worse than leave Old England for a few months."

They turned in soon after twelve.

"You oughtn't to feel cold, Saunders," said Eustace, "when you can afford to sport a great fur-lined coat like this. You do yourself very well, all things considered. Look at those gloves, for instance. Who could possibly feel cold when wearing them?"

"They are far too clumsy, though, for driving. Try them on and see"; and he tossed them through the door on to Eustace's bed and went on with his unpacking. A minute later he heard a shrill cry of terror. "Oh, Lord," he heard, "it's in the glove! Quick, Saunders, quick!" Then came a smacking thud. Eustace had thrown it from him. "I've chucked it into the bathroom," he gasped; "it's hit the wall and fallen into the bath. Come now, if you want to help." Saunders, with a lighted candle in his hand, looked over the edge of the bath. There it was, old and maimed, dumb and blind, with a ragged hole in the middle, crawling, staggering, trying to creep up the slippery sides, only to fall back helpless.

"Stay there," said Saunders, "I'll empty a collar-box or something, and we'll jam it in. It can't get out while I'm away."

"Yes, it can," shouted Eustace. "It's getting out now; it's climbing up the plug-chain. No, you brute, you filthy brute, you don't! Come back, Saunders; it's getting away from me. I can't hold it; it's all slippery. Curse its claws! Shut the window, you idiot! It's got out!" There was the sound of something dropping on to the hard flag-stones below, and Eustace fell back fainting.

* * *

For a fortnight he was ill.

"I don't know what to make of it," the doctor said to Saunders. "I can only suppose that Mr. Borlsover has suffered some great emotional shock. You had better let me send someone to help you nurse him. And by all means indulge that whim of his never to be left alone in the dark. I would keep a light burning all night, if I were you. But he *must* have more fresh air. It's perfectly absurd, this hatred of open windows."

Eustace would have no one with him but Saunders. "I don't want the other man," he said. "They'd smuggle it in somehow. I know they would."

"Don't worry about it, old chap. This sort of thing can't go on indefinitely. You know I saw it this time as well as you. It wasn't half so active. It won't go on living much longer, especially after that fall. I heard it hit the flags myself. As soon as you're a bit stronger, we'll leave this place, not bag and baggage, but with only the clothes on our back, so that it won't be able to hide anywhere. We'll escape it that way. We won't give any address, and we won't have any parcels sent after us. Cheer up, Eustace! You'll be well enough to leave in a day or two. The doctor says I can take you out in a chair to-morrow."

"What have I done?" asked Eustace. "Why does it come after me? I'm no worse than other men. I'm no worse than you, Saunders; you know I'm not. It was you who was at the bottom of that dirty business in San Diego, and that was fifteen years ago."

"It's not that, of course," said Saunders. "We are in the twentieth century, and even the parsons have dropped the idea of your old sins finding you out. Before you caught the hand in the library, it was filled with pure malevolence—to you and all mankind. After you spiked it through with that nail, it naturally forgot about other people and concentrated its attention on you. It was shut up in that safe, you know, for nearly six months. That gives plenty of time for thinking of revenge."

Eustace Borlsover would not leave his room, but he thought there might be something in Saunders's suggestion of a sudden departure from Brighton. He began rapidly to regain his strength.

"We'll go on the first of September," he said.

The evening of the thirty-first of August was oppressively warm. Though at midday the windows had been wide open, they had been shut an hour or so before dusk. Mrs. Prince had long since ceased to wonder at the strange habits of the gentlemen on the first floor. Soon after their arrival she had been told to take down the heavy window curtains in the two bedrooms, and day by day the rooms had seemed to grow more bare. Nothing was left lying about.

"Mr. Borlsover doesn't like to have any place where dirt can collect," Saunders had said as an excuse. "He likes to see into all the corners of the room."

"Couldn't I open the window just a little?" he said to Eustace that evening. "We're simply roasting in here, you know."

"No, leave well alone. We're not a couple of boarding-school misses fresh from a course of hygiene lectures. Get the chess-board out."

They sat down and played. At ten o'clock Mrs. Prince came to the door with a note. "I am sorry I didn't bring it before," she said, "but it was left in the letter-box."

"Open it, Saunders, and see if it wants answering."

It was very brief. There was neither address nor signature.

"Will eleven o'clock to-night be suitable for our last appointment?"

"Who is it from?" asked Borlsover.

"It was meant for me," said Saunders. "There's no answer, Mrs. Prince," and he put the paper into his pocket.

"A dunning letter from a tailor; I suppose he must have got wind of our leaving."

It was a clever lie, and Eustace asked no more questions. They went on with their game.

On the landing outside Saunders could hear the grandfather's clock whispering the seconds, blurting out the quarter-hours.

"Check," said Eustace. The clock struck eleven. At the same time there was a gentle knocking on the door; it seemed to come from the bottom panel.

"Who's there?" asked Eustace.

There was no answer.

"Mrs. Prince, is that you?"

"She is up above," said Saunders; "I can hear her walking about the room."

"Then lock the door; bolt it too. Your move, Saunders."

While Saunders sat with his eyes on the chess-board, Eustace walked over to the window and examined the fastenings. He did the same in Saunders's room, and the bath-room. There were no doors between the three rooms, or he would have shut and locked them. too.

"Now, Saunders," he said, "don't stay all night over your move. I've had time to smoke one cigarette already. It's bad to keep an invalid waiting. There's only one possible thing for you to do. What was that?"

"The ivy blowing against the window. There, it's your move now, Eustace."

"It wasn't the ivy, you idiot! It was someone tapping at the window"; and he pulled up the blind. On the outer side of the window, clinging to the sash, was the hand.

"What is it that it's holding?"

"It's a pocket-knife. It's going to try to open the window by pushing back the fastener with the blade."

"Well, let it try," said Eustace. "Those fasteners screw down; they can't be opened that way. Anyhow, we'll close the shutters. It's your move, Saunders. I've played."

But Saunders found it impossible to fix his attention on the game. He could not understand Eustace, who seemed all at once to have lost his fear. "What do you say to some wine?" he asked. "You seem to be taking things coolly, but I don't mind confessing that I'm in a blessed funk."

"You've no need to be. There's nothing supernatural about that hand, Saunders. I mean, it seems to be governed by the laws of time and space. It's not the sort of thing that vanishes into thin air or slides through oaken doors. And since that's so, I defy it to get in here. We'll leave the place in the morning. I for one have bottomed the depths of fear. Fill your glass, man! The windows are all shuttered; the door is locked and bolted. Pledge me my Uncle Adrian! Drink, man! What are you waiting for?"

Saunders was standing with his glass half raised. "It can get in," he said hoarsely; "it can get in! We've forgotten. There's the fire-place in my bed-room. It will come down the chimney."

"Quick!" said Eustace, as he rushed into the other room; "we haven't a minute to lose. What can we do? Light the fire, Saunders. Give me a match, quick!"

"They must be all in the other room. I'll get them."

"Hurry, man, for goodness' sake! Look in the bookcase! Look in the bath-room! Here, come and stand here; I'll look."

"Be quick!" shouted Saunders. "I can hear something!"

"Then plug a sheet from your bed up the chimney. No, here's a match!" He had found one at last, that had slipped into a crack in the floor.

"Is the fire laid? Good, but it may not burn. I know—the oil from that old reading-lamp and this cotton wool. Now the match, quick! Pull the sheet away, you fool! We don't want it now."

There was a great roar from the grate, as the flames shot up. Saunders had been a fraction of a second too late with the sheet. The oil had fallen on to it. It, too, was burning.

"The whole place will be on fire!" cried Eustace, as he tried to beat out the flames with a blanket. "It's no good! I can't manage it. You must open the door, Saunders, and get help."

Saunders ran to the door and fumbled with the bolts. The key was stiff in the lock. "Hurry," shouted Eustace, "or the heat will be too much for me." The key turned in the lock at last. For half a second Saunders stopped to look back. Afterwards he could never be quite sure as to what he had seen, but at the time he thought that something black and charred was creeping slowly, very slowly, from the mass of flames towards Eustace Borlsover. For a moment he thought of returning to his friend; but the noise and the smell of the burning sent him running down the passage, crying: "Fire! Fire!" He rushed to the telephone to summon help, and then back to the bathroom—he should have thought of that before—for water. As he burst into the bedroom there came a scream of terror which ended suddenly, and then the sound of a heavy fall.

This is the story which I heard on successive Saturday evenings from the senior mathematical master at a second-rate suburban school. For Saunders has had to earn a living in a way which other men might reckon less congenial than his old manner of life. I had mentioned by chance the name of Adrian Borlsover, and wondered at the time why he changed the conversation with such unusual abruptness. A week later Saunders began to tell me something of his own history; sordid enough, though shielded with a reserve I could well understand, for it had to cover not only his failings, but those of a dead friend. Of the final tragedy he was at first especially loath to speak; and it was only gradually that I was able to piece together the narrative of the preceding pages. Saunders was reluctant to draw any conclusions. At one time he thought that the fingered beast had been animated by the spirit of Sigismund Borlsover, a sinister eighteenth-century ancestor, who, according to legend, built and worshipped in the ugly pagan temple that overlooked the lake. At another time Saunders believed the spirit to belong to a man whom Eustace had once employed as a laboratory assistant, "a black-haired, spiteful little brute," he said, "who died cursing his doctor, because the fellow couldn't help him to live to settle some paltry score with Borlsover."

From the point of view of direct contemporary evidence, Saunders's story is practically uncorroborated. All the letters mentioned in the narrative were destroyed, with the exception of the last note which Eustace received, or rather which he would have received, had not Saunders intercepted it. That I have seen myself. The handwriting was thin and shaky, the handwriting of an old man. I remember the Greek "e" was used in "appointment." A little thing that amused me at the time was that Saunders seemed to keep the note pressed between the pages of his Bible.

I had seen Adrian Borlsover once. Saunders I learnt to know well. It was by chance, however, and not by design, that I met a third person of the story, Morton, the butler. Saunders and I were walking in the Zoological Gardens one Sunday afternoon, when he called my attention to an old man who was standing before the door of the Reptile House.

"Why, Morton," he said, clapping him on the back, "how is the world treating you?"

"Poorly, Mr. Saunders," said the old fellow, though his face lighted up at the greeting. "The winters drag terribly nowadays. There don't seem no summers or springs."

"You haven't found what you were looking for, I suppose?"

"No, sir, not yet; but I shall some day. I always told them that Mr. Borlsover kept some queer animals."

"And what is he looking for?" I asked, when we had parted from him.

"A beast with five fingers," said Saunders. "This afternoon, since he has been in the Reptile House, I suppose it will be a reptile with a hand. Next week it will be a monkey with practically no body. The poor old chap is a born materialist."

Q is for Quarry

E. and H. Heron were pseudonyms for the British mother-and-son writing team of Kate Prichard (1851–1935) and Hesketh Prichard (1876–1922), best known for their tales of occult detective Flaxman Low. In this story, which first appeared in the March 1898 issue of *Pearson's Magazine*, "quarry" refers not only to the quarry in which the supernatural phenomena begins, but also to something that is hunted.

E. AND H. HERON

The Story of the Moor Road

"The medical profession must always have its own peculiar offshoots," said Mr. Flaxman Low, "some are trades, some mere hobbies, others, again, are allied subjects of a serious and profound nature. Now, as a student of psychical phenomena, I account myself only two degrees removed from the ordinary general practitioner."

"How do you make that out?" returned Colonel Daimley, pushing the decanter of old port invitingly across the table.

"The nerve and brain specialist is the link between myself and the man you would send for if you had a touch of lumbago," replied Low with a slight smile. "Each division is but a higher grade of the same ladder—a step upwards into the unknown. I consider that I stand just one step above the specialist who makes a study of brain disease and insanity; he is at work on the disorders of the embodied spirit, while I deal with abnormal conditions of the free and detached spirit."

Colonel Daimley laughed aloud.

"That won't do, Low! No, no! First prove that your ghosts are sick."

"Certainly," replied Low gravely. "A very small proportion of spirits return as apparitions after the death of the body. Hence we may conclude that a ghost is a spirit in an abnormal condition. Abnormal conditions of the body usually indicate disease; why not of the spirit also?"

"That sounds fair enough," observed Lane Chaddam, the third man present. "Has the Colonel told you of our spook?"

The Colonel shook his handsome grey head in some irritation.

"You haven't convinced me yet, Lane, that it is a spook," he said drily. "Human nature is at the bottom of most things in this world according to my opinion."

"What spook is this?" asked Flaxman Low. "I heard nothing of it when I was down with you last year."

"It's a recent acquisition," replied Lane Chaddam. "I wish we were rid of it for my part."

"Have you seen it?" asked Low as he relit his long German pipe.

"Yes, and felt it!"

"What is it?"

"That's for you to say. He nearly broke my neck for me—that's all I can swear to."

Low knew Chaddam well. He was a long-limbed, athletic young fellow, with a good show of cups in his rooms, and was one of the various short-distance runners mentioned in the Badminton as having done the hundred in level time, and not the sort of man whose neck is easy to break.

"How did it happen?" asked Flaxman Low.

"About a fortnight ago," replied Chaddam. "I was flight-shooting near the burn where the hounds killed the otter last year. When the light began to fail, I thought I would come home by the old quarry, and pot anything that showed itself. As I walked along the far bank of the burn, I saw a man on the near side standing on the patch of sand below the reeds and watching me. As I came nearer I heard him coughing; it sounded like a sick cow. He stood still as if waiting for me. I thought it odd, because amongst the meres and water-meadows down there one never meets a stranger."

"Could you see him pretty clearly?"

"I saw his outline clearly, but not his face, because his back was towards the west. He was tall and jerry-built, so to speak, and had a little head no bigger than a child's, and he wore a fur cap with queer upstanding ears. When I came close, he suddenly slipped away; he jumped behind a big dyke, and I lost sight of him. But I didn't pay much attention; I had my gun, and I concluded it was a tramp."

"Tramps don't follow men of your size," observed Low with a smile.

"This fellow did, at any rate. When I got across to the spot where he had been standing—the sand is soft there—I looked for his tracks. I knew he was bound to have a big foot of his own considering his height. But there were no footprints!"

"No footprints? You mean it was too dark for you to see them?" broke in Colonel Daimley.

"I am sure I should have seen them had there been any," persisted Chaddam quietly. "Besides, a man can't take a leap as he did without leaving a good hole behind him. The sand was perfectly smooth, because there had been a strong east wind all day. After looking about and seeing no marks, I went on to the top of the knoll above the quarry. After a bit I felt I was followed, though I couldn't see anyone. You remember the thorn bush that overhangs the quarry pool? I stopped there and bent over the edge of the cliff to see if there was anything in the pool. As I stooped I felt a point like a steel puncheon catch me in the small of the back. I kicked off from the quarry wall as well as I could, so as to avoid the broken rocks below, and I just managed to clear them, but I fell into the water with a flop that knocked the wind out of me. However, I held on to the gun, and, after a minute, I climbed to a ledge under the cliff and waited to see what my friend on top would do next. He waited, too. I couldn't see him, but I heard him—he coughed up there in the dusk, the most ghastly noise I ever heard. The Colonel laughs at me, but it was about as nasty a half-hour as I care to have. In the end, I swam out across the pool and got home."

"I laugh at Lane," said the Colonel, " but all the same, it's a bad spot for a fall."

"You say he struck you in the back?" asked Flaxman Low, turning to Chaddam.

"Yes, and his finger was like a steel punch."

"What does Mrs. Daimley say to this affair?" went on Low presently.

"Not a word to my wife or Olivia, my dear Low!" exclaimed Colonel Daimley. "It would frighten them needlessly; besides, there would be an infernal fuss if we wanted to go flighting or anything after dark. I only fear for them, as they often drive into Nerbury by the Moor Road, which passes close by the quarry."

"Do they go in for their letters every evening as they used to do?"

"Just the same. And they won't take Stubbs with them, in spite of advice." The Colonel looked disconsolately at Low. "Women are angels, bless them! But they are the dickens to deal with because they always want to know why?"

"And now, Low, what have you to say about it?" asked Chaddam.

"Have you told me all?"

"Yes. The only other thing is that Livy says she hears someone coughing in the spinney most nights."

"If all is as you say, Chaddam—pardon me, but in cases like this imagination is apt to play an unsuspected part—I should think that you have come upon a unique experience. What you have told me is not to be explained upon the lines of any ordinary theory."

After this they followed the ladies into the drawing-room, where they found Mrs. Daimley immersed in a novel as usual, and Livy looking pretty enough to account for the frequent presence of Lane Chaddam at Low Riddings. He was a distant cousin of the Colonel, and took advantage of his relationship to pay protracted visits to Northumberland.

Some years previous to the date of the above events, Colonel Daimley had bought and enlarged a substantial farmhouse which stood in a dip south of a lonely sweep of Northumbrian moors. It was a land of pale blue skies and far off fringes of black and ragged pine trees.

From the house a lane led over the wind-swept shoulder of the upland down to a hollow spanned by a railway bridge, then up again across the high levels of the moors until at length it lost itself in the outskirts of the little town of Nerbury. This Moor Road was peculiarly lonely; it approached but one cottage the whole way, and ran very nearly over the doorstep of that one—a deserted-looking slip of a place between the railway bridge and the quarry. Beyond the quarry stretched acres of marshland, meadows and reedy meres, all of which had been manipulated with such ability by the Colonel, that the duck shooting on his land was the envy of the neighbourhood.

In spite of its loneliness the Moor Road was much frequented by the Daimleys, who preferred it to the high road, which was uninteresting and much longer. Mrs. Daimley and Olivia drove in of an evening to fetch their letters—being people with nothing on earth to do, they were naturally always in a hurry to get their letters—and they perpetually had parcels waiting for them at the station which required to be called for at all sorts of hours. Thus it will be seen that the fact of the quarry being haunted by Lane Chaddam's assailant, formed a very real danger to the inhabitants of Low Riddings.

At breakfast next day Livy said the tramp had been coughing in the spinney half the night.

"In what direction?" asked Flaxman Low.

Livy pointed to the window which looked on to the gate and the thick boundary hedge, the last still full of crisp ruddy leaves.

"You feel an interest in your tramp, Miss Daimley?"

"Of course, poor creature! I wanted to go out to look for him the other night, but they would not allow me."

"That was before we knew he was so interesting," said Chaddam. "I promise we'll catch him for you next time he comes."

And this was in fact the programme they tried to carry out, but although the coughing was heard in the spinney, no one even caught a glimpse of any living thing moving or hiding among the trees.

The next stage of the affair happened to be an experience of Livy. In some excitement she told the assembled family at dinner that she had just seen the coughing tramp.

Lane Chaddam changed colour. "You don't mean to say, Livy, that you went to search for him alone?" he exclaimed half-angrily.

Flaxman Low and the Colonel wisely went on eating oyster patties without taking any apparent notice of the girl's news.

"Why shouldn't I?" asked Livy quickly, "but as it happens I saw him in Scully's cottage by the quarry this evening."

"What?" exclaimed Colonel Daimley, "in Scully's cottage. I'll see to that."

"Why? Are you all so prejudiced against my poor tramp?"

"On the contrary," replied Flaxman Low, "we all want to know what he's like."

"So odd-looking! I was driving home alone from the post when, as I passed the quarry cottage, I heard the cough. You know it is quite unmistakable; I looked up at the window and there he was. I have never seen anybody in the least like him. His face is ghastly pale and perfectly hairless, and he has such a little head. He stared at me so threateningly that I whipped up Lorelie."

"Were you frightened, then?"

"Not exactly, but he had such a wicked face that I drove away as fast as I could."

"I understood that you had arranged to send Stubbs for the letters?" said Colonel Daimley with some annoyance. "Why can't girls say what they mean?"

Livy made no reply, and after a pause Chaddam put a question.

"You must have passed along the Moor Road about seven o'clock?"

"Yes, it was after six when I left the Post-Office," replied Livy. "Why?"

"It was quite dark—how did you see the hairless man so plainly? I was round on the marshes all the evening, and I am quite certain there was no light at any time in Scully's cottage."

"I don't remember whether there was any light behind him in the room," returned Livy after a moment's consideration; "I only know that I saw his head and face quite plainly."

There was no more said on the subject at the time, though the Colonel forbade Livy to run any further risks by going alone on the Moor Road. After this, the three men paraded the lane and lay in wait for the hairless tramp or ghost. On the second evening their watch was rewarded, when Chaddam came hurriedly into the smoking-room to say that the coughing could at that instant be heard in the hedge by the dining-room. It was still early, although the evening had closed in with clouds, and all outside was dark.

"I'll deal with him this time effectually!" exclaimed the Colonel. "I'll slip out the back way, and lie in the hedge down the road by the field gate. You two must chivy him out to me, and when he comes along, I'll have him against the sky-line and give him a charge of No. 4 if he shows fight."

The Colonel stole down the lane while the others beat the spinney and hedge, Flaxman Low very much chagrined at being forced to deal with an interesting problem in this rough and ready fashion. However, he saw that on this occasion at least it would be useless to oppose the Colonel's notions. When he and Chaddam met after beating the hedge they saw a tall figure shamble away rapidly down the lane towards the Colonel's hiding-place.

They stood still and waited for developments, but the minutes followed each other in intense stillness. Then they went to find the Colonel.

"Hullo, Colonel, anything wrong?" asked Chaddam on nearing the field gate.

The Colonel straightened himself with the help of Chaddam's arm.

"Did you see him?" he whispered.

"We thought so. Why did you not fire?"

"Because," said the Colonel in a husky voice, "I had no gun!"

"But you took it with you?"

"Yes."

Flaxman Low opened the lantern he carried, and, as the light swept round in a wide circle, something glinted on the grass. It was the stock of the Colonel's gun. A little further off they came upon the Damascus barrels bent and twisted into a ball like so much fine wire. Presently the Colonel explained.

"I saw him coming and meant to meet him, but I seemed dazed—I couldn't move! The gun was snatched from me, and I made no resistance—I don't know why." He took the gunbarrels and examined them slowly, "I give in. Low, no human hand did that."

During dinner Flaxman Low said abruptly: "I suspect you have lately had an earthquake down here."

"How did you know?" asked Livy. "Have you been to the quarry?"

Low said he had not.

"It was such a poor little earthquake that even the papers did not think it worth while to mention it!" went on Livy. "We didn't feel any shock, and, in fact, knew nothing about it until Dr. Petterped told us."

"You had a landslip though?" went on Low.

Livy opened her pretty eyes.

"But you know all about it," she said. "Yes, the landslip was just by the old quarry."

"I should like to see the place to-morrow," observed Low.

Next day, therefore, when the Colonel went off to the coverts with a couple of neighbours, whom he had invited to join him, Flaxman Low accompanied Chaddam to examine the scene of the landslip.

From the edge of the upland, looking across the hollow crowded with reedy pools, they could see in the torn, reddish flank of the opposite slope the sharp tilt of the broken strata. To the right of this lay the old quarry, and about a hundred yards to the left the lonely house and the curving road.

Low descended into the hollow and spent a long time in the spongy ground between the back of the quarry and the lower edge of the newly-uncovered strata, using his little hammer freely, especially about one narrow black fissure, round which he sniffed and pottered in absorbed silence. Presently he called to Chaddam.

"There has been a slight explosion of gas—a rare gas, here," he said. "I hardly hoped to find traces of it, but it is unmistakeable."

"Very unmistakeable," agreed Chaddam, with a laugh. "You'd have said so had you been here when it happened."

"Ah, very satisfactory indeed. And that was a fortnight ago, you say?"

"Rather more now. It took place a couple of days before my fall into the quarry pool."

"Anyone ill near by—at that cottage for instance?" asked Low, as he joined Chaddam.

"Why? Was that gas poisonous? There's a man in the Colonel's employ named Scully in that cottage, who has had pneumonia, but he was on the mend when the landslip occurred. Since then he has grown steadily worse."

"Is there anyone with him?"

"Yes, the Daimleys sent for a woman to look after him. Scully's a very decent man. I often go in to see him."

"And so does the hairless man apparently," added Low.

"No, that's the queer part of it. Neither he nor the woman in charge have ever seen such a person as Livy described. I don't know what to think."

"The first thing to be done is to get the man from here at once," said Low decidedly. "Let's go in and see him."

They found Scully low and drowsy. The nurse shook her head at the two visitors in a despondent way.

"He grows weaker day by day," she said.

"Get him away from here at once," repeated Low, as they went out.

"We might have him up at Low Riddings, but he seems almost too weak to be moved," replied Chaddam doubtfully.

"My dear fellow, it's his only chance of life."

The Daimleys made arrangements for the reception of Scully, provided Dr. Thomson of Nerbury gave his consent to the removal. In the afternoon, therefore, Chaddam bicycled into Nerbury to see the doctor on the subject. "If I were you, Chaddam," said Low before he started, "I'd be back by daylight."

Unfortunately Dr. Thomson was on his rounds, and did not return until after dark, by which time it was too late to remove Scully that evening. After leaving the doctor's house Chaddam went to the station to inquire about a box from Mudie's. The books having arrived, he took out a couple of volumes for Mrs. Daimley's present consumption, and was strapping them on in front of his bicycle, when it struck him that unless he went home by the Moor Road he would be late for dinner.

Accordingly he branched off into the bare track which led over the moors. The twilight had deepened into a fine, cold night, and a moon was swinging up into a pale, clear sky. The spread of heather, purple in the daytime, appeared jet black by moonlight, and across it he could see the white ribbon of road stretching ahead into the distance. The scents of the night were fresh in his nostrils, as he ran easily along the level with the breeze behind him.

He soon reached the incline past Scully's cottage. Well away to the left lay the quarry pool like a blotch of ink under its shadowing cliff. There was no light in the cottage, and it seemed even more deserted-looking than usual.

As Chaddam flashed under the bridge, he heard a cough, and glanced back over his shoulder.

A tall, loose-jointed form he had seen once before, was rearing itself up upon the railway bridge. There was something curiously unhuman about the lank outlines and the cant of the small head with its prick-eared cap showing out so clearly against the lighter sky behind.

When Chaddam looked again, he saw the thing on the bridge fling up its long arms and leap down on to the road some thirty feet below.

Then Chaddam rode. He began to think he had been a fool to come, and he counted that he was a good mile from home. At first he fancied he heard footfalls, then he fancied there were none. The hard road flew under him, all thoughts of economising his strength were lost, his single aim was to make the pace.

Suddenly his bicycle jerked violently, and he was shot over into the road. As he fell, he turned his head and was conscious of a little, bleached, bestial face, wet with fury, not ten yards behind!

He sprang to his feet, and ran up the road as he had never run before. He ran wonderfully, but he might as well have tried to race a cheetah. It was not a question of speed, the game was in the hands of this thing with the limbs of a starved Hercules, whose bony knees seemed to leap into its ghastly face at every stride. Chaddam topped the slope with a sickening sense of his own powerlessness. Already he saw Low Riddings in the distance, and a dim light came creeping along the road towards him. Another frantic spurt, and he had almost reached the light, when a hand closed like a vice on his shoulder, and seemed to fasten on the flesh. He rushed blindly on towards the house. He saw the door-handle gleam, and in another second he had pitched head foremost on to the knotted matting in the hall.

When he recovered his senses, his first question was: "Where is Low?"

"Didn't you meet him?" asked Livy, "I—that is, we were anxious about you as you were so late, and I was just going to meet you when Mr. Low came downstairs and insisted on going instead."

Chaddam stood up.

"I must follow him."

But as he spoke the front door opened, and Flaxman Low entered, and looked up at the clock.

"Eight-twenty," he said, "You're late, Chaddam."

Afterwards in the smoking-room he gave an account of what he had seen.

"I saw Chaddam racing up the road with a tall figure behind him. It stretched out its hand and grasped his shoulder. The next instant it stopped short as if it had been shot. It seemed to reel back and collapse, and then limped off into the hedge like a disappointed dog."

Chaddam stood up and began to take off his coat.

"Whatever the thing is, it is something out of the common. Look here!" he said, turning up his shirtsleeve over the point of his shoulder, where three singular marks were visible, irregularly placed as the fingers of a hand might fall. They were oblong in shape, about the size of a bean, and swollen in purple lumps well above the surface of the skin.

"Looks as if someone had been using a small cupping glass on you," remarked the Colonel uneasily. "What do you say to it, Low?"

"I say that since Chaddam has escaped with his life, I have only to congratulate him on what, in Europe certainly, is a unique adventure."

The Colonel threw his cigar into the fire.

"Such adventures are too dangerous for my taste," he said. "This creature has on two occasions murderously attacked Lane Chaddam, and it would, no doubt, have attacked Livy if it had had the chance. We must leave this place at once, or we shall be murdered in our beds!"

"I don't think, Colonel, that you will be troubled with this mysterious visitant again," replied Flaxman Low.

"Why not? Who or what is this horrible thing?"

"I believe it to be an Elemental Earth Spirit," returned Low. "No other solution fits the facts of the case."

"What is an Elemental?" resumed the Colonel irritably. "Remember, Low, I expect you to prove your theories so that a plain man may understand, if I am to stay on at Low Riddings."

"Eastern occultists describe wandering tribes of earth spirits, evil intelligences, possessing spirit as distinct from soul—all inimical to man."

"But how do you know that the thing on the Moor Road is an Elemental?"

"Because the points of resemblance are curiously remarkable. The occultists say that when these spirits materialise, they appear in grotesque and uncouth forms; secondly, that they are invariably bloodless and hairless; thirdly, they move with extraordinary rapidity, and leave no footprints; and, lastly, their agility and strength is superhuman. All these peculiarities have been observed in connection with the figure on the Moor Road."

"I admit that no man I have ever met with," commented Colonel Daimley, "could jump uninjured from a height of thirty feet, race a bicycle, and twist up gunbarrels like so much soft paper. So perhaps you're right. But can you tell me why or how it came here?"

"My conclusions," began Low, "may seem to you far-fetched and ridiculous, but you must give them the benefit of the fact that they precisely account for the otherwise unaccountable features which mark this affair. I connect this appearance with the earthquake and the sick man."

"What? Scully in league with the devil?" exclaimed the Colonel bluntly. "Why the man is too weak to leave his bed; besides, he is a short, thick-set fellow, entirely unlike our haunting friend."

"You mistake me, Colonel," said Low, in his quiet tones. "These Elementals cannot take form without drawing upon the resources of the living. They absorb the vitality of any ailing person until it is exhausted, and the person dies."

"Then they begin operations upon a fresh victim? A pleasant look-out to know we keep a well-attested vampire in the neighbourhood!"

"Vampires are a distinct race, with different methods; one being that the Elemental is a wanderer, and goes far afield to search for a new victim."

"But why should it want to kill me?" put in Chaddam.

"As I have told you, they are animated solely by a blind malignity to the human race, and you happened to be handy."

"But the earthquake, Low; where is the connection there?" demanded the Colonel, with the air of a man who intends to corner his opponent.

Flaxman Low lit one cigar at the end of another before he replied.

"At this point," he said, "my own theories and observations and those of the old occultists overlap. The occultists held that some of these spirits are imprisoned in the interior of the earth, but may be set free in consequence of those shiftings and disturbances which take place during an earthquake. This in more modern language simply means that Elementals are in some manner connected with certain of the primary strata. Now, my own researches have led me to conclude that atmospheric influences are intimately associated with spiritual phenomena. Some gases appear to be productive of such phenomena. One of these is generated when certain of the primary formations are newly exposed to the common air."

"This is almost beyond belief—I don't understand you," said the Colonel.

"I am sorry that I cannot give you all the links in my own chain of reasoning," returned Low. "Much is still obscure, but the evidence is sufficiently strong to convince me that in such a case of earthquake and landslip as has lately taken place here the phenomenon of an embodied Elemental might possibly be expected to follow, given the one necessary adjunct of a sick person in the near neighbourhood of the disturbance."

"But when this brute got hold of me, why didn't it finish me off?" asked Chaddam. "Or was it your coming that prevented it?"

Flaxman Low considered.

"No, I don't think I can flatter myself that my coming had anything to do with your escape. It was a near thing—how near you will understand when we hear further news of Scully in the morning."

A servant entered the room at this moment.

"The woman has come up from the cottage, sir, to say that Scully is dead."

"At what hour did he die?" asked Low.

"About ten minutes past eight, sir, she says."

"The hour agrees exactly," commented Low, when the man had left the room. "The figure stopped and collapsed so suddenly that I believed something of this kind must have happened."

"But surely this is a very unprecedented occurrence?"

"It is," said Flaxman Low. "But I can assure you that if you take the trouble to glance through the pages of the psychical periodicals you will find many statements at least as wonderful."

"But are they true?"

Flaxman Low shrugged his shoulders.

"At any rate," said he, "we know this is."

The Daimleys have spent many pleasant days at Low Riddings since then, but Chaddam—who has acquired a right to control Miss Livy's actions more or less—persists in his objection to any solitary expeditions to Nerbury along the Moor Road. For, although the figure has never been seen about Low Riddings since, some strange stories have lately appeared in the papers of a similar mysterious figure which has been met with more than once in the lonelier spots about North London. If it be true that this nameless wandering spirit, with the strength and activity of twenty men, still haunts our lonely roads, the sooner Mr. Flaxman Low exorcises it the better.

R is for Revenant

Revenant is an all encompassing term used to describe things that return from the dead, and in the tales of Irish ghost-story master J. Sheridan Le Fanu (1814–1873), those who return assume a wide variety of guises and forms. This story, which first appeared in the January 1868 issue of *Temple Bar,* is subtitled "a ghost story," though the ghostly presence it features is far from conventional.

J. Sheridan Le Fanu

Squire Toby's Will

A Ghost Story

Many persons accustomed to travel the old York and London road, in the days of stage-coaches, will remember passing, in the afternoon, say, of an autumn day, in their journey to the capital, about three miles south of the town of Applebury, and a mile and a half before you reach the old Angel Inn, a large black-and-white house, as those old-fashioned cage-work habitations are termed, dilapidated and weather-stained, with broad lattice windows glimmering all over in the evening sun with little diamond panes, and thrown into relief by a dense background of ancient elms. A wide avenue, now overgrown like a churchyard with grass and weeds, and flanked by double rows of the same dark trees, old and gigantic, with here and there a gap in their solemn files, and sometimes a fallen tree lying across on the avenue, leads up to the halldoor.

Looking up its sombre and lifeless avenue from the top of the London coach, as I have often done, you are struck with so many signs of desertion and decay,—the tufted grass sprouting in the chinks of the steps and window-stones, the smokeless chimneys over which the jackdaws are wheeling, the absence of human life and all its evidence, that you conclude at once that the place is uninhabited and abandoned to decay. The name of this ancient house is Gylingden Hall. Tall hedges and old timber quickly shroud the old place from view, and about a quarter of a mile further on you pass, embowered in melancholy trees, a small and ruinous Saxon chapel, which, time out of mind, has been the burying-place of the family of Marston, and partakes of the neglect and desolation which brood over their ancient dwelling-place.

The grand melancholy of the secluded valley of Gylingden, lonely as an enchanted forest, in which the crows returning to their roosts among the trees, and the straggling deer who peep from beneath their branches, seem to hold a wild and undisturbed dominion, heightens the forlorn aspect of Gylingden Hall.

Of late years repairs have been neglected, and here and there the roof is stripped, and "the stitch in time" has been wanting. At the side of the house exposed to the gales that sweep through the valley like a torrent through its channel, there is not a perfect window left, and the shutters but imperfectly exclude the rain. The ceilings and walls are mildewed and green with damp stains. Here and there, where the drip falls from the ceiling, the floors are rotting. On stormy nights, as the guard described, you can hear the doors clapping in the old house, as far away as old Gryston bridge, and the howl and sobbing of the wind through its empty galleries.

About seventy years ago died the old Squire, Toby Marston, famous in that part of the world for his hounds, his hospitality, and his vices. He had done kind things, and he had fought duels: he had given away money and he had horse-whipped people. He carried with him some blessings and a good many curses, and left behind him an amount of debts and charges upon the estates which appalled his two sons, who had no taste for business or accounts, and had never suspected, till that wicked, openhanded, and swearing old gentleman died, how very nearly he had run the estates into insolvency.

They met at Gylingden Hall. They had the will before them, and lawyers to interpret, and information without stint, as to the encumbrances with which the deceased had saddled them. The will was so framed as to set the two brothers instantly at deadly feud.

These brothers differed in some points; but in one material characteristic they resembled one another, and also their departed father. They never went into a quarrel by halves, and once in, they did not stick at trifles.

The elder, Scroope Marston, the more dangerous man of the two, had never been a favourite of the old Squire. He had no taste for the sports of the field and the pleasures of a rustic life. He was no athlete, and he certainly was not handsome. All this the Squire resented. The young man, who had no respect for him, and outgrew his fear of his violence as he came to manhood, retorted. This aversion, therefore, in the ill-conditioned old man grew into positive hatred. He used to wish that d——d pippin-squeezing, hump-backed rascal Scroope, out of the way of better men—meaning his younger son Charles; and in his cups would talk in a way which even the old and young fellows who followed his hounds, and drank his port, and could stand a reasonable amount of brutality, did not like.

Scroope Marston was slightly deformed, and he had the lean sallow face, piercing black eyes, and black lank hair, which sometimes accompany deformity.

"I'm no feyther o' that hog-backed creature. I'm no sire of hisn, d——n him! I'd as soon call that tongs son o' mine," the old man used to bawl, in allusion to his son's long, lank limbs: "Charlie's a man, but that's a jack-an-ape. He has no good-nature; there's nothing handy, nor manly, nor no one turn of a Marston in him."

And when he was pretty drunk, the old Squire used to swear he should never "sit at the head o' that board; nor frighten away folk from Gylingden Hall wi' his d——d hatchet-face—the black loon!"

"Handsome Charlie was the man for his money. He knew what a horse was, and could sit to his bottle; and the lasses were all clean *wad* about him. He was a Marston every inch of his six foot two."

Handsome Charlie and he, however, had also had a row or two. The old Squire was free with his horsewhip as with his tongue, and on occasion when neither weapon was quite practicable, had been known to give a fellow "a tap o' his knuckles." Handsome Charlie, however, thought there was a period at which personal chastisement should cease; and one night, when the port was flowing, there was some allusion to Marion Hayward, the miller's daughter, which for some reason the old gentleman did not like. Being "in liquor," and having clearer ideas about pugilism than self-government, he struck out, to the surprise of all present, at Handsome Charlie. The youth threw back his head scientifically, and nothing followed but the crash of a decanter on the floor. But the old Squire's blood was up, and he bounced from his chair. Up jumped Handsome Charlie, resolved to stand no nonsense. Drunken Squire Lilbourne, intending to mediate, fell flat on the floor, and cut his ear among the glasses. Handsome Charlie caught the thump which the old Squire discharged at him upon his open hand, and catching him by the cravat, swung him with his back to the wall. They said the old man never looked so purple, nor his eyes so goggle before; and then Handsome Charlie pinioned him tight to the wall by both arms.

"Well, I say—come, don't you talk no more nonsense o' that sort, and I won't lick you," croaked the old Squire. "You stopped that un clever, you did. Didn't he? Come, Charlie, man, gie us your hand, I say, and sit down again, lad." And so the battle ended; and I believe it was the last time the Squire raised his hand to Handsome Charlie.

But those days were over. Old Toby Marston lay cold and quiet enough now, under the drip of the mighty ash-tree within the Saxon ruin where so many of the old Marston race returned to dust, and were forgotten. The weather-stained top-boots and leather-breeches, the three-cornered cocked hat to which old gentlemen of that day still clung, and the well-known red waistcoat that reached below his hips, and the fierce pug face of the old Squire, were now but a picture of memory. And the brothers between whom he had planted an irreconcilable quarrel, were now in their new mourning suits, with the gloss still on, debating furiously across the table in the great oak parlour, which had so often resounded to the banter and coarse songs, the oaths and laughter of the congenial neighbours whom the old Squire of Gylingden Hall loved to assemble there.

These young gentlemen, who had grown up in Gylingden Hall, were not accustomed to bridle their tongues, nor, if need be, to hesitate about a blow. Neither had been at the old man's funeral. His death had been sudden. Having been helped to his bed in that hilarious and quarrelsome state which was induced by port and punch, he was found dead in the morning,—his head hanging over the side of the bed, and his face very black and swollen.

Now the Squire's will despoiled his eldest son of Gylingden, which had descended to the heir time out of mind. Scroope Marston was furious. His deep stern voice was heard inveighing against his dead father and living brother, and the heavy thumps on the table with which he enforced his stormy recriminations resounded through the large chamber. Then broke in Charles's rougher voice, and then came a quick alternation of short sentences, and then both voices together in growing loudness and anger, and at last, swelling the tumult, the expostulations of pacific and frightened lawyers, and at last a sudden break up of the conference. Scroope broke out of the room, his pale furious face showing whiter against his long black hair, his dark fierce eyes blazing, his hands clenched, and looking more ungainly and deformed than ever in the convulsions of his fury.

Very violent words must have passed between them; for Charlie, though he was the winning man, was almost as angry as Scroope. The elder brother was for holding possession of the house, and putting his rival to legal process to oust him. But his legal advisers were clearly against it. So, with a heart boiling over with gall, up he went to London, and found the firm who had managed his father's business fair and communicative enough. They looked into the settlements, and found that Gylingden was excepted. It was very odd, but so it was, specially excepted; so that the right of the old Squire to deal with it by his will could not be questioned.

Notwithstanding all this, Scroope, breathing vengeance and aggression, and quite willing to wreck himself provided he could run his brother down, assailed Handsome Charlie, and battered old Squire Toby's will in the Prerogative Court and also at common law, and the feud between the brothers was knit, and every month their exasperation was heightened.

Scroope was beaten, and defeat did not soften him. Charles might have forgiven hard words; but he had been himself worsted during the long campaign in some of those skirmishes, special motions, and so forth, that constitute the episodes of a legal epic like that in which the Marston brothers figured as opposing combatants; and the blight of the law costs had touched him, too, with the usual effect upon the temper of a man of embarrassed means.

Years flew, and brought no healing on their wings. On the contrary, the deep corrosion of this hatred bit deeper by time. Neither brother married. But an accident of a different kind befell the younger, Charles Marston, which abridged his enjoyments very materially.

This was a bad fall from his hunter. There were severe fractures, and there was concussion of the brain. For some time it was thought that he could not recover. He disappointed these evil auguries, however. He did recover, but changed in two essential particulars. He had received an injury to his hip, which doomed him never more to sit in the saddle. And the rollicking animal spirits which hitherto had never failed him, had now taken flight for ever.

He had been for five days in a state of coma—absolute insensibility—and when he recovered consciousness he was haunted by an indescribable anxiety.

Tom Cooper, who had been butler in the palmy days of Gylingden Hall, under old Squire Toby, still maintained his post with old-fashioned fidelity, in these days of faded splendour and frugal housekeeping. Twenty years had passed since the death of his old master. He had grown lean, and stooped, and his face, dark with the peculiar brown of age, furrowed and gnarled, and his temper, except with his master, had waxed surly.

His master had visited Bath and Buxton, and came back, as he went, lame, and halting gloomily about with the aid of a stick. When the hunter was sold, the last tradition of the old life at Gylingden disappeared. The young Squire, as he was still called, excluded by his mischance from the hunting-field, dropped into a solitary way of life, and halted slowly and solitarily about the old place, seldom raising his eyes, and with an appearance of indescribable gloom.

Old Cooper could talk freely on occasion with his master; and one day he said, as he handed him his hat and stick in the hall:

"You should rouse yourself up a bit, Master Charles!"

"It's past rousing with me, old Cooper."

"It's just this, I'm thinking: there's something on your mind, and you won't tell no one. There's no good keeping it on your stomach. You'll be a deal lighter if you tell it. Come, now, what is it, Master Charlie?"

The Squire looked with his round grey eyes straight into Cooper's eyes. He felt that there was a sort of spell broken. It was like the old rule of the ghost who can't speak till it is spoken to. He looked earnestly into old Cooper's face for some seconds, and sighed deeply.

"It ain't the first good guess you've made in your day, old Cooper, and I'm glad you've spoke. It's bin on my mind, sure enough, ever since I had that fall. Come in here after me, and shut the door."

The Squire pushed open the door of the oak parlour, and looked round on the pictures abstractedly. He had not been there for some time, and, seating himself on the table, he looked again for a while in Cooper's face before he spoke.

"It's not a great deal, Cooper, but it troubles me, and I would not tell it to the parson nor the doctor; for, God knows what they'd say, though there's nothing to signify in it. But you were always true to the family, and I don't mind if I tell you."

" 'Tis as safe with Cooper, Master Charles, as if 'twas locked in a chest, and sunk in a well."

"It's only this," said Charles Marston, looking down on the end of his stick, with which he was tracing lines and circles, "all the time I was lying like dead, as you thought, after that fall, I was with the old master." He raised his eyes to Cooper's again as he spoke, and with an awful oath he repeated—"I was with him, Cooper!"

"He was a good man, sir, in his way," repeated old Cooper, returning his gaze with awe. "He was a good master to me, and a good father to you, and I hope he's happy. May God rest him!"

"Well," said Squire Charles, "it's only this: the whole of that time I was with him, or he was with me—I don't know which. The upshot is, we were together, and I thought I'd never get out of his hands again, and all the time he was bullying me about some one thing; and if it was to save my life, Tom Cooper, by —— from the time I waked I never could call to mind what it was; and I think I'd give that hand to know; and if you can think of anything it might be—for God's sake! don't be afraid, Tom Cooper, but speak it out, for he threatened me hard, and it was surely him."

Here ensued a silence.

"And what did you think it might be yourself, Master Charles?" said Cooper.

"I han't thought of aught that's likely. I'll never hit on't—*never*. I thought it might happen he knew something about that d—— hump-backed villain, Scroope, that swore before Lawyer Gingham I made away with a paper of settlements—me and father; and, as I hope to be saved, Tom Cooper, there never was a bigger lie! I'd a had the law of him for them identical words, and cast him for more than he's worth; only Lawyer Gingham never goes into nothing for me since money grew scarce in Gylingden; and I can't change my lawyer, I owe him such a hatful of money. But he did, he swore he'd hang me yet for it. He said it in them identical words—he'd never rest till he *hanged* me for it, and I think it was, like enough, something about *that,* the old master was troubled; but it's enough to drive a man mad. I *can't* bring it to mind—I can't remember a word he said, only he threatened awful, and looked—Lord a mercy on us!—frightful bad."

"There's no need he should. May the Lord a-mercy on him!" said the old butler.

"No, of course; and you're not to tell a soul, Cooper—not a living soul, mind, that I said he looked bad, nor nothing about it."

"God forbid!" said old Cooper, shaking his head. "But I was thinking, sir, it might ha' been about the slight that's bin so long put on him by having no stone over him, and never a scratch o' a chisel to say who he is."

"Ay! Well, I didn't think o' that. Put on your hat, old Cooper, and come down wi' me; for I'll look after that, at any rate."

There is a bye-path leading by a turnstile to the park, and thence to the picturesque old burying-place, which lies in a nook by the roadside, embowered in ancient trees. It was a fine autumnal sunset, and melancholy lights and long shadows spread their peculiar effects over the landscape as "Handsome Charlie" and the old butler made their way slowly toward the place where Handsome Charlie was himself to lie at last.

"Which of the dogs made that howling all last night?" asked the Squire, when they had got on a little way.

"'Twas a strange dog, Master Charlie, in front of the house; ours was all in the yard—a white dog wi' a black head, he looked to be, and he was smelling round them mounting-steps the old master, God be wi' him! set up, the time his knee was bad. When the tyke got up a' top of them, howlin' up at the windows, I'd a liked to shy something at him."

"Hullo! Is that like him?" said the Squire, stopping short, and pointing with his stick at a dirty-white dog, with a large black head, which was scampering round them in a wide circle, half crouching with that air of uncertainty and deprecation which dogs so well know how to assume.

He whistled the dog up. He was a large, half-starved bull-dog.

"That fellow has made a long journey—thin as a whipping-post, and stained all over, and his claws worn to the stumps," said the Squire, musingly.

"He isn't a bad dog, Cooper. My poor father liked a good bull-dog, and knew a cur from a good 'un."

The dog was looking up into the Squire's face with the peculiar grim visage of his kind, and the Squire was thinking irreverently how strong a likeness it presented to the character of his father's fierce pug features when he was clutching his horsewhip and swearing at a keeper.

"If I did right I'd shoot him. He'll worry the cattle, and kill our dogs," said the Squire. "Hey, Cooper? I'll tell the keeper to look after him. That fellow could pull down a sheep, and he shan't live on my mutton."

But the dog was not to be shaken off. He looked wistfully after the Squire, and after they had got a little way on, he followed timidly.

It was vain trying to drive him off. The dog ran round them in wide circles, like the infernal dog in "Faust"; only he left no track of thin flame behind him. These manoeuvres were executed with a sort of beseeching air, which flattered and touched the object of this odd preference. So he called him up again, patted him, and then and there in a manner adopted him.

The dog now followed their steps dutifully, as if he had belonged to Handsome Charlie all his days. Cooper unlocked the little iron door, and the dog walked in close behind their heels, and followed them as they visited the roofless chapel.

The Marstons were lying under the floor of this little building in rows. There is not a vault. Each has his distinct grave enclosed in a lining of masonry. Each is surmounted by a stone kist, on the upper flag of which is enclosed his epitaph, except that of poor old Squire Toby. Over him was nothing but the grass and the line of masonry which indicate the site of the kist, whenever his family should afford him one like the rest.

"Well, it does look shabby. It's the elder brother's business; but if he won't, I'll see to it myself, and I'll take care, old boy, to cut sharp and deep in it, that the elder son having refused to lend a hand the stone was put there by the younger."

They strolled round this little burial ground. The sun was now below the horizon, and the red metallic glow from the clouds, still illuminated by the departed sun, mingled luridly with the twilight. When Charlie peeped again into the little chapel, he saw the ugly dog stretched upon Squire Toby's grave, looking at least twice his natural length, and performing such antics as made the young Squire stare. If you have ever seen a cat stretched on the floor, with a bunch of Valerian, straining, writhing, rubbing its jaws in long-drawn caresses, and in the absorption of a sensual ecstasy, you have seen a phenomenon resembling that which Handsome Charlie witnessed on looking in.

The head of the brute looked so large, its body so long and thin, and its joints so ungainly and dislocated, that the Squire, with old Cooper beside him, looked on with a feeling of disgust and astonishment, which, in a moment or two more, brought the Squire's stick down upon him with a couple of heavy thumps. The beast awakened from his ecstasy, sprang to the head of the grave, and there on a sudden, thick and bandy as before, confronted the Squire, who stood at its foot, with a terrible grin, and eyes that glared with the peculiar green of canine fury.

The next moment the dog was crouching abjectly at the Squire's feet.

"Well, he's a rum 'un!" said old Cooper, looking hard at him.

"I like him," said the Squire.

"I don't," said Cooper.

"But he shan't come in here again," said the Squire.

"I shouldn't wonder if he was a witch," said old Cooper, who remembered more tales of witchcraft than are now current in that part of the world.

"He's a good dog," said the Squire, dreamily. "I remember the time I'd a given a handful for him—but I'll never be good for nothing again. Come along."

And he stooped down and patted him. So up jumped the dog and looked up in his face, as if watching for some sign, ever so slight, which he might obey.

Cooper did not like a bone in that dog's skin. He could not imagine what his master saw to admire in him. He kept him all night in the gun-room, and the dog accompanied him in his halting rambles about the place. The fonder his master grew of him, the less did Cooper and the other servants like him.

"He hasn't a point of a good dog about him," Cooper would growl. "I think Master Charlie be blind. And old Captain (an old red parrot, who sat chained to a perch in the oak parlour, and conversed with himself, and nibbled at his claws and bit his perch all day),—old Captain, the only living thing, except one or two of us, and the Squire himself, that remembers the old master, the minute he saw the dog, screeched as if he was struck, shakin' his feathers out quite wild, and drops down, poor old soul, a-hangin' by his foot, in a fit."

But there is no accounting for fancies, and the Squire was one of those dogged persons who persist more obstinately in their whims the more they are opposed. But Charles Marston's health suffered by his lameness. The transition from habitual and violent exercise to such a life as his privation now consigned him to, was never made without a risk to health; and a host of dyspeptic annoyances, the existence of which he had never dreamed of before, now beset him in sad earnest. Among these was the now not unfrequent troubling of his sleep with dreams and nightmares. In these his canine favourite invariably had a part and was generally a central, and sometimes a solitary figure. In these visions the dog seemed to stretch himself up the side of the Squire's bed, and in dilated proportions to sit at his feet, with a horrible likeness to the pug features of old Squire Toby, with his tricks of wagging his head and throwing up his chin; and then he would talk to him about Scroope, and tell him "all wasn't straight," and that he "must make it up wi' Scroope," that he, the old Squire, had "served him an ill turn," that "time was nigh up," and that "fair was fair," and he was "troubled where he was, about Scroope."

Then in his dream this semi-human brute would approach his face to his, crawling and crouching up his body, heavy as lead, till the face of the beast was laid on his, with the same odious caresses and stretchings and writhings which he had seen over the old Squire's grave. Then Charlie would wake up with a gasp and a howl, and start upright in the bed, bathed in a cold moisture, and fancy he saw something white sliding off the foot of the bed. Sometimes he thought it might be the curtain with white lining that slipped down, or the coverlet disturbed by his uneasy turnings; but he always fancied, at such moments, that he saw something white sliding hastily off the bed; and always when he had been visited by such dreams the dog next morning was more than usually caressing and servile, as if to obliterate, by a more than ordinary welcome, the sentiment of disgust which the horror of the night had left behind it.

The doctor half-satisfied the Squire that there was nothing in these dreams, which, in one shape or another, invariably attended forms of indigestion such as he was suffering from.

For a while, as if to corroborate this theory, the dog ceased altogether to figure in them. But at last there came a vision in which, more unpleasantly than before, he did resume his old place.

In his nightmare the room seemed all but dark; he heard what he knew to be the dog walking from the door round his bed slowly, to the side from which he always had come upon it. A portion of the room was uncarpeted, and he said he distinctly heard the peculiar tread of a dog, in which the faint clatter of the claws is audible. It was a light stealthy step, but at every tread the whole room shook heavily; he felt something place itself at the foot of his bed, and saw a pair of green eyes staring at him in the dark, from which he could not remove his own. Then he heard, as he thought, the old Squire Toby say—"The eleventh hour be passed, Charlie, and ye've done nothing—you and I 'a done Scroope a wrong!" and then came a good deal more, and then—"The time's nigh up, it's going to strike." And with a long low growl, the thing began to creep up upon his feet; the growl continued, and he saw the reflection of the up-turned green eyes upon the bed-clothes, as it began slowly to stretch itself up his body towards his face. With a loud scream, he waked. The light, which of late the Squire was accustomed to have in his bed-room, had accidentally gone out. He was afraid to get up, or even to look about the room for some time; so sure did he feel of seeing the green eyes in the dark fixed on him from some corner. He had hardly recovered from the first agony which nightmare leaves behind it, and was beginning to collect his thoughts, when he heard the clock strike twelve. And he bethought him of the words "the eleventh hour be passed—time's nigh up—it's going to strike!" and he almost feared that he would hear the voice reopening the subject.

Next morning the Squire came down looking ill.

"Do you know a room, old Cooper," said he, "they used to call King Herod's Chamber?"

"Ay, sir; the story of King Herod was on the walls o't when I was a boy."

"There's a closet off it—is there?"

"I can't be sure o' that; but 'tisn't worth your looking at, now; the hangings was rotten, and took off the walls, before you was born; and there's nou't there but some old broken things and lumber. I seed them put there myself by poor Twinks; he was blind of an eye, and footman afterwards. You'll remember Twinks? He died here, about the time o' the great snow. There was a deal o' work to bury him, poor fellow!"

"Get the key, old Cooper; I'll look at the room," said the Squire.

"And what the devil can you want to look at it for?" said Cooper, with the old-world privilege of a rustic butler.

"And what the devil's that to you? But I don't mind if I tell you. I don't want that dog in the gun-room, and I'll put him somewhere else; and I don't care if I put him there."

"A bull-dog in a bedroom! Oons, sir! the folks 'ill say you're clean mad!"

"Well, let them; get you the key, and let us look at the room."

"You'd shoot him if you did right, Master Charlie. You never heard what a noise he kept up all last night in the gun-room, walking to and fro growling like a tiger in a show; and, say what you like, the dog's not worth his feed; he hasn't a point of a dog; he's a bad dog."

"I know a dog better than you—and he's a good dog!" said the Squire, testily.

"If you was a judge of a dog you'd hang that 'un," said Cooper.

"I'm not going to hang him, so there's an end. Go you, and get the key; and don't be talking, mind, when you go down. I may change my mind."

Now this freak of visiting King Herod's room had, in truth, a totally different object from that pretended by the Squire. The voice in his nightmare had uttered a particular direction, which haunted him, and would give him no peace until he had tested it. So far from liking that dog to-day, he was beginning to regard it with a horrible suspicion; and if old Cooper had not stirred his obstinate temper by seeming to dictate, I dare say he would have got rid of that inmate effectually before evening.

Up to the third storey, long disused, he and old Cooper mounted. At the end of a dusty gallery, the room lay. The old tapestry, from which the spacious chamber had taken its name, had long given place to modern paper, and this was mildewed, and in some places hanging from the walls. A thick mantle of dust lay over the floor. Some broken chairs and boards, thick with dust, lay, along with other lumber, piled together at one end of the room.

They entered the closet, which was quite empty. The Squire looked round, and you could hardly have said whether he was relieved or disappointed.

"No furniture here," said the Squire, and looked through the dusty window. "Did you say anything to me lately—I don't mean this morning—about this room, or the closet—or anything—I forget—"

"Lor' bless you! Not I. I han't been thinkin' o' this room this forty year."

"Is there any sort of old furniture called a *buffet*—do you remember?" asked the Squire.

"A buffet? why, yes—to be sure—there was a buffet, sure enough, in this closet, now you bring it to my mind," said Cooper. "But it's papered over."

"And what is it?"

"A little cupboard in the wall," answered the old man.

"Ho—I see—and there's such a thing here, is there, under the paper? Show me whereabouts it was."

"Well—I think it was somewhere about here," answered he, rapping his knuckles along the wall opposite the window. "Ay, there it is," he added, as the hollow sound of a wooden door was returned to his knock.

The Squire pulled the loose paper from the wall, and disclosed the doors of a small press, about two feet square, fixed in the wall.

"The very thing for my buckles and pistols, and the rest of my gimcracks," said the Squire. "Come away, we'll leave the dog where he is. Have you the key of that little press?"

No, he had not. The old master had emptied and locked it up, and desired that it should be papered over, and that was the history of it.

Down came the Squire, and took a strong turn-screw from his gun-case; and quietly reascended to King Herod's room, and with little trouble, forced the door of the small press in the closet wall. There were in it some letters and cancelled leases, and also a parchment deed which he took to the window and read with much agitation. It was a supplemental deed executed about a fortnight after the others, and previously to his father's marriage, placing Gylingden under strict settlement to the elder son, in what is called "tail male." Handsome Charlie, in his fraternal litigation, had acquired a smattering of technical knowledge, and he perfectly well knew that the effect of this would be not only to transfer the house and lands to his brother Scroope, but to leave him at the mercy of that exasperated brother, who might recover from him personally every guinea he had ever received by way of rent, from the date of his father's death.

It was a dismal, clouded day, with something threatening in its aspect, and the darkness, where he stood, was made deeper by the top of one of the huge old trees overhanging the window.

In a state of awful confusion he attempted to think over his position. He placed the deed in his pocket, and nearly made up his mind to destroy it. A short time ago he would not have hesitated for a moment under such circumstances; but now his health and his nerves were shattered, and he was under a supernatural alarm which the strange discovery of this deed had powerfully confirmed.

In this state of profound agitation he heard a sniffing at the closet-door, and then an impatient scratch and a long low growl. He screwed his courage up, and, not knowing what to expect, threw the door open and saw the dog, not in his dream-shape, but wriggling with joy, and crouching and fawning with eager submission; and then wandering about the closet, the brute growled awfully into the corners of it, and seemed in an unappeasable agitation.

Then the dog returned and fawned and crouched again at his feet.

After the first moment was over, the sensations of abhorrence and fear began to subside, and he almost reproached himself for requiting the affection of this poor friendless brute with the antipathy which he had really done nothing to earn.

The dog pattered after him down the stairs. Oddly enough, the sight of this animal, after the first revulsion, reassured him; in his eyes, so attached, so good-natured, and palpably so mere a dog.

By the hour of evening the Squire had resolved on a middle course; he would not inform his brother of his discovery, nor yet would he destroy the deed. He would never marry. He was past that time. He would leave a letter, explaining the discovery of the deed, addressed to the only surviving trustee—who had probably forgotten everything about it—and having seen out his own tenure, he would provide that all should be set right after his death. Was not that fair? at all events it quite satisfied what he called his conscience, and he thought it a devilish good compromise for his brother; and he went out, towards sunset, to take his usual walk.

Returning in the darkening twilight, the dog, as usual attending him, began to grow frisky and wild, at first scampering round him in great circles, as before, nearly at the top of his speed, his great head between his paws as he raced. Gradually more excited grew the pace and narrower his circuit, louder and fiercer his continuous growl, and the Squire stopped and grasped his stick hard, for the lurid eyes and grin of the brute threatened an attack. Turning round and round as the excited brute encircled him, and striking vainly at him with his stick, he grew at last so tired that he almost despaired of keeping him longer at bay; when on a sudden the dog stopped short and crawled up to his feet wriggling and crouching submissively.

Nothing could be more apologetic and abject; and when the Squire dealt him two heavy thumps with his stick, the dog whimpered only, and writhed and licked his feet. The Squire sat down on a prostrate tree; and his dumb companion, recovering his wonted spirits immediately, began to sniff and nuzzle among the roots. The Squire felt in his breast-pocket for the deed—it was safe; and again he pondered, in this loneliest of spots, on the question whether he should preserve it for restoration after his death to his brother, or destroy it forthwith. He began rather to lean toward the latter solution, when the long low growl of the dog not far off startled him.

He was sitting in a melancholy grove of old trees, that slants gently westward. Exactly the same odd effect of light I have before described—a faint red glow reflected downward from the upper sky, after the sun had set, now gave to the growing darkness a lurid uncertainty. This grove, which lies in a gentle hollow, owing to its circumscribed horizon on all but one side, has a peculiar character of loneliness.

He got up and peeped over a sort of barrier, accidentally formed of the trunks of felled trees laid one over the other, and saw the dog straining up the other side of it, and hideously stretched out, his ugly head looking in consequence twice the natural size. His dream was coming over him again. And now between the trunks the brute's ungainly head was thrust, and the long neck came straining through, and the body, twining after it like a huge white lizard; and as it came striving and twisting through, it growled and glared as if it would devour him.

As swiftly as his lameness would allow, the Squire hurried from this solitary spot towards the house. What thoughts exactly passed through his mind as he did so, I am sure he could not have told. But when the dog came up with him it seemed appeased, and even in high good-humour, and no longer resembled the brute that haunted his dreams.

That night, near ten o'clock, the Squire, a good deal agitated, sent for the keeper, and told him that he believed the dog was mad, and that he must shoot him. He might shoot the dog in the gun-room, where he was—a grain of shot or two in the wainscot did not matter, and the dog must not have a chance of getting out.

The Squire gave the gamekeeper his double-barrelled gun, loaded with heavy shot. He did not go with him beyond the hall. He placed his hand on the keeper's arm; the keeper said his hand trembled, and that he looked "as white as curds."

"Listen a bit!" said the Squire under his breath.

They heard the dog in a state of high excitement in the room—growling ominously, jumping on the window-stool and down again, and running round the room.

"You'll need to be sharp, mind—don't give him a chance—slip in edgeways, d'ye see? and give him both barrels!"

"Not the first mad dog I've knocked over, sir," said the man, looking very serious as he cocked the gun.

As the keeper opened the door, the dog had sprung into the empty grate. He said he "never see sich a stark, staring devil." The beast made a twist round, as if, he thought, to jump up the chimney—"but that wasn't to be done at no price,"—and he made a yell—not like a dog—like a man caught in a mill-crank, and before he could spring at the keeper, he fired one barrel into him. The dog leaped towards him, and rolled over, receiving the second barrel in his head, as he lay snorting at the keeper's feet!

"I never seed the like; I never heard a screech like that!" said the keeper, recoiling. "It makes a fellow feel queer."

"Quite dead?" asked the Squire.

"Not a stir in him, sir," said the man, pulling him along the floor by the neck.

"Throw him outside the hall-door now," said the Squire; "and mind you pitch him outside the gate to-night—old Cooper says he's a witch," and the pale Squire smiled, "so he shan't lie in Gylingden."

Never was man more relieved than the Squire, and he slept better for a week after this than he had done for many weeks before.

It behooves us all to act promptly on our good resolutions. There is a determined gravitation towards evil, which, if left to itself, will bear down first intentions. If at one moment of superstitious fear, the Squire had made up his mind to a great sacrifice, and resolved in the matter of that deed so strangely recovered, to act honestly by his brother, that resolution very soon gave place to the compromise with fraud, which so conveniently postponed the restitution to the period when further enjoyment on his part was impossible. Then came more tidings of Scroope's violent and minatory language, with always the same burthen—that he would leave no stone unturned to show that there had existed a deed which Charles had either secreted or destroyed, and that he would never rest till he had hanged him.

This of course was wild talk. At first it had only enraged him; but, with his recent guilty knowledge and suppression, had come fear. His danger was the existence of the deed, and little by little he brought himself to a resolution to destroy it. There were many falterings and recoils before he could bring himself to commit this crime. At length, however, he did it, and got rid of the custody of that which at any time might become the instrument of disgrace and ruin. There was relief in this, but also the new and terrible sense of actual guilt.

He had got pretty well rid of his supernatural qualms. It was a different kind of trouble that agitated him now.

But this night, he imagined, he was awakened by a violent shaking of his bed. He could see, in the very imperfect light, two figures at the foot of it, holding each a bed-post. One of these he half-fancied was his brother Scroope, but the other was the old Squire—of that he was sure—and he fancied that they had shaken him up from his sleep. Squire Toby was talking as Charlie wakened, and he heard him say:

"Put out of our own house by you! It won't hold for long. We'll come in together, friendly, and stay. Forewarned, wi' yer eyes open, ye did it; and now Scroope'll hang you! We'll hang you together! Look at me, you devil's limb."

And the old Squire tremblingly stretched his face, torn with shot and bloody, and growing every moment more and more into the likeness of the dog, and began to stretch himself out and climb the bed over the foot-board; and he saw the figure at the other side, little more than a black shadow, begin also to scale the bed; and there was instantly a dreadful confusion and uproar in the room, and such a gabbling and laughing; he could not catch the words; but, with a scream, he woke, and found himself standing on the floor. The phantoms and the clamour were gone, but a crash and ringing of fragments was in his ears. The great china bowl, from which for generations the Marstons of Gylingden had been baptized, had fallen from the mantelpiece, and was smashed on the hearth-stone.

"I've bin dreamin' all night about Mr. Scroope, and I wouldn't wonder, old Cooper, if he was dead," said the Squire, when he came down in the morning.

"God forbid! I was adreamed about him, too, sir: I dreamed he was dammin' and sinkin' about a hole was burnt in his coat, and the old master, God be wi' him! said—quite plain—I'd 'a swore 'twas himself—'Cooper, get up, ye d——d land-loupin' thief, and lend a hand to hang him—for he's a daft cur, and no dog o' mine.' 'Twas the dog shot over night, I do suppose, as was runnin' in my old head. I thought old master gied me a punch wi' his knuckles, and says I, wakenin' up, 'At yer service, sir'; and for a while I couldn't get it out o' my head, master was in the room still."

Letters from town soon convinced the Squire that his brother Scroope, so far from being dead, was particularly active; and Charlie's attorney wrote to say, in serious alarm, that he had heard, accidentally, that he intended setting up a case, of a supplementary deed of settlement, of which he had secondary evidence, which would give him Gylingden. And at this menace Handsome Charlie snapped his fingers, and wrote courageously to his attorney; abiding what might follow with, however, a secret foreboding.

Scroope threatened loudly now, and swore after his bitter fashion, and reiterated his old promise of hanging that cheat at last. In the midst of these menaces and preparations, however, a sudden peace proclaimed itself: Scroope died, without time even to make provisions for a posthumous attack upon his brother. It was one of those cases of disease of the heart in which death is as sudden as by a bullet.

Charlie's exultation was undisguised. It was shocking. Not, of course, altogether malignant. For there was the expansion consequent on the removal of a secret fear. There was also the comic piece of luck, that only the day before Scroope had destroyed his old will, which left to a stranger every farthing he possessed, intending in a day or two to execute another to the same person, charged with the express condition of prosecuting the suit against Charlie.

The result was, that all his possessions went unconditionally to his brother Charles as his heir. Here were grounds for abundance of savage elation. But there was also the deep-seated hatred of half a life of mutual and persistent aggression and revilings; and Handsome Charlie was capable of nursing a grudge, and enjoying a revenge with his whole heart.

He would gladly have prevented his brother's being buried in the old Gylingden chapel, where he wished to lie; but his lawyers doubted his power, and he was not quite proof against the scandal which would attend his turning back the funeral, which would, he knew, be attended by some of the country gentry and others, with an hereditary regard for the Marstons.

But he warned his servants that not one of them were to attend it; promising, with oaths and curses not to be disregarded, that any one of them who did so, should find the door shut in his face on his return.

I don't think, with the exception of old Cooper, that the servants cared for this prohibition, except as it baulked a curiosity always strong in the solitude of the country. Cooper was very much vexed that the eldest son of the old Squire should be buried in the old family chapel, and no sign of decent respect from Gylingden Hall. He asked his master, whether he would not, at least, have some wine and refreshments in the oak parlour, in case any of the country gentlemen who paid this respect to the old family should come up to the house? But the Squire only swore at him, told him to mind his own business, and ordered him to say, if such a thing happened, that he was out, and no preparations made, and, in fact, to send them away as they came. Cooper expostulated stoutly, and the Squire grew angrier; and after a tempestuous scene, took his hat and stick and walked out, just as the funeral descending the valley from the direction of the "Old Angel Inn" came in sight.

Old Cooper prowled about disconsolately, and counted the carriages as well as he could from the gate. When the funeral was over, and they began to drive away, he returned to the hall, the door of which lay open, and as usual deserted. Before he reached it quite, a mourning coach drove up, and two gentlemen in black cloaks, and with crapes to their hats, got out, and without looking to the right or the left, went up the steps into the house. Cooper followed them slowly. The carriage had, he supposed, gone round to the yard, for, when he reached the door, it was no longer there.

So he followed the two mourners into the house. In the hall he found a fellow-servant, who said he had seen two gentlemen, in black cloaks, pass through the hall, and go up the stairs without removing their hats, or asking leave of anyone. This was very odd, old Cooper thought, and a great liberty; so upstairs he went to make them out.

But he could not find them then, nor ever. And from that hour the house was troubled.

In a little time there was not one of the servants who had not something to tell. Steps and voices followed them sometimes in the passages, and tittering whispers, always minatory, scared them at corners of the galleries, or from dark recesses; so that they would return panic-stricken to be rebuked by thin Mrs. Beckett, who looked on such stories as worse than idle. But Mrs Beckett herself, a short time after, took a very different view of the matter.

She had herself begun to hear these voices, and with this formidable aggravation, that they came always when she was at her prayers, which she had been punctual in saying all her life, and utterly interrupted them. She was scared at such moments by dropping words and sentences, which grew, as she persisted, into threats and blasphemies.

These voices were not always in the room. They called, as she fancied, through the walls, very thick in that old house, from the neighbouring apartments, sometimes on one side, sometimes on the other; sometimes they seemed to holloa from distant lobbies, and came muffled, but threateningly, through the long panelled passages. As they approached they grew furious, as if several voices were speaking together. Whenever, as I said, this worthy woman applied herself to her devotions, these horrible sentences came hurrying towards the door, and, in panic, she would start from her knees, and all then would subside except the thumping of her heart against her stays, and the dreadful tremors of her nerves.

What these voices said, Mrs. Beckett never could quite remember one minute after they had ceased speaking; one sentence chased another away; gibe and menace and impious denunciation, each hideously articulate, were lost as soon as heard. And this added to the effect of these terrifying mockeries and invectives, that she could not, by any effort, retain their exact import, although their horrible character remained vividly present to her mind.

For a long time the Squire seemed to be the only person in the house absolutely unconscious of these annoyances. Mrs. Beckett had twice made up her mind within the week to leave. A prudent woman, however, who has been comfortable for more than twenty years in a place, thinks oftener than twice before she leaves it. She and old Cooper were the only servants in the house who remembered the good old housekeeping in Squire Toby's day. The others were few, and such as could hardly be accounted regular servants. Meg Dobbs, who acted as housemaid, would not sleep in the house, but walked home, in trepidation, to her father's, at the gatehouse, under the escort of her little brother, every night. Old Mrs. Beckett, who was high and mighty with the make-shift servants of fallen Gylingden, let herself down all at once, and made Mrs. Kymes and the kitchen-maid move their beds into her large and faded room, and there, very frankly, shared her nightly terrors with them.

Old Cooper was testy and captious about these stories. He was already uncomfortable enough by reason of the entrance of the two muffled figures into the house, about which there could be no mistake. His own eyes had seen them. He refused to credit the stories of the women, and affected to think that the two mourners might have left the house and driven away, on finding no one to receive them.

Old Cooper was summoned at night to the oak parlour, where the Squire was smoking.

"I say, Cooper," said the Squire, looking pale and angry, "what for ha' you been frightenin' they crazy women wi' your plaguy stories? d—— me, if you see ghosts here it's no place for you, and it's time you should pack. I won't be left without servants. Here has been old Beckett, wi' the cook and the kitchenmaid, as white as pipe-clay, all in a row, to tell me I must have a parson to sleep among them, and preach down the devil! Upon my soul, you're a wise old body, filling their heads wi' maggots! and Meg goes down to the lodge every night, afeared to lie in the house—all your doing, wi' your old wives' stories,—ye withered old Tom o' Bedlam!"

"I'm not to blame, Master Charles. 'Tisn't along o' no stories o' mine, for I'm never done telling 'em it's all vanity and vapours. Mrs. Beckett 'ill tell you that, and there's been many a wry word betwixt us on the head o't. Whate'er I may *think*," said old Cooper, significantly, and looking askance, with the sternness of fear in the Squire's face.

The Squire averted his eyes, and muttered angrily to himself, and turned away to knock the ashes out of his pipe on the hob, and then turning suddenly round upon Cooper again, he spoke, with a pale face, but not quite so angrily as before.

"I know you're no fool, old Cooper, when you like. Suppose there was such a thing as a ghost here, don't you see, it ain't to them snipe-headed women it 'id go to tell its story. What ails you, man, that you should think aught about it, but just what *I* think? You had a good headpiece o' yer own once, Cooper, don't be you clappin' a goosecap over it, as my poor father used to say; d——it, old boy, you mustn't let 'em be fools, settin' one another wild wi' their blether, and makin' the folks talk what they shouldn't, about Gylingden and the family. I don't think ye'd like that, old Cooper, I'm sure ye wouldn't. The women has gone out o' the kitchen, make up a bit o' fire, and get your pipe. I'll go to you, when I finish this one, and we'll smoke a bit together, and a glass o' brandy and water."

Down went the old butler, not altogether unused to such condescensions in that disorderly and lonely household; and let not those who can choose their company, be too hard on the Squire who couldn't.

When he had got things tidy, as he said, he sat down in that big old kitchen, with his feet on the fender, the kitchen candle burning in a great brass candlestick, which stood on the deal table at his elbow, with the brandy bottle and tumblers beside it, and Cooper's pipe also in readiness. And these preparations completed, the old butler, who had remembered other generations and better times, fell into rumination, and so, gradually, into a deep sleep.

Old Cooper was half awakened by some one laughing low, near his head. He was dreaming of old times in the Hall, and fancied one of "the young gentlemen" going to play him a trick, and he mumbled something in his sleep, from which he was awakened by a stern deep voice, saying, "You wern't at the funeral; I might take your life, I'll take your ear." At the same moment, the side of his head received a violent push, and he started to his feet. The fire had gone down, and he was chilled. The candle was expiring in the socket, and threw on the white wall long shadows, that danced up and down from the ceiling to the ground, and their black outlines he fancied resembled the two men in cloaks, whom he remembered with a profound horror.

He took the candle, with all the haste he could, getting along the passage, on whose walls the same dance of black shadows was continued, very anxious to reach his room before the light should go out. He was startled half out of his wits by the sudden clang of his master's bell, close over his head, ringing furiously.

"Ha, ha! There it goes—yes, sure enough," said Cooper, reassuring himself with the sound of his own voice, as he hastened on, hearing more and more distinct every moment the same furious ringing. "He's fell asleep, like me; that's it, and his lights is out, I lay you fifty——"

When he turned the handle of the door of the oak parlour, the Squire wildly called, "Who's *there?*" in the tone of a man who expects a robber.

"It's me, old Cooper, all right, Master Charlie, you didn't come to the kitchen after all, sir."

"I'm very bad, Cooper; I don't know how I've been. Did you meet anything?" asked the Squire.

"No," said Cooper.

They stared on one another.

"Come here—stay here! Don't you leave me! Look round the room, and say is all right; and gie us your hand, old Cooper, for I must hold it." The Squire's was damp and cold, and trembled very much. It was not very far from day-break now.

After a time he spoke again: "I 'a done many a thing I shouldn't; I'm not fit to go, and wi' God's blessin' I'll look to it—why shouldn't I? I'm as lame as old Billy—I'll never be able to do any good no more, and I'll give over drinking, and marry, as I ought to 'a done long ago—none o' yer fine ladies, but a good homely wench; there's Farmer Crump's youngest daughter, a good lass, and discreet. What for shouldn't I take her? She'd take care o' me, and wouldn't bring a head full o' romances here, and mantua-makers' trumpery, and I'll talk with the parson, and I'll do what's fair wi' everyone; and mind, I said I'm sorry for many a thing I 'a done."

A wild cold dawn had by this time broken. The Squire, Cooper said, looked "awful bad," as he got his hat and stick, and sallied out for a walk, instead of going to his bed, as Cooper besought him, looking so wild and distracted, that it was plain his object was simply to escape from the house. It was twelve o'clock when the Squire walked into the kitchen, where he was sure of finding some of the servants, looking as if ten years had passed over him since yesterday. He pulled a stool by the fire, without speaking a word, and sat down. Cooper had sent to Applebury for the doctor, who had just arrived, but the Squire would not go to him. "If he wants to see me, he may come here," he muttered as often as Cooper urged him. So the doctor did come, charily enough, and found the Squire very much worse than he had expected.

The Squire resisted the order to get to his bed. But the doctor insisted under a threat of death, at which his patient quailed.

"Well, I'll do what you say—only this—you must let old Cooper and Dick Keeper stay wi' me. I mustn't be left alone, and they must keep awake o' nights; and stay a while, do *you*. When I get round a bit, I'll go and live in a town. It's dull livin' here, now that I can't do nou't, as I used, and I'll live a better life, mind ye; ye heard me say that, and I don't care who laughs, and I'll talk wi' the parson. I like 'em to laugh, hang 'em, it's a sign I'm doin' right, at last."

The doctor sent a couple of nurses from the County Hospital, not choosing to trust his patient to the management he had selected, and he went down himself to Gylingden to meet them in the evening. Old Cooper was ordered to occupy the dressing-room, and sit up at night, which satisfied the Squire, who was in a strangely excited state, very low, and threatened, the doctor said, with fever.

The clergyman came, an old, gentle, "book-learned" man, and talked and prayed with him late that evening. After he had gone the Squire called the nurses to his bedside, and said:

"There's a fellow sometimes comes; you'll never mind him. He looks in at the door and beckons,—a thin, hump-backed chap in mourning, wi' black gloves on; ye'll know him by his lean face, as brown as the wainscot: don't ye mind his smilin'. You don't go out to him, nor ask him in; he won't say nout; and if he grows anger'd and looks awry at ye, don't ye be afeared, for he can't hurt ye, and he'll grow tired waitin', and go away; and for God's sake mind ye don't ask him in, nor go out after him!"

The nurses put their heads together when this was over, and held afterwards a whispering conference with old Cooper. "Law bless ye!—no, there's no madman in the house," he protested; "not a soul but what ye saw,—it's just a trifle o' the fever in his head—no more."

The Squire grew worse as the night wore on. He was heavy and delirious, talking of all sorts of things—of wine, and dogs, and lawyers; and then he began to talk, as it were, to his brother Scroope. As he did so, Mrs. Oliver, the nurse, who was sitting up alone with him, heard, as she thought, a hand softly laid on the door-handle outside, and a stealthy attempt to turn it. "Lord bless us! who's there?" she cried, and her heart jumped into her mouth, as she thought of the hump-backed man in black, who was to put in his head smiling and beckoning—"Mr. Cooper! sir! are you there?" she cried. "Come here, Mr. Cooper, please—do, sir, quick!"

Old Cooper, called up from his doze by the fire, stumbled in from the dressing-room, and Mrs. Oliver seized him tightly as he emerged.

"The man with the hump has been atryin' the door, Mr. Cooper, as sure as I am here." The Squire was moaning and mumbling in his fever, understanding nothing, as she spoke. "No, no! Mrs. Oliver, ma'am, it's impossible, for there's no sich man in the house: what is Master Charlie sayin'?"

"He's saying *Scroope* every minute, whatever he means by that, and—and—hisht!—listen—there's the handle again," and, with a loud scream, she added—"Look at his head and neck in at the door!" and in her tremour she strained old Cooper in an agonizing embrace.

The candle was flaring, and there was a wavering shadow at the door that looked like the head of a man with a long neck, and a longish sharp nose, peeping in and drawing back.

"Don't be a d—— fool, ma'am!" cried Cooper, very white, and shaking her with all his might. "It's only the candle, I tell you—nothing in life but that. Don't you see?" and he raised the light; "and I'm sure there was no one at the door, and I'll try, if you let me go."

The other nurse was asleep on a sofa, and Mrs. Oliver called her up in a panic, for company, as old Cooper opened the door. There was no one near it, but at the angle of the gallery was a shadow resembling that which he had seen in the room. He raised the candle a little, and it seemed to beckon with a long hand as the head drew back. "Shadow from the candle!" exclaimed Cooper aloud, resolved not to yield to Mrs. Oliver's panic; and, candle in hand, he walked to the corner. There was nothing. He could not forbear peeping down the long gallery from this point, and as he moved the light, he saw precisely the same sort of shadow, a little further down, and as he advanced the same withdrawal, and beckon. "Gammon!" said he; "it is nout but the candle." And on he went, growing half angry and half frightened at the persistency with which this ugly shadow—a literal shadow he was sure it was—presented itself. As he drew near the point where it now appeared, it seemed to collect itself, and nearly dissolve in the central panel of an old carved cabinet which he was now approaching.

In the centre panel of this is a sort of boss carved into a wolf's head. The light fell oddly upon this, and the fugitive shadow seemed to be breaking up, and re-arranging itself as oddly. The eye-ball gleamed with a point of reflected light, which glittered also upon the grinning mouth, and he saw the long, sharp nose of Scroope Marston, and his fierce eye looking at him, he thought, with a steadfast meaning.

Old Cooper stood gazing upon this sight, unable to move, till he saw the face, and the figure that belonged to it, begin gradually to emerge from the wood. At the same time he heard voices approaching rapidly up a side gallery, and Cooper, with a loud "Lord a-mercy on us!" turned and ran back again, pursued by a sound that seemed to shake the old house like a mighty gust of wind.

Into his master's room burst old Cooper, half wild with fear, and clapped the door and turned the key in a twinkling, looking as if he had been pursued by murderers.

"Did you hear it?" whispered Cooper, now standing near the dressing-room door. They all listened, but not a sound from without disturbed the utter stillness of night. "God bless us! I doubt it's my old head that's gone crazy!" exclaimed Cooper.

He would tell them nothing but that he was himself "an old fool," to be frightened by their talk, and that "the rattle of a window, or the dropping o' a pin" was enough to scare him now; and so he helped himself through that night with brandy, and sat up talking by his master's fire.

The Squire recovered slowly from his brain fever, but not perfectly. A very little thing, the doctor said, would suffice to upset him. He was not yet sufficiently strong to remove for change of scene and air, which were necessary for his complete restoration.

Cooper slept in the dressing-room, and was now his only nightly attendant. The ways of the invalid were odd: he liked, half sitting up in his bed, to smoke his churchwarden o' nights, and made old Cooper smoke, for company, at the fireside. As the Squire and his humble friend indulged in it, smoking is a taciturn pleasure, and it was not until the Master of Gylingden had finished his third pipe that he essayed conversation, and when he did, the subject was not such as Cooper would have chosen.

"I say, old Cooper, look in my face, and don't be afeared to speak out," said the Squire, looking at him with a steady, cunning smile; "you know all this time, as well as I do, who's in the house. You needn't deny—hey?—Scroope and my father?"

"Don't you be talking like that, Charlie," said old Cooper, rather sternly and frightened, after a long silence; still looking in his face, which did not change.

"What's the good o' shammin', Cooper? Scroope's took the hearin' o' yer right ear—you know he did. He's looking angry. He's nigh took my life wi' this fever. But he's not done wi' me yet, and he looks awful wicked. Ye saw him—ye know ye did."

Cooper was awfully frightened, and the odd smile on the Squire's lips frightened him still more. He dropped his pipe, and stood gazing in silence at his master, and feeling as if he were in a dream.

"If ye think so, ye should not be smiling like that," said Cooper, grimly.

"I'm tired, Cooper, and it's as well to smile as t'other thing; so I'll even smile while I can. You know what they mean to do wi' me. That's all I wanted to say. Now, lad, go on wi' yer pipe—I'm goin' asleep."

So the Squire turned over in his bed, and lay down serenely, with his head on the pillow. Old Cooper looked at him, and glanced at the door, and then half-filled his tumbler with brandy, and drank it off, and felt better, and got to his bed in the dressing-room.

In the dead of night he was suddenly awakened by the Squire, who was standing, in his dressing-gown and slippers, by his bed.

"I've brought you a bit o' a present. I got the rents o' Hazelden yesterday, and ye'll keep that for yourself—it's a fifty—and give t'other to Nelly Carwell, to-morrow; I'll sleep the sounder; and I saw Scroope since; he's not such a bad 'un after all, old fellow! He's got a crape over his face—for I told him I couldn't bear it; and I'd do many a thing for him now. I never could stand shilly-shally. Good-night, old Cooper!"

And the Squire laid his trembling hand kindly on the old man's shoulder, and returned to his own room.

"I don't half like how he is. Doctor don't come half often enough. I don't like that queer smile o' his, and his hand was as cold as death. I hope in God his brain's not a-turnin'!" With these reflections, he turned to the pleasanter subject of his present, and at last fell asleep.

In the morning, when he went into the Squire's room, the Squire had left his bed. "Never mind; he'll come back, like a bad shillin'," thought old Cooper, preparing the room as usual. But he did not return. Then began an uneasiness, succeeded by a panic, when it began to be plain that the Squire was not in the house. What had become of him? None of his clothes, but his dressing-gown and slippers, were missing. Had he left the house, in his present sickly state, in that garb? and, if so, could he be in his right senses; and was there a chance of his surviving a cold, damp night, so passed, in the open air?

Tom Edwards was up to the house, and told them, that, walking a mile or so that morning, at four o'clock—there being no moon—along with Farmer Nokes, who was driving his cart to market, in the dark, three men walked, in front of the horse, not twenty yards before them, all the way from near Gylingden Lodge to the burial ground, the gate of which was opened for them from within, and the three men entered, and the gate was shut. Tom Edwards thought they were gone in to make preparation for a funeral of some member of the Marston family. But the occurrence seemed to Cooper, who knew there was no such thing, horribly ominous.

He now commenced a careful search, and at last bethought him of the lonely upper storey, and King Herod's chamber. He saw nothing changed there, but the closet door was shut, and, dark as was the morning, something, like a large white knot sticking out over the door, caught his eye.

The door resisted his efforts to open it for a time; some great weight forced it down against the floor; at length, however, it did yield a little, and a heavy crash, shaking the whole floor, and sending an echo flying through all the silent corridors, with a sound like receding laughter, half stunned him.

When he pushed open the door, his master was lying dead upon the floor. His cravat was drawn halter-wise tight round his throat, and had done its work well. The body was cold, and had been long dead.

In due course the coroner held his inquest, and the jury pronounced, "that the deceased, Charles Marston, had died by his own hand, in a state of temporary insanity." But old Cooper had his own opinion about the Squire's death, though his lips were sealed, and he never spoke about it. He went and lived for the residue of his days in York, where there are still people who remember him, a taciturn and surly old man, who attended church regularly, and also drank a little, and was known to have saved some money.

S *is for* Spider

For many horror readers, spiders are the creepiest of creepy crawlies. In this story, first published in the March 1903 issue of *Pearson's,* British writer H.G. Wells (1866–1946) imagines how horrifying it would be for ill-equipped humans to blunder into *terra icognita* where the spiders outnumber the humans, and are just a bit larger than usual.

H.G. Wells

The Valley of Spiders

Towards mid-day the three pursuers came abruptly round a bend in the torrent bed upon the sight of a very broad and spacious valley. The difficult and winding trench of pebbles along which they had tracked the fugitives for so long, expanded to a broad slope, and with a common impulse the three men left the trail, and rode to a little eminence set with olive-dun trees, and there halted, the two others, as became them, a little behind the man with the silver-studded bridle.

For a space they scanned the great expanse below them with eager eyes. It spread remoter and remoter, with only a few clusters of sere thorn bushes here and there, and the dim suggestions of some now waterless ravine, to break its desolation of yellow grass. Its purple distances melted at last into the bluish slopes of the further hills—hills it might be of a greener kind—and above them invisibly supported, and seeming indeed to hang in the blue, were the snowclad summits of mountains that grew larger and bolder to the north-westward as the sides of the valley drew together. And westward the valley opened until a distant darkness under the sky told where the forests began. But the three men looked neither east nor west, but only steadfastly across the valley.

The gaunt man with the scarred lip was the first to speak. "Nowhere," he said, with a sigh of disappointment in his voice. "But after all, they had a full day's start."

"They don't know we are after them," said the little man on the white horse.

"*She* would know," said the leader bitterly, as if speaking to himself.

"Even then they can't go fast. They've got no beast but the mule, and all to-day the girl's foot has been bleeding—"

The man with the silver bridle flashed a quick intensity of rage on him. "Do you think I haven't seen that?" he snarled.

"It helps, anyhow," whispered the little man to himself.

The gaunt man with the scarred lip stared impassively. "They can't be over the valley," he said. "If we ride hard—"

He glanced at the white horse and paused.

"Curse all white horses!" said the man with the silver bridle, and turned to scan the beast his curse included.

The little man looked down between the melancholy ears of his steed.

"I did my best," he said.

The two others stared again across the valley for a space. The gaunt man passed the back of his hand across the scarred lip.

"Come up!" said the man who owned the silver bridle, suddenly. The little man started and jerked his rein, and the horse hoofs of the three made a multitudinous faint pattering upon the withered grass as they turned back towards the trail. . . .

They rode cautiously down the long slope before them, and so came through a waste of prickly, twisted bushes and strange dry shapes of horny branches that grew amongst the rocks, into the levels below. And there the trail grew faint, for the soil was scanty, and the only herbage was this scorched dead straw that lay upon the ground. Still, by hard scanning, by leaning beside the horses' necks and pausing ever and again, even these white men could contrive to follow after their prey.

There were trodden places, bent and broken blades of the coarse grass, and ever and again the sufficient intimation of a footmark. And once the leader saw a brown smear of blood where the half-caste girl may have trod. And at that under his breath he cursed her for a fool.

The gaunt man checked his leader's tracking, and the little man on the white horse rode behind, a man lost in a dream. They rode one after another, the man with the silver bridle led the way, and they spoke never a word. After a time it came to the little man on the white horse that the world was very still. He started out of his dream. Besides the little noises of their horses and equipment, the whole great valley kept the brooding quiet of a painted scene.

Before him went his master and his fellow, each intently leaning forward to the left, each impassively moving with the paces of his horse; their shadows went before them—still, noiseless, tapering attendants; and nearer a crouched cool shape was his own. He looked about him. What was it had gone? Then he remembered the reverberation from the banks of the gorge and the perpetual accompaniment of shifting, jostling pebbles. And, moreover—? There was no breeze. That was it! What a vast, still place it was, a monotonous afternoon slumber. And the sky open and blank, except for a sombre veil of haze that had gathered in the upper valley.

He straightened his back, fretted with his bridle, puckered his lips to whistle, and simply sighed. He turned in his saddle for a time, and stared at the throat of the mountain gorge out of which they had come. Blank! Blank slopes on either side, with never a sign of a decent beast or tree—much less a man. What a land it was! What a wilderness! He dropped again into his former pose.

It filled him with a momentary pleasure to see a wry stick of purple black flash out into the form of a snake, and vanish amidst the brown. After all, the infernal valley *was* alive. And then, to rejoice him still more, came a little breath across his face, a whisper that came and went, the faintest inclination of a stiff black-antlered bush upon a little crest, the first intimations of a possible breeze. Idly he wetted his finger, and held it up.

He pulled up sharply to avoid a collision with the gaunt man, who had stopped at fault upon the trail. Just at that guilty moment he caught his master's eye looking towards him.

For a time he forced an interest in the tracking. Then, as they rode on again, he studied his master's shadow and hat and shoulder, appearing and disappearing behind the gaunt man's nearer contours. They had ridden four days out of the very limits of the world into this desolate place, short of water, with nothing but a strip of dried meat under their saddles, over rocks and mountains, where surely none but these fugitives had ever been before—for *that!*

And all this was for a girl, a mere wilful child! And the man had whole cityfuls of people to do his basest bidding—girls, women! Why in the name of passionate folly *this* one in particular? asked the little man, and scowled at the world, and licked his parched lips with a blackened tongue. It was the way of the master, and that was all he knew. Just because she sought to evade him. . . .

His eye caught a whole row of high plumed canes bending in unison, and then the tails of silk that hung before his neck flapped and fell. The breeze was growing stronger. Somehow it took the stiff stillness out of things—and that was well.

"Hullo!" said the gaunt man.

All three stopped abruptly.

"What?" asked the master. "What?"

"Over there," said the gaunt man, pointing up the valley.

"What?"

"Something coming towards us."

And as he spoke a yellow animal crested a rise and came bearing down upon them. It was a big wild dog, coming before the wind, tongue out, at a steady pace, and running with such an intensity of purpose that he did not seem to see the horsemen he approached. He ran with his nose up, following, it was plain, neither scent nor quarry. As he drew nearer the little man felt for his sword. "He's mad," said the gaunt rider.

"Shout!" said the little man, and shouted.

The dog came on. Then when the little man's blade was already out, it swerved aside and went panting by them and past. The eyes of the little man followed its flight. "There was no foam," he said. For a space the man with the silver-studded bridle stared up the valley. "Oh, come on!" he cried at last. "What does it matter?" and jerked his horse into movement again.

The little man left the insoluble mystery of a dog that fled from nothing but the wind, and lapsed into profound musings on human character. "Come on!" he whispered to himself. "Why should it be given to one man to say 'Come on!' with that stupendous violence of effect. Always, all his life, the man with the silver bridle has been saying that. If *I* said it—!" thought the little man. But people marvelled when the master was disobeyed even in the wildest things. This half-caste girl seemed to him, seemed to every one, mad—blasphemous almost. The little man, by way of comparison, reflected on the gaunt rider with the scarred lip, as stalwart as his master, as brave and, indeed, perhaps braver, and yet for him there was obedience, nothing but to give obedience duly and stoutly. . .

Certain sensations of the hands and knees called the little man back to more immediate things. He became aware of something. He rode up beside his gaunt fellow. "Do you notice the horses?" he said in an undertone.

The gaunt face looked interrogation.

"They don't like this wind," said the little man, and dropped behind as the man with the silver bridle turned upon him.

"It's all right," said the gaunt-faced man.

They rode on again for a space in silence. The foremost two rode downcast upon the trail, the hindmost man watched the haze that crept down the vastness of the valley, nearer and nearer, and noted how the wind grew in strength moment by moment. Far away on the left he saw a line of dark bulks—wild hog perhaps, galloping down the valley, but of that he said nothing, nor did he remark again upon the uneasiness of the horses.

And then he saw first one and then a second great white ball, a great shining white ball like a gigantic head of thistle-down, that drove before the wind athwart the path. These balls soared high in the air, and dropped and rose again and caught for a moment, and hurried on and passed, but at the sight of them the restlessness of the horses increased.

Then presently he saw that more of these drifting globes—and then soon very many more—were hurrying towards him down the valley.

They became aware of a squealing. Athwart the path a huge boar rushed, turning his head but for one instant to glance at them, and then hurling on down the valley again. And at that, all three stopped and sat in their saddles, staring into the thickening haze that was coming upon them.

"If it were not for this thistle-down—" began the leader.

But now a big globe came drifting past within a score of yards of them. It was really not an even sphere at all, but a vast, soft, ragged, filmy thing, a sheet gathered by the corners, an aerial jelly-fish, as it were, but rolling over and over as it advanced, and trailing long, cobwebby threads and streamers that floated in its wake.

"It isn't thistle-down," said the little man.

"I don't like the stuff," said the gaunt man.

And they looked at one another.

"Curse it!" cried the leader. "The air's full of it up there. If it keeps on at this pace long, it will stop us altogether."

An instinctive feeling, such as lines out a herd of deer at the approach of some ambiguous thing, prompted them to turn their horses to the wind, ride forward for a few paces, and stare at that advancing multitude of floating masses. They came on before the wind with a sort of smooth swiftness, rising and falling noiselessly, sinking to earth, rebounding high, soaring—all with a perfect unanimity, with a still, deliberate assurance.

Right and left of the horsemen the pioneers of this strange army passed. At one that rolled along the ground, breaking shapelessly and trailing out reluctantly into long grappling ribbons and bands, all three horses began to shy and dance. The master was seized with a sudden unreasonable impatience. He cursed the drifting globes roundly. "Get on!" he cried; "get on! What do these things matter? How *can* they matter? Back to the trail!" He fell swearing at his horse and sawed the bit across its mouth.

He shouted aloud with rage. "I will follow that trail, I tell you!" he cried. "Where is the trail?"

He gripped the bridle of his prancing horse and searched amidst the grass. A long and clinging thread fell across his face, a grey streamer dropped about his bridle-arm, some big, active thing with many legs ran down the back of his head. He looked up to discover one of those grey masses anchored as it were above him by these things and flapping out ends as a sail flaps when a boat comes, about—but noiselessly.

He had an impression of many eyes, of a dense crew of squat bodies, of long, many-jointed limbs hauling at their mooring ropes to bring the thing down upon him. For a space he stared up, reining in his prancing horse with the instinct born of years of horsemanship. Then the flat of a sword smote his back, and a blade flashed overhead and cut the drifting balloon of spider-web free, and the whole mass lifted softly and drove clear and away.

"Spiders!" cried the voice of the gaunt man. "The things are full of big spiders! Look, my lord!"

The man with the silver bridle still followed the mass that drove away.

"Look, my lord!"

The master found himself staring down at a red, smashed thing on the ground that, in spite of partial obliteration, could still wriggle unavailing legs. Then when the gaunt man pointed to another mass that bore down upon them, he drew his sword hastily. Up the valley now it was like a fog bank torn to rags. He tried to grasp the situation.

"Ride for it!" the little man was shouting. "Ride for it down the valley."

What happened then was like the confusion of a battle. The man with the silver bridle saw the little man go past him slashing furiously at imaginary cobwebs, saw him cannon into the horse of the gaunt man and hurl it and its rider to earth. His own horse went a dozen paces before he could rein it in. Then he looked up to avoid imaginary dangers, and then back again to see a horse rolling on the ground, the gaunt man standing and slashing over it at a rent and fluttering mass of grey that streamed and wrapped about them both. And thick and fast as thistle-down on waste land on a windy day in July, the cobweb masses were coming on.

The little man had dismounted, but he dared not release his horse. He was endeavouring to lug the struggling brute back with the strength of one arm, while with the other he slashed aimlessly, The tentacles of a second grey mass had entangled themselves with the struggle, and this second grey mass came to its moorings, and slowly sank.

The master set his teeth, gripped his bridle, lowered his head, and spurred his horse forward. The horse on the ground rolled over, there were blood and moving shapes upon the flanks, and the gaunt man, suddenly leaving it, ran forward towards his master, perhaps ten paces. His legs were swathed and encumbered with grey; he made ineffectual movements with his sword. Grey streamers waved from him; there was a thin veil of grey across his face. With his left hand he beat at something on his body, and suddenly he stumbled and fell. He struggled to rise, and fell again, and suddenly, horribly, began to howl, "Oh—ohoo, ohooh!"

The master could see the great spiders upon him, and others upon the ground.

As he strove to force his horse nearer to this gesticulating, screaming grey object that struggled up and down, there came a clatter of hoofs, and the little man, in act of mounting, swordless, balanced on his belly athwart the white horse, and clutching its mane, whirled past. And again a clinging thread of grey gossamer swept across the master's face. All about him, and over him, it seemed this drifting, noiseless cobweb circled and drew nearer him. . . .

To the day of his death he never knew just how the event of that moment happened. Did he, indeed, turn his horse, or did it really of its own accord stampede after its fellow? Suffice it that in another second he was galloping full tilt down the valley with his sword whirling furiously overhead. And all about him on the quickening breeze, the spiders' airships, their air bundles and air sheets, seemed to him to hurry in a conscious pursuit.

Clatter, clatter, thud, thud—the man with the silver bridle rode, heedless of his direction, with his fearful face looking up now right, now left, and his sword arm ready to slash. And a few hundred yards ahead of him, with a tail of torn cobweb trailing behind him, rode the little man on the white horse, still but imperfectly in the saddle. The reeds bent before them, the wind blew fresh and strong, over his shoulder the master could see the webs hurrying to overtake. . . .

He was so intent to escape the spiders' webs that only as his horse gathered together for a leap did he realise the ravine ahead. And then he realised it only to misunderstand and interfere. He was leaning forward on his horse's neck and sat up and back all too late.

But if in his excitement he had failed to leap, at any rate he had not forgotten how to fall. He was horseman again in mid-air. He came off clear with a mere bruise upon his shoulder, and his horse rolled, kicking spasmodic legs, and lay still. But the master's sword drove its point into the hard soil, and snapped clean across, as though Chance refused him any longer as her Knight, and the splintered end missed his face by an inch or so.

He was on his feet in a moment, breathlessly scanning the onrushing spider-webs. For a moment he was minded to run, and then thought of the ravine, and turned back. He ran aside once to dodge one drifting terror, and then he was swiftly clambering down the precipitous sides, and out of the touch of the gale.

There under the lee of the dry torrent's steeper banks he might crouch, and watch these strange, grey masses pass and pass in safety till the wind fell, and it became possible to escape. And there for a long time he crouched, watching the strange, grey, ragged masses trail their streamers across his narrowed sky.

Once a stray spider fell into the ravine close beside him—a full foot it measured from leg to leg, and its body was half a man's hand—and after he had watched its monstrous alacrity of search and escape for a little while, and tempted it to bite his broken sword, he lifted up his iron-heeled boot and smashed it into a pulp. He swore as he did so, and for a time sought up and down for another.

Then presently, when he was surer these spider swarms could not drop into the ravine, he found a place where he could sit down, and sat and fell into deep thought and began after his manner to gnaw his knuckles and bite his nails. And from this he was moved by the coming of the man with the white horse.

He heard him long before he saw him, as a clattering of hoofs, stumbling footsteps, and a reassuring voice. Then the little man appeared, a rueful figure, still with a tail of white cobweb trailing behind him. They approached each other without speaking, without a salutation. The little man was fatigued and shamed to the pitch of hopeless bitterness, and came to a stop at last, face to face with his seated master. The latter winced a little under his dependant's eye. "Well?" he said at last, with no pretence of authority.

"You left him?"

"My horse bolted."

"I know. So did mine."

He laughed at his master mirthlessly.

"I say my horse bolted," said the man who once had a silver-studded bridle.

"Cowards both," said the little man.

The other gnawed his knuckle through some meditative moments, with his eye on his inferior.

"Don't call me a coward," he said at length.

"You are a coward like myself."

"A coward possibly. There is a limit beyond which every man must fear. That I have learnt at last. But not like yourself. That is where the difference comes in."

"I never could have dreamt you would have left him. He saved your life two minutes before. . . . Why are you our lord?"

The master gnawed his knuckles again, and his countenance was dark.

"No man calls me a coward," he said. "No. . . . A broken sword is better than none. . . . One spavined white horse cannot be expected to carry two men a four days' journey. I hate white horses, but this time it cannot be helped. You begin to understand me?. . . I perceive that you are minded, on the strength of what you have seen and fancy, to taint my reputation. It is men of your sort who unmake kings. Besides which—I never liked you."

"My lord!" said the little man.

"No," said the master. *"No!"*

He stood up sharply as the little man moved. For a minute perhaps they faced one another. Overhead the spiders' balls went driving. There was a quick movement among the pebbles; a running of feet, a cry of despair, a gasp and a blow. . . .

Towards nightfall the wind fell. The sun set in a calm serenity, and the man who had once possessed the silver bridle came at last very cautiously and by an easy slope out of the ravine again; but now he led the white horse that once belonged to the little man. He would have gone back to his horse to get his silver-mounted bridle again, but he feared night and a quickening breeze might still find him in the valley, and besides he disliked greatly to think he might discover his horse all swathed in cobwebs and perhaps unpleasantly eaten.

And as he thought of those cobwebs and of all the dangers he had been through, and the manner in which he had been preserved that day, his hand sought a little reliquary that hung about his neck, and he clasped it for a moment with heartfelt gratitude. As he did so his eyes went across the valley.

"I was hot with passion," he said, "and now she has met her reward. They also, no doubt—"

And behold! Far away out of the wooded slopes across the valley, but in the clearness of the sunset distinct and unmistakable, he saw a little spire of smoke.

At that his expression of serene resignation changed to an amazed anger. Smoke? He turned the head of the white horse about, and hesitated. And as he did so a little rustle of air went through the grass about him. Far away upon some reeds swayed a tattered sheet of grey. He looked at the cobwebs; he looked at the smoke.

"Perhaps, after all, it is not them," he said at last.

But he knew better.

After he had stared at the smoke for some time, he mounted the white horse.

As he rode, he picked his way amidst stranded masses of web. For some reason there were many dead spiders on the ground, and those that lived feasted guiltily on their fellows. At the sound of his horse's hoofs they fled.

Their time had passed. From the ground without either a wind to carry them or a winding sheet ready, these things, for all their poison, could do him little evil.

He flicked with his belt at those he fancied came too near. Once, where a number ran together over a bare place, he was minded to dismount and trample them with his boots, but this impulse he overcame. Ever and again he turned in his saddle, and looked back at the smoke.

"Spiders," he muttered over and over again. "Spiders! Well, well. . . . The next time I must spin a web."

T
is for
Transformed

Terrifying transformations are a staple of supernatural horror fiction. In this tale, first published in the January 14, 1832, edition of the *Philadelphia Saturday Courier,* American master of the macabre, Edgar Allan Poe (1809–1849), suggests an unholy metempsychosis that binds together two rivals in life and, inevitably, death.

EDGAR ALLAN POE

Metzengerstein

Pestis eram vivus—moriens tua mors ero.
MARTIN LUTHER

Horror and fatality have been stalking abroad in all ages. Why then give a date to the story I have to tell? Let it suffice to say, that at the period of which I speak, there existed, in the interior of Hungary, a settled although hidden belief in the doctrines of the Metempsychosis. Of the doctrines themselves—that is, of their falsity, or of their probability—I say nothing. I assert, however, that much of our incredulity (as La Bruyere says of all our unhappiness) *"vient de ne pouvoir être seuls."**

*Mercier, in *"L'an deux mille quarte cents quarante,"* seriously maintains the doctrines of Metempsychosis, and I. D'Israeli says that "no system is so simple and so little repugnant to the understanding." Colonel Ethan Allen, the "Green Mountain Boy," is also said to have been a serious metempsychosist.

But there are some points in the Hungarian superstition which were fast verging to absurdity. They—the Hungarians—differed very essentially from their Eastern authorities. For example, *"The soul,"* said the former—I give the words of an acute and intelligent Parisian—*"ne demeure qu'un seul fois dans un corps sensible: au reste—un cheval, un chien, un homme meme, n'est que la ressemblance peu tangible de ces animaux."*

The families of Berlifitzing and Metzengerstein had been at variance for centuries. Never before were two houses so illustrious, mutually embittered by hostility so deadly. The origin of this enmity seems to be found in the words of an ancient prophecy—"A lofty name shall have a fearful fall when, as the rider over his horse, the mortality of Metzengerstein shall triumph over the immortality of Berlifitzing."

To be sure the words themselves had little or no meaning. But more trivial causes have given rise—and that no long while ago—to consequences equally eventful. Besides, the estates, which were contiguous, had long exercised a rival influence in the affairs of a busy government. Moreover, near neighbors are seldom friends; and the inhabitants of the Castle Berlifitzing might look, from their lofty buttresses, into the very windows of the Palace Metzengerstein. Least of all had the more than feudal magnificence, thus discovered, a tendency to allay the irritable feelings of the less ancient and less wealthy Berlifitzings. What wonder, then, that the words, however silly, of that prediction, should have succeeded in setting and keeping at variance two families already predisposed to quarrel by every instigation of hereditary jealousy? The prophecy seemed to imply—if it implied anything—a final triumph on the part of the already more powerful house; and was of course remembered with the more bitter animosity by the weaker and less influential.

Wilhelm, Count Berlifitzing, although loftily descended, was, at the epoch of this narrative, an infirm and doting old man, remarkable for nothing but an inordinate and inveterate personal antipathy to the family of his rival, and so passionate a love of horses, and of hunting, that neither bodily infirmity, great age, nor mental incapacity, prevented his daily participation in the dangers of the chase.

Frederick, Baron Metzengerstein, was, on the other hand, not yet of age. His father, the Minister G——, died young. His mother, the Lady Mary, followed him quickly. Frederick was, at that time, in his eighteenth year. In a city, eighteen years are no long period; but in a wilderness—in so magnificent a wilderness as that old principality, the pendulum vibrates with a deeper meaning.

From some peculiar circumstances attending the administration of his father, the young Baron, at the decease of the former, entered immediately upon his vast possessions. Such estates were seldom held before by a nobleman of Hungary. His castles were without number. The chief in point of splendor and extent was the "Palace Metzengerstein." The boundary line of his dominions was never clearly defined; but his principal park embraced a circuit of fifty miles.

Upon the succession of a proprietor so young, with a character so well known, to a fortune so unparalleled, little speculation was afloat in regard to his probable course of conduct. And, indeed, for the space of three days, the behavior of the heir out-heroded Herod, and fairly surpassed the expectations of his most enthusiastic admirers. Shameful debaucheries—flagrant treacheries—unheard-of atrocities—gave his trembling vassals quickly to understand that no servile submission on their part—no punctilios of conscience on his own—were thenceforward to prove any security against the remorseless fangs of a petty Caligula. On the night of the fourth day, the stables of the Castle Berlifitzing were discovered to be on fire; and the unanimous opinion of the neighborhood added the crime of the incendiary to the already hideous list of the Baron's misdemeanors and enormities.

But during the tumult occasioned by this occurrence, the young nobleman himself sat apparently buried in meditation, in a vast and desolate upper apartment of the family palace of Metzengerstein. The rich although faded tapestry hangings which swung gloomily upon the walls, represented the shadowy and majestic forms of a thousand illustrious ancestors. *Here,* rich-ermined priests, and pontifical dignitaries, familiarly seated with the autocrat and the sovereign, put a veto on the wishes of a temporal king, or restrained with the fiat of papal supremacy the rebellious sceptre of the Arch-enemy. *There,* the dark, tall statures of the Princes Metzengerstein—their muscular war-coursers plunging over the carcasses of fallen foes—startled the steadiest nerves with their vigorous expression; and *here,* again, the voluptuous and swan-like figures of the dames of days gone by, floated away in the mazes of an unreal dance to the strains of imaginary melody.

But as the Baron listened, or affected to listen, to the gradually increasing uproar in the stables of Berlifitzing—or perhaps pondered upon some more novel, some more decided act of audacity—his eyes were turned unwittingly to the figure of an enormous, and unnaturally colored horse, represented in the tapestry as belonging to a Saracen ancestor of the family of his rival. The horse itself, in the fore-ground of the design, stood motionless and statue-like—while, farther back, its discomfited rider perished by the dagger of a Metzengerstein.

On Frederick's lip arose a fiendish expression, as he became aware of the direction which his glance had, without his consciousness, assumed. Yet he did not remove it. On the contrary, he could by no means account for the overwhelming anxiety which appeared falling like a pall upon his senses. It was with difficulty that he reconciled his dreamy and incoherent feelings with the certainty of being awake. The longer he gazed, the more absorbing became the spell—the more impossible did it appear that he could ever withdraw his glance from the fascination of that tapestry. But the tumult without becoming suddenly more violent, with a compulsory exertion he diverted his attention to the glare of ruddy light thrown full by the flaming stables upon the windows of the apartment.

The action, however, was but momentary; his gaze returned mechanically to the wall. To his extreme horror and astonishment, the head of the gigantic steed had, in the meantime, altered its position. The neck of the animal, before arched, as if in compassion, over the prostrate body of its lord, was now extended, at full length, in the direction of the Baron. The eyes, before invisible, now wore an energetic and human expression, while they gleamed with a fiery and unusual red; and the distended lips of the apparently enraged horse left in full view his sepulchral and disgusting teeth.

Stupified with terror, the young nobleman tottered to the door. As he threw it open, a flash of red light, streaming far into the chamber, flung his shadow with a clear outline against the quivering tapestry; and he shuddered to perceive that shadow—as he staggered awhile upon the threshold—assuming the exact position, and precisely filling up the contour, of the relentless and triumphant murderer of the Saracen Berlifitzing.

To lighten the depression of his spirits, the Baron hurried into the open air. At the principal gate of the palace he encountered three equerries. With much difficulty, and at the imminent peril of their lives, they were restraining the convulsive plunges of a gigantic and fiery-colored horse.

"Whose horse? Where did you get him?" demanded the youth, in a querulous and husky tone, as he became instantly aware that the mysterious steed in the tapestried chamber was the very counterpart of the furious animal before his eyes.

"He is your own property, sire," replied one of the equerries, "at least he is claimed by no other owner. We caught him flying, all smoking and foaming with rage, from the burning stables of the Castle Berlifitzing. Supposing him to have belonged to the old Count's stud of foreign horses, we led him back as an estray. But the grooms there disclaim any title to the creature; which is strange, since he bears evident marks of having made a narrow escape from the flames."

"The letters W. V. B. are also branded very distinctly on his forehead," interrupted a second equerry; "I supposed them, of course, to be the initials of Wilhelm Von Berlifitzing—but all at the castle are positive in denying any knowledge of the horse."

"Extremely singular!" said the young Baron, with a musing air, and apparently unconscious of the meaning of his words. "He is, as you say, a remarkable horse—a prodigious horse! although, as you very justly observe, of a suspicious and untractable character; let him be mine, however," he added, after a pause, "perhaps a rider like Frederick of Metzengerstein, may tame even the devil from the stables of Berlifitzing."

"You are mistaken, my lord; the horse, as I think we mentioned, is *not* from the stables of the Count. If such had been the case, we know our duty better than to bring him into the presence of a noble of your family."

"True!" observed the Baron, drily; and at that instant a page of the bedchamber came from the palace with a heightened color, and a precipitate step. He whispered into his master's ear an account of the sudden disappearance of a small portion of the tapestry, in an apartment which he designated; entering, at the same time, into particulars of a minute and circumstantial character; but from the low tone of voice in which these latter were communicated, nothing escaped to gratify the excited curiosity of the equerries.

The young Frederick, during the conference, seemed agitated by a variety of emotions. He soon, however, recovered his composure, and an expression of determined malignancy settled upon his countenance, as he gave peremptory orders that the apartment in question should be immediately locked up, and the key placed in his own possession.

"Have you heard of the unhappy death of the old hunter Berlifitzing?" said one of his vassals to the Baron, as, after the departure of the page, the huge steed which that nobleman had adopted as his own, plunged and curveted, with redoubled fury, down the long avenue which extended from the palace to the stables of Metzengerstein.

"No!" said the Baron, turning abruptly toward the speaker, "dead! say you?"

"It is indeed true, my lord; and, to the noble of your name, will be, I imagine, no unwelcome intelligence."

A rapid smile shot over the countenance of the listener. "How died he?"

"In his rash exertions to rescue a favorite portion of his hunting stud, he has himself perished miserably in the flames."

"I-n-d-e-e-d-!" ejaculated the Baron, as if slowly and deliberately impressed with the truth of some exciting idea

"Indeed;" repeated the vassal.

"Shocking!" said the youth, calmly, and turned quietly into the palace.

From this date a marked alteration took place in the outward demeanor of the dissolute young Baron Frederick Von Metzengerstein. Indeed, his behavior disappointed every expectation, and proved little in accordance with the views of many a manœuvering mamma; while his habits and manner, still less than formerly, offered anything congenial with those of the neighboring aristocracy. He was never to be seen beyond the limits of his own domain, and, in this wide and social world, was utterly companionless—unless, indeed, that unnatural, impetuous, and fiery-colored horse, which he henceforward continually bestrode, had any mysterious right to the title of his friend.

Numerous invitations on the part of the neighborhood for a long time, however, periodically came in. "Will the Baron honor our festivals with his presence?" "Will the Baron join us in a hunting of the boar?"—"Metzengerstein does not hunt"; "Metzengerstein will not attend," were the haughty and laconic answers.

These repeated insults were not to be endured by an imperious nobility. Such invitations became less cordial—less frequent—in time they ceased altogether. The widow of the unfortunate Count Berlifitzing was even heard to express a hope "that the Baron might be at home when he did not wish to be at home, since he disdained the company of his equals; and ride when he did not wish to ride, since he preferred the society of a horse." This to be sure was a very silly explosion of hereditary pique; and merely proved how singularly unmeaning our sayings are apt to become, when we desire to be unusually energetic.

The charitable, nevertheless, attributed the alteration in the conduct of the young nobleman to the natural sorrow of a son for the untimely loss of his parents;—forgetting, however, his atrocious and reckless behavior during the short period immediately succeeding that bereavement. Some there were, indeed, who suggested a too haughty idea of self-consequence and dignity. Others again (among whom may be mentioned the family physician) did not hesitate in speaking of morbid melancholy, and hereditary ill-health; while dark hints, of a more equivocal nature, were current among the multitude.

Indeed, the Baron's perverse attachment to his lately-acquired charger—an attachment which seemed to attain new strength from every fresh example of the animal's ferocious and demon-like propensities—at length became, in the eyes of all reasonable men, a hideous and unnatural fervor. In the glare of noon—at the dead hour of night—in sickness or in health—in calm or in tempest—the young Metzengerstein seemed riveted to the saddle of that colossal horse, whose intractable audacities so well accorded with his own spirit.

There were circumstances, moreover, which coupled with late events, gave an unearthly and portentous character to the mania of the rider, and to the capabilities of the steed. The space passed over in a single leap had been accurately measured, and was found to exceed by an astounding difference, the wildest expectations of the most imaginative. The Baron, besides, had no particular *name* for the animal, although all the rest in his collection were distinguished by characteristic appellations. His stable, too, was appointed at a distance from the rest; and with regard to grooming and other necessary offices, none but the owner in person had ventured to officiate, or even to enter the enclosure of that particular stall. It was also to be observed, that although the three grooms, who had caught the steed as he fled from the conflagration at Berlifitzing, had succeeded in arresting his course, by means of a chain-bridle and noose—yet no one of the three could with any certainty affirm that he had, during that dangerous struggle, or at any period thereafter, actually placed his hand upon the body of the beast. Instances of peculiar intelligence in the demeanor of a noble and high-spirited horse are not to be supposed capable of exciting unreasonable attention, but there were certain circumstances which intruded themselves per force upon the most skeptical and phlegmatic; and it is said there were times when the animal caused the gaping crowd who stood around to recoil in horror from the deep and impressive meaning of his terrible stamp—times when the young Metzengerstein turned pale and shrunk away from the rapid and searching expression of his earnest and human-looking eye.

Among all the retinue of the Baron, however, none were found to doubt the ardor of that extraordinary affection which existed on the part of the young nobleman for the fiery qualities of his horse; at least, none but an insignificant and misshapen little page, whose deformities were in every body's way, and whose opinions were of the least possible importance. He (if his ideas are worth mentioning at all), had the effrontery to assert that his master never vaulted into the saddle without an unaccountable and almost imperceptible shudder; and that, upon his return from every long-continued and habitual ride, an expression of triumphant malignity distorted every muscle in his countenance.

One tempestuous night, Metzengerstein, awaking from a heavy slumber, descended like a maniac from his chamber, and, mounting in hot haste, bounded away into the mazes of the forest. An occurrence so common attracted no particular attention, but his return was looked for with intense anxiety on the part of his domestics, when, after some hours' absence, the stupendous and magnificent battlements of the Palace Metzengerstein, were discovered crackling and rocking to their very foundation, under the influence of a dense and livid mass of ungovernable fire.

As the flames, when first seen, had already made so terrible a progress that all efforts to save any portion of the building were evidently futile, the astonished neighborhood stood idly around in silent, if not apathetic wonder. But a new and fearful object soon riveted the attention of the multitude, and proved how much more intense is the excitement wrought in the feelings of a crowd by the contemplation of human agony, than that brought about by the most appalling spectacles of inanimate matter.

Up the long avenue of aged oaks which led from the forest to the main entrance of the Palace Metzengerstein, a steed, bearing an unbonneted and disordered rider, was seen leaping with an impetuosity which outstripped the very Demon of the Tempest.

The career of the horseman was indisputably, on his own part, uncontrollable. The agony of his countenance, the convulsive struggle of his frame, gave evidence of superhuman exertion: but no sound, save a solitary shriek, escaped from his lacerated lips, which were bitten through and through in the intensity of terror. One instant, and the clattering of hoofs resounded sharply and shrilly above the roaring of the flames and the shrieking of the winds—another, and, clearing at a single plunge the gate-way and the moat, the steed bounded far up the tottering staircases of the palace, and, with its rider, disappeared amid the whirlwind of chaotic fire.

The fury of the tempest immediately died away, and a dead calm sullenly succeeded. A white flame still enveloped the building like a shroud, and, streaming far away into the quiet atmosphere, shot forth a glare of preternatural light; while a cloud of smoke settled heavily over the battlements in the distinct colossal figure of—*a horse.*

U *is for* Unknown

By their very nature, tales of supernatural horror attempt to impose shape and substance upon the Unknown. In this story, first published in his 1911 collection *Here and Hereafter,* British writer Barry Pain (1864–1928) gives intimidating physicality to an uncanny presence whose nature remains just beyond the pale of human comprehension.

BARRY PAIN

The Tower

In the billiard room of the Cabinet Club, shortly after midnight, two men had just finished a game. A third had been watching it from the lounge at the end of the room. The winner put up his cue. slipped on his coat, and with a brief "Good-night" passed out of the room. He was tall, dark, clean-shaven and foreign in appearance. It would not have been easy to guess his nationality, but he did not look English.

The loser, a fair-haired boy of twenty-five, came over to the lounge and dropped down by the side of the elderly man who had been watching the billiards.

"Silly game, ain't it, doctor?" he said cheerfully. The doctor smiled.

"Yes," he said, "Vyse is a bit too hot for you, Bill."

"A bit too hot for anything," said the boy. "He never takes any trouble; he never hesitates; he never thinks; he never takes an easy shot when there's a brilliant one to be pulled off. It's almost uncanny."

"Ah," said the doctor, reflectively, "it's a queer thing. You're the third man whom I heard say that about Vyse within the last week."

"I believe he's quite alright—good sort of chap, you know. He's frightfully clever too—speaks a lot of beastly difficult Oriental languages—does well at any game he takes up."

"Yes," said the doctor, "he is clever; and he is also a fool."

"What do you mean? He's eccentric, of course. Fancy his buying that rotten tower—a sweet place to spend Christmas in all alone, I don't think."

"Why does he say he's going there?"

"Says he hates the conventional Christmas, and wants to be out of it; says also that he wants to shoot duck."

"That won't do," said the doctor. "He may hate the conventional Christmas. He may, and probably will, shoot duck. But that's not his reason for going there."

"Then what is it?" asked the boy.

"Nothing that would interest you much, Bill. Vyse is one of the chaps that want to know too much. He's playing about in a way that every medical man knows to be a rotten, dangerous way. Mind, he may get at something; if the stories are true he has already got at a good deal. I believe it is possible for a man to develop in himself certain powers at a certain price."

"What's the price?"

"Insanity, often as not. Here, let's talk about something pleasanter. Where are you yourself going this Christmas, by the way?"

"My sister has taken compassion upon this lone bachelor. And you?"

"I shall be out of England," said the doctor. "Cairo, probably."

The two men passed out into the hall of the club.

"Has Mr. Vyse gone yet," the boy asked the porter.

"Not yet, Sir William. Mr. Vyse is changing in one of the dressing rooms. His car is outside."

The two men passed the car in the street, and noticed the luggage in the tonneau. The driver, in his long leather coat, stood motionless beside it, waiting for his master. The powerful headlight raked the dusk of the street; you could see the paint on a tired woman's cheek as she passed through it on her way home at last.

"See his game?" said Bill.

"Of course," said the doctor. "He's off to the marshes and that blessed tower of his tonight."

"Well, I don't envy him—holy sort of amusement it must be driving all that way on a cold night like this. I wonder if the beggar ever goes to sleep at all?"

They had reached Bill's chambers in Jermyn Street.

"You must come in and have a drink," said Bill.

"Don't think so, thanks," said the doctor; "it's late, you know."

"You'd better," said Bill, and the doctor followed him in.

A letter and a telegram were lying on the table in the diminutive hall. The letter had been sent by messenger, and was addressed to Sir William Orsley, Bart., in a remarkably small handwriting. Bill picked it up, and thrust it into his pocket at once, unopened. He took the telegram with him into the room where the drinks had been put out, and opened it as he sipped his whisky-and-soda.

"Great Scot!" he exclaimed.

"Nothing serious, I hope," said the doctor.

"I hope not. I suppose all the children have got to have the measles some time or another; but it's just a bit unlucky that my sister's three should all go down with it just now. That does for her house-party at Christmas, of course."

A few minutes later, when the doctor had gone, Bill took the letter from his pocket and tore it open. A cheque fell from the envelope and fluttered to the ground. The letter ran as follows:

> "Dear Bill,—I could not talk to you tonight, as the doctor, who happens to disapprove of me, was in the billiard-room. Of course, I can let you have the hundred you want, and enclose it herewith with the utmost pleasure. The time you mention for repayment would suit me all right, and so would any other time. Suit your own convenience entirely.
>
> "I have a favour to ask of you. I know you are intending to go down to the Leylands' for Christmas. I think you will be prevented from doing so. If that is the case, and you have no better engagement, would you hold yourself at my disposal for a week? It is just possible that I may want a man like you pretty badly. There ought to be plenty of duck this weather, but I don't know that I can offer any other attraction—Very sincerely yours,
>
> "Edward Vyse."

Bill picked up the cheque and thrust it into the drawer with a feeling of relief. It was a queer invitation, he thought—funnily worded, with the usual intimations of time and place missing. He switched off the electric lights and went into his bedroom. As he was undressing a thought struck him suddenly.

"How the deuce," he said aloud, "did he know that I should be prevented from going to Polly's place?" Then he looked round quickly. He thought that he had heard a faint laugh just behind him. No one was there, and Bill's nerves were good enough. In twenty minutes he was fast asleep.

The cottage, built of grey stone, stood some thirty yards back from the road, from which it was screened by a shrubbery. It was an ordinary eight-roomed cottage, and it did well enough for Vyse and his servants and one guest—if Vyse happened to want a guest. There was a pleasant little walled garden of a couple of acres behind the cottage. Through a doorway in the further wall one passed into a stunted and dismal plantation, and in the middle of this rose the tower, far higher than any of the trees that surrounded it.

Sir William Orsley had arrived just in time to change before dinner. Talk at dinner had been of indifferent subjects—the queer characters of the village, and the chances of sport on the morrow. Bill had mentioned the tower, and his host had hastened to talk of other things. But now that dinner was over, and the man who had waited on them had left the room, Vyse of his own accord returned to the subject.

"Danvers is a superstitious ass," he observed, "and he's in quite enough of a funk about that tower as it is; that's why I wouldn't give you the story of it while he was in the room. According to the village tradition, a witch was burned on the site where the tower now stands, and she declared that where she burned the devil should have his house. The lord of the manor at that time, hearing what the old lady had said, and wishing to discourage house-building on that particular site, had it covered with a plantation, and made it a condition of his will that this plantation should be kept up."

Bill lit a cigar. "Looks like checkmate," he said. "However, seeing that the tower is actually there—"

"Quite so. This man's son came no end of a cropper, and the property changed hands several times. It was divided and sub-divided. I, for instance, only own about twenty acres of it. Presently there came along a scientific old gentleman and bought the piece that I now have. Whether he knew of the story, or whether he didn't, I cannot say, but he set to work to build the tower that is now standing in the middle of the plantation. He may have intended it as an observatory. He got the stone for it on the spot from his own quarry, but he had to import his labour, as the people in these parts didn't think the work healthy. Then one fine morning before the tower was finished they found the old gentleman at the bottom of his quarry with his neck broken."

"So," said Bill, "they say of course that the tower is haunted. What is it that they think they see?"

"Nothing. You can't see it. But there are people who think they have touched it and have heard it."

"Rot, ain't it?"

"I don't know exactly. You see, I happen to be one of those people."

"Then, if you think so, there's something in it. This is interesting. I say, can't we go across there now?"

"Certainly, if you like. Sure you won't have any more wine? Come along, then."

The two men slipped on their coats and caps. Vyse carried a lighted stable-lantern. It was a frosty moonlit night, and the path was crisp and hard beneath their feet. As Vyse slid back the bolts of the gate in the garden wall, Bill said suddenly, "By the way, Vyse, how did you know that I shouldn't be at the Leylands' this Christmas? I told you I was going there."

"I don't know. I had a feeling that you were going to be with me. It might have been wrong. Anyhow, I'm very glad you're here. You are just exactly the man I want. We've only a few steps to go now. The path is ours. That cart-track leads away to the quarry where the scientific gentleman took the short cut to further knowledge. And here is the door of the tower."

They walked round the tower before entering. The night was so still that, unconsciously, they spoke in lowered voices and trod as softly as possible. The lock of the heavy door groaned and screeched as the key turned. The light of the lantern fell now on the white sand of the floor and on a broken spiral staircase on the further side. Far up above one saw a tangle of beams and the stars beyond them. Bill heard Vyse saying that it was left like that after the death in the quarry.

"It's a good solid bit of masonry," said Bill, "but it ain't a cheerful spot exactly. And, by Jove! It smells like a menagerie."

"It does," said Vyse, who was examining the sand on the floor.

Bill also looked down at the prints in the sand. "Some dog's been in here."

"No," said Vyse, thoughtfully. "Dogs won't come in here, and you can't make them. Also, there were no marks on the sand when I left the place and locked the door this afternoon. Queer, isn't it?"

"But the thing's a blank impossibility. Unless, of course, we are to suppose that—"

He did not finish his sentence, and, if he had finished it, it would not have been audible. A chorus of grunting, growling, and squealing broke out almost from under his feet, and he sprang backwards. It lasted for a few seconds, and then died slowly away.

"Did you hear that," Vyse asked quietly.

"I should rather think so."

"Good; then it was not subjective. What was it?"

"Only one kind of beast makes that row. Pigs, of course—a whole drove of them. It sounded like they were in here, close to us. But as they obviously are not, they must be outside."

"But they are not outside," said Vyse. "Come and see."

They hunted the plantation through and through with no result, and then locked the tower door and went back to the cottage. Bill said very little. He was not capable of much self-analysis, but he was conscious of a sudden dislike of Vyse. He was angry that he had ever put himself under an obligation to this man. He had wanted the money for a gambling debt, and he had already repaid it. Now he saw Vyse in the light of a man with whom one should have no dealings, and the last man from whom one should accept a kindness. The strange experience that he had just been through filled him with a loathing far more than with fear or wonder. There was something unclean and diabolical about the whole thing that made a decent man reluctant to question or investigate. The filthy smell of the brutes seemed still to linger in his nostrils. He was determined that on no account would he enter the tower again, and that as soon as he could find a decent excuse he would leave the place altogether.

A little later, as he sat before the log fire and filled his pipe, he turned to his host with a sudden question: "I say, Vyse, why did you want me to come down here? What's the meaning of it all?"

"My dear fellow," said Vyse, "I wanted you for the pleasure of your society. Now, don't get impatient. I also wanted you because you are the most normal man I know. Your confirmation of my experiences in the tower is most valuable to me. Also, you have good nerves, and, if you will forgive me for saying so, no imagination. I may want help that only a man with good nerves would be able to give."

"Why don't you leave the thing alone? It's too beastly."

Vyse laughed. "I'm afraid my hobby bores you. We won't talk about it. After all, there's no reason why you should help me?"

"Tell me just what it is that you wanted."

"I wanted you if you heard this whistle"—he took an ordinary police whistle down from the mantelpiece—"any time tonight or tomorrow night, to come over to the tower at once and bring a revolver with you. The whistle would be a sign that I was in a tight place—that my life, in fact, was in danger. You see, we are dealing here with something preternatural, but it is also something material; in addition to other risks, one risks ordinary physical destruction. However, I could see that you were repelled by the sight and sound of those beasts, whatever they may be; and I can tell you from my own experience that the touch of them is even worse. There is no reason why you should bother yourself any further about the thing."

"You can take the whistle with you," said Bill. "If I hear it I will come."

"Thanks," said Vyse, and immediately changed the subject. He did not say why he was spending the night in the tower, or what it was he proposed to do there.

It was three in the morning when Bill was suddenly startled out of his sleep. He heard the whistle being blown repeatedly. He hurried on some clothes and dashed down into the hall, where his lantern lay all ready for him. He ran along the garden path and through the door in the wall until he got to the tower. The sound of the whistle had ceased now, and everything was horribly still. The door of the tower stood wide open, and without hesitation Bill entered, holding his lantern high.

The tower was absolutely empty. Not a sound was to be heard. Bill called Vyse by name twice loudly, and then again the awful silence spread over the place.

Then, as if guided by some unseen hand, he took the track that led to the quarry, well knowing what he would find at the bottom of it.

The jury assigned the death of Vyse as an accident, and said that the quarry should be fenced in. They had no explanation to offer of the mutilation of the face, as if by the teeth of some savage beast.

V is for Vampire

If you think all vampires are fanged figures of the un-dead who prowl by night to feast on the blood of the living—think again. This story, by British writer Ulric Daubeny (1888–1922), appeared more than a century ago in his 1919 collection *The Elemental*, and it features an ingenious variation on a theme from vampire folklore, inspired by observation of the plant world.

ULRIC DAUBENY

The Sumach

"How red that Sumach is!"

Irene Barton murmured something commonplace, for to her the tree brought painful recollections. Her visitor, unconscious of this fact, proceeded to elaborate.

"Do you know, Irene, that tree gives me the creeps! I can't explain, except that it is not a nice tree, not a *good* tree. For instance, why should its leaves be red in August, when they are not supposed to turn until October?"

"What queer ideas you have, May! The tree is right enough, although its significance to me is sad. Poor Spot, you know; we buried him beneath it two days ago. Come and see his grave."

The two women left the terrace, where this conversation had been taking place, and leisurely strolled across the lawn, at the end of which, in almost startling isolation, grew the Sumach. At least, Mrs. Watcombe, who evinced so great an interest in the tree, questioned whether it actually was a Sumach, for the foliage was unusual, and the branches gnarled and twisted beyond recognition. Just now, the leaves were stained with splashes of dull crimson, but rather than droop, they had a bloated appearance, as if the luxuriance of the growth were not altogether healthy.

For several moments they stood regarding the pathetic little grave, and the silence was only broken when Mrs. Watcombe darted beneath the tree and came back with something in her hand.

"Irene, look at this dead thrush. Poor little thing! Such splendid plumage, yet it hardly weighs a sugar plum!"

Mrs. Barton regarded it with wrinkled brows.

"I cannot understand what happens to the birds, May—unless someone lays poison. We continually find them dead about the garden, and usually beneath, or very near this tree."

It is doubtful whether Mrs. Watcombe listened. Her attention seemed to wander that morning, and she was studying the twisted branches of the Sumach with a thoughtful scrutiny.

"Curious that the leaves should turn at this time of year," she murmured. "It brings to mind poor Geraldine's illness. This tree had an extraordinary fascination for her, you know. It was quite scarlet then, yet that was only June, and it had barely finished shooting."

"My dear May! You have red leaves on the brain this morning!" Irene retorted, uncertain whether to be irritated or amused. "I can't think why you are so concerned about the colour. It is only the result of two days' excessive heat, for scarcely a leaf was touched, when I buried poor old Spot."

The conversation seemed absurdly trivial, yet, Mrs. Watcombe gone, Irene could not keep her mind from dwelling on her cousin's fatal illness. The news had reached them with the shock of the absolutely unexpected. Poor Geraldine, who had always been so strong, to have fallen victim to acute anæmia! It was almost unbelievable, that heart failure should have put an end to her sweet young life, after a few days' ailing. Of course, the sad event had wrought a wonderful change for Irene and her husband, giving them, in place of a cramped suburban villa, this beautiful country home, Cleeve Grange. Everything for her was filled with the delight of novelty, for she had ruled as mistress over the charmed abode for only one short week. Hilary, her husband, was yet a stranger to the more intimate of its attractions, being detained in London by the winding up of business affairs.

Several days elapsed, for the most part given solely to the keen pleasure of arranging and re-arranging the new home. As went by, the crimson splashes on the Sumach faded, the leaves becoming green again, though drooping as if from want of moisture. Irene noticed this when she paid her daily visits to the pathetic little dog grave, trying to induce flowers to take root upon it, but do what she might, they invariably faded. Nothing, not even grass, would grow beneath the Sumach. Only death seemed to thrive there, she mused in a fleeting moment of depression, as she searched around for more dead birds. But none had fallen since the thrush, picked up by Mrs. Watcombe.

One evening, the heat inside the house becoming insupportable, Irene wandered into the garden, her steps mechanically leading her to the little grave beneath the Sumach. In the uncertain moonlight, the twisted trunk and branches of the old tree were suggestive of a rustic seat, and feeling tired, she lifted herself into the natural bower, and lolled back, joyously inhaling the cool night air. Presently she dropped asleep, and in a curiously vivid manner, dreamt of Hilary; that he had completed his business in London, and was coming home. They met at evening, near the garden gate, and Hilary spread wide his arms, and eagerly folded them about her. Swiftly the dream began to change, assuming the characteristics of a nightmare. The sky grew strangely dark, the arms fiercely masterful, while the face which bent to kiss her neck was not that of her young husband: it was leering, wicked, gnarled like the trunk of some weather-beaten tree. Chilled with horror, Irene fought long and desperately against the vision, to be at last awakened by her own frightened whimpering. Yet returning to consciousness did not immediately dissipate the nightmare. In imagination she was still held by rigid brutal arms, and it was only after a blind, half-waking struggle the she freed herself, and went speeding across the lawn, towards the lighted doorway.

Next morning Mrs. Watcombe called, and subjected her to a puzzled scrutiny.

"How pale you look Irene. Do you feel ill?"

"Ill? No, only a little languid. I find this hot weather very trying."

Mrs. Watcombe studied her with care, for the pallor of Irene's face was very marked. In contrast, a vivid spot of red showed on the slender neck an inch or so below the ear. Intuitively a hand went up, as Irene turned to her friend in explanation.

"It feels so sore. I think I must have grazed the skin, last night, while sitting in the Sumach."

"Sitting in the Sumach!" echoed Mrs. Watcombe in surprise. "How curious you should do that. Poor Geraldine used to do the same, just before she was taken ill, and yet at the last she was seized with a perfect horror of the tree. Goodness, but it is quite red again this morning!"

Irene swung round in the direction of the tree, filled with a vague repugnance. Sure enough, the leaves no longer drooped, nor were they green. They had become flecked once more with crimson, and the growth had quite regained its former vigor.

"Eugh!" she breathed, hurriedly turning towards the house. "It reminds me of a horrid nightmare. I have rather a head this morning; let's go in, and talk of something else!"

As the day advanced, the heat grew more oppressive, and night brought with it a curious stillness, the stillness which so often presages a heavy thunderstorm. No bird had offered up its evening hymn, no breeze came sufficient to stir a single leaf: everything was pervaded by the silence of expectancy.

The interval between dinner and bedtime is always a dreary one for those accustomed to companionship, and left all alone, Irene's restlessness momentarily increased. First the ceiling, then the very atmosphere seemed to weigh heavy upon her head. Although windows and doors were all flung wide, the airlessness of the house grew less and less endurable, until from sheer desperation she made her escape into the garden, where a sudden illumination of the horizon gave warning of the approaching storm. Feeling somewhat at a loss, she roamed aimlessly awhile, pausing sometimes to catch the echoes of distant thunder, until at last she found herself standing over Spot's desolate little grave. The sight struck her with a sense of utter loneliness, and the tears sprang to her eyes, in poignant longing for the companionship of her faithful pet.

Moved by she knew not what, Irene swung herself into the comfortable branches of old Sumach, and soothed by the reposeful attitude, her head soon began to nod in slumber. Afterwards it was a doubtful memory whether she actually did sleep, or whether the whole experience was not a kind of waking nightmare. Something of the previous evening's dream returned to her, but this time with added horror, for it commenced with no pleasurable vision of her husband. Instead, relentless stick-like arms immediately closed in upon her, their vice-like grip so tight that she could barely breathe. Down darted the awful head, rugged and lined by every sin, darting at the fair, white neck as a wild beast on its prey. The foul lips began to eat into her skin. . . . She struggled desperately, madly, for to her swooning senses the very branches of the tree became endowed with active life, coiling unmercifully around her, tenaciously clinging to her limbs, and tearing at her dress. Pain at last spurred her to an heroic effort, the pain of something—perhaps a twig—digging deep into her unprotected neck. With a choking cry she freed herself, and nerved by a sudden burst of thunder, ran tottering towards the shelter of the house.

Having gained the cosy lounge-hall, Irene sank into an armchair, gasping hysterically for breath. Gusts of refreshing wind came through the open windows, but although the atmosphere rapidly grew less stagnant, an hour passed before she could make sufficient effort to crawl upstairs to bed. In her room, a further shock awaited her. The bloodless, drawn face reflected in the mirror was scarcely recognisable. The eyes lacked lustre, the lips were white, the skin hung flabby on the shrunken flesh, giving it a look of premature old age. A tiny trickle of dry blood, the solitary smudge of colour, stained the chalky pallor of her neck. Taking up a hand-glass, she examined this with momentary concern. It was the old wound re-opened, an angry-looking sore, almost like the bite of some small, or very sharp-toothed animal. It smarted painfully. . . .

Mrs. Watcombe, bursting into the breakfast room next morning, with suggestions of an expedition to the neighbouring town, was shocked at Irene's looks, and insisted on going at once to fetch the doctor. Mrs. Watcombe fussed continually throughout the interview, and insisted on an examination of the scar upon Irene's neck. Patient and doctor had regarded this as a negligible detail, but finally the latter subjected it to a slightly puzzled scrutiny, advising that it should be kept bandaged. He suggested that Irene was suffering from anæmia, and would do well to keep as quiet as possible, building up her strength with food, open windows, and a genererous selection of pills and tonics. But despite these comforting arrangements, no one was entirely satisfied. The doctor lacked something in assurance, Irene was certain that she could not really be anæmic, while Mrs. Watcombe was obsessed by inward misgivings, perfectly indefinable, yet none the less disturbing. She left the house as a woman bent under a load of care. Passing up the lane, her glance lighted on the old Sumach, more crimson now, more flourishing in its growth than she had seen it since the time of Geraldine's fatal illness.

"I loathe that horrid old tree!" she murmured, then added, struck by a nameless premonition, "Her husband ought to know. I shall wire him at once."

Irene, womanlike, put to use her enforced idleness, by instituting a re-arrangement of the box-room, the only part of her new home which yet remained unexplored. Among the odds and ends of the rubbish to be thrown away, there was a little note book apparently unused. In idle curiosity, Irene picked it up, and was surprised to learn, from an inscription, that her cousin Geraldine had intended to use it as a diary. A date appeared—only a few days prior to the poor girl's death—but no entries had been made, though the first two pages of the book had certainly been removed. As Irene put it down, there fluttered to the ground a torn scrap of writing. She stooped, and continued stooping, breathlessly staring at the words that had been written by her cousin's hand—*Sumach fascinates m*——

In some unaccountable manner this applied to her. It was obvious what tree was meant, the old Sumach at the end of the lawn; and it fascinated her, Irene, though not until that moment had she openly recognised the fact. Searching hurriedly through the note book, she discovered, near the end, a heap of torn paper evidently the first two pages of a diary. She turned the pieces in eager haste. Most of them bore no more than one short word, or portions of a longer one, but a few bigger fragments proved more enlightening, and filled with nervous apprehension, she carried the book to her escritoire, and spent the remainder of the afternoon in trying to piece together the torn-up pages.

Meanwhile, Mrs. Watcombe was worrying and fretting over Irene's unexpected illness. Her pallor, her listlessness, even the curious mark upon her neck, gave cause for positive alarm, so exactly did they correspond with symptoms exhibited by her cousin Geraldine during the few days prior to her death. She wished that the village doctor, who had attended the earlier case, would return soon from his holiday, as his *locum tenens* seemed sadly wanting in that authoritative decision which is so consoling to patients, relatives, and friends. Feeling, as an old friend, responsible for the welfare of Irene, she wired to Hilary, telling him of the sudden illness, and advising him to return without delay.

The urgency of the telegram alarmed him, so much so that he left London by the next train, arriving at Cleeve Grange shortly after dark.

"Where is your mistress?" was his first enquiry, as the maid met him in the hall.

"Upstairs, Sir. She complained of feeling tired, and said she would go to bed."

He hurried to her room, only to find it empty. He called, he rang for the servants; in a moment the whole house was astir, yet nowhere was Irene to be found. Deeming it possible that she might have gone to see Mrs. Watcombe, Hilary was about to follow, when that lady herself was ushered in.

"I saw the lights of your cab——" she commenced, cutting short the sentence, as she met his questioning glance.

"Where is Irene?"

"Irene? My dear Hilary, is she not here?"

"No. We can't find her anywhere. I thought she might have been with you."

For the space of half a second, Mrs. Watcombe's face presented a picture of astonishment; then the expression changed to one of dismayed concern.

"She's in that tree! I'm certain of it! Hilary, we must fetch her in at once!"

Completely at a loss to understand, he followed the excited woman into the garden, stumbling blindly in her wake across the lawn. The darkness was intense, and a terrific wind beat them back as if with living hands. Irene's white dress at length became discernible, dimly thrown up against the pitchy background, and obscured in places by the twists and coils of the old Sumach. Between them they grasped the sleeping body, but the branches swung wildly in the gale, and to Hilary's confused imagination it was as if they had literally to tear it from the tree's embrace. At last they regained the shelter of the house, and laid their inanimate burden upon the sofa. She was quite unconscious, pale as death, and her face painfully contorted, as if with fear. The old wound on the neck, now bereft of bandages, had been reopened and was wet with blood.

Hilary rushed off to fetch the doctor, while Mrs. Watcombe and the servants carried Irene to her room. Several hours passed before she recovered consciousness, and during that time Hilary was gently but firmly excluded from the sick room. Bewildered and disconsolate, he wandered restlessly about the house, until his attention was arrested by the unusual array of torn-up bits of paper on Irene's desk. He saw that she had been sorting out the pieces, and sticking them together as the sentences became complete. The work was barely half finished, yet what there was to read, struck him as exceedingly strange:

> The seat in the old Sumach fascinates me. I find myself going back to it unconsciously, nay, even against my will. Oh, but the nightmare visions it always brings me! In them I seem to plumb the very depths of terror. Their memory preys upon my mind, and every day my strength grows less.
>
> Dr. H. speaks of anæmia . . .

That was as far as Irene had proceeded. Hardly knowing why he did so, Hilary resolved to complete the task, but the chill of early morning was in the air before it was finished. Cramped and stiff, he was pushing back his chair when a footstep sounded in the doorway, and Mrs. Watcombe entered.

"Irene is better," she volunteered immediately. "She is sleeping naturally, and Doctor Thompson says there is no longer any immediate danger. The poor child is terribly weak and bloodless."

"May—tell me—what is the meaning of all this? Why has Irene suddenly become so ill? I can't understand it!"

Mrs. Watcombe's face was preternaturally grave.

"Even the doctor admits that he is puzzled," she answered very quietly. "The symptoms all point to a sudden and excessive loss of blood, though in cases of acute anæmia—"

"God! But—not like Geraldine? I can't believe it!"

"Neither can I. Oh, Hilary, you may think me mad, but I can't help feeling that there is some unknown, some awful influence at work. Irene was perfectly well three days ago, and it was the same with Geraldine before she was taken ill. The cases are so exactly similar. . . Irene was trying to tell me something about a diary, but the poor girl was too exhausted to make herself properly understood."

"Diary? Geraldine's diary, do you think? She must mean that. I have just finished piecing it together, but frankly, I can't make head or tail of it!"

Mrs. Watcombe rapidly scanned the writing, then studied it again with greater care. Finally she read the second part aloud.

"Listen, Hilary! This seems important."

> Dr. H. speaks of anæmia. Pray heaven, he may be correct, for my thoughts sometimes move in a direction which foreshadows nothing short of lunacy—or so people would tell me, if I could bring myself to confide these things. I must fight alone, clinging to the knowledge that it is unusual for anæmic persons to be obsessed by unhealthy fancies. If only I had not read those horribly suggestive words in Barrett. . .

"Barrett? What can she mean, May?"

"Wait a moment. Barrett? Barrett's *Traditions of the Country,* perhaps. I have noticed a copy in the library. Let us go there; it may give the clue!"

The book was quickly found, and a marker indicated the passage to which Geraldine apparently referred.

> At Cleeve, I was reminded of another of those traditions, so rapidly disappearing before the spread of education. It concerned the old belief in vampires, spirits of the evil dead, who by night, could assume a human form, and scour the countryside in search of victims. Suspected vampires, if caught, were buried with the mouth stuffed full of garlic, and a stake plunged through the heart, whereby they were rendered harmless, or, at least, confined to that one particular locality.
>
> Some thirty years ago, an old man pointed out a tree which was said to have grown from such a stake. So far as I can recollect, it was an unusual variety of Sumach, and had been enclosed during a recent extension of the garden to the old Grange . . .

"Come outside," said Mrs. Watcombe, breaking a long and solemn silence. "I want you to see that tree."

The sky was suffused with the blush of early dawn, and the shrubs, the flowers, even the dew upon the grass caught and reflected something of the pink effulgence. The Sumach alone stood out, dark and menacing. During the night its leaves had become a hideous, mottled purple; its growth was oily, bloated, unnaturally vigorous, like that of some rank and poisonous weed.

Mrs. Watcombe, looking from afar, spoke in frightened, husky tones.

"See, Hilary! It was exactly like that when—when Geraldine died."

When evening fell, the end of the lawn was strangely bare. In place of the old tree, there lay an enormous heap of smouldering embers—enormous, because the Sumach had been too sodden with dark and sticky sap, to burn without the assistance of large quantities of other timber.

Many weeks elapsed before Irene was sufficiently recovered to walk as far as Spot's little grave. She was surprised to find it almost hidden in a bed of garlic. Hilary explained that it was the only plant they could induce to grow there.

W *is for* Werewolf

Werewolves—humans who shift shape into wolf form by the light of the full moon and prey on human flesh—are among the most famous of all supernatural monsters. In this story, British writer Bernard Capes (1854–1918), who mixed tales of the supernatural with non-supernatural in several collections—including his 1915 compilation *The Fabulists,* where this story first appeared—delivers a werewolf tale that is as oblique as it is brief.

BERNARD CAPES

The Thing in the Forest

Into the snow-locked forests of Upper Hungary steal wolves in winter; but there is a footfall worse than theirs to knock upon the heart of the lonely traveller.

One December evening Elspet, the young newly wedded wife of the woodman Stefan, came hurrying over the lower slopes of the White Mountains from the town where she had been all day marketing. She carried a basket with provisions on her arm; her plump cheeks were like a couple of cold apples; her breath spoke short but more from nervousness than exhaustion. It was nearing dusk, and she was glad to see the little lonely church in the hollow below, the hub, as it were, of many radiating paths through the trees, one of which was the road to her own warm cottage yet a half-mile away.

She paused a moment at the foot of the slope, undecided about entertaining the little chill, silent building and making her plea for protection to the great battered stone image of Our Lady of Succour which stood within by the confessional box; but the stillness and the growing darkness decided her, and she went on. A spark of fire glowing through the presbytery window seemed to repel rather than attract her, and she was glad when the convolutions of the path hid it from her sight. Being new to the district, she had seen little of Father Ruhl as yet, and somehow the penetrating knowledge and burning eyes of the pastor made her feel uncomfortable.

The soft drift, the lane of tall, motionless pines stretched on in a quiet like death. Somewhere the sun, like a dead fire, had fallen into opalescent embers faintly luminous: they were enough only to touch the shadows with a ghastlier pallor. It was so still that the light crunch of the snow in the girl's own footfalls trod on her heart like a desecration.

Suddenly there was something near her that had not been before. It had come like a shadow without more sound or warning. It was here—there—behind her. She turned, in mortal panic, and saw a wolf. With a strangled cry and trembling limbs she strove to hurry on her way; and always she knew, though there was no whisper of pursuit, that the gliding shadow followed in her wake. Desperate in her terror, she stopped once more and faced it.

A wolf!—was it a wolf? O who could doubt it! Yet the wild expression in those famished eyes, so lost, so pitiful, so mingled of unsatiable hunger and human need! Condemned, for its unspeakable sins, to take this form at sunset, and so howl and snuffle about the doors of men until the blessed day released it. A werewolf—not a wolf.

That terrific realization of the truth smote the girl as with a knife out of darkness: for an instant she came near fainting. And then a low moan broke into her heart and flooded it with pity. So lost, so infinitely hopeless. And so pitiful—yes, in spite of all, so pitiful. It had sinned beyond any sinning that her innocence knew or her experience could gauge; but she was a woman, very blest, very happy, in her store of comforts and her surety of love. She knew that it was forbidden to succour these damned and nameless outcasts, to help or sympathize with them in any way. But—

There was good store of meat in her basket, and who need ever know or tell? With shaking hands she found and threw a sop to the desolate brute—then, turning, sped upon her way.

But at home her secret sin stood up before her, and, interposing between her husband and herself, threw its shadow upon both their faces. What had she dared—what done? By her own act forfeited her birthright of innocence; by her own act placed herself in the power of the evil to which she had ministered. All that night she lay in shame and horror, and all the next day, until Stefan had come about his dinner and gone again, she moved in a dumb agony. Then, driven unendurably by the memory of his troubled, bewildered face, as twilight threatened she put on her cloak and went down to the little church in the hollow to confess her sin.

"Mother, forgive and save me," she whispered, as she passed the statue.

After ringing the bell for the confessor, she had not knelt long at the confessional box in the dim chapel, cold and empty as a waiting vault, when the chancel rail clicked, and the footsteps of Father Ruhl were heard rustling over the stones. He came, he took his seat behind the grating; and with many sighs and falterings, Elspet avowed her guilt. And as, with bowed head, she ended, a strange sound answered her—it was like a little laugh, and yet not so much like a laugh as a snarl. With a shock as of death she raised her face. It was Father Ruhl who sat there—and yet it was not Father Ruhl. In that time of twilight, his face was already changing, narrowing, becoming wolfish—the eyes rounded and the jaw slavered. She gasped, and shrunk back; and at that, barking and snapping at the grating, with a wicked look he dropped—and she heard him coming. Sheer horror leant her wings. With a scream she sprang to her feet and fled. Her cloak caught in something—there was a wrench and crash and, like a flood, oblivion overswept her.

It was the old deaf and near senile sacristan who found them lying there, the woman unhurt but insensible, the priest crushed out of life by the fall of the ancient statue, long tottering to its collapse. She recovered, for her part: for his, no one knows where he lies buried. But there were dark stories of a baying pack that night, and of an empty bloodstained pavement when they came to seek for the body.

X
is for
X-Rayed

X-rays were a relatively new form of medical technology when British writer George Griffith (1857–1906), author of a number of early works of science fiction, published this tale in the April 1896 issue of *Pearson's.* Many writers since have written tales of the monstrous mutations x-ray exposure can cause, but here, with tongue in cheek, Griffith suggests how monstrous a look inside ourselves must have seemed to those unfamiliar with x-ray images.

GEORGE GRIFFITH

A Photograph of the Invisible

"Why, what is this, Denton, my friend?" said the Professor. "Your holiday doesn't seem to have done you much good. Have you had a fever or anything of that sort? You were looking a little worn out and run down when you went away, but, God bless me, you look more as if you had got up from a bed of sickness, than come back from a three month's yachting cruise in the Mediterranean."

"I dare say I do," said his visitor, taking his hand out of the Professor's and pulling from his pocket a little gilt-edged sheet of note paper. The Professor saw that it had been crushed up and smoothed out again. There was a pretty monogram in the top left-hand corner, and a faint sweet scent as of dried rose-leaves and violets rose from it as the pale, haggard, bright-eyed young fellow before him put it into his hands, and said:

"Read that, and tell me if you don't think it's about enough to knock a man over. May God—"

"Hush, my friend, hush!" said the Professor, laying his left hand on the other's shoulder, and holding the little letter in his right about six inches from his spectacles. "It is bad, but not bad enough for that, and gentlemen and men of science don't do that sort of thing, you know. So she has sold you, as the man in the street would say. Ah, well—"

"Sold me, sold herself you mean! Sold herself body and soul to that German Jew brute and his millions. Sold herself more vilely and basely than the most wretched outcast of the streets, for she has cold and hunger as her excuses, and Edith had a good home, an ample income, and a man who has loved her all his life to come to whenever she would, and she had promised to come, too. Is there any forgiveness for a sin like that, do you think?"

"That is not our business, my friend," said the Professor quietly; "and then you know I am enough of a pagan not to believe in the forgiveness of sins. Not here at least; the hereafter is another matter which is beyond our discussion. But in this world I have never seen sin and punishment as anything else than cause and effect, the one following the other as logically and as inevitably as a shock follows a blow."

"Good logic," said Denton with a short, savage laugh. "Capital logic from the physical point of view, but a trifle cold for my present frame of mind. Is that all the consolation you can give me?"

"I cannot give you any consolation, my friend; nothing but time and hard work can give that to a man in your state, but I might give you something else that would be more to your mind just now."

"What is that?"

"Your revenge. An idea that is something like an inspiration has just come to me. I can give you a revenge that shall be purely scientific, beyond the reach of all human law, and, I think I may say, absolutely unique. What do you say to that?"

"Tell me what it is; quick! I have been thinking all night and all day of nothing else. This thing has brought all the savage in me to the surface, and if I had all the arts of a Borgia, I believe I could use them just now without ruth or scruple. Now what is it?"

"Light a cigar and help yourself to whiskey and soda, and let me prescribe for once in a way to my own doctor. A combination of sedative and tonic is just what your present state of mind indicates," said the Professor, still in his dry, quiet voice, and pointing to a wide, deep arm chair on the other side of the library fire. It is not a thing that I can make you understand in a minute, and, besides, a little enforced quiet, and a turn of your attention to something else, would do you all the good in the world."

"Very well. I'll be patient and you doctor for a bit, go ahead! Something new to think about would be a Godsend to me just now."

When they were settled in their chairs, and the smoke of their cigars was mingling about the mantelpiece, the Professor began:

"Of course you've heard something about this new photography of the invisible, as they call it, Röntgen's discovery, you know, with Crooke's vacuum tubes?"

"No, I can't say that I have, at least, nothing beyond mere rumours and newspaper paragraphs. I think it's all happened while I've been away. I did mean to look into it when I got home, and when I did I got *this*."

"Ah, well, that's no matter. I can soon make you understand all you need to know about it. It has been discovered, to put it shortly, that there are rays other than what we call light rays, to which some transparent substances are opaque, and some opaque substances transparent, and it has also been found that the photographic plate is sensitive to these rays. Ergo, by proper management it is possible to obtain a photograph of things invisible either to the eye or to the microscope."

"Wonderful, but hardly relevant, as far as I can see. What has the photography of the invisible got to do with my case and Edith's —Mrs. Goldsberg's, I mean? Oh, look here, Grantham, I can't stand science now, I want revenge, and if you can give it me, just tell me what to do straight out."

"Very well, my friend, very well. I can see you are impatient, and no doubt naturally. We'll let the explanation go for the present. After all, it's no good trying to explain a thing like this to a man who can't sit still for a minute in his chair, and lets his cigar out before he's taken half a dozen whiffs. Come into the studio and I'll give you an object-lesson."

This will be a convenient place to say that Professor Grantham, though a chemist and physical investigator by profession, was a photographer by hobby. Not a photographer in the ordinary sense of the word, but rather an excursionist in the outer and least known realms of the science.

He had practically solved the fascinating problem of chromatic photography, and as soon as he had perfected a few details of his invention he was going to astonish the world and make his fortune with it. He could photograph people with a ghostly double of themselves looking over their shoulder, and by means of photographs of a man, and his parents, and his grandparents, he had produced a composite picture that was an excellent likeness of a remote ancestor, as proved by an ivory miniature that he had never seen.

Of course he never did this kind of thing for money, but as a matter of favour; and, for the sake of his pet art, he had now and then taken the photographs of some of the most noted beauties of Society by his unknown process, and the results, with their exquisite blending of light and shade and tinting, were the pride and glory of their originals and the envy and despair of every professional in the world. It was a natural consequence that these favours should be most eagerly sought after, all the more eagerly because they were so few and far between.

When they got into the studio, the Professor turned a switch just inside the door, and lit a single electric light. In the middle of the room there was a camera, and in front of it, on another tripod just level with the lens, was a little black wooden box standing on its end. The camera had a cap of ebonite, and two curly electric wires ran up to each side of it from a battery on the floor. The Professor went to the box, and drew a sliding lid off the top. Then he said to Denton:

"Come and put your hand inside here, and keep it there until I tell you to move."

"What are you going to do?"

"Take a photograph of your hand, that's all, but such a photograph! Ah, wait till you see it!"

The young doctor did as he was told, and the Professor took out his watch and turned a switch in the side of the camera.

"Now mind you don't move your hand; ten minutes will do it."

"Rather a long exposure, isn't it?"

"Yes, but necessary."

When the Professor's watch had ticked off the tenth minute, he said:

"Now you can take your hand out and go back into the library, and have another smoke and amuse yourself thinking about the justice of revenge while I develop the plate. Then you shall see the results."

Denton did as he was told; but when he got back to the library, instead of sitting down and trying to take things quietly, he only strode up and down the room with his hands clenched behind his back, chewing the end of his cigar and the cud of his bitter reflections, until the door from the studio opened and the Professor came in with a little square of glass in his hand.

He put it behind him, and as Denton stopped in front of him he said, much more seriously than he had spoken so far:

"My friend, do you remember what I told you after you had saved my little girl's life at the risk of your own by drawing the diphtheritic membrane from her throat through a quill? I told you if ever I could serve you, you were but to ask and to have.

"Now you are in sorrow and in trouble, you have suffered the greatest wrong save one that an honourable man can suffer, and you have asked me for revenge. Very well, you shall have it, but in such a form that it shall be a just and merited punishment. This woman has commited a crime against herself and all true womanhood, and to punish her you shall wound her in the tenderest spot in such a woman's being, her vanity and the vainglory which she takes in the beauty she has sold. You shall teach her, in a word—yes, and that millionaire purchaser of hers too, that that beauty is but skin deep."

"What in heaven's name do you mean, man? I've scarcely understood a word you've said to-night. For goodness sake speak a little more plainly and let me see what you are driving at."

"This!" said the Professor, holding up the glass plate between Denton and the light of the electric chandelier that hung over the table. "There is your hand! Now, how do you think Mr. Joel Goldsberg would like a photograph of his wife done in that style, and how would *she* like it?"

Denton craned his neck upward for a moment, to look more closely at the object on the plate. Then he started back, and stared at the Professor with a look of wonder that was near akin to horror in his eyes.

"Is that a fact, Grantham?" he almost whispered. "Is that really the photograph of my hand, and could you—Oh, my God, no! It would be too horrible. She has done enough to make me hate her, and I do hate and despise her as much as I loved her a couple of days ago; but if I saw that thing I believe I should go mad."

"There will be no need for you to see it, and on the presumably coarser natures of Mr. and Mrs. Goldsberg the effect would probably be nothing like so serious. She will be one of the beauties of England now that she is a millionairess. She will be only too glad of a suggestion, which can easily be managed, that I am willing to photograph her by a novel process. I will make a vignette of her—just the head and shoulders and bust, you know."

"Stop, man, for God's sake, stop! That's enough. If you tell me any more I shall relent and forbid you to do it—and yet she deserves it. After all, it will only be a sort of scientific practical joke, I suppose."

"Yes, and I can easily say that some unforeseen accident that happened in the process has resulted in a scientific curiosity, and send it to her husband with my apologies and an offer to take her in colours, as compensation for the disappointment," said the Professor.

As Professor Grantham had shrewdly anticipated, Mrs. Joel Goldsberg, who had so unexpectedly scandalised her most intimate friends, and astonished the London world at large by developing, after an exceedingly brief courtship, into the mistress of many millions and the wife of an almost phenomenally homely and vulgar financier, jumped at the chance of having her undeniable and now universally lauded beauty portrayed in that wonderful guise which only he could give to it.

It is true that when the time for the *séance* arrived she was not a little mystified, not to say frightened, by the singularity of the methods adopted by the Professor, for she was photographed in absolute darkness, and the fact that the process seemed to take an unconscionably long time by no means made the ordeal easier.

But still she recognised that she was receiving a favour, and so, of course, there was nothing to be said beyond a few pretty little expostulations and expressions of wonder when the *séance* was over. Then she went away, taking with her the Professor's promise to send her the result of the experiment, as he called it, as soon as the operations of developing and printing off were finished.

It was about a week later that a small flat parcel, marked "Private and with care," was brought to Mr. Joel Goldsberg as he sat at breakfast with "his young and lovely bride," as the newspaper reports of their wedding had justly, if tritely, styled her.

"I think this is the Professor's writing, my dear," said the millionaire as he looked the packet over; "so I suppose it will be that new photograph of yours."

"Oh, yes, I daresay it will," she said. "Let us see what it is like." And she got up and went and leant over her husband's shoulder.

He took off the brown paper cover; then a white paper one inside that, and then he raised the sheet of tissue paper that was gummed along the top of the card.

Neither of them said anything when they first saw what was underneath, but the blood rushed to his face till it was almost purple, and died out of hers till it was grey and white and ghastly—the face of a corpse, but for the two bright, glaring eyes that stared out of it, and this is what those eyes saw.

The photograph seemed, as it were, to be in three layers—all transparent save the third. It was a vignette, just showing the head and neck and shoulders. The dress, a most dainty morning costume, in which she had elected to be taken, was perfect in pattern, but diaphanous and transparent. Under this were the skin and flesh, transparent also.

Above were her features, perfect in their likeness, and the wreathed crown of golden brown hair of which she was so proud, but they were the face and hair not of a living woman, but of a ghost, and, beneath all, sharp in outline and perfect in every hideous detail, a fleshless skull—her own skull—poised on the jagged vertebrae of her neck, and supported on the bare bones of her chest and shoulders, grinned at her through the transparent veil of flesh, and seemed to stare at her out of the sockets in which two ghostly eyes appeared to float.

A day or two afterwards Society was startled by an amazing piece of news concerning the golden idols which it had most recently set up. Mr. Joel Goldsberg had been suddenly struck down by some mysterious malady of a nervous character, and his newly-wedded bride had vanished utterly from the gaze of her worshippers. Later still it transpired, through the agency of an indefatigable society journalist, that her reason had suddenly given way from some unknown cause, and that she was now an inmate of a private lunatic asylum.

"I have it on the best authority," concluded the paragraph in which the *Gutter Gazette* gave this piquant detail to the world, "that the unhappy lady's malady is of a most singular description. She imagines that she is a skeleton, and that her clothing and skin and flesh are nothing more than transparent shadows which everybody can see through. As a consequence her physicians are obliged at present to allow her to live day and night in a dark room, since the presence of the faintest light drives her instantly into a condition of the most violent hysterics."

[NOTE.—*Although this is of course a purely imaginative story, it may be as well to say that such photographs as that of Mrs. Goldsberg have been shown by actual experiment to be possible. It is hardly necessary to add that what the Professor showed Denton was a photograph of his own skeleton hand in a shadowy outline of transparent flesh.*]

Y *is for* Yeti

The four collections of horror tales that Edward Fredric Benson (1867–1940) published in his lifetime feature some of the most monstrous manifestations to appear in weird fiction in the first half of the twentieth century. This story, first published in the September 1922 issue of *Hutchinson's* magazine, is one of the first published works of fiction to feature an anthropoid monster that, despite its Alps setting, we recognize as the yeti, a creature out of Tibetan folklore more commonly known as the Abominable Snowman of the Himalayas.

E.F. BENSON

The Horror-Horn

For the past ten days Alhubel had basked in the radiant midwinter weather proper to its eminence of over 6,000 feet. From rising to setting the sun (so surprising to those who have hitherto associated it with a pale, tepid plate indistinctly shining through the murky air of England) had blazed its way across the sparkling blue, and every night the serene and windless frost had made the stars sparkle like illuminated diamond dust. Sufficient snow had fallen before Christmas to content the skiers, and the big rink, sprinkled every evening, had given the skaters each morning a fresh surface on which to perform their slippery antics. Bridge and dancing served to while away the greater part of the night, and to me, now for the first time tasting the joys of a winter in the Engadine, it seemed that a new heaven and a new earth had been lighted, warmed, and refrigerated for the special benefit of those who like myself had been wise enough to save up their days of holiday for the winter.

But a break came in these ideal conditions: one afternoon the sun grew vapour-veiled and up the valley from the north-west a wind frozen with miles of travel over ice-bound hill-sides began scouting through the calm halls of the heavens. Soon it grew dusted with snow, first in small flakes driven almost horizontally before its congealing breath and then in larger tufts as of swansdown. And though all day for a fortnight before the fate of nations and life and death had seemed to me of far less importance than to get certain tracings of the skate-blades on the ice of proper shape and size, it now seemed that the one paramount consideration was to hurry back to the hotel for shelter: it was wiser to leave rocking-turns alone than to be frozen in their quest.

I had come out here with my cousin, Professor Ingram, the celebrated physiologist and Alpine climber. During the serenity of the last fortnight he had made a couple of notable winter ascents, but this morning his weather-wisdom had mistrusted the signs of the heavens, and instead of attempting the ascent of the Piz Passug he had waited to see whether his misgivings justified themselves. So there he sat now in the hall of the admirable hotel with his feet on the hot-water pipes and the latest delivery of the English post in his hands. This contained a pamphlet concerning the result of the Mount Everest expedition, of which he had just finished the perusal when I entered.

"A very interesting report," he said, passing it to me, "and they certainly deserve to succeed next year. But who can tell, what that final six thousand feet may entail? Six thousand feet more when you have already accomplished twenty-three thousand does not seem much, but at present no one knows whether the human frame can stand exertion at such a height. It may affect not the lungs and heart only, but possibly the brain. Delirious hallucinations may occur. In fact, if I did not know better, I should have said that one such hallucination had occurred to the climbers already."

"And what was that?" I asked.

"You will find that they thought they came across the tracks of some naked human foot at a great altitude. That looks at first sight like an hallucination. What more natural than that a brain excited and exhilarated by the extreme height should have interpreted certain marks in the snow as the footprints of a human being? Every bodily organ at these altitudes is exerting itself to the utmost to do its work, and the brain seizes on those marks in the snow and says 'Yes, I'm all right, I'm doing my job, and I perceive marks in the snow which I affirm are human footprints.' You know, even at this altitude, how restless and eager the brain is, how vividly, as you told me, you dream at night. Multiply that stimulus and that consequent eagerness and restlessness by three, and how natural that the brain should harbour illusions! What after all is the delirium which often accompanies high fever but the effort of the brain to do its work under the pressure of feverish conditions? It is so eager to continue perceiving that it perceives things which have no existence!"

"And yet you don't think that these naked human footprints were illusions," said I. "You told me you would have thought so, if you had not known better."

He shifted in his chair and looked out of the window a moment. The air was thick now with the density of the big snow-flakes that were driven along by the squealing north-west gale.

"Quite so," he said. "In all probability the human footprints were real human footprints. I expect that they were the footprints, anyhow, of a being more nearly a man than anything else. My reason for saying so is that I know such beings exist. I have even seen quite near at hand—and I assure you I did not wish to be nearer in spite of my intense curiosity—the creature, shall we say, which would make such footprints. And if the snow was not so dense, I could show you the place where I saw him."

He pointed straight out of the window, where across the valley lies the huge tower of the Ungeheuerhorn with the carved pinnacle of rock at the top like some gigantic rhinoceros-horn. On one side only, as I knew, was the mountain practicable, and that for none but the finest climbers; on the other three a succession of ledges and precipices rendered it unscalable. Two thousand feet of sheer rock form the tower; below are five hundred feet of fallen boulders, up to the edge of which grow dense woods of larch and pine.

"Upon the Ungeheuerhorn?" I asked.

"Yes. Up till twenty years ago it had never been ascended, and I, like several others, spent a lot of time in trying to find a route up it. My guide and I sometimes spent three nights together at the hut beside the Blumen glacier, prowling round it, and it was by luck really that we found the route, for the mountain looks even more impracticable from the far side than it does from this. But one day we found a long, transverse fissure in the side which led to a negotiable ledge; then there came a slanting ice couloir which you could not see till you got to the foot of it. However, I need not go into that."

The big room where we sat was filling up with cheerful groups driven indoors by this sudden gale and snowfall, and the cackle of merry tongues grew loud. The band, too, that invariable appanage of tea-time at Swiss resorts, had begun to tune up for the usual potpourri from the works of Puccini. Next moment the sugary, sentimental melodies began.

"Strange contrast!" said Ingram. "Here are we sitting warm and cosy, our ears pleasantly tickled with these little baby tunes and outside is the great storm growing more violent every moment, and swirling round the austere cliffs of the Ungeheuerhorn: the Horror-horn, as indeed it was to me."

"I want to hear all about it," I said. "Every detail: make a short story long, if it's short. I want to know why it's *your* Horror-horn?"

"Well, Chanton and I (he was my guide) used to spend days prowling about the cliffs, making a little progress on one side and then being stopped, and gaining perhaps five hundred feet on another side and then being confronted by some insuperable obstacle, till the day when by luck we found the route. Chanton never liked the job, for some reason that I could not fathom. It was not because of the difficulty or danger of the climbing, for he was the most fearless man I have ever met when dealing with rocks and ice, but he was always insistent that we should get off the mountain and back to the Blumen hut before sunset. He was scarcely easy even when we had got back to shelter and locked and barred the door, and I well remember one night when, as we ate our supper, we heard some animal, a wolf probably, howling somewhere out in the night. A positive panic seized him, and I don't think he closed his eyes till morning. It struck me then that there might be some grisly legend about the mountain, connected possibly with its name, and next day I asked him why the peak was called the Horror-horn. He put the question off at first, and said that, like the Schreckhorn, its name was due to its precipices and falling stones; but when I pressed him further he acknowledged that there was a legend about it, which his father had told him. There were creatures, so it was supposed, that lived in its caves, things human in shape, and covered, except for the face and hands, with long black hair. They were dwarfs in size, four feet high or thereabouts, but of prodigious strength and agility, remnants of some wild primeval race. It seemed that they were still in an upward stage of evolution, or so I guessed, for the story ran that sometimes girls had been carried off by them, not as prey, and not for any such fate as for those captured by cannibals, but to be bred from. Young men also had been raped by them, to be mated with the females of their tribe. All this looked as if the creatures, as I said, were tending towards humanity. But naturally I did not believe a word of it, as applied to the conditions of the present day. Centuries ago, conceivably, there may have been such beings, and, with the extraordinary tenacity of tradition, the news of this had been handed down and was still current round the hearths of the peasants. As for their numbers, Chanton told me that three had been once seen together by a man who owing to his swiftness on skis had escaped to tell the tale. This man, he averred, was no other than his grandfather, who had been benighted one winter evening as he passed through the dense woods below the Ungeheuerhorn, and Chanton supposed that they had been driven down to these lower altitudes in search of food during severe winter weather, for otherwise the recorded sights of them had always taken place among the rocks of the peak itself. They had pursued his grandfather, then a young man, at an extraordinarily swift canter, running sometimes upright as men run, sometimes on all-fours in the manner of beasts, and their howls were just such as that we had heard that night in the Blumen hut. Such at any rate was the story Chanton told me, and, like you, I regarded it as the very moonshine of superstition. But the very next day I had reason to reconsider my judgment about it.

"It was on that day that after a week of exploration we hit on the only route at present known to the top of our peak. We started as soon as there was light enough to climb by, for, as you may guess, on very difficult rocks it is impossible to climb by lantern or moonlight. We hit on the long fissure I have spoken of, we explored the ledge which from below seemed to end in nothingness, and with an hour's stepcutting ascended the couloir which led upwards from it. From there onwards it was a rock-climb, certainly of considerable difficulty, but with no heart-breaking discoveries ahead, and it was about nine in the morning that we stood on the top. We did not wait there long, for that side of the mountain is raked by falling stones loosened, when the sun grows hot, from the ice that holds them, and we made haste to pass the ledge where the falls are most frequent. After that there was the long fissure to descend, a matter of no great difficulty, and we were at the end of our work by midday, both of us, as you may imagine, in the state of the highest elation.

"A long and tiresome scramble among the huge boulders at the foot of the cliff then lay before us. Here the hill-side is very porous and great caves extend far into the mountain. We had unroped at the base of the fissure, and were picking our way as seemed good to either of us among these fallen rocks, many of them bigger than an ordinary house, when, on coming round the corner of one of these, I saw that which made it clear that the stories Chanton had told me were no figment of traditional superstition.

"Not twenty yards in front of me lay one of the beings of which he had spoken. There it sprawled naked and basking on its back with face turned up to the sun, which its narrow eyes regarded unwinking. In form it was completely human, but the growth of hair that covered limbs and trunk alike almost completely hid the sun-tanned skin beneath. But its face, save for the down on its cheeks and chin, was hairless, and I looked on a countenance the sensual and malevolent bestiality of which froze me with horror. Had the creature been an animal, one would have felt scarcely a shudder at the gross animalism of it; the horror lay in the fact that it was a man. There lay by it a couple of gnawed bones, and, its meal finished, it was lazily licking its protuberant lips, from which came a purring murmur of content. With one hand it scratched the thick hair on its belly, in the other it held one of these bones, which presently split in half beneath the pressure of its finger and thumb. But my horror was not based on the information of what happened to those men whom these creatures caught, it was due only to my proximity to a thing so human and so infernal. The peak, of which the ascent had a moment ago filled us with such elated satisfaction, became to me an Ungeheuerhorn indeed, for it was the home of beings more awful than the delirium of nightmare could ever have conceived.

"Chanton was a dozen paces behind me, and with a backward wave of my hand I caused him to halt. Then withdrawing myself with infinite precaution, so as not to attract the gaze of that basking creature, I slipped back round the rock, whispered to him what I had seen, and with blanched faces we made a long detour, peering round every corner, and crouching low, not knowing that at any step we might not come upon another of these beings, or that from the mouth of one of these caves in the mountain-side there might not appear another of those hairless and dreadful faces, with perhaps this time the breasts and insignia of womanhood. That would have been the worst of all.

"Luck favoured us, for we made our way among the boulders and shifting stones, the rattle of which might at any moment have betrayed us, without a repetition of my experience, and once among the trees we ran as if the Furies themselves were in pursuit. Well now did I understand, though I dare say I cannot convey, the qualms of Chanton's mind when he spoke to me of these creatures. Their very humanity was what made them so terrible, the fact that they were of the same race as ourselves, but of a type so abysmally degraded that the most brutal and inhuman of men would have seemed angelic in comparison."

The music of the small band was over before he had finished the narrative, and the chattering groups round the tea-table had dispersed. He paused a moment.

"There was a horror of the spirit," he said, "which I experienced then, from which, I verily believe, I have never entirely recovered. I saw then how terrible a living thing could be, and how terrible, in consequence, was life itself. In us all I suppose lurks some inherited germ of that ineffable bestiality, and who knows whether, sterile as it has apparently become in the course of centuries, it might not fructify again. When I saw that creature sun itself, I looked into the abyss out of which we have crawled. And these creatures are trying to crawl out of it now, if they exist any longer. Certainly for the last twenty years there has been no record of their being seen, until we come to this story of the footprint seen by the climbers on Everest. If that is authentic, if the party did not mistake the footprint of some bear, or what not, for a human tread, it seems as if still this bestranded remnant of mankind is in existence."

Now, Ingram, had told his story well; but sitting in this warm and civilised room, the horror which he had clearly felt had not communicated itself to me in any very vivid manner. Intellectually, I agreed, I could appreciate his horror, but certainly my spirit felt no shudder of interior comprehension.

"But it is odd," I said, "that your keen interest in physiology did not disperse your qualms. You were looking, so I take it, at some form of man more remote probably than the earliest human remains. Did not something inside you say 'This is of absorbing significance'?"

He shook his head.

"No: I only wanted to get away," said he. "It was not, as I have told you, the terror of what according to Chanton's story, might await us if we were captured; it was sheer horror at the creature itself. I quaked at it."

The snowstorm and the gale increased in violence that night, and I slept uneasily, plucked again and again from slumber by the fierce battling of the wind that shook my windows as if with an imperious demand for admittance. It came in billowy gusts, with strange noises intermingled with it as for a moment it abated, with flutings and moanings that rose to shrieks as the fury of it returned. These noises, no doubt, mingled themselves with my drowsed and sleepy consciousness, and once I tore myself out of nightmare, imagining that the creatures of the Horror-horn had gained footing on my balcony and were rattling at the window-bolts. But before morning the gale had died away, and I awoke to see the snow falling dense and fast in a windless air. For three days it continued, without intermission, and with its cessation there came a frost such as I have never felt before. Fifty degrees were registered one night, and more the next, and what the cold must have been on the cliffs of the Ungeheuerhorn I cannot imagine. Sufficient, so I thought, to have made an end altogether of its secret inhabitants: my cousin, on that day twenty years ago, had missed an opportunity for study which would probably never fall again either to him or another.

I received one morning a letter from a friend saying that he had arrived at the neighbouring winter resort of St. Luigi, and proposing that I should come over for a morning's skating and lunch afterwards. The place was not more than a couple of miles off, if one took the path over the low, pine-clad foot-hills above which lay the steep woods below the first rocky slopes of the Ungeheuerhorn; and accordingly, with a knapsack containing skates on my back, I went on skis over the wooded slopes and down by an easy descent again on to St. Luigi. The day was overcast, clouds entirely obscured the higher peaks though the sun was visible, pale and unluminous, through the mists. But as the morning went on, it gained the upper hand, and I slid down into St. Luigi beneath a sparkling firmament. We skated and lunched, and then, since it looked as if thick weather was coming up again, I set out early about three o'clock for my return journey.

Hardly had I got into the woods when the clouds gathered thick above, and streamers and skeins of them began to descend among the pines through which my path threaded its way. In ten minutes more their opacity had so increased that I could hardly see a couple of yards in front of me. Very soon I became aware that I must have got off the path, for snow-cowled shrubs lay directly in my way, and, casting back to find it again, I got altogether confused as to direction. But, though progress was difficult, I knew I had only to keep on the ascent, and presently I should come to the brow of these low foot-hills, and descend into the open valley where Alhubel stood. So on I went, stumbling and sliding over obstacles, and unable, owing to the thickness of the snow, to take off my skis, for I should have sunk over the knees at each step. Still the ascent continued, and looking at my watch I saw that I had already been near an hour on my way from St. Luigi, a period more than sufficient to complete my whole journey. But still I stuck to my idea that though I had certainly strayed far from my proper route a few minutes more must surely see me over the top of the upward way, and I should find the ground declining into the next valley. About now, too, I noticed that the mists were growing suffused with rose-colour, and, though the inference was that it must be close on sunset, there was consolation in the fact that they were there and might lift at any moment and disclose to me my whereabouts. But the fact that night would soon be on me made it needful to bar my mind against that despair of loneliness which so eats out the heart of a man who is lost in woods or on mountain-side, that, though still there is plenty of vigour in his limbs, his nervous force is sapped, and he can do no more than lie down and abandon himself to whatever fate may await him. . . . And then I heard that which made the thought of loneliness seem bliss indeed, for there was a worse fate than loneliness. What I heard resembled the howl of a wolf, and it came from not far in front of me where the ridge—was it a ridge?—still rose higher in vestment of pines.

From behind me came a sudden puff of wind, which shook the frozen snow from the drooping pine-branches, and swept away the mists as a broom sweeps the dust from the floor. Radiant above me were the unclouded skies, already charged with the red of the sunset, and in front I saw that I had come to the very edge of the wood through which I had wandered so long. But it was no valley into which I had penetrated, for there right ahead of me rose the steep slope of boulders and rocks soaring upwards to the foot of the Ungeheuerhorn. What, then, was that cry of a wolf which had made my heart stand still? I saw.

Not twenty yards from me was a fallen tree, and leaning against the trunk of it was one of the denizens of the Horror-horn, and it was a woman. She was enveloped in a thick growth of hair grey and tufted, and from her head it streamed down over her shoulders and her bosom, from which hung withered and pendulous breasts. And looking on her face I comprehended not with my mind alone, but with a shudder of my spirit, what Ingram had felt. Never had nightmare fashioned so terrible a countenance; the beauty of sun and stars and of the beasts of the field and the kindly race of men could not atone for so hellish an incarnation of the spirit of life. A fathomless bestiality modelled the slavering mouth and the narrow eyes; I looked into the abyss itself and knew that out of that abyss on the edge of which I leaned the generations of men had climbed. What if that ledge crumbled in front of me and pitched me headlong into its nethermost depths?. . .

In one hand she held by the horns a chamois that kicked and struggled. A blow from its hindleg caught her withered thigh, and with a grunt of anger she seized the leg in her other hand, and, as a man may pull from its sheath a stem of meadow-grass, she plucked it off the body, leaving the torn skin hanging round the gaping wound. Then putting the red, bleeding member to her mouth she sucked at it as a child sucks a stick of sweetmeat. Through flesh and gristle her short, brown teeth penetrated, and she licked her lips with a sound of purring. Then dropping the leg by her side, she looked again at the body of the prey now quivering in its death-convulsion, and with finger and thumb gouged out one of its eyes. She snapped her teeth on it, and it cracked like a soft-shelled nut.

It must have been but a few seconds that I stood watching her, in some indescribable catalepsy of terror, while through my brain there pealed the panic-command of my mind to my stricken limbs "Begone, begone, while there is time." Then, recovering the power of my joints and muscles, I tried to slip behind a tree and hide myself from this apparition. But the woman—shall we say?—must have caught my stir of movement, for she raised her eyes from her living feast and saw me. She craned forward her neck, she dropped her prey, and half rising began to move towards me. As she did this, she opened her mouth, and gave forth a howl such as I had heard a moment before. It was answered by another, but faintly and distantly.

Sliding and slipping, with the toes of my skis tripping in the obstacles below the snow, I plunged forward down the hill between the pine-trunks.

The low sun already sinking behind some rampart of mountain in the west reddened the snow and the pines with its ultimate rays. My knapsack with the skates in it swung to and fro on my back, one ski-stick had already been twitched out of my hand by a fallen branch of pine, but not a second's pause could I allow myself to recover it. I gave no glance behind, and I knew not at what pace my pursuer was on my track, or indeed whether any pursued at all, for my whole mind and energy, now working at full power again under the stress of my panic, was devoted to getting away down the hill and out of the wood as swiftly as my limbs could bear me. For a little while I heard nothing but the hissing snow of my headlong passage, and the rustle of the covered undergrowth beneath my feet, and then, from close at hand behind me, once more the wolf-howl sounded and I heard the plunging of footsteps other than my own.

The strap of my knapsack had shifted, and as my skates swung to and fro on my back it chafed and pressed on my throat, hindering free passage of air, of which, God knew, my labouring lungs were in dire need, and without pausing I slipped it free from my neck, and held it in the hand from which my ski-stick had been jerked. I seemed to go a little more easily for this adjustment, and now, not so far distant, I could see below me the path from which I had strayed. If only I could reach that, the smoother going would surely enable me to out-distance my pursuer, who even on the rougher ground was but slowly overhauling me, and at the sight of that riband stretching unimpeded downhill, a ray of hope pierced the black panic of my soul. With that came the desire, keen and insistent, to see who or what it was that was on my tracks, and I spared a backward glance. It was she, the hag whom I had seen at her gruesome meal; her long grey hair flew out behind her, her mouth chattered and gibbered, her fingers made grabbing movements, as if already they closed on me.

But the path was now at hand, and the nearness of it I suppose made me incautious. A hump of snow-covered bush lay in my path, and, thinking I could jump over it, I tripped and fell, smothering myself in snow. I heard a maniac noise, half scream, half laugh, from close behind, and before I could recover myself the grabbing fingers were at my neck, as if a steel vice had closed there. But my right hand in which I held my knapsack of skates was free, and with a blind back-handed movement I whirled it behind me at the full length of its strap, and knew that my desperate blow had found its billet somewhere. Even before I could look round I felt the grip on my neck relax, and something subsided into the very bush which had entangled me. I recovered my feet and turned.

There she lay, twitching and quivering. The heel of one of my skates piercing the thin alpaca of the knapsack had hit her full on the temple, from which the blood was pouring, but a hundred yards away I could see another such figure coming downwards on my tracks, leaping and bounding. At that panic rose again within me, and I sped off down the white smooth path that led to the lights of the village already beckoning. Never once did I pause in my headlong going: there was no safety until I was back among the haunts of men. I flung myself against the door of the hotel, and screamed for admittance, though I had but to turn the handle and enter; and once more as when Ingram had told his tale, there was the sound of the band, and the chatter of voices, and there, too, was he himself, who looked up and then rose swiftly to his feet as I made my clattering entrance.

"I have seen them too," I cried. "Look at my knapsack. Is there not blood on it? It is the blood of one of them, a woman, a hag, who tore off the leg of a chamois as I looked, and pursued me through the accursed wood. I—"

Whether it was I who spun round, or the room which seemed to spin me, I knew not, but I heard myself falling, collapsed on the floor, and the next time that I was conscious at all I was in bed. There was Ingram there, who told me that I was quite safe, and another man, a stranger, who pricked my arm with the nozzle of a syringe, and reassured me. . . .

A day or two later I gave a coherent account of my adventure, and three or four men, armed with guns, went over my traces. They found the bush in which I had stumbled, with a pool of blood which had soaked into the snow, and, still following my ski-tracks, they came on the body of a chamois, from which had been torn one of its hindlegs and one eye-socket was empty. That is all the corroboration of my story that I can give the reader, and for myself I imagine that the creature which pursued me was either not killed by my blow or that her fellows removed her body. . . . Anyhow, it is open to the incredulous to prowl about the caves of the Ungeheuerhorn, and see if anything occurs that may convince them.

Z *is for* Zombie

Long before they became the living dead who feast on flesh in contemporary film and fiction, zombies were traditional figures of West African folklore: corpses raised through sorcery to provide cheap labor for humans unscrupulous enough to resurrect them. This story by British writer Vivian Meik (1894–1955), from his 1933 collection *Devils' Drums,* is one of the first short zombie stories to be published.

VIVIAN MEIK

White Zombie

Geoffrey Aylett, acting commissioner of the district of Nswadzi, was frightened. During his twenty years in Africa never before had he experienced the sensation of being so definitely baffled. He felt as if something was pressing against him, something that he could neither see nor locate, but, nevertheless, something that seemed to envelop him, and, in some inexplicable way, threatened to stifle him. Lately he had begun to wake suddenly at nights, struggling for breath and almost overcome by a feeling of nausea. After the nausea had disappeared there still remained a strange suggestion of some nameless, horrible odour, an odour that was strongly reminiscent of the aftermath of the earlier battles of the Mesopotamia campaign. Those had been days of foul disease, when cholera and dysentery, sunstroke, typhoid and gangrene, had raged unchecked; where hundreds had lain where they had fallen; when, pressed by enemies and forgotten by friends, the survivors were forced to let even the elementary decencies of death go by the board. . . . He remembered the flies and the corruption, and the temperature of a hundred and twenty degrees. . . .

And now, eighteen years later, that same smell of fœtid corruption seemed to hover about him like some evil invisible presence when he awoke at nights.

Aylett was, first and foremost, a rational man accustomed to face facts. His knowledge of the mystery of Africa, of its depths and jungles, of its eerie atmosphere, was as complete as that of any white man—he smiled whimsically as he emphasized to himself how little that was—and he looked for some concrete reason that would explain the bridging of the years by this horrible harmonic. Failing a satisfactory solution he would be forced to conclude that it was about time he went home on a long leave.

Carefully, as befitted of a man of his experience of the ways of the dark gods, he searched his innermost soul, but failed to find the answer he sought.

There was only one connection in the district between him and the Mesopotamia of 1915—a certain John Sinclair, late of the Indian Army—but that connection was already a broken link long before the first occurrence of these nauseating nightmares.

Sinclair had been a brother officer in the old days, and, mainly on Aylett's advice, had taken up a few thousand acres of virgin country in the comparatively unknown Nswadzi district immediately after the war. But he had died more than a year previously—and, what was more to the point, had died a natural death. Aylett himself had been present at the passing of his friend.

Being both a mystic as a result of his knowledge of Africa, and a logician as a result of his Western upbringing, Aylett methodically considered the platitudinous truth that there are more things in heaven and earth than are dreamed of in our philosophy, and went over the entire period of his association with Sinclair in every detail.

At the end of it all, he was forced to admit failure, and, indeed, judged either logically or mystically, there was no adequate reason for linking Sinclair with his present troubles. Sinclair had died peacefully. He even remembered the utter content of the last sigh. . .as if some great burden had been lifted.

It was true that before this, Sinclair—and Aylett himself for that matter—during the first two years of the War, had been through a hell that only those who had experienced it could appreciate. It was also true that Sinclair had saved Aylett's life at a great risk to his own, on a certain memorable occasion, when Aylett, left for dead, had been lying badly wounded. . .in the sun. Aylett had, naturally, never forgotten that, but being a typical Englishman, had done very little more than shake his friend's hand, and mumble something to the effect that he hoped that one day there would be an opportunity to repay. Sinclair had waved the matter aside, with a laugh, as one of no account—merely a job in the day's work. There the incident had ended, and each went about his own lawful occasions.

As a settler, Sinclair had been a complete success. In due course, he had married a very capable woman, who, it appeared to Aylett, whenever he had broken journey at the homestead, was eminently suited to the hard existence of a planter's wife.

At first Sinclair had seemed very happy, but as the years went by Aylett had not been quite so sure. He had had occasion more than once to notice the subtle change for the worse in his old friend. Staleness, he diagnosed, and recommended a holiday in England. Lonely plantations, far from one's own kind, are apt to get on the nerves. Nothing came of his suggestion, however, and the Sinclairs stayed on. They had grown to love the place too well, they said, though he thought that Sinclair's enthusiasm did not ring true. Anyway, it had not been his business.

That was all that he could recall in his contemplation, and he repeated again how it had all finished over a year ago. But old memories cling. He found himself living over again that ghastly day after Ctesiphon, when Sinclair had literally brought him back to life.

He began to wonder—idly, fantastically. The afternoon dimmed to sundown, sundown gave way to the magic of the night. Still Aylett made no move to leave the camp-chair under the awning of his tent and go to bed. After a while, the last of his "boys" came up to ask whether he might retire. Aylett answered him absently, his eyes on the glowing logs of camp-fire.

As the hours wore on he could hear the sound of the night drums more distinctly. From all the points of the compass the sounds came and went, drum answering drum. . .the telegraph of the trackless miles that the world calls Africa. Lazily he wondered what they were saying, and how exactly they transmitted their news. Strange, he thought, that no white man had ever mastered the secret of the drums.

Subconsciously he followed their throbbing monotony. He gradually became aware that the beat had changed. No more were simple news or opinions being transmitted. That much he could understand. There was something else being sent out, something of importance. He suddenly realized that whatever this was, it was apparently regarded as being of vital urgency, and that, at least for an hour, the same short rhythm had been repeated. North, south, east and west, the echoes throbbed and throbbed again.

The drums began to madden him, but there was no way to stop them. He decided to go to bed, but he had been listening too long, and the rhythm followed him. Eventually he dropped into a listless disturbed sleep, during which the implacable staccato throbbing kept hammering away its unreadable message into his subconscious.

It seemed only a moment later that he awoke. A malarious mist had rolled up from the swamps below and had pervaded his camp. He found himself gasping for breath. He tried to sit up, but the mist seemed to be pressing him down where he lay. No sound issued from his lips when he endeavoured to call his "boys." He felt himself being steadily submerged—down, down, down and still down. Just before he lost consciousness he realized that he was being suffocated, not by the heavy mist, but by a foul miasma reeking with all the horror of corruption. . . .

Aylett looked about him in a bewildered fashion when he opened his eyes again. A kindly bearded face was bending over him, and heard a voice that seemed to be coming from a great distance that encouraged him to drink something. His head was throbbing violently, and his breath came in deep gasps. But the cool water cleared in some measure the foul odour that seemed to cling to his brain.

"Ah, *mon ami, c'est bon.* We thought you were dead when the 'boys' brought you in." The bearded face broke into a grin: "but now you will be well, *hein?* You are—what you say?—a tough, *hein.*"

Aylett laughed in spite of himself. Why, of course, this was the mission station of the White Fathers, and his old friend, Padre Vaneken, placid and reliable, was looking after him. He closed his eyes happily. Now there was nothing more to fear, everything would soon be well. Then, as suddenly as it had come, that terrible clinging odour of death and decay left him. . . .

"But, padre man," he discussed his horrible experience later, "what could have happened? We are both men of some experience of Africa—"

The missionary shrugged his shoulders. "*Mon ami,* as you imply, this is Africa. . .and I have no evidence that the curse on Ham, the son of Noah, has ever been lifted. The dark forests, they are the stronghold of such whose unconscious spirits have rebelled and have not yet come out to serve as was first ordained. Who knows?. . . We—I—do not look too deeply there. When I first came out, in my early idealism I sought but the convert, now I—I am content to do mostly the cures for fevers and wounds, and hope that *le bon Dieu* will understand. It is the same everywhere where the curse of Noah carries. Civilization counts not. Regard Hayti—I spent twelve years there—Sierra Leone, the Congo, and here. What can I say about your attack by the mist? Nothing, *hein?* You—you thank God you live, for here, *mon ami*—here is the cradle of Africa, the oldest stronghold of the sons of Ham. . . ."

Aylett regarded the missionary intently. "Padre," he spoke deliberately, "what exactly are you trying to make me understand?"

The two men, old in the ways of the black jungle, faced each other steadily. "*Mon ami,*" the priest said quietly, "you are my old friend. On the forms of religion we think differently, you and I, but this is not conventional Europe, thank God, and side by side, we have done our best according to our lights. God himself cannot do more. So I will tell you. *I have seen the mist before. . .twice. Once in Hayti and once in this district.*"

"Here?"

The padre nodded. "I was in camp at the catechumen's school by Mrs. Sinclair's estate—"

"Go on." Aylett's voice was low.

"As you know, Mrs. Sinclair has run the plantation since her husband's death. She refused to go home. At first you, I—all the countryside—thought she was mad to stay there alone, but—" the missionary shrugged his shoulders, "*que voulez-vous?* A woman is a law to herself. Anyway, she has made it a greater success than ever, and we are silent, *hein?*"

"But the mist?"

"I was coming to that. It caught me by the throat that night. I was living at the house, as we all do who pass that way—Central Africa is not a cathedral close—but beyond not knowing anything of what happened for several hours, nothing happened to me." He touched the emblem of his faith on the rosary that was part of his dress. "Mrs. Sinclair said that I had been overcome by the heat, but to me that explanation would not do. . . ."

"But that doesn't explain anything."

"Perhaps not—*but Mrs. Sinclair said that she had not noticed anything peculiar*. . . ."

"How was that?"

The priest shrugged his shoulders. "I am not Mrs. Sinclair," he said abruptly, and Aylett knew that not another word about her would the missionary say.

"Tell me about Hayti, padre," he asked.

The priest replied quietly. "We understood it there to mean that it was artificially produced by *voodoo* black magic—a very real thing, *mon ami,* which my church readily admits as you probably know—and there they call it 'the breath of the dead.' Why?. . ." He shrugged his shoulders again.

Aylett turned away and looked out steadily into the distance. For a long time he fixed his gaze on the line of distant hills, thinking deeply. He recalled a picture where just such hills appeared in the background—a photograph taken by a man who had been almost beyond the border-line to give truth to the world. But he had failed. The picture showed a group of figures. That was all until one studied them, and even then no one would believe that this was a photograph of dead men—*who were not allowed to die*.

For hours the two men sat silently, each busy with his own thoughts. Night mantled the tiny mission station, and from afar the sound of drums came through on the soft breeze. Aylett turned suddenly to the missionary. "Padre man," he said quietly, "it's only twenty miles from here to the Sinclair estate. . . ."

The padre nodded. "I understand, *mon ami,*" he replied. Then after a moment, "Would you think it an impertinence if I asked you to keep this in your pocket—till you come back?" He produced a small silver crucifix.

Aylett held out his hand. "Thank you," he said simply.

The sun had set when Aylett's *machila** was set down on Mrs. Sinclair's verandah. She came forward to welcome him. "I wondered if I should ever see you

* *Machila*—a stretcher slung on a pole—the standard means of transport in the "bush."

again." She looked at him quietly. "You haven't been here since—for over a year now." Then she changed her tone. She laughed. "As a district officer," she said, "you've neglected your duties shamefully!"

Aylett smilingly pleaded guilty, excusing himself on the ground that everything had gone so well in this section, that he had hesitated to intrude on perfection.

"Has it fallen from perfection now?" she countered.

"Not at all," he replied, "this visit is merely routine."

"Er—thank you," she said dryly. "Anyway, come in and make yourself comfortable, and to-morrow I'll show you a perfect estate."

Aylett studied his hostess carefully through dinner. He felt uneasy at what he saw whenever he caught her off her guard. He could hardly believe that this was the same woman whom he had welcomed as a bride a few years ago. The lonely life had hardened her, but he had expected that. There was something more, though—a kind of bitter hardness, he called it, for want of a better term.

After her formal welcome Mrs. Sinclair spoke very little. She seemed preoccupied with the affairs of the plantation. "My very own stake in Africa," she said. "Oh, how I love the country, its magic and mystery and its vast grandeur." She reminded him how she had refused to go home. But to-morrow, she said, when he saw *her* Africa—the plantation—he would understand.

Aylett retired early, distinctly puzzled. He had noticed her looking over the swept and garnished tidiness of the plantation before she had said good-night. She had unconsciously stretched out her hands to it a kind of adoring supplication, and yet in the brilliant moonlight under this sensual adoration, he distinctly noticed the contrast of the hard lines on her face and the bitterness of the mouth. Africa. . .

Exhausted as he was, he slept well. Whether the little cross the padre had given him had anything to do with it or not, he did not know, but in the morning he had waked more refreshed than he had been for weeks. He looked forward to the visit over the estate.

Mrs. Sinclair had not exaggerated when she had used the word perfection. Fields had been hoed till not a stray blade of grass grew among the crops; barns stood in serried rows; wood fuel was stacked in the neatest of "cords"; the orchard and the kitchen garden were luxurious, and the pasture in the miniature home farm was the greenest he had seen in the tropics.

"For what?" his subconscious brain kept hammering at him. "Why—and above all, *how?*"

Aylett had noticed what only an expert would have seen. There was a great shortage of labour, though such workers as were dotted about seemed to be very busy.

As if she divined his thoughts, Mrs. Sinclair answered them. "My 'boys' *work*," she said, in even tones as she flicked the hippo hide whip she carried.

Aylett raised his eyebrows. "Portuguese methods?" he asked quietly, and looked at the whip.

Mrs. Sinclair turned to him. For the first time he noticed her deliberate antagonism. "Not at all," she said evenly, "a knowledge of how to get the most out of a native, a faculty which I notice officialdom has not yet acquired."

The district official took the rapier-like thrust without faltering. *"Touché,"* he answered, but nevertheless he knew he had not been wrong about the labour. "Queer," he thought, "damnably queer. . . ."

Mrs. Sinclair took no notice of his acknowledgment of her point. Her lips were set hard and she spoke coldly. She continued. "It's only a matter of getting to the heart of Africa—the throbbing beating heart below all this—Africa has no use for those who do not join their own souls." Suddenly she realized what she was saying, but before she could change the subject Aylett took up the question. He matched her tone.

"Very interesting. . ." he said, "but we don't encourage Europeans, especially European women, to go 'native.' "

The last word, however, was with the woman. "All the perspicacity of officialdom!" she murmured. Then she looked Aylett full in the face. "Do I sound *native*," she said harshly, "or *look* native?"

Aylett was hardly listening. He was staring at her. Her eyes belied her words, for if ever he saw an expression of masterful, baleful perversion in any human face, he saw it then. He began to understand. . . .

He was thankful when the inspection was over, and felt relieved that she did not offer the formal suggestion that he should stay a little longer.

Five miles beyond her boundary he had a bivouac tent pitched behind a thorn-bush, and stored two days' rations in the shade. He sent his *safari* on at the double to the mission station, and watched it till it was out of sight. Then he sat down to wait for the night.

"The heart of Africa..." he repeated to himself, but his voice was grim, and his eyes flashed in cold anger.

It was not till he heard the news drums throb that Aylett retraced his steps along the ill-defined track to the plantation. At the edge of the estate he merged himself in the shadows of the forest fringe, and gradually worked his way along the eucalyptus wind breaks. He crawled noiselessly as far as the tree that grew in the garden before the homestead.

In a little while he saw Mrs. Sinclair come out on to the verandah. Beside her stood a gigantic native who looked like some obscene devil, a witch doctor, sinister and grotesque, and naked but for a necklace of human bones dangling and rattling on his enormous chest. Daubs of white clay and red ochre plastered his face.

Only partly covered by a magnificent leopard skin, the white woman stepped down into the clearing and snapped the whip she had in her hands. It sounded like a revolver shot. As if it were a signal, Aylett heard the roll of drums near at hand. From one of the barns began the most grotesque procession he had ever seen. The drums throbbed malevolently—the short staccato throb that had preceded the fœtid mist which had almost suffocated him. Louder they grew and louder. The message rolled through the jungles, was caught up and answered again. There was no doubt as to its meaning.

He crouched lower as the drums approached, his eyes fixed on the macabre scene before him. Following the drums, as regularly as a column on the march, moved the men who worked the perfect plantation. In columns of four they moved, heavy footed and automatic—but they moved. Every now and then the crack of that terrible whip sounded like a pistol shot through the roll of drums, and every now and then Aylett could see that cruel thong cut through naked flesh, and a figure drop silently, only to pick itself up again and rejoin the column.

They marched round the garden. As they came near Aylett held his breath. He had to strain every nerve in his body to prevent himself screaming. Almost as if he were hypnotized he looked on the dull, expressionless faces of the silent, slow-moving automatons—faces on which there was not even despair. They simply moved to the command of that merciless whip, as they would shortly move off to their allotted task in the fields. Bowed and crushed, they passed by him without a sound.

The nervous tension nearly broke Aylett. Then the realization came to him—*these pitiful automatons were dead—and they were not allowed to die. . . .*

The figures in the unbelievable photograph came back to him; the padre's words; the magic of the *voodoo* acknowledged as fact by the greatest Christian Church in history. The dead. . .who were not allowed to die. . . Zombies, the natives called them in hushed voices, wherever the curse of Noah was borne. . .and *she* called it knowing Africa.

A cold terror came over Aylett. The long column was nearing its end. Mrs. Sinclair was walking down the line, her whip cracking mercilessly, her face distorted with perverted lust, the foul witch doctor leering over her naked shoulder. She stopped by the tree behind which he crouched. A single bent figure followed the column. With a gasp of horror Aylett recognized Sinclair. Sinclair. The whip crashed against the poor thing who had once died in his arms.

"My God!" Aylett muttered helplessly. "It's not possible—" but he knew that the witch doctor's *voodoo* had thrown the impossibility in his face. The whip cracked again, hurling the lone white Zombie to the ground. Slowly, it picked itself up—without a sound, without expression—and automatically followed the column. He heard, as in a nightmare, unbelievably foul obscenities fall from the woman's lips—cruel taunts. . . . And the whip cracked and bit and tore, again and yet again. At the head of the column the drums throbbed on.

Horror gave way at last. Aylett found himself desperately clutching the tiny cross the padre had given him. With the other hand he found his revolver and took aim with icy coolness. . . . Four times he fired at a point above the leopard skin, and twice into the ochred face of the witch doctor. . . . Then he leapt forward, cross in hand, to what had once died as Sinclair.

The figure was standing silently, bent and expressionless. It made no sign as Aylett approached, but as the crucifix touched it a tremor shook the frame. The drooping eyelids lifted and the lips moved. "You have repaid," they whispered gently. The body swayed slightly and toppled over. "Dust to dust. . . ." Aylett prayed. In a few moments all that remained was a grayish powder. A tropical year had passed, Aylett remembered with a shudder. . . . Then he turned, and, crucifix in hand, walked along the column. . . .